John Suchet is an award-winning television journalist and news-caster. As an ITN foreign correspondent he has reported from every country in Western Europe, as well as America, Africa, the Middle East and the Far East. In 1986 he was awarded the Royal Television Society's Journalist of the Year Award for his reporting from the Philippines, and in 1996 was voted Newscaster of the Year by the Television and Radio Industries Club. He is now the regular presenter of the *Early Evening News* and frequently presents *News at Ten*. *The Last Master* is his first novel.

The Last Master

Passion & Anger

Volume one of a fictional biography of
LUDWIG VAN BEETHOVEN

John Suchet

WARNER BOOKS

A *Warner* Book

First published in Great Britain in 1996
by Little, Brown and Company
This edition published in 1997 by Warner Books

A CIP catalogue record for this book
is available from the British Library.

ISBN 0 7515 1980 4

Typeset in Bembo by
Palimpsest Book Production Limited,
Polmont, Stirlingshire
Printed and bound in Great Britain by
Clays Ltd, St Ives plc

Warner Books
A Division of
Little, Brown and Company (UK)
Brettenham House
Lancaster Place
London WC2E 7EN

For Bonnie my wife who encouraged and inspired

You will ask me where I get my ideas. That I cannot tell you with certainty; they come unsummoned, directly, indirectly – I could seize them with my hands – out in the open air; in the woods; while walking; in the silence of the nights; early in the morning; incited by moods, which are translated by the poet into words, by me into tones that sound and roar and storm about me until I have set them down in notes.

Ludwig van Beethoven, 1822

The last master of tuneful song, the organ of soulful concord, the heir and enhancer of Handel and Bach, of Haydn and Mozart's immortal fame is now no more, and we stand weeping over the riven strings of the harp that is hushed.

The harp that is hushed! Let me call him so! For he was an artist, and all that was his, was his through art alone. He was an artist – and who shall arise to stand beside him?

The Funeral Oration
by Franz Grillparzer, 1827

Contents

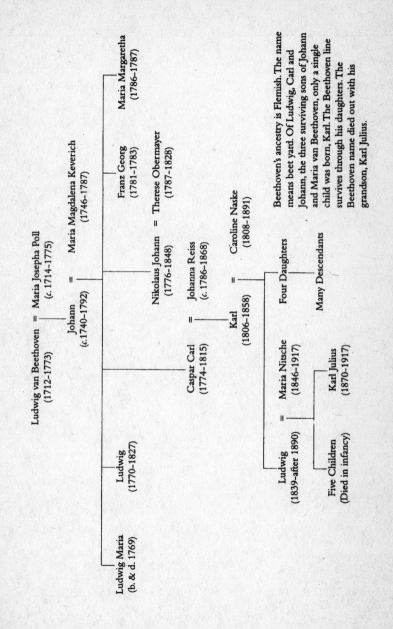

Ludwig van Beethoven = Maria Josepha Poll
(1712-1773)   (c. 1714-1775)

Johann = Maria Magdalena Keverich
(c. 1740-1792)   (1746-1787)

Ludwig Maria
(b. & d. 1769)

Ludwig
(1770-1827)

Caspar Carl
(1774-1815)

Nikolaus Johann = Therese Obermayer
(1776-1848)   (1787-1828)

Franz Georg
(1781-1783)

Maria Margaretha
(1786-1787)

Karl = Johanna Reiss
(1806-1858)   (c. 1786-1868)

Karl = Caroline Naske
(1806-1858)   (1808-1891)

Ludwig = Maria Nitsche
(1839-after 1890)   (1846-1917)

Four Daughters

Many Descendants

Karl Julius
(1870-1917)

Five Children
(Died in infancy)

Beethoven's ancestry is Flemish. The name
means beet yard. Of Ludwig, Carl and
Johann, the three surviving sons of Johann
and Maria van Beethoven, only a single
child was born, Karl. The Beethoven line
survives through his daughters. The
Beethoven name died out with his
grandson, Karl Julius.

Cast of Characters

These are the main characters who came into contact with Beethoven during the first thirty-two years of his life:

Beethoven, Caspar Carl van (1774–1815). Elder of Beethoven's two younger brothers. Followed Ludwig to Vienna in 1794. Tried to earn a living teaching music, but eventually took a job as clerk in the Finance Department of the Hofburg palace.

Beethoven, Johann van (c. 1740–92). Beethoven's father. Tenor at the Electoral court at Bonn, but failed to succeed his father as Kapellmeister. Became an alcoholic and was dismissed from court service in 1789.

Beethoven, Ludwig van (1712–73). Beethoven's beloved grand-father. Born in Malines, Belgium. Moved to Bonn in 1733 where he became Kapellmeister in 1761. Beethoven was only three when he died, but he remained devoted to him for the rest of his life.

Beethoven, Maria Magdalena van (1746–87). Beethoven's mother. Her first husband died soon after the marriage and the child she bore him died in infancy. She married Johann van Beethoven on 12 November 1767. Three of their children survived into adulthood. She died of consumption at the age of forty.

Beethoven, Nikolaus Johann van (1776–1848). Younger of Beethoven's two younger brothers. Trained as a pharmacist in Bonn. Followed Beethoven to Vienna in 1795, where he worked as a pharmacist's assistant.

Breuning, Eleonore von (1771–1841). Daughter of Helene

(*q.v.*). Childhood friend of Beethoven's in Bonn. He taught her piano. She married Franz Gerhard Wegeler in 1802.

Breuning, Helene von (1750–1838). Head of one of Bonn's most prominent families, after her husband died in the palace fire of 1777. Made her house and piano available to young Ludwig and employed him to teach piano to two of her children.

Breuning, Stephan von (1774–1827). Beethoven's closest friend in Bonn, a friendship which was renewed in Vienna when Stephan moved there. Outside musical circles, Stephan remained Beethoven's closest friend – with periodic interruptions caused by arguments – for the whole of Beethoven's life. Stephan at first worked for the Teutonic Order, then as an official in the War Department at the Hofburg palace.

Czerny, Carl (1791–1857). Taken on as a pupil by Beethoven in 1801, later becoming close to him. He was renowned for his intimate knowledge of Beethoven's piano works, and his ability to play them as Beethoven had instructed.

Dragonetti, Domenico (1763–1846). Virtuoso double-bass player. Made Beethoven aware of the potential of the double-bass when he performed one of Beethoven's Cello Sonatas on it, accompanied by the composer. The result was a more important role for the instrument in Beethoven's Symphonies (particularly numbers 3, 5 and 9) than any other composer had hitherto given it.

Gelinek, Abbé Joseph (1758–1825). Priest and pianist from Bohemia. Soon after his arrival in Vienna, Beethoven trounced him in an improvisation contest.

Guicciardi, Countess Giulietta (1784–1856). Acquaintance of Beethoven, with whom he fell in love and intended marrying. He composed the 'Moonlight' Sonata for her and dedicated it to her. In 1803 she married Count Gallenberg.

Haydn, Franz Joseph (1732–1809). Beethoven first met Haydn in Bonn, when Haydn was on his way to England. Generally regarded as Europe's greatest living composer after Mozart's death, Haydn agreed to take the young Beethoven on as a pupil on his return to Vienna. Relations between the two were variable. Haydn criticised the Opus 1 Trios, but Beethoven dedicated his first three Piano Sonatas (Op. 2) to him, and always held him in high regard.

Hummel, Johann Nepomuk (1778–1837). Composer and pianist. He and Beethoven were rivals, but soon developed a mutual respect. Friends noted how different their styles were: Hummel's compositions and playing delicate and refined, Beethoven's stormy and unpredictable.

Kinsky, Prince Ferdinand (1781–1812). Professional soldier. Still in his teens when he first met Beethoven and heard his music. Instantly became an admirer and supporter of the composer and advocate of his music.

Lichnowsky, Prince Karl (1756–1814). One of Beethoven's earliest and most influential patrons in Vienna. For a while, shortly after his arrival in Vienna, Beethoven lived with the Prince and Princess in their apartment. The Prince retained his own Quartet and gave regular Friday matinées at which Beethoven often performed his music. Beethoven dedicated his Opus 1, the Piano Trios, to the Prince, as well as the Second Symphony and several piano pieces.

Lobkowitz, Prince Franz Joseph (1772–1816). Great music lover, capable violinist and patron of the arts. He converted a room of his palace into a concert hall and retained his own orchestra. An early admirer of Beethoven's music, he made his concert hall available to him. Among Beethoven's dedications to him were his first String Quartets Op. 18, as well as the Third, Fifth and Sixth Symphonies. The Prince was born with a deformed hip and walked all his life with the aid of a crutch.

Maximilian Franz, Elector of Cologne (1756–1801). Youngest son of Empress Maria Theresa, brother of two Habsburg Emperors and uncle of a third, brother of Marie Antoinette. He ruled his principality from Bonn, where he fostered the musical career of the young Beethoven. He made possible Beethoven's first visit to Vienna to meet Mozart. An enlightened ruler and great patron of the arts.

Mozart, Wolfgang Amadeus (1756–91). From as early as he could remember Beethoven admired Mozart's music, studying the scores as soon as they reached Bonn. He achieved his ambition to meet Mozart when he went to Vienna in 1787 and Mozart agreed to take him on as a pupil.

Neefe, Christian Gottlob (1748–98). First full-time teacher of the young Beethoven in Bonn. He recognised Beethoven's extraordinary talent, securing for him the post of assistant organist as well as instrumentalist with the court theatre orchestra. Worked hard to persuade the Elector to allow Beethoven to travel to Vienna to meet Mozart.

Ries, Franz (1755–1846) was a senior court musician who showed much kindness to Beethoven after Frau Beethoven's early death, and Beethoven never forgot the kindness. Beethoven taught Ries' son Ferdinand (1784–1838), piano and later took him under his wing in Vienna, where the young man was his willing assistant.

Rudolph, Archduke of Austria (1788–1831). Brother of Emperor Franz. First heard Beethoven's music at the composer's benefit concert at the Burgtheater, in the company of his mother the Empress. Was a devotee of Beethoven's music from that moment on and became his only composition pupil. An excellent pianist and accomplished composer, he was to become Beethoven's leading and most influential patron. Beethoven dedicated far more compositions to him than to anyone else, including the *Missa Solemnis*, the Emperor Piano Concerto, numerous Piano Sonatas and other chamber music.

Schmidt, Dr Johann Adam (1759–1809). Beethoven's doctor, whose advice to him regarding his deafness largely consisted of going to the country to rest his ears, which was welcome after the drastic and failed remedies of earlier doctors. It was on his recommendation that Beethoven spent the fateful summer of 1802 in Heiligenstadt. Beethoven had a high regard for him.

Schuppanzigh, Ignaz (1776–1830). Violinist and leader of Prince Lichnowsky's Quartet. Great friend of Beethoven and admirer of his music. Regularly the first to play his compositions for violin. Beethoven made much fun of his fatness, composing a piece for him for chorus and male solo voices entitled 'In Praise of the Fat One'.

Streicher, Johann Andreas (1761–1833) and Nanette, *née* Stein (1769–1833). Andreas was a piano maker from Stuttgart. After he married Nanette, from Augsburg, the couple moved to Vienna where they set up a piano factory. Andreas developed more robust instruments with wider keyboards to accommodate Beethoven's needs. Nanette was solicitous for his well-being, finding him suitable accommodation and frequently taking care of his housekeeping needs.

Swieten, Baron Gottfried van (1733–1803). One of Beethoven's earliest patrons in Vienna. The composer dedicated the First Symphony to him. Swieten wrote the text for Haydn's oratorio *The Creation*.

Waldstein, Count Ferdinand von (1762–1823). Friend of Elector Max Franz in Bonn and leading patron of the young Beethoven. He was instrumental in securing Beethoven's second and conclusive trip to Vienna, writing prophetically in Beethoven's autograph book that he would receive 'Mozart's spirit from Haydn's hands'. Beethoven was to immortalise his name with the Waldstein Sonata.

Wegeler, Dr Franz Gerhard (1765–1848). Close friend of the young Beethoven in Bonn, introducing him to the Breuning family. The two met again when Wegeler came to Vienna. It was in a letter to Wegeler in 1801 that Beethoven first mentioned his problem with hearing. Wegeler married Eleonore von Breuning in 1802.

Zmeskall, Nikolaus von (1759–1833). Official in the Hungarian Chancellery in Vienna, and capable amateur cellist. Became a close friend of Beethoven, often providing him with distractions when problems with work – and his hearing – threatened to overwhelm him. Provided him with a ready supply of quills from his office.

Preface

This is the story of Ludwig van Beethoven. It is written as a novel, but it is true. I set myself a rule at the outset, a rule which I have not once knowingly broken: nothing in this book could not have happened. I prefer to state the rule in the negative, rather than to say that everything in this book happened, because it is a novel. But my intention has been to weave the known facts and my imagination together – the latter filling in the gaps left by the former – in such a way that the reader will not know where one stops and the other begins. On numerous occasions where later research showed I had unwittingly broken my rule, I went back and rewrote whole passages. I believe – based on extensive and painstaking research – that everything in the book is in accordance with the known facts.

There is no shortage of known facts about Beethoven's life – a glance down any library list will show hundreds of books about the man and his music. Although there are many more about the music than the man – whole books, even, devoted to a single composition – there is abundant information about his life. On my own shelves I have around fifty books which I have consulted regularly. The total number I have used – including general history books – must run to over a hundred. And I have a cupboard full of pamphlets and articles published by the two most important research institutions, the Beethoven-Archiv in Bonn and the Centre for Beethoven Studies at San José State University, California.

I made several research trips to Bonn, Vienna and Prague, and the Austrian countryside that Beethoven spent so many summers in. In the Postscript I give more details both of the research material I used and the form my own research took. I also compare the main locations in the book with how they are today, and will do the same with later volumes, in the hope that I have stimulated readers' interest.

Certainly there is no shortage of interest in Beethoven, as I discovered for myself. When I revealed to friends that I was writing a trilogy on his life, I was surprised at their desire to know more. Several friends – who did not know each other – told me they had books on Beethoven and offered to lend them to me. One friend, who I did not know had any interest in music, had bought an entire set of the Symphonies the week before I told her about my book. And it was always rewarding to see how raptly friends listened when I related the stories behind some of the compositions.

While writing the book I amassed a pile of newspaper cuttings about Beethoven, from DNA testing of a lock of his hair to theories about the inspiration behind his music. And in a six-month period in 1995–6, the London concert-goer could hear the complete cycle of symphonies, piano concertos, string quartets, piano trios – and *Fidelio* – with not an anniversary in sight.

Most people know two facts about Beethoven: that he wrote the 'fate knocking at the door' motif at the opening of the Fifth Symphony – surely the most famous bars in all music – and that he went deaf. It will, I am sure, surprise them to discover just what a fascinating life Beethoven's was. It surprised me too. There were twists and turns I had no idea were there; elation and despair, love and enmity, unexpected drama, promises made and broken . . . set against the natural drama of the Napoleonic wars. Often in my research I found myself using the same methods I use as a journalist, sometimes shaking my head in disbelief at what I found. In journalistic terms, Beethoven's life is a good story.

My own feelings towards Beethoven metamorphosed over a decade or so of researching and writing. Early drafts of the novel were written from the perspective of a bystander. Not surprisingly – and to my disappointment – I found that I did not like him as much as I expected. I was not as tolerant of his moods and his unpredictability as some others around him.

Slowly, though, I came to understand him better. And as I came to understand him I grew fond of him. I began to experience his emotions; I knew how he would react to given situations because I was thinking like him. I was now writing his story through his eyes.

It is easy to admire Beethoven; less easy, as I discovered, to like him. I have come to know him intimately, and in so doing to like him. I hope the reader will come to like him too.

Prologue

The small boy stood by the side of the bed and shook the old man's shoulder.

'Wake up, Grandpa. Wake up. Talk to me more about those men.'

He shook him again but he knew he would not move.

'Tell me those names again, Grandpa. Bach. Handel. Mozart.'

He leaned forward and put his mouth to the old man's ear. The hairs tickled his lips.

'Bach. Handel. Mozart,' he whispered.

Still the old man did not move. A wave of anger swept over the boy and he frowned. He went to shake the shoulder again, but instead he stroked his grandfather's hair. It was thick and white and slightly coarse. He leaned forward and kissed the forehead, which was still warm.

'Grandpa. Grandpa. Don't go. I need you to be here.'

He looked at his grandfather's head but could not understood why it was smaller than it had been. It seemed to have shrunk. And although his eyelids were tightly closed the eyes seemed larger underneath, like round marbles trying to push through the thin, translucent skin. The cheeks were shrunken and the chin hung slackly down.

The boy, who was just a week past his third birthday, sank to his knees. He clasped his hands in front of him. Silently he sobbed, tasting the saltiness of his tears as they ran round the corners of his mouth.

Ludwig was asleep, his tousled dark hair spread out on the pillow. His breathing was deep but his sleep was troubled. It was a sleep which he knew would be disturbed at any moment. Each time its warm comfort enveloped him, he consciously woke himself up. That way he would be more prepared when the awful moment came.

Ludwig heard the noise in his subconscious before it truly reached him; an irregular, raucous noise which hurt his ears even as he slept. It was the sound of a drunkard in the street outside. A man singing. The voice was high with a pronounced vibrato. There was a silkiness to it which suggested it was a finer voice than the average man might possess. But this man seemed determined not to let it show. A strong, high note was immediately followed by a rough, hoarse growl. The words he sang were slurred and crude.

Ludwig pulled the bedclothes round his shoulders and brought his knees up tightly into his stomach. He wished he could shrink his body even further, more and more until it disappeared altogether. He wished it was all a dream, that he could keep his eyes closed and the noise would go away.

He wished his grandfather was still there. Ludwig van Beethoven. Kapellmeister. The man after whom he had been named. He wished he could smell again the exotic pungent smell of the Turkish tobacco which permeated his clothes. Hear the deep, resonant voice that talked to him of music, feel the strong arm round his shoulder, the large muscular hand that held his as they walked together in the gardens of the Elector's palace.

He winced as the door of his room flew open. He counted the four heavy steps before the hand shook him roughly.

'Come on, my genius. Up and play for me.'

The smell of alcohol hit Ludwig and made him nauseous. His body shivered at the sudden cold. He did not look at his father. He did not want to see his face.

Pushed by his father, he stumbled into the front room towards the piano, the old piano he had heard his grandfather play on so often. There was the familiar portrait on the wall, his grandfather in a velvet gown with tassels on the lapel and cuffs, a rich matching velvet turban on his head. The face was unsmiling, but sensitive and with a warmth which was almost tangible. In his hands he held a book of music. Where was his dear grandfather, now that he needed him so?

A low bench stood in front of the piano. Ludwig did not need to be told to stand on it.

'Now, my little genius. Play for your father. My little Wolfgang Amadeus. Show me you are as good as him.'

Ludwig began playing, stretching his small fingers to reach the notes. Every time he missed, his father brought a stick down on to his wrists. It was not hard and it did not hurt but it made Ludwig wince.

He wished his mother would walk in. But he knew she would not. She had tried to intervene once and had borne the marks round her eyes for several weeks afterwards.

Ludwig did not know what time it was, only that it was the middle of the night and that he would have to stand on the bench and play until dawn. He only hoped his father would fall asleep so he would stop using the stick.

Maria van Beethoven looked at her son and shook her head gently. What boy would not thrill to be where he was now, on the deck of a sailing ship gliding slowly down the busy Rhine towards Rotterdam? Sailors bustling hither and thither, trimming sails, coiling rope; on the banks people waving, farmers in the field, hay wagons rolling by . . .

Ludwig just stood, his hands thrust into his pockets, staring into the distance with a serious look on his face. His eyes seemed to be looking straight through everything that was happening around him. He was a young boy, little more than a child, yet his shoulders sagged as if he already carried the cares of middle age upon them.

She wondered if she should ever have agreed to bring him on this trip. It had been her husband Johann's suggestion and came so unexpectedly she barely had time to muster any resistance. 'It might lead to something,' he had said. But she feared it would not and she already dreaded returning to Bonn to tell him.

Both she and Johann were well aware of their son's musical talent, but both knew too how unpredictable he was about displaying it. The day was still talked about in Bonn when Ludwig refused to play in front of the Elector. Refused to play! If his grandfather could have seen him . . .

Maria had liked old Ludwig, despite an unpromising start to their relationship. Slowly, they had grown closer. She knew why. Both recognised that Johann, a court singer, was slowly throwing his career away.

She had not seen the destructive qualities in Johann when she had married him, and she now cursed herself for her blindness. She should have known. He always drank a lot, but had seemed to be able to control it. Those days were gone now.

Really it was only history repeating itself. His own mother had been an alcoholic and been placed in an institution. It was

the greatest sadness of her father-in-law's life. Marriage, Maria
said to herself for the thousandth time, what is it but a chain of
sorrows?

The sound the seagulls made was harsh and Ludwig looked
up at them reproachfully. He wanted to scream at them that
their squawking was ugly, that they were making a horrible
noise. Instead he clenched his fists in frustration.

He was not really sure where his mother was taking him,
except that it was to the country where his grandfather had been
born. He certainly knew why they were going there. He would
have to perform, play the piano, demonstrate his talent. As he
had just done for his father in towns all along the Rhine.

He had heard his parents arguing about him. His father had
shouted that his skill at the piano was the only way the family
could earn some extra income. He had the talent; he should be
made to display it. His mother had said he was too young. He
had entered the room and both had turned to look at him. But
neither had moved. He wanted his mother to envelop him, but
she had just stood there.

He wanted to walk towards her now, but he could not. He
knew she was looking at him. He sensed it, felt it. People always
looked at him. They knew he could play the piano like an adult
– 'Just wait till his little hands grow bigger,' they always said –
and they stared at him in wonder.

But when his mother looked at him there was always an
expression of incomprehension on her face. He had always
sensed he was different from other children. He had to be –
why else did they seem to stay away from him, as if they were
frightened of him? – but he wanted his mother to tell him it
was not true. That he was not really different.

Instead she reinforced it. 'Why can't you be more like your
brothers? They're normal.' *Normal.* So he was not normal. His
own mother had as good as told him so.

He did not hear her voice at first through the noise of the
seagulls and the flapping sails. When he heard it he saw that she
was gesturing to him to come and sit with her on the bench.

'Are you cold?'

'A little. Just my feet.'

'Here. Put them under my blanket.' She leaned forward and
took his shoes off and lifted his feet on to her lap.

Ludwig, supported by the arm of the bench, watched his
mother as she rubbed warmth into his feet. He wanted her to

turn to him and smile, say something encouraging. But she said nothing.

He wanted to say to her that he would play the piano as best he could wherever it was they were going. But the words would not come.

BOOK ONE

Chapter 1

Johann van Beethoven thought of himself as a likeable man. He was not short of friends; there was always someone he could call on to spend a couple of hours with him at the tavern. He resented his wife calling them cronies; she'd be the first to complain if he never left the house. And who could blame him for wanting to get out? Johann was a sociable man; he liked to tell a good joke and listen to a good story. And Heaven knows there was little enough of that in the house.

Johann had married Maria Magdalena Leym fifteen years before, because he had genuinely fallen in love with her. She had a handsome rather than pretty face, which might have been unduly stern but for the soft, slightly unfocused look of her eyes. She was a serious woman, perhaps a little more serious than he would have liked. But he was sure that would change. He would be able to change it.

What Johann failed to see was the sadness which lay deep behind her eyes. Maria Magdalena Keverich had married one Johann Leym, valet to the Elector of Trèves, at the age of sixteen. She bore him a son who died an infant. Within three years her husband too had died. She had therefore lost a child and been widowed before she was nineteen years of age. And as if that were not enough grief for a young woman, her close friends sometimes wondered if she had ever really recovered from her father's sudden death when she was only twelve years old.

Johann first saw Maria one fine summer's day when in an idle moment he decided to take a boat trip up the Rhine to the small town of Ehrenbreitstein. Over the next few months he slipped away several times to catch further glimpses of the young widow in black. His absences did not go unnoticed, and his good friend Theodor Fischer the baker soon established their purpose from Johann and lost no time in informing their circle of friends. Many a time in the tavern Johann was at the receiving end of ribald remarks from his friends. 'The widow Leym, unaware of what fate awaits her the day she sheds her widow's weeds . . .'

With due deference Johann avoided contact with Maria until she came out of mourning. Then, he was pleasantly surprised at the ease with which he wooed and won her. He flattered himself that he was an eligible young man, and that Maria had not failed to be impressed by his striking looks and good career prospects. He was already earning a hundred florins a month as a court musician; his fine tenor voice was much admired, and it was generally assumed – by Johann as much as anyone – that with practice he would improve his musical skills and be able to assume the mantle of Kapellmeister when his father retired.

But his relationship with his new wife immediately ran into trouble. Indeed it had run into trouble before she even became his wife, and from the source he least expected. From the day Johann had turned twenty-one, his father had pestered him to marry. 'Johann the Sprinter, that's what you are,' he mocked him. 'Always running around and achieving nothing, while the world passes you by. But remember this. You have been born into a family with a musical dynasty. You are a musician yourself, but that is only because I taught you. Now you must marry and have children, who themselves will be musicians, so that the name of Beethoven will be forever associated with the noblest art . . .'

But now Johann had found his bride, and without a word to his father had secured from her the promise of marriage. It was therefore with high expectations that he brought her to Bonn to present her to his father. Johann knew immediately that all was not well when he saw his father standing before the fire with his face grim and his hands folded behind his back and under his tailcoat.

Johann's first thought was how ridiculous his father looked: the short, muscular frame, with the large, cavernous chest brought on from years of bass singing causing the tight jacket to strain at the clasp. And above him on the wall, the portrait in oils of him by the court painter Radoux, of which he was so proud, showing him in a velvet robe with ornamental tassels and a fur turban on his head. Johann had long ago vowed to get rid of the painting, but now it hung defiantly in place in silent support of its subject.

'Father, I wish to present to you Maria Magdalena Keverich Leym, my intended bride.'

'Leave the room, young lady, while I talk to my son.'

'Father . . .'

'Hold your tongue, boy. Now, Frau Leym . . .' and he put emphasis on the word 'Frau', 'if you would be so good as to wait in the entrance hall.' The old man took Maria by the arm and firmly but without undue force walked her to the door.

Maria gone, the Kapellmeister stood looking at his son for a full minute. Finally, almost as a splutter, he said: 'A chambermaid, a housemaid. The daughter of a cook. You, a court musician, in the service of His Most Gracious Lord the Elector of Cologne, and son of the Kapellmeister, you bring home a . . . a . . . a servant girl! And a widow too. Already married and a mother. And . . . and . . . not even from your own home town. Are the women of Bonn perhaps beneath you? Whatever happens, your poor mother must not be told. She has enough sadness already on her shoulders. It would be the last straw, poor woman.'

Johann felt the anger rise in him. Why did his father talk to him like this, as if he was still a child? And could he not see how ridiculous he looked? Between his teeth he clenched a small narrow-stemmed clay pipe, and every word he stressed sent a puff of smoke out of the bowl. Johann wanted to laugh but he knew it would be a mistake; so would a sudden burst of anger. He decided instead to reason with his father.

'Father, you have been misinformed. Maria's father was overseer of the kitchen at the palace of His Most Gracious Lord the Elector of Trèves. And Maria was never a housemaid. I don't know where you got that information from.'

'She has been married before.'

'Her husband died. He was valet to the Elector. A senior post in the Prince's household.'

'Her family are tradesmen.'

'Father, her family are merchants. She has an uncle who is a court councillor. They are a highly respected family, one of the leading families of Ehrenbreitstein.'

Old Ludwig did not continue the conversation, but his son noticed that he did not at any point expressly forbid the match. Johann's battle to secure Maria as his wife was not over, however.

The Keverich family had been gratified at the speed with which Maria appeared to recover from the double tragedy of losing her child and her husband. At least now she could rebuild her life, regain her strength and morale, before marrying again, say, in five years' time.

It was with profound disquiet that they heard she was showing signs of responding to the attentions of a court musician from Bonn. A family meeting was convened and it was unanimously decided that action needed to be taken. The result was that Johann van Beethoven found himself facing a formidable array of Keverichs, just as he had recently faced his own father.

'You are a singer,' said one with barely disguised contempt, fingering the rich fur collar of his long frock coat, 'a singer. And what income does that yield to you, pray?'

'I have a monthly salary of a hundred florins,' Johann replied in a steady voice, adding, 'and I have been assured by His Most Gracious Lord the Elector himself that my prospects in his service are excellent. I think it is assured, only a matter of time, that I shall one day succeed my father as Kapellmeister.'

'He is Flemish, is he not? He is not a German. Were you born in Germany, Herr van Beethoven?'

'I was, yes. I am German. As German as you are.'

The Keverichs were not impressed, by either Johann's proclamation of his nationality or his optimistic predictions for his career. The hallmark of the family was hard work. They had become one of the foremost families in Ehrenbreitstein by working all hours. When Heinrich Keverich had died, his wife Anna, despite being a member of the Westorff merchant family, did not hesitate to take a position as cook at the court, to supplement the family income. The job of 'singer', they made quite clear to Johann, was not one for a respectable man.

Nevertheless to Johann's relief they said they would not stand in Maria's way, if marriage to Johann was what she really wanted. But there was a condition, though it was not presented as such. It would be helpful, said Herr Westorff, if the marriage were not to take place in Ehrenbreitstein.

Johann congratulated himself on the way events had turned out. When, armed with the Keverichs' albeit reluctant acceptance of his suit, he again confronted his father, the old man said he would not stand in his son's way – 'At least you will be married. Off my hands.' But as with the Keverichs there was a condition, and it dovetailed perfectly with theirs.

'Do not expect me to travel to Ehrenbreitstein,' he told his son with finality. 'The marriage, if it has to take place, will take place here in Bonn.'

*   *   *

Within a month of their marriage, while all Bonn was caught up in Christmas festivities, Johann and his young wife tramped the streets in search of humbler lodgings. They discovered that inexpensive rooms were available in the Bonngasse, at the rear of number 515, the house owned by the lace-dealer Clasen.

The house itself had a moderately imposing frontage on the Bonngasse, but the lodging to let lay through an arch in the main building. Its advantage was that it looked out not on to the street but over a small garden. However, Herr Clasen made it clear that the garden was not for the use of tenants – 'Indeed if I could prevent you from overlooking it, I would,' he had said with ill grace. The rooms were small, with no provision for heating. The newly married couple placed their bed against the single wall the lodgings had in common with the main house, so that they could profit from the small amount of warmth that came through.

In the first weeks of 1768, far from rejoicing in his marriage, Johann van Beethoven was a bitter man. His wife, from the day they had married, had become a sour woman. The levity he so longed for, that he was sure lay beneath the surface, never showed. Maria kept her feelings to herself, but Johann knew she resented the fact that he had taken her away from her family against their wishes. He suspected too that she shared at least part of their misgivings about his profession. And he knew, because she had said as much, that she was hurt and angry that his father had so comprehensively rejected her.

Well, there was another way of looking at it, he told himself angrily. He had been rejected by her family, so he had just as much cause to be resentful. And instead of being hurt by her father-in-law's rejection of her, why didn't she instead feel gratitude towards her husband for the way he had stood up to his father on her behalf? Living as they did in cold and cramped lodgings, their mutual resentment of circumstances prevented any of the joy and warmth one would expect to pass between a newly married couple. At night, the extra warmth they should have enjoyed from each other was sadly absent.

On top of all these problems Johann, for the first time in his life, was truly poor. One hundred florins a month was simply not enough to sustain two people, even in vastly less expensive lodgings than before. And it was certainly not enough to allow Johann to continue his regular visits to the tavern to drink with his old friend, the fish-dealer Klein.

In February 1768, three months after his marriage and without a word to his wife, Johann van Beethoven left home early one morning and took the boat upriver to Ehrenbreitstein. Without announcing himself he entered the house of his mother-in-law. To his dying day Johann never revealed to a soul what transpired in the two hours he spent in the Keverich house alone with the old lady. All anyone knew was that Anna Clara Westorff Keverich suffered a mental breakdown shortly afterwards; Johann van Beethoven came away with certificates in his pockets worth three hundred thalers, representing Frau Keverich's entire savings. And the official report which the Keverich family ordered into the incident stated simply: 'Through an ill-turned marriage of her only daughter, Frau Keverich was relieved of three hundred thalers.'

Those charitable to Johann concluded that the old lady had settled a substantial dowry on her daughter; those less charitable kept their views to themselves. In September of that year Frau Keverich died and any whiff of impropriety on the part of Johann van Beethoven died with her.

By the time of her mother's death, Maria Magdalena van Beethoven was expecting her second child, her first by Johann. The pregnancy brought the couple closer together. Johann's situation had improved. His drinking was not yet causing a problem; he was living within his means and in the new year received a salary increase of twenty-five florins a month from the Elector. As well as his duties at court, he had a number of music pupils, who brought a welcome addition to his income.

On 1 April 1769, Maria gave birth to a boy. The next day he was baptised Ludwig Maria. The infant's godparents were his grandfather Ludwig, for whom he was named, and the wife of the Beethovens' next-door neighbours, from whom he took his second name. Old Ludwig held the baby in his arms at the baptismal service, his normally stern countenance softened as he gazed down at the tiny wrinkled face. Very quietly he hummed as he gently rocked the swaddled figure. His mind was calm, safe in the knowledge that the Beethoven line was secure and that this child would one day cause the world to wonder at his musical genius.

Ludwig Maria van Beethoven lived for six days. Johann remembered how surprised he had been by his wife's calmness when she reported to him that the child was dead in its cot. He had gazed down at the tiny discoloured face. With the corner of his handkerchief he had wiped the flecks of white foam from the silent open mouth. Then the tears had come, quietly at first and then out loud. With a cluck of her tongue Maria had turned on her heel and left the room.

Johann knew his wife had undergone tragedy in her life, but he was unprepared for what he saw as a streak of callousness in her character. How else to explain her attitude of near indifference when she became pregnant again almost a year later?

Gone this time was the rosy flush that had marked her cheeks during her last pregnancy. And her insistence on moving into the small room at the back of the house dumbfounded him. It meant the baby would be born in the coldest room in their lodgings, with two outside walls, one of them sloping, and just one small window which let in as much cold air as light. And the ceiling was so low Johann could not stand upright in the room.

Johann forced himself to remember that this was in fact the third time Maria Magdalena had carried a child. Perhaps her fatalistic attitude this time was a form of defence against yet another tragedy. It was too subtle for him. Why couldn't she at least show some enthusiasm? Behave normally, for God's sake?

When the child was born, though, the parents' attitudes were curiously reversed. Maria seemed to love the infant, cuddling him and talking to him softly. She came close to ignoring Johann, behaving at times almost as if he wasn't there. When Johann approached the child she would turn its face away, throwing a resentful look at her husband.

Perhaps, thought Johann, he had brought her disdain upon himself when he had remarked, within hours of the child's birth, that it certainly had not inherited the fine looks of the Beethovens. For of one fact, he thought to himself, there was no doubt. The child had not a single trace of charm in its crumpled face. He found it difficult to feel affection towards his son, and more and more difficult to feel any love towards his wife.

Immediately the child was born there was a family disagreement. Johann found himself lined up against the curious and unexpected alliance of his father and his wife. The loss of the first child, Ludwig Maria, seemed to have drawn the two of them together. Maybe it was because the infant had carried both their names. Johann did not know; he could not fathom it. But he was determined to stand up for himself.

'The child will be called Ludwig, after you, Father. But there will be no other name.'

'Why no second name? Like his poor dead brother?'

'A single name was good enough for me, and it was good enough for you.'

'Yes, but . . .'

'He will have no second name.'

'Does that mean no second godparent? Why can't he have a second godparent?' asked Maria.

'He will have one godparent. You, Father. And one name. Just Ludwig. Nothing else. Ludwig van Beethoven.'

Chapter 2

'Look what I've got for him,' said old Ludwig, holding the tiny wig proudly for Maria to see.

'You'll spoil him.' Maria clucked her tongue in disgust. 'I'm going to the kitchen. Don't be long.'

Ludwig beckoned to his grandson to stand in front of him and, smiling broadly, he placed the wig carefully on the small head. He pulled the sides down over the ears and sat back.

The child immediately scratched both ears, pushing the wig out of position. 'I don't like it. It scratches.'

Ludwig laughed. 'You're right. But see how smart you look. Look at me in my wig. It's the mark of a gentleman. Now, put this on.'

He held out a small blue tailcoat and the child slipped his arms in the sleeves, looking up into his grandfather's eyes as the old man did up the shiny buttons.

'Now this. The final touch.' With both hands he held out a black velvet tricorn hat and placed it firmly on the child's head.

He looked at the boy, pride suffusing his face. 'Maria. Come. Look at your son.' But he heard her bustling continue in the kitchen. He even thought she banged a pan with a little extra force to act as a reply.

'Ah, my grandson. Ludwig. How proud I am of you.'

Old Ludwig got up from the chair, grimacing as he did so and pressing his hands behind his hips to ease his aching bones. He steadied himself on the chair. The child reached forward instinctively and old Ludwig smiled gratefully.

'These old bones. This old body. Old before their time. At least the voice is still strong. Come, Ludwig. Let's go. Walk with me.'

Ludwig adjusted his wig and put on his own coat and hat, picking up his cane as he walked through the front door with his grandson.

Together they walked down the Bonngasse and into the Marktplatz. Old Ludwig frequently acknowledged acquaintances, bowing his head slightly and saying each time, 'My grandson. Ludwig.'

They stopped before the ornate building at the top of the square.

'The late Elector's palace, Ludwig. Prince Clemens August, God rest his soul. He it was who brought me here to Bonn. From Flanders. That is where the Beethoven family is from. It was 1733. Forty years ago. A lifetime. Come, I'll show you the new palace, where the Elector lives now.'

They walked through the narrow street at the end of the square and as they emerged from the shadow of the old palace, beautifully laid out gardens stretched before them. A high-walled path ran round the top of the gardens to the magnificent new Elector's palace, painted entirely white.

Two straight rows of linden trees just coming into bud lined the path. The scent of spring was in the air. Ludwig took his grandson's hand.

'Beautiful, isn't it, Ludwig? So much beauty.' But he was having difficulty speaking and his breathing had grown heavier. 'Come, let us sit on a bench. I must catch my breath.'

He nodded – more cursorily this time – to more familiar faces as he walked towards the shade of the trees. He noticed that his small grandson was holding his arm with both hands and helping to guide him to the seat.

He sat down heavily and breathed steadily for several minutes without speaking. He pulled a handkerchief from his sleeve and dabbed his forehead.

'Grandpa? Grandpa? Tell me those names again. Talk to me about them.'

Old Ludwig nodded and took off his hat. He lifted the front of his wig and wiped his forehead.

'You're right about these wretched wigs, Ludwig. They're hot and they scratch.'

The boy let out a little cry of joy and took his off. 'There. Come on, Grandpa. Take yours off too.'

Ludwig looked quickly round and his face flashed with mischief. He whipped his hands up and took his wig off. He leaned back and let the cool air wash over his face.

'Ah yes. That feels good. I am better now. I think we walked too far. I just needed to sit down.'

'Bach,' said his grandson. 'It's a stream, isn't it?'

'Yes.' Old Ludwig laughed. 'We used to make fun of our teacher over that. When I was at school. We used to say, "He is a stream and full of flowing water", and we played his preludes as if they were flowing water, all the notes slurred and running into each other. "No no!" he would say. "Not like that. Separate the notes." He got so angry.'

'There were many "streams".'

'Yes. The Bach family. Johann Sebastian. Carl Philipp Emanuel. Johann Christian. Those last two are still alive, one in Hamburg, one in London, I think. Johann Christoph. What a great family. But Johann Sebastian is the greatest. He died a little over twenty years ago.'

'Will I play his music one day?'

Ludwig turned to his grandson. 'You will, my boy, you will. Here, show me your hands.'

The child held out his hands and his grandfather took them. 'See, look what a musician's hands you have. Your fingers' – and he waggled them, making the child smile – 'are a pianist's fingers. Strong and firm, and look at the ends. Square. That's so you can hit the keys firmly. And strong palms.' He turned the child's hands over. 'Yes, look. Wide palms, so you will be able to reach across a whole octave and more. One day. One day. I only wish I could live to see it. My grandson, Ludwig van Beethoven.'

He lapsed into a moment's silence, but the child broke it. 'Show me what you do with your thumb, Grandpa. Go on. Show me, show me. Take it off. Make it come off.'

Old Ludwig smiled. 'Now watch carefully. Very carefully.' He held up both his hands, palms outwards, then quickly folded the thumbs in, covering them with his fingers. 'Watch. Here it goes. My thumb comes off.'

The child squealed with delight as he watched his grandfather perform the trick. He appeared to be pulling his thumb off one hand with the other hand. Together, apart; together, apart.

'Ooh, it hurts so,' he said, pulling a face of mock pain. 'My poor thumb. There it goes. Right off my hand. Oh, the pain!'

'Stop, Grandpa! Stop! Is it all right? Show me it's all right.'

Laughing, Old Ludwig suddenly unfolded his hands and held them up to show each one complete with its thumb.

The two of them laughed together. Kapellmeister Ludwig van Beethoven, the most senior musician in Bonn, sixty-one years of age, but bent with bones that ached and seemed to befit a man of seventy. And his grandson, not quite three years of age, in whom he saw the future, who he knew instinctively would be a musician like himself.

He knew it, but the boy's own parents did not. Ludwig could forgive Maria for not seeing it. What did she know of music? But his own son Johann, a musician himself, should recognise it. He should be talking to his small son about music, singing to him, playing the piano for him, developing the interest that any musician could see was there.

But his son was worthless, old Ludwig knew that. A tenor at court, but only because he, the Kapellmeister, had made it possible. There would be no advancement for him. That was obvious to anyone, to everyone it seemed except Johann himself. But he had a son of his own now and he should be nurturing him, encouraging him. Instead he seemed to take little notice of him.

A wave of depression engulfed old Ludwig. He wished he could see into the future, to know what would become of the Beethoven family. It was obvious now he had been right about his son's marriage. It was loveless, and he blamed Johann as much for it as Maria. He was an indolent, uncaring husband. Maria had obviously realised that very quickly, and realised too that there was little she could do about it.

The tragedy of the lost baby obviously was partly responsible. Old Ludwig had hoped it might bring them closer together, but it did not. He had been sure that with the safe delivery of the second child named Ludwig all would be well. Again it was not.

He thought of his own wife, languishing in a clinic, her life destroyed by alcohol, and he felt a pang of guilt. Maybe he was partly responsible. If he had not bothered with the wine trade . . . Maybe his own son was destined for the same fate.

He looked down at his small grandson's face. In it he saw determination. The future of the family would one day depend on him. God give him strength, he thought.

He smiled at his grandson, dug into his pocket and brought out a bar of marzipan which he knew the child adored. He smiled with pleasure as he saw little Ludwig's face light up.

Then he reached into his other pocket and brought out his clay pipe. He filled it with Turkish tobacco and lit it with a taper which he scratched on the gravel. The pungent exotic cloud enveloped his head and he half closed his eyes, enjoying the relaxation it brought him.

Maria knew she was pregnant again but was glad that with a judicious choice of clothes she was still able to hide it. Johann would be furious, she knew that. Another mouth to feed, with so little money coming into the house. It was not that he earned a poor salary; it could have been adequate, especially with the extra income from teaching, except that he spent a large part of it in the tavern. He would have to know sooner or later. The later the better.

Maria herself had mixed feelings. This was the fourth child she had carried. Only one of the previous three she had given birth to had survived. Ludwig. Strange Ludwig. He only ever seemed to smile when he saw his grandfather. At first she had loved him, been protective towards him particularly when Johann taunted him about his ugliness. But he seemed to give nothing in return.

How many times she had looked deep into his eyes. But she had seen nothing there. The truth was that she could not look deep. There was something unfathomable about his eyes, his face. She would look down at him in her arms and smile and talk to him. He would stare up at her, not lovingly, not questioningly. Defiantly, almost. That was the word. As if he was saying that he did not need that kind of love.

Why, then, did he behave so differently towards his grandfather? She did not know. But as a mother she knew instinctively it was not natural. At first she had tried to fight it. But she came to realise that it was not such a bad thing. The child was, after all, showing affection to someone. If he chose not to show it to her, so be it.

As for the old man, somewhat to her own surprise she had developed a fondness for him. After his overt opposition to the marriage she had decided to have as little to do with him as possible. But as Johann's behaviour became more unreasonable, she and her father-in-law formed an odd alliance. She had been genuinely touched when he instituted the custom of celebrating her birthday. And she had to admit that in predicting the marriage would not be a success, he had not been entirely wrong.

But old Ludwig's health was failing. It was plain to see. Maria feared he did not have long to live. And then what would happen, with Johann the head of the family? She would be living with a husband she did not love and who clearly cared little for her, and a son who would have lost his dearest friend. Perhaps Ludwig would turn instead to her, or less likely to his father. She doubted it.

Now she was pregnant again. She remembered when it had happened. One of the few occasions Johann had not been too drunk to make love to her. He had come at her like an elephant. Perhaps the new child would be different. She forced herself to say the word. *Normal*. And perhaps with a brother or sister Ludwig would become more . . . more normal too. Again – and she felt a twinge of guilt at the thought – she doubted it.

Maria's heart sank when she heard the musicians gingerly tuning up their instruments. She should be grateful, but really there was so little cause for celebration. She rather wished Johann had cancelled it this year, but she knew that would upset old Ludwig.

It had been his idea in the first place, to celebrate her birthday by assembling a small group of court musicians to play for her late on the eve of the day itself, which was 19 December, the feast of St Mary Magdalene.

It had been so joyous in past years. Johann always drank too much, but the atmosphere was jolly and boisterous, with Christmas only a week away and the rooms already decorated with flowers, leaves and laurel. Ludwig, as Kapellmeister, would conduct with due solemnity and the musicians – two violins, a cello and a horn – would play for two hours. Neighbours and friends called in, enjoying the hot wine and cold meats that were laid out, and dancing as best they could in the small room.

Maria smoothed her smock and ran her hands yet again through her hair. At exactly ten o'clock there was a knock on the bedroom door. She opened the door and feigned surprise as Theodor Fischer and his wife threw open their arms and led her to the festivities.

Her entrance was greeted with laughter and applause and she returned the affectionate greetings as best she could. She quickly saw that Johann was already drunk, leaning unsteadily against the food table with a glass of wine in his hand.

Her eyes swept round the small, crowded room and found old Ludwig. She could scarcely contain her shock. He sat in his usual chair, which was high-winged and covered in tapestry wool, and from which in the past he had so often made authoritative pronouncements. It stood slightly away from the wall.

Now he sat deep in it like a sunken shell. It was only two days since she had last seen him, but he seemed to have aged a year. His skin hung below his chin, his cheeks were sunken and his eyes seemed to have retreated into his head. His mouth hung slightly open and he breathed laboriously.

She went quickly over to him and kissed him on the forehead. It was slightly clammy and colder than she expected.

'Good evening, Father-in-law. What a wonderful surprise all this is. You are so kind.'

Old Ludwig managed a slight smile and looked up at her. His eyes were moist.

'Where's my Ludwig? Where's my boy?' he said in a hoarse voice.

'I'll find him. I'll bring him to you.'

Even in such a small room it took her a moment to find Ludwig. He was standing behind the high-winged chair, effectively hidden from the company. He was looking up at the portrait of old Ludwig in his fur turban and velvet robe. Flowers were entwined around its frame.

Maria put her hands on his shoulders but he did not turn to look at her.

'Why doesn't Grandfather look like that any more?'

'Come, Ludwig. He wants to see you.'

Ludwig shook her hands off him. 'Leave me. I will go to him myself.'

Maria smiled sadly. She felt Theodor Fischer take her by the arm. He began to dance. Maria tried to move, grateful that the crush of people did not allow her too much room.

Fischer's wife came quickly over to intercede.

'No, Theodor. Leave her. I don't think . . . I really don't think . . .' She looked knowingly at Maria. 'I am right, my dear. Aren't I?' she said conspiratorially, with an expectant smile on her face.

Maria smiled wanly and gave her head the slightest nod. There was a resigned look on her face.

Frau Fischer clapped her hands insistently until the music stopped.

'Everyone. Listen to me. Good news. Our dear friend, whose birthday and name day we are celebrating tonight, has happy joyous news. She is to have another baby. Let us drink to Maria and Johann.'

Maria looked quickly across at her husband. She registered a fleeting look of horror on his face and saw him reach for a bottle and refill his glass.

After the general congratulations Theodor Fischer said to her, 'I think the rooms on the second floor of our house in the Rheingasse will soon be vacant. Come and live with us there. Johann will be happy. It's the same house he and I grew up in. You will need the space,' he said, laughing.

Maria nodded her head weakly, knowing Johann would accept the offer but wondering how they would find the money.

Five days later, on Christmas Eve, old Ludwig the Kapellmeister died. Johann van Beethoven knew his moment had come. Kapellmeister Johann van Beethoven. How the appointment would transform his life! The senior musician at court, in charge of all musical activities; the final arbiter in making appointments to the orchestra and choir. And think of the status it would give him. Looked up to by all the musicians, his advice constantly sought.

His pupils would see him in a new light, treat him with new respect – if he decided to keep them on.

And his family. He felt a small measure at guilt at so clearly exulting in his father's demise, but really the old man's influence on the family had been too much. His wife Maria, at first so resistant to him, had clearly grown fond of him. As for his son Ludwig . . . At first Johann had hugely resented the way his son had practically ignored him and treated his grandfather as if he was his father. In time, though, he had come to see some benefit in it.

The child was not like other children. There was something remote about him. Johann did not fully understand it and found it difficult to explain. He had tried to talk to Maria about it but she had just shrugged it off. But he was in no doubt: Ludwig was simply not like other children. The Fischer children, for instance. Normal, boisterous, playful children. Why could Ludwig not be like them? Even when he was with his grandfather, which he was most of the time, he was serious. Music. That was all they talked about. Not normal childish subjects. Just music.

*   *   *

Johann was slightly surprised that when he asked Belderbusch how long it would be before his appointment as Kapellmeister was announced, the First Minister advised him to apply to the Elector in writing.

'But is it really necessary? Why should it be necessary?'

'It is the proper way of doing things, Beethoven. Others will have to do the same.'

'Others? What others? There are no others.'

'I strongly advise you to do as I say, Beethoven.'

Johann wrote the petition, rewrote it and rewrote it again. At first he demanded the job, then requested it. Finally he decided the right tone was one of dignified restraint. He was the son of the former Kapellmeister; he had been a court singer for eighteen years; he was a respected teacher. The petition should really be no more than a reminder to the Elector, a hint almost; accompanied, of course, by a certain measure of appropriate flattery.

> Most Reverend Archbishop,
> Most Gracious Elector and Lord, Lord
>   Will Your Electoral Grace be pleased to hear that my father has passed away from this world, to whom it was granted to serve his Electoral Grace Clemens August and Your Electoral Grace and gloriously reigning Lord, Lord for forty-two years, as Kapellmeister with great honour, whose position I have found capable of filling, but nevertheless I would not venture to offer my capacity to Your Electoral Grace . . .

Johann settled back to wait, in the meantime gladly taking up Fischer's invitation to rent the rooms on the second floor of his house on the Rheingasse. A sizeable apartment, befitting his new status as Kapellmeister. The increase in salary that the post of Kapellmeister would bring was very timely, the money he had secretly secured from his late mother-in-law having long since been exhausted.

In April Maria gave birth to a son, Caspar Carl. 'At last, a normal child,' Johann told Klein, his regular drinking companion, in the tavern. 'And he is named after Belderbusch. Clever, eh?'

When Klein told Johann a little later that an Italian musician had been appointed Kapellmeister, Johann refused to believe him.

'You do not understand the workings of the court, Klein. I can assure you the last thing they would do is appoint a foreigner to such a senior position.'

Klein shrugged. 'That's what I heard. From someone who had heard it from Ries. I think that was his name. Or Reiss. No, Ries.'

Johann's stomach turned over. Franz Ries was a senior musician at court, a violinist of many years' service who was universally held in high regard. Klein would not know of him. It meant that there might be some truth in the report.

Johann demanded to see the First Minister and was quickly – surprisingly quickly – given an appointment by the usually protective secretary.

'I . . . I simply do not understand it. My father was . . . he was Kapellmeister. I watched him at work, I saw what his duties were, he discussed them with me. I already know what the duties are. I . . .'

'Beethoven, listen to me,' said Belderbusch with an edge to his voice. 'I am sorry it has not worked out the way you wished. But it has happened. And you must come to terms with it. Signor Lucchesi is the new Kapellmeister.'

'Lucchesi? An Italian? How can that be? He is not even employed at court. He has no experience of court matters.'

'Signor Lucchesi is a highly accomplished musician. You know as well as I do his reputation in the city.' He pulled a piece of paper towards him. 'He has composed nine operas, two of them since he has been here in Bonn. In one of them, as you know, your late father frequently sang. As well as writing for the theatre he has also composed sacred works for the church, cantatas, masses and vespers. Recital pieces too, six sonatas for piano and violin, four piano quartets, as well as several piano concertos. What is more, he is a fine organist. He is, as I said, a highly accomplished and well-respected musician.'

'But what will I do? What will happen to my family? We have a new child . . .'

'Johann,' said Belderbusch with a more kindly tone to his voice, 'you still have your position as court tenor, which provides you with an income. And take on more pupils. I have heard you are a good teacher. That will supplement your income.'

'But they will see me as a failure. If I am not Kapellmeister . . .'

'Nonsense, Johann. If you were Kapellmeister you would

not have time for teaching so you would lose them anyway. No, stress to them how fortunate it is for you – and them – that you can continue to teach them.'

Johann van Beethoven's world had collapsed. All his ambition was gone. Perhaps he should have been able to foresee what would happen. He was a singer. Traditionally singers did not become Kapellmeister. Instrumentalists who composed, better still composers who were instrumentalists . . . Lucchesi, in fact, had the ideal qualifications.

But his father had not been an instrumentalist and he was Kapellmeister. It was all so unfair. Why had Belderbusch not warned him? He had even gone so far as to advise him to apply for the post. He was obviously trying to humiliate him; there could be no other reason.

Johann found his comfort in alcohol. He spent more and more time in the tavern with Klein and various other drinking companions. And Klein it was who, one cold winter evening, made a remark which set Johann thinking.

He ignored the comment at first. In fact the next day he did not even remember it. But it had lodged itself at the back of his mind, where it stayed.

'What about that son of yours? The one who plays the piano. I hear he's pretty good. Make him practise and put him out to work. He could earn you money. Like that Austrian boy. That's what his father did to him. I forget his name.'

'Mozart,' Johann replied.

Chapter 3

Ludwig tossed in bed, sweat coating his face and body. His nightshirt stuck to his skin and felt cold. He shivered uncontrollably and his head throbbed with pain.

The daylight filtered through the thin curtains and Ludwig knew he should get up. But he could not. He knew if he got out of bed the cold air would be too much for him. He doubted his legs would hold him.

He wanted his mother to come to see him. He desperately wanted her to come and mop his forehead and tell him he would be all right.

When finally she came to see him, she sat on the bed, a look almost of anger on her face.

'Why are you ill? You have a fever. Who have you been with? Who do you know who has a fever? You must have caught it from somebody. Well, you'll have to stay here. I can't risk catching it with a new baby in the family.'

Later in the day she brought him a bowl of soup. He smiled at her with gratitude. She put it just inside the door and said, 'I won't come near you. I don't want to catch it. Here's an extra cloth to mop your face with.'

The next morning, after what seemed an interminable night of sleeplessness, he was aware that his skin was sore. Slowly the soreness became more and more painful. Braving the cold air, he took off his nightshirt. His stomach turned as he saw that his body was covered in an angry rash.

His first thought was to hide it from his mother. He knew she would be angry if it turned out he had more than a simple fever. But he could feel his face burning and he knew it was only a matter of time before his mother found out.

Maria gasped when she saw the rash on Ludwig's face. 'Is it on your body as well?'

Ludwig nodded and began pulling up his nightshirt.

'No, no. Don't do that. Leave it. I'll get the doctor. I just hope . . .'

The doctor took very little time to confirm Maria's worst fears. He looked at the rash but avoided touching it. He lifted Ludwig's eyelids and looked closely at his eyes, nodding as he did so. He looked into the boy's mouth, pressing down his tongue with a wooden spatula.

Finally he turned to Maria. 'Smallpox. Keep him isolated. Keep the baby away. And the other child. I'll give you some cream to rub into his body. Use gloves. He'll develop blisters in a few days. Don't scratch them, Ludwig, do you hear? Whatever you do, don't scratch them, or they'll burst and leave scars which will never go.'

Maria and the doctor left the room quickly. Ludwig turned his face to the wall. He felt more wretched than he had ever felt. His mother had given birth again. He had another brother, Nikolaus Johann – Johann, to carry his father's name. He knew what the coming days and weeks would bring. He would be alone. He must fight the disease alone.

His fears were accurate. A knock on the door signalled that a small plate of food, usually soup that was never quite hot enough, was outside. Always with the food was an extra plate with a small amount of cream in it, which Ludwig rubbed gratefully into the parts of his body that hurt most.

The blisters, when they came, were less bad than he expected. He knew they signalled the worst was over. He avoided touching them, but in his sleep he scratched, and he knew that he would bear the scars for life.

He lost count of how long he was in his room alone. He knew only that he did not see his mother for at least a week. When finally she came to see him, she called from behind the closed door to make sure he was in bed, and then she did not come into the room by more than a pace.

At last the disease left him. The doctor confirmed that he was no longer infectious, but clucked and shook his head when he saw the tiny scars on Ludwig's face.

How he longed for his grandfather, but he was not there. If he closed his eyes he could see his grandfather's face, smell the Turkish tobacco. But when he opened them again it all vanished.

He buried his face in the pillow. He realised he had never felt more alone in his life.

*   *   *

Ludwig sat at the piano gazing out of the window and wrinkling his nose at the acrid smell. The night sky was red and the air was filled with the sounds of screaming. He wondered if he could leave the piano and go up to the attic room to get a better view, but the thought that his father would find him frightened him too much.

He did not understand why his father was treating him so mercilessly, particularly since it was only a short time since he had shaken off the smallpox. The disease had left him feeling weak in body and isolated in mind. Isolated from his family. More than the effects of the disease itself, he remembered most being alone.

His father now made him sit at the piano for hours on end, practising scales, chords, arpeggios. Sometimes he dragged him from his bed in the middle of the night and made him practise until dawn.

The worst sin Ludwig could commit was to do what he wanted to do most: play a tune of his own invention and then weave variations around it. His father would not hear of it.

'What is that nonsense you are playing? What are you splashing around at?' he said once. 'One more note like that and I will box your ears.'

Ludwig had tried to talk to his mother about it, to enlist her support. But he had been unable to. A distance had developed between mother and son since Ludwig's smallpox. Ludwig felt as if his mother blamed him for contracting the disease, as if it were yet one more manifestation of his strangeness, his distance from the rest of the family. Whenever he looked at her she would turn a confused and bewildered look on him and it rendered him unable to speak. The result was that she seemed even more bewildered by him and there was no communication between them.

There were more screams outside. In his frustration Ludwig pounded the keys. From the tumult of notes a tune emerged, struggling to make itself heard. But each time it seemed about to take flight, Ludwig stopped it with a welter of trills, like an angry crowd silencing what they know to be a single voice of reason.

Suddenly the door burst open. Ludwig's fingers froze above the keys.

'Quick, Ludwig, come and look. The Elector's palace is on fire!'

It was the two Fischer children, Cäcilie and Hans. Ludwig needed no further encouragement. Together the three ran to the attic room in the high gable at the top of the house. By the side of the little window stood a large telescope.

'I'm the eldest. I'll look first,' said Cäcilie commandingly. She gasped as she put her eye to the glass. 'It's awful . . . the whole building . . . people running everywhere . . . they're passing buckets of water . . .'

'Let me see! let me see!' shrieked her younger brother.

Ludwig felt his breathing become deeper. He knew he would have to look through the telescope, but he did not want to. He did not want to see the dreadful scenes of panic, the destruction, the chaos. It would all be disorder; there would be no control and he did not want to see that.

But most of all he did not want to look because he knew he would see where he used to go with his grandfather. The path lined with linden trees where they walked and sat would be where everyone was running and shouting. It was always so calm and beautiful there, no one ever hurrying or talking loudly, as if they were respectful of the fact that they were within the palace precincts. It would be so dreadfully different now.

Cäcilie almost had to hold him against the telescope. 'Look, Ludwig. Do you see what's happening? Isn't it awful?'

Ludwig started as he saw the scale of the destruction. The wall behind the row of linden trees, the outer wall of the palace, had collapsed. There were piles of bricks and rubble, men carrying buckets clambering over them. Flames were licking out of windows, lighting up the night sky.

'A man's hurt,' he said almost to himself. 'They're carrying him out.'

Ludwig swung the telescope to the left, away from the palace and up.

'What are you doing, Ludwig?' asked Cäcilie. 'Oh, I know, you're looking at that horrid hill again. Well, you can't see it in the dark anyway. And if you don't want to watch the fire, give the telescope back to Hans and me.'

The next day the whole of Bonn, it seemed, was caught up in the great disaster of the fire which destroyed the Electoral palace. Nobody knew how it had started; the most likely cause was a spark thrown out by a fire, setting alight a carpet or curtain. The sumptuous furniture and thick tapestries and curtains which adorned nearly all the rooms gave the flames all the fuel they needed.

There was much mutual congratulation that the speedy action by so many citizens meant a greater disaster had been averted. The building had been quickly evacuated; it seemed no one had been trapped inside. Injuries were small in number; nothing worse than a few twisted ankles among the firefighters.

One man, though, had died. Councillor Joseph von Breuning, head of one of the most prominent families in Bonn. And he had died because he insisted on going into the burning building to save important state documents, not once but three times. He was almost at the palace gate after his third dash into the building, his arms piled high with documents, when a beam crashed down on him. He was already being hailed as a hero.

Ludwig took advantage of the confusion to slip out into the street. He knew his father was at the palace. His mother was fully occupied with the two younger children, Caspar now nearly three and Nikolaus, known as Nikola, just three months.

Ludwig gave the baby scant regard. He noticed immediately that one of its eyes pointed outwards. He thought it made the baby's face look sinister. He knew he would not like this youngest brother any more than he liked Caspar.

Pulling a coat around him he turned right into the Rheingasse and walked down to the river. There he turned right again and walked along the river bank. He barely glanced at the blackened building which stood on raised land with figures swarming over it. Instead his eyes searched the mist upriver.

At first he was frightened by the lights which emerged eerily from the mist. But they were just boats – barges mostly, working their way downriver, helped by the current.

On the opposite banks he saw the twinkling lights of Oberkassel and Königswinter. On he walked, his eyes still searching.

Finally, far ahead, he saw what he was looking for, the great looming shadows of the Siebengebirge, the seven hills which stretched back from the opposite bank into the distance. He could barely see them, just their huge shapes. The light filtering through the mist played tricks with him, allowing him to see the hills that were further away better than those close to the bank.

Strain his eyes and peer as he might, he could not see what he knew was there: the massive pile of rock which was the first of the seven hills and which came right down to the water's edge. The Drachenfels. The Dragon Rock.

He shivered and pulled his coat tighter around him. He turned and quickly, running almost, retraced his steps along the river bank back to the city. The mud of the bank splashed around his shoes, feeling cold as it seeped over the top of his boots and around his feet. Several times he hit a muddy puddle and the water splashed up and stung his face.

He wanted to feel the warmth of home, to hurry to his mother's side, tell her how frightening it was out there and wallow in her comforting words.

He heard his mother's voice before he reached the second floor of the Fischer house. It was shrill and shot through with panic. A baby was screaming too. Just as he entered the door of the apartment, he heard his mother cry, 'I don't know. I've no idea where he is.'

Both mother and father saw Ludwig at the same moment. He stood there like a statue. His clothes were oozing mud and water was dripping off them on to the floor. His hair was sodden and plastered on his forehead. He was breathing heavily from the exertion of climbing the stairs. His eyes were wide open with trepidation.

Ludwig looked quickly at his father and saw the anger there. He turned to his mother, his eyebrows raised in silent supplication.

'Where . . . ? What have you . . . ? We've been worried to death . . .'

She strode the few paces to him, tore his coat off his shoulders and gave him a stinging slap behind his knees. His father leaned down and put his face almost to his son's. Ludwig could smell the stale alcohol as he spoke.

'You useless child. Good-for-nothing, worthless child. Thank the Lord there are two other Beethoven sons. Otherwise God knows what would become of this family.'

Ludwig felt his lower lip begin to quiver and the sting of tears prickle behind his eyes. But he was determined not to cry.

'I'm not worthless,' he said in a small voice.

His father stood back, his hands on his hips. 'No? Well, we'll soon find out. We'll soon know what you're made of.'

Johann van Beethoven had made a decision, a decision which he knew would be crucial to his son's future. Ludwig was just past his seventh birthday. It was time, Johann had decided, to test the boy's musical talent in public.

Johann knew Ludwig was unusually gifted. Musical talent ran in the family; it was not such an extraordinary thing. But how gifted was he really? Could it be possible he was a child prodigy, as gifted as the young Wolfgang Mozart had been?

There were those who thought he might be. Several of the court musicians had heard him play and had spoken to Johann about it. This was a rare talent which he must nurture and encourage, they told him. Franz Ries had urged him to place Ludwig with a qualified music teacher, and even gave him some names.

Johann had considered it. But that was before he learned he would not be Kapellmeister. Now it was out of the question. He did not have the money to pay for lessons. But if Ludwig already possessed enough talent to demonstrate it in public, then it was possible he could start earning money for the family. Much-needed money.

Johann decided to approach a certain Doktor Franz Klaren, manager of a small concert room in the Sternengasse in Cologne. Doktor Klaren was well known and respected in the musical world. He had a sizeable and loyal following in Cologne; music-lovers there attended his recitals whoever was performing or whatever the music was to be. They trusted his judgement. Several of the court musicians from Bonn had performed there, always to an enthusiastic response from a sophisticated audience.

Before he made the short journey to Cologne, Johann told his wife what he had in mind.

'But he is so young. Isn't it too soon to make him play in public?'

'But that's the whole point. Because he's so young, he'll attract attention. That's what Mozart's father did with him. Even took him on tour to other countries. To London, for instance, when he wasn't much older than Ludwig is now.'

'I don't know. I'm not sure he's ready for that sort of thing. You know how . . . how . . . unpredictable he can be.'

'Well, he's going to have to learn not to be. If he's going to be a musician he's got to learn discipline.'

Maria smiled wanly. 'I'm not sure that's an easy task. I've tried talking to him about being more . . . more . . . Oh, I don't know, just not being off in a dream all the time. But he just shrugs it off.'

'Maybe a recital in public will make him concentrate. If Doktor Klaren agrees to let him perform.'

Johann's doubt was not misplaced. Klaren was less than enthusiastic.

'My dear Beethoven, I have of course heard of your son's talent. Word has reached me here in Cologne. But from what I hear he is no Wolfgang Mozart.'

'How do you know that? You have not heard him play.'

'Allow me to point out, Herr Beethoven, that while still a child Mozart already had a number of public performances – not to mention several worthwhile compositions – to his name. Your son – forgive me – has nothing as yet. What age is he?'

Johann was about to answer, but held momentarily back. What had Klein said to him the other day? 'Small your son, isn't he? Looks younger than he is.'

'Six,' said Johann in a firm voice.

'Six? Is he really? I thought he was rather older than that. And he can play pieces by Bach, J.S. and C.P.E., without music, from what I have heard?'

Johann nodded vigorously.

'But I am not sure that at the tender age of six he could sustain a complete recital. No child could.'

Johann thought fast. 'I have an excellent pupil, Herr Doktor. Her name is Averdonck. Helene Averdonck. She has a fine contralto voice, as well as being, how shall I put it, a very attractive young lady. She has sung solo several times at court and received many compliments.'

Klaren smiled. 'I know of Fräulein Averdonck, Herr Beethoven. Her father is an employee of the Electoral Bureau of Accounts. He has spoken to me of his daughter. Also of his son Severin, who composes. They are both, I believe, very promising young musicians.'

Johann smiled, knowing his objective was achieved.

'You shall have your recital, Herr Beethoven. A six-year-old pianist and a beautiful young contralto will, I believe, be enough to sell all the seats. Let me see now . . .' He consulted a large book on his desk. 'This March the twenty-sixth we shall have it. Two weeks from tomorrow. Agreed?'

'Agreed.'

★　　★　　★

'I will not play, Papa. I will not play for them.'

'You will do as I say, my boy. And I say you will play.'

'They will laugh at me. They won't understand what I am trying . . .'

Johann leaned towards his son and changed the tone of his voice.

'You want to be a musician, Ludwig, don't you? Like your father and grandfather. You remember your grandfather, don't you? What a fine musician he was. He would be so proud if he knew you were to play in public.'

Ludwig looked at his father. He knew with a child's instinct that his father was not being sincere. But he also knew that what his father said was true. Old Ludwig would be proud.

'You must let me play what I want.'

'Yes. The Bach prelude you have been playing. And a minuet by Mozart. And a piece by C.P.E. Bach. Three pieces. Perfect. And you must prepare an encore. Another piece by Mozart. To remind the audience you are his successor.'

'No! I will invent a tune at the piano. Something simple. Then I will play variations on it. And . . .'

'No! Ludwig, you must listen to me. Doktor Klaren was very specific. He told me what he wanted. And he will announce the pieces you are to play. There is to be none of your . . . your . . . splashing about. Both Bachs and Mozart. We can add a piece by Helmuth if you wish. There is not much time. You must practise.'

Ludwig was surprised that he did not feel nervous as he stood at the back of the concert hall listening to Helene Averdonck singing her arias. It was not a large hall, but every seat was taken. Ludwig looked at the backs of the heads in front of him. Most of them were tilted slightly one way or another. Some nodded gently with the beat of the music.

They looked faintly ridiculous, Ludwig thought. He wondered if they knew. Like soldiers, all facing in the same direction, looking at the same objective, moving as if to an invisible command. They were clearly appreciating the music, but what did they really know of it? he wondered. To them it was just so many tunes. How could they understand the pain of the artist, what it meant to stand there and make this art, the art of music, intelligible to them?

He looked at poor Helene, singing with her pure, small

voice, her arms held out as if in supplication to the audience, pain etched on her face. Yet she, as the artist, was worth more than all of them. She had a gift, a gift given to so few: the gift of music.

And he had it too. Just a boy, but he knew. His eyes fixed on the piano as he walked to it, that instrument that to so many people was just a box with keys which could be made to sound pleasant, but which to him was like an extension of his hands. And when he placed his hands over the keys and pressed them, the sounds were what he wished his voice to be. Music in place of words. You want me to answer your question? Here is my answer, made with my hands on these keys.

He heard his father's voice, which irritated him.

'. . . my son, Bonn's own Wolfgang Mozart, just six years of age, blessed with the same genius and surely destined to be . . .'

Words. Just words. Words his father had never used to him at home. What use were words? There was no truth in words. Ever. Only in music.

He began the Mozart minuet before his father had finished speaking, which brought a ripple of amusement from the audience and sent Johann scurrying back to his seat on the far aisle.

Such simple music, he thought as he played. That's what the audience will be thinking. A simple piece, written by a child and now played by one. Nothing to it. Just notes, pretty notes. But if that is so, why does Mozart suddenly throw it into the minor key?

He does it to say that life is never simple, never straight-forward. Just when you think it is, that you have mastered life, that nothing can go wrong . . . He struck the minor chord and played it as Mozart wrote it, not *forte* as he had so often heard it played by court musicians, but *pianissimo* as Mozart intended.

He crouched low over the keys. He sensed the audience lean forward with anticipation. They did not know what that single chord meant, as he did, but they knew from the way he had played it that it was portentous. It drew them into the music in a way that played *forte* it would not have done.

Mozart. The master. Living in Vienna. So far from here. One day . . . Maybe one day . . .

The Bach prelude was the perfect contrast. Complex and flowing, like the water of the composer's name. Ludwig played it faster than was usual, revelling in the way the notes interwove with each other, a discord constantly threatened but always, by a hair's breadth, avoided.

He knew he should rise to acknowledge the applause. His father had told him to stand with one hand on the piano and bow deeply. But he did not want to move away from the piano, the instrument that was his voice. He was part of it; if he stood it would break the bond between them.

He began the partita by Helmuth. It annoyed him that his father had made him play this. He knew why. It was noisy, boisterous music which gave the impression of virtuosity. But really it was empty music, like a banal conversation compared with the philosophising of Mozart and Bach.

On a sudden whim he stopped playing. In the middle of a bar, without bringing the phrase to a conclusion, he stopped playing. Oblivious to the audience, not hearing the gasps of surprise and chuckles, he sat with his hands on his thighs, looking at the keys.

'No, not Helmuth,' he said too quietly for any but the front row to hear. 'Mozart. His is the music I want to play.'

Holding his head up and closing his eyes, he began playing the minuet again, only this time he transposed it to the distant key of A flat. He loved the gentle sonority of the black keys, the warmth they had which the white keys did not.

When he came to the first chord he played it as an arpeggio, relishing the sounds of the notes overlapping. He played a new arpeggio in another key. There was now no key signature to the notes he was playing, no regular time. He was playing for himself, not the audience. Many among them were no longer listening and had begun talking quietly while he played.

Although his eyes were half closed Ludwig became aware of movement in the room. He looked up, his reverie broken. His father was walking quickly towards him.

'My son Ludwig's recital will end there, ladies and gentlemen. I am sure you will agree . . . appreciate . . . fine young musician . . .'

Ludwig felt his father grip his arm and dig his fingers in and half carry him from the room.

Word of the recital quickly spread to Bonn and Johann van Beethoven was gratified to hear that the reports were not as bad as he had feared.

The Bach prelude was talked of as a great success, the general opinion being that young Ludwig had played it as well as many an adult musician. If there was any criticism, it was that he had taken a little too much liberty with the tempo and dynamic markings. The same was said of the Mozart minuet. But then, the critics added wisely, from a six-year-old boy one must not expect perfection. In time, with the proper teaching . . .

With the proper teaching. Franz Ries, who was taking an almost fatherly interest in the young musician, broached the matter again with Johann.

'Formal teaching is what he requires, Johann. You really must place him with a teacher. All that fire and spirit. It needs controlling and developing.'

'I can't afford a teacher. You know that, Ries. I have three sons to support.'

'Listen, there is a fine young musician who I know is shortly coming to live here in Bonn. At the moment he is on tour with Seyler's theatrical company. But he is leaving them to join the Grossman company, which will be based here. And he is to be given a position at court as chapel organist, such is his reputation.'

'He will be expensive then.'

'I think not. From what I have heard he is a good teacher, and he particularly enjoys encouraging young musicians.'

'What is his name.'

'Neefe. Gottlob Neefe.'

'What do you think of Pfeiffer, the tenor singer? He is also an oboist. He has been recommended to me.'

Ries smiled weakly. 'From what I hear he spends more time in the tavern than the music room. But I do not wish to be critical of a man I do not know.'

'I will speak to him.'

'Johann. Another question. Forgive my intrusiveness. But should young Ludwig not start attending school soon? Other children of his age are already being taught elementary studies. Ludwig's musical prowess should not lead you to neglect his general education. Do forgive my boldness in saying so.'

Chapter 4

Ludwig could find no outlet for his misery. Tobias Pfeiffer was an unsympathetic teacher. His technique was to select a piece of music for the piano and make Ludwig learn it, note perfect, so that he could play it without music.

'Remember,' he said, 'you have to impress your audience. That is how you will advance.'

Ludwig wanted to argue with him, to tell him that it was not impressing the audience that mattered, but understanding the music. He wanted Pfeiffer to take him behind the notes, talk to him of the composers and what they were trying to say, why they had chosen to write in a particular way.

But Pfeiffer, clumping up and down the room in the heavy boots that were the latest fashion, was only interested in accurate playing.

'Repeat that passage. Again. Now without the music.'

There was no escape for Ludwig, because Pfeiffer had rented a room in the building next door to the Fischer house, and he and Johann van Beethoven had developed a close relationship. More and more they spent the evenings together at the tavern.

Often, when Johann dragged Ludwig from his bed and forced him to play the piano, Pfeiffer was his willing accomplice. Worst of all, both men forbade Ludwig to play music other than that which Pfeiffer had specifically ordered him to learn. And ask as he might, the music of Mozart was banned.

'They call it revolutionary,' Pfeiffer said with contempt. 'I call it claptrap.'

The misery Ludwig felt at home was compounded by the institution know as the Tirocinium, the lower grade school run by the dictatorial Doktor Krengel. The dark, dank building was like a prison, and each time he entered it Ludwig felt a wave of panic sweep over him.

Reading, writing, Latin and arithmetic. Try as he might he could master none of them. Always he tried to sit at the back of the class where he would not be noticed; always Doktor Krengel moved him to the front to make an example of him. Very quickly his fellow pupils recognised as a target this awkward boy who seemed to lack all intelligence and whose dark face bore the marks of smallpox, and they joined forces to taunt him.

'Spaniard-with-the-pox-face. Spaniard-with-the-pox-face. Can't read. Can't write,' they chanted at him in the mid-morning break, pushing him as they encircled him.

Krengel knew Ludwig was being made a victim, but did nothing to stop it. In his stern Germanic way he thought some good might come out of it. He knew Ludwig's head was wrapped constantly in thoughts of music; he believed – at least in Ludwig's early days at the school – that his fellow pupils' taunts might have some beneficial effect, might make him concentrate more on his work.

What worried Krengel most was Ludwig's writing. His ineptitude at Latin and arithmetic could be dealt with in time, but he ought to be able to write legibly at the age of nearly eight. Ludwig's writing, compared with the other boys', was an illegible scrawl and Krengel did not know what to do about it.

His solution was to make Ludwig write with chalk on the blackboard, providing the class with much amusement. That might shock him into a greater effort.

Ludwig desperately wanted a friend at the school, someone he could turn to. He found him in Ferdinand Würzer, whose father ran a meat stall in the Marktplatz. His humble origins put him apart from the other boys and he turned to Ludwig.

'Why do they call you a Spaniard, Ludwig? Is that where your family is from? Is that why you have a "van" in front of your name and not a "von"?'

Ludwig could not help a smile crossing his face. There was no malice in Ferdinand Würzer's question.

'My grandfather came from Flanders. They call me a . . . a . . . Spaniard because my skin is darker than theirs. I don't know why it is.' He shrugged his shoulders.

'Do you mind them calling you that?'

'I'm different to them. Like I'm different to my brothers. Maybe I'll always be called something. I don't know. I don't care.' He shrugged again.

'Is it true you are a musician, Ludwig?' Ferdinand asked one morning in between classes.

Ludwig nodded.

'Will you let me hear you play?'

'One day.'

'Will you let me be your friend?'

Ludwig nodded, but did not know what to say.

One of the older boys, surrounded by several younger acolytes, pushed Würzer out of the way.

'Beet garden. That's what your name means, doesn't it?'

There was a roar of laughter from the other boys.

'I know, because my father has a Flemish friend and he told me. It's true, isn't it? That means you must have been born in a beet yard.'

There was more laughter.

'Is your mother dead?' another boy asked.

'Yes,' several said. 'Is she dead? Beet garden's mother's dead. Beet garden's mother's dead,' they chanted.

Ludwig felt the tears rising, but he clenched his fists to hold them in.

'Why do you ask that?' It was Würzer's voice from behind the boys.

'What's it to you?' one said.

'Look how untidy he is,' said another. 'Jacket all creased and dirty. Buttons missing. Boots with only one lace. His mother must be dead. She'd never send him to school like that otherwise.'

This time Ludwig could not hold the tears back.

'Mama, why are my clothes dirty?'

Maria gave an exasperated sigh. 'Ludwig, I have two other sons. Look at my stomach. There is another coming. God knows how I will cope. Anyway I did clean your clothes. But you don't look after them. I can't keep doing it.'

'The boys at school said you were dead.'

Maria's head whipped round. There was a look of profound sorrow on her face. 'Sometimes, Ludwig, I think it would be better if I were. Now go and find your brothers. Play with them in the sandpit down by the river. Go on. I have work to do.'

'I don't want to. I want to be alone.'

*   *   *

In time Ludwig's tormentors tired of their sport and found other, fresh targets. Doktor Krengel too realised that his martinet approach was having little effect. He decided Ludwig's inability to learn was not due to any wilful obstinacy on his part; he simply was not capable of assimilating what he was taught. Krengel began to wonder whether he shouldn't speak to the boy's father about it.

Matters came to a head when Ludwig began appearing late for classes. Only once a week, and then not every week. In fact it was some time before Krengel noticed. And even then he was disinclined to do anything about it, since it was accompanied by an obvious improvement in Ludwig's demeanour. He decided to monitor the situation.

Ludwig had discovered the organ at the Münsterkirche, and he owed it to his friend Ferdinand Würzer. The chief organist at the church, Gustav Zenser, was a friend of the Würzer family, and Ferdinand offered to take Ludwig to meet him.

Zenser was a tall, thin man with a haughty demeanour, at first impatient to have his time taken up with two boys.

'I am delighted to make your acquaintances, young gentlemen, but I do not have time right now to let you hear the great organ. I have vespers to prepare for. Come tomorrow morning, after Mass. I will be giving my organ pupil a lesson then, and you can hear him play.'

The next morning the two boys sat patiently in the front pew while Zenser took his student through a Bach toccata. One passage was causing the student a particular problem, a run of semiquavers over an offbeat sequence of quavers in the bass.

Ludwig soon became oblivious to his surroundings. His eyes were fixed on the organ and he leaned forward with concentration. The fumbling of the student and the frequent wrong notes were upsetting him, and he wished Zenser would let him sit there instead.

Finally he could contain himself no longer. He did not see Würzer's hand stretch out to restrain him. With determined tread he walked up the three steps to the organ platform.

'Young man, return to your seat. I am giving Theissen a lesson and I do not wish to be interrupted.'

'Sir. Permit me. I can play that passage. Please will you let me?'

Zenser smiled. 'I admire your confidence. Now return to the pew or I shall ask you to leave.'

'It is the timing. Count eight to the bar instead of four and the bass section becomes easy.'

'Show us then,' said Theissen. 'If you permit, sir. It will give me confidence to hear someone play it worse than me.'

He moved aside and Ludwig sat at the organ. He played the piece from the beginning, accomplishing the difficult passage with such speed and ease that at first neither man realised he had heard it.

Ludwig played on, grateful that Theissen was now turning the pages for him. After several minutes of faultless playing he brought the piece to an end and sat silent, looking down at his hands which rested on his thighs.

'Remarkable, Beethoven. Remarkable,' said Zenser. 'How long have you been playing that toccata?'

'I have not played it before. I was sight-reading.'

At Ludwig's request Zenser allowed him to play the organ at six o'clock Mass. After that he played once a week, though not every week. It was on those mornings that he arrived late at the Tirocinium. It was not long before Krengel discovered the reason for Ludwig's late arrival – and his less surly demeanour.

He allowed it to continue for a period of time, then after giving it considerable thought he decided to speak to Ludwig's father.

'It is my recommendation, Herr Beethoven, that you remove your son from my school. His talents clearly lie in another direction, and I think it is one that you should foster.'

'How?'

'It really is not for me to say. Music is not my area. But certainly he should have, in my view, a proper teacher. You should nurture his talent. I have spoken to Zenser at the Münsterkirche and apparently your son really is possessed of remarkable talent. I can only say that he does not display it at school.'

Johann thought hard about Krengel's advice. The point was not lost on him that it dovetailed with what Ries had said. Could it be that with the proper tuition Ludwig really could soon start performing and earning money for the family?

The recital in Cologne may not have gone precisely to plan, but it had hardly been a failure. Klaren had sold every seat and made a profit, and had passed on a modest amount to Johann.

Several people who were there had told Johann that he ought to foster his son's musical career.

There was another development which accorded with the advice Johann was receiving. Tobias Pfeiffer, who although a good drinking companion was clearly not furthering Ludwig's musical education, had suddenly left Bonn to become conductor of the Bavarian military band in Düsseldorf.

Maybe Johann should see this man Ries had recommended, Gottlob Neefe.

But first Johann decided he needed to know what the people who really mattered thought of Ludwig's prowess. The men who were patrons of the arts and who spent large amounts of their considerable wealth commissioning pieces of music. Could they be persuaded to take an interest – a financial interest – in Ludwig?

Ludwig knew his father was surprised when he readily agreed to accompany him on a tour of a number of towns on both banks of the Rhine, particularly since Johann made it clear he wanted Ludwig to play the piano for certain very important personages.

But for Ludwig it meant release from the pressures of school and home. There would be no standing in front of his fellow pupils, giving them sport at his inability to write legibly on the blackboard, and no Doktor Krengel driving him mercilessly.

Even more attractive from Ludwig's point of view, he would be away from home, even if it meant being with his father. As he grew older he spent as much time out of the house as he could. What was there for him there? It had begun when he contracted smallpox. Shut away by his mother, his brothers kept from him, even the doctor saying there was nothing he could do and that the disease must take its course. His isolation was complete.

He recognised from a very early age that he was a being apart. In the simplest terms, no boy of his age in the whole of Bonn could play the piano as he did. That gift alone might have brought admiration. Instead, given his other failings, it brought only loneliness.

Ludwig did not get on with his brothers Caspar and Nikola. Even they had teased him about his pockmarked face, Caspar with his ridiculous red hair and pink skin and Nikola with the one eye that always looked out to the side. He did not tease them back. He just walked away from them. He found them shallow, their greatest joy being to play in the sandpit by the river. The two younger boys clearly enjoyed each other's company, with the result that they were always together and Ludwig was alone.

The arrival of the new baby, Franz Georg, had not helped matters. Maria, Caspar and Nikola clustered round the crib, talking infantile nonsense to the baby. There was no place there for Ludwig, and it did not sadden him.

When the family was involved in that way, Ludwig would pull a coat over his shoulders, put his thick boots on and leave the house. For hours he would walk, content to be alone. Sometimes he went just along the banks of the Rhine. More often, if he had a few coins in his pocket, he walked upriver until he was opposite the little town of Königswinter and the great heap of rock that was the Drachenfels and took the ferry across.

He walked always around the base of the Drachenfels and strode off into the foothills of the Siebengebirge. What glorious countryside lay so close to Bonn, and how little its residents knew of it! There in the open spaces, Bonn just a cluster of roofs and spires below in the distance, he could breathe freely.

How he wished he knew more about the countryside. Instead of the dreadful Doktor Krengel trying to teach him Latin, why did he not instead teach him about nature? On his walks Ludwig found he could look at a single tree for an hour and not tire of it. And while he examined its bark and leaves, birds in its upper branches sang to him.

He listened to birdsong on his walks in the Siebengebirge foothills. It was not just there in the background as it might have been for anyone else. He really listened to it. Sometimes he pulled a scrap of paper from his pocket and tried to re-create the birdsong in notes. But he found he could not. He smiled at his amateurish attempts to do what the bird could do effortlessly.

He listened to the sounds of the countryside. The running of a stream, the rustle of wind through leaves, the croak of a frog, even sometimes in the distance the harsh bark of a deer. And always the singing of birds, whatever the time of day, whatever the season of the year. The constant harmony of the countryside.

The little carriage Johann had hired took them west from Bonn through the gentle green hills. To begin with Ludwig was ill at ease with his father; he had never known how to talk to him. Even now there was a certain distance to him, as if he too did not know how to communicate with his son.

But for the first time that Ludwig could remember, his father listened when he spoke to him and responded with interest. If Ludwig pointed out a clump of trees, or cattle in a field, Johann was enthusiastic and asked Ludwig questions. If Ludwig wanted to show his father a particular tree or plant, Johann unhesitatingly ordered the carriage to stop. Though he never said so, it was clear that Johann too was enjoying the freedom of being away from the Rheingasse and the demands of family.

Possibly for the first time in his life Ludwig felt pride in his father as they called on the nobility and civic dignitaries first in the little town of Rheinbach, then a few kilometres south-east in the larger town of Ahrweiler. There they were received with some pomp by the mayor himself, Bürgermeister Schopp.

Across the Rhine father and son visited the towns of Hennef, Bensberg and Oberkassel. In the latter Johann introduced his son to Rudolf von Meinertzhagen, the wealthy head of a large estate. This well-known music lover promised – 'one day' – to commission a composition from Ludwig, 'when you have undergone some training in composition, of course'. 'Of course,' replied Johann, who later bemoaned to his son the fact that no one ever earned a living on promises.

On to Siegburg, the beautiful walled town on the banks of the Sieg, a tributary of the Rhine. Here for the first time on the trip Ludwig had cause for concern. Johann renewed a friendship with an old acquaintance in the tavern by the river bank.

'Father, we must be at the abbey by six. That's right, isn't it?'

Johann nodded. 'Two hours from now. I'll be here. Take a walk. I want to talk to an old friend of mine. Haven't seen him for years.'

Ludwig felt the familiar dread sweep over him. Could this be where the trip would come to an abrupt end? In humiliation and failure? He wanted to tell his father not to drink, not to spoil what lay ahead. The abbey in Siegburg had the finest organ in the region. Johann had written to the Prelate and secured his permission for Ludwig to play on it.

If he returned to the tavern and found his father drunk, that would be the end. There would be no playing on the abbey organ. The trip would be over and word would quickly spread about what had happened.

He walked along the banks of the Rhine – so different out here in the country to Bonn; so much gentler, greener, more sloping, and the river itself less grey, less menacing – trying to concentrate on the sights and sounds of nature. But he could not rid his mind of the image of his father drunk again.

With a pounding heart Ludwig returned to the tavern. He heard his father's raucous laugh before he even entered the room.

'Ah, Ludwig! My boy.' Johann turned to his companion and clapped him on the shoulder. 'We have an appointment. Here. Finish my beer. No more for me.'

Together they climbed the hill to the abbey, Ludwig exultant in the knowledge that his father was sober and that at the top of the hill, in the austere grey building, sat an organ more sophisticated and more tuneful than any he had played on.

The Prelate was a rotund and jovial man. 'Your reputation, young man, has reached us. It will be a pleasure to hear you demonstrate what you are capable of on our instrument here.'

Ludwig smiled and sat at the huge organ, with its two keyboards, stops on either side and an array of pedals below. Before playing he glanced round at the front pew, where the Prelate sat with Johann next to him.

Johann's arms were folded in front of him and he was looking straight at his son, a look of pride suffusing his face.

Ludwig played that day for his father, as he had never done before. He played to make his father proud of him, and afterwards Johann put his arm round his son as he shook the Prelate's hand. There were tears in his eyes, and he just nodded his thanks.

'Your son is a fine musician, Herr Beethoven. I wish him every success in life.'

Ludwig felt a real twinge of sadness when his father announced that the small town of Flammersheim near the river Wied would be their last stop. 'But it will be our most important. We are to be received by no less a personage than His Excellency the Chamberlain of the District of Utrecht.' Ludwig felt a feeling of fear sweep over him as they disembarked from the carriage at the entrance to the Chamberlain's castle.

In an anteroom Ludwig watched as his father adjusted his wig and straightened the knot of his cravat. Anyone seeing father and son standing there, side by side, could not fail to be struck by the physical similarity between them. The son may not have resembled his father in his first years, but he had now developed a considerable likeness to him. Both were short and stocky, with large head and heavy-jowled face, a wide expanse of forehead and prominent eyebrows.

Ludwig looked up at his father and registered the older man's nervousness. Instead of the nervousness communicating itself to the boy, Ludwig felt instead that he possessed the means to help his father overcome it. He had the talent which everyone wanted to see. He would use it on behalf of his father, both to make his father proud and to express his gratitude in the only way he knew how for the marvellous trip Johann had given him.

And so Ludwig played for Baron Friedrich Wilhelm of Dalwigk, Chamberlain of Utrecht. And he, as much as his father, was saddened and hurt when the Baron sent them away with nothing firmer than fine words.

As the carriage left the castle and turned on to the road for Bonn, Johann had looked at his son, his eyes moist with emotion. 'You are a good son, Ludwig. You have done your best. Now we must see what more we can do.' He put his arm round Ludwig's shoulder. Ludwig looked up at his father. He wondered if he would ever enjoy such closeness to him again.

Johann kept his promise by sending Ludwig with his mother to Rotterdam to stay with family friends who arranged for him to play before influential audiences; but this trip, like the tour of Rhineland towns, yielded nothing but promises and paltry gifts. No one, it seemed, was prepared to make a financial commitment to the young musician.

Johann was in a quandary. He needed to make a decision about his eldest son's future. He discussed it with Maria, whose opinion was that Ludwig should stay at school.

'What if he's not good enough – never good enough – to earn a living as a musician? He won't have been properly educated, and he'll suffer from it.'

He discussed it, naturally, with Klein the fish-dealer in the tavern – over many evenings and copious quantities of cheap wine.

'It's simple,' said Klein. 'The boy's got talent. Put him out to work.'

'But what if no one'll employ him?'

'Train him until he's good enough. Then they'll employ him.'

'How can I afford a teacher?'

'Sell something.'

Ludwig looked at his father, his fists gripped at his sides and tears stinging his eyes.

'Where is it? You've taken it, haven't you? Tell me! Tell me!'

'Don't you shout at me. It's for your own good anyway. I did it for you.'

'What do you mean? I don't want anything. I want you to get it back.'

Ludwig turned and looked at the wall above the high-winged armchair. The pale rectangle where the portrait of his grandfather had hung – the portrait he had known for as long as he could remember – threw the rest of the wall into dirty relief.

'You've sold it, haven't you? Haven't you? How could you do that?' Ludwig began to sob.

'Now you listen to me,' said Johann in a harsh voice, and he seized Ludwig by the shoulders and pushed him into old Ludwig's chair. 'If it wasn't for you I wouldn't have had to do anything. But I needed money. For you. I'm taking you out of school and getting you a teacher . . .'

'I don't want a teacher.'

'Then you can give up trying to be a musician. You're not good enough yet, you know that. Fine words. That's all you've earned. Once I thought maybe, just maybe, you have genius. Now I know it's not true. You're no Mozart. But I'm still prepared to do what I can. So now you've got this . . . this . . . Neefe man to teach you. And I expect results. Do you hear me?'

Ludwig looked his father in the eyes. 'Why? So you don't have to work any more? So you can spend more time in the tavern?'

'Don't you dare talk to me like that, you impudent . . . you . . . you . . .'

Johann drew his hand back to strike Ludwig, but at that moment Maria came running into the room.

'Stop it, Johann! Stop it! Enough. Leave the child alone.'

'Bah!' Johann exclaimed. 'Women. Children. You're all

useless. I'm the only one in this household worth anything,' and he strode out of the room. Both listened for his heavy tread on the stairs and the slamming of the door which gave out on to the Rheingasse.

'Your father is not an easy man, Ludwig. But he means well. And he hasn't sold the picture. Just pawned it. He'll get it back one day.'

Ludwig looked at his mother. How he wished she would put her arm around him. Instead she clenched her lips and moved her head slightly from side to side, as if out of pity for her son.

Ludwig stayed in his grandfather's chair after his mother had left the room. He shifted his body so he sat back in the chair. His legs stood out beyond the seat. His arms rested on the arms of the chair, which were higher than in a normal chair. His head did not come as much as halfway up the back.

He closed his eyes and felt the bulk of the chair surround him. He thought of his grandfather, how often he had seen him sitting here; how often he had sat on his lap and heard him talk of music.

In his mind's eye he saw his grandfather's face and smelled the Turkish tobacco which always surrounded him. He heard his voice talking to him, gently and insistently. He heard the names again. Bach. Handel. Mozart.

And it was his grandfather's voice which he heard saying, '. . . I'm taking you out of school. You'll have a teacher. And with his help you'll become a fine musician. Like me. Another Ludwig van Beethoven.'

Chapter 5

'The boy must go to Vienna.'

'The boy is a fool and an imbecile and I will have none of it.'

'The boy, Herr Beethoven, must go to Vienna.'

Johann van Beethoven looked at the young man he had engaged as his son's music teacher. He did not like Gottlob Neefe, with his smug Protestant ways; and from what he had heard, Neefe was a little more involved in political activities than was good for him. Johann would have to keep an eye on him. But at least he clearly had Ludwig's interests at heart, even if he was letting his enthusiasm run away with him.

Johann decided he needed to exert his authority. He stood up for dramatic effect and walked to the window. He looked down at the Rheingasse, where figures hurried to or from the river which ran along the bottom of it.

'This is a fine apartment, is it not, Neefe? I rent the whole floor. Fischer gives me a special rate because I have known him so long. Grew up with him, in fact. But it is still expensive. I have no choice. I am a senior court musician and I often give lessons here. And I have a young family to support. Four sons, as you know. Life is expensive.'

He sat down at the table again and leaned across to Neefe.

'Let me be candid with you, young man. I simply do not have the money to send Ludwig to Vienna. I cannot afford it. And anyway, if you want my opinion, it would be money thrown away. I told you what happened in Rotterdam. A waste of money. I dread to think what it cost me. And what did he bring back to show for it? A Meerschaum pipe and a snuff box. I expected him to earn money. But what did they give him? Gifts. And useless ones at that. A pipe and a snuff box for a boy. The Dutch. Idiots, all of them.'

'Vienna is different, Herr Beethoven. There they appreciate

music and understand it. They live and breathe it. And a certain Wolfgang Mozart is now making his mark there.'

'Mozart. I thought he was in ... Where was it? ... Salzburg?'

'He was. But he resigned from the court. Apparently he had a furious row with the Archbishop. Now he is living in Vienna and making a name for himself. It is not surprising, Herr Beethoven. He is in my opinion the most talented musician in Europe. And I want your son to meet him.'

Johann waved his hand dismissively in the air. 'My son is no Mozart, Neefe. I am a musician too. Do not forget that. I can recognise talent. Ludwig has talent. But he is no Mozart.'

'Herr Beethoven, I will choose my words carefully. Please do not dismiss what I say. Mozart has more than talent. He has genius. He is a genius. Of that there is no question. It is my opinion that your son Ludwig is touched with genius too.'

Johann shook his head and there was a note of sadness in his voice. 'No, Neefe. I thought so once too. But it is not so. Talent yes, but not genius. The question is whether the talent is enough for him to make a living. Earn money. Contribute ...'

'Sir, he is just a boy,' said Neefe with indignation in his voice. 'You must not expect ... He is still learning ... You must allow him to develop his ... his ... genius.'

'Neefe, I will be blunt. If I offend you I apologise. But what is your training? Your musical training? You have said it yourself. You have never had a complete course in composition. The pieces you have composed, what are they? They are pretty. But they will not endure. What are you? An organist by day; a theatre musician by night. So do not talk to me of geniuses, Herr Neefe. You are not one; I am not one. No one here is one!'

'Tell me, Herr Beethoven,' said Neefe gently, 'do you ever talk to Ludwig? I mean, really talk to him?'

A look of sadness passed over Johann's face, as he momentarily pursed his lips. He spoke in slower, more measured tones. 'No, I do not talk to him. I have tried. From the earliest days. But I cannot talk to him. He ... he never responds. Even about music. I once said to him – he was about five or six years old – "You make nice music on the piano." He looked at me with a look so full of anger ... "Nice music, nice music" ... he spat the words back to me. "What do you know of music? You are ignorant, stupid." He used those words to me, his own father. So what is the point, Neefe? What is the point?'

'The point, Herr van Beethoven, is that music is Ludwig's language. I talk to him because I am his teacher, but his words are awkward. Yet I watch him play the piano and I marvel. For when he plays, he is speaking to me, in the one language he truly understands.'

Neefe leaned forward and clasped his hands with enthusiasm. 'Herr Beethoven, I have a suggestion. Will you allow me to speak to First Minister Belderbusch? He has the Elector's ear. He may not be a man I particularly admire, given the rod of iron he rules this city with, but he is close to the Elector. None closer. And the Elector is a great patron of the arts. Music he loves above all. I know he admires Mozart. He might even agree to—'

Johann brought his fist down on the table. 'Enough! I have heard enough. You will not speak to Belderbusch, and I will not have His Excellency the Elector brought into this. No, Neefe. You continue teaching my son. Develop his talent. One day it will have to earn him his living. God knows he has no other talent. And let me hear no more talk of geniuses.'

Ludwig shuffled in the seat of the carriage, trying to get comfortable in the stiff, formal clothes he was wearing. The jacket was tight across his chest and the woollen trousers irritated the backs of his legs. He was only grateful that he had persuaded Neefe not to make him wear a wig.

He looked across at his teacher. How nervous he looked, staring out of the window with his fist clenched under his chin. A grown man. Yet I, he thought, am a mere boy not yet thirteen years of age. We are going to see the Elector and his First Minister. What is so special about them? Are they musicians? Artists?

Ludwig knew his teacher had worked hard to secure this audience at the palace, not least because of the opposition of his father. His father. Ludwig grimaced at the thought of Johann and his nose wrinkled as he recalled the stale smell of alcohol, the stale rancid smell that he would for ever associate with him.

A shadow crossed the interior of the carriage as it passed under the arch and into the driveway leading to the Electoral palace, now rebuilt and gleaming white after the dreadful fire.

Ludwig looked at his teacher again and found that Neefe was looking at him, apprehension on his face.

'Are you nervous?' Neefe asked.

Ludwig shook his head and shrugged his shoulders slightly.

'If you are going to become a musician, you will constantly be performing before an audience. You'll soon learn not to have nerves.'

Ludwig said, 'I'm not nervous.'

'Put your hands like this,' Neefe said, spreading his hands out on his thighs. 'Work your fingers. Like this. It'll keep them supple.'

Ludwig smiled, thinking how silly the two of them looked, sitting in the carriage playing imaginary piano keys on their thighs.

He knew he should feel nervous as the courtier, eyes down-cast in deference, swung open the ornately carved wooden doors and stepped to one side to allow Ludwig and Neefe in.

Ludwig's eyes swept round the room. It was the biggest he had ever stood in, and certainly the most sumptuously appointed. Twelve tapestries from the Gobelins factory in Paris hung round the four walls, each one depicting a hunting scene in a different month of the year. At one end of the room was a suite of furniture, covered in gold cloth, at the other a large desk with a high-backed chair behind it. In front of the desk and slightly to one side stood two smaller chairs.

Ludwig followed Neefe to these two chairs and they sat. Neefe shot his pupil a look of encouragement. They were alone in the room. Ludwig, instead of sitting calmly in respectful anticipation, swivelled round in his chair, his eyes scanning the room.

'What are you doing?' Neefe asked him in an urgent whisper. 'Sit still. They'll be coming in at any moment.'

'Where's the piano? There's no piano.'

As he spoke, smaller double doors along a side wall opened and two courtiers, without looking up, pushed a small, elaborately decorated piano into the room. They angled it so the keyboard was visible from the desk. Before leaving, one placed a chair in front of it and raised the keyboard cover.

Ludwig breathed deeply and visibly relaxed. There was a piano in the room. He now felt the equal of any man, no matter how exalted.

He heard footsteps behind him and two men walked past him to the other side of the desk. One, small and slightly built, immediately sat. He had an encrusted silver cross around his neck.

The other stood at the seated man's shoulder and slightly behind him. He was tall and portly, his wig very slightly askew.

Neefe motioned to Ludwig to stand and as they did so the second man announced, 'His Most Gracious Lord the Elector of Cologne and Most Reverend Archbishop of Cologne and Münster.'

Ludwig watched Neefe and imitated his slight incline of the head before, like him, sitting down again.

He looked at the two men confronting him, the two highest personages in the land. Instinctively he crossed his arms and hooked one leg behind the other, looking straight at them and waiting for one of them to speak.

Belderbusch spoke first.

'His Most Gracious Lord grants you fifteen minutes of his very precious time. After that he must return to affairs of state. And I with him. Now, Neefe. What is it you have to say?'

'I shall then come straight to the point. My Lord, Your Excellency, you have both, I know, heard my pupil Ludwig van Beethoven play the organ. I allowed him to stand in for me at Christmas Eve Mass. If I may say so, I have considerable experience of young musicians, having taught music in my home town of Chemnitz. I have never come across one as remarkable as young Ludwig here. He is, I believe, touched with genius.'

'Quite a word to use of one so young,' said the Elector. 'You must not let this go to your head, young man,' he added looking directly at Ludwig.

Ludwig spoke in a clear, firm voice. 'Sir, I have a gift that people say comes from God. I believe that to be true.'

'Well now, let us hope your confidence in yourself is not misplaced. Otherwise you will be sorely disappointed.'

'Sire,' said Neefe, 'Ludwig does not wish to sound arrogant. I can confirm that he does indeed have a remarkable talent, and you shall shortly hear it for yourself.'

'What is it you want, Neefe?' asked Belderbusch with irritation in his voice. 'We do not have much time.'

'Sire. Your Excellency. It is my urgent desire that Ludwig be allowed to travel to Vienna to meet the foremost composer of the age, Herr Wolfgang Mozart. I believe that such . . .'

The Elector smiled wryly. 'But, Neefe, how old is your pupil? Surely he is too young to undertake such a journey. What does his father say?'

'Sire, I believe that if his father were to be told it was your desire that he go . . .'

Belderbusch leaned forward and put his clenched fists on the desk. 'There is more to your request, is there not, Neefe? It is all to do with your wretched little band of subversives, the so-called Illuminati. Mozart is the same, only in Vienna it is called Freemasonry. Traitorous rot, I call it.'

'Anton, calm yourself,' said the Elector soothingly. 'Do you take my point, Neefe? Is he not too young?'

'I believe not, sire. At his age Mozart was already well travelled . . .'

'With his father.'

'But, sire, if he were given a room in the palace alongside His Imperial Highness the Archduke—'

'What has His Imperial Highness the Archduke got to do with it?' These was just a touch of irony in the way the Elector pronounced the words 'His Imperial Highness'. It was not lost on Neefe.

Neefe cleared his throat. 'Your chosen successor, sire, when the dreadful day comes that you . . . The Archduke Maximilian Franz, younger brother of his Imperial Highness the Emperor. A member of the illustrious family of Habsburg. An Austrian.'

Ludwig did not follow what his teacher was talking about and wondered why he seemed to have stopped talking of music. But he saw Belderbusch shoot an unmistakable look of warning at Neefe.

'Why do you choose to tell me what I already know, Neefe?' asked the Elector.

'Sire, forgive my presumptuousness. It is only to point out that whereas you are descended from the great German family of Königseck-Rothenfels, Lords of Swabia, your chosen successor is Austrian, and it is therefore not surprising that he in his turn has chosen . . .'

'Chosen what, Neefe? Chosen what?'

'Well, my colleagues in the imperial capital tell me that His Royal Highness the Archduke intends – when, of course, in the fullness of time he succeeds to your illustrious position – intends to appoint Wolfgang Mozart as his Kapellmeister here in Bonn, Herr Mozart of course also being an Austrian.'

Belderbusch began to speak but a wave of the Elector's arm quieted him.

'I think I understand what you are trying to tell me, Neefe.'

'Again, sire, forgive my presumptuousness.'

'But I do not see the relevance of all this to the question in hand, namely the future of your young pupil here.'

'Only this, sire. That I am well aware of your great love of the arts and your desire to foster them among your people. It is my belief – my honest belief – that Ludwig van Beethoven is destined to be as great a musician as Mozart, or even Bach. Possibly greater. If you, beginning at his tender age now, were to be his patron, you will be remembered for that for many years to come. For centuries to come. By Germany. A German prince, patron of Germany's great – possibly greatest – composer.'

Ludwig looked at his teacher and there was gratitude in his eyes. He might not have understood much of what Neefe had said. But this last speech he understood completely, and he wanted to tell his teacher how much he appreciated it.

He saw Belderbusch bend down and whisper in the Elector's ear. The Elector nodded.

Belderbusch spoke. 'Neefe, it is His Grace's belief that you may have allowed yourself to become rather . . . rather . . . carried away. We are talking of a boy here. We all know he has talent. But the Elector feels that now is not the time to disrupt his education. The matter is closed.'

Ludwig heard the words but had to let them resound in his ears again to understand what they meant. He was aware that Neefe was saying something, but he could not hear the words, just the despair in his voice.

He wanted to tell Neefe not to worry, that they were both musicians and that they understood this language they shared; that the two men on the other side of the desk knew nothing of it; that he had tried his best; that for the moment it didn't matter. In time . . . in time . . .

He became aware that the Elector was speaking to him.

'Boy? Young man? I am addressing you. You must pay attention when I speak to you. Now, it is my wish to hear you play. What will you play for me?'

Ludwig was aware that all three men were looking at him. He tried to speak but the words would not come. He turned to his teacher.

Neefe spoke. His voice sounded tired. 'Ludwig will play for you first a movement from Emanuel Bach's cantata "Morning Song of Creation". He will then play you a work he has himself composed, which is a set of nine variations on a march by Ernst Dressler.'

'One work I think will suffice, Neefe,' said Belderbusch.

The Elector waved his hand again. 'A work you have yourself composed, Ludwig? Nine variations? Nine? Well, I shall listen with great interest. Play me that piece. Your piece. We shall forgo the Bach this time. And who knows? Maybe one day, when you are older . . . maybe three or four years from now . . . There you are. The piano is in that corner.' He pointed over Ludwig's shoulder.

Ludwig looked at the wall above the Elector's head and saw for the first time the painting hanging there. In the foreground a stag stood proudly, its antlers held high in the air. Behind it a brook meandered through a pasture. On the far side of the brook a herd of deer grazed.

Ludwig looked at the stag. So proud, so free. He thought of Mozart and how he had argued with the Archbishop of Salzburg and how he was now in Vienna, and free. A musician, an artist who had said no and set himself free. He looked at Neefe and saw the hurt on his face.

He wished his grandfather were here, sitting next to him. He wanted to ask him what he should do. He wanted his advice. Why did you have to die, Grandpa, when I was still so young? He felt the emotion well up in him. He forced it down and clenched the muscles in his face.

He could see the face of his grandfather clearly: loving, reassuring, encouraging, trusting, and above all full of faith in him. That he would be Ludwig van Beethoven, composer.

He sat straight in his chair, drawing his shoulders up, and looked directly at the Elector.

'No. I will not play the piano today.'

BOOK TWO

Chapter 1

'Ludwig? Do you mind if we come in?'

Ludwig sighed and reluctantly swivelled the telescope away from his eye.

'Were you looking at that dreadful gloomy rock again? I don't know why it fascinates you so much.'

Cäcilie stood in the doorway of the tiny attic room. A tall, thin young man was alongside her.

'Ludwig, this is Franz Wegeler. I'd like you to meet him. He's studying to be a doctor.'

The young man walked towards Ludwig, his hand outstretched. Ludwig noticed immediately that he had a kind, open face and a genuine smile.

'Sir, I cannot tell you what a pleasure it is to meet you. I have heard of your musical genius and when Cäcilie told me she lived in the same building as you, I was bold enough to ask her to introduce me to you.'

Ludwig did not know what to say. He could tell the young man was at least five years older than him, his voice already deep.

'May we sit with you a few minutes, Ludwig?' asked Cäcilie.

Ludwig nodded, making room on the sill. Cäcilie sat next to him. Wegeler noticed a stool in the corner and brought it over. He leaned forward.

'Is it true you refused to play the piano for the Elector?' he asked eagerly.

'Yes, is it true, Ludwig?' Cäcilie echoed. 'Everyone is talking about it.'

Ludwig nodded. He liked the smiles that were directed at him, as if they classified Franz and Cäcilie as co-conspirators. So different from his father, who had shouted at him and scolded him when he had heard.

John Suchet

'Tell us, Ludwig. What did the Elector say?'

'He . . . he just looked angry. And the man with him looked angry too. But I looked at my teacher, and he said if I didn't want to play, it was all right.'

'Ha! He's a brave man, your teacher. And so are you!'

A cloud flitted across Ludwig's face. 'They upset Herr Neefe, my teacher. And it made me angry.'

'How? What did they say to upset him?'

'He wants me to go to Vienna to meet Herr Mozart and he was asking the Elector's permission. The Elector said I was too young.'

'How old are you?'

Ludwig hesitated. 'I'm twelve. My father says I must tell people I'm eleven because it'll make them think I'm more like Mozart.'

'Well, you are young.'

A spark came into Ludwig's voice. 'Yes. But I must meet Mozart. He is the greatest composer of them all. Only Bach is as good. Johann Sebastian, not the others. If I could meet him . . . if I could play the piano for him . . . If only I could go to Vienna . . .'

'Is that what you are trying to see through the telescope?' asked Franz, smiling. 'Vienna? It's in the right direction but a little too far, I fear.'

'No,' said Cäcilie. 'He looks at the gloomy old rock up the river. What's it called, Ludwig?'

'The Drachenfels.'

'Ah, yes,' said Wegeler. 'The Dragon Rock. Do you know why it's called that?'

Ludwig shook his head but his eyes were open wide. 'Do you know? There's a legend, isn't there? Do you know what it is?'

'Yes. We read about it in school. Did you know that apparently, in other parts of Germany, we Rhinelanders are regarded as somehow different? My teacher was from Hamburg in the north. He said all Rhinelanders are mystical people, wrapped up in the legends of the Rhine. He said they imagine us creeping out of the Rhine like prehistoric beasts, emerging from the mists which hang low over the water . . .' he wove shapes in the air with his hands, 'and heading for the nearest tavern and drinking mugfuls of beer.'

All three laughed out loud. Ludwig said, 'What is the legend of the Drachenfels? Tell me.'

'I can't remember every detail. But it's about Siegfried, the hero of the Rhine, and how he saves the maidens from the dragon whose lair is in the rock that stands at the edge of the Rhine. The Drachenfels.'

'How does he do it?'

Franz smiled. 'In his hand he has Balmung, the magic sword given to him by the gods of the river. On his feet are the magic boots, seven-league boots bequeathed to him by the seven giants who built the seven mountains, the Siebengebirge. With one leap he crosses the Rhine and climbs the rock to the dragon's lair.'

Warming to his theme, he leaned forward slightly on the stool and continued. 'At the entrance to the lair he hears the maidens' plaintive song, pure and sweet, urging him to rescue them from the dragon. With two swift sweeps from Balmung he dispatches the dragon's two guards who fly at him, their bodies tumbling into the raging river below. He enters the cave and is blinded by the brightness of the flame shooting forth from the dragon's mouth. The heat of it knocks him over.'

All three started at a sudden scratching at the door. Cäcilie quickly opened it, bent down and swept up her tiny poodle Mitzi into her arms.

'Go on,' she said. 'Go on.'

'Suddenly Siegfried sees the dragon looming over him, a huge monster, half beast, half serpent, its scales shiny like a fish, flames coming from its mouth and smoke from its nostrils. Behind it, at the back of the cave, he can dimly hear the singing of the maidens. Siegfried struggles to his feet and wields his trusty magic sword. He thrusts it at the dragon's scaly flank, but it slides off. The dragon, sensing victory, rears up to kill Siegfried, but as it does so he again stabs with the sword. Again it slides off, but this time as it slides the tip catches a tiny fold in the flesh and a small trickle of blood weaves its way down the scales. The beast is suddenly aware the sword has pierced its flesh and the full pain of the wound hits home. Again it rears up, and this time Siegfried darts right under the dragon's head and with a mighty effort thrusts Balmung deep into the base of its long neck.'

Cäcilie and Ludwig both gasped. 'So he rescues the maidens,' said Cäcilie.

'Wait,' said Franz, 'it is not over yet. The blood from the dragon's neck gushes over Siegfried and covers him. But as the dragon dies, from its snout come the words of a man. "I am

Hagen, your sworn enemy. You have killed me but I will have my revenge," it says. But then Siegfried hears the sweet voices of the maidens. "Siegfried, you have saved us," they say, "and we offer you this gift. If you bathe in the dragon's blood you will become invincible. No sword will be able to pierce you." So Siegfried bathes in the blood, cupping his hands and pouring it over his shoulders. But as he does so, from high up in the cave a linden leaf falls slowly down, coming to rest between Siegfried's shoulder blades. His sweat causes it to stick there, and as he continues to bathe in the dragon's blood, it parts and runs down either side of the linden leaf.'

'So it doesn't cover that spot?'

'No, just that spot remains uncovered and when later Siegfried goes into battle his wife, thinking she is doing the right thing, sews a cross on the back of his tunic and asks his great ally to watch over him in battle and make sure that no weapon ever touches him where the cross is. And do you know who the great ally is?'

Cäcilie and Ludwig shook their heads.

'Hagen, who before they go into battle urges Siegfried to kneel at the edge of the Rhine and drink the refreshing water. And as he does so Hagen brings his sword crashing down on the cross Siegfried's wife has sewn on his tunic, and Siegfried, hero of the Rhine, falls into its magic waters. And deep in the water lies the Nibelung treasure, guarded by the dwarf Alberich . . . But no, enough of that for now. I think I can understand why other Germans think we Rhinelanders are different from them!'

Cäcilie sat saying nothing, her eyes wide open, clutching Mitzi to her chest.

Ludwig looked serious for a moment. 'Siegfried, hero of the Rhine. What a fine opera that would make.'

Gottlob Neefe found that the incident at the Electoral palace had not improved his reputation. An outsider – if not exactly a foreigner – by birth and upbringing, a Protestant to make matters worse, the word now was that he had come close to insulting the Elector. No one knew exactly what it was he had said, and he was not offering to elaborate. But he knew his Illuminati activities already rendered him an object of some suspicion.

He only hoped his reputation as a teacher of music had not suffered by one particular pupil's decision to defy the most important personage in the land. He doubted it. In fact he suspected that most of the musicians at court secretly admired Ludwig's demonstration of independence.

At any rate he had his own position to consider: court organist at a respectable salary of four hundred florins – and with a wife and two infant daughters to support, he could not afford to put this at risk. Perhaps he had been a little over-bold to suggest, by implication, that the choice of the Elector's successor – made by the Empress Maria Theresa in Vienna – had been politically inspired. Well, he had said it. It could not be unsaid. He would tread a little more carefully now.

But what to do about Ludwig van Beethoven, this wilful and extraordinarily talented boy? Maybe he had been a little ambitious in taking his case for Ludwig to go to Vienna to the Elector. Certainly his wife had thought so. He should have listened. Ironically it was his wife who came up with a suggestion for what he might do next.

They were sitting round the table in the kitchen of the small apartment Neefe rented close to the Electoral palace. Their two daughters were in bed. Clara Neefe was a petite woman with fair hair. Her face seemed to exude calm restraint and common sense.

'I knew it was a mistake for you to go to see the Elector, Gotti. They're all so suspicious at the palace. Especially that awful man Belderbusch.'

'He doesn't like me because I'm a Protestant. And he knows about the Illuminati. Mind you, their faces when Ludwig refused to play . . .'

'Tell me about him. Is he really as good a musician as I have heard?'

Neefe sighed. 'Yes. I really have never come across anybody like him before. He plays the piano like . . . like . . . well, like a grown man. I know without any doubt that he will one day overtake me, and it will not be long before he reaches the age I am now. At the moment we are studying Bach's "Well-Tempered Klavier". He loves it. You know how long it is, how many pieces are in it? The first time I showed him the music he played the first six pieces at sight. There were wrong notes, but he did not stop and they did not seem to matter. He had captured the spirit of the thing. At sight!'

'It just comes naturally . . .'

Neefe jumped up. 'Well, that's the extraordinary thing. It

doesn't seem to. You know what they say about Mozart? He sits at the piano, a sweet smile on his face, his body barely moving, yet his long, slim fingers racing up and down the keyboard, and this beautiful sound emerges. As if it has come from God straight through the body of Mozart to his fingertips. It's not like that with Ludwig. Everything for him is a struggle. His face contorts, his shoulders hunch, his fingers pound the keys. Short and stocky they are. Not a pianist's fingers. And this angry sound emerges. Sometimes it is not beautiful to watch, or even to hear. And yet, and yet . . . From a boy whose voice has not yet changed. It is a gift from somewhere. But divine? Not if it comes from the same God as Mozart's gift.'

'What will you do now about him? Maybe you don't need to do anything. It seems everybody knows about what happened at the palace. His fame has gone before him.'

Neefe smiled wryly. 'I don't know, I really don't. I know people think I'm . . . I'm . . . Oh, I don't know, that I'm obsessed with him. But I honestly believe if he could go to Vienna and meet Mozart . . . He talks about his music all the time. He knows it intimately. He sees things in it that I . . . that other musicians – adult professional musicians – don't.'

Neefe sat down again and leaned towards his wife. 'The truth is, Clara, it is my belief that one day – one day – the world will know this boy's name. It will talk of him in the same breath as Bach and Handel. And here he is in my care. For the moment, to help him forget what happened at the palace, I have appointed him my assistant organist. But it's unofficial. There's no salary. It's just between him and me. But I want to encourage him. More to the point, I want to encourage other people to see in him what I can see.'

'Why don't you put an announcement in Cramer's journal. What is it called? You are always reading it. All musicians read it. *Das Magazin der Musik.* Describe this pupil of yours. Some wealthy patron of the arts might see it. And who knows?'

His Excellency Count Kaspar Anton von Belderbusch, First Minister to His Most Gracious Lord the Elector and Archbishop of Cologne, swallowed hard to keep down the heartburn. Why did he always get these awful pains in his chest whenever he thought of the Illuminati? Damned traitors, that's what they are. Damned, disloyal traitors. They are fools if they think I do not know what is going on. And Neefe is their leader. Court organist

Neefe, leader of the Illuminati. Well, I will take matters into my own hands, Belderbusch thought. Neefe needs to be taught a lesson. For him, a lowly musician, given the unique opportunity of sitting across the desk from the Elector himself – whatever the motives behind the meeting – and then to talk like that . . . and to allow his pupil to insult the Elector by refusing to play.

His hand went suddenly to his chest as he felt the familiar pain spread through it. He swallowed several times, thumping gently between his lungs.

It came to him in a flash. He would recruit a new spy to his network of informants.

And I know just the man, he thought. A man who will welcome the money, who will be loyal to me, who I know dislikes Neefe and yet who has unrivalled access to him. Through his son.

Chapter 2

'What use is this? I mean, really, has the man gone mad? He's mocking me, that's what he's doing. Trying to make a fool of this family. Here, read it.'

Johann van Beethoven tossed the journal on to the table, the corners of several pages catching the dish of meat and turning instantly dark with the stain of gravy.

Maria Magdalena carried on eating, ignoring her husband's outburst. Caspar and Nikola looked up briefly to check on their mother and, taking their cue from her, went on eating likewise. Only Ludwig seemed to hear his father. He sat motionless, holding his spoon and fork above his food. In a crudely built and battered high chair, set away from the table, the infant Franz Georg moaned.

'Why don't you shut the child up, woman? His groaning is enough to drive a man insane. On and on he goes, whining every minute of the day. And half the night. Is he in pain or something? You should know, you're his mother. Maybe he's hungry. Give him some food, for God's sake.'

Maria Magdalena, stung by her husband's tone, put her knife and fork down noisily and walked over to the chair.

'I fed him only an hour ago,' she said, more to herself than her husband. 'I don't know why he cries so.' She put a spoon to his mouth but he pushed it angrily away, sharpening his moaning with a shrill cry and pounding the small table in front of him with his fist.

'Read it, for God's sake, woman,' said Johann, gesturing to the journal. Maria ignored him.

'I'll read it myself,' said Johann, 'to you all. The journal in question is Cramer's learned and well-respected *Magazin der Musik*. The edition is dated March 1783 and the author is none other than the court organist himself, and teacher to our young "genius" here, Herr Christian Gottlob Neefe. He writes as follows. Pay attention, good wife, worthy sons and the genius here who honours us with his presence.

'"Louis van Beethoven" – Louis indeed. Is the good old-fashioned German name of Ludwig not good enough for our Herr Neefe, I wonder? – "Louis van Beethoven, son of the tenor singer mentioned" – so, no name at all for me. Well, what else can a mere singer . . .'

'Johann, for goodness' sake, I cannot stand this sarcasm. Read it if you must. But for the love of God just read it.'

'Very well. Read it I shall: "Louis van Beethoven, son of the tenor singer mentioned, a boy of eleven years"' – he coughed nervously at the mention of Ludwig's age and read rapidly on – '"and of most promising talent. He plays the piano very skilfully and with power, reads at sight very well, and – to put it in a nutshell – he plays chiefly 'The Well-Tempered Klavier' of Sebastian Bach, which Herr Neefe put into his hands. Whoever knows this collection of preludes and fugues in all the keys – which might almost be called the *non plus ultra* of our art – will know what this means. So far as his duties permitted, Herr Neefe has also given him instruction in thorough-bass. He is now training him in composition and for his encouragement has had nine variations for the pianoforte, written by him on a march – by Ernst Christoph Dressler – engraved at Mannheim. This youthful genius"' – Johann paused to look up, his eyes sweeping the room to ensure the words were not lost on anyone present. He repeated them, just in case – '"this youthful genius is deserving of help to enable him to travel."' Johann now emphasised his words with deliberate stress and read more slowly. '"He would surely become a second Wolfgang Amadeus Mozart were he to continue as he has begun."'

His words hung in the air, no one daring to speak. Ludwig sat with eyes downcast, his lower lip trembling slightly.

'For goodness' sake, Johann, leave the boy . . .'

'This youthful genius, a second Wolfgang Mozart indeed. I thought so once too. But since then I've come to my senses.' Johann pushed his chair roughly back. Maria pulled the infant from her breast and hurriedly put him in his high chair, ignoring the crying that began instantly. But she was too late to stop Johann cuffing Ludwig across the back of the head with the rolled-up journal.

'This Neefe is a fool. A fool and a Protestant, what's more.

I've heard a thing or two about him. He's going to have to watch his step.'

As quickly as it had come upon him, Johann's temper seemed to pass. He slumped in his chair. 'What will we do with you, Ludwig? Will you be a genius like the Austrian? Will your talent earn you a living, even? What happened with those variations you composed? You dedicated them to some high-powered lady, didn't you? Well?'

Ludwig nodded slowly. 'Who was she, Ludwig? Answer me, boy. Has the cat got your tongue?'

'She was the Countess Wolff-Metternich,' Ludwig said quietly. 'Her husband, the Count, is a judge.'

'And what have you got to show for it? Did she pay you any money?'

Ludwig shook his head without raising it.

'I don't see the point, then,' his father said.

Ludwig snapped his head up. 'The point is, I am twelve years of age. I have to start somewhere. I am not the head of this household. Why should I have to earn the money?' His shoulders heaved and he could not suppress the sobs that followed.

'Why, I'll teach you to insult me, you—'

'Johann. Stop.' Maria's voice had a harsh edge to it that her family had rarely heard.

Johann stood and directed his angry gaze at the high chair. 'Can no one stop that damned child crying?' he shouted, as he raised his hands to his ears to shut out the noise.

The Elector Maximilian Friedrich was in high good humour. Unhesitatingly he returned the waves of his subjects as the ornate carriage, decorated in the livery of the royal family, turned into the Marktplatz and made its way across the black lava cobbles past the ornate and gilded town hall (another of his predecessor's extravagances) towards the palace entrance. The cause of his good spirits was not the conclusion of his trip to Münster, a trip he had been long dreading, but his successful journey back. Successful in that he, in his role as Archbishop of Cologne and Münster, had managed to arrange an overnight stay on the return journey at the home of the Abbess of Vilich. How easy it had been for him to send his courtiers on to Bonn, explaining that he intended to pay a courtesy call on the Abbess to discuss religious matters with her.

Religious, indeed! He chuckled as he conjured up in his mind the delights of the night he had just spent with the Abbess of Vilich, otherwise known as the Countess Caroline von Satzenhofen, mistress these last ten years to the Elector of Cologne, and – yes, there was no hiding it – to his First Minister, Count von Belderbusch. But there was no jealousy in the Elector's mind. In fact, quite the reverse. It was he, the Elector, who had first introduced Belderbusch to the Countess. More than that, it was he, the Elector, who had subtly encouraged Belderbusch to avail himself of the Countess's charms.

He had known from the start how useful such an arrangement would be. He was no youngster, and more to the point as Elector he would not have at his disposal all the time he might want to indulge in such earthly matters. Belderbusch would therefore fulfil two functions: he would add some variety to the Countess's life; and by being, as it were, a partner in love with the Elector, he would enable him to pursue his relationship with the Countess to the fullest extent possible, and with the maximum discretion.

And indeed, what a lady! He felt the familiar tight feeling in his chest and the rush of blood to his loins as he remembered – merely remembered! – the night he had just spent. Here was a woman past her fiftieth year, who had borne two children, who led a cloistered life of prayer, and yet who threw herself into the pleasures of love as if her very life depended on it. What on earth did she see in a little old man of more than seventy years? What on earth was there to see in such a man? It was simple to suggest that she was in love with his power, with the fact that he was the most powerful man in the region. But how could that explain the sheer abandon with which she made love to him, the unabashed pleasure she clearly derived from seeing his naked body, stroking it, kissing it, loving it, and at the same time giving every part of her body completely to him?

He allowed the rhythmic swaying of the carriage to lull his mind and body as images from the night before swam in and out of his subconscious. But the sudden darkening of the carriage as it went under the arch into the palace courtyard reminded him that in less than a minute he would be surrounded by courtiers, advisers, officials; he would have to make decisions, sign documents, chair meetings.

Dismounting from the carriage he walked swiftly along the

corridor to his chambers, an official at his side reading the day's engagements from a file he carried in front of him.

'What's first again? Tell me what's first.'

'A delegation, Your Majesty, from the Federation of Tailors.'

'When are they due and what do they want?'

'They have an appointment to see you at ten o'clock, my lord. It should have been earlier, but we knew that you wouldn't be back from Münster in time, since you stopped for the night . . .'

'Yes, yes, all right. What do they want?'

'It's to do with the recent increase in taxes, my lord. The President of the Federation will be bringing a petition to you signed by more than a hundred tailors and master cutters, calling on you . . .'

The Elector wasn't listening. He had picked up a copy of a journal lying on his desk, with a marker directing him to a certain page. The official fell quiet while the Elector read. He skimmed through it twice, taking no more than a minute to do so.

'Get me Belderbusch. Send him to me, and don't allow anyone in until I'm finished with him.'

'Yes, my lord. Of course.'

The Elector read the article for a third time, a small smile spreading across his face. He swivelled his chair and gazed out of the tall double window. He contrived to be in the same position when he heard the small knock on the door, followed by the sound of Belderbusch entering. The two men had been close colleagues and confidants for more than twenty years, but a little touch of insouciance, the Elector felt, would serve to remind his minister, should there be the smallest need to do so, of their relative positions in government. He heard Belderbusch walk quietly the few steps to the desk. He knew full well that it was Belderbusch who had entered; the First Minister was the only person in the land whom he allowed to enter after a mere knock, without first hearing a sharp 'Komm!' from himself.

Maximilian Friedrich turned back from the window and could scarcely conceal his sharp intake of breath as his eyes took in the sight of Belderbusch standing before him.

'My dear Anton,' the Elector said, with genuine concern in his voice. 'Do sit down, for heaven's sake.' And he walked swiftly round his desk to move a chair up for the younger man.

'No, please, I'm perfectly all right,' said Belderbusch, but he did not move to stop the Elector and sat gratefully and heavily in the chair the Elector put in place for him.

Maximilian walked back round his desk and sat down. For a few moments he studied his minister's face. It was drawn in a way he had not seen before, almost haggard. And there was an unhealthy grey pallor to it.

'Anton, you look dreadful. You do not need me to tell you. You are working too hard. Take some days off.' He leaned forward and a sparkle came into his eyes. 'I will tell everyone you have gone to Münster! To a certain Abbess we both know. Why not, Anton? Why not?'

Belderbusch shook his head. 'Thank you, my lord. I will be all right. It's the wretched pain in my chest. It will soon go. I cannot leave. There is too much work to do.'

Maximilian said, 'I've read the article in Cramer's journal. Very interesting.'

A small smile crossed Belderbusch's face. 'I thought that would intrigue you.'

'What do you think is behind it?'

'I presume Neefe has given up his attempt to interest you in the boy, after that infamous meeting. By the way, word has got out about it. Not what Neefe said, and he is not volunteering the information. But the fact that the boy refused to play for you.'

'Really? What are they saying? That I was humiliated by a boy?'

'I wouldn't put it that strongly. Just that you were somewhat surprised to find that your most rebellious subject is a young boy.'

'Mm.' The Elector thought for a moment. 'Tell me, Anton. What do you think the reaction would be if I sent the boy to Vienna? As Neefe wants.'

Belderbusch frowned. 'Sir, I know you want to do the best for the boy. My concern is Neefe. To do what he wants – such generosity – it might be misinterpreted. Or more likely, be seen as acquiescence in—'

'Would that be so bad?'

'Do not forget, my lord. Neefe is head of the Illuminati chapter here in Bonn. I am having him watched. I am worried about their activities . . .'

'My dear Anton. You are obsessed with this wretched little group. I have told you before. They are harmless.'

'Maybe, sir. But still I—'

'What are they, Anton? A dozen men? Fifteen? Not even enough to form a small orchestra.'

'It does not take many to foment unrest. My informants tell me they are in secret contact with revolutionaries in France, and there they are now talking openly of revolution, of overthrowing the monarchy . . .'

Maximilian Friedrich laughed. 'It will take more than a handful of hotheads to do that! And remember, France is just France. The Holy Roman Empire is somewhat different. It has existed for nearly a thousand years, and it is not going to be destroyed by a handful of men discussing Voltaire and Rousseau in the city of Bonn!'

Belderbusch said nothing. 'Now, back to more pleasant matters. What is your opinion of this Beethoven boy, Anton? You have heard him play more often than I have. I've only heard him once or twice. Is he as good as they say?'

'He is good, yes. Very good.'

'Is he another Mozart?'

'I don't know. It's possible. But he's . . . he's . . . wilder. He has no grace. Even at this tender age he pounds on the piano. Sometimes it can be quite ugly. But in ten years from now, who knows?'

'In ten years from now, I will no longer be on this earth to hear him,' the Elector said with humour in his voice. 'But what if I sponsor him and he does fulfil his promise? I will be remembered for that, will I not?'

Belderbusch nodded.

'Well, go and see Neefe, Anton. Not right away. When you think the moment is right. Tell him I am considering fulfilling his wish. Gauge his reaction. I leave it in your hands. But I am inclined to send the boy to Vienna. Just for six months, say.'

Belderbusch nodded wearily.

Neefe sat in front of Belderbusch's desk in the First Minister's office. Belderbusch himself stood at the tall window, looking out, his hands clasped behind his back. How Neefe loathed the man! The Elector's mouthpiece.

Neefe knew the moment he was elected leader of the local chapter of the Illuminati that his problems would increase. He suspected Belderbusch would put a spy on to him. He did not communicate his fears to his wife; he decided to wait and see how serious the problem became. Only when he realised – very quickly – that the spy was Johann van Beethoven did he relax somewhat.

He even had some fun at Johann's expense. Leaving the printer's shop where he regularly picked up musical manuscripts, he made an elaborate play of half hiding his face with his cloak and looking carefully before leaving – making sure Johann, poorly hidden across the street, could see him.

Nor was he concerned to receive the summons to come to the palace to see the First Minister. He knew he was guilty of nothing.

'Tell me, Neefe,' Belderbusch said in a firm, matter-of-fact voice, 'that announcement you put in Cramer's magazine. Did it yield results?'

'It caused much comment. Several musicians here at court – senior musicians, Herr Ries for example – said it was the right thing to do, if only because it drew people's attention to the boy. But an offer of sponsorship? Regrettably not.'

'Then what I have to say will no doubt cause you particular pleasure. I decided to show His Grace the Elector your announcement, which given your young pupil's behaviour in His Grace's presence was, you might agree, a somewhat bold move on my part.'

Neefe folded his arms tightly across his chest, his scepticism at Belderbusch's role in the affair visible on his face.

'His Grace,' Belderbusch continued, 'is, as you know, well disposed to the arts. Why else would he have agreed to see your pupil? He has, in his benevolence, expressed a willingness to help him travel to Vienna.'

'Then His Grace is most . . . most . . .'

'It is not quite as straightforward as that. His Grace has instructed me to tell you that he wants further proof of the boy's genius. If indeed he has genius.'

'What further proof?'

'I do not question the Elector, Neefe. Nor should you. It is for you and the boy to decide what is appropriate.'

'But he has heard him play in the court chapel. He knows for himself . . .'

Belderbusch leaned forward and clasped his hands on the desk. 'What does the boy do now, apart from take lessons from you?'

'He is assistant court organist, appointed – without salary – by me. For certain less well-attended services I allow him to be sole organist. I have also introduced him to Madame Grossman of the Grossman theatrical company, and she allows him to deputise for me as répétiteur at company rehearsals. I can assure you he is a young musician with a burgeoning reputation.'

'Then between you, you and he should not find it too difficult to satisfy His Grace's desire. You may go.'

Neefe stood. 'Should I bring him to play again for the Elector?'

'Again?' asked Belderbusch with a thin smile. 'I do not remember the last performance. No. I rather think something more is required. But I confess I do not know what. As I said, it is your problem.'

Neefe turned to leave. For a brief moment he considered telling Belderbusch he knew that Johann van Beethoven was spying on him. But he thought better of it and left the room.

Chapter 3

Ludwig looked at his mother and did not know what to say. Caspar and Nikola stood on either side of her, as if they were guarding her and defying him to come nearer. She sat in a chair, gently rocking. In her arms lay the child Franz Georg, wrapped tightly in a blanket. She looked down beatifically at his small, pinched face, the corners of the mouth drawn unnaturally in, the eyes neither fully open nor fully closed.

'Shall I find Papa?' asked Caspar. Maria shook her head.

Ludwig looked down at his youngest brother and wondered what it was that had made him give up his fight. His firmest memory of him was that he was always crying, always pounding his little fists. What was he fighting against? Ludwig wondered if he too had been like that when he was a baby. He knew he had cried a lot, because his mother had so often told him.

He remembered how she had shunned him when he had smallpox, as if somehow it was wilful on his part, that he could control it. But he couldn't, any more than Franz Georg could. Ludwig had harboured the hope that in time he would develop a relationship with his youngest brother, in a way that he had been unable to with Caspar and Nikola.

'I have to see my teacher,' Ludwig said quietly. His mother continued to gaze at the child, but his brothers gave him looks of resentment mingled with triumph, as if to say that there was no place for him here anyway.

Ludwig gathered up some manuscript papers and carefully put them in a firm folder. Then he threw a coat over his shoulders and left the room.

He was early for his lesson with Neefe but he did not want to stay in the house for a moment longer. He wanted to be alone, to allow his emotions and aspirations free rein. He was sad about his brother, but he saw no cause to fight it. Fate had ruled the infant's life. It was not something any amount of mourning could reverse.

And there was another matter occupying his mind, one that made him want to shout with joy. He knew Neefe had good news for him. He had sent a note to him by courier – something he had never done before – telling him there was a possibility the Elector would allow him to go to Vienna, and that he would tell him more at the next lesson.

How could he stay in the house after such a tragedy, when all he wanted to do was smile and say that his one great dream was about to be granted?

He hardly noticed the rain, which was falling in great vertical shafts like an impenetrable curtain. Careless of his own dryness, he slipped the folder under his coat to protect it from the rain.

He walked down the Rheingasse to the river and turned to walk along its banks. The water lapped around his feet, which it never normally did. In the pouring rain he stood and looked at the water. It had a swirl to it that he had not seen before. It seemed to pull one way then immediately another. He watched a cluster of leaves being thrown around as if there were several unseen hands below the water. Suddenly a hidden whirlpool pulled them under. He waited for them to reappear, but they did not.

As he realised at last the strength of the rain, he increased his pace and ten minutes later arrived at the room in a wing of the palace where Neefe gave him lessons.

Ludwig was surprised to find Neefe in contemplative mood.

'Come in, Ludwig. Sit down. We'll talk about Vienna in a minute. I may have misled you in my note. It's not straight-forward. But first let's talk.'

Ludwig sensed it would be a wrong move on his part to show dissent. He laid down the folder, wiping it with his sleeve to remove any residue of rain that had seeped through his coat.

'The Bach. "The Well-Tempered Klavier". Are you making progress?'

Ludwig nodded. 'There are certain passages . . . Some are difficult. But I can see why he wrote them as he did. I'll get them right. It won't be a problem.'

'No,' said Neefe, smiling faintly. 'I am sure it won't.'

'I . . . I should tell you. My brother Franz Georg has died. Just now. Today.'

'Oh, my dear boy, I'm so sorry. Look, do you want to go home to be with your family?'

'No,' Ludwig said quickly. 'I want to have my lesson and hear what you have to tell me.'

Neefe looked out of the window for a few moments, a serious expression on his face. Ludwig wondered if he should play some of the Bach. But he sensed he should wait.

'Ludwig,' Neefe said finally, 'why do we make music?'

Ludwig did not reply, but Neefe had his attention.

'Do we make music because we want to, or because we like to? Or perhaps because it amuses us? *We* don't, Ludwig. Some people do. Most people do. But we don't. So why do we make music? We make music for the same reason we breathe in the air. Because if we do not, we die.'

Ludwig nodded. He did not know whether Neefe expected him to say anything. So he nodded again.

Neefe touched the tips of his fingers to his lips. 'If music is our life, what form should it take? How do we express our life in music? How can we express it? That is the question all artists ask. If a painter paints a picture, he shows us himself. But he shows us more than that. He shows us life too. If all he shows us is what he sees, then he is not a true artist. So with us musicians. If all we write is music, then that is not enough. Our music must express life. How do we achieve that, Ludwig? I shall tell you. We achieve it through nature. We achieve it by studying nature, and all natural things around us. Only in that way can the true musician learn to depict every shade of emotion. You must study nature, Ludwig. And as you study it you will learn that man, the human being, alone in all nature is rational and free. It is the natural state of man to be free. Without his freedom man is in chains.'

Neefe leaped up from his chair and talked on as he paced the room. Now, though, he made a deliberate effort to keep his voice low.

'You must read the philosophers, Ludwig. Listen to what Rousseau says: "Man is born free but is everywhere in chains." And Voltaire, one of the great writers of our century. Do you know what happened to him, Ludwig? He challenged a nobleman and was thrown into the Bastille. That was more than half a century ago, and is life so different now? If I challenged the Elector, really challenged him, not like that talk about his successor, but really questioned his authority, his right to rule, do you think he would smile and clap me on the shoulder? No, I too would end up in jail. But it will change, Ludwig, it will change. It is already changing here in Germany. You cannot stop a writer like Goethe from writing the truth. And Schiller. I will give you Schiller to read, Ludwig, and you will begin to understand the highest aspirations of man. You will learn that all men are free and equal under God.'

Ludwig frowned, trying to assimilate what his teacher was saying. He knew he was talking about important truths, and he knew also that so far as he understood them, he agreed with them. But he would have much rather Neefe stopped and asked him to play the Bach.

'But, Ludwig,' Neefe continued, 'all men are *not* free under God. We all know that. But it will change, and do you know who will change it? We artists, Ludwig. With our art we can illuminate people's minds. Ours is the highest calling. And that is what I strive every day of my life to do. And one day you will do it too. Illuminate people's minds with your art.'

Neefe sat down and spoke more quietly. 'You may have heard of this organisation I belong to. The Illuminati. I have been elected its leader here in Bonn. We try to illuminate people's minds through our art. Unfortunately some people fear us, but we are not dangerous. We do not hurt people. We do not preach revolution. In France they are beginning to preach revolution. Violent revolution.'

Ludwig decided he should speak. 'I would like to play the Bach now. May I?'

Neefe smiled. 'Of course. Maybe I shouldn't talk like this to you. You are too young. But it is my belief, Ludwig, that one day you will be a great artist. Like Mozart. The man you might soon be going to see.'

Ludwig's eyes opened. 'When can I go? Has the Elector said I can go to Vienna?'

'Apparently so. But there is a condition. Belderbusch has told me the Elector wants further proof of your genius. I have told him you will play for the Elector – as often as he wants and any music he chooses. Belderbusch says that is not enough. And I do not know what else I can suggest. I have racked my brain, but I cannot come up with a solution.'

Neefe leaned forward on the small table, a look of defeat on his face. 'I suppose that is what prompted my lecture to you just now. At the moment we musicians, we artists, are at the beck and call of our leaders, to do as they wish. One day we will all break away, as Mozart has done. But for the moment . . .'

Ludwig smiled. It was a smile of confidence, the confidence that comes of knowing you have a better understanding of a situation than one much older and more experienced than you.

'I know what I should do. I know what the Elector wants.'

Neefe looked at him expectantly, but the look on his face did not show great confidence.

Ludwig opened the folder he had brought with him. 'I have composed three sonatas for the piano. Here they are. There is still work to do on the third. There are three movements in each. I will dedicate them to the Elector.'

Neefe spoke slowly. 'You have composed three sonatas?'

Ludwig nodded. 'While I was studying the Bach. I found it helped.'

'Will you play them to me. Let me hear them?'

Ludwig nodded enthusiastically.

There was pandemonium in the streets of Bonn. Town officials, their cloaks dragging in the mud and their boots squelching heavily as they ran in different directions, one arm ringing a large bell, the other waving manically in the air, shouted: 'Evacuate your homes! Hurry, hurry! Leave everything behind! Get out while you have time! The Rhine has burst its banks! We're flooded! Leave your homes! Hurry!'

Maria ran into the children's nursery, where Caspar and Nikola were playing with a set of tin soldiers. She took each of them by the hand and hurried quickly down the stairs. Cäcilie Fischer was already coming out of her room on to the landing.

'Is it serious? Must we leave?'

'Yes,' said Maria. 'Get Gottfried quickly. Wrap him up in a blanket. Leave everything else behind.'

Maria went quickly down the stairs to the front hall. When she was only halfway down the flight she already knew it was too late. Water was seeping in under the door and the entrance hall was flooded. She knew if she tried to open the door the water would gush in. She turned and went back up the stairs, instinctively pulling the two boys closer to her. Cäcilie ran out, her baby brother wrapped tightly in her arms.

'It's too late,' Maria said. 'We'll have to get out of the window.'

'Oh my God, I can't,' said Cäcilie. 'I'll fall.'

'You won't,' snapped Maria. 'You'll be strong.'

'Where's Ludwig?'

'With Herr Neefe at the palace. He's having a lesson. Thank goodness I don't have to worry about him. Thank the Lord you're here, Cäcilie. I couldn't manage without you. Not with all these children.'

'Where's Herr Beeth—'

'Oh, Heaven knows. Certainly not where he ought to be. Probably in the tavern where he spends most of his time.'

She stopped on the stairs, suddenly out of breath. She felt Cäcilie's hand firm on her shoulder.

'Don't worry, Frau Beethoven. We'll be all right. We'll take the children to safety.'

They hurried up the remaining stairs to the second floor and into the Beethovens' back room. The window was at the level of the roof of the house across the narrow alley. The roof was flat. Maria threw open the window and looked down. The alley was so narrow there was no daylight in it, but Maria could see it was flowing with water. She knew the roof opposite was their only chance.

She looked at the small group huddled close to her. Cäcilie was crouched by the open window. The baby in her arms mercifully was asleep. Nikola, now seven years of age, sobbed quietly and rubbed his eyes with closed fists. His brother Caspar had a look of excitement on his face.

Maria's eyes swept quickly round the room, resting gratefully on the narrow trestle table in the corner. She walked quickly over to it, praying as she moved that it would not be too heavy for her. Standing at one of the narrow ends, she levered the table top off the trestle legs and let it slide to the ground. She tested its weight, grimaced, closed her eyes and lifted it clear of the ground. She half carried, half dragged it to the window.

Cäcilie moved the children back as Maria allowed the table to crash down on to the window sill. Then she pushed it out through the window, keeping her end pressed down so that the other end would clear the edge of the roof opposite. When she thought the table was far enough out of the window, she let her end go, hoping it would be long enough. She gave a silent prayer of thanks as the far end crashed down on to the roof opposite.

'Now, Cäcilie, you must walk across with the baby, and I will walk the children across to you. It's better if you don't look down. Are you all right? Can you be strong?'

'Yes, Frau Beethoven. I will do it.' As best she could while holding the baby, Cäcilie crossed herself and her lips moved in silent prayer. Then, without a look back, she clambered up on to the table top. She ducked under the window, and once outside, stood slowly upright, the infant clasped firmly to her chest. Looking straight ahead she walked purposefully forward. Four paces saw her to the other side and she dropped off the table top on to the roof.

'Good, Cäcilie,' called Maria. 'Now here comes Caspar.' Muttering words of encouragement to her son, Maria helped him up on to the table top. 'Now, keep looking at Cäcilie. Don't take your eyes off her. Go, Caspar.'

With a look that was a mixture of exhilaration and panic on his face, the boy walked hesitantly forward. Cäcilie held out her free hand and helped him jump down on to the roof.

'Now, Nikola, do what Mama tells you. Be a good brave boy. Up you go. There. Now walk to Cäcilie. See, she's waiting for you.'

Maria's stomach turned over as the small boy gave a sudden yelp and ran across, causing the table top to reverberate under his feet.

Relieved that Cäcilie and all the children were safely across, Maria climbed up on to the table herself and walked across, praying it would take her weight. For a fleeting moment the table sagged in the middle, but it held. Gratefully she stepped on to the roof.

Without a backward glance, they all ran across to the adjoining roof. By luck there were several roofs which adjoined without a break. They hurried across them until they came to the farthest edge.

Maria heard the babble of voices below. She motioned the group of Cäcilie and the children to stay back and she walked to the edge. Again luck was with them. Below the final roof the ground was much higher. She called out for help. Several men ran forward with ladders. One by one she guided the children down into the welcoming hands waiting below. Then it was Cäcilie's turn.

Finally, when Maria was sure every one of the group was safe, she herself climbed down the ladder. Two men took her by the arms as she stepped off the final rung into the street she recognised as the Giergasse. She began to thank them, but suddenly her legs could no longer support her and she sank to the ground unconscious.

Chapter 4

Ludwig felt a large measure of guilt that he had been absent when the Rhine burst its banks and flooded the lower part of the town. He heard from Cäcilie how brave his mother had been, but when he tried to talk to Maria about it she just shook her head dismissively.

'It's a good thing you weren't there as well,' was all she said, 'otherwise goodness only knows how we would have coped. And the same goes for your father.'

The near disaster the family had suffered had the effect of drawing those who had been directly involved more closely together. Ludwig found his brothers even more reluctant to communicate with him, and between them and their mother there existed a new deeper bond. They had faced the danger together and come through it.

The same empathy did not occur between the two members of the family who had not been involved – Ludwig and his father. Johann was becoming an ever more pitiful man, drinking ever more heavily.

The sudden death of First Minister Belderbusch, coming shortly before the dreadful floods, had thrown the city into some confusion. If he had been alive, it was said, at least the fight to contain the floodwaters would have been efficient and organised. With his influence, he might even have ordered the mighty Rhine not to burst its banks. But even as the populace mourned his death, they realised that a new state of freedom had dawned.

Everyone knew that Belderbusch had operated a network of spies, and with his death these citizens suddenly found themselves out of work. Many of them were – like Johann van Beethoven – local men recruited for the sole purpose of allowing Belderbusch to keep abreast of what was being said in the streets.

Rarely had any report made by one of these spies led to arrest or even interrogation. Most of them had been known to the people; some of them had even boasted about it. 'You'd better be careful what you say' was an expression often heard in the taverns.

The spies themselves had found that Belderbusch's promise of good pay had not been forthcoming. Nevertheless their activities had brought them a certain amount of status, given their access to Belderbusch or at least his staff.

With Belderbusch's death, though, these spies – Johann van Beethoven included – found themselves not only out of work, but held in contempt by their former friends. In Johann's case, his only true, reliable, uncomplaining friend was the wine bottle.

Gottlob Neefe had cause to be grateful for the First Minister's untimely death. Although Johann van Beethoven's efforts to follow him had been laughable, there had been at the back of Neefe's mind the nagging suspicion that Belderbusch was being more subtle than he gave him credit for, and that Johann was merely a diversion for a more professional spy, maybe even within the Illuminati.

With Belderbusch's death – and the Elector's known tolerance of the Illuminati – Neefe was able to enjoy peace of mind for the first time since coming to Bonn. He had a full workload. Kapellmeister Lucchesi was temporarily absent from Bonn and Neefe had assumed his role. Gratefully he delegated more and more of his duties – both at the court organ and with the Grossman Company – to his young pupil, Ludwig. He also began to think again of making it possible for Ludwig to travel to Vienna.

Neefe remembered his surprise at Ludwig's suggestion that he should dedicate his three sonatas to the Elector. What an extraordinarily mature suggestion from one so young! There was nothing new about composers dedicating works to secure reward; Mozart had done it at Salzburg, Haydn at Esterhaz and Philipp Telemann at Bayreuth and Eisenach. But a boy not yet in his teenage years? With the express intention of securing his ambition?

More remarkable still, Neefe had to concede, was the fact that Ludwig had actually composed three sonatas for piano. Three! With three movements each, and all full length.

Neefe had sat there as Ludwig played them through, all three with barely a pause between them. He had marvelled at the clarity of thought in them and the features which he already knew characterised Ludwig's music: the sudden transposition to an unrelated key, the stresses off the beat.

Ludwig had already composed a number of songs and some small pieces for piano. Neefe was used to hearing his pupil break rules. He had given up asking why Ludwig had chosen such and such a key, or a combination of notes that were practically a discord. Ludwig did not always have an explanation, but always he was adamant about not changing it, as if every note was predestined to be exactly where it was.

Take the first song Ludwig had shown to him, 'Portrait of a Young Girl', a popular poem he had set to music.

It was short, a mere nineteen bars long. The song was pretty enough, yet in the fourteenth bar, as the words compared the young girl's eyes to the stars which sparkle on a winter's night, Ludwig had written an astonishing sequence of notes for the piano accompaniment: four demisemiquavers, four semiquavers and a dotted crotchet, over a dotted crotchet, two semiquavers and two quavers in the bass.

It was an extraordinary change in tempo which entirely threw out the regular sequence of quavers that preceded it. More than that, the notes in this notorious bar were off the established and conventional key of G in which the song was written. In just two beats of the bar there were no fewer than five accidentals – three flats, a sharp and a natural! The effect of that single bar was like lobbing a heavy stone into a still pond.

'Ludwig,' Neefe exploded, 'why have you done that? You have written a nice song, yet you have ruined it. And for what? Why? It is unnecessary.' But nothing Neefe could say would make the boy alter what he had written.

Neefe was pleased that the three piano sonatas which Ludwig intended dedicating to the Elector contained nothing so startling, nothing which was liable to make the Elector react unfavourably. And they contained several passages which required sparkling virtuosity, something he knew their young creator was well capable of executing.

Neefe decided the time was right to pen a diplomatic and polite letter to the Elector, reminding him of the promise conveyed by his deeply lamented late First Minister to consider allowing Ludwig van Beethoven to travel to Vienna.

'. . . My young pupil', he wrote, 'would greatly welcome the opportunity to make a gift to Your Grace of his latest compositions, which he earnestly wishes will meet with your esteemed approval . . .'

Ludwig hoped he was emerging from a period of unhappiness and instability. The Fischer house had been dried out and repainted and the Beethovens were now back in their apartment, but the move had increased the tension within the family.

Instinctively Ludwig sought out acquaintances other than his brothers, who continued to exclude him from their games. Cäcilie often came to talk to him in the attic room, where he spent much of his time. Indeed she put a small table and chair in there for him to sit and compose.

'Why don't you sit at the piano downstairs?' she asked one day. 'How can you write music without a piano? Not that you could have one in here even if you wanted. There's no room.'

'I can hear the music in my head,' he said.

He spent more time with Franz Wegeler, the medical student. Ludwig liked Franz. The student's parents had come to Bonn – where Franz was born – from Alsace. The two had discussed how it felt to have parents or grandparents who were not natives of Bonn. Despite being born in the city themselves, it made them feel to a certain extent outsiders. Ludwig had often said how he wished his family name was more German, like Franz's, and less Flemish. For one thing it would have made his brief school career less painful.

On a fine early-spring morning in 1784 they walked together along the banks of the Rhine, upriver towards the Siebengebirge.

'Hard to believe this docile river became so angry,' Franz said.

They walked on in silence, turning their heads to watch an occasional boat coast downriver, or making way for a horse-drawn barge.

After an hour the massive dark shape of the Drachenfels loomed ahead.

'That fascinates you, doesn't it?' asked Franz. 'Why? Is it the legends?'

Ludwig shook his head. 'I don't know. I suppose it's just the . . . the . . . permanence of it. It's been there for thousands of years and it'll be there for thousands to come. And it hasn't changed. It hasn't been tamed by man. It's nature.'

He stood still, looking at it in the distance. 'I've walked in the Siebengebirge hills. But I've never climbed the Drachenfels. I'd like to climb it one day.'

'Well, not now. Come on, I have to get back.'

They turned and began walking back towards the city. 'Do you know Stephan von Breuning?' Franz asked.

Ludwig shook his head.

'He lives in the big house in the Münsterplatz. His father was the one who died in the fire at the Electoral palace. His mother is very kind to me. She lets me visit a lot.' Franz paused a moment, then said, 'Stephan has a sister. Eleonore. She's called Lorchen. I'll take you to the house. They have a big piano.'

Ludwig nodded. To have friends in the Münsterplatz – especially with a piano – would give him more cause to keep away from the house in the Rheingasse.

'What about the opera you said you would write? About the Rhine legends? Have you started it yet?' Franz asked, smiling.

Ludwig smiled too as he shook his head. 'I've been working on something different. For the Elector. Franz, I think he's going to let me go to Vienna.'

'So, young man,' said Maximilian Friedrich, 'we meet again. Will I have the pleasure of hearing you play this time?'

Ludwig nodded.

'Your Grace, may I first of all thank you on behalf of myself and my pupil for graciously according us your valuable time. May I too offer my condolences on the passing of your First Minister.'

'Thank you, Neefe. Now, Ludwig, am I right in thinking it is still your desire to go to Vienna and meet with Herr Mozart?'

Ludwig nodded enthusiastically, as aware as the two men of the palpable lack of tension in the room, compared to the last time he had sat in this chair.

'Well, who knows? Maybe. We shall see. What do you have for me today?'

Ludwig glanced at Neefe, who nodded encouragingly.

Ludwig opened the folder he was holding on his lap and stood up. In a firm voice, he read from the top sheet of manuscript:

'Three sonatas for pianoforte dedicated to the most worthy Archbishop and Prince Elector of Cologne, Maximilian Friedrich, my Most Gracious Lord. Dedicated and composed by Ludwig van Beethoven, aged eleven.'

As Ludwig walked with determined tread to the piano, which was in position as it had been on the last occasion he was in the ornate room, Neefe spoke in a restrained voice.

'Sire, I should tell you that these three sonatas have been accepted for publication by the house of Bossler in the city of Speyer. Although my pupil published last year a set of variations on a well-known march, these are the first compositions entirely of his own creation to be published. And the title page will bear the dedication he has just read to you.'

The Elector sat back in his chair and allowed the sounds from the piano to wash over him. How like Mozart, he thought, as he listened to the ornate theme that opened the first sonata. But he knew, even as he listened, how difficult it was to play such deceptively simple-sounding music without making mistakes. Try as he might in his own dilettante fashion, the number of Mozart pieces he could play numbered no more than the fingers of one hand, and those all early and undemanding pieces. He knew the music he was listening to now was beyond his capabilities.

With the opening to the second sonata, with its plaintive minor chords, the Elector knew beyond doubt that Bonn had its own Wolfgang Mozart, a musician who would surely one day bring renown to the small city on the banks of the Rhine.

On the evening of 15 April 1784, the Beethoven family sat round the table eating dinner. It was the same table that in the awful floods had saved so many lives.

'So, son, it seems you are to be congratulated on two counts. Tell us first about your appointment.'

'Herr Neefe . . . Herr Neefe said after I played for the Elector that he would ask him – His Grace – to appoint me assistant court organist. Officially. The Elector agreed to let me take the examination. My teacher heard today that I passed. So now I am assistant court organist.'

'And your salary?'

'I . . . I don't know yet. They haven't . . .'

'Bah! Whenever it come to money, they . . . they . . .'

'For goodness' sake, Johann,' said Maria, 'leave the boy alone. He's done well. Now stop criticising him.'

'And Vienna?' asked Johann. 'When, might I ask, are you travelling to the imperial capital?'

'I don't know. The Elector's office . . .'

'Don't know! Don't you know anything?'

'The Elector's office . . .'

'The Elector's office,' Johann mimicked. 'How old are you? Mmm. Well, anyway,' he went on hurriedly, 'you are certainly going up in the world. On nodding terms with the Elector, no less.'

Ludwig heard his two brothers snigger on the other side of the table.

'And I take it your good friend the Elector will pay for this trip, this piece of extravagance being undertaken against my express wishes?'

'Johann . . .'

Ludwig felt his temper rising, the pent-up anger against his father welling up inside him. Unable to restrain himself, he brought his fists down on the table. A glass fell over, spilling water on to the wood.

'Look, I don't know. I only know I am going, that's all.'

'Don't you raise your voice to me, you little . . .'

They were all distracted by the sound of heavy and urgent footsteps on the staircase. There was a knock on the door. Without waiting for an answer, Gottlob Neefe walked into the room.

'I . . . I . . . I'm sorry for disturbing you. But there's been a tragedy. An absolute tragedy. The Elector has died. Suddenly. It happened barely two hours ago. Already the exchequer has ordered all expenses to be stopped immediately. The Grossman company is dismissed. Ludwig, you cannot go to Vienna.'

BOOK THREE

Chapter 1

Ludwig stood motionless in the centre of the Münsterplatz. He stared at the house; so often he had walked past it on his way to the Münsterkirche, but never before had he stopped and really looked at it. Only two storeys high, but with no fewer than nine windows on the first floor, its breadth giving a commanding view of the square. Eight windows spread across the ground floor, four on either side of the front door, and each framed by green shutters. More windows were set into the high roof, the group of three in the centre making it evident that these were no mere attic rooms. Three chimneys rose from the neatly tiled slate roof. A garden separated the front of the house from the street; in it a number of mature bushes stood, their height designed to obscure the interior of the front rooms from the eyes of passers-by. Iron railings, low and shaped in a gentle curve, bordered the front of the garden; in their centre a gate, closed. The railings and gate were raised off the street and two steps led up to the gate. And high above the front door, reaching over the sill of the first-floor window, a cardinal's hat set in stone to commemorate the man for whom the house was originally built, Cardinal Barmann.

In short the house emitted an air of grandeur that to Ludwig, untidily dressed and of a naturally nervous disposition, was overwhelmingly forbidding.

'Come on, Ludwig,' said Franz Wegeler. 'It'll be all right, I promise you. You'll like them a lot. They're such nice people.'

Together they went through the gate, up to the immense front door, and pulled the long bell chain that hung to its right.

Wegeler turned to look at his friend, and a slight feeling of apprehension went through him as he saw the face set in the familiar frown, the eyebrows heavy and the mouth tightly closed, giving the whole visage an air of defiance.

Together they were ushered into the drawing room of the magnificent house, to be met by a tableau of elegantly clad personages. Before Ludwig's eyes could take in the scene – and while they were still desperately scanning the room for a piano – he became aware of a rustling and he involuntarily stepped a small pace backwards as he saw a woman walking towards him and Franz.

'My dear Franz,' she said, 'it is so nice to see you again. I'm so pleased you have come. And . . .' She turned and looked down at Ludwig. A wave of panic swept over him; he tried to open his mouth to speak but couldn't; he tried to step back but his feet seemed to be weighted down with lead.

'Frau Breuning, this is my good friend Ludwig van Beethoven.'

Ludwig felt the woman take his hands in hers and his nose caught the scent of her perfume as she looked at him and spoke.

'Ludwig. I cannot tell you how delighted I am to welcome you to our home. We have heard such a lot about you from Franz. Now, my name is Helene von Breuning, and I would so like you to meet my children. Come.'

She led him into the room and began to introduce him. 'I will begin with my youngest. This is Lorenz, he is now seven years of age; we call him Lenz. Next is Stephan, he is ten. We call him Steffen. Steffen is taking lessons on the violin from Herr Ries, whom I am sure you know. He is a senior member of the court orchestra. Steffen, this is Ludwig. Now, this is my eldest son, Christoph, aged eleven.'

The whole time Frau Breuning kept hold of Ludwig's hand. Now she led him a little away from the group of three boys and said: 'Ludwig, I'd like you to meet my eldest child. This is my daughter Eleonore. She is now thirteen and quite a young lady. Eleonore, will you allow Ludwig to call you Lorchen, as we do?'

Ludwig looked at the girl and felt an instant antipathy towards her. There was something about the way her face was set that made him feel unwanted, unwelcome. He felt the silence as Eleonore let her mother's question hang in the air.

'Lorchen? Will you answer my question? May Ludwig call you Lorchen? I am sure you will say yes.'

Ludwig was surprised to see the young girl's face transform into a radiant smile in no more time than it took to blink. And he was surprised to find himself smiling back, drawn irresistibly by the obvious sincerity of her reaction.

'Of course, Mama. Ludwig, my name is Lorchen. I am pleased to make your acquaintance.' Ludwig felt Frau Breuning release him to allow him to take Lorchen's proffered hand. He barely touched it, before quickly seeking refuge back in the firm and safe grip of her mother.

'So, Ludwig, now you have met the Breuning family. Come, sit here and let us talk. Franz, tell us first, how does it go with our young doctor?'

At first Ludwig listened intently, as his friend explained that his medical studies were progressing favourably at the new university of Bonn, but after a few minutes, his hands thrust underneath him on the chair, he began to gaze round the room. He looked first at the face of Frau Breuning, and found in it warmth and kindness as she listened intently to Franz Wegeler. His eyes then skipped over Christoph and Lorenz, and came to rest on Stephan. He instinctively liked the boy.

Stephan, of the three boys, had by far the most interesting face. His nose was sharp and prominent, the small hump in the middle preventing it from being fine; his eyes were large and full, and his mouth, with a slightly prominent upper lip, was wide and curved. In short, Stephan's face, like his mother's, was kindly. But what struck Ludwig before any of that was the boy's hair. It was absolutely straight and hung round his face as if the head of a mop had simply been placed on his head. It gave him a slightly comical appearance, and made Ludwig want to smile.

He looked then at Eleonore. He saw her turn quickly away and knew she had been looking at him. Her face was strong and to a degree frightening. Ludwing instinctively wanted to look away, but found he couldn't. He was drawn to the face, but it was not because of any beauty in it. He wanted to talk to her, he wanted to ask her if . . .

'Ludwig? Ludwig, I am talking to you.' Frau Breuning's voice was soft but insistent, with a quizzical note. Ludwig frowned, and instinctively braced himself for the strong words which he was used to hearing from adults when he was caught in a reverie. Instead Frau Breuning laughed gently and smiled as she spoke.

'My young friend Franz tells me you are making your way in the world and that you already have quite a reputation as a musician.'

Ludwig listened but said nothing. He knew the words were

complimentary, but of more interest to him was the cadence of Frau Breuning's voice. It was as if the words were coming towards him on an undulating wave of air.

'So, Ludwig. You are assistant court organist in the city of Bonn. What an honour for one so young. Tell us how you achieved it. Children. Pay attention. Listen to Ludwig.'

Ludwig looked quickly round the group. He turned to his friend Franz, who smiled and nodded at him in encouragement.

'I . . . I had to take an examination. Four men, all musicians from the court, sat in the front row of the church. My teacher Herr Neefe was there also. The rain made a lot of noise on the roof of the church. They asked me what I was going to play. I told them I would play my Organ Fugue in D.'

'*Your* Organ Fugue in D?' asked Frau Breuning.

'Yes. I wrote it last year. It's better than any of the other pieces I had to play. So I played it first. Then I played the others.'

Ludwig was aware of more laughter from one of the children, ineffectually stifled with a hand in front of the mouth. But he continued.

'My teacher received a notice from the Elector's office saying I had passed and appointing me assistant court organist. But then, before I was due to start and earn a salary, the Elector died.'

'God rest his soul,' said Frau Breuning, crossing herself. The children muttered the same words in unison.

'Also,' said Ludwig, 'I was due to go to Vienna. The Elector said I could go there to meet Herr Mozart. But he died – the Elector, I mean – and it was cancelled.'

'How sad for you, you poor boy. So what happened then?'

'Just a week ago I received notice from the new Elector's office that I could take up my appointment. They've given me a salary of a hundred and fifty gulden a year. My father says it's practically nothing but that without it, we'd starve.'

'You see, children, the life of an artist is not an easy one.'

'But I cannot go to Vienna. More than anything I want to go there to meet Herr Mozart.'

'Maybe one day, Ludwig. When you are older. Do not give up, if you really want to do it. At any rate, you are now officially the assistant court organist to His Most Gracious Lord the new Elector Maximilian Franz, brother of the Emperor himself. I am so pleased for you. Now, my dear Franz, tell me some more about how your medical studies are going.'

Ludwig allowed the conversation to resume, pleased to be left alone for a moment. Again his eyes began to sweep the room, though not this time to examine faces. He could not find what he sought, though he knew it would be there because Franz had told him so. Finally he turned fully round in his chair to examine the one corner of the room hidden totally from his view. There stood the piano, more ornate than any he had seen.

Without a word Ludwig stood and walked towards the instrument. He ran his fingers over the fine golden filigree inlaid in the rich wooden sides and allowed his fingers to stroke the ivory keys, now yellowing slightly with age.

'It's a Stein,' he said in a voice barely audible. 'From Augsburg. I've never played on a Stein.' And he sat on the plush, velvet-covered stool, looked up quickly to make sure that the others were all involved in conversation and began to play, softly at first then progressively louder.

For fully ten minutes he played, without stopping. He allowed the closing notes to reverberate round the piano's wooden frame and finally evaporate before lifting his fingers from the keys, standing up and quietly returning to his chair.

There was a moment's silence. It was broken softly by Frau Breuning. 'Bravo, Ludwig. That was a very fine rendering. I confess I am not sure of what, though. Sebastian Bach, I would think, or another of that illustrious family. You are truly a most accomplished player. Do you not think so, children?'

Ludwig looked towards the children and saw them nod silently, their eyes on him all the time. 'It was the Piano Concerto in E flat,' he said. 'It is only the first. I will write more.'

'You mean, Ludwig, that you wrote that? Now, young man, you would not be playing a little joke on us, I hope?'

Ludwig looked at Frau Breuning and the innocence in his eyes told her he meant what he said.

There was again silence in the room. Frau Breuning coughed slightly and said, 'You certainly must not take offence if I say so, Ludwig, but you play with a very firm style. I have not seen our dear old piano shake so.'

Ludwig frowned and looked up. But the frown became a smile and he said, 'It is because I play the organ too much. On the organ I have to bend my fingers the wrong way at the joints. It is bad for my piano-playing. I should play the piano more,' and he held out his hands and demonstrated with his fingers what he meant.

'Ludwig!' said Frau Breuning, clapping her hands with glee. 'I can do you a service in more ways than one. First, you will teach Lenz and Lorchen to play the piano. For that I will of course remunerate you. You agree, of course, don't you, Ludwig?'

'Mama. He's too young. I will not take lessons from a boy.'

'Lorchen!' For the first time there was a note of anger in Frau Breuning's voice. 'In the first place, kindly do not speak in those terms when there are honoured guests in our house. And secondly, my question was addressed to Ludwig, not to you. Now, Ludwig?'

Ludwig looked at Lorchen. He continued to look at her until she smiled. 'Why do you stare at me, Ludwig?' she asked.

Ludwig looked back at her mother. 'Yes, I will teach them.'

'Good. And in gratitude for that, I shall make you a promise. You may come to this house whenever you please to play on our piano. You need not await an invitation. You may treat the piano as if it belonged to you. Ah,' she added wistfully, 'how my dear husband would have enjoyed hearing you play. He quite prided himself on his musical talents.'

Involuntarily, in a gesture she would remember for many years, Ludwig rushed to Frau Breuning. At the last instant he restrained himself and stood before her, looking up into her face from under his heavy brow. The words would not come and he said nothing.

Helene von Breuning looked down into that complex face and her heart went out to the awkward but brilliantly talented boy.

The Elector Maximilian Franz sat stolidly in the ornate chair at the head of the long, wide table and surveyed the councillors seated around it. He noticed how each of them was engaged in hushed conversation with his immediate neighbour and it irked him. He knew full well that if his predecessor had been in his place, no such insubordination would have occurred. All eyes would have been turned to him, waiting for him to declare the meeting open. But then his predecessor had had the authority of years and the unsurpassable advantage that he personally had appointed each man around the table.

I know, he thought, why they are doing this. They consider me a mere twenty-eight-year-old, whose appointment to Bonn was engineered by my mother. If that's what they believe, they are seriously underestimating me and the Habsburg family, just as the French are underestimating my sister Marie Antoinette.

He coughed slightly; it made no impression on those present. He began to derive some amusement from the circumstances. If I were truly the fool I know these men take me for, he thought, I would allow anger to affect my judgement. I would bang my fist on the table, I would shout. And then I would be doomed; it would take me years to establish my authority. What do these men know of me? Nothing, except what their spies at the imperial court have told them, and that, no doubt, is that I am possessed of little brain. They would do well to remember, he thought, that I was once a soldier, and have been well schooled in the art of tactics.

Quietly Max Franz slid back his chair, rose from it and, limping slightly from a damaged knee suffered on the battlefield, left the room. He waited a few moments on the other side of the door, then opened it, entered, closed the door sharply and walked to his chair.

'Gentlemen, good morning,' he said in a loud voice. 'I am grateful to you for making your valuable time available to me. This is, as you will be aware, my first council meeting, and I beg you to indulge me should I fail to meet the standards of excellence set by my illustrious predecessor, God rest his soul.'

There were mutterings around the table, and a number of men crossed themselves.

'My Most Gracious Lord,' said a voice to his immediate right, 'I know I speak on behalf of my fellow councillors when I say that you are truly welcome to this fair city of ours. Here in Bonn we take some pride in the fact that our city is the finest on the Rhine. One has only to look at Mainz or Cologne, at the immorality of the people and the darkness in their souls that matches the darkness in the streets, to know that in Bonn there exists all that is pure, that the citizens of this great city carry in their hearts a love for God, just as they will always carry a love for their great benefactor, Maximilian Friedrich.'

'Councillor, I am grateful for your words. There is none more grateful than I for the achievements of the late Elector, and none more aware than I of the tasks that lie ahead. For that reason I propose—'

'My Lord,' said another voice, 'if I—'

Max Franz held up his hand. 'By way of introduction let me say I have heard words in the palace corridor that I have decided to take advantage of the Papal bull obtained for me by my mother the Empress and defer my assumption of priestly vows for ten years. Lest any of you here fear I shall neglect my holy office of Archbishop, let me inform you I shall enter the seminary in Cologne at the end of November; I shall expect the Nuntius to ordain me subdeacon eight days later, deacon eight days after that, then priest before Christmas. It is my intention to read my first Mass on Christmas Eve in the Florian chapel. Now . . .' and he waved down the mutterings around the table, 'to business at hand. In order that I may properly be able to conduct the affairs of state, gentlemen, I require you to prepare for me full and detailed reports concerning all branches of administration. I wish you to lay before me the salaries of all those in the court's employ, including of course your own. I wish to know the expenditure of the court on public services, on the theatre and music. In short, gentlemen, I wish to know the exact state of the court's revenues.'

He paused a moment and enjoyed the total silence with which his words were received. Then he spoke again.

'Furthermore, gentlemen, from each of you I require pro-posals of how savings of fifty per cent in your respective departments can be made. The next council meeting will be a week from now at this time. I expect you to present your reports to me then. I bid you all good morning.'

Max Franz left the room, giving his limp an added emphasis, knowing they would be aware it was a battlefield wound. He smiled at the cacophony of voices that began the moment he closed the door behind him. He walked along the corridor as briskly as his injured knee would allow him, ignoring the portraits staring down at him, to his private apartment. Entering his study he sat at the desk, pulling a sheet of notepaper towards him. He dipped his quill in the inkpot and began to write.

Bonn, June 1784

My dear Count

Since I am now installed in the Electoral palace here in Bonn and have begun my governance, I feel the moment is appropriate to express my gratitude for the worthy and valuable advice you offered me before I left Vienna. Heavy as my heart was to be leaving the bosom of my family, it was considerably lightened by your words of encouragement.

Rest assured that by a separate missive I have relayed your kind words also to my dear sister in Paris, whose daily travail as Queen of that foreign country puts my own slight apprehensions to shame.

As for my duties, I began them this morning, with the same effect on the worthy councillors as a cat set amongst birds! Unbeknown to them I have studied a confidential report on the exchequer prepared by First Minister Belderbusch shortly before he died. What a parlous picture it presents. My predecessor's rule was known for its thrift, but it seems that in the last years great sums of money were spent to fight, as the Minister put it, 'the forces of subversion'. A network of spies was in operation, whose chief function, it seems to me, was milking the court of its funds.

I believe, as did my predecessor, the threat of subversion to be greatly exaggerated. The Illuminati, so-called, are nothing worse than worthy citizens with misguided intentions. As such they are easy to deal with. It is no secret that the leader of the movement here in Bonn is the court organist. He is a Saxon and is also a member of the Calvinist religion. But he has a fine assistant, little more than a boy, who this year past has performed at church services with enormous accomplishment. He is from a poor family. I have not yet heard him play, but I am told he is a prodigy in the mould of the Austrian Wolfgang Mozart. If that is so, I shall encourage him.

Meanwhile I still have it in my mind to invite Mozart to come to Bonn as Kapellmeister. (The simple expedient of reducing Lucchesi's salary should create the vacancy!) You must understand that it is my profound desire to turn Bonn into the cultural capital of Germany, to be to this country what Vienna is to my own. And for that, my dear Count, I require your help.

As a member of one of the most aristocratic families of Austria, in whose veins flows even the blood of the Austrian monarchy, and whose love for the arts is as fulsome as my own, you have a contribution to make to this city that none can match. I am asking you, indeed I implore you, to put behind you thoughts of war and glory on the battlefield, and come instead to Bonn. It would be my privilege to instal you in this very same palace, and as Grand Master of the Teutonic Order I would actively seek to enrol you in that illustrious band.

Give what I have written careful consideration, my dear Count. I shall shortly be entering the seminary at Cologne to prepare for holy orders, in order that I may assume the mantle of Archbishop of Cologne and Münster. If now you and your safety are in my thoughts, know that when I am ordained you will be constantly in my prayers.

Max Franz signed the letter, sprinkled sand on the wet ink and folded the paper. Lifting the lighted candle he dropped hot red wax on the reverse and made the seal with the Electoral ring on the fourth finger of his right hand.

Picking up his quill again, he addressed the letter to Count Ferdinand Ernst Waldstein, at the headquarters of the imperial army in Valletta, Malta.

The two friends strolled aimlessly along the banks of the stream, soaking up the warm sun of the midsummer day. The only sounds were of the water as it broke on the stones, the birds high above and the brush of the long grass against the leather boots of the walkers.

Franz Wegeler broke the reverie the two young men had fallen into. 'Is it not a good day to be alive, Ludwig?'

Ludwig said nothing. Franz walked on a few paces and it was some seconds before he realised Ludwig was no longer with him. He looked back. Ludwig had sat down in the tall grass on the edge of the stream. His knees supported his elbows and his head was in his hands.

'Come on, young friend, the world is not about to end. You'll survive.'

There was silence for a few moments. Ludwig looked up, his eyes red from rubbing. 'I was a fool. But, Franz, I could not help myself. That man Heller is so pompous. He calls himself a singer, an artist. Listen to the birds, Franz. Listen! They are more of an artist than that man.'

'You still should not have done it, Ludwig. Heller is a highly respected court singer,' Franz said, walking back to join his friend.

'Highly respected! I'll tell you why he's highly respected. Because he is tedious and boring. He has no ... no ... no spark. Why else is he always chosen to sing the Lamentations of Jeremiah in Holy Week? And you know how tedious they are – each vocal line just four consecutive notes. Tedious. Until' – and his eyes sparkled – 'the third line. That's the interesting one because that's where the singer can improvise. And improvisation is what makes a real musician. After the improvisation a few notes from me on the organ to bring him back to the key for the fourth and final line.'

'But, Ludwig, the Lamentations are sung in Holy Week. It's a solemn time. You're supposed to be—'

'I know, Franz, I know. I had no intention of being anything else. The rehearsal was perfect, so I asked Herr Heller if, when he came to recite the Lamentations before the congregation, I might vary the accompaniment.'

After a few moments of deliberate silence, Franz said, 'That is not quite all you said to Heller, is it, Ludwig?'

Ludwig allowed a smile of mischief to break through the lines of depression which had set upon his face. 'It is true I asked his permission to try and throw him off the note with my accompaniment. But, Franz, I asked his permission and he readily gave it. He even said, "It will take more than a child musician to throw Heller off the note."'

'I wish I had been there,' Franz said. 'Tell me again what happened, Ludwig. I shall enjoy it just as much, although it will be the tenth time I have heard it!'

Ludwig said nothing for a few moments. Then the words burst from him. 'He's a fool, Franz, a fool!' and as he said 'fool' for the second time he stamped his foot down in the water, sending a spray of drops over both of them. 'I even made it easy for him to begin with. Just small variations. And it gave him no difficulty. So I allowed my fingers to wander some more. But, Franz, always I played solemnly and with dignity. And I stayed in the same key. Any good musician would have had no trouble at all. But as I made the variations more and more complex, I heard his voice begin to waver. First he stumbled over the text and then he could not find the note again. But I actually helped him, Franz. Far from enjoying his misfortune, as I was accused of later, I actually helped him. With my little finger I kept striking the note he should sing . . .' and he struck the air with his little finger to emphasise the point, 'and still he could not find it. In the end he just stood there. I brought the music to a solemn close. Heller resumed his seat. But I could hear some laughter from somewhere and I could feel his anger.'

Franz laughed out loud. 'You should not have done it, Ludwig. Of that there is no doubt. But I still would have given anything to see Heller's face. And what of Kapellmeister Lucchesi? He was there, wasn't he? And he was impressed with your playing, is that not true?'

'He called me to his room the next day and said he had not heard such skilful playing ever from one so young. He was nervous. He kept drumming the table with his fingers. Then he said my behaviour was atrocious, and that if I ever attempted to make a fool of a court musician again, he would ensure I was dismissed from my position as assistant organist.'

'Ludwig, I am afraid tact is not—'

'Lucchesi is a fool as well. He calls himself a musician. Where will he be fifty years from now? Dead and forgotten. And his music, his operas? Dead and forgotten too. What use is it being a musician if your music doesn't live on after your death?'

'I suppose Our Most Gracious Lord the Elector is a fool too, Ludwig?'

Ludwig smiled and thought for a moment. 'I like Max Franz. He is also a better musician than people give him credit for.'

'How on earth can you know that, Ludwig?'

'Because we talked of music when he called me to see him.'

'But he called you because Heller made an official complaint about you. He called you to punish you.'

Ludwig chuckled. 'The first thing he said to me was "I hear you humbled the great Heller." He was as surprised as I was that the stupid man had made an official complaint. He said that in order to allow Heller to save face, he would command that in future only the simple accompaniment be played to the Lamentations. Then we talked about music and Mozart. And Vienna.'

'Did you tell him you were going to go . . . ?'

Ludwig nodded. 'I told him only the late Elector's death prevented it. And I asked him if he would send me. He said the expense made it impossible. But he said one day I could become Kapellmeister, like my grandfather. But, Franz, I want more than that.'

'And you, a boy, told His Grace the Elector that?'

'I liked him. We spoke easily together.'

'He sings, the Elector, does he not?'

'He sings. But he is also a good viola player. I have heard

him in the court chamber orchestra several times. He is a good musician. There is no doubt about that. I told him so. He denied it. Not just out of modesty. He argued with me and reasoned as to why he was of no use to the world of music. I find that an attractive quality in a man. Arrogance is what I cannot abide, Franz. More than anything it is arrogance which makes me angry. That is why I threw Heller off the note.'

Franz laughed. 'Ludwig, you must not take offence, but I have heard that word used also to describe you.'

Ludwig shot Franz an angry look. Then his features softened. 'Arrogance is being proud of something you do not have,' he said quietly.

The two young men sat in silence, watching the water flow by. The sun had gone behind a cloud, causing a slight chill in the air.

'Come on, let's walk home,' said Franz, standing up. They began to walk. Franz grasped Ludwig's arm and said enthusiastically, 'Tell me about Lorchen, Ludwig. How do you enjoy teaching her the piano? Eh? Come on, Ludwig, tell me. Does she smile at you? Do you flirt with her? Ludwig,' he said, lowering his voice, 'have you kissed her?'

Ludwig shook his arm free. His face was set in a scowl as the two of them walked on.

Chapter 2

Maria Magdalena lay quietly for a moment, allowing the peacefulness of early dawn to wash over her. It was still dark, and she could see from the opaque patterns on the outside of the window panes that there had been a heavy frost. She felt the chill air on her face and knew that the moment she got out of bed the familiar shivering would start. And then she would cough. At first the irritation low in her throat had not worried her. After the damp summer when autumn brought a lowering of the temperature, everybody had complained of ailments. But hers had persisted. And a week ago she had begun dislodging phlegm when she coughed. She was sure it would pass. But it was just another worry to add to many.

She half turned and felt rather than saw Johann's massive back, his fleshy body incongruously lying in the foetal position. He was breathing deeply and silently, which did not surprise her, since she knew he had come to bed only three or four hours ago, and was therefore in the deepest part of his sleep. The alcohol he had consumed the night before would ensure he would stay that way for some hours yet. She had long ago given up waking him prematurely.

What contempt she now felt for the man she had married! Why, oh why, had he thrown everything away? Look at his father. A fine man; a fine musician. No one could fault him for the way in which he had brought up his son. He'd encouraged him, taught him. But where had it led? At the same time that she despised her husband, she also felt pity for him. The tragedy was that he had inherited his mother's character, and she had ended up in an institution. There was no fibre, no backbone on that side of the family. And to think that old Ludwig had opposed her own marriage because she had come from a family of merchants. A family, though, with backbone. Without me, Maria thought ruefully, this family would simply have disintegrated.

She it was who had known things would change with a change of Elector. She had warned Johann. At first she hadn't realised how accurate her fears were. It was only in a drunken depression that Johann had confessed to her that with the death of Belderbusch a portion of his income had disappeared. Johann claimed that the First Minister had used him 'to gather vital information'. She had called it spying, and had said if that was how he had earned money, she'd just as soon not have it.

But what else could Johann do? She knew, because unkind tongues had made sure she knew, that in the report submitted to the new Elector on court employees, her husband had been described as having 'a very stale voice' and as being 'very poor'. She knew both were accurate, and she alone of the two of them knew how fortunate Johann had been not to lose his job at court. Only his length of service, twenty-eight years, had prevented him becoming unemployed. But what sort of salary was three hundred and fifteen florins? It was barely enough to keep him supplied with alcohol, let alone to support a family. Now there was this silly business where he was deluding himself he was owed money by the family of the late First Minister, Belderbusch. He had promised her it would be the end of their problems but she knew there was not the remotest possibility of that.

Maria slid out of the bed and stood up. A wave of weakness swept over her. She swayed slightly and remained still for a few seconds until the dizziness passed. It was long enough for the cold air to penetrate her nightgown. She shivered, at first slightly, then uncontrollably. She pulled the woollen shawl she kept by the bed tightly around her shoulders and walked unsteadily into the next room. Gratefully she slumped into a chair. Now she gave into the cough she had suppressed in the bedroom. She was sick, she knew that. She only prayed it was nothing serious.

Slowly, quietly, she began to sob. 'A chain of sorrows' was how she had once described marriage to Cäcilie Fischer. A death sentence would be more accurate, she now thought. She rested her head in her hands and fought to hold back the tears of despair. The tiniest movement in her stomach added to her misery.

She had kept it secret from Johann for a month now, but she knew she could not keep it from him much longer. Her fear was that the knowledge there would be another mouth to feed in the family might be the final blow needed to break him. Then what would happen to the Beethovens? Starvation? Silently she prayed that the baby might be born dead. Then the full horror of that thought swept over her, and she prayed out loud for forgiveness.

Johann van Beethoven stood naked in front of the full-length mirror and ran his hands briskly through the thick hair that coated his chest and stomach.

'Revenge at last on Belderbusch,' he said under his breath.

Playfully he slapped his stomach, weighed it with both hands and smiled a satisfied smile. He reached for the large stiff-haired brush he kept by the bed and began to scrub his body. Beginning with his chest, he moved down to his stomach and down further to his thighs and legs; then his arms and shoulders and finally, lifting his penis with one hand, he scrubbed his scrotum vigorously.

With a deep exhalation of breath he sat down on the edge of the bed, enjoying the burning sensation that emanated from his skin and watching the more tender parts of his body turn deep red, the brush marks showing up as white lines. A shiver passed through him and he muttered a quick prayer to keep out the devil. But he knew it would take more than the devil to spoil the day. His day. The day he had waited for these past two years. At last the chance to get even with Belderbusch, to settle the score for not being appointed Kapellmeister. He knew it was Belderbusch who had poisoned the Elector's mind against him. Now I get my revenge, he thought. If only the old fool was still alive to witness my victory.

He snatched up the glass from the bedside table and sucked the raw egg into his mouth. He juggled it with his tongue until it broke and he enjoyed feeling the slimy yolk spread over his tongue and trickle down its sides. Then, as he had done for years on days when he would be singing solo, he let the yolk slide slowly down his throat. He would not be singing solo today but he would, he knew, be using his voice to great effect.

He belched. The taste of last night's alcohol came into his mouth, but it did not have its usual effect of causing him to stick out his tongue and grimace with disgust. Instead he allowed it to flow up through his nose and it whetted his appetite for the celebratory drinking he knew was just a few short hours away. He had left Klein with instructions to have the wine on ice at the tavern for three o'clock in the afternoon.

For two minutes he sat still, his eyes closed, his chest moving rhythmically to his steady breathing, contemplating his victory.

A burst of childish giggles from the next room shook him back to reality. Quickly and without fuss he dressed in his finest clothes, a white cravat knotted at the neck, black breeches buckled below the knee over white stockings, and the double-buttoned, high-collared black tailcoat he had not worn since his wedding day. He removed his wig from its stand, positioned it on his head, adjusting it until the fit was perfect. Finally he took hold of the curled sides and pulled them down firmly over the top of his ears. Cursing quietly, he remembered he had forgotten to powder it. He snatched up the pot, sprinkled some powder on to the top of the wig, and cursed louder when the residue fell on to his shoulders. He brushed the flecks off, adjusted the sit of the coat, and strode out of the room.

His heart sank, as it always seemed to, when he looked at Maria. Now, he thought, she looked more pitiful than ever. Her skin was grey and the fullness of her face, which he used to find so attractive, had simply evaporated. Her swollen stomach accounted for it, no doubt – as well as giving me another wretched mouth to feed, he thought.

'Well, boys, what do you think of your father?'

Caspar, now in his thirteenth year, feigned disinterest. He was the elder of the two brothers, but his physique and appearance belied it, and he was determined to show it by his behaviour. His red hair had become more tightly curled as he had grown, but its auburn lustre had become a dull red. But of more disappointment to Caspar was that he was smaller and stockier than his younger brother. Every night he prayed to God to make him grow more quickly than Nikola.

Nikola, two and a half years younger, was a fine-looking boy and he knew it. He could not doubt it – friends of the family were constantly patting him on the head and telling him how handsome he would one day be. He was tall for his age and already had a good physique. The only blemish he had was that his right eye which slipped outwards had not yet corrected itself as his mother had assured him it would. But he was young yet. He was not worried.

Unlike his brother, Nikola was determined to garner his

father's favour. He let out a little shriek and ran to Johann's side, tugging at his sleeve. Johann pushed him away with a playful tap on his bottom and readjusted the coat. Ludwig was not in the room.

Johann glanced at his wife and it irritated him that she was looking at the boys and not at him. 'Maria, will you not compliment your husband?'

Maria turned a tired look on him and said in a quiet voice: 'What's the use, Johann? You're simply deluding yourself.'

A flash of anger shot through him. 'Maria! You have no right to say that. Maria the pessimist. Always miserable. And with you in that condition, you should be cheering for me. How else could we possibly manage?' He caught the doleful look both boys assumed, and said more quietly: 'Where is the laughing Maria I once knew?'

'Gone, Johann. Gone. Gone for ever.' Her eyes moistened and she lifted a finger to wipe away the tear before it could fall.

'By tonight she will be back again. Mark my words. By tonight our problems will be over. Over, Maria. Do you hear me?'

'Oh, Johann, you're such a fool.' Despite herself she could not stop the words pouring out. 'Even if you were to get the money it wouldn't be the end of our problems. You'll drink it away. Don't tell me you won't. I know you, Johann. You'll go to the tavern and that will be that.'

'Maria, I—'

'But that won't arise anyway. You are not going to get the money. I know that. And if you were honest with yourself, Johann, truly honest, you too would know that.' She was angry that the familiar irritation in her lungs had caused her to start coughing again. She had so much more she wanted to say, but she knew her coughing would give Johann the opportunity to interrupt.

Johann banged his fist on the table. 'You tell me to be honest with myself. Well, now it's the turn of the state to be honest with me. Do you think I would petition the Elector for no reason? I have a list, Maria, a signed list. Now it is in the hands of the court. Do you think the Elector would have passed it on to the court if he had not believed it was . . .' He stopped himself, then added, 'if he had not been impressed by my claim?'

Maria looked away and sighed, Johann's litany all too familiar.

She ordered the two boys to run off and play, which they did without a moment's hesitation.

Johann continued. 'I was wronged by Belderbusch, Maria. He made me a promise. I was to be appointed Kapellmeister. The whole court knew that. All he asked in return were gifts for himself and the Countess. And who was I to refuse the First Minister? And the mistress he shared with the Elector? I sent them cases of wine, jewellery, silver ornaments, gifts for those young brats Belderbusch had sired on her—'

'Oh, Johann, stop. Do you expect me to believe you had that much money to throw around?'

'The list, Maria. Do not forget the list. All the gifts are written there, and the First Minister signed it, Maria. He signed it. Oh, yes. Do you think I would be foolish enough to give so many gifts and not have proof of it? A signed list, now in the hands of the court. Today the court will deliver judgement, and tomorrow the Count's heirs will repay me.'

'You ask me to believe the Count bribed you and then signed a document proving the corruption? Johann, why do you take everyone for a fool? Maybe I am a fool. Certainly you treat me like one. But the Elector, the court. You take them all for fools also. But they are not, Johann.' She set her jaw to force the last words out before having to give way once more to coughing. '*You* are the fool, Johann. *You*. And a dishonest fool too.'

Johann raised his hand to slap her. She continued to look at him defiantly. He lowered his hand, pulled a handkerchief from his cuff and mopped the perspiration from his brow. Then, straightening his coat one last time, he walked from the room, down the stairs and on to the street, and strode off in the direction of the courthouse.

The senior court musician Franz Ries, greatly respected at court and instantly recognisable by his small eccentricity of always wearing a velvet tasselled cap, was now taking more than the usual interest he had for some years past in Ludwig.

At Ludwig's request he was teaching him the violin, along with Stephan von Breuning. Ries did not ask for payment from Ludwig. He said he regarded it as a pleasure. His side of the bargain, he said, was that he would ask Ludwig to teach his baby son Ferdinand the piano when he was a little older. Ludwig happily agreed.

The atmosphere at court – with an Elector who had made

it clear he would keep on the entire complement of court musicians – was more relaxed than it had been for some years. For Ludwig the environs of the Electoral palace, where as a child he had walked with his grandfather, were a preferable place to be than the house on the Rheingasse.

Ludwig had a new sibling, Maria Margaretha Josepha. He hoped that a baby girl would help lift his mother from the depressed mood that seemed to envelop her. But it was not to be so. He watched as she clasped the baby to her chest, looking down at it with pity, as if she had accepted that the child's life would be unhappy. Or it could have been guilt on her face, guilt at bringing another child into the world. Ludwig did not know. He knew he could not ask.

He no longer spoke to his father unless it was unavoidable. Johann van Beethoven had become a figure of fun in the town and of contempt in his own house after his disastrous attempt to obtain money from the estate of the late First Minister.

The magistrate had much fun at Johann's expense. He had held up to the court Johann's list of gifts he claimed to have given to Belderbusch, and pointing to the signature at the bottom, he had invited comparison between it and the First Minister's signature at the foot of at least a dozen state documents he had before him.

'You will note,' the magistrate had declaimed, 'how consistent are the signatures of the late Count von Belderbusch on these state papers. Compare them with this signature on the Beethoven document, and you will ask yourself, as I have asked myself, whether the court musician standing before us is attempting to play a practical joke. So many are the discrepancies between this signature and the others that I am forced to . . . to . . . congratulate Herr van Beethoven on at least spelling the late First Minister's name correctly!'

The magistrate had stilled the laughter that ensued by raising his hand and adopting a grave tone. He looked straight across the small room at Johann van Beethoven and said: 'You may consider yourself fortunate, my good sir, that I have decided not to invoke the law against you. You may attribute my leniency solely to the many years of service you and your revered father have given to the court. Forgery is a serious crime. I attribute it to a momentary lapse of judgement on your part. Now I suggest you leave this court forthwith and it is my earnest counsel to you that you do not attempt to involve yourself with the law again. If you do, you cannot expect similar leniency next time.'

The magistrate's words, and the speed with which they had circulated around the city, had broken Johann's spirit. For several weeks he could not bear to be seen in public, even eschewing his visits to the tavern. Not that that had lessened his drinking; he simply remained at home, locked in an upper room, in a state of ceaseless inebriation.

Ludwig thought often about his father's downfall. He had once been a competent musician, of that there was no doubt. So why had his father thrown it away? Obviously the failure to follow his own father and become Kapellmeister had hurt him deeply, but Ludwig believed the reason lay in the actual make-up of the man. So often he remembered that tour of the Rhine towns his father had taken him on; then he had behaved like a gentleman, like a member of the Bonn court, and Ludwig had been proud of him. But he simply could not maintain it and Ludwig was forced to recognise that the flaw lay in his father's character: he was a weak man.

When he was neither at home nor at the court, Ludwig was at the Breunings' house on the Münsterplatz. He was teaching Eleonore and her younger brother the piano, as Frau Breuning had requested. He also took seriously her invitation to use their piano whenever he wished.

The servants were accustomed to opening the door to the untidily dressed boy clutching a folder under his arms bursting with sheets of manuscript paper. Without a word Ludwig would walk straight into the salon, pull a table across to the piano and begin work, oblivious to who might be in the room. Frau Breuning had issued instructions to children and servants alike that when Ludwig was at the piano he was to be given privacy.

But as he widened his musical skills, Ludwig became increasingly frustrated with life in Bonn. He was in no doubt that in a very short time the city and its musicians would have nothing left to teach him. Here he was, a mere boy, and yet he knew instinctively that he was a being apart.

There was only one musician who could teach him anything, and he was five hundred miles away in Vienna. Ludwig still felt frustration that the death of Maximilian Friedrich had prevented him from going to Vienna and meeting Wolfgang Mozart. He had discussed it with Neefe, who had said that with the drastic economies the new Elector had implemented, there was no prospect of Ludwig being allowed to go to Vienna. Yet, as the year 1786 drew to a close, he became obsessed once again with the desire to go to Vienna.

For many weeks he wrestled with the problem. His father's pecuniary circumstances and his duties at court made it in practical terms impossible. Finally he decided he could do no better than repeat the tactic which had proved successful with the previous Elector.

Chapter 3

Ludwig had completed a piano concerto, but he was not satisfied with it. It would not do for Maximilian Franz. What then? A new work for solo viola? No. On reflection he made the decision that the three quartets for piano and strings were more appropriate, since he had written them in the style of Mozart.

He had composed the quartets more than a year previously, but had shown them to no one, except Neefe. He was aware that they were unconventional and that the musicians at court, if they were allowed to play the score, would take great delight in criticising them. Even Neefe had been strongly critical of his choice of instruments.

'A piano and three strings, Ludwig? Why? It's unknown. It's eccentric even. No one has done it. Not even your revered Mozart.'

'Does that mean it can't be done?'

'Yes, it does. Because if it could be done, it would have been done. There is a very good reason why a piano cannot play with three strings. Because the three strings would not be heard. The piano alone would be heard. Why do you not adapt the piano part for a second violin? Then you would have a string quartet?'

Ludwig shook his head. 'No. Not yet. The string quartet is different. It will be a long time before I turn to four strings.'

The very fact that he had chosen an unusual combination of instruments was, Ludwig felt, another reason for dedicating the piano quartets to the Elector. He was a man of music and he would appreciate their singular quality.

The piano quartets needed a little revision. He could not work on the piano at home; he did not want to work on them at the court, for fear of attracting attention. It was naturally to the Breuning house that Ludwig turned, and to the Münsterplatz that he directed his footsteps one evening at the beginning of the new year.

Head down and with the familiar bundle of manuscripts under his arm, Ludwig rang the bell that hung to the side of the huge door, walked silently past the servant who admitted him and turned into the drawing room which contained the piano.

Within a matter of minutes he was deeply involved in reworking a passage of the first piano quartet, oblivious of his surroundings. It was several seconds before the gentle voice of Helene von Breuning registered with him.

'Well, what a fine collection of musicians I have at my house tonight. Ludwig, come and bid good evening to my guests. I know they are no strangers to you.'

Ludwig looked up and saw the familiar face of Franz Ries, and with him was Joseph Reicha, musical conductor at court and solo cellist. Reicha had only recently joined the Bonn court from Wallerstein, where the orchestra was said to be the best in Bavaria.

Ludwig, rather resenting the interruption, nodded unsmilingly to both.

'So serious for one so young,' said Reicha.

'Herr Ries, Herr Reicha, you must forgive me, but I was totally absorbed in what I was doing.'

Reicha nodded. 'Well, to us professionals, music is a serious business.'

Ludwig turned and began to walk towards the door.

'Ludwig,' cried Frau Breuning, 'you cannot be intending to leave us, surely?'

'I do not wish to intrude.'

'Not at all, dear Ludwig. You know well that I never consider your visits an intrusion.' And she walked across to him and led him to a chair.

'Now, gentlemen, with three such talented musicians in my house, together with their instruments I am glad to say, I will not let the moment pass. But first let me summon the children, so they can hear fine music being made.'

The two older men demurred, but to no avail. Ludwig sat quietly, clutching his folder, regretting that he had chosen this evening to come to the Breuning house. He sensed where it would lead, rather wishing it would not.

Franz Ries spoke. 'Ludwig, tell us how you are progressing. What are you working on? I must say, your playing at court at the moment is most impressive. I trust you're finding time to practise the violin? Just a little.'

Ludwig smiled at Ries. He liked the older man perhaps better than any other of the senior court musicians. 'Yes, sir. But right now I am revising some quartets I wrote. I . . . I . . . I want to dedicate them to the Elector.'

'Quartets? For what purpose? Normally there is a reason for a dedication. Or is it just flattery?' asked Reicha.

'I want to go to Vienna. I want to meet Herr Mozart. The late Elector agreed . . .'

'Ah, yes,' said Ries, 'I had forgotten. The three piano sonatas you published. They were dedicated to Maximilian Friedrich, were they not?' Ludwig nodded. 'And he was going to send you to Vienna.'

'But he died. It was unfortunate.'

'More unfortunate for him,' said Reicha, with a laugh, but he stifled it quickly as Frau Breuning registered disapproval of his humour. She had re-entered the room, Eleonore in front of her, her hands on the girl's shoulders.

'Just my Lorchen and I to be your audience, gentlemen.'

Ludwig felt a shaft of nervousness go through him. He glanced up to find Eleonore looking directly at him. He dropped a sheet of manuscript paper and cursed under his breath. He did not look at her again, but busied himself with his papers. He knew that in a few moments he would be playing the piano, and then he would be her equal.

'Now, gentlemen,' said Frau Breuning, 'I will order the refreshments of your choice in a moment. But first, what will you play for us?'

Reicha said: 'Young Ludwig here tells us he has some quartets he has written. Shall we play those? We will be missing one part, of course, since there are only three of us. And we will be playing at sight. But I am sure we will not find it too difficult, eh, Ludwig?'

Ries interjected: 'Yes. But first we must ask your permission, Ludwig. Will you allow us to play your music?'

There was silence. Ries continued: 'I ask, because with only three of us, we will not be able to do justice to what you have written.'

'I hardly think—' Reicha began.

'Here is what I suggest,' said Ries quickly. 'I will take the first violin part. You, Ludwig, can play viola; and Joseph, of course, cello. We are missing only the second violin. Now, Ludwig, will you agree?'

Ludwig shook his head. 'They are *piano* quartets. For piano and strings, violin, viola and cello.'

Reicha laughed out loud; Ries frowned. There were stifled giggles from the sofa.

'Piano and strings, did you say? Piano and strings? Ludwig, that is a very strange combination of instruments,' said Reicha. 'In fact . . .' he thought for a moment, 'I know of none of the great composers who have used it. Not even, to my knowledge, Mozart, although I may be mistaken. So why have you, a young musician at the start of his career . . . ?'

'Ludwig,' said Ries, again in a kindly tone, 'it is indeed an unknown combination.' He walked across and laid a hand on Ludwig's shoulder. 'But you must not think that because it is unknown, it has also been unthought of. It *has* been thought of. Discussed. But always it has been rejected. And do you know why, Ludwig? Because the piano is a strong instrument, so strong it can fill a concert hall just on its own. What chance do three feeble strings have against it? It hurts me to admit it, Ludwig, it hurts me, since I am a violinist myself. But my poor instrument is no match for the mighty piano.'

Ludwig sat quietly while Ries returned to his chair. After a few moments he lifted his head. 'My teacher Herr Neefe has said the same thing. But I believe it is not so impossible. I believe the balance can be right. Can we play the first of the three quartets, the one in E flat major? I would like you to hear it, even without the viola part.'

'Yes, gentlemen, play it for us,' said Frau von Breuning. 'I myself would very much like to hear it, and so would Lorchen here.'

Without further words the two older musicians quickly tuned their instruments to Ludwig's A from the piano and arranged the manuscripts on music stands that the servants had hurriedly placed in front of them.

They were barely ready when Ludwig threw his head up and brought it instantly down, signifying the start. Reicha began fractionally late, and after a few bars called: 'Slower, Ludwig, remember this is our first reading.' But Ludwig played on and the two men struggled to keep up with him.

At one moment both men stopped playing, and when Ludwig stopped too, several bars later, both complained – Reicha more vehemently than Ries – that the score was so untidily written that it was impossible to read at sight. Without a word, Ludwig resumed playing and both men kept up as best they could.

Ludwig played with speed and power. Sometimes he looked at the music propped up in front of him, but mostly he played from memory, the heavy features of his face reflecting the deep concentration of his mind.

Several times he called out, '*Allegro! Allegro con spirito!*'

The first movement ended, the three players reaching the final note respectably together. Frau Breuning and Lorchen applauded. Ludwig made as if to play on, but Reicha said: 'Enough, enough. That will do for now,' and he laid his cello horizontally on the floor. 'Young man, no one can accuse you of writing dull music. But do you understand now what Ries and I meant about the strength of the piano? Our feeble strings were barely audible above all your crashing. And you have not helped matters by writing such a strong piano part. In fact the piano dominates the entire movement. You have made a fundamental error in the balancing of your instrumentation—'

'Joseph, Joseph,' said Ries, with the kindly smile that seemed permanently on his face, 'you are talking to a young man less than half our age. Ludwig, you have written a fine piece of music, and your playing for one so young is remarkable. Now, if I had to make one small criticism it would be only that you have clearly modelled your work closely on Wolfgang Mozart, perhaps too closely. Once or twice I heard a theme that perhaps I have heard in a Mozart work. You are learning, of course, and who better to learn from than that master himself? But be careful to develop at the same time your own style.'

'My own style! My own style!' Ludwig threw his hands up. 'Do you wish to hear my own style? Here is the theme you referred to, Herr Ries,' and he picked it out with the fingers of his right hand. 'You are right. It is Mozart. From a violin sonata. That is Mozart. This is Beethoven.'

And he played the theme again, this time weaving harmonies around it with his left hand. Then another variation, slow at first, then becoming quicker; a fugue followed; a march; a minuet . . . and always the theme was recognisable within the harmonies.

For ten minutes Ludwig played. Not once did he strike a discord. He brought the music to a graceful close and sat looking down at the keys, breathing heavily.

'Bravo!' cried Frau Breuning, and again she and Lorchen clapped.

Joseph Reicha sat with his arms folded, his chin deep into his chest. From his lowered eyes he looked across at the boy still seated at the piano. 'That was most impressive, Ludwig. Why did you not tell us you had composed that? A set of variations on a theme of Mozart. To my mind, if I am to be totally honest with you, it is a more substantial piece of work than your . . . your . . . quartet for strange instruments. When did you compose it?'

Ries said quietly: 'I am not entirely sure that he did.'

'Then who did compose it? Mozart himself?'

'No, no,' said Ries. 'That is not what I meant. Ludwig, am I right? You did not sit down and compose that, did you?'

Ludwig shook his head. 'The theme was Mozart. But the rest . . . I invented it, just now, as I was playing it.'

There was silence. Then Ludwig said: 'That was improvisation. I believe that in improvisation lies the true spirit of music. When a musician improvises he is showing you his soul. It is not music that is written down, that the pianist or violinist reads with his eyes and transfers to his fingers. It . . . it . . . comes from his soul.'

Ludwig snapped his head up as he heard Eleonore cough.

'Impressive words and impressive music, if I might say so,' said Reicha. 'More so, in my view, than the quartets.'

'But the quartets . . . If I dedicate them to the Elector . . .'

'There may not be any need for that, Ludwig,' said Ries. 'If I am not mistaken, you did not compose your quartets recently. Is that correct?'

Ludwig nodded. 'I wrote them some time ago.'

'Yes. Ludwig, believe me when I say you are already a considerably more accomplished musician than when you wrote them. Put them away and move on to better things. As for Vienna, leave that to me. I will speak to the Elector. You never know. He is a reasonable man. He might be persuaded.'

Three weeks later Ludwig sat at the dining table in the kitchen, wishing he could blot out the sound of his father's voice.

'Do you hear me, Ludwig? It's your fault and yours alone. The upheaval will be dreadful. Worse than after the floods. And with your mother sick as well. I don't know how we'll cope.'

'Oh, do hush, Johann,' said Maria with exasperation in her voice. 'If we have to do it we'll manage somehow.'

Ludwig looked at his mother, his face expressing his thanks. But she had turned away. Ludwig was sad for her. Since the birth of the baby Maria Margaretha she seemed to have become even more withdrawn, more remote. If the baby, now nearly a year old, cried in her cot, Maria was less inclined to go to her, clucking with irritation and walking into the adjoining room.

But it was her physical appearance which struck him most. In the last year she had thinned dramatically. Her cheeks were hollow and her skin sallow. She stooped when she stood, her shoulders seeming to sag under an invisible weight.

He wondered how she would cope with this latest crisis, a crisis which his father was unfairly laying at his feet.

With great reluctance Theodor Fischer had told his old friend Johann that the Beethoven family would have to leave the house on the Rheingasse. He made apologies, saying that another family had offered to pay a much higher rent, and of course the Beethovens did not have to move until they had found alternative accommodation.

Johann was in no doubt as to what lay behind it. It was Ludwig's pounding on the piano at all hours of the day and night. The neighbours had had enough, and who could blame them?

Although Ludwig knew that there was no justification to this complaint since he was spending less and less time in the house, the accusation still caused him great pain. Cäcilie, upset for her friend, told him the real reason. Johann had fallen behind with the rent, and had now not paid it for three months. Also, he was returning to the house increasingly late at night and noisily drunk. The neighbours were indeed complaining, but about the father not the son.

Johann, having not taken Herr Fischer's threat seriously at first, had finally realised he needed to take action. He secured rooms in the same house on the Wenzelgasse to which the family had temporarily moved after the flood. There were fewer rooms this time, and smaller, but the house was a pleasant one and in a higher and therefore more fashionable area of the town.

Now Ludwig decided that rather than ignore his father's attack, the best way to handle it was to talk about the house in the Wenzelgasse.

'It's nice there. Maybe it'll be better than here, so close to the river.'

'It'll hardly matter to you, you seem to spend all your time at the palace, with your important friends. And talking of important friends, how is His Grace the . . . ?'

Johann's words were stilled by the sound of footsteps coming up the staircase. His face paled. 'It'll be Fischer. I . . . I'll deal with him. I'll tell him . . .'

There was a gentle but insistent knock on the door and a head with a tasselled velvet cap on it looked round.

Ludwig's face lit up. 'Herr Ries. Here, let me get you a chair. How is Ferdi?'

'He's well, thank you. Very well. No sign of musical promise yet. But we have not given up. And when he's ready you shall teach him his first notes.'

Ludwig smiled. Ries sat in the chair and laid his hands palm-down on the table.

'So, Johann, I bring you good news about your son.'

'He is to get a pay rise. He is to become chief organist. He is to be Kapellmeister.'

'Maybe all that lies in the future. But one step at a time. I am very pleased to tell you – to tell you all – that His Grace the Elector has agreed to send Ludwig to Vienna. There he will meet Wolfgang Mozart who, it is hoped, will take him under his wing.'

Ludwig looked up, trying to suppress the look of pure pleasure on his face, but unable to eradicate the broad smile that suffused it. His mother was looking at him aghast, as if the news Ries had imparted were final proof that her son was a being apart, beyond her comprehension.

His father snorted. 'Impossible. We need him here. To help us with the move. Anyway, I cannot do without his salary, meagre though it is.'

Ries's voice took on a hard edge. 'Johann, the matter is decided. The Elector has ordered it. The financial arrangements are made. It will cost you nothing. In fact you will lose nothing either. Ludwig's salary will be paid to him in Vienna, less that part of it which he gives you, which will be added to your own salary here.'

Maria spoke for the first time since Ries had entered the room. It was a small voice and her face registered the strain of forming the words.

'How long will he be in Vienna for? Who will look after him? His clothes?'

'Do not worry, Maria. We have thought of everything. You

know the court musician Andreas Bamberger? You do, I know, Johann. The horn-player. His wife has a relative in Vienna, a cousin. A musician too. Ludwig is to stay at his house, where his wife will look after him – give him meals, wash his clothes and so on.'

'How long?' she repeated weakly.

'Two months initially. But the Elector is prepared to extend it if he receives good reports. I would imagine a maximum of six months.'

Johann said gruffly, 'What's the difference? We see little enough of him already. He is never here. He might as well go.' He stood and left the room. His heavy footsteps sounded as he went down the stairs and out of the front door.

Maria too got up from her chair, coughing as she did so.

'Are you all right, Maria, my dear?' said Ries. 'You seem . . .'

'I've got a chill. It's gone to my chest. It'll pass.' She looked at Ludwig, then Ries. 'Will he be all right? Will he—?'

'Of course,' said Ries, laughing. 'He's a fine young man. You can be very proud of him.'

Ludwig looked at his mother and flinched slightly as she came towards him. She kissed him fleetingly on the forehead and left the room. Ludwig noticed that her lips were cool.

'Right, my young friend,' said Ries, 'now for the details. You must concentrate.' He pulled a bundle of papers from his pocket. 'We are not sending you direct to Vienna. You are to go to Augsburg first, where you will stay with Councillor Schaden and his wife. Then on to Munich, where you'll stay at the Hotel Zum Schwarzen Adler. From there you'll take the stage east to the Austrian border, via Linz, to Vienna. I'll go through the details with you more throughly later. It's not the most direct route, but it's the most economical. You'll return the same way.'

Ludwig looked at the documents. 'Thank you, Herr Ries. I do not know what . . . I am grateful.'

'So you see, your friends have been diligent on your behalf. But before you let it all go too much to your head, let me tell you what the Elector himself said.'

Ludwig looked straight at Ries, concentrating.

'Do not be offended. All criticism is good if it is constructive. He said, "The boy plays exceedingly well, but his playing is heavy and rough, without finesse. I know Herr Mozart will cure him of that."'

Ludwig smiled. 'Mozart . . . Mozart . . . his compositions . . .'

'To return to practical matters. As I said to your father, you will draw your salary from the Elector's office at the imperial palace in Vienna. It will not be much for you to live on, with the deduction here for your father. But it is enough. Now, the most important thing of all. Here are two letters which as you can see are from the Elector himself. See the seal. This one is from the Elector to his brother, the Emperor Joseph. It introduces you to him and explains why he has sent you to Vienna. It also asks him to arrange for you to meet Wolfgang Mozart. If you take it to the Electoral office in the palace they will arrange for the Emperor to receive it. And this letter . . . this one, see who it is addressed to? To Herr W.A. Mozart himself. It too will inform the illustrious musician of your circumstances; and it begs him to give you some instruction while you are in Vienna.'

Chapter 4

Ludwig watched the rain streaming down the window of the carriage, peering through the irregular rivulets to try to give some form to the shapes beyond. But all he could see was the dark mass of buildings pushing up into an equally dark sky, with the occasional street lamp flickering as it slowly passed, causing him to screw up his eyes against the sudden glare.

But this was Vienna. Ludwig felt the excitement again well up in him. At last he was in the musical capital of Europe and home to Wolfgang Mozart. Two months at least lay ahead of him – the most important two months of his life. Here he would meet real musicians, listen to real orchestras. He would learn from true artists, not the provincial players of Bonn who barely deserved to be called musicians. Music, he thought, the highest art, coming directly from God. How many men have such a calling? In Bonn one alone. In Vienna one alone. And now I will meet him. At last.

He leaned back against the seat and thought again of Wolfgang Mozart. Why am I practically alone in understanding the man's true genius? In the court in Bonn they talk of him in the same breath as Grétry, or Benda, or Paisiello. They simply cannot see that in many years to come his name will be remembered while theirs will have long since vanished. There are others whose music is worthy: there is Gluck, for instance, or Salieri. And of course there is Haydn. But there is no genius amongst them like the genius of Mozart. His music will endure. Why? Because the emotion in his music is real. We share the tragedy, the joy. We do not just listen; we are involved. What happens in Mozart's music happens *to* us. But how does he achieve that? Ludwig thrilled again at the thought that he would soon be able to put the question directly to the composer himself.

As he had done so many times previously on the journey, Ludwig reached inside his jacket and felt the familiar bulk of the two letters against his chest; already they were a little grubby and creased from Ludwig's constant handling of them. He imagined the scene that surely awaited him in Vienna . . . In the music room of the imperial palace, the Emperor in attendance with Herr Mozart at his side, he, Ludwig van Beethoven from Bonn, would play the piano for them. He would play first Mozart's music, then his own. He would ask Mozart for a theme and improvise on it. On and on he would play until finally, overwhelmed with admiration, the Emperor would congratulate him and Mozart would deem him his worthy successor. Without further ado Mozart would take him on as a pupil, promising to keep the Emperor informed of his progress. Over the ensuing weeks he would play in the salons of Vienna's nobility, creating a reputation second only to that of the great Mozart himself. He would return briefly to Bonn to settle his affairs, terminate his employ at court and leave again for Vienna where he would make his career.

A jolt as the carriage passed over uneven cobbles awoke him from his reverie. He glowered at the faces opposite him, as if they were somehow responsible for interrupting his thoughts. Austrians, he thought, barely suppressing a guilty smile at the realisation that their faces matched their reputation. Serious, unsmiling, so unlike us Rhinelanders. And where were the great men to rival those whom Germany had produced: Dürer, Bach, Handel, Goethe, the young playwright Schiller? Remembering always the single great exception, Wolfgang Amadeus Mozart.

Purkersdorf had been the last stop before Vienna, where the three unsmiling, overweight and red-faced men with their green hunting hats had boarded the stage. If they had been Rhinelanders they would have been laughing, clapping each other on the shoulder. *Die drei Männer von Purkersdorf*, now there's a good title for a song, or an opera even, thought Ludwig, smiling to himself.

Things began badly. Bamberger's wife's cousin, a court musician named Herr Wuschel, had a temperament to match his pinched face. His eyes were dull and watery, his nose long and thin, the tip turning suddenly down, and his lips, which stretched tight across his teeth, barely moved when he spoke. He showed Ludwig to his room with ill grace, warning him he should be careful with his clothes, because his wife would not wash them more than once every two weeks.

He was small of stature, and seemed to acquire a spring in his step as he continued his litany of unwelcome news.

'See the Emperor? You, a boy from Germany? Well, it'd be difficult enough under normal circumstances, but you'll find it impossible. Don't you know what His Imperial Majesty is about to undertake? Where are we now, Saturday the seventh of April. Tomorrow is Easter Day. Well, I can tell you this. Tomorrow the Emperor will attend High Mass in the Hofpfarrkirche. On Monday evening he'll be going to the opera. There's a new soprano singing in Gugliemi's *L'Inganno Amoroso*. But other than those two excursions he'll be locked up in the Hofburg palace day and night. Why? Because on the eleventh he leaves for the Crimea to meet none other than the Empress Catherine of Russia. I can tell you this. He's so busy he's given all of us musicians the week off. Music's the last thing on his mind. Oh yes, and one other thing. All the imperial offices are closed now till after he gets back. That includes your − what is it? − Electoral office. So as for meeting the Emperor, young man, or even getting your letter to him, I think you might as well put it out of your mind.'

The next morning Ludwig joined the crowd that had gathered outside the Hofpfarrkirche and watched the imperial retinue arrive for the Easter service. The Emperor, resplendent in his uniform, his plumed hat giving him extra height and dignity, walked the short distance to the church entrance, acknowledging the cheers. Ludwig stood rooted to the spot. He felt the letter in his pocket, as he watched the Emperor turn in his direction and smile. Ludwig opened his mouth but no words came. Then the Emperor entered the church, the heavy wooden doors swung shut and the crowd dispersed.

For several minutes Ludwig remained where he was, his face wreathed with disappointment. Then slowly he began to walk.

As he made his way through the city he could not resist the infectious throb of excitement the place instilled in him. Vienna, the city that breathed music. He gazed in wonder at the tall spire of St Stephansdom which soared above the tightly packed buildings below. He walked along the banks of the Wien river which ran round the east side of the city, sat on the wooden seats in the great Augarten public park, and strolled through the wide meadows and woods of the Prater. But more than anywhere else he spent his time in the Michaelerplatz, the broad square set directly in front of the ornate entrance to the imperial palace.

Carriages swarmed through the square, entering and leaving under one of the arches set around it. Noblemen and women were carried sedately through it in sedan chairs; stall-holders sold freshly baked delicacies from ornately decorated tables set around the edge of the square; army officers dressed in the elegant uniforms of the imperial regiments strolled imperiously through, their high-cockaded hats and swords at their sides joining their erect bearing to set them apart from the ordinary mortals who thronged the square.

Ludwig drank in the atmosphere, so different from the small provincial town he had grown up in. Even the dust, whipped up by the sudden sharp winds that traversed the square and the carriage wheels which clattered unevenly across the cobbles, failed to dull his enthusiasm. In the Michaelerplatz he stood outside the imperial palace, the Hofburg, knowing his host was right and that he would never walk through the door. The solid grey building stood massive and ornate, the pillared portico adorned with winged statues, the central of which portrayed a winged warrior with sword and shield standing astride his defeated enemy. A member of the Imperial Guard stood on each side of the pillars, eyes fixed unwaveringly ahead.

Adjacent to the palace was a second building, less grand, less ornate, but which held him in greater thrall. It was the Burgtheater which, although it was similarly adorned with imperial symbols, the centrepiece being an eagle with wings outstretched astride a golden orb and topped with a dome which was itself crowned with a globe tilted on its axis, was a building which belonged to the people. Here the citizens of Vienna gathered nightly to hear concerts and the opera. It was here, as Ludwig well knew, that a little under a year ago Mozart's new opera, *The Marriage of Figaro*, was first presented to an adoring public.

Word had soon reached Bonn that the work itself, which should have lasted around four hours, had run to the length of three operas on the first night, due to the fact that the audience demanded an encore of every piece in it, and that the Emperor himself was forced to issue an order the next day that no further encores were to be given during the performance! How astounded then were the musical circles of Bonn when word reached them that the opera was withdrawn after only nine performances, to be replaced by a new work, *Una Cosa Rara*, by the young Spanish sensation, Martin Solar, whose career was sponsored in Vienna by the wife of the Spanish ambassador. They were less astounded, though, when they listened to the music of that work. The tunes were easy to play, easy to sing and instantly memorable. The opera was the first to contain a waltz, and very soon the operatic cognoscenti of Vienna began to vie with one another to see who could attend the most performances of *Una Cosa Rara*. *The Marriage of Figaro* was soon forgotten.

Not by young Ludwig, though, who had studied the score bar by bar, note by note. Against the protestations of more senior musicians at the Electoral court in Bonn, he argued that Mozart's opera was by far the better and more enduring work. He had been proved correct when, a few months later, the Bohemian city of Prague – long a musical rival of Vienna and by general agreement (at least in Vienna) inferior to the imperial capital – proclaimed *The Marriage of Figaro* to be a masterpiece. The city echoed to the melodies from the opera, and very soon the Prague authorities implored Mozart and his wife Constanze to do them the honour of visiting their city. Mozart accepted and was received in Prague as a hero. Ludwig knew this, and knew too that Mozart had only recently returned to Vienna, where he was determined now to win the same accolade from the musically more mature imperial capital.

And so Ludwig stared longingly and often at the Burgtheater, knowing with certainty that Mozart would triumph again there, and knowing too – again with that inexplicable conviction – that he too would one day hear his works performed there.

He was also only too aware that his only chance of handing his letter to the Emperor was when he came to the performance at the Burgtheater of *L'Inganno Amoroso* the following evening.

But the Fates which had withheld their help so far from the young Rhinelander were no kinder to him the next day. That night, after another failed attempt to attract the Emperor's attention, he sat on the edge of his bed and felt the tears of frustration come. He threw the two letters on to the floor and buried his head in his hands. This boy, who had always felt himself apart from others but had accepted it as his fate, now sobbed uncontrollably at his isolation. Not since the smallpox of his childhood had he felt so alone.

He did not hear his host Herr Wuschel enter his room. There

was that same pinched look on his face. His lips barely moved as he spoke, as if he was trying to hold the words back.'You must have influence. Don't understand how. Note here from the Electoral office. You are to see Herr Mozart. Two o'clock tomorrow afternoon.'

'You are ugly and I detest ugliness. Let me look at you more closely. What are those marks on your face? Ugh! Disease marks. Yes, you are ugly. Truly ugly.' He laughed a high-pitched laugh and skipped happily round the room, coming to a halt again in front of the boy. In an instant the smile vanished from his face and was replaced by a severe frown. He lowered his voice a register. 'Music is a thing of beauty. Music *is* beauty. Of all the arts music gives most beauty to the world.' He thrust his face closer to the boy. 'Music cannot exist where ugliness lives.'

Ludwig studied the face which was now so close to his. He registered the slender nose, the full lips, the small chin which almost receded. He took in the fine full hair, powdered and tied in a queue at the back. But most of all he studied the eyes, quick-moving as they darted between his own eyes, yet heavy-lidded and fleshy underneath. Ludwig's thick eyebrows came down low as his mind concentrated and his own eyes strove to see a spark of recognition in the face looking at him, a common trait that he could instantly identify as the bond which would link the two of them together as musicians. He saw tiny pockmarks on the cheeks. Was that all they would have in common?

In those eyes, although so active, he saw a dullness, as if a veil had been drawn across the brightness which he knew had to exist beneath. And as the face drew back from him, Ludwig saw for the first time how the skin, pallid and sallow, was covered with a film of sweat. He saw how the sharpness of the face was more an impression created by the fine, straight nose, and that in fact the cheeks were fleshier than they should have been and beneath the chin the skin hung lower than was normal.

The face drew back, and Ludwig flinched as he saw the stab of pain shoot across it.

'I'm not well, you see. I have this pain. In my stomach, mostly, and here.' He put his hand flat against his side, towards his back. He laughed suddenly. 'Why must artists always suffer? Did God decree it? All artists must suffer,' he said ponderously in imitation of the Almighty. He walked swiftly across the room. 'I have to leave. It is my usual problem. One I cannot ignore.' He laughed, a series of short bursts on a single high level, accompanied by a smile of embarrassment. 'I forget why you are here. But I expect you will be gone when I return.' He left the room hurriedly.

Ludwig did not move from his chair. The frown remained on his face as he tried to recall the words he had just heard. But he could not. He tried to recall the face that had stared at his. But he could not. He sat calmly for another minute and then a sudden wave of panic flowed over him. He had met the Master and had not spoken to him! He could barely remember what Mozart had said. Except for the word 'music'. He had heard that, he knew. But what had he said about music? The words had gone.

Then something came back to Ludwig, an impression, something that he knew was inescapably true. Whatever he had said, Herr Mozart had clearly not liked him. He had said something abusive to him. He knew that, though he could not remember what. It saddened him. He hit the arms of his chair with clenched fists. He knew Mozart would not return. He knew the meeting was over. He knew he had to leave.

The sudden sound of voices and high-pitched laughter brought his mind rushing back to the moment. He heard quick footsteps approaching. The door opened abruptly and a woman walked in. She was petite, with dark hair in ringlets framing an alert and lively face. Her whole being gave off a feeling of energy. She looked straight at him, registering no surprise at his presence.

'Where is Wolfi, do you know? Have you seen him? Anyway, what are you sitting there for? Why aren't you at the piano? Is he wasting time again, talking all his nonsense at you? I've told him. If he doesn't give better lessons he'll soon have no pupils to teach. And then what will we do? Where did he go?'

Ludwig sat still, saying nothing.

'All the same, you musicians,' the woman said. 'There's only one language you speak and it's made up of little black dots on lined sheets of paper. There's no point in asking your name, you've probably forgotten it.' She turned abruptly on her heel and almost collided with her husband as he came into the room.

'Wolfi! Sometimes I think you are quite stupid, sometimes I think you are malicious. The Katzenbergs are in the salon waiting for you. You promised to join us for a game of bowling. Now I find you have a pupil waiting for you. Will you explain to me? What exactly are your immediate intentions?'

Wolfgang slumped into a chair. Ludwig noticed how his appearance had changed since he had last been in the room. His face, already sallow, now appeared to be drained of whatever colour had been there. Beads of perspiration shone on his forehead and white flecks on his lips. Ludwig watched as Mozart drew the heavily embroidered sleeve of his coat across his mouth.

'I have been unwell again, Stanzi. It must have been the food at lunch. Anyway, I cannot come to the skittle ground. My feet are hurting. So are my legs.'

Ludwig was concentrating hard, listening, determined to hear, understand and remember what Mozart said. He looked down and saw how Mozart's ankles bulged over the top of his tight lacquered shoes, and he noticed for the first time how Mozart's swollen legs filled the white stockings to the extent that the fabric was stretched unnaturally.

'Then stick to your music. Give your lesson. God knows we need the money.' Constanze turned on her heel and left the room, closing the door noisily behind her.

Then there was silence. Mozart sat slumped in the chair, staring in front of him. Ludwig watched him, not daring to speak. He feared that if he reminded Mozart of his presence, the great musician would instantly dismiss him, or simply leave.

His stomach turned in panic as, a moment later, Mozart turned and looked at him. The composer smiled weakly. 'I remember now. Yes, I remember. You are from Germany, are you not? The principality of . . . by the Rhine? Is that not right?'

Ludwig nodded with as slight a movement as he could, afraid to break the spell. Mozart continued, 'One of the musicians at court asked me to see you. He said the Emperor knew you were here. His Apostolic Majesty, interested in an ugly youth like you? It was probably all lies. I should have refused. What is your name?'

'Beethoven. Ludwig van Beethoven. The Emperor . . . I tried . . . But he . . .'

'How I hate the way you Germans talk. So . . . so rough. So harsh. All from the back of the throat. There is no beauty in how you speak. You are a music student?'

'I am a musician and composer.'

'Ha! So we are both musicians and composers. You have a fine arrogance, young man. I assure you we have nothing in common. Nothing.' He laughed. 'Well, not quite nothing. Even from here I can see you have pockmarks on your face. You have an ugly face. You must leave now. I will tell the Emperor I have seen you. He will be satisfied. The man is a fool, anyway.'

Ludwig stood and walked, not towards the door, but towards the piano. He expected to hear an angry tirade behind him, but there was nothing. Emboldened, he sat on the stool, throwing his tailcoat out behind him. Oblivious of the stern gaze from the portrait of Constanze's mother on the wall, he removed the sheets of manuscript propped up on the stand in front of him. Briefly he turned to make sure Mozart had not, by some act of magic, left the room. He started to play, beginning with single notes in the bass register.

'Not the introduction!' shouted Mozart. 'That's the introduction for orchestra. Play the piano part.'

Ludwig stopped playing. He shot a look at Mozart, composed himself, then launched into the piano opening of the Concerto in C major. He played the notes lightly, as the music demanded. As his playing progressed, it became firmer, more assured. He played on, his fingers, even in the most difficult passages, unerringly flying across the keys. The sound filled the room.

'Stop, stop!' cried Mozart. Abruptly the boy withdrew his hands from the keys and placed them, fingers spread, on his thighs. He looked across at Mozart, his face tense with anxiety.

'You play the piano the way you speak. You are rough and harsh. You flatter me by playing my own music and then you attempt to beat it to death.' He paused. 'But I confess I did not hear a wrong note, which is more than I can say for some pianists twice your age. You are competent, but you are young. You have no . . . You lack . . . finesse. Hummel is better than you. He is my best student. No, you are no match for him. Now I suggest you return to wherever you are from and continue your studies. Tell your teacher he must make you lighten your touch.'

'Herr Mozart,' said the boy, emboldened by his own playing, 'you are right. I played your own music to flatter you. Now I will play some more and I will not leave until you have heard me. I have come to Vienna to see you, because you are the only musician in Europe I can learn from. In Bonn they have nothing more to teach me. Only you . . . I have studied your scores. I understand what you are writing. My teachers tell me to learn from your scores, and in the end I teach them. When a key change takes them by surprise, or you bring in the oboe, say, at an unexpected moment, I explain to them why you have done it. To me it is logical.'

Mozart was silent, his chin cupped in his hand, looking intently at the boy seated at the piano.

'Now,' Ludwig continued, 'I will play some more for you. First, Herr Mozart, please come here and play a theme, any theme you choose.'

Mozart laughed and rose slowly from his chair. He walked stiffly and painfully to the piano. He began playing before he had even fully sat down on the stool. For a full minute he played. Then he returned to his chair.

'What is that you played? I have not heard it before. Will you play something I am familiar with? Your Sonata in C minor, for instance?'

Mozart said nothing.

Ludwig sat at the piano and played exactly what Mozart had just played. Every note was in its place. Mozart, intrigued, looked at Ludwig. 'I do not believe you, my boy. That was my Fantasia in D minor. I wrote it five years ago. You have clearly studied it.'

Again, with effort, he rose from his chair and walked across to the piano. Ludwig again yielded the stool to him.

'Now. I am working on a new opera. It is based on the life of the great lover Don Giovanni. I have this in mind for an aria. No one else has heard this, so now we shall see exactly what you are capable of.'

Lightly, he picked out a theme in the soprano register, embellishing it first with chords, then with arpeggios. Again, he played for a full minute. 'A simple theme, is it not? That is the secret of great music,' he said, almost to himself. 'The main themes must always be simple.'

Ludwig took his place at the piano. 'Yes, that was a simple theme, Herr Mozart. Simple and beautiful. This is what I can do with it.' And instead of repeating the music, as he had done with the Fantasia, he immediately set about playing variations on the theme. The first variation consisted of a series of chords, expressing the theme's harmonic structure. The second began with an abrupt change of key, and as Ludwig reproduced the theme in chords with the left hand, his right hand flew across the keys in a seemingly unending series of semiquavers. He played on without interruption, varying the theme sometimes in subtle ways, sometimes with complex combinations of notes.

After several minutes, Ludwig shouted, 'And now this!' While his left hand unerringly picked out the theme, his right played a series of discords, discords which threatened to break the theme down. Yet instead of destroying it, they seemed somehow to enhance it, as if to show the theme could survive even this! Then by contrast a variation with more silence than notes, an abstraction of the theme, a disintegration almost. And finally the original theme, played now in full for the first time by Ludwig, just as Mozart had played it. Quietly and peacefully, Ludwig brought it to a conclusion. The final chord hung in the air.

Mozart did not speak, but quietly returned to his chair. Ludwig, his face flushed with effort, said, 'In *The Marriage of Figaro*, Herr Mozart, near the beginning, you have an aria for Figaro. It is in the form of a cavatina, "Se vuol ballare". It is a simple and instantly memorable melody.' And he played it. 'I have it in mind one day soon to write variations on it, perhaps for piano and violin. But now to my music. This is the rondo from my Piano Concerto in E flat.' Again Ludwig played, the sounds filling the room. Finally his fingers came to a rest. As they did so, the door opened and Constanze, looking in, said, 'You were playing such furious music a few moments ago, Wolfi. Our guests remarked on it. I told them it was not in your style. They said I should come and ask you . . .'

'It was not me playing, Stanzi. It was this boy. His name is Beethoven. Ludwig Beethoven. Von Beethoven. Watch out for him. One day he will give the world something to talk about.'

'How can you say that? He is just a boy.'

'I have just heard him play on the piano in a remarkable way. Truly remarkable. I am telling you. His name will one day be known.'

'Hm. Unlike ours. Mozart. No, the name does not have the ring of greatness. Nor his. It is too harsh.'

'Leave us now, Stanzi. We must talk.'

Constanze closed the door behind her.

'Come and sit here, Ludwig.' The boy did as he was bidden.

'Do not write opera. It does not pay well. Do you hear?'
Ludwig nodded as Mozart talked on, excitedly and barely
pausing. 'Look what happened to my Figaro. All that work.
First that fool Rosenberg tried to take the ballet out. Then they
take the whole opera off to make way for that nonsense by . . .
by . . . some Spanish idiot. Ha! Only the Bohemians have the
sense . . . They have asked me to write another opera. I do not
want to. But I must. It will be called *Don Giovanni*. I already told
you that. Da Ponte has written the libretto again for me. He is a
fine poet. He seems to understand . . . You must find yourself a
good librettist, Ludwig, or else you . . . No no no, I told you,
you must not write opera. Do you know why? Do you know
why? Because if you do you will remain poor. There are no
copyright laws for music. Can you understand that? An author
writes a book and no one else is allowed to copy it. But music
is different. There are no laws. And so in Germany they print
my music and play it, and I am not paid a single florin. And
opera is expensive to perform. Singers, costumes, the theatre
must be hired. So write your piano concertos. They are cheap
to perform and you will be paid. And you must get yourself a
position at court. It is the only way to ensure you will be paid
regularly. But do not depend too heavily on only one patron.
When I think of the Archbishop of Salzburg, that evil man . . .
If I had not finally engineered my own dismissal . . . Soon I hope
to have a position at court. Old Christoph Gluck is seventy-three
years old now, and his health is failing. When he dies the post
of Kammermusikus will be vacant. I must secure it. I must . . .
But Kapellmeister to the Emperor. That is . . . that is . . . It is
said Salieri will be the next to hold that post. Salieri . . . Salieri
. . . people believe he is a better composer than I . . . Even the
Emperor . . .'

Ludwig frowned. 'Salieri is a good composer. But he is not
your equal. I have studied his scores too. There is not the . . .
the . . . they are more ordinary.'

'I am worried about my father's health,' Mozart said, looking
away from Ludwig. It was as if he was thinking aloud, the
progression of his thoughts following no clear pattern. 'I have
written to him. I have told him that death is the greatest friend
of mankind. I should go to see him, but Salzburg is a long way
from Vienna, and I have to continue work on *Don Giovanni*.
Maybe in the summer. Yes, I will visit him in the summer. But
maybe he will not live till then.'

He turned to Ludwig, as if suddenly realising the boy was still there. He smiled, the sadness wiped away by an unexpected alertness. 'Do you know I could have been Kapellmeister to the Elector of Cologne?'

Ludwig looked up sharply. 'I know. The Elector Maximilian Franz told me.'

'The very same. When I left Salzburg and that brutal Arch-bishop, the Archduke Maximilian summoned me, I remember it as if it were yesterday. I went to the Hofburg to see him and he was standing in an ante-room in front of a stove. He had his hands under his tailcoat, flapping it. He was warming his arse.' He gave a high-pitched laugh. 'He said when he became Elector of Cologne he would appoint me as his Kapellmeister. Now he is Elector in Cologne and I am in Vienna.' He laughed again. 'Since he took holy orders the man has become a fool. Before he was witty and clever. Now he is stupid. Anyway, what is Cologne compared to Vienna?'

'His palace is in Bonn. It is where I—'

'Do you know the music of Haydn? Joseph Haydn? Do you?'

Ludwig pursed his lips. 'Yes. Some of his scores have come to Bonn. I don't think—'

'You are wrong. You are wrong. His music is wonderful. His themes are so simple. He is a genius. We must all learn from him. He is my great friend too. But I weep for him. I escaped from Salzburg. But for him there is no escape from Esterhaz Castle. Prince Nicolaus has him entombed there. He will not even let him come here to Vienna for twenty-four hours. But his music. Ah. When I listen to it, it is as if I am reaching back into the past, back even before him to Bach and Handel. But he has done new things. Things they were not capable of. In harmony, counterpoint. You must study his music.'

'His music. It is very . . . very structured. Somehow, the inspiration that I expect is not there. It is pretty. It is . . . formal.'

'No, Ludwig, no. His music is great and it will endure. Because it is simple. You must study it. Just as you study my music, you must study Haydn's music too. Above all you must study his quartets. I have learned from them. The quartet, you know, it is the purest music. Just four voices, but those four voices can carry a greater meaning than a full orchestra. Ah, there is so much to learn, and so little time left. Who is your teacher?'

'Herr Neefe, the court organist.'

'Don't know the name.'

'Herr Mozart, will you teach me? Will you teach me to compose music? Will you ... will you open my ears and my heart?'

Mozart let out a shrill laugh. 'We are musicians, you and I. I know it by the words you just used. You know, a week or two ago, a young boy came to see me, about your age. "Maestro," he said, "Maestro, will you recommend a book to me that will teach me to compose?" I said to him, "These are your books," and I pointed to his ears and his heart. Then I pinched his arse and propelled him out of the door.'

For several seconds there was silence. 'You are a fine musician, Ludwig. There is a lot I could teach you. But my work is already too great a burden to me. And my health is not good.'

Ludwig slammed his fists on the arms of the chair. 'You must teach me! You will teach me! I will not leave Vienna. Say you will teach me, Herr Mozart. Say you will teach me.'

Mozart frowned. Taking a lace handkerchief from his sleeve he wiped beads of perspiration from his brow. He moved in the chair and winced as the familiar pain shot through his side. He straightened his back and pushed his hands into his sides. Finally he slumped back.

'Yes, Ludwig. I will teach you. You are an extraordinary musician, a fine pianist. I will teach you. Who knows? Maybe you too will teach me. Go over to that desk in the corner. Open it and bring me the sheets of music lying inside.'

Ludwig did as he was told. 'These are some serenades, some divertimenti. There are five, I think. I have scored them for two basset horns and one bassoon. An unusual combination. But wind instruments have one great advantage over strings. Do you know what it is? They can be heard clearly out of doors. In the open air. So these pieces will be played in the stand in the Hofburg gardens while His Majesty entertains, and everyone will be able to hear the music. Unless someone farts and the wind carries the music off!' and he laughed with the same infectious high-pitched monotone. 'Now take the manuscripts back to your lodgings and study them. Come back in two or three days and we will discuss them.'

In obvious pain, Wolfgang Mozart rose from his chair and unsteadily walked to the door and opened it. He turned and said,

'Remember. Simple themes. It is not the theme that counts, but what you do with it.' He left the room.

For a few moments Ludwig sat motionless, gripping the sheaves of manuscript with such force his knuckles were white. Suddenly, realising he was creasing the paper, he relaxed his grip. He stared at the sheets, the proof that he had not imagined the events of the last hour. He turned and looked at the piano, and, unable to resist the temptation, walked across to it. He looked at the keys, the keys on which he had played for Wolfgang Mozart. Wolfgang Mozart! Gently, still standing, he caressed the keys with his fingers. The keys on which Wolfgang Mozart plays. The piano at which Wolfgang Mozart composes his divine music.

Now, in the weeks to come, he, Ludwig van Beethoven, would play at the same piano for Wolfgang Mozart. He felt the surge of joy within him. He wanted to shout, cry out to vent the joy. Instead his face became serious. An observer seeing that face would have read in it anger and bitterness. But that would have been a misreading. Ludwig glanced at the keys, then at the music he gripped, marvelling at the neatness with which Mozart had written the notes. No scratching out, no evidence of an inner struggle. Ludwig knew instinctively the notes had come from Mozart's head on to the paper with barely a pause for thought. He looked at the piano keys again.

At that precise moment Ludwig knew for the first time in his short life total happiness.

As he returned to his lodgings, Ludwig's mind was filled with the thoughts of the great Master. Exhausted from the day's excitement he climbed the stairs to his room, laid the manuscript sheets carefully on the table by his bed, climbed on to the bed without removing his shoes or any clothing, and fell into a deep sleep.

He woke up some hours later. There was total darkness outside the small window and no sounds from the street. It was the middle of the night. Sitting on the edge of the bed he fumbled with a wooden taper, managing to light it. He held it to the single candle by the bed. In the dim light he removed his jacket, cursing as he saw the letter from the Elector to Mozart still in the inside pocket. He would give it to him the next time he saw him.

Immediately he reached for the sheets of manuscript lying

on the table and touched them, as if to reassure himself that
they were real. He lifted them to look at them more closely.
It was only then that he saw the envelope that had been lying
underneath them. He picked it up and held it in the light of the
candle. He recognised his father's handwriting and a feeling of
dread swept over him.

Unsteadily and with jerky movements he tore the envelope
open and took out the single folded sheet of paper. His father
had written simply:

Bonn, 8 April 1787

Ludwig

Your mother fares badly. Her health has worsened. The
doctors believe she will shortly die. You must return by
the first available stage. Do not delay.

Your Father

Ludwig clenched his fists, screwing up the letter as he did so. He
set his teeth, jutting his jaw forward. His eyebrows came down
low over his eyes. He felt the tears well up but he suppressed
them. His breathing became stronger and deeper. Suddenly he
turned and pummelled the bed with both fists, forcing the anger
out through his clenched teeth, the bedclothes muffling the cry
that accompanied it.

BOOK FOUR

Chapter 1

Councillor von Schaden and his wife, of Augsburg, friends of
Franz Ries in Bonn, looked at Ludwig, concern on their faces.
'You poor dear boy, how dreadful for you.'

Ludwig wanted to ask Frau von Schaden to take her arm
off his shoulder, to stop expressing her sympathy for him. He
feared her concern would break through the flimsy defences he
had put in place.

'Do you have any more news of your mother?'

Ludwig shook his head. He looked at Councillor Schaden and
sighed with relief when the Councillor appeared to understand
his unspoken message.

'Enough, I think, my dear. Let us not dwell on sad matters.
Tell us about Vienna, Ludwig. How was the great city?'

'I saw the Burgtheater, where *The Marriage of Figaro* was
performed. The Hofburg palace. I tried to see the Emperor.
I had a letter for him . . .'

'I would have been surprised if—'

'And Mozart. Wolfgang Mozart. That was the purpose of
your trip, was it not?'

Ludwig nodded. 'I saw him only once. I played for him. He
said he would take me on as his pupil. But then I had to leave
suddenly because of my mother.'

'Well, I am sure you will be allowed to go back soon. If he
agreed . . .'

'Willi,' said Anna Schaden enthusiastically, 'didn't Andreas
Stein's daughter also play for Mozart? When he came here some
years ago?' Without waiting for an answer she turned to Ludwig.
'My dear Ludwig, I have something to tell you which will please
and delight you. One of the most famous piano-makers in all of
Europe lives here in our city.'

'Stein,' said Ludwig, smiling. 'The piano I play on at Frau
Breuning's is a Stein. Made in Augsburg.'

'And I am sure you would not turn down an opportunity of meeting Herr Stein. And his daughter Nanette. She is a fine pianist, and if my memory serves, she, like you, has played for Herr Mozart.'

The building which housed one of Europe's most prestigious piano manufacturers was not impressive from the outside. The house in which Stein, a widower, lived with his young children had a dilapidated air, the paint peeling off the woodwork. Joined on to it was a large, ramshackle barn where Stein built his pianos – and the organs which first established his reputation.

The elderly craftsman, famed throughout Germany and as far away as Vienna and London, welcomed Ludwig warmly and showed him with pride his array of instruments.

'I have heard of you, young man. Your fame as a virtuoso has spread even here to Bavaria. And I hear from Frau Schaden that you have been to Vienna and played before Mozart, as my daughter has done. You shall meet her presently. Now, come and look at my instruments and tell me what you think.' He took Ludwig into a huge shed, replete with pianos in various stages of construction and repair. Organ pipes stood against the wall and the aroma of polished wood filled the air. Ludwig walked slowly between the instruments, stroking them as he passed, playing an occasional note.

Herr Stein bustled up to him. 'Come and look at this one, Ludwig,' he said, leading the young man to an instrument apart from the others. 'This is my latest development. See how it has five octaves and two notes, like Walter is building in Vienna. But look here inside. Individually hinged levers so the hammers cannot jam against the strings. And Walter cannot match my tone. See here,' and he leaned over the edge of the instrument, 'have you ever seen hammers like that? I am experimenting with buckskin, using several layers of different thickness. The sound is more . . . more . . . I cannot describe it,' he said with a laugh. 'Here, play on it. See what you think.'

Without sitting, Ludwig played several chords. The sound was unlike anything he had heard before. It resonated and seemed to hang in the air. He pulled up a chair and played more chords, then scales and arpeggios, using both hands with equal strength. 'It's wonderful!' he cried. 'Listen to how the high notes balance the low notes without being smothered by them. I have never heard . . . always I have the problem of balance . . .

the bass smothers . . .' And he played on. For several minutes he played, improvising as he went along. Finally he stopped and said to Herr Stein, 'This is a fine instrument. You are an excellent craftsman, because you understand music.'

'Ludwig,' the older man replied in a kindly voice, 'you play in such a determined manner for one so young. You will not, I am sure, take it amiss if I offer a little advice?' Ludwig shook his head. 'You must play more gently, more smoothly, not so rude and hard. Otherwise,' and he laughed again, 'my poor instruments will not last a week.'

As he spoke the sound of running footsteps drew near. 'Ha!' said Stein, removing his heavy leather apron. 'My children. My young prodigies. My young geniuses. Now, boys, you will show a little respect to our guest. This is Herr Ludwig van Beethoven from Bonn, and he is as fine a piano player as I have heard. Ludwig, these are my sons, Matthäus who's eleven, and little Friedrich who's—'

'I'm not little,' the small boy cried. 'I'm three and I can play the piano too.' Before his father could stop him, the small child clambered on to the stool, stretched out his tiny hands and began playing. Ludwig listened bemused. When the child finally stopped Ludwig said, 'That was good, Friedrich. Very good.'

'Come now, children,' Herr Stein said. 'Where is Nanette? Let us go and find her and introduce this young man to her.' The sound of china cups and plates being laid out drew them to Nanette in the salon.

'Now, Ludwig,' said Herr Stein, 'I would like you to meet my daughter Anna Maria. We call her Nanette. She too is a fine pianist. Indeed, when she was just eight and a half years old she too played for Herr Mozart here in Augsburg. He professed himself to be entranced.'

Nanette's sleek dark hair framed her face demurely, her eyes were wide, her nose fine and straight and her lips full. She had tied her hair at the back, giving prominence to her high cheekbones. Her face was not beautiful, but it had a gentleness that was immediately attractive.

Ludwig felt the familiar feeling well over him that always seemed to render him timid in the presence of attractive young women. It was happening just as it had when he met Eleonore von Breuning for the first time. But this time he sensed it was different. He realised immediately that Nanette Stein was not a threatening person, not someone who was aware of her own charm and used it to unsettle her chosen victim. With Eleonore he had felt ill at ease, as if that was somehow her intention. It was not like that with Nanette. Instead of looking down at his feet to hide his unease, he found himself looking at her face as she walked towards him.

'Dear Ludwig,' she said, her voice gentle and suffused with kindness, 'you cannot know what an honour I feel to meet you. I have heard my father speak of you often. I wondered if I would ever meet you, and here you are in my own home!' She laughed, and involuntarily Ludwig found himself laughing with her, infected by the gaiety in her voice.

For fully an hour Ludwig sat with the Steins – father, daughter and son (the infant Friedrich having run off to his nursery) – telling them of his frustrations in Bonn, his ambition to become a great composer, and his abortive trip to Vienna. Nanette was visibly shocked at Ludwig's description of Mozart. 'When he came to Augsburg he seemed so young and healthy, at any rate to an eight-year-old,' she said. When Ludwig explained why he had had to cut short his trip and how he feared he might not reach home in time to find his mother still alive, Nanette leaned forward and placed her hand reassuringly on his, a movement that seemed so natural Ludwig made no attempt to withdraw it.

Herr Stein said it was a pity he had to leave so soon. 'Otherwise you could have given us all a concert. It would have provided us with something to talk of for some time. Will you come and visit us again?'

Ludwig nodded, his face etched with sadness and the heavy frown on his forehead. For a moment there was silence.

Then Nanette, with genuine concern in her voice, said: 'Poor Ludwig. I wish you could stay with us here a little longer. I would look after you. See how your coat is grimy from your travels. I would clean it for you. I would wash your shirts for you and make them tidy. Dear Ludwig, you must hurry home now to be with your mother. But we will meet again. I know it. And when we do I will take care of you. I will look after you so you may devote yourself to your music.'

She smiled at Ludwig, and so genuine and winning was her expression that Ludwig, despite his overwhelming sadness at events, smiled back.

★   ★   ★

Ludwig had been away from Bonn for almost two months but now, as he trudged up towards the Münsterplatz, dragging his bag on the cobbles, it was as if he had not been away at all. Familiar sights loomed in front of him. On the west side of the square was the residence of the Austrian ambassador, who through Frau Breuning had requested piano lessons from Ludwig but whom Ludwig had refused.

Nearer to him stood the Breuning house where he had spent so many happy hours, its front windows now shielded by the newly blossomed linden trees, allowing him to pass close by unnoticed. He entered the Remigiusplatz and his eyes fell upon the comforting sight of the Minorite church, whose organ he so loved. For a brief moment, he thought of going into the church, feeling the organ pedals under his feet and the three keyboards under his hands. But with a sudden churn of emptiness in his stomach he remembered he was on his way home to see his dying mother.

The incline had made him hot and breathless. He stopped walking and let his bag fall to the cobbles. For several minutes he breathed heavily, gulping down air as if he could not get enough to fill his lungs. A wave of fatigue swept over him and he wished only that he could climb on to his bed and fall asleep. Finally, as his breathing steadied, he picked up his bag and dragged it across the Marktplatz and into the Wenzelgasse.

He stopped outside number 462, familiar to him from the days following the flood. Grasping his bag and breathing deeply, he climbed the stairs to the upper floor. It was late afternoon. Caspar and Nikola would shortly be home from school. He hoped his father would be in the house with his mother, but he doubted it. He dropped his bag and walked to the room where he knew his mother would be. Clenching his fists, he entered.

In years to come Ludwig would often remember this precise moment of his youth. Expecting to see his mother in bed and near to death, he found her instead sitting in a chair, a shawl round her shoulders and a blanket over her knees. She was asleep, her head lowered and inclined slightly to one side. Her face – and this was what he would remember most – was utterly at peace. Her skin was unlined and milky soft, and her high cheekbones were flushed pink.

Conflicting emotions swept over him. He was sad to see his mother, who always seemed preoccupied as she tirelessly went about her domestic business, sitting motionless and asleep.

She did not look ill, but she had to be. Why else would she be sitting asleep? It was not something he had ever seen her do before.

But he felt angry too. Angry that he had been forced to leave Vienna, leave Mozart, to find that his mother was clearly not in the terminal stages of her illness, as his father had implied in the brief letter he had sent.

And then guilt. A quiet sobbing came from the cot in the corner of the room. It was the infant Maria Margaretha. Ludwig looked intently at his mother and saw movement behind her eyelids. He wanted to turn and run out of the room, but he knew he could not. As her eyes slowly and hesitatingly opened, his mother's features underwent a transformation. Her mouth fell open, pulling down her cheeks and creating a deep hollow on either side of her face. In an instant she had metamorphosed from a woman in a peaceful sleep to a woman who was clearly very sick.

Ludwig felt the emotion well up in him at the realisation that his mother was seriously ill. Maria's eyes slowly focused on her eldest son but she did not smile at him. Her breathing quickened as she summoned the strength to speak.

'Ah, Ludwig. The strange one. You left me. Why? I wish I understood.'

The effort of speech caused her to cough. The coughing intensified and she held a crumpled handkerchief to her mouth. In the last spasm of the cough she threw her head forward and Ludwig knew before he saw it that the handkerchief would be stained red.

He wanted to walk to his mother's chair, but his legs were immovable. Instead he spoke.

'Dear Mother. I am sorry you are unwell. Father wrote to me in Vienna. Can I tell you what I—?'

'Bring me my baby,' his mother said. 'Bring me my Maria.' And with renewed strength, 'Take care as you lift her. She is frail.'

Ludwig turned and walked to the cot. Tenderly he lifted the child out, taking care not to let the blanket fall from her. He placed her in his mother's outstretched arms.

Taking a step back, he again said, 'Dear Mother.' He repeated it, but his mother was looking down into Maria's eyes. Her breathing had become harsh, and Ludwig could see from the frown on her face that she was struggling to restrain the cough she knew was welling up in her throat. Turning to leave the room, Ludwig took a last look at mother and child. He noticed how the infant's cheeks were flushed, just like her mother's.

Gottlob Neefe was worried for his pupil, and he wondered if he shared part of the blame.

'Musically, I mean. Have I done enough for him musically?'

'No one has done more, Gotti. No one,' said his wife, who had just put their two daughters to bed. 'You have done everything possible for the boy.'

'Have I really? I rather neglected him when Lucchesi was away.'

Clara laughed reassuringly. 'Gotti, you were acting Kapell-meister! You had more work than you could cope with. In fact you kept telling me how Ludwig was helping you.'

'You're right. But I'm thinking artistically. Musically. Have I really done enough for him?'

'Of course you have. For one thing, I know it was Herr Ries who persuaded the Elector to let him go to Vienna, but he could not have achieved it without your help, your support.'

'Yes. Such a pity. So sad he had to come back.'

'Look, Gotti,' said Clara. 'Stop torturing yourself. At the moment Ludwig is a very unhappy young man. He's been forced to come back from Vienna because his mother is dying. That's enough for anyone to have to cope with. The fact that Mozart agreed to take him on as pupil is proof of his skill, so why are you concerned?'

Neefe stood and paced round the small kitchen. 'I don't know. It's just . . . A year or two ago, even less, I would have said to you that this boy was an undoubted genius and that by now everyone would know it. We would not only be listening to him play, but we would performing his music.'

'But he has composed, hasn't he? I've heard you play some of his music.'

'But it's . . . it's . . . It's so different. As if he is deliberately . . . Remember that song I told you about? "Portrait of a Young Girl", I think he called it. A pretty song. Just the sort of song to be performed at court by one of the young tenors. But there's that wild passage on the piano, which completely goes against the tender words of the song. I tried to tell him it was wrong, but he was absolutely adamant.' He thrust his hands into his pockets. 'Then there were the quartets. The *piano* quartets,' he said, stressing the word with some irony. 'The ones Herr Ries, even, advised him to put to one side.'

'He's experimenting. You've often said that. That he likes to . . . to . . .'

'And there's another song he's written,' said Neefe, a smile spreading across his face. 'I could hardly stop myself laughing when he showed it to me. I've got it here somewhere.' He looked through some papers on a side table. 'Here. Yes, this is the one. It's called "For an Infant". Let me read the first verse to you. Just as he read it to me.'

Neefe cleared his throat and assumed a grave look. He held one hand out in a declamatory gesture.

> '"Yet know ye not whose child ye be,
> Who clotheth thee, that thou might'st live?
> Who guardeth thee both night and day,
> And warmth and milk to thee doth give?"

'It's portentous, isn't it? Pretty serious. Implying the child does not know its own mother. But do you know how he has written it? He has given it a pretty little tune, so memorable that I still hear it in my head. And do you know what voice he has written it for? Wouldn't you expect a soprano or tenor? An adult consoling this infant? He's given it to the boy trebles of the court choir. Not just one, but all of them!'

'As I said, he's experimenting.'

Neefe sat down again, his smile gone. 'It's just that if he keeps experimenting, he'll be left behind. Take Mozart, his great idol. By the time he was Ludwig's age he had already written symphonies, piano concertos – even operas. They weren't his greatest. But he had written them. And he had been to Brussels, Paris, London. And here in Bonn Ludwig's not the only talent. There's the young Reicha. A flautist. He's the same age as Ludwig and he's already composing pieces for the choir and orchestra. There are the Rombergs, cousins. Violin and cello. They've already been to Paris to perform.'

'Gotti,' said Clara with kindly finality. 'Ludwig has a lot of unhappiness in his life at the moment. It's bound to affect his work.'

'You're right, my love. I know you're right. You know . . .' he leaned forward and put his hands on hers, 'I sometimes wonder why I think so long and hard about Ludwig, why

I worry so much on his behalf. But there's something . . . something about him.' He paused a moment. 'I know what he needs. I know exactly what he needs. And it's something I cannot give him. He needs a patron. A benefactor. A wealthy nobleman who loves the arts and is prepared to sponsor him. Someone to give him an entrée into the salons of Europe. That way he will achieve the greatness that I am sure is within him. By then he'll have left me far behind. I only hope they remember that his first teacher was your husband.'

He smiled at Clara and squeezed her hands.

Ferdinand Ernst Gabriel, Count von Waldstein, stood solidly, legs apart, hands on hips. He looked at the portrait and smiled. He thought it had captured his aristocratic looks exactly, even – though he would never say so aloud – improved on them slightly. The small bump which prevented his nose from being perfectly straight had been excised by the artist as surely as with a surgeon's knife. His face undoubtedly looked sensitive and artistic, intelligent even. But best of all was the uniform: the splendid white tunic with red collar and ruff, and the magnificent silver-trimmed bicorn hat which sat majestically across his head.

'There, Father, Mother. A suitable memento. You will feel as if I am in the room with you, instead of being at the outermost frontier of our great empire.'

'You will take care, dear, won't you? Is it true about the French, that they covet the Rhineland?'

'Ha!' laughed Waldstein's father. 'They can covet it, but they cannot have it. The Emperor's own brother is Elector there. He has the forces of the empire at his disposal. No, you are a lucky young man, Gabi. With your pedigree and the settlement I am making on you, you will have a comfortable life. People will respect and look up to you. Friend of the Elector and knight of the most noble Teutonic Order. You have a bright future. Your dear mother and I will, we know, one day have cause to be proud of our youngest son.'

If the young Count von Waldstein had been first-born to his illustrious parents, instead of fourth, it was probable he would never have set foot in Bonn, or even on German soil, in his entire life. Instead he would in time have succeeded to the family title and taken his elevated place among the Austrian nobility in Vienna.

How he wished that could have been the case! The Hofburg palace, confidant of the Emperor, a senior rank in the imperial army. Instead of what? The small provincial town of Bonn, confidant of the Elector, member of the Teutonic Order.

'Are you seriously leaving us to live among the savages on the banks of the Rhine?' one of his young nobleman friends had asked him incredulously.

'I shall be at the centre of government,' he had replied, 'at the right hand of the Emperor's younger brother. Far closer than you are to the Emperor himself. I shall be a member of the court.'

'You can hardly call it a court, my dear Gabi. More a council. And the Teutonic Order. It's not the force it once was.'

'There you are mistaken. Here in Vienna maybe not. But in Germany . . . And the Elector himself has personally pledged to install me as a knight. He wrote to me in Malta.'

'Well, if I were you, Gabi, I would make my mark in other areas. If you try to influence government, you will be accused of interfering, of being an outsider from Vienna. Friend of the Elector or not. You know what these provincials are like. No. Involve yourself in gentler pursuits. The arts, for example. Be a patron of the arts. For that you will receive nothing but gratitude.'

Chapter 2

Ludwig pulled a chair to his mother's bedside and wondered where his father was? And where were Caspar and Nikola? Could they not see that the end was imminent? He looked round the room. Nothing. The infant Margaretha's cot had been moved into another room. He was at least grateful for that.

Maybe the doctor had told his father and brothers that it might be many hours yet. If so, he was wrong. That was obvious. Ludwig looked at his mother. Her head, propped up on the pillow, had slipped slightly to the side. Her jaw hung down and her mouth was open. Her hair, still the dark and lustrous hair of a woman under fifty, was tangled and matted. Her cheekbones had a roseate glow to them. He felt her hand. It was no longer warm and he sensed it become colder even as he held it.

He reached forward to lift her jaw and close her mouth. As he released it, it immediately fell open again and a rivulet of saliva ran down her chin. He quickly dabbed it dry with a cloth. Her eyelids were tightly closed and her eyes underneath seemed to have swollen. He thought of his grandfather, and how he had sat by old Ludwig's head and marvelled at the transformation death had wrought. Now he was watching his mother undergo the same ravages.

Suddenly she breathed deeply, her chest rising as she did so. Immediately she exhaled the air and was still. Her hand was cold but her pulse still gave a tiny, tremulous flutter. On her forehead beads of sweat stood out. He dabbed them dry and they did not return.

'Mother,' he said quietly, 'I remember how you warmed my feet on the boat. There is so much more I want to tell you. But it is too late.'

Maria breathed deeply again, but this time it was more of a gasp.

He heard voices from downstairs and knew his father had

returned. He stood and leaned forward. Gently he kissed his mother's forehead. It was icy cold. Her eyelids had now opened slightly. He knew she was dead and was grateful that the moment of her passing had been peaceful.

He descended the stairs and walked out, avoiding his father. The cool evening air bathed his face like fresh water.

He walked down through the Marktplatz to the Rheingasse. He passed the Fischer house, not looking at it as he did so. At the bottom he turned and began walking along the river. Far ahead the mighty Drachenfels loomed, but he looked only at his feet.

What would become of the Beethoven family now? His mother, who had held the family together, was gone. His father was descending ever more into drunkenness. Ludwig knew Johann would sooner or later lose his position as tenor singer. Caspar and Nikola were young, just thirteen and eleven. Margaretha was only a year.

And he, Ludwig, was almost seventeen, earning a salary as assistant court organist. He was now composing, which he knew to be his life's work. There were the piano quartets and the sonatas he had dedicated to the late elector. There were songs and rondos for piano. But those were only beginnings.

He sat on the bank and held his head in his hands. He prayed to God to allow him to continue his work, not to burden him with responsibilities he could not fulfil. He thought of his grandfather. His dear grandfather. How he wished he were still alive, that he could hear his comforting voice, smell the familiar Turkish tobacco . . . talk about music with him.

But he was dead. And now his mother was dead too. Try as he might, Ludwig could not stop the tears welling up in him.

Ludwig watched the small boy with dark curly hair press the piano keys with his little fingers.

'Maybe, Herr Ries. Maybe one day he'll be a musician, and a fine one too.'

Franz Ries smiled. 'He certainly loves standing on the stool and making dreadful noises. Remember your promise. When he's old enough I'll ask you to give him his first lessons.' He turned to the child. 'Run along, Ferdi. Find Mama. I must speak to this young man.'

He guided Ludwig to a chair and sat beside him. 'Your poor dear Mama. I'm so sad for you, Ludwig. She did not have an easy life. Your father did not . . . He is not an easy man to live with. How is he taking her death?'

'He is drinking more and more. His voice is deteriorating. It is only a matter of time before he is dismissed and then I don't know what we'll do.'

Ries put his hand on Ludwig's shoulder. 'Is money a problem, Ludwig? Do you have enough to live on?

Ludwig nodded. 'It's all right at the moment. When I've paid back what I owe it'll be better. And Caspar might soon be able to earn a little, which will help. And in a year or two he'll have left school and . . .'

'What do you mean, money you owe?'

'I . . . I . . . Because I had to leave Vienna suddenly I didn't have time to draw any money. So Herr Schaden in Augsburg lent me some. I spoke to the exchequer's office here and they said that since I didn't stay in Vienna I was not entitled to my salary there. So I'll have to wait until . . .'

Ries nodded and sat down again opposite Ludwig. 'I know that already. I just wanted to hear it from you. Well, I've spoken to the exchequer's office on your behalf and you'll be pleased to hear that order has been reversed. The salary that was sent to Vienna is being paid to you here right away. Two months' money, to compensate for the disruption. So you'll be able to clear your debt and have some left over.'

Ludwig smiled and thanked Ries.

'Don't say another word, young man. And let me know how you get on. If you have any problems, I want to know. Do you hear?'

It was the housekeeper who discovered the infant Maria Margaretha's lifeless body in the cot. She offered up a silent prayer for the child, then briskly went about the necessary business, summoning the doctor to certify death and arrange for the little body to be taken away. Like her mother, Margaretha had died of consumption.

Ludwig returned from the Electoral palace that evening to be confronted by an angry trio of his father and brothers.

'Damn you. You're worthless. Where have you been all day? Your sister's dead.'

'I . . . I've been working.'

'You splash away with your stupid music while your sister dies. Do you not care?'

'Yes,' echoed Caspar, 'do you not care?'

'Yes,' said Nikola with important finality.

Ludwig slumped into a chair. He felt all the weight of family pressures descend upon his shoulders. With a measure of relief he saw his father lurch towards the door and leave the room. Nikola hurried after him, not wanting to remain in the room if his father was not going to be there.

'You've never cared, have you? All you care about is your music,' said Caspar accusingly.

For a moment Ludwig said nothing, then he could not restrain the anger that rose up within him.

'How can you say that? You! What have you ever done? You just go to school all day and when you're not at school you're in the sandpit. But I work. I earn money.'

'What do you earn? Nothing. Father says you're worthless. He says you could have earned much more. But you won't, because instead of playing for important people all you do is write your stupid stuff down.'

'Don't say that! Don't say that!'

'It's Father who says that. And he's right.'

Ludwig sprang from the chair and stood face to face with his brother, breathing hard. Suddenly he could look no longer at the arrogance which was written on Caspar's face and he grabbed him by the shoulders, wrestling him to the ground.

The two boys pummelled each other. The housekeeper, who was leaving for the day when she heard the commotion, hurried back up the stairs and separated them.

'Come on, you two. Enough of that. Enough!'

Caspar ran from the room. Ludwig sat down, breathing heavily. As he regained his composure he was secretly proud that he had stood up to his brother.

Curiously, Ludwig was less affected by his infant sister's death than he expected to be. He was sad, as he kept telling himself. But he came to realise that he had always assumed his sister was doomed. Maybe it was because his mother had loved her so, clung to her when the consumption took hold, so that Ludwig could hardly think of his sister without thinking of his mother.

Now that she had gone, he felt a certain freedom. There was no longer an infant in the household who needed constant attention. His brothers at least – given that the housekeeper cooked the meals and washed clothes – could look after themselves. As for his father, Ludwig could hardly be expected to look after him.

More and more Ludwig spent time on his own, walking sometimes for hours on end. He crossed the river and walked purposefully in the Siebengebirge hills, seeing the sights and hearing the sounds of nature.

'You and your walks,' Stephan said to him one day. 'If walking were a profession and nature your employer, you would be a wealthy man.'

'And a happy one,' Ludwig replied.

Soon after the turn of the year, at the end of a lesson with Neefe, his teacher turned to him.

'Your friend Stephan Breuning was here a little earlier. He left a note for you.'

Ludwig unfolded the paper and read the message. Stephan was relaying an invitation from his mother to come to the house at seven in the evening. 'She asks, if it does not inconvenience you, if you would wear your best jacket.'

He looked up to see Neefe smiling at him. 'For a young man, Ludwig, you are moving in exalted circles. You can call the Elector himself a friend, and now you are to meet the second most important person in Bonn. No, no, I did not read your note. Stephan told me. And I can assure you of one thing. You will be called upon to play the piano. So let us take another look at the Bach preludes.'

'Ludwig, do come in. How kind of you to respond to my invitation. I'd like you to meet a new resident of our city, Count Waldstein. He is from Vienna. His family is related to the Emperor himself.'

'Distantly, distantly, I assure you,' said Waldstein, standing and walking towards Ludwig, his hand outstretched.

Ludwig looked up into the face of the twenty-six-year-old Count and took an instant liking to him. By now well used to meeting people of a considerably higher social standing than himself, he was not awed by the powdered wig or finely tailored clothes the Count was wearing. What he saw was a kindly, open face and a smile of genuine pleasure.

'Young man, your fame has travelled before you. I know of your visit to Vienna. In fact, I can tell you that it was talked of afterwards for quite some time, and how sad you had to leave. Herr Mozart had words of praise for you.'

Ludwig gasped. 'He did? He remembered me?'

'He most certainly did. He kept saying . . . what was it he said? . . . Yes. "Remember that boy. One day he will give the world something to talk about." Similar words to that, anyway.'

Ludwig nodded. 'He said the same thing to his wife while I was there.' He looked quickly down to hide his immodesty.

'How nice for you, dear Ludwig,' said Frau Breuning. 'To have heard from the Count of the impression you made. The Count has come to live here in Bonn, to be adviser to His Grace the Elector, and he asked me if he could meet you.'

Ludwig looked at the Count. 'Are you a musician? Do you know music?'

'Well, I am forced to answer no to your first question, but yes to your second. I am a soldier by training, but for the moment my services are of more use to His Imperial Majesty as a diplomat. When not acting in that capacity I am bound to say that the pursuit of music is my greatest pleasure. Truth to tell, I can play the piano, but only for my own enjoyment. I would not inflict it on others. But at the Hofburg palace in Vienna I arrange concerts, choose music. And . . . well . . . I have tried my hand at a little composition. But with very amateurish results, I regret to say.'

'The Count has told me he wishes to be involved in the musical activities of our town, as a patron of music.'

'Of all the arts, if I might say so. But of music more than any of them.'

'How long will you be here in Bonn?' Ludwig asked.

'It depends on what happens on the other side of the Rhine. I am afraid the French are giving us plenty to think about at the moment. Our embassy in Paris reports that revolution is in the air. It is talked of openly in the streets. The end of the monarchy, even. The creation of a republic.'

'How dreadful,' said Frau Breuning. 'There would be bloodshed, that is certain.'

'You may be right. And King Louis is married to the sister of our Emperor, the Archduchess Marie Antoinette. I fear for her. I am afraid – though I implore you not to repeat my words outside this room – her husband the King is . . . well . . . not as aware as he might be of what is happening around him.'

'Will there be war?'

'I profoundly hope not. But there are firebrands in Paris already talking about it. A lawyer from Arras in the north, Robespierre, I think his name is. And a peasant who can barely write his own name. Danton. They are talking of revolution and war. And ridding Europe of what they call Habsburg domination. It does not bode well for the future.'

'Let us talk no more of such things. Ludwig, will you do us the honour of playing the piano for us?'

Ludwig looked at the two eager faces, both with eyebrows raised in anticipation. He felt – as he had done that day when he faced the late Elector across the desk – a power. He possessed a talent, a skill, with which he knew he could impress them. He had the power too to refuse their request, as he had done the Elector's. But he liked both Frau Breuning and the Count.

He sat at the piano and looked at the ivory keys for a moment. 'Count, would you play me a theme, a simple theme, of your own invention? And then I will show you what that theme is capable of becoming.'

The Count sat in the chair Ludwig had vacated. 'This will not be very good, Ludwig. But it is all I am capable of.' He played a simple theme in the right hand, just eight bars long, accompanied by chords in the left. 'Do not ask me to repeat it,' he said, smiling. 'I could not.'

Ludwig sat at the piano and played the theme exactly as Waldstein had played it. Then, still playing the same chords with the left hand, he embellished the theme with the right, introducing runs of quavers where before there had been crotchets, and introducing trills and grace notes. Now it was the turn of the bass register, throwing the theme into the minor key, while the right hand played chords. The two hands contrapuntally; a fugue; a march played with chords in both hands. *Piano*, *pianissimo*, the theme played in fragments, disintegrating, yet retaining its essentials. Finally a flourish in both hands, bringing the variations to a stirring climax and finish.

Frau Breuning and Count Waldstein clapped. 'That was my theme?' asked the Count incredulously. 'With the theme I composed you can do all that? It must have been a remarkably fine theme!' he said, and both he and Frau Breuning, as well as Ludwig, laughed.

Chapter 3

The talk in the Zehrgarten tavern in the Markplatz was of only one topic: revolution in France. The mob had stormed the Bastille and liberated its prisoners. The revolution had begun. Who was to say where it would end?

'It will end nowhere. The rabble is undisciplined and disunited. One detachment of French guards will be enough to quell them.'

'You are wrong. The Bastille is the symbol of repression. It was supposed to be invincible. With that gone, the whole country will rise up.'

The first speaker laughed, banging a carafe of wine on the table for emphasis. 'My dear friend, you are a dreamer. Do you know how many prisoners were set free in this famous attack? Shall I tell you? Precisely seven, and two of them were madmen. No, I don't believe it will lead to anything.'

'But the King is weak,' said a third voice. 'He could have quelled it quickly, and then I believe you would be right. But he recognised the citizens' militia. The National Guard, it's called now. It means the people are in control of Paris. The King cannot govern without their consent.'

'And I heard there are riots spreading across the country,' said another. 'And rumours of aristocrats being attacked. Châteaux burned.'

'Exaggeration,' said the first speaker. 'Wild rumours. You see, in a few weeks all will return to normal and the French will get back to their most important task. Producing the wine we all love so much!'

There was general laughter. At a round table in the corner of the tavern, Ludwig sat with Stephan Breuning and Franz Wegeler.

'What do you think, Ludwig?' asked Stephan. 'Will there be revolution in France?'

Ludwig shrugged. 'At court they don't seem to think so. But the Elector is worried. Count Waldstein and he are always holding meetings with the council to discuss the situation.'

'It's because of his sister, isn't it? Marie Antoinette?' Wegeler asked.

Ludwig nodded. 'He knows how unpopular she is in Paris. He is worried for her safety. He thinks his brother the Emperor should do something. Some expression of support for Louis. So the rabble will know that if they attack the King, they will have the imperial family of Habsburg to deal with too.'

'The Emperor has more to worry about than just his sister,' said Stephan, instinctively lowering his voice. 'He may not be under attack in the way King Louis is, but the empire is far from being a haven of tranquillity. In the Netherlands they're close to revolt, apparently. The nationalists in Bohemia are sowing dissent. This disturbance in France will encourage other firebrands, that's my worry.'

Ludwig was about to reply, but his face fell as he saw his brother Caspar come into the large open room and start looking round the tables. He knew from the way his brother stood – his body tensed and leaning slightly forward – and the look of clear anguish on his face that there was a problem. It had to be his father. Ludwig held his breath as Caspar, seeing him, came hurrying over.

'Ludwig. You've got to come quickly. It's Papa.'

'What's happened? Has he . . . ? Is he all right?'

'He's . . . he's been drinking. The police have arrested him. They're threatening to put him prison.'

The three hurriedly left the tavern with Caspar and walked up the Bonngasse and into the Kölnstrasse. They heard Johann shouting before they had entered the police station.

'Don't you know who I am? I am a member of the court. My father was Kapellmeister. I am a senior musician. You will have His Grace himself to answer to for this.'

Ludwig looked at his father. He was a pitiful sight, sitting in a chair with his wrists strapped to its arms. The upper half of his body was slumped forward. Saliva ran down the corner of his chin.

'Ludwig. Tell these damned fools—'

'Quiet, Father. Don't say any more. Let me deal with this.' He turned to the two policemen standing by the door. 'Who's the senior policeman here?'

'I am, young man,' said one. 'This your father? The night patrol arrested him for drunken behaviour in the street.'

'Let me take him home. I'll look after him. I'll make sure it doesn't happen again.'

'This is not the first time, young man. You know that, don't you?'

'I'll take him home. With my brother. And friends here.'

'By rights he should stay the night here and appear in court tomorrow.'

'Look,' Ludwig said, his voice raised in exasperation, 'it's not necessary. I will look after him.' Stephan put his arm on Ludwig's shoulder to calm him.

'Officer,' said Stephan, 'my name is Breuning. Von Breuning. My father was the Court Councillor. He died in the fire at the palace. This is my friend Dr Wegeler. He recently qualified to practise medicine. We can vouch for what our friend here says. If you let us take Herr Beethoven home, we will ensure there is no repeat of this.'

'You'll need to sign the release papers. You'll be held responsible if it happens again.'

Ludwig told Franz Ries about what had happened to his father, but found he already knew.

'I am so sorry about it. I am glad you were with your friends when it happened.'

'Steffen persuaded the policeman to let my father go. I was so angry, I . . . I . . . He stopped me losing my temper. It would have been awful if I had made matters worse.'

'It's over now. I don't think it will happen again. I've spoken to your father and he is contrite. Ashamed. He realises what pain he has caused to you and your brothers. I am worried for him, though. I am afraid his behaviour is now general knowledge. The Elector is said to be displeased, since your father is an employee of the court.'

Ludwig's shoulders slumped. 'He will be dismissed soon. I know it. I have known it for a long time.'

Ries nodded. 'Ludwig, I have given the matter a lot of thought. Will you let me advise you?' Ludwig nodded, and Ries continued. 'I believe you are right and that if something is not done your father will be dismissed. That will cause him enormous humiliation. More importantly, it will affect his pension. If he is dismissed he will not be entitled to the full amount.'

'But what . . . what can we do?'

'My advice is that you should petition the Elector – I will help you write it – and ask him to release your father from duty so that he can retire, on the grounds that his health is deteriorating. He is fifty now and his voice is not as good as it was. He is perfectly entitled to retire. I have seen others do it. And you should state that you wish half his pension to be paid to you to help you care for him and your brothers. That too is not an unusual request.'

'Would . . . would the Elector grant it? It's not . . .'

Ries nodded. 'Ludwig, believe me, I would not be advising this rather drastic course of action if I had not first undertaken a little research on your behalf. I have spoken to the right people. Your petition will be granted.'

Ries had laid the ground for Ludwig's petition better than he realised. The Elector's reply contained, almost buried in it, ten words which when he read them caused the tears to well up in Ludwig's eyes.

> . . . His Electoral Highness having graciously granted the prayer of the petitioner and dispensed henceforth wholly with the services of his father, who is to withdraw to a village in the Electorate . . .

Who is to withdraw to a village in the Electorate . . . They were banishing his father. He ignored the rest of the reply, which granted his request that half his father's pension be paid to him, and hurried to see Herr Ries.

'Can they do this? Why must they do this? It will . . . will . . . destroy him.'

Ries put a comforting arm round Ludwig's shoulder. 'Don't worry. I knew they were considering saying that, but I wasn't sure so I didn't want to alarm you. It's only a precaution. The feeling is that it will convince your father of the seriousness of the situation. It'll help make sure he doesn't transgress again. And by the way, I've had a quiet word with Klein the fish-dealer. He has promised me he will not tempt your father to go to the tavern with him.'

The crisis over Johann's behaviour passed, and it seemed as if he had understood the gravity of what had happened. No longer employed, and under threat of imprisonment – even banishment

– if he was arrested again, Johann controlled his drinking in public at least, although he continued drinking heavily within the confines of the apartment on the Wenzelgasse.

Johann knew that the Elector had ordered him to leave Bonn, and he was grateful to his son for not insisting this ultimate humiliation be inflicted on him. Nor did he resent the fact that half his pension was being paid directly to Ludwig; in fact he was relieved that he was no longer required to sing at court. With retirement came a welcome release from responsibilities.

The duties that correspondingly fell on Ludwig's shoulders were also less onerous that he feared. Both Caspar and Nikola had now left school. Caspar was studying music and Nikola was apprenticed to an apothecary. The extra one hundred thalers Ludwig now received from his father's pension covered the costs of both his brothers. Caspar's musical instruction would shortly be coming to an end, after which he was promised salaried employment at court. And Nikola, when he finished his apprenticeship, would also earn a small salary as an apothecary's assistant.

For Ludwig too there was a sudden upturn in his fortune, and the cause of it was an event which rocked the Austrian Empire.

Ludwig wanted to talk about Wolfgang Mozart's latest opera, *Così fan Tutte*, which had opened to huge acclaim in Vienna. But the only topic of conversation in Bonn, whether in the taverns, on the street or at the palace, was the death of the Emperor Joseph.

Bonn went into mourning. Prayers for Joseph were offered in every little church. The Elector, in his capacity as Archbishop of Cologne and Münster, officiated at Requiem Masses to his brother in Cologne Cathedral, attended by his fellow Electors from other German principalities.

In Bonn the musicians at court were learning and performing sacred works, it seemed, from morning until night. The court organist Gottlob Neefe and his assistant Ludwig van Beethoven took it in turns to rehearse the choir. When he was not working with the choir, Ludwig took his place in the court orchestra as violinist. Because of sickness Stephan Breuning was also given a place in the orchestra. He and Ludwig shared a desk at the back of the first violins, Stephan grateful that Ludwig's firm playing eclipsed his own rather faltering efforts.

A week after the Emperor's death Ludwig received a summons to see the Elector, 'To discuss a matter of musical importance.' Ludwig let out a slight sigh of exasperation when he read the note. He was certain he knew what the Elector wanted. Max Franz would have made a decision to perform personally at one of the services, either as singer or on his favourite instrument the viola, and he wanted Ludwig to give him some personal tuition.

Many court musicians would feel honoured and flattered to be summoned by the highest personage in the land to perform such a duty. Ludwig's reluctance was due not just to the heavy workload occasioned by the Emperor's death, which itself prevented him working on his own compositions – he had recently begun sketching an ambitiously large set of piano variations – but by his natural aversion to teaching.

He had realised very quickly that teaching music was not an activity that he enjoyed. Nor did it come to him naturally. His piano pupils Eleonore Breuning and her younger brother Lenz had both received harsh words from him at their failure to progress at the speed he had hoped for. On more than one occasion Stephan had had to speak to Ludwig, reminding him that patience was required and that he could not expect everyone to share his prodigious talent.

He knew he lacked the patience required of a teacher, a quality that Gottlob Neefe, for instance, seemed to have naturally within him. He also knew, though, that teaching earned money and that it gave him access to influential people, people who were in a position to further his own art.

'Come in, Ludwig. Come in. Sit over here.' He was ushered to a firmly upholstered but comfortable chair, not by the Elector, but by Count Waldstein, who himself sat in one of the other two empty chairs which stood around a long, low table on which a number of papers were spread.

How well Ludwig knew this room, and how apprehensive he had been when he had first swept his eyes round it, ignoring the opulent tapestries and rich furnishings, looking only for the piano. He was a child then and he still smiled when he remembered his protest, his refusal to play for Maximilian Friedrich.

'His Grace will be with us in a few moments,' said Waldstein. 'So sad about His Imperial Majesty. Did you meet him when you were in Vienna?'

Ludwig shook his head. 'Who will be Emperor now?'

'His younger brother Leopold. He rules in Milan. It is a difficult time for him to become the head of the empire. His late brother's death really was most untimely.'

'Why?'

Waldstein smiled. 'The French. What is happening only a short distance west of here is of great concern to the empire. A revolution against the established order. Against the monarchy.'

'But Europe is ruled by monarchies. Prussia, Spain, England . . .'

'Yes. You are right. There is no danger in the long term. But there are disturbing reports coming from our agents in Paris. The French are building their forces. Units of so-called National Guards are springing up all over the country. They're made up of ordinary citizens, that's the worry. Not professional soldiers. The country is rising up. And there is talk of France expanding its borders. And if they come east . . . to the Rhine . . .'

The door at the far end of the room opened and Maximilian Franz came in. Ludwig noticed how corpulent he had become, the flesh beneath his chin swinging as he walked. His limp was now more pronounced, and the rapid loss of his hair contributed to the image of an unhealthy man who looked much older than his thirty-four years.

'I do apologise for keeping you waiting. Count. Ludwig. How is your father, Ludwig? Good. Dear me, such sad times. I was fond of my brother. Very fond.' He sat down alongside Waldstein and opposite Ludwig. He leaned forward and tidied the papers on the low table in front of him. 'So unexpected. Such a short illness.'

'Will you return to Vienna, sir?' asked Waldstein.

'Yes, at some stage. I'll have to. For the funeral. And of course for the coronation. But I don't want to leave Bonn, with so much going on. These wretched French. One thing's certain now. The Bastille was no isolated act. The whole country is in revolt. My poor, poor sister. How I fear for her. And, listen to this, a slogan being distributed by pamphlet. Our agent sent us one.' He shuffled through the papers until he found the one he wanted. '"All mortals are equal. It is not by birth but by virtue that we are distinguished. In every state the law must be universal and mortals, whosoever they be, are equal before it." I wonder what they will make of that at the Hofburg palace.' He threw the paper down with a contemptuous gesture.

'We will resist the French, sir. The empire cannot be challenged by an undisciplined rabble. A thousand years of history will not be wiped out by a mob. If they choose to challenge us, they will receive a bloody nose.'

'I wish I had your confidence, Waldstein. What you say may be true of Vienna, the seat of empire. The heart. With a city wall that is impregnable, which held off the Ottoman invaders. But here on the banks of the Rhine . . . Take a carriage ride to the west and in a short while you can practically see into France. No,' he shook his head, 'I fear for the future.'

Ludwig listened to the two men discussing affairs of state, the future of Europe. 'All mortals are equal.' Yes, he thought. How could anyone argue with that? It is self-evident. He remembered Neefe had once said something similar to him. It is a birth right, and is that not what I want to express in my music? Not in words, like in that pamphlet, but in music, in notes.

At first Ludwig did not hear the Elector addressing him. It was Waldstein's insistent voice which he heard.

'Ludwig. The Elector is talking to you. His Grace.'

'Now, Ludwig. Let me tell you why I have asked you to come to see me. Shall I proceed, Count, or would you, as a member of the Lesegesellschaft . . . ?'

'No, sir, please. I beg of you, do go ahead.'

'Ludwig,' the Elector said, a look of sadness replacing the smile, 'I was very close to my eldest brother, the Emperor, despite our difference in age. He was a good man and I believe history will judge him to have been a great Emperor. He himself was too modest to admit it. When I last spoke to him all he could talk about was how he had not yet accomplished all he wanted to. But he believed very deeply in reform.'

Warming to his theme the Elector rose from his chair, rubbed his damaged knee and flexed the leg a little, then walked stiffly in a small circle. 'In my own small way I have tried to effect similar reforms here in Bonn. Most of all the Emperor believed in free thought, and I do too. That was why I gave the city a university. That is why you and your friends can now read Aristotle, Plato, Plutarch. Even the French writers and philosophers that the mindless rabble in France hold in such awe. Rousseau, Voltaire. And you are in no danger of arrest, as you might once have been. No, First Minister Belderbusch, from what I hear of him, would not recognise the city now. Don't you agree, Count?'

'Sir, I did not know this city before it was fortunate enough to become your seat of government. Certainly now it is the . . . the . . . jewel of the Rhine.'

Ludwig coughed slightly. 'What music is it you would like me to go through with you, sir?'

The Elector sat down again heavily, his weight shifting the chair on the smooth floor. 'Hah!' he laughed. 'Not the Lamentations of Jeremiah, I can assure you of that! Have you heard the story, Waldstein? Of how our young genius here humbled the great Ferdinand Heller? Remind me to tell you about it. No, it is rather more important than that. It concerns my late brother the Emperor, and my other brother soon to become Emperor.'

Ludwig suddenly sat bolt upright. 'Vienna?' he asked tremulously. 'Am I to go to . . . am I . . . ?'

Simultaneously both the Elector and Waldstein shook their heads. 'No, no, Ludwig,' said Max Franz, 'I am sorry to disappoint you. But your disappointment may not last when you hear what I have to say to you. The Lesegesellschaft, the Reading Society, of which the good Count here is of course a member, wishes to hold a memorial funeral service to my late brother. It has in its possession a poem by a young . . . I forget his name . . . a poet . . .'

'Averdonck, sir,' said Waldstein. 'Severin Anton Averdonck. A monk at the Bethlemite Monastery in Ehrenbreitstein. His sister is a singer here at court.'

'She sang at my first concert,' said Ludwig. 'In Cologne. I was a child.'

'Yes. Well, the Society wishes the poem to be set to music. A cantata. There was much discussion as to who should be chosen for this honour. And . . . well, Waldstein, you were at the meeting. Why do you not explain what happened?'

'Professor Schneider put forward the idea for a cantata to be played, after he himself has read the funeral oration. He then recited the poem by Averdonck, which received universal admiration. As His Grace says, there was much discussion as to the choice of composer to set it to music. Some favoured Herr Neefe, others Herr Reicha. It was the Professor's view that something new and entirely original was required for so important an occasion, and he favoured your name above all others. I have to admit to my own small part. I agreed with him wholeheartedly.'

Ludwig was listening intently, his mouth slightly open.

'To begin with,' Waldstein continued, 'there was not universal acceptance. The point put against you, Ludwig, was your lack of experience as a composer. The fact that you have not yet published any works for full orchestra. But I am pleased to say that in the end Schneider and I carried the day. And I was asked to convey the decision to His Grace for his approval.'

'Which I give with very great pleasure. So, Ludwig, it is now up to you. Do you accept the commission to compose a cantata, a "Cantata on the Death of His Imperial Majesty, Joseph"? A task for which you will, of course, be recompensed.'

Ludwig nodded. 'Yes. Yes. I will compose it.'

'Good!' said the Elector, clapping his hands. 'Then let me give you another little piece of news. I would very much like you, when you have completed the work, to compose another. In a different . . . shall we say . . . mood. A second cantata, but, I hope, a rather more joyous one. A "Cantata on the Elevation of Leopold to the Imperial Dignity". You accept, of course, don't you?'

Ludwig smiled, and nodded again.

Chapter 4

'Professor Schneider,' said Sebastian Pfau, 'this is not a decision we have taken lightly.'

'We have worked hard at it. But there is no more we can do.' The speaker was the court clarinettist Joseph Pachmeyer. He and the flautist Pfau had been chosen to represent the wind section of the court orchestra.

The strings were represented by the violinists Ernst Riedel and Christoph Brandt. 'The piece is unbalanced,' said Brandt. 'The winds dominate. The strings merely accompany.'

'Except in the lower strings,' said Riedel, 'and we do not have enough cellists or double bass players to give it the weight it needs.'

'There's another problem,' said Pachmeyer. 'There are passages for the wind sections that are unplayable. Unplayable. It's not just that they are difficult and that we lack the skill. They are unplayable. It is almost as if he has written them to make us look incompetent.'

'You should tell him that if he expects a flautist to play what he has written, he should find one with six fingers on each hand,' said Pfau tetchily.

'Gentlemen, gentlemen,' said Schneider in a conciliatory voice. 'Let us remain calm, and try to be constructive over this. The memorial service is just three days away. There is obviously a problem. What can we do about it?'

Clemens von Schall, a leading member of the Lesegesellschaft, though not himself a musician, spoke. 'If we ask him to correct the balance that you are complaining about, and perhaps simplify certain passages, would that . . . ?'

'It's not a question of simplifying them,' said Pfau. 'I am not asking for simple music to play. What he needs to do is rewrite it. I do not want to be technical, but he has written chromatic passages, with octave leaps. Unnecessary, and not within the capability of our instruments. By writing them he has demonstrated ignorance of what our instruments can and cannot do. He needs to rewrite it. Turn it into proper music, the sort we would have got if someone else had written it. Herr Neefe or Herr Reicha, for instance.'

'There is one other solution. The only other solution. Get the full orchestra from Cologne to swell our numbers. That will solve the problem of balance. And with that number of players we can simply not play the impossible passages and no one will notice. Particularly since the piece has not been heard before. No one will know there are passages missing.'

Schneider shook his head. 'The Lesegesellschaft's coffers would not stretch to that, I am afraid, gentlemen. And with only three days to go, even if he were to rewrite it, which I doubt would be possible, there would be no time for you to rehearse it.'

There was silence for a few moments. Schneider turned to Schall. 'I think we have no choice but to abandon it. Will you prepare a statement? The handbills have already gone out, so I think we have to correct them.' He turned to the musicians. 'The other musical pieces, I take it, are no problem?' They shook their heads. 'And the choir?'

'No. They'll be as relieved as we are at your decision. Believe me, to have performed the piece would have risked major embarrassment at what is supposed to be a solemn occasion.'

'Do we need to give a reason for the cancellation?' asked Schall.

'No,' said Schneider. 'Just say the Cantata by Ludwig van Beethoven cannot be performed for various reasons.'

'How did Ludwig take it?' Ries asked Neefe anxiously the next day.

'To be honest with you, I was most surprised. He shrugged his shoulders and said he had expected it.'

'Did you suggest he might want to . . . to . . . recast certain sections?'

'I didn't need to. Before I could say any more he said, "I'm not changing a note. If they can't play it, I'll wait until there are musicians who can."'

Ries smiled and shook his head slowly. 'Yes, I rather thought that might be his attitude. What about the second cantata? Is he going ahead with it?'

'Yes. He even said he would make it a little easier. "For the amateur musicians of Bonn." Tell me, Herr Ries. The cantata they wouldn't play. Have you seen the score?'

'Yes,' Ries said slowly. 'I have. And Ludwig has played me passages on the piano.'

'What's your view?'

Ries clenched his jaw. 'At first . . . at first I thought . . . I didn't quite know what to make of it. But the more I heard it, thought about it even . . . I began to realise . . . The soprano aria, for instance. It's one of the most beautiful . . . Deceptive . . . It sounds simple but if you look at the score . . .'

Neefe nodded vigorously. 'Do you know what it reminds me of? The whole cantata? Handel's music. Some of his oratorios. It's shorter, obviously. Less dramatic. But there's the same . . . intensity. In my view it's great music. And written by, what, a twenty-year-old?'

Ries smiled. 'To be honest I am not surprised some of the musicians have reacted the way they have. It must have been unlike anything they have seen. After all, when was the last time they were called on to play anything by Handel? Even Mozart frightens them. They're far happier with Martin, Paisiello, Sacchini . . .'

'. . . and Neefe,' said Neefe, smiling.

'My dear man, I did not mean to . . .'

'Not at all. Not at all. The reason they enjoy playing my music is that I write to their strengths. I know what they are capable of. Even I would not claim my music is the most challenging there is. But of its kind . . . But it does not compare with what young Ludwig is writing. I am well aware of that.'

'Yes. The truth of it is that this cantata which has caused all the trouble is an extraordinary piece of music. It might even be considered to be great. I don't know. But I am sure that one day he will start composing music which will be considered great. And I don't mean by our musicians here in Bonn!'

'Such a pity about Vienna. Such a pity. It's even possible he might never have come back, and that under Mozart's guidance he could even now be composing great works.'

'I agree. And I see no prospect of him returning. For one thing he is now too important . . . too valuable a court musician for the Elector to let go. For another, with all this trouble in France, even talk of war, the Elector is clamping down on all finances.

And the fortunes of a single twenty-year-old are not uppermost in his mind.'

'No. It would take something totally unexpected. A miracle almost. I cannot think what. Anyway, let us be grateful he is here in Bonn. One day we might be proud to say we were the first to recognise his genius!'

On the day after Christmas in 1790, two men of very contrasting demeanour walked into the court chapel in Bonn and took their places in the centre of a pew near the rear of the chapel, the better to preserve some anonymity.

The older man was small in stature but held himself erect, which gave him the appearance of being taller than he was. A fine aquiline nose and full mouth gave his face an air of sensitivity and distinction. His grey powdered wig was perfectly in place with not a hair astray, and his ruffed collar and cuffs set off his well-cut black coat. There was nothing in his appearance to suggest that this man, now only three months off his fifty-ninth birthday, had just endured ten days' travel from Vienna.

His companion, smaller and stockier, his wig pushed back from a high forehead, perhaps showed it more; not in the manner of his dress, but in the tiredness around his eyes and the somewhat unhealthy pallor of his cheeks. Although thirteen years the other man's junior, he had sustained the ordeal less well.

As the first chords of High Mass sounded, Joseph Haydn shook his head gently from side to side and smiled. He lowered his head in embarrassment, although he admitted to himself he was flattered to hear his own music played. His younger companion, Johann Peter Salomon, gave him a look that could best be described as a smile tinged with mischief. As he weighed up a number of factors in his mind, Haydn concluded rather regretfully that the quiet, anonymous stay he had wanted in Bonn was not to be.

Peter Salomon was, of course, at the root of it. A native of Bonn, he was well connected in court and musical circles, despite having been away for many years, and had obviously alerted the court to his companion's impending arrival.

Confirmation of this was to come even sooner than Haydn expected. As the last notes of his *Missa Sancti Nicolai* sounded, he was approached by a court servant who begged the two men to follow him to the oratory. Salomon hung back slightly, allowing Haydn to enter the small chapel first. Passing through the narrow doorway, Haydn did not at first see the figure awaiting him. When he looked up, his face registered genuine astonishment at finding himself in the company of the Elector Maximilian Franz.

'My dear Haydn,' said Maximilian, grasping Haydn's hand with both his, 'how honoured I am that you are here. For me it is a great personal pleasure . . .'

Haydn motioned to the Elector to stop, rather embarrassed at the effusive welcome after the strictures of the Hungarian court.

'Your Excellency, 'tis I who am flattered by your kind attention. I shall have words with my colleague Herr Salomon later. Had I known I would be ushered into your presence, I should have ensured my entry was a little more appropriate, a little more, ah, formal.'

'Not a bit of it, my good Haydn. I would think you are well pleased to be rid of all that stuffy protocol,' said Maximilian, a twinkle in his eye.

'Well, I, er, I am certainly looking forward to my trip to London.'

'Indeed, and I must not detain you now, since you must still be tired from your trip from Vienna. One final word. I would be most flattered if you two gentlemen would join me for dinner at the palace this evening. Say, at seven o'clock, two hours from now?'

Haydn was flustered. As he and Salomon had left their lodgings earlier that afternoon, they had asked for a quiet dinner to be served for them in the small dining room at the back. Haydn knew it was too late to prevent the landlord's wife preparing the meal. Yet, how to turn down an invitation from the Elector?

Salomon came to the rescue. 'Your Excellency, I beg your indulgence. Our journey was a long and tiring one, and Herr Haydn will I am sure not be offended if I tell you that only this afternoon as we left our lodgings he expressed to me his desire to retire to his room early tonight. He wishes to check some of the manuscripts he is taking to London, before himself retiring to bed as early as he can.'

Maximilian threw his hands up. 'Of course, of course. I quite understand. How selfish of me. Gentlemen, allow me to introduce you briefly to my choir and orchestra and

I shall then let you take your leave – for a well-earned rest.'

Haydn thought he caught that same mischievous smile on Salomon's face again, but thought no more about it. The truth was, he was enjoying his new-found freedom brought about by the death of his unbending patron, Prince Nicolaus Esterhazy. He was flattered that the Elector – as well as ensuring his own music was played – had come to meet him personally, and although he feigned annoyance with Salomon for plotting to make all that happen, he did so with a twinkle in his eye.

Ludwig sat at the long, narrow table between Gottlob Neefe and Franz Ries. Around the table sat the leading musicians from the court. Ludwig was pleased none of those who had refused to play his cantata were there, particularly since, at Neefe's urging, he had brought the scores of both cantatas with him. The second, 'On the Elevation of Leopold', had been played at the Emperor's coronation in Frankfurt, though Ludwig had not been there. The Elector himself – now seated at the head of the table – had told him it was a success and thanked him for making it somewhat easier to play than the first.

There was an air of anticipation in the room, a low hum of conversation punctuated by the occasional hissed 'Shhh!' The Elector, Count Waldstein and his senior musicians had come to the lodgings in the Fürstenstrasse, close to the palace, where Haydn and Salomon were staying. The Elector was aware of Haydn's reluctance to attend a formal dinner at the palace, and it was he who had surprised Salomon with his suggestion that if Haydn would rather not come to him, he – and his musicians – would come to Haydn.

Ludwig felt surprisingly at ease in the august company, the Elector at one end of the table, Count Waldstein at the other. He had long since decided that he liked the Elector, and felt no nervousness in his company. He was aware that he was a different kind of musician to any man in the room. It was not that he felt superior to them – though that was inevitably part of it – but different.

The composition of the two cantatas had had a profound effect on him. They were his first full-scale works and he had brought them to a successful conclusion. Of the two, he knew the first was the more significant. He had written it as he wanted to. It was Beethoven's music. The fact that the musicians of

Bonn could not play it, he thought mischievously, was proof of it. The second he had adapted so that it could be performed. He was still proud of it. But it was the first, 'On the Death of the Emperor Joseph', that had left him convinced, in a way that nothing before had, that he had found his role in life. Yes, he would be a musical performer. But first and foremost he was to be a composer.

He thought now of Haydn, a composer whose music was well known in Bonn and whose reputation was established. He remembered what Mozart had said to him in Vienna. 'Study Haydn's music . . . His themes are so simple . . . He is a genius.' Ludwig had been reluctant, believing that Haydn's music was not as great as Mozart's. But he had done as Mozart advised. He had studied Haydn's scores. And it was the quartets more than anything else that had convinced him of Haydn's genius, just as Mozart had said.

Now he was to meet him. At any moment he would walk through the door into the dining room. A frisson of nervousness ran through Ludwig. He was glad he was seated between Neefe and Ries, two men who he knew were his firmest advocates at court.

His initial impression of a formal, aloof man as Haydn entered the room with a look almost of disdain on his face was immediately dispelled as Haydn's cheeks turned deep red and his face crumpled with embarrassment.

'Gentlemen, gentlemen,' he said, arms outstretched and shaking his head from side to side, 'You do me too much honour.'

The Elector himself was leading the applause, as every man in the room stood.

'Your Grace,' Haydn said insistently, 'may I be so bold as to ask Your Grace please to be seated. Gentlemen, I beg you . . . Then I shall sit quickly and beg you to do likewise.'

He sat in the empty chair at the Elector's right hand. Salomon, who had followed him into the room, sat at the other end of the table, next to Count Waldstein. The Elector motioned everyone to sit and then spoke.

'My dear Herr Haydn, may I on behalf of myself and the senior musicians of the court welcome you to our fair city on the Rhine. We are more honoured by your presence among us than you know. We also know that you and Herr Salomon have had a long and tiring journey. So let me just say that there will be no formality tonight. We ask you to eat and drink as our guests. We wish you both a pleasant and convivial evening.'

He sat down, motioned to the landlord to begin serving the food and wine, and after a few moments of near silence, conversation began, growing to a steady hum as the wine had its relaxing effect on the company.

Ludwig looked at the tall, thin man sitting on the Elector's right. A composer! A renowned composer, whose music was universally recognised. Spoken of in the same breath as Mozart. How he wished he could talk to the great man about music. Just the two of them. Never mind that Joseph Haydn was more than thirty years older than he, bewigged and befrocked and with a lifetime of loyal court service behind him. Music was common to both of them. Music would bring them together.

Ludwig felt a hand on his shoulder. He turned, to see the friendly face of Herr Salomon smiling down at him.

'You are Ludwig van Beethoven, aren't you? So good to see you after so many years, though I confess I would not have recognised you. I was so sorry to hear about your dear mother. I knew her, you know. I knew your father too. You won't remember me, but my family lived in the house of Clasen the lace-dealer in the Bonngasse. The same one you were born in. We were at the front of the house. I remember quite clearly when you were born, though it must be twenty years ago now.'

Ludwig asked, 'Did you know my grandfather? The Kapellmeister?'

'Indeed I did. Fine man. In fact I can remember seeing him walking with you in the grounds of the palace. He was very proud of you, you know. He used to tell everyone you would one day be a fine musician.'

Ludwig felt a wave of emotion sweep over him. His throat tightened and his eyes prickled. He said nothing.

'"The future Kapellmeister", he used to call you. "The second Kapellmeister Ludwig van Beethoven." And from what I hear, his predictions are so far going according to plan. Your colleagues here have been telling me you are making quite a name for yourself.'

'I do not want to be Kapellmeister. I wish to compose my own music. Not because I am instructed to do so because of a particular event.'

'Yet I understand that is precisely what you have done this

year – twice – and rather successfully, even if not all the instrumentalists agreed.'

Ludwig smiled, acknowledging the inconsistency of his argument. 'That is now. I am twenty. I hope when I am older . . .'

'Always remember, a musician – player or composer – has to earn a living, and it is not easy. Herr Haydn here spent many years—'

'But now he is free. As Herr Mozart is free. The Archbishop of Salzburg no longer—'

'Did someone mention Mozart's name,' said Haydn from across the table.

'Yes. This young man here,' said Salomon as he returned to his seat. 'Let me introduce him to you, Joseph. His name is Beethoven. Ludwig van Beethoven. I knew his family when we too lived here in Bonn. We had lodgings in the same house.'

'Delighted, young sir. And may I say I have heard your name in Vienna from Mozart. You made a great impression on him, apparently, with your piano-playing.'

Ludwig looked at Haydn, his eyes shining, but he said nothing.

Nikolaus Simrock, the horn-player, spoke. 'Tell us of Mozart, Herr Haydn. His music is much appreciated here in Bonn.'

Haydn pursed his lips and shook his head slightly. 'Ah, poor dear Mozart.'

'Why poor? He is not unwell, is he?'

Haydn looked at Salomon, who took up the story. 'I arranged a dinner on the fourteenth of this month, the eve of our departure, for Herr Haydn and Mozart. He was in a strange mood – Mozart, I mean. Wouldn't you agree, Joseph?'

Haydn nodded slowly. Salomon continued.

'He was distressed that Joseph was leaving. "Papa!" he said. He always calls Joseph "Papa". It's rather nice, do you not think? "Papa, you must not go," he said. "You are no longer a young man. And what knowledge do you have of the great world? You have never travelled; you speak no other language but German." "Ah," said Joseph, "my language is understood the whole world over."'

There was laughter and applause around the table. 'But that is not all,' Salomon continued. 'The next day, the day of our departure from Vienna, Mozart would not leave Haydn's side. He followed him as we prepared our bags, as a puppy would follow its master. Finally, when the moment came for us to board our coach, Mozart threw his arms round Joseph and embraced him fondly. Then he said, "Papa, I fear that this will be our last farewell." And I saw there were tears in his eyes.'

There was silence around the table. Everyone looked at Haydn, who took a handkerchief from his sleeve and dabbed his own eyes. Suddenly he smiled.

'Come now. Let us not be sad. I will prove Wolfgang wrong. I have yet to reach sixty, despite my wrinkled skin and my hair, which I assure you is as grey as my wig! There is still so much work to be done. I may not be young, but I will return in one piece to Vienna and put him to shame with my vitality!' His joviality had the desired effect on those present, and more wine was poured.

Haydn turned to Ludwig. 'Now, young man, as I was saying, your name is not unknown in the imperial capital. My good friend Mozart has spoken of you, as I said. And I hear from His Grace here that your talent at the piano is not the only one with which you have been bestowed. You also compose, is that not so?'

'It is what I wish to do more than anything,' Ludwig said. 'I composed two cantatas this year for the Emperors. The funeral and coronation. But . . . but . . .'

'There was a problem with the first,' the Elector said. 'Some of our musicians – none here this evening, I might say – who considered some of the music to be a little beyond the capability of their instruments.'

Haydn laughed aloud. 'Ah, yes! The musician's excuse. I have heard it so often. "My instrument is not capable of it. You do not understand the limitations of my instrument, Herr Kapellmeister Haydn!" When what they mean is, "I am not capable of playing it. It is too difficult for me."'

There was laughter around the table.

'Herr Haydn,' said Franz Ries, 'the cantatas our young friend here has written are, in my humble opinion, truly remarkable works. And I know I am not alone in believing that.' He turned to Neefe, who nodded his agreement. Several other heads nodded, including those of the two most influential men at the table, the Elector and Count Waldstein. 'On my instruction – and, I should add, very much against his own modest wishes – he has brought the scores with him tonight. Would you care to see them?'

'Herr Ries, Herr Haydn is tired. He has a long journey behind him and an even longer one ahead of him, including a sea crossing, which at this time of the year . . . I am sure he would rather . . .'

Haydn waved his hand. 'Your Grace, I am most grateful for your kind concern. But it would give me enormous pleasure to see the work of one so young and . . . so determined.'

Ludwig walked round the table and handed the scores to Haydn, who took them with a genuine smile of gratitude. He put a pair of pince-nez on his nose, pushed his chair back, propped the folders on the edge of the table and settled down to look at them.

Ludwig thought, as he returned to his chair, that Haydn might even be a little grateful to be occupied with looking at music, and thereby not be called upon by the company to speak. Under similar circumstances he was sure that was how he would feel.

The conversation around the table continued, shifting from musical matters to political events in France. Ludwig did not participate. From under his eyebrows he watched Haydn, trying to read from the composer's face what he felt about the cantatas. But Haydn's face was impassive.

'If the King doesn't soon reimpose his authority . . .'; 'Who's this man Robespierre? I don't trust him'; 'Lafayette and Mirabeau, they are the only ones . . .'

Only Ludwig saw Haydn remove his pince-nez and close the folder. He wanted to draw attention to the fact that the composer had finished looking at the scores, but the conversation around him was too strong. He felt his stomach churn as Haydn looked directly at him, his face still impassive and rather stern.

'So, Herr Haydn, what do you think?' The voice belonged to Count Waldstein, who, since he was sitting at the other end of the table from Haydn, spoke loudly and brought silence.

Haydn spoke. 'This really is quite extraordinary music. The harmonies. I have not seen harmonies like this. Does it work? Yes, it must work. And the tempi. They are so varied. One moment fast and furious, the next slow and dignified. And so many stresses off the beat. You cross the bar lines as if they were not there, the emphasis . . .'

'No, no,' cried Ludwig. 'They must be there. That is what throws the emphasis off the beat.'

'Yes, yes, I see,' said Haydn. 'It must have the effect of . . . of driving the music forward, pushing it on. Ludwig, this is exciting composition. And you wrote it?' He looked up questioningly.

Heads nodded in confirmation. Franz Ries smiled.

'Herr Haydn,' said Neefe, 'as his teacher I can vouch for it. I can confirm too that what you say is correct. It is a very dynamic form of music.'

'Yes. This one I think is the better of the two.' Haydn held up the first cantata. 'Even if certain passages owe a little too much to Handel. You have scored no timpani. You have achieved your effect in more subtle ways. The soprano aria "Da stiegen die Menschen an's Licht . . ." You call it a cavatina, and I can see why. It is beautiful. Lyrical. Yet it makes demands on the soloist. It is not easy. And you integrate the chorus more successfully with the solo voices in this cantata than in the other. Not that the other is without merit,' he said, lifting the second score. 'But there are fewer arias in it. You rely more on the broad effect of the chorus, and this time you use timpani for added weight . . .'

'How . . . how can you see all that so quickly?' asked Ludwig. 'And . . . and I know you are right. The second I had to make easier. For the musicians who complained about the first. But it is the first that is . . . that is . . . the better of the two.'

Haydn nodded. 'When you have lived as long as I have and seen as many scores as I have . . .' He smiled. 'I am glad to have seen these, Ludwig. You are a very remarkable young man. Tell me, do you have any plans to come again to Vienna?'

Ludwig shot a quick look at the Elector and then at Neefe. He shook his head. 'No. It is not possible at the moment.'

'Well, if ever you do – and I hope you do before too long – it would give me very great pleasure to teach you. Now that I am no longer, as it were, required at Esterhaz, it is in Vienna that I will make my home. So maybe one day, one day, you and I will be involved in the pursuit of music together.'

BOOK FIVE

BOOK FIVE

Chapter 1

'I'm sorry I'm late. I'm really sorry. I . . .'

Ludwig knew there was sweat on his brow and his hair was uncombed. He cursed his forgetfulness which meant he had arrived at the Breuning house hot, untidy and thirty minutes late to give Eleonore her piano lesson.

She sat at the piano, playing the keys gently and ignoring him. He recognised the piece as a sonatina he had written and told her she could have. She was playing the second movement, at the top of which he had written *Romanze*.

With his hands he tried to smooth down his hair, at the same time trying to control his breathing. Hoping Eleonore would not turn round, he drew the sleeve of his jacket across his forehead then brushed it with his hand.

As she reached the end of the jaunty little phrase, played in quick three-four time, she deliberately hit a wrong key with her right hand.

'I know what you've been doing. You don't even have to tell me.'

Ludwig pulled a chair towards the piano. He wished she would take that angry frown off her face. He so wanted her to smile. 'Look at you. So untidy. You've been walking in the hills again, haven't you?'

He nodded. 'How could you do it, Ludwig? You must have known you'd be late for my lesson.'

'I'm sorry. I . . . I . . . It was such a lovely day and I needed to . . . I was writing some music and . . . it was so lovely outside . . .'

'Oh, Ludwig. Always in a dream. Such a lovely day, so everything else can just be forgotten and you can go and walk in the hills.'

He raised his eyes to meet hers and hoped the penitent look on his face would quell her anger. But she had not quite finished reproaching him.

'I know what the truth of it is, Ludwig. You don't have to tell me. You hate teaching, don't you? You really hate teaching.'

He nodded. 'But it's not ι . . it's not . . .'

'No, no. I know it's not me. My brother Lenz has told me the same thing. And Mama told me about the Austrian ambassador.' She could not suppress a slight grin lifting the corners of her mouth. 'Is it true, Ludwig? Did you really refuse to teach him?'

'He . . . When your mother introduced him to me, he just . . . just . . . took it for granted that I would teach him. He was arrogant.'

'But you were impolite to him. And Mama said that was bad.'

'I'm sorry I upset her. But I apologised to her later. But I'm not apologising to him.'

At last she smiled, fully and openly. He smiled back at her. Really, he thought to himself, she did have a lovely face. More than anything in the world he would like to lean forward, take it in his hands . . .

'Why did you call this movement *Romanze*, Ludwig? Were you in love when you wrote it?'

He felt his breathing quicken. What did she mean? Was she teasing him or was she . . . ? 'It . . . I can't really remember. I thought it was a good description.'

'It is. You are a musician, Ludwig, and I admire you for it. But don't you think it's wonderful to be a doctor? To devote yourself to healing other people. Like Franz Wegeler. I admire him so much. It's the most important thing you can do, don't you think? It's more important than making music, isn't it? Isn't it? Don't you think so?'

Ludwig wanted to say no. He wanted to shout no. He wanted to tell her that the body was an imperfect instrument. That it was always imperfect, whatever doctors tried to do to heal it. That it was in the mind that a human being's true health lay. And that art, music, was the doctor of the mind. The healer of the mind.

He looked at her. Her eyebrows were raised in anticipation of his reply. Her slight smile told him she knew he was about to agree with her. How could he do otherwise? If he tried to explain to her what he really thought, she would mock him, he knew that. Anyway, he knew he would not be able to explain it adequately.

He nodded. 'Yes.'

'There. I knew you would agree with me,' she said.

The people of Bonn were in a state of high excitement. The plans for Carnival Sunday were more elaborate than they had been for many years, and they had Count Waldstein to thank for it. Now installed as a member of the Teutonic Order, he decided a pageant was called for, a pageant that would remind the citizens of Germany's heritage.

It would also, he quietly pointed out to the Elector, serve as a useful antidote to the heretical and anti-royalist goings-on across the border in France.

He secured the Elector's permission to use the Ridotto room in the old palace built by his illustrious predecessor Elector Clemens August at the top of the Market Square. He then engaged the dancing master Heinrich Haben from Aachen to choreograph a series of tableaux, and he asked Ludwig van Beethoven to compose the music.

'It will be a series of pieces,' he told both of them when he summoned them to his office at the Electoral palace, 'intended to conjure up images of German folklore. Here's a list I've drawn up.' He handed each of them a piece of paper.

'As you can see, it will open with a march. Then I want a hunting song, a war song, a German dance and a romance. And, of course, a drinking song. I haven't decided the order yet. But, Ludwig, you write the music. And, Habich, I want the scenes to be staged in original dress. And I will organise the parade which will precede the performance.'

Ludwig enjoyed working on the commission. From the headquarters of the Teutonic Order at Mergentheim, Count Waldstein acquired for him copies of medieval German songs, which he adapted for the spectacle which Waldstein had given the name of Ritterballet, Pageant of the Knights.

He was particularly pleased with the hunting song, in which he gave a virtuoso passage to the horns, which were led by Nikolaus Simrock, who had supported him loyally against other wind players over the two cantatas.

Carnival Sunday was a brilliantly sunny early spring day, and the people of Bonn lined the Marktplatz for the procession. They cheered and waved their hats as the senior nobility of the city, headed by the Elector himself, paraded through the square in traditional costumes – the men in balloon britches and armoured breastplates, feathers clustered in their hunting hats; the women in low-cut and long-flowing dresses, tall, thin conical hats trailing fantastically woven lace.

Last into the square was Siegfried, hero of the Rhine. He was a tall young man with a mane of blond hair which swept backwards. His armour glinted in the sun, as did the huge sword which he waved in the air. On his head was a crown to denote his royal lineage. In front of him two small boys ran, crouched over, the one behind the other and holding on to his hips, the green scaly costume that covered them both symbolising the dragon that dwelt in the Drachenfels. And gathered around him, alternately paying him homage and acknowledging the cheers of the crowd, was a cluster of young girls, dancing as they walked. They were the Rhine maidens.

Inside the Ridotto room all was ready for the pageant. Ludwig, composer of the music, played in the violin section. Joseph Reicha conducted.

As each tableau unfolded, the audience – the nobility occupying the best seats, ordinary citizens crowded in the back and on the balcony – exploded into applause. And when the final tableau was reached a cry of 'Encore!' went up and several pieces were played again.

When the curtain fell for the last time, Count Waldstein appeared on stage in front of the dancers to acknowledge the applause. He turned and swept his arm around the semicircle formed by the performers. Then he bent forward and gestured to the orchestra with both arms.

Finally he stood alone on the stage and bowed to the audience. Four times the audience called him back out. He was the undisputed hero of the moment. Just as the applause began to wane, a voice at the back of the hall called out, 'Speech! Speech!' It was taken up around the hall.

Waldstein needed little encouragement. He stepped forward to the edge of the stage.

'Your Grace,' he began, bowing slightly to the Elector seated in the centre of the front row, 'most noble burghers of the city of Bonn. If my humble efforts have pleased you, I am most gratified. If I have succeeded in reminding you of Germany's glorious past, while around us today there is so much turmoil, then I can ask no more. You, who unlike me were born by the banks of the mighty Rhine, in whose veins the magical waters of that great river flows, you who can trace your ancestry to Siegfried and his royal parents Siegmund and Sieglind, should be proud of your illustrious past and fight always to preserve your freedom, whatever the threat from outside. If my pageant this day, my music and my ballet, have helped in that noble endeavour, then I am indeed the most fortunate of men.'

Gottlob Neefe was rather surprised to read the report of the pageant two weeks later in the news sheet *Theaterkalender*.

'Listen to this, Clara,' he said to his wife as they both sat at the kitchen table drinking morning coffee. '"On Quinquagesima Sunday the local nobility performed in the Ridotto room a characteristic ballet in old German costume. The author, His Excellency Count Waldstein, to whom the ballet and music do honour, had shown in it consideration for the deep love of our ancestors for war, the hunt, love and drinking." It goes on to say how splendid everyone looked in the old costumes.'

'I'm so glad it was a success. But why do you sound so put out?'

'"The author, His Excellency Count Waldstein, to whom the ballet and music do honour . . ." What about Habich? And more to the point, since he is a native of this city and the Count professed himself so in awe of Rhinelanders, what about Beethoven? He is the one to whom the music does honour. He's not going to be pleased when he reads this.'

To his enormous surprise, Neefe was wrong. When he drew his attention to it, Ludwig merely shrugged his shoulders.

'It doesn't matter. It was not great music anyway. I just took what I was given and reworked it.'

'But it was so well received, and Waldstein is getting the credit for writing it.'

'It will soon be forgotten. Like the pageant.'

Count Waldstein, when he realised what had happened, was as keen to talk to Ludwig as Neefe.

'My dear boy, such a success. And you played such a large part in it.'

'The people liked it. That is what is important. The orchestra played well.'

'Yes. Ah, Ludwig, by cruel coincidence I see that the *Theaterkalender* is reporting it as if it was I who composed the music. I don't know if . . .'

Ludwig nodded.

'I hope you are not angry. I had no idea . . . It is very remiss of them. I shall be protesting . . .'

'No need. I did not put my name to the music. That is why they . . .'

'Do you intend publishing it?'

'No.'

'Ludwig,' Waldstein said, somewhat emboldened, 'since I pro-cured the ancient songs for you from the Teutonic Order, and since the pageant was my . . . my conception, would you take it amiss if I acknowledged the many expressions of congratulations without . . . without . . . ? Of course I would never say that I composed the music. But the congratulations are for the event as a whole and . . .'

'Count, has there been any word from Herr Haydn in London? Is there any information on when he is returning?'

Waldstein nodded, relieved that Ludwig had changed the subject. 'I have heard from Salomon that the visit is a great success. So much so that the stay is being prolonged. He is unlikely to return before the autumn. Maybe not this year.'

'I do not want him to forget what he said to me about studying with him in Vienna. Two composers have now both offered to teach me. Herr Mozart and Herr Haydn. All that is needed is for me to go to Vienna.'

'My dear boy, are you still hankering after that? Look, here your reputation is steadily growing. You will one day be Kapellmeister, of that there is no doubt. As your grandfather was. In Vienna, you would be . . . forgive me for putting it like this, but you would be a small fish in a very large pond. It would be difficult for you to make your reputation. Impossible, even. As a virtuoso performer, maybe, after many years. But certainly not as a composer. In a city which already boasts Haydn and Mozart.'

'My future is in Vienna, Count Waldstein. With Mozart. I know that as surely as I know anything. Will you help me get there? Will you?'

'I don't know . . . I'm not sure . . . The Elector would never . . .'

'Count,' said Ludwig, leaning forward and lowering his voice, 'I am helping your reputation. As a patron of the arts and as a musician. The Ritterballet is yours. I make a present of the music to you. Will you now help me?'

Waldstein looked at Ludwig. Slowly a smile crossed his face. 'You will need to be patient. I have heard that Mozart is unwell. Very unwell. He would not be able to take on a new pupil. So I cannot do anything until Haydn returns from London. Salomon told me they will come back through Bonn on their way to Vienna. If he is still prepared to take you on as a student, that might make a difference. I will see what I can do. But be patient. Will you?'

Ludwig nodded. 'Thank you,' he said.

Chapter 2

The summer of 1791 was one of the loveliest anyone could remember, the warm sun ripening the corn in the fields and swelling the grapes on the vine. The Rhine sparkled mischievously, never flowing too fast for the boats which used it for both business and pleasure. The hills around Bonn, bathed in sunlight, offered delicious refuge from the bustle of the city, the air crisp but still warm the higher one climbed. People seemed to feel the sun in their hearts as well as on their skin. Rarely did strangers pass without at least a nod or a congenial 'Good day'. And everywhere, it seemed, there was a chorus of birdsong as accompaniment.

Ludwig spent as much time outside Bonn as his duties allowed. Fortuitously his duties were light, not just because in the summer months the court calendar was at its least busy, but because in a matter of weeks the court musicians were to leave Bonn for Mergentheim.

The Elector, as Grand Master of the Teutonic Order, needed to be in Mergentheim to chair a grand meeting of Knights and Commanders of the Order. At the last such meeting, two years before, the affair had dragged on – to the Elector's irritation – for three whole months, with no entertainment of any kind to alleviate the schedule.

This time, the Elector had decided he would take a selection of court musicians with him – those who wished to go and whose family commitments allowed them to be absent from Bonn for up to a month.

There was no shortage of volunteers, and in the end Franz Ries, in consultation with Count Waldstein, had drawn up a list of twenty musicians. Ludwig's name was on it. It would mean several weeks away from court, away from official functions. Away, too, from the house on the Wenzelgasse. He found himself looking forward to it from the moment he was told he would be going.

Until then, every day, if he could, he walked in the fields to the north and west of the city, or south along the Rhine, across to Königswinter and into the lower slopes of the Siebengebirge. How different the massive Drachenfels looked in the sunshine; no longer brooding, no longer menacing.

One afternoon, as the sun had just begun to lose its strength, instead of striding on out of Königswinter he turned to the right and began climbing the Drachenfels. It was not a conscious decision, nor was it that he felt irresistibly drawn to this rock, so steeped in Rhine legend, that he had gazed at for so many hours since his childhood. He simply wanted to escape the summer heat and the thick green foliage seemed inviting.

Very quickly he found himself out of breath. The lower slope of the rock, which looked so gradual from across the Rhine, was steeper than he had imagined, and the foliage, which again from a distance looked like a smooth protective carpet, was irregular and jagged.

He climbed on, pushing branches out of his way, aware that their sharp points were snagging his sleeves. Several times he nearly lost his footing, feeling the strain on his ankle as his foot slipped on a stone concealed in the undergrowth.

He was grateful for the coolness, but he was also aware of the darkness. It was as if night had suddenly fallen. Above him a roof of leaves blocked out the summer sky, with only the tiniest pinpricks of light filtering through.

Soon he lost all sense of direction. He stood quite still and listened for the sound he prayed he could still hear. The gentle lapping of water. He turned towards it, hoping he would be able to carve his way through to it. The noise of rustling leaves and snapping twigs blotted everything else out, but soon he could smell what he sought: the slightly stale and pungent aroma of the Rhine.

He forced his way through the last curtain of leaves and emerged suddenly into the light. He was dazzled for a moment and stood with his eyes closed, breathing heavily. Then he looked around him. In front and below the water flowed; on the other side of the river were the gentle paths and woods that he had so often walked; to the right and downriver, shimmering in the distance, were the spires of Bonn. He turned to the left and looked up. All he could see above him was more thick foliage, the medieval castle ruins that sat atop the rock hidden from view.

He looked down again at the river. He wished it was clear and blue, but it was a dirty brown and he could not see into it. He thought of Siegfried and the Nibelung treasure that legend said lay on the river bed. With a shiver he thought of the dragon whose lair must be only a short distance above his head. If he closed his eyes tight, would he hear the plaintive song of the maidens imprisoned there?

Siegfried, and his magic sword Balmung. Alberich, the dwarf who guards the treasure. Hagen, the enemy who betrays Siegfried and drives Balmung between his shoulder blades on the spot where his wife Kriemhild lovingly sewed the cross, where the linden leaf lay . . .

Ludwig sat on a rock and looked at the river. He allowed his eyes to follow the flow of water. In his ears he heard the lapping of the tiny waves. Above him the rustle of leaves in the gentle breeze, the buzz of insects. Deeper and deeper he tried to look into the water, but his eyes could only see the brown surface.

The noise of the river seemed to grow louder in his head, as if the water was rushing faster. But he knew it was not. Or was it the insects that were gathered in a cloud above him? Or perhaps the dragon? Or Siegfried's last cry when he realised Kriemhild's love for him had caused his death . . . ?

He reached into his pocket and took out a notebook; from his other pocket he pulled a pencil. Hurriedly he scribbled a sequence of notes. He looked at them for a few moments then crossed them out. He wrote more notes and crossed them out again. He looked down at the water. The sudden turbulence he had imagined had gone, and with it the rushing noise.

In his head now he clearly heard the maidens' song, gentle, lyrical. 'Siegfried,' they called, 'Siegfried. Come and save us.' He wrote a new sequence of notes, a rising theme followed by a falling one. Like water flowing. He wrote it a second time, though this time with more notes. Quavers. He covered the whole sequence with a single slur.

At the top of the paper he wrote, 'Siegfried, Hero of the Rhine'. He looked back down at the river, his eyes following the water downriver, and he saw again the city of Bonn, on the opposite bank and in the distance.

At the front and dominating the view was the broad white expanse of the Elector's palace, seeming to dance in the heat haze. Suddenly the image of his grandfather came into Ludwig's mind. He remembered how together they had walked along the path that ran round the palace gardens.

Old Ludwig would not recognise the palace now, Ludwig thought, a pang of sadness hitting his stomach. Rebuilt and painted after the fire, the onion domes which had stood for so long gone. How he wished he had been able to know his grandfather better. He could only remember that he was Kapellmeister, and that he had talked to him of music.

He remembered too, quite distinctly, how his grandfather had told him he would one day be a great musician. Ludwig van Beethoven. Named for his grandfather and destined to give his name to great music, as Bach had done. And Handel, and Mozart.

A whiff of Turkish tobacco fleetingly passed under his nose. He tried to seize it, breathe it in, but it had already gone. In his head he heard laughter, childish laughter. 'Stop, Grandpa! Stop!' And just as he thought the worst had happened, his grandfather's thumb was back on his hand. Safe. Secure. And he felt his grandfather's strong, comforting arm around him.

Two weeks later, on an August evening, the sun still warm though now low in the sky, Ludwig was walking with Stephan and Lenz von Breuning in Godesburg, just outside Bonn. Franz Wegeler had wanted to come on the evening walk with them, but had been detained at the hospital. They were discussing the Elector and the reports that were circulating of his apparently eccentric behaviour.

'I believe he's just trying to prove he's one of the people,' said Lenz.

'But he's not one of the people, that's just the point,' said Stephan. 'You or I can walk around the streets of Bonn in a shabby old overcoat, but the Elector can't.'

'Well, I heard he was in the Gangolfstrasse when he saw an old woman struggling with a heavy bundle, and he picked it up and carried it for her. When someone told her who it was who had helped her, she went running after him and kissed his hand. I don't call that eccentric behaviour. It's just—'

They were interrupted by the shouts of a young man. 'Hey, Ludwig! Remember me?'

'Würzer! Is it you? My old friend? My only school friend?'

'Yes. The Tirocinium and that awful teacher Krengel –

remember him? I'd have recognised you anywhere. Your clothes still don't fit!'

Ludwig laughed, although he had winced at the name of Krengel, remembering how the martinet schoolmaster had chastised him.

Würzer continued, 'I hear you are making quite a name for yourself in musical circles. I don't suppose anyone calls you the Spaniard any more!' He greeted Ludwig's friends. 'The Breuning brothers, Stephan and Lorenz. Are you well? Your sister? Your dear mother?'

'We are indeed, Ferd'nand,' said Stephan.

'And, Ludwig. Your brothers? What are they doing now?'

'Caspar is trying to be a musician and Nikola is apprenticed to Grimm the apothecary.'

'Another musician in the Beethoven family!'

'He is not . . . I don't think . . .'

'Are you going to Mergentheim, Ludwig? My father says the trip is the talk of the court. He was told it by one of the musicians who buys his meat from us. Are you going?'

Ludwig smiled and nodded. 'Yes. It'll be good to be away for a while. Just with musicians.'

'We're all envious of him,' said Stephan. 'What brings you to Godesburg, Ferd'nand?'

'Making a delivery for my father. They needed some meat at the Wild Boar inn. I didn't object. On an evening like this it's a pleasure to be outside the city.'

Würzer suddenly exclaimed and put his hands on his hips. 'Ludwig. I remember once at school, you—'

'No, Würzer. The one subject I do not want to talk about is school. They were not the happiest days of my childhood. Why darken this beautiful evening . . . ?'

'No, no, don't worry. I wasn't going to talk about any of that. What I was going to say was that once, I distinctly remember, you promised that one day you would let me hear you play your music.'

Ludwig shook his head. 'I am sure I didn't.'

'Oh, yes,' said Würzer, nodding. 'We were friends. You were being teased about your name. I felt sorry for you, because the other boys were always teasing me about my father being just a humble stall-holder. And we said we would be friends. And you said one day you'd let me hear you play.'

'You're very honoured then, Ferdi,' said Stephan. 'Ludwig

does not often make such promises. In fact, such promises are as rare and valuable as the Nibelung treasure!'

They all laughed, including Ludwig.

'Listen, Ludwig,' said Würzer, 'let's all go up to the church at Marienforst. It's not far. Just behind the woods up there. They've just renovated the church, and I've been told that they've repaired and rebuilt the organ. You can play for us.'

Ludwig demurred but allowed himself to be persuaded. Würzer walked over to his cart and checked that the mare was firmly tethered to a tree. Then the four young men walked up in silence through the woods in the dying sun and emerged to a view that took their breath away.

The steeple of the Marienforst church, so long in disrepair, now shone in the crimson sunlight, the old stone, carefully preserved by the masons, absorbing the light as if it were its natural colour. The young men approached the church, but found the heavy arched oak door locked. They walked round to the back of the church where they found the priest tidying some stones. The priest led them to a side door and they went in.

The air inside was cool and rich with the aroma of new wood and stone. But the church was not empty, as they had expected. Half a dozen workmen were clearing away the debris left from the renovation work. They were working swiftly, keen to get the job finished and go home. A couple of them shot the young men disgruntled looks, unhappy at the interruption which they feared would delay their departure.

Ignoring them, the four walked up the centre aisle to the chancel. The altar was covered with a new deep-purple cloth, and the silver cross atop it reflected the light. Behind the altar the reredos gleamed darkly, its intricate wooden carvings newly cleaned and repaired.

At first Ludwig resisted their pleadings but then, yielding, he walked to the organ, adjusted the height of the stool, looked for a few moments at the layout of the keys, and began playing. He played uninterrupted for several minutes, oblivious of the noise from the labourers.

Calling out to the others, he said, 'Siegfried's theme.' He played the sequence he had written on his notepad while he sat on the edge of the Drachenfels. He played it again, this time with a chord accompaniment in the left hand.

Then he paused slightly and began to vary the theme. Sometimes he would pick it out in the pedals, or in the bass register, while his right hand played the variation. Then with barely a pause he would invert the procedure.

The three young men stood entranced. The priest stood with them, marvelling at Ludwig's skill. And slowly, one by one, the labourers put down their tools and stood listening, amazed at what they heard.

On a cool morning in early September a large yacht with the Electoral seal on its bow stood tied up at the quayside. The musicians and singers, around twenty of them, filed on board, after joyous farewells to families and friends. Amid much cheering and waving of handkerchiefs the yacht set sail. Knots of people formed, leaning against the railing which ran round the flat deck, as the sails searched for wind and the boat plied valiantly but slowly against the current of the mighty Rhine.

Ludwig stood on his own, drinking in the scenery which meandered slowly past. Godesberg on the right bank, the new steeple of Marienforst pointing out of the woods. A few minutes later, on the left, the Siebengebirge hills. And there, looming out of the water, the Drachenfels.

How different it looked from the middle of the river. Instead of a huge rock, part of the Siebengebirge hills reaching down to the river, it looked now as if the river were its source, as if it belonged to the river. And somehow, seeing it like that, it lost its menace; it was the river that held the power, not the rock.

A burst of laughter made Ludwig turn round. Joseph Lux, bass singer with the court theatre, who at the farewell party the night before had been elected Great King of the Journey, stood in the middle of the deck, a crown upon his head.

'Bring me the maiden,' he cried in a tremulous voice. 'Quick, before it is too late.'

He was handed a lifesize bundle of straw, tied at the top and bottom. Its arms were smaller, thinner bundles of straw which stuck out from the body.

Lux took it, turned to the Drachenfels and held it out. 'Oh great dragon of the Drachenfels. We offer you this sacrifice. This young maiden to satisfy your hunger. We ask in return that you do not take any more of our maidens from us . . .' He turned round quickly, put his hand to his mouth and whispered to the group so that the dragon would not hear, 'Otherwise how could we perform with no sopranos or contraltos?' and promptly hushed the laughter which followed.

'Here, great dragon. We offer you . . . we offer you . . .' He turned again. 'What's her name? What's her name?'

'Brunhild,' someone said. 'Kriemhild,' said another.

'We offer you this maiden of many names, renowned for her beauty. Our sacrifice to you, oh great dragon.'

With a mighty thrust he cast the maiden on to the water. A cheer went up from the deck. Immediately the churning water loosened the ties that held the bundle together and strands of straw began floating away. By the time the boat was past the rock there was no more straw to be seen.

'There,' said Lux, wiping his hands together, 'that should keep the dragon quiet. And we can be sure none of the ladies we are honoured to have among us will be snatched away.'

There was more laughter and embarrassed smiles from the small number of women on the deck as the men turned to them and applauded.

'And now it is time,' Lux boomed, 'to distribute the high offices of my court.'

He unfurled a document and read out the name of each member of the party. Franz Ries and Joseph Reicha, by virtue of their seniority, escaped any menial tasks. Others less fortunate were assigned cleaning duties on deck and in the public rooms. All complained with loud groans as their chores were announced, but smiling and laughing all the while at Lux's antics.

'And now,' he boomed, 'lest they think King Lux has forgotten them, I turn to the most junior in our band. And to them I assign the most menial, the most awful, the most ghastly tasks on board.' Loud cheers mingled with groans.

'Step forward those fine practitioners of our divine art, Master Bernhard Romberg and Master Ludwig van Beethoven.' The two young men, the first now twenty-four years of age and a cellist in the court orchestra, the second not yet twenty-one, walked through the crowd to much cheering and clapping on the back.

'Gentlemen, I the Great King Lux hereby confer upon you both the title of scullion, kitchen boy, washer of pots and pans.' In an aside and to much laughter, he added, 'And who washes and who dries I leave to you to decide.'

Ludwig laughed, and he and Romberg shook hands. Romberg, tall and fine-featured, was a popular young man with an easy nature. His musical reputation had been sealed by a trip to Paris where he had performed with his cousin, a violinist, to much acclaim.

The crowd broke up into small chattering groups, laughter echoing around the deck.

'Come, Ludwig,' said Romberg, 'I want you to meet a friend of mine.'

He led Ludwig to a small group of young women. Ludwig knew them all by sight – they were singers at the court – but he had never spoken to them.

'Magdalena, this is Ludwig van Beethoven. I told you about him.'

'Hello, Ludwig. There is no need to introduce us, Bernhard. I know Ludwig well. By reputation, of course.'

Ludwig smiled. He had seen Magdalena many times at court but never realised before how beautiful she was. Her eyes seemed to dance in her face and her lips were full and round. The breeze coming off the river caressed her hair and moved it back from her cheeks.

'I know you too. You sing well.'

'Oh, but that is nothing. I have heard you play the piano and you are already a master of it.' She turned to the other young women with her. 'This is Anna. And Klara and Gertrude.'

Ludwig nodded at the other women but turned back to Magdalena. 'A musician I may be, but for the moment I am just a kitchen boy.' The whole group laughed.

Ludwig had never before felt so free of care. For the first time in his life, it seemed, there were no pressures bearing down upon him. Added to that he was in the company of musicians, the only people with whom he ever felt totally at ease. And then there was Magdalena Willman, who would slip her arm through his and walk around the deck with him, talking lightly of music, Bonn and her family.

One evening, late, as they stood against the railing, she said, 'I do like you so, Ludwig,' and kissed him gently on the cheek. He felt fire shoot through his body. For a moment he hesitated, then turned his face abruptly to hers. Their lips met, but almost in the instant they touched, Magdalena drew her head back, smiling at him and touching his cheek with her hand as she did so.

'Good night, Ludwig,' she said, still smiling, and turned away to go to her cabin.

Soon there was more laughter at the court of the Great King

Lux. As they passed the imposing Lorelei rock, Lux, dressed in a flowing robe and wig, seductively stroked the long blond tresses which cascaded on to his mighty chest, while he extended his other arm to entice the musicians to come to him, just as the beautiful but lethal mermaids of the Lorelei had done for centuries, all the while singing falsetto.

Then as the Mäuseturm, the Mouse Tower, came into view, its miniature turrets seeming to thrust from the water itself, Lux became the Archbishop of Mainz, feasting, as legend had it, off an imaginary banquet while his subjects, played with much laughter by the musicians, writhed with hunger pains around him. But then, as they moved nearer to him, his self-satisfied look became one of panic as he realised they had turned into mice and were circling him. In desperation he mimed the Archbishop's flight to the top turrets of the tower, but in swarms the mice followed him there, finally satisfying their hunger with his flesh.

Amid cries of delight the musicians helped an exhausted Lux to his feet.

Immediately after the Mouse Tower the great river narrowed, to flow swiftly and dangerously past the rocks and reefs of the Bingerloch. Here the water, compressed into a narrow passage, swirled and crashed on to the rocks. It was too dangerous for boats laden with passengers to navigate. And so the Elector's yacht pulled into the bank just past the town of Bingen, and while the yacht's crew navigated the treacherous passage, the company of musicians and players climbed the craggy rocks to the heights above Rüdesheim.

There the irrepressible Lux once more entertained the company. Reading from a roll of honour, he handed out awards to those who it was considered had been particularly diligent in the tasks allotted to them.

'And finally,' boomed the King, 'to the kitchen boy and scullion Ludwig van Beethoven, I offer the congratulations of the royal court and announce the said Beethoven's promotion from kitchen boy to server at table, a most honourable post and most richly deserved. To that end I do hereby present him with this diploma.'

To applause and laughter Lux then handed Ludwig the document, which was attached to a small wooden box by a seal in pitch from which hung several threads of twine from the ship's rigging. Ludwig took the prized parchment and gazed lovingly at it. He held the seal to his nose and sniffed it, relishing the pungency of the tar. He folded the document, which fitted perfectly into the box, and walked back through the company looking at it all the while.

'Congratulations, Ludwig. I cannot tell you how envious I am. Must I now wash the dishes alone?' asked Bernhard Romberg.

'Yes, congratulations, Ludwig,' echoed Magdalena Willman.

Ludwig smiled. Had he ever felt so free? he wondered. Away from Bonn; away from his father and brothers. Just musicians for company.

Soon after Wiesbaden, at the great confluence of the Rhine and the Main, the yacht sailed east, leaving the mighty Rhine behind. The next and last stop before Mergentheim was to be Aschaffenburg, where the Elector of Mainz kept his large summer palace. While the members of the orchestra planned to spend a few hours strolling round the picturesque town, a small number of them, Ludwig included, headed to the palace. Neefe, in teaching Ludwig keyboard technique, had often talked of the renowned Abbé Franz Sterkel, one of the foremost pianists and composers of the day. Now a man of forty, he was said to be without rival in much of Germany, perhaps all of it.

Franz Ries and Nikolaus Simrock took their younger colleagues Andreas and Bernhard Romberg, together with Ludwig, to the palace where the Abbé had his quarters. Ludwig stared as the tall man with his mane of white hair and flowing robe came forward to meet them. He was thin and moved with a certain grace, and his innate seriousness contrasted with the naturally more jovial and easy-going Rhinelanders. There was a haughtiness about the way he held his head, and his overall demeanour was forbidding. Ludwig felt a measure of tension rise in him.

'So, my good friends from Bonn. I received word you were coming. How good of you to include me in your busy schedule.'

If there was a certain air of condescension in his voice, it was that of a master musician revered throughout Germany towards orchestral players from a small provincial city. He led them through to a vast vaulted hall, where warm drinks and snacks had been laid on low tables for them. A fire smouldered gently in the grate, necessary since the late-summer sun no longer had the strength to warm the thick stone walls. As his eyes swept the room, Ludwig saw, under a tall stained-glass window, a grand piano. It was the largest he had seen.

The party ate and drank and conversed politely until, in a lull in the conversation, Franz Ries asked the Abbé to play the piano for them. Sterkel politely demurred, but in response to Simrock's heartfelt 'Abbé, if you do not, we shall not consider our journey complete, no matter what musical treasures lie ahead of us,' he reluctantly agreed.

'In fact,' said the Abbé, 'in honour of our young friend here, Herr Beethoven, of whom I have heard good reports, shall I not play his Righini variations?'

There was a chorus of approval, though Ludwig said nothing. 'I think it is particularly appropriate,' the Abbé continued, 'since Kapellmeister Righini is a colleague of mine in the service of His Excellency the Elector of Mainz. I must say, young man,' he said, turning to Ludwig, 'I sent for the manuscript as soon as the good Götz of Mannheim published it just a month ago. I was somewhat surprised that you chose to make no fewer than twenty-four variations on my friend's arietta, "Vieni Amore". After all, he himself chose to write only five.'

'His were for voice, so there was a limit to what he could do. I wanted to show . . . how . . . how . . .' Ludwig struggled to find the words to express his musical ideas.

Sterkel leaned back, opened his robe to cross his legs, then folded it back again. 'Yes, quite. Frankly, I was never that impressed with the aria myself, though I wouldn't tell Righini so. These Italians become so emotional, do you not think? Really, the tune is quite a simple little affair.'

'No. I mean yes. That is exactly it. It is a simple tune. But it is no less good music for that. That is the mistake so many musicians make. Bach showed the way. And Handel. A tune does not have to be complicated to be good. The great themes in music are small and simple. Mozart told me that.'

'Since you mention Mozart, my dear Beethoven, though I am not sure you are worthy to do so, allow me to remind you that that great master has never written more than twelve variations on any subject, yet you—'

'Yes, yes,' said Ludwig, a touch of exasperation creeping into his voice, 'but listen to Mozart's variations. His technique is . . . is . . . He adorns the melody, he embellishes it, but the melody is always there. You can hear it.'

'That is somehow a mistake?'

'No, no. It is not a mistake. But it is only half of what you can do with a melody. I . . . what I have tried to do is . . . is take the melody, the tune,' his hands were now illustrating his words, 'and undo it, unweave it, take it apart, reduce it to nothing. So that the only link left is in the . . . the . . . structure of . . . its harmonic structure. The tune, the theme, has gone. It has vanished. But it is still there.'

His words, vehemently spoken, echoed round the chamber. Sterkel leaned forward with a serious look on his face. 'What intensity in one so young. Well, let us see how this tune disappears,' and he walked to the piano, adjusted the stool and began playing Beethoven's Righini variations from memory. Ludwig leaped up from his chair, walked swiftly to Sterkel's side and watched him intently as he played.

'And now,' cried Sterkel above his playing, 'variation fourteen.' At the end he stopped. 'Now, young man, I have thought a lot about that particular variation, and I have to tell you I have come to the conclusion that you have made a mistake. Either that, or Götz has. Surely you mean this.' And he played some more.

'No no no. It is as you played it the first time. It is a double variation, don't you see? First *allegretto*, then *adagio*. Play it again, then continue with the variations.'

Sterkel, raising an eyebrow, played, but stopped again after the fourteenth variation. 'I have rarely played beyond this point, so certain was I that you had made a mistake. I confess I cannot play on from memory. I have the music somewhere, but I must have misplaced it. Come now, young man, let us see something of what you are capable of playing. Since I do not have the music you will have to play from memory. Let us see how many of your own variations you can recall.'

He yielded the stool, but Ludwig walked back to his chair and rejoined his colleagues, who had been following every word with rapt attention. Now, to a man, they encouraged him to play.

'I fear,' said the Abbé Sterkel resuming his seat, 'that our young man is rather more confident with his theories than his playing. Perhaps from memory he can play no more than fragments of his own piece. Such a pity I have mislaid the music.'

Ludwig looked at his friends and found them all smiling. He sat still for a moment, then smiled with them.

'I will play the variations. Right through. I will play them as they should be played. Then I shall play them as you played them. And where you stopped I shall continue – with new variations.'

Ludwig did exactly as he promised, remaining at the piano for nearly an hour, during which not a single word was spoken by any man in the room. When he had finished he resumed his seat and broke the silence.

'You have a style that is refined and cultivated, Abbé Sterkel. But there are passages in my music that need . . . need . . . attack. You heard the difference when I played just now. But I have learned from the way you play. I will use it to improve my own style.'

'You should,' the Abbé said. 'You are a fine pianist and I should not have doubted you. But allow me to say that at times your playing is rude and hard. The piano, young man, is an instrument of beauty to be caressed, not a weapon to be fired. But you are young. In time there is no doubt you will make your mark. And when you do, I will be pleased to say I made your acquaintance.'

Chapter 3

Ludwig looked at his father. There was no room for pity in his heart. Johann van Beethoven was slumped in old Ludwig's chair, his head resting against one of the high wings. Saliva was trickling from the corner of Johann's mouth, down his chin, and dripping on to the chair. There was a pungent smell of stale alcohol.

Ludwig wanted to tell his father to get out of the chair, that it belonged to his grandfather and he was defiling it. He thought, as he often had, of his grandfather's portrait, still languishing in the pawn shop. The portrait he had gazed at so often as a child, of the man he had loved and who was still his inspiration. One day, he thought . . . one day . . .

He decided to leave his father asleep; to awaken him would only unleash a torrent of drunken abuse. He had wanted to tell him about the stay at Mergentheim, how successful it had been. That the orchestra had played his compositions and that everyone, from the Elector down, had praised them.

He had written several songs – two arias for bass and one for soprano – which received their first performance in the Elector's summer palace. At Max Franz's personal request the orchestra and chorus had given several performances of the Cantata 'On the Elevation of the Emperor Leopold', and each time the Elector professed himself delighted with the work.

He wanted his father to be proud of him, but he knew it was an impossible hope. It was more likely he would criticise than praise him. His own career was now over. A failure. Far from being pleased that his son was forging a successful musical career, he resented that Ludwig was already a better musician than he had ever been, even in the days when he was a solo singer.

Ludwig left the room, walked down the stairs and out into the Wenzelgasse. Franz Ries had sent word to him to come to the music rooms in the palace; he had something to show him.

As he walked towards the palace Ludwig thought of Magdalena Willman. During the stay in Mergentheim he had found himself becoming drawn towards her. He wanted to tell her, but he could not bring himself to. He noticed that she smiled often at him, and she was always among the first to congratulate him after the performance of one of his works.

Could it be that she was drawn to him too? He could not bring himself to hope it was so. Soon after they had all returned to Bonn, Ludwig decided to seek Bernhard Romberg's advice. He was a worldly young man and Ludwig had noticed how much time he spent in Magdalena's company.

Bernhard had imparted the news he secretly expected: yes, of course Magdalena liked him, but there was no one she did not like. In fact there was a particular young man she was drawn to, and it was he – Bernhard. They had declared their love for each other and they were considering becoming engaged.

Ludwig had expected the news to devastate him. In fact, to his surprise, it had not. He wanted to compose music. He wanted to do nothing but compose music. Soon, he would begin in earnest on a new and major project which had been revolving in his mind but which he knew he had not been ready for. An opera, Siegfried, Hero of the Rhine. If he fell in love, if he devoted his energies – and emotions – to pursuing the object of his love, he would not be able to devote himself to his work. He knew that, and he accepted it.

He was a musician, a composer. Nothing must be allowed to get in the way of that.

He found Franz Ries, once again wearing the familiar tasselled cap he had abandoned for the stay in Mergentheim.

'Ah, dear boy, come in, come in. How are you?'

'Well, sir. And you, and your family?'

'Excellent. So good to see them again. Little Ferdi grew so much, although we were away only five weeks. I hardly recognised him. And I have to tell you, Ludwig, it is my opinion he is ready for his first piano lesson. Will you keep your promise and teach him?'

'Of course.'

'But I know – I have heard from certain unimpeachable witnesses – that you have developed an intense dislike of teaching. Not for you the life of the pedagogue, eh?'

'The life, no, sir. But it will give me great pleasure to teach Ferdinand.'

'Good. I shall watch his progress with interest. My Ferdi. The youngest pupil of the youngest teacher in Bonn! Now . . .' He stood up and walked over to the table on which a journal lay. 'Now, have you seen this?'

'What is it? The *Musikalische Zeitung*?'

'No, rather more rarefied than that, but of excellent repute I assure you. It's Bossler's *Musikalische Correspondenz*, published in Speyer near Mannheim. Do you remember the chaplain who came to hear us play at Mergentheim? The chaplain from Kirchberg. Carl Ludwig Junker was his name.'

'Yes. Didn't I play the piano for him? In private?'

'That's right. You weren't too pleased at first, but you finally agreed.'

Ludwig smiled.

'Well, I think you will not regret the decision. He has written a piece for Bossler's magazine here. Let me read it to you. Sit down. Sit down. It's a long piece, but I'll just read you the bit that concerns us. Here we are. He begins by talking about the whole orchestra. "I was eyewitness of the court orchestra from Bonn's surpassing excellence. It was not possible to hear a higher degree of exactness. Such perfection in the *pianos*, *fortes*, *rinforzandos* – such a swelling and gradual increase of tone and then such an almost imperceptible dying away, from the most powerful to the lightest accents – all this was formerly to be heard only in Mannheim . . ." He's right there. The Mannheim orchestra is excellent, but it appears we are now better. "It would be difficult to find another orchestra", he says, "in which the violins and basses are throughout in such excellent hands. The players, almost without exception, are in their best years, glowing with health" – I wonder if he counts me as an exception! – "men of culture and fine personal appearance . . ." He obviously hasn't seen me in my tasselled cap! "They form a truly fine sight, when one adds the splendid uniform in which the Elector has clothed them – red, and richly trimmed with gold."'

Ludwig laughed. 'I am glad someone appreciated those uniforms. The cloth was so tight. It did not exactly make it easier to play on our instruments.'

'Now we come to the passage that concerns you, Ludwig. He writes, "I heard also one of the greatest of pianists – the dear, good Bethofen." I'm afraid he hasn't spelled your name correctly, but I think we can forgive him that, given what he goes on to say. "I heard him extemporise in private; yes, I was even invited to propose a theme for him to vary . . ."'

'I remember. A banal theme it was too.'

'". . . The greatness of this amiable, light-hearted man . . ." Well, that's the first time I've ever heard anyone use that description of you, Ludwig!'

'Light-hearted? Light-hearted? Maybe he's confusing me with somebody else.'

'No. Listen. "His greatness may in my opinion be safely estimated from his almost inexhaustible wealth of ideas, the altogether characteristic style of expression in his playing, and the great execution which he displays." Is that not good, Ludwig? Has he not described you perfectly?'

Ludwig lowered his head in modesty. At that moment the door opened and Joseph Reicha came in. His face was dark and severe. He immediately walked to an empty chair, limping slightly as he did so.

'Joseph, my poor friend. The wretched gout again? You must hear what I'm reading to Ludwig. It will cheer you up.' Reicha did not smile. He was about to speak but Ries continued.

'It's a piece about our trip to Mergentheim in Bossler's, written by Chaplain Junker. Do you remember him? First he praises us, the orchestra, then he writes about our young friend in the most glowing terms. Listen. "Even the members of this remarkable orchestra are, without exception, this young musician's admirers. Yet he is exceedingly modest and free from pretension."'

Ries looked up, his face wreathed in a smile. 'First amiable and light-hearted. Now modest and free from pretension.' Ludwig had again lowered his head. Reicha was looking straight ahead, his face still stern and unsmiling. He gave no indication he was listening.

'"His style of treating his instrument is so different from that usually adopted that it impresses one with the idea that by a path of his own discovery he has attained that height of excellence whereon he now stands. I know, therefore, of no one thing which this great Bethofen lacks, that conduces to the greatness of an artist." There. I would say, Ludwig, that you have never been more favourably described.'

'He calls me an artist. That was the final word. That is all that matters.'

'What do you think, Joseph? Should we not be proud of our fellow musician here? Read the whole piece. It is written in the most glowing terms.' He put the journal on the table next to where Reicha sat.

Reicha looked up and nodded, but still he did not smile. 'Franz. Ludwig. You must forgive my mood. But I have just heard some terrible news. News that I know will have the same profound effect on you as it has had on me.' He paused for a moment, then lowered his head as he spoke. His voice trembled with emotion. 'Wolfgang Mozart has died.'

Ludwig gasped. 'Died? Mozart? No, it's impossible. He was only . . . only . . .'

'Thirty-five. Just thirty-five. But it's as if . . . as if . . . he knew. He was working on a Requiem Mass when he died. It's unfinished.'

'Mozart,' Ludwig said quietly. 'Mozart. Dead. I can never . . . He will never . . .' He looked up at the two older men. 'Now there is only Haydn.'

The Elector Max Franz paced the floor. The old wound to his knee had worsened with his increasing bulk, the pain causing his face to contort. But it was not his knee alone that was causing him distress. Count Waldstein looked at him. Only thirty-five, and yet he looked at least ten years older. He had swollen in size and carried his weight with difficulty. The anxiety which now enveloped him caused the fleshy skin which hung below his chin to quiver every time he shook his head.

'They have gone mad. Collectively mad. As a nation, I mean. First they destroy themselves. Now they seek to destroy everyone else.'

'I see it differently from you. It is welcome news. They have declared war on the Holy Roman Empire. They will be defeated. It is inevitable. It will put an end to this so-called revolution. France will return to peace and stability.'

'If only my poor brother . . . my poor brother . . . So sudden.'

'It was an awful shock to you, sir. And you have my sympathy. But – and forgive me for saying so – the Emperor Leopold was a cautious man. Even more so than his illustrious predecessor Joseph. In my view there is only one way to deal with the French, and that is to stand up to them.'

Max Franz sat down heavily and rubbed his knee. 'Still the warrior, eh, Waldstein? Fight, fight, fight. Don't you see why the French have done this? Precisely because the Emperor is dead. Another emperor dead. Two emperors dead in two years. And who is Emperor now? My nephew Franz. I barely know him. But I do know this. He is twenty-three. That is all. Barely . . .'

'But Austria is allied with Prussia. They will overwhelm the French. Disciplined, well-ordered troops against a revolutionary rabble.'

'And if you are wrong, Waldstein? If you are wrong? What then? I will tell you what will happen then. It will be the end of the monarchy in France. My poor sister. They will overthrow her and Louis and who knows what will happen to them? And then how long do you think we would survive here? How long do you think it would be before the French armies pour across the Rhine?'

'Sir,' said Waldstein, shaking his head, 'you are naturally concerned for your own family. But you are a Habsburg. You are a member of the most illustrious family in all Europe. A family of Emperors and Kings. You have armies at your disposal and loyal subjects in their millions. Your sister is Queen of France. If there the people are abusing the honour of having a Habsburg on their throne, then it is up to the rest of Europe to teach them a lesson.'

'It will not be that simple, Waldstein. I know it. I feel it in my blood. Something has been unleashed that will not be easily stopped. It may not be possible to stop it at all.'

Ludwig wanted to work but external pressures were getting in the way. The city of Bonn was in turmoil. Rumours were rife. The French were about to invade. No, the Austrian and Prussian armies had defeated them. The new Emperor Franz was determined to crush the French. Whatever he decided was irrelevant anyway; it was Chancellor Kaunitz who was making the decisions.

Ludwig was trying to make progress on his opera but he was making no headway. He had Siegfried's theme and had written a short musical introduction, which was intended to conjure up an image of the Rhine. A flowing motif in the strings suggested water and he had incorporated one of the old German themes he had used in the Ritterballet. But he was not happy with what he had written.

While all his friends, it seemed, wanted to talk only of war and revolution and the premature death of Emperor Leopold, he wanted to talk of what he considered to be a much more profound loss. A loss not only to Austria, but to mankind. The death of Wolfgang Mozart.

Ludwig was finding it difficult – almost impossible – to come to terms with the fact that Mozart was dead, that there would be no more scores of the Great Master's music arriving in Bonn for him to devour. How could that be? A man of thirty-five? Ludwig had always taken it for granted that he would be studying new works by Mozart for decades to come – and that he would one day – one day – go to Vienna to meet him again.

In the immediate term Ludwig knew he had to abandon this desire. He wanted to raise the matter again with Count Waldstein, to remind him of the conversation they had had after the Ritterballet and to tell him that despite Mozart's death his desire to go to Vienna was as strong as ever. Vienna was a city where the people lived and breathed music, where talk in the salons, coffee houses, even in the streets, was of music. And it was a city to which the musicians of Europe gravitated, as if pulled by an invisible force. There he would find kindred minds, other men who had given their lives to music. And he would be challenged. If he stayed in Bonn he would stultify.

But with Mozart gone he knew exactly what Waldstein would say. And anyway, Waldstein surely had other matters on his mind, far removed from music. Revolution and war.

Joseph Haydn was disappointed to find that the Elector was not in Bonn – and just as disappointed to find that he had taken most of the court musicians with him to Frankfurt for the coronation of his nephew Franz as Emperor. But Count Waldstein had stayed in Bonn and Haydn lost no time in seeing him.

'I was due to stay another six months, but in London the talk is of war against the French, and I thought I had better leave while I could.'

'And by all accounts a very successful stay. We heard from Salomon that your new symphonies were exceedingly well received.'

'It would appear so, though I am not the best judge. I am delighted to say, though, that I have been invited to go to London again, which pleases me enormously. I suppose my music must have given some little pleasure.'

'Always so modest, Herr Haydn. You heard of course of the sad news of your great musical colleague, Wolfgang Mozart.'

Haydn's face fell. 'Indeed I did. It was the talk of London. He visited there as a small boy. They remember him with great affection.' There was a moment's silence. Haydn looked up and said sadly, 'You know, Count, sometimes it seems to me that I am always mourning the loss of great musicians. I was just eighteen when Johann Sebastian Bach died. I remember it so well. And then barely ten years later Georg Handel died. I had just been appointed Kapellmeister to Count Morzin, and my joy was tempered by his death. Now, my happiness at being well received in London is clouded by my friend's Mozart's death. You know, at our last meeting he implied it would be the final time we met. I thought he was concerned about my advancing years. I wonder if he . . . sensed something.'

'But, sir, tragic as circumstances are, you are now indisputably the senior musician in all of Europe. There is no one who can match your prowess.'

'I am getting on, Count. My best work is done. It is to the next generation that we must look now. And that reminds me. What of that young man I met last time I was here? He had written two remarkable cantatas. Beethoven, Ludwig von Beethoven.'

'*Van* Beethoven. He continues to astound us with his virtuosity. He has told me he is working on an opera.'

'An opera! Already?' Haydn frowned. 'A mistake. It is a mistake. It is too soon. You know, Count, I would very much like to teach that young man. He needs instruction. He has extraordinary talent. Genius even. But at the moment he perhaps cannot control it. Who instructs him here?'

'Neefe, the court organist. At least he did, but I am not sure if he still does. He has told me often there is nothing more he can teach Beethoven. He says the young man already plays and composes better than he does.'

Haydn nodded vigorously. 'Just as I suspected. He has a natural gift. Innate. I confess to barely having the time to take on a pupil, but I believe this young man will repay the effort. Certainly Mozart thought so; he was willing to teach him. I feel I must continue what Mozart started. A musician's obligation if you like. What possibility is there, do you think, that the Elector would release him from his duties here so he can come to Vienna?'

Waldstein rubbed his jaw. 'I might be able to persuade him. Actually I have a small obligation to Ludwig myself. I will talk to the Elector. If you are guaranteeing to take him on . . .'

Haydn nodded again. Waldstein continued, 'But the new musical season begins soon and does not end until next spring. He would not be able to leave until then, at the earliest.'

'That would be fine. It would give me time . . .'

'I honestly cannot speak for the Elector. But I know he too admires the young man and wants the best for him. I just might be able to persuade him.'

Chapter 4

Ludwig could not find Stephan. He practically ran to the house on the Münsterplatz, but Frau Breuning did not know where her son was. Maybe he was in the music rooms at the palace, practising the violin.

He was not there, nor was he in the university building. The Zehrgarten tavern in the Marktplatz. Of course. That was where he would be. That was where all the students were. Talking, discussing, arguing. With such momentous events unfolding, it was hardly surprising they spent more time there than anywhere else.

Ludwig clutched the folder under his arm as his eyes swept the crowded room. He quickly spotted Stephan, sitting with Franz Wegeler and some other students at a table to the right. There was an empty chair and Ludwig took it, nodding to his friends but not yet wanting to interrupt the intense conversation.

'The turning point was when they stormed the Tuileries Palace and imprisoned the King and Queen. After that there was no going back.'

'It was a symbolic gesture. You cannot keep the King under lock and key. You just cannot.'

'They are proving you wrong. And as long as that is where he is and the mob rules, there is no telling what will happen next.'

'Valmy,' said another voice. 'That is what did it. Our armies were too complacent and the French won the day. That battle was the decisive moment. It gave the revolutionaries the respectability they craved. They defeated the famed Prussian army. No one could call them a rabble any more.'

'And now,' said Stephan wearily, 'they have invaded the Rhineland and occupied it. How far will they go?'

'They've gone as far as Worms and Mainz already,' said

Wegeler. 'It's only a matter of time before they take Frankfurt and then Bonn. Our own fair city.'

'Is it true the Elector is going to move his court to Münster? That he's ordered all state documents to be packed up ready for shipment? Have you just come from the court, Ludwig? Have you heard anything?'

'That's what Count Waldstein told me, yes. That it wouldn't be safe for the Elector to stay if the French invaded. Steffen, are you busy at the moment? Could I speak to you?'

Stephan stood and made his farewells. Ludwig was already walking towards the door.

'What is it, Ludwig?' said Stephan as they stepped outside. He shivered slightly. 'Autumn is definitely here. You can feel it in the air.'

'Steffen, would you walk with me? I want to walk.'

'All right, but not far. I think it's going to get chilly later this afternoon. How is the composition going?'

Ludwig did not reply, but lengthened his stride and headed down the Brudergasse, into the Rheingasse and down to the river. At the bank he turned right and began to walk upriver.

'Ludwig, what exactly do you have in mind? Would you be so good as to tell me?'

Ludwig did not speak. Stephan walked along beside him, finding it difficult to keep up with his determined stride. For the moment he decided not to ask any more questions.

On they walked, the only sounds those of lapping water made by the occasional barge coasting downriver or yacht struggling upriver against the current, and the alarm calls of birds whose tranquillity they were disturbing. Stephan cursed as a fine rain began to fall.

Finally Ludwig spoke. 'There it is in the distance, Steffen. And we are going to climb it.'

'The Drachenfels? Are you mad? For one thing it's raining, for another it'll start getting dark soon. Ludwig, I'm turning back.'

'Steffen, please. Come with me. I want to talk to you. I *need* to talk to you.'

After nearly two hours walking the two young men stood opposite the mighty rock, hands on hips, breathing heavily and gazing at it. It was half veiled by a curtain of light rain, seeming to dance behind it; on its summit the ruined medieval castle swayed in the mist. Ludwig clutched his folder more tightly under his arm and waved to the ferryman.

'Can't cross now, my fine fellows. Look for yourself. Barely see in front of your nose.'

Even as he spoke a pale sun came out from behind a cloud and bathed the Rhine in a watery light. 'Well, in all my years . . . I could have sworn we wouldn't see the sun again until tomorrow. Come on then. Mind you get back in good time, though. It won't be light for much longer.'

On the other side, the two young men walked swiftly up the hill through Königswinter and on to the lower slopes of the Drachenfels. Ludwig seemed tireless. Stephan had trouble keeping up with him as he climbed the irregular hill, stepping over or round jagged rocks, one arm clutching the folder, the other pushing twigs and leaves out of the way.

Soon they could see no light at all as they struggled through the dense undergrowth. Stephan desperately wanted to stop to catch his breath, but at the same time he knew that the sooner they reached the summit, the sooner they would be able to come down again. And he had long since abandoned any attempt to persuade Ludwig to turn back.

There was still a dim light in the sky when finally they emerged near the summit of the hill, on a ridge below the ruined medieval castle.

Ludwig was breathing heavily. 'Come on. We're going up to it.'

'The castle? Ludwig, for Heaven's sake . . .' But Ludwig had already begun the final ascent.

At last the two of them stood inside the stone walls. The light was fading, the rain threatening again. The air was damp and chilly.

Ludwig walked to the edge where the ground suddenly dropped away.

'Look, Steffen. The river. The Rhine. How beautiful it looks. Mighty. Majestic.'

'Ludwig, if we've come all this way so you can admire the river . . .'

'Steffen,' said Ludwig, turning to face him, 'I am going to Vienna. At last I am going to Vienna.'

'I'm very pleased for you, Ludwig. Delighted. But could you not have told me that in the warmth of the Zehrgarten? Did we have to come to the top of the biggest, roughest hill on the Rhine so that you could impart to me your good news?'

'The Drachenfels, Steffen. My Drachenfels. There is something about this rock, Steffen. Its wildness, ruggedness. People are frightened of it. The darkness, the legend. But I . . . I seem to . . . I understand it. Thank you for coming here with me, Steffen. You know, of all my friendships yours is the one I value most. I wanted to tell you that.'

Stephan could not help returning Ludwig's smile. He had always found himself drawn to this strange young man, whom his mother had first invited into the house on the Münsterplatz so many years before. He found him unpredictable, irritating, headstrong, but he knew from the beginning that Ludwig possessed a gift that set him apart from other people, affected his temperament, and that required patience and understanding.

Stephan remembered the first time he had seen Ludwig pick up the violin, the instrument he himself worked so hard to master. Ludwig was a superb pianist, but his approach to the smaller, more refined instrument was extraordinary. He picked it up roughly, clamped it under his chin and brought the bow down on the strings like a fiddler in a tavern.

Stephan saw immediately that Ludwig's left wrist was too high, which meant that he could not reach up the strings with his fingers, that he flattened the top joints of his fingers so he could not produce a proper vibrato, and that his right hand held the bow too high so it was not balanced properly. But it was Ludwig's face that struck him most. He played as if in a trance, his eyes half closed and his mouth open, his jaw working against the chin rest. He breathed heavily, sometimes in short gasps, the sound quite audible alongside the music.

Franz Ries, Stephan remembered, had tried initially to correct Ludwig's technique. 'No, no, that'll come,' Ludwig said. 'The technique is unimportant. I want to understand the violin. I want to know what it can do.' And when he had satisfied that desire, he stopped taking lessons and went to Nikolaus Simrock, whom he asked to teach him the fundamentals of the horn.

Stephan was a young man with political ambitions, who loved music and enjoyed playing it. Ludwig was a musician, who thought rarely of anything else. It was Stephan's innate understanding of this that had led him to become Ludwig's closest friend.

'What are you carrying, Ludwig? What is in that folder? I hope it's nothing important.'

Ludwig looked at the folder he had been carrying under his

left arm. His grip had crumpled it and the rain had soaked it through. The brown dye that coloured the covers was running, trickling down Ludwig's hand. He smiled.

'Shall I tell you what this is, Steffen? This is my *magnum opus*. My opera. *Siegfried, Hero of the Rhine*. Here, let me show it to you.'

He opened the folder and the rain, which was falling steadily, spattered on to the pages. Immediately the notes Ludwig had scribbled in the staves began to run. The ink trickled in rivulets to the edge of the page and dripped off the paper on to the ground.

'But, Ludwig . . .'

'Ha! My great masterpiece. Buried for ever in the soil of the Drachenfels.'

'I don't understand. Why . . . ?'

'I am going to Vienna, Steffen. Count Waldstein has told me. To study with Haydn. Vienna, the city of music. There I will compose. New works. Siegfried belongs to the Rhine. One day, when I return, maybe I will take up his story again. For the moment I must look forward, not back. I will go to Vienna and continue what Mozart started.'

The two young men stood facing each other, two rain-sodden figures, their hair matted to their foreheads, their clothes hanging on them heavily; one looking quizzically, the other smiling more broadly than he ever had, conscious that he had achieved his long-held ambition, that he had reached a defining moment in his life.

Above them the ruined castle stood, its jagged edges thrusting up into the darkening sky.

'Listen, Steffen,' said Ludwig, holding up his hand. 'Do you hear the roar? The dragon's roar? And listen carefully. Very carefully. The maidens' song . . .'

'That's it,' said Stephan gruffly. 'I've had enough. We've probably both caught our death of colds up here. We're going back down. Right now.'

'You poor boy. What a state you're in!' said Franz Ries. 'But I don't suppose it will dampen your excitement.'

Ludwig shook his head, holding a handkerchief to his nose and eyes. 'Just a cold,' he said hoarsely. 'It won't get any worse.'

'I'm so pleased for you, my boy. You must be the only

person in Bonn to benefit from the terrible events that are happening to us.'

Ludwig nodded. 'With the Elector moving to Münster and the court being disbanded, there was no need for me to stay.'

'Yes. Dreadful times. Who knows where it will end? Where's Ferdi? I want him to say goodbye to you. Here he comes. I can hear him.'

Ferdinand Ries, now eight years of age, came into the room, his hair as black and curly and tousled as ever. 'No lesson today,' he said. 'I'm going to Hansi's house to play.'

'No, my boy. No lesson today. In fact no lesson with Herr Beethoven for some time. How long will it be, Ludwig?'

'Count Waldstein didn't say. And he's gone to Münster now so I can't ask him. But he implied at least a year. Maybe two. It depends on what happens here.'

'But you'll come back, of course.'

Ludwig nodded. 'The Count said I can draw my salary in Vienna for a year and then they'll review it. But the Elector wants me back to rejoin the court orchestra when things have settled down.'

'So, Ferdi, you'll have to practise hard while Herr Beethoven is away. I've asked Herr Neefe to take Ferdi on, Ludwig. He said he would be delighted.'

'Where is Herr Neefe? I have to see him.'

'He had to return suddenly to Chemnitz. His mother is ailing. I believe. But he knew about your trip. Count Waldstein spoke to him. He was so pleased for you.'

'I'll write to him. Thank you for everything you have done for me, Herr Ries. I wish there was some way . . .'

'Think nothing of it, Ludwig. Maybe one day I will ask you to do something for me. And by then you will be an important musician in Vienna and you won't even remember me.'

'No, no . . .'

'Don't forget us, Ludwig. We'll be following your progress, you know. And be sure to see Frau Breuning before you leave. I know there's something she wants to show you,' he said with a twinkle in his eye.

Ludwig walked across the Münsterplatz and stopped to look at the imposing building he had first approached with Franz Wegeler so many years before. He had no fear of it now.

He rang the bell and asked the servant to tell Frau Breuning he was there.

He heard the rustle of her copious dress before he saw her. He smiled at her as she came into the room.

'Ludwig. At last. I was so glad when I heard. Sit down. Sit down. Let me ring for some coffee. Or would you—?'

'Forgive me, Frau Breuning. But I leave in the morning. Early. And I still have—'

'Of course. You will go and see Lorchen before you go, won't you? She's in her room. She wants to see you.'

Ludwig looked down and gripped his hands together. 'Is she . . . ? Will she . . . ?'

Frau Breuning smiled. 'I think it'll be all right. But she's a little upset with you, you know. You'll have to speak very nicely to her. Tell me, Ludwig, why did you stop giving her lessons?'

'I . . . I . . . There were always so many other things to do.'

'You should really have come and explained to her. I think that's what upset her most. Lenz was a different matter. He's a boy, and rather less sensitive, but I'm afraid Lorchen took it rather to heart.'

'I'll go and see her. I'll apologise.'

'That would be good. Now, I have some nice things to tell you. First, I have to give you this. Count Waldstein gave it to me for you before he left. It's an autograph book. Some of your best friends have written in it for you. To wish you luck. But you mustn't open it until you have left Bonn.'

Ludwig took it with a smile and put it in his bag.

'Frau Breuning. Thank you for everything you have done for me. Especially . . .' He stood and walked to the piano. He stroked the keys and the ornate wooden frame. 'When I met Herr Stein in Augsburg I told him what a beautiful piano it was. Thank you for letting me play on it.'

'Oh, you will have your pick of the finest pianos in Vienna. You will soon forget this one. But come back here and sit down. I have something for you.' She walked to the bell cord that hung to one side of the fireplace and pulled it.

Moments later a servant entered carrying something flat and rectangular, covered with a sheet.

'Just put it against my chair, Müller. Thank you.'

Carefully she removed the sheet, watching Ludwig's face as she did so. Ludwig was overwhelmed to see the familiar face of his grandfather looking up at him. He felt tears in his eyes; his lips trembled. His grandfather's portrait.

'I will look after it for you here until you return. It will be safe. Now,' she said hurriedly, 'off you go to see Lorchen. And I wish you well in Vienna, Ludwig. Stay in touch with us.'

He stood and she embraced him quickly. Then he left the room and walked to the back of the house, where Eleonore was working on some embroidery in a small drawing room.

The door was open, and Ludwig knocked and walked in. Eleonore did not look up.

'Eleonore. Lorchen. I have come to say goodbye. I leave tomorrow morning. For Vienna.'

Eleonore worked on for several seconds, then put down her embroidery with a heavy sigh and looked at him.

'Ludwig. Do you know how long it is since I last saw you? Let me tell you. Three weeks and two days. That's three piano lessons you missed. Three times that I have sat patiently waiting for you. And when finally you do come to see me, it is not to say sorry. Oh no. It is to say goodbye. As if what is happening to you is the only thing of importance in the world. Sometimes, Ludwig, you can be quite selfish.'

'I've been busy, Eleonore. Herr Neefe has been giving me a lot of work to do as his assistant, and I've had orchestral work at court, as well as my own composing. And now I'm going to Vienna.'

'I know, Ludwig. I'm so pleased for you. It's what you've always wanted, isn't it?'

Ludwig nodded, smiling.

Eleonore handed him a small, soft package, wrapped in brown paper. 'Here. A gift for you. Something I made. It will fit at the bottom of your bag. Keep it wrapped up to protect it. When you wear it, it will remind you of me.'

Ludwig took it. 'Thank you, Lorchen. I will miss you. You and your brothers. Will you say goodbye to them for me?'

Eleonore nodded. Ludwig leaned forward. Eleonore turned her face quickly, offering him her cheek. He kissed it lightly.

'You will come back and see us, won't you?'

'Of course,' Ludwig said.

There was one more farewell Ludwig wanted to make. From the Münsterplatz he walked along the Sternstrasse to the edge of the town. It was late afternoon and the light was fading, making the heavy black gates all the more forbidding. Suppressing a desire to turn back, he pulled on one of the gates and entered the cemetery.

A sharper chill than outside hung over the cemetery, held there by the high wall which ran round its perimeter. He pulled his coat tightly around him. Pausing to establish his bearings in the half-light, he turned to the right and walked along the path which ran round the wall. On his left stood the ornate and imposing headstone to the Belderbusch family, the most recent engraving commemorating the late First Minister.

He walked on into the cemetery and finally stopped by a plain headstone which stood by the wall. The earth around it was soft and it leaned back, supported by the wall. There were patches of moss on the stone, on which was carved simply:

MARIA MAGDALENA KEVERICH BEETHOVEN
1746–1787

There were no flowers on the grave and what had once been a neat mound had now fallen to the level of the ground. The grass growing on it needed trimming.

Ludwig thrust his hands deep into his pockets and stared at his mother's grave. He wanted to tell her he was going to Vienna. He wanted to tell her that this time he was going to stay; that although Count Waldstein had told him it would be a year or two, and although everyone was talking about how they looked forward to seeing him on his return, he would not come back for a long time. Not until he was a famous composer; not until the whole of Europe knew his music and knew his name.

Vienna was his home. He had known it since he was a child. Since he had first heard the name of Wolfgang Mozart from his grandfather.

'Goodbye, Mother,' he said softly. 'When I return I will come and see you again and you will be proud of me.'

He turned quickly and retraced his steps, unable to see the path in the darkness.

His father was not in the house on the Wenzelgasse when Ludwig returned from the cemetery. Caspar and Nikola were being given their dinner by the housekeeper. She asked Ludwig if he wanted to eat. He shook his head.

'I must get my things together. Where's Father?'

'With Klein,' said Caspar. 'He won't be back till late. What time are you leaving?'

'The stage departs at five thirty in the morning. I have to catch it or I will miss the connecting stage at Koblenz.'

'I wish I was going with you,' said Nikola. 'When are you coming back?'

Ludwig shrugged his shoulders.

Caspar said, 'I might try to come and see you. If the opportunities for musicians are good, will you let me know?'

'You can't leave Father,' said Nikola. 'You'll be in charge while Ludwig's gone. Anyway, if you go, I'm coming with you.'

'Stop talking like that, both of you,' said Ludwig sharply. 'I'll be back soon anyway.'

The next morning he rose in the darkness before dawn. As he left the house on the Wenzelgasse, he heard his father's snoring as he passed his room, but he did not stop. He carried a bag in one hand and a folder of papers in the other. He walked through the Marktplatz, along the Remigiusstrasse and into the Münsterplatz. He glanced up at the Breuning house in which he had spent so many hours. Head down, he walked on.

He boarded the carriage, and settled down for the journey, his folder and bag on his lap. He tried to sleep but the jolting of the uneven cobbles made it impossible. Three hours later he changed to a larger carriage at Koblenz, which crossed by ferry to Ehrenbreitstein.

It was fully daylight, and Ludwig had his first sight of the small river town, dominated by a ruined medieval castle, where his father had wooed his mother a quarter of a century before. He looked down at the river below. The great rushing Rhine. He turned his head so his eyes could linger on the ceaselessly moving water until the very last moment, when the carriage turned away to the east.

They were on country roads now, and Ludwig relaxed into the rhythm of the swaying carriage.

Carefully, he put his hand down into his bag and brought out the album Count Waldstein had asked Frau Breuning to give him. He opened the front cover and turned the first page. On the left was a silhouette of the Count. On the right, in carefully measured script, he had written:

Dear Beethoven!

At last you are going to Vienna in fulfilment of a wish that has for so long been frustrated. The GENIUS of Mozart still mourns and weeps over the death of her pupil. She found a refuge but no occupation with the inexhaustible Haydn; through him she desires again to form a union with another. Through your unceasing toil, may you receive *Mozart's spirit from Haydn's hands*.

Your true friend, Waldstein.

BOOK SIX

Chapter 1

Ludwig van Beethoven stood at the small window of the attic room and looked out across the north-western suburbs of Vienna to the hills beyond. Wiping the condensation on the glass pane with his sleeve, he could see over the tightly packed houses of the village of Grinzing, its narrow lanes and their steep inclines yielding to the spacious vineyards beyond. With another wipe of his sleeve and straining his eyes to peer through the damp atmosphere, Ludwig could see the dark outline of the Vienna woods which curved in a great scythe-like sweep from the west, and there at their northern tip, barely visible in the distance, the Kahlenberg.

A knot of loneliness tightened in Ludwig's stomach as he gazed at the hill which had dominated the Viennese skyline for centuries past. How ridiculous it was! Such a neat, manicured hill, with its slim, erect beech trees; on its summit the walls which once housed monks now providing a hermitage for the wealthy wishing to escape from the bustle of the city below.

So different from the Drachenfels, Ludwig thought. There is nature in the raw. The rough and jagged rock with the crumbling stones of an ancient castle atop it. Are not people moulded by the force of nature? Am I not a product of the Drachenfels; just as the Viennese, who gaze daily at the Kahlenberg, are moulded by it? The Viennese, sophisticated, with an air of arrogance, smartly turned out, neat, tidy. Like their hill. Look once at the Kahlenberg and you have understood all there is to understand about them.

But the Drachenfels. One could gaze at it for a lifetime and not see its inner secrets. Ludwig clenched his fists. That is how my music will be. Dark, secret. Like the Drachenfels. They will hear it and think they know it. But when they listen to it again they will hear something different. Each layer they strip away will reveal another layer. They will say they understand my music, but they will not. Only those who listen and wonder and know that they cannot understand . . . Only those people will know.

On a late morning in December Ludwig left his cramped room. He remained there only because it was in the house where Prince Lichnowsky, to whom Ludwig carried a letter of introduction, had an apartment. He hoped that the Prince would introduce him to a wealth of musicians, but so far the Prince had failed to return from his country residence in Silesia, and Ludwig was growing impatient.

He walked down the Alstergasse and on to the Glacis, the wide expanse of green beyond which lay the Bastion, the huge fortified city wall that encircled Vienna. He could see the tall Gothic spire of St Stephansdom, the great medieval cathedral, rising above the city. The Bastion, which had twice protected the city from the besieging Turks, was high and forbidding, and had long since turned a dark and dirty black. The grass of the Glacis, covered in a thin frost, crunched underfoot. Ludwig pulled his collar around his neck. People crisscrossed the Glacis, some on their way into the city, others with packages hurrying to their homes in the suburbs for their midday meal. A few stopped in the cold air to watch a small detachment of soldiers drilling under the city wall, the officer's commands carrying on the chill December air.

Ludwig shivered as he came under the shadow of the huge Bastion and walked through the Schottentor, the Scottish gate. The air was still and icy and his footsteps echoed on the stone ground. He emerged from under the Bastion into the city, and it was as if he had entered another world. Gone was the calm of the Glacis; in its place noise and bustle.

It reminded him suddenly of his first trip to Vienna five years before. He had never seen or heard such crowds of people. Now, as then, they moved in all directions, always, it seemed, with purpose. The intermittent cries of street vendors selling their wares cut through the air; horses' hooves clopped on the cobbles and iron-rimmed carriage wheels clattered. There was an aroma of roasting food; chestnuts glowed on braziers and a strong winter punch simmered on outdoor stoves. There was also the sweet smell of Christmas cakes baking on hot plates. Shop windows sparkled with candles and tinsel; small figures depicted the birth of Christ.

Small groups of people, some in military uniform, stood talking. They were animated, their arms emphasising their words, their breath turning instantly white as it hit the air. On all their faces there were expressions of dismay and foreboding.

Ludwig turned round and climbed the steps that led to the top of the Bastion. The broad boulevard which ran along the top of the city wall and which in the summer would be crowded with promenaders and sideshows, was practically deserted. A few people hurried along it. A man with a tricorn hat and a musket over his shoulder strode slowly, confident his patrol was unlikely to be interrupted.

By the raised wall which bordered the walkway, a forlorn figure stood behind an upended box, his neck muffled with a scarf and a hat pulled down nearly to his eyes. His voice quivered with cold as he called out, 'Imperial army defeated. Imperial army defeated.'

Ludwig dug into his pocket for a coin and took a newssheet from the grateful vendor.

IMPERIAL TROOPS BRAVELY DEFEND JEMAPPES

A brave force of Austrian infantry, resplendent in their white uniforms, were unable to resist the French forces and were forced to yield to them the town of Jemappes in the Imperial Netherlands.

Repeatedly our supporting cavalry counter-attacked, only to see victory snatched from them by superior numbers of French forces.

It is our sad duty to report that around four thousand brave soldiers of the imperial army perished on the battlefield.

Ludwig descended the steps again, the cold penetrating his coat. He headed along the Herrengasse, turned into the Wallner-strasse, up the Kohlmarkt and into the wide Graben, where the ornate monument to the plague of a hundred years ago stood. The cold was now cutting through to his skin. He saw a coffee house, its window misted with heat, and he went in.

As he sipped the warming liquid, he listened to the hum of conversation around him. It was of only two topics: the defeat at Jemappes, and the fate of the French King.

'He is imprisoned. His trial is about to begin.'

'They dare not. They simply dare not. The royalists will rise up against them.'

John Suchet

'Not only will he stand trial, but he will be found guilty of whatever it is they have charged him with, and he will be the guest of Madame Guillotine.'

'Impossible. For the simple reason they do not need to do that. The revolution is won . . .'

Politics, war, revolution. It reminded Ludwig of the Zehrgarten in the familiar Marktplatz in Bonn. There, too, that was all anybody seemed to talk about. Where can I go to talk about music? Ludwig wondered.

As he finished his coffee, Ludwig thrust his hand into his coat pocket and brought out a crumpled piece of paper. He had torn it out of an inside page of the *Wiener Zeitung* the day before. He read the address again, although he already knew it by heart: 'Im Kramerschen Breihaus Nr. 257 im Schlossergassel, am Graben'.

He weaved his way round the tables and went out again into the chill air. He quickly found the Schlossergassel, a narrow alley which ran off the Graben, walked along it until he stood outside number 257 and entered the dark premises.

He paused to allow his eyes to adjust to the light and then looked round the room. It was more spacious than he had imagined and seemed at first sight to be empty. Then he saw a table and chair against one wall, the tabletop covered with a disorganised pile of paper.

More urgently this time his eyes swept the room again, a knot of disappointment already forming in his stomach. Then he saw the object of his quest.

It was smaller than he wanted, unsteadily poised on irregular legs and coated in dust. But it was a piano. The piece of board propped on its music stand read, 'For rent, half a sovereign: or 6 florins, 40 kreutzer'. Without sitting down Ludwig played a few chords, ran some scales up and down the keyboard, smiled quietly to himself and set off to find the proprietor.

Chapter 2

Ludwig looked at the letter with a sense of foreboding, as he recognised his brother's handwriting. How pleasant it would be, he thought, if Caspar were writing to him to enquire after his health and to wish him prosperity for the new year. But that was a forlorn hope.

He tore open the letter and read the spidery handwriting with a sinking heart. The final paragraph compounded his misery.

Brother Ludwig

Our dear father passed away one week before Christmas. He was in his bed and his soul was at peace with the world before he breathed his last. Nikolaus held one hand and I the other. He blessed us both. He blessed your name too when I reminded him. Since we are short of funds he will not be buried alongside Mama but in the public cemetery.

His Grace the Elector has abandoned this city and moved the court to Münster. We are at the mercy of the French. You must of course return immediately. Nikola and I await you.

Your brother Caspar

Ludwig's mind raced back to that fateful day when a letter from his father had ended his first visit to Vienna. Why did fate conspire so remorselessly against him? Each time it seemed he had achieved his desire, his hopes were dashed. He was to come to Vienna over a decade ago but then Elector Maximilian Friedrich died; then he came to Vienna and Mozart agreed to take him on as a pupil but his mother died; then it was Mozart himself who died. And now his father's death threatened his future.

He was not going to let that happen, of that he was absolutely sure. In any case his father was already dead; there was no point in returning. And if he left, the same fate awaited him as before. It might be many years before he could return to Vienna, particularly given the likely invasion by the French forces and the removal of the court to Münster. And with war impending, what chances were there of pursuing his musical ambitions?

He had now begun lessons in Vienna with Haydn, and they were studying Johann Sebastian Bach's massive set of piano exercises, the preludes and fugues of the *Wohl-Temperierte Klavier*. Two sets of twenty-four preludes and fugues, each set covering every major and minor key.

From the day Bach had completed the second set half a century before, they had become the standard work to which every piano student aspired. Ludwig had studied the pieces with Gottlob Neefe in Bonn, but Neefe had regarded them fundamentally as exercises; some more elaborate and difficult than others, but exercises nonetheless. Haydn saw them differently.

'Do not make the mistake, Ludwig,' he said at one lesson, 'of thinking of the forty-eight as mere practice pieces. They are works for the piano, each one independent of its predecessor.'

Patiently he showed Ludwig how each prelude and fugue was a small – but complete – work, its tiny structure totally logical and precise. 'Like a perfect miniature portrait,' Haydn said. 'Why else would Bach have written two sets, and twenty years apart? He was saying to us, "I have shown you how every key is tuneful and how every key has its own individual temperament. To prove it to you I am showing you twice." He was telling us, Ludwig, that the art we practise, the art of music, is infinite.'

Haydn opened Ludwig's eyes and ears to the music of Bach in a way that Neefe, competent musician that he was, had not and could not do. Under Haydn's guidance Ludwig began to play the preludes and fugues in a new way, not understating the simple passages, not overstating the virtuosic passages. He treated each piece as a musical whole, not as a stepping stone to the next.

Soon Haydn began allowing Ludwig to play pieces from the Well-Tempered Klavier at salon soirées. Introducing Ludwig always as his pupil, 'who one day soon is destined to surpass my meagre attainments', he was effusive in his praise of Ludwig's playing and modestly dismissive of his own contribution. Already it was being said that Ludwig's playing of the Well-Tempered Klavier was the most accomplished that had been heard since the time of Bach himself.

Could he leave all this behind and return to Bonn? It was impossible. Once again Ludwig reassured himself that as his father was already dead there would be no point. As for his brothers, Caspar was nearly nineteen years of age and Nikolaus only two years younger. While Caspar's musical talents were by no means as great as those of his elder brother, he was a capable pianist and earned money from teaching – never failing to point out to potential students that his illustrious brother, now conquering the salons of Vienna, had instructed him personally. And Nikolaus was now earning a small but regular income as an apothecary. If his brothers had to leave the house on the Wenzelgasse and move to something smaller, that would not be too great a hardship.

If he were to return to Bonn now he would be sacrificing his musical future just as he had before. No, Ludwig decided emphatically, it would not happen a second time.

He looked at the letter from Caspar again, screwed it up and threw it into the fire grate. He had no intention of replying to it; that alone should convey to Caspar his intention to remain in Vienna.

It was to be many months before Ludwig realised that he had not once grieved for his father. In making the decision not to return to Bonn but to continue his studies with Haydn, all he was conscious of was a great weight having been lifted from his shoulders. The problems that he had had to deal with because of his father's drunkenness were gone. And any vestige of guilt that he might have had at leaving Caspar to inherit the problem was gone too.

He did not even inform Haydn of his father's death. There seemed no need.

As if in final acceptance of the fact that the first phase of his life was over, that he had left Bonn – and his youth – behind, he wrote a letter to Gottlob Neefe in which he made it clear he no longer considered himself as his student.

> . . . I thank you for the advice you have very often given me about making progress in my divine art. Should I ever become a great man, you too will have a share in my success . . .

*   *   *

Ludwig walked through the doorway of the long, low house on the Wasserkunstbastei in the southern part of the city, clutching the folder of manuscripts firmly under his arm and not noticing the carriage that stood outside. He climbed the stairs to the first floor, hearing the sounds of Bach in his head and not the voices that came from the front room.

'I . . . I'm sorry, Herr Haydn, I didn't realise you—'

'Come in, dear boy, come in. I'd like you to meet His Excellency Baron Swieten. The Baron is director of the imperial court library and second to none in his love – and I might say support – for the noble art you and I pursue. His salon ranks with the finest in the city, and he is no mean musician himself.'

'My dear Haydn, you flatter me too much. I am a humble dilettante. My musical ambitions far outstrip my meagre talents. But I declare you have not overstated my love for your art. Now, young man,' he said, turning to Ludwig, 'I have heard much about you.'

Initially, Ludwig felt ill at ease, as he always did when meeting new people, particularly when, like Baron Swieten, they were immaculately coiffed and dressed, with the sophistication which seemed to come naturally to the nobility of Vienna.

But the Baron was unlike other aristocrats Ludwig had been introduced to by Haydn. There was a naturalness about him which Ludwig was immediately drawn to. He was a large man with an avuncular demeanour. His fleshy face, with a broad, misshapen nose, radiated warmth and kindness. He immediately stood up and walked towards Ludwig, carrying his weight with surprising ease.

'How good to meet you, Ludwig. I may call you that, may I?'

Ludwig nodded, returned the Baron's bow, waited for him to sit down again and followed suit. He looked quickly at Haydn, who was smiling at him and nodding slowly and confidently.

'In fact you and I share a small mark of distinction,' Swieten continued. 'You are *Van* Beethoven, are you not? Just as I am *Van* Swieten. You must be of Flemish descent, as I am.'

'Yes. My grandfather came from Flanders. To Bonn in the Rhineland. He was Kapellmeister there.'

'Ah, a musical family. How fortunate you are. My father was merely a doctor . . .'

'To the Empress Maria Theresa, no less,' said Haydn, laughing.

'And he too came from Flanders. We Flemish must stick together, eh, Ludwig? Bring some culture to these Austrians. Always excepting you, of course, Joseph.'

All three laughed. 'Joseph here has told me of your remarkable achievements,' Swieten continued. 'I only regret that my absence from Vienna has meant you have not yet graced my salon – a lamentable state of affairs that I hope you will allow me to rectify soon.'

Ludwig looked towards his teacher for guidance. Haydn nodded more vigorously and spoke.

'As I said, Ludwig, the Baron is a fine musician himself. How many symphonies is it, Baron? Twelve?'

A look of pride shot across Swieten's face, to be instantly replaced by one of self-mockery. 'Twelve in number, yes. But not a single one worthy of comparison with any of yours. The works of a mere dabbler. No,' his face turned serious, 'if I have any claim to be a friend of music, it is because of my services to the late, dearly missed Herr Mozart.'

Ludwig leaned forward. 'You knew him?'

'More than that. I was fortunate enough for him to count me a friend. It was I, although I ask you to forgive my immodesty, who spent more hours at his deathbed than anyone other than Constanze, and I who arranged his funeral. My profoundest regret is that I was unable to prevent his precious body from being buried in a common grave. But I was able to make some amends. I was responsible for arranging the first performance of the great master's requiem, after it was completed by Süssmayr.'

Ludwig nodded slowly. 'I played for him. I was to be his pupil. But I . . .'

'I know. Joseph here has told me. But now you are the pupil of Europe's greatest composer—'

'No, no, Gottfried. Enough! You are kind, but . . .'

'And let me remind you, Joseph, it is my firm intention to provide you with a text for a great oratorio. I will take it from the Holy Bible. Only you are capable of writing music befitting such sacred words.'

Haydn shook his head. 'You flatter me too much, Baron. No, my work is all but done.'

'Come now, in my opinion the best work is still to come. Look at Bach and Handel. They both improved with age. I shall start work soon and you will have your text. And then we shall see.'

Haydn clapped his hands. 'Enough of that. Now, Baron, let us come to the matter in hand. Why don't you tell Ludwig the reason for your visit?

'Indeed I shall. Now, Ludwig, have you heard of our famous improvisation contests here in Vienna?'

'Improvisation contests? No. What are they?'

'Well, in some other countries, for their amusement, the nobility put two wrestlers on the mat and place their money on who they think will unbalance the other. Or two sprinters and who will be the swiftest. I believe the English enjoy watching two cockerels fighting to the death. The French are more sophisticated – or were before the present troubles. I have heard they have poetry-reading contests. Here in Vienna, where we pride ourselves on our artistic achievements, we boast a greater number of piano virtuosos than anywhere else in Europe. And it would appear, dear Ludwig, that you have added to their number.'

'What are you asking me to do?' There was disquiet in his voice.

'Forgive me for my absurd comparisons. I do not mean for one moment to diminish your great artistry. Here in Vienna it is common practice for two piano virtuosos to play against each other in an improvisation contest. One will play a theme and the other will improvise on it. Then the second pianist will set a theme and the first will improvise on it. The themes will be new, of course. To test each player to the full. If the audience desires it, a second round is heard with new themes. The audience is the judge of who is deemed to have performed better. Often if a certain player has particularly pleased, he will be asked to play more.'

Haydn, noticing Ludwig's unease, interjected. 'Actually, Ludwig, it is a very interesting musical exercise. Not just interesting, but instructive. You are forced to make an immediate judgement about a theme, see into its structure instantly and break it down. In front of a demanding audience! In my earlier days I took part in a few such contests myself and came to regard them as highly challenging. You, as I have told you, have a natural aptitude for improvisation. It is a great gift. I believe you would acquit yourself admirably.'

Ludwig looked from one man to the other, not knowing what to say. Instinctively he rebelled against the entire notion. He wanted to tell them that it was putting musicians on display, asking them to perform like . . . like . . . circus animals. At the same time he knew Haydn was right. Improvisation was an area in which he excelled. Could this be the way to make his mark in Vienna?

'And there's another thing to be said for it,' Haydn continued. 'Such contests attract the most important people in Vienna. Patrons of the arts. There is no quicker way for you to establish yourself.'

'But what are you . . . ? Are you saying you want me to do this soon? When are you . . . ?'

'There is a very fine pianist in the city at the moment,' Swieten said. 'His name is Gelinek. Abbé Josef Gelinek. He is from Bohemia. He is a stern gentleman, as you might gather from his calling, and he is . . . How can I put it without wishing to be unkind? . . . A formal pianist. Strict and correct. Is that fair, Joseph?'

Haydn nodded. 'Very different from you, Ludwig. A different approach. I think it would interest you greatly to hear him.'

'The Abbé is the guest here of Prince Kinsky. He is tutoring the Prince's children. The Prince has a fine salon. Ludwig,' said Swieten, his voice rising with enthusiasm, 'will you allow me to champion you against Gelinek?'

Ludwig found himself looking forward to the improvisation contest. He tried to examine why. It was precisely the kind of event he revolted against. So often in Bonn he had been called on to perform for astonished audiences. Ignorant audiences. When they applauded and shook his hand and wondered at his talent, what did they really know of music? Of him?

He had not always performed to order. On occasion, as if to remind them of his talent, he refused to play. Or he would reach a point in a performance and refuse to continue. His genius was not at their bidding. He thought back many years to the day when as a child he had refused to play for the Elector Maximilian Friedrich. Why had he made that sudden decision – a decision which could have blighted his musical prospects irretrievably?

It was seeing the stag that did it. The huge beast looked so defiant, so proud, his head held high, his eye gazing down at the onlooker almost in contempt. You cannot make me do anything I do not wish, he seemed to be saying. Behind him a herd of deer. His herd. His subjects. His audience.

Yet here he was, in Vienna at last, about to allow himself

to be manipulated, to play to order, to satisfy another ignorant audience. And he was looking forward to it! Looking deeply into his own thoughts, he knew why. For the simple reason that he had not a shred of doubt that he would emerge triumphant, his reputation established.

Chapter 3

Ludwig wished Haydn were present – any gathering he attended seemed to acquire an added air of respectability – but he had to go to Esterhaz to see the young Prince Anton, to whom he owed his freedom from court service. Swieten, though, was in buoyant mood, moving among his guests with ease and enthusiasm. He had welcomed Ludwig effusively, assuring him the evening would be a great success, whatever the outcome. He told him some of the most notable patrons of the arts in Vienna were to be present. The only exception, sadly, was Prince Lichnowsky, who had still not returned from his country estate to Vienna.

Ludwig had nodded. It was ironic that the one member of the aristocracy to whom he had an introductory letter from Count Waldstein, and in the same building as whom he had his rooms – again, specifically arranged by Waldstein – had still not returned to Vienna. But Ludwig was assured by Swieten that the Prince would not be away for much longer. 'And he will, I am sure, be most happy to make your acquaintance. As will the Princess,' he had added.

'Come now, Ludwig. You shall meet His Excellency Prince Kinsky.'

Swieten guided Ludwig to a large man of middle age, his starched military uniform straining against the gleaming silver belt which attempted to hold in his girth.

'Your Excellency. Allow me to introduce my young friend, Herr Ludwig van Beethoven. Like me of Flemish origin, and a truly remarkable musician, as you shall shortly hear.'

'Honoured. Honoured. You're dreadfully young. You don't look Viennese. Not smart enough. Ha! Where are you from?'

'Bonn, sir. In Germany. By the Rhine.'

'Yes. Excellent. Excellent. No doubt that's why you talk in a strange way. Meet my son. Ferdinand.'

Ludwig looked at Prince Ferdinand Kinsky and almost gasped

at the likeness between father and son. The boy could not have been much more than in his early teenage years, yet he was a smaller, younger replica of his father. Unusually, and immediately noticeable, both men had their hair brushed forward, not just on the top of their heads but at the sides too. It gave them both a startled, nervous look, compounded by a slight jerking forward of the head, like a cockerel straining to reach his brood. In the father the sense of unpredictability was compounded by an untidy moustache which perched precariously on his upper lip. In the boy there was already a swelling of the girth which portended a figure to match his father's rotundity.

'Ferdi's to follow me into the army, at the service of His Imperial Majesty. Eh, Ferdi? Eh?'

'Sir!' said the boy, bringing his heels together and turning sharply towards Ludwig. 'Great pleasure to meet you, sir. Damned odd uniform. Maybe one day you'll allow me to kit you out.'

Prince Kinsky and Swieten laughed in astonishment at the boy's precociousness. Ludwig, to his surprise, found himself laughing too. There was a disarming frankness to the boy's face which he liked.

'Hear you're going to play against my man,' said the Prince. 'Ha! Better watch yourself. He's got a more powerful patron than me. The Lord Himself!'

'Is . . . is he here yet?' Ludwig asked.

'No, no! He likes to make a grand entrance. You'll know when he's here. Watch out, young man. Watch out!'

The young Prince took Ludwig's arm and leaned towards him. 'He's teaching me while he's in Vienna. The Abbé. He has a perfectly correct style. But I think it's boring.'

'What's that?' said his father. 'What's that? What are you saying?'

Ludwig felt Swieten's hand on his arm. He smiled at the boy as he turned away.

'Come, Ludwig. I want you to meet another important person. He's one of the city's most influential patrons of the arts. After Prince Lichnowsky, of course. Much more so than me. He's from Bohemia. Very wealthy. Spends much of it putting on musical recitals and dramatic performances. Too much for his wife, it's said. Come. His name is Lobkowitz. Prince Franz Joseph Lobkowitz.'

Ludwig found himself looking at a young man of about his

own age, but with an appearance which added ten years to him.

He was slightly built, with shoulders that sloped, and his body leaned forward to be supported under the right arm by a leather-topped crutch. His right leg was shorter than his left and his boot built up by a thick sole and heel. He was lively but walked with a pronounced limp, and the cost of every movement registered on his face. His hair – unexpectedly for one so smartly dressed – stood out thickly in all directions and was already whitening. To a tall, fit man it would have given a forbidding appearance. To Prince Lobkowitz, though, it gave an air of vulnerability.

'Prince. May I introduce my young champion? Ludwig van Beethoven. From the German city of Bonn.'

Lobkowitz smiled broadly and it transformed his appearance. He stood up straight and opened his arms, for a moment lifting the crutch clear of the ground.

'Yes, yes! I have heard of you. From one of Herr Haydn's pupils. He teaches you too, doesn't he?' Ludwig nodded. 'So, I gather we are to have the pleasure of hearing you play tonight?'

'And Abbé Gelinek too, who I am told is . . .'

Lobkowitz waved his crutch in the air dismissively. 'Kinsky thinks so. But he is the only one. From what I hear of your skills, you will consume the holy man with tongues of flame!' He laughed at the aptness of his words, and immediately winced with pain.

'Damned hip. The cross I bear. Do you know, Ludwig, I call myself a musician too. Violin. I play the violin. Competently too, if I might say so. Played it since I was a child. Can you guess why? No, of course you can't. Well, I'll tell you. Born with this damned hip, I was. Malformed, gave me a withered leg. See, it's shorter than the other one.' He tapped his foot with the crutch. 'Aches all the time. Always has, so I have to keep moving to exercise it. Trouble is, as a child, I kept bumping into things and knocking them over! So my father said, "Give the boy a violin. That'll tie him down." And it did!'

Ludwig laughed. He was drawn to Prince Lobkowitz by his open face. He also felt a curious envy of the Prince's physical disability. It was evident, there for all to see. The Prince had his crutch under his arm at all times and walked with an undisguised limp. People could see immediately that he was different from them.

That was how Ludwig so often felt. Different from any company he was with. He knew people found him difficult to talk to, awkward in his manners. He wanted to tell them that it was because he was different. But there was no physical evidence of it. That was why he had been teased so mercilessly at school; why even in his later years in Bonn there had been so few people he could really regard as close friends. Stephan Breuning, Wegeler, some of the musicians at court. But a brief spell attending lectures at the university, for instance, had brought him no new friends.

Respect, though, that was different. He knew he could command that, just by sitting at the piano. It was about to happen tonight. He knew he was going to win the contest; he was in no doubt about it. And everyone in the room, from the highest-born down, would respect him. But everyone, he knew, would regard him as a being apart. Not quite *normal*. And it pained him.

There was a sudden buzz of conversation from across the room. Ludwig turned and saw the tall figure of a man who could be only Abbé Gelinek. His head held higher than any other around him.

Ludwig looked at the Abbé and his mind raced back to the cold stone walls of the castle at Aschaffenberg, where he had met – and played for – Abbé Sterkel. Why did men of the church always look so similar? he wondered. Not just the long, flowing black robe and silver cross about the neck, but the same tall, thin, upright figure, the sharp nose set in an imperious face. Gelinek's hair was a lustrous brown, unlike the white mane of Sterkel, but it still hung long, covering his ears completely, the waves in it giving the impression that if the hair had not been cut, it would have flowed uninterrupted to the ground.

Swieten took Ludwig's arm. 'Let me introduce you,' he said quietly. 'Do not let his appearance intimidate you.'

Gelinek did not offer his hand but inclined his head slightly to acknowledge Ludwig. 'Reports of your skills have reached me, young man. I look forward to judging them for myself.'

Ludwig said nothing. Instead he looked at Gelinek's hands, which were clasped across his chest. They were long and slender, with slim fingers and perfectly manicured nails. The skin was smooth and pure white, as if without veins. They reminded

Ludwig of the kind of hands he had seen in Italian Renaissance paintings. He knew from looking at them exactly how Gelinek would play the piano.

Swieten looked quickly at both Gelinek and Ludwig, registered the nod from the Abbé, then clapped his hands.

'Ladies and gentlemen. Your Imperial Highnesses. Most honoured guests. May I welcome you to my salon. Your presence does more credit to my humble abode than I deserve. On behalf of His Imperial Highness Prince Kinsky and myself, we invite you this evening to judge the skills of two artists, two formidable artists, who are to demonstrate their powers on the piano for you.'

He turned to make sure Gelinek and Ludwig were standing close to him. 'One, of course, is already known to most of you. The Venerable Abbé Joseph Gelinek has had the honour of playing for you before, though not in my salon, and it gives me great pleasure to rectify that tonight. You will also hear this young man, whom I believe you do not know. His name is Ludwig van Beethoven, whose family, like mine, is of Flemish origin. He is descended from a distinguished line of musicians and until recently was a player at the court of His Grace the Elector Maximilian Franz – brother of our dear departed Emperor – in Bonn in the Rhineland, of which he is a native. His style . . . his manner of playing . . . you may find unlike what you are used to hearing. Suffice it to say in his recommendation that my good friend Joseph Haydn – a musician of the greatest distinction and without peer in our city – has gladly taken him on as a pupil, and speaks of him in the most glowing terms.'

There was polite applause. 'And now, Abbé, may I ask you to open proceedings. After we have heard from our artists, and you have been good enough to deliver your verdict, I will ask you all to adjourn to the dining room where you will find food and wine laid out.'

Gelinek walked to the piano and waited while the audience took their seats. He sat with his back absolutely straight, his head held high and his eyes closed. His hands lay on his thighs. He breathed deeply. After a few moments there was total silence. Still the Abbé held his position and did not move.

A full minute later he slowly extended his hands, held them for a moment over the keys, opened his eyes only very slightly, and began playing the familiar rising notes of the first prelude of Bach's Well-Tempered Klavier.

Ludwig gasped under his breath. It was exactly what he had intended playing. But he had never heard the piece performed in this way. Gelinek was racing through it at double speed, a furious pace. It was immediately obvious that the audience was delighted. Feet began tapping and heads nodding.

Ludwig wanted to shout at Gelinek to stop, that he was not playing the music in the way Bach intended. What he was doing had no other purpose than to show off his own virtuosity. Instead he smiled at his own naïveté. What other purpose was there, if not to demonstrate virtuosity? Bach's piece provided the perfect means to do so.

Ludwig was pleased Gelinek had gone to the piano first. He himself would have offered a perfect rendering of the prelude, but the audience would not have been particularly impressed. Gelinek slowed as the piece approached its end and he exaggerated the ornamental notes in the final bars. He lifted his hands a little above the keys and held them there until the notes had completely died away, before placing them again on his thighs and allowing the applause to sound.

He stood, acknowledged the applause with several nods of the head, and took his seat.

Ludwig walked to the piano, his coat flapping open, wondering what he should play. He decided on the ninth prelude, a short but virtuosic piece. Chords in the left hand, a *perpetuum mobile* of flying notes in the right. He played them slightly faster than he would otherwise have done. He paused only slightly over the double-handed arpeggio which brought the music to a stop, before a vigorous run in both hands and the chords that ended the piece.

The applause was polite and slightly more sustained than that for Gelinek, but that was only because the music was designed to elicit an enthusiastic response.

Gelinek walked slowly to the piano, sat, turned to the audience and said, 'I feel Herr Bach might have preferred to hear his prelude played so.'

He reached forward and played what Ludwig had played, only nearly twice as fast. His hands seemed barely to move, but his fingers flew across the keys until they were almost a blur. The applause, accompanied by one or two shouts of 'Bravo!', began before the final chords had finished.

He turned again to the audience. 'I now offer my young competitor this theme upon which to improvise. It is in the key of A major.' He played a short, bright sequence, a mixture of chords and several short runs.

He returned to his seat and Ludwig went to the piano. He looked at the keys for a few moments, reached his hands forward and began playing.

There was an immediate murmur in the audience. At first they thought Ludwig must have misheard what Gelinek had said and that he, in turn, was offering Gelinek a theme to improvise on. Then they realised that what they were hearing was indeed Gelinek's theme, but inverted and transposed to a new key. Ludwig was varying the theme without having first stated it!

He continued to improvise on the theme, expanding it, contracting it, in a variety of keys, one moment favouring the right hand, the next the left. Suddenly he played the theme in *fortissimo* minor chords, giving it a profundity it had not seemed capable of possessing. This he followed with a skeletal variation in which the theme was stripped almost to nothing. Notes which seemed to float in the air and disintegrate.

For a final variation, while he picked out the main notes of the theme in the bass, his right hand flew over the treble keys – even faster than Gelinek's had done in the Bach prelude – and in the last few bars he crossed his left hand over his right and played the closing chords of the variation in the high treble.

Finally he played – for the first time – the theme exactly as Gelinek had played it; only now he played it as a jaunty tune, simple and trite. His message was clear and understood immediately by the audience. The theme was banal, Ludwig was saying, yet I have made great music out of it.

Prince Lobkowitz was first to his feet, clapping and cheering, the crutch taking the weight of his body. Others took his lead and stood and applauded.

Ludwig turned to the audience, breathing heavily. 'This is the Presto from the second sonata I dedicated to the Elector Maximilian Friedrich.'

It was in the minor key, with furious runs in the right hand. He remembered as he played how the Elector had at first refused to believe that he – little more than a child – had composed it. Playing it now reminded him of Bonn, of all he had left behind. He closed his eyes, allowing his right hand to move over the keys, the sounds so familiar to him from his childhood.

He barely heard the renewed applause. With scarcely a pause

he played again. More gently this time, but every dilettante pianist in the audience understood the technical difficulty of what he was playing.

After the applause he said, 'That is the opening of the piano concerto I am writing. The piano opening. After an orchestral *tutti*.'

There was a gasp from the audience. A piano concerto! 'Bravo!' cried Lobkowitz, banging his crutch on the floor.

Abbé Gelinek stood and walked to the piano. Ludwig looked up at him. 'Forgive me. I . . . I . . . I must now give you a theme, is that right? For you to improvise on?'

Gelinek shook his head and turned to the audience. 'Gentlemen. Your Imperial Highnesses. Ladies. I wish to say a few words. You will forgive me if I do not play any more for you this evening. I have just heard playing which is in the highest degree astonishing. The theme I gave this young man, he has not heard before. No one has heard it before. Yet in his hands, it became . . . it became . . . Well, suffice it to say I was not aware I was capable of writing such an important theme!'

The audience laughed. 'In all humility,' he continued, 'I yield the evening to this young man. His name is Betthoffen. Were I not a religious man, I would say his playing was full of the very devil. And none the worse for it!'

Joseph Haydn was beside himself. He stood by the piano, hopping from one foot to the other, one hand on the piano frame to steady himself. He was smiling more broadly than Ludwig had ever seen.

Ludwig looked at his teacher and for the first time realised how small he was. Always he had perceived him as tall and thin. He was thin, certainly, but really quite small. His breeches were buckled below the knee and his hopping movements caused his calf muscles to bulge against the tight black stockings he was wearing. His wig, always so immaculately positioned, was slightly askew and some of the powder had dropped on to the dark velvet shoulders of his coat.

Ludwig was aware that he was looking at Europe's best-known and most respected composer, who was welcomed into not just the finest salons but royal drawing rooms too. Looking at him now he found him faintly absurd. It was not a feeling he had experienced before.

'Tell me, Ludwig. Tell me again. What did Gelinek say?'

'That I had the devil in me.'

'Hah! Yes, I know. Swieten told me. He told me everything. Ludwig, you made quite an impact.'

'Gelinek played in the old style. Pretty playing, but—'

'And I too am guilty of it, am I not?'

'I . . . I . . . I prefer to play more—'

'And quite right too, Ludwig. You are a new generation of musician. You must carry our art forward. Look at me. My life's work is done. Or the best of it, anyway. But in London they will be kind to me.'

'When do you leave?'

'A little over a month from now, and still the symphonies Salomon has demanded are not ready. Six! Six new symphonies for the audiences of London. Will I be a slave all my life?' he asked, smiling.

'I would like to go to London one day. I have heard they hold more concerts there than here in Vienna.'

Haydn nodded. 'And different. There are music-lovers in all levels of society. At a concert you will find a tradesman sitting next to a lord, or a . . . a . . . housekeeper next to a duchess. They are united by their love of music. Here concerts attract the same audiences all the time. Always upper class and wealthy, who want to be seen at the concert, who want people to know they have subscribed. But our music has not yet reached the levels of ordinary citizens.'

'The music I compose is for all people. All levels.'

'Ludwig. Take my advice. Develop your artistry on the piano. That way you will make your name, and earn a good living too. Compose, and you will be disappointed. Your music will be criticised and your name along with it. And if the music does not survive, your name will not survive either.'

Ludwig wanted to argue, to tell Haydn he was wrong; that he knew what his life's work was. That it was not to perform before an audience, but to create new music. Music that would endure beyond his lifetime. Music for all people, all mankind.

Instead he decided to broach a subject that had been on his mind for some time, but that the victory over Gelinek gave him the confidence to mention.

'Herr Haydn, I find myself short of money. After my father's death, the Elector's office stopped paying me that part of my father's pension that I used to receive. The amount I draw now is not enough to live on, with the rent I have to pay.'

'Ah, Ludwig, you are learning the first lesson of the artist. That a life of poverty lies ahead of you—'

'No.' There was a sharpness in Ludwig's voice that he had not used to his teacher before. 'I . . . I have established myself. I have proved myself. I believe the Elector should increase my salary.'

Haydn had not missed the tone of Ludwig's voice and looked at him, the smile now gone from his face. 'Ah, you young men. You have the confidence I lacked. If I had spoken like that of Prince Nikolaus . . . Well, what do you suggest? Will you write to His Grace?'

'Herr Haydn, I would like you to write to him for me. He will listen to you. Will you do that?'

'Times are hard for Maximilian Franz. I heard he had to leave Bonn for a second time. The court moved again to Münster, though it may be back in Bonn by now. You know his sister followed her husband to the guillotine? Poor Marie Antoinette. It is said her body was thrown into a common grave.'

'Herr Haydn, I want you to write to him for me.'

'You are a demanding young man, Ludwig. What shall I tell him? That you play the piano well? He already knows that. That you defeated Gelinek? He will want to hear more than that, if he listens at all.'

Ludwig took a pile of papers from his bag and put them on the table.

'I know that. Look. Here. Compositions. An oboe concerto. A quintet. A partita, for eight voices. Variations for the piano. A fugue.'

Haydn's eyes widened. 'But, Ludwig . . . I did not know . . . Why did you not tell me? You have been working hard, my boy. Very hard indeed.'

'These are proof. Will you tell the Elector that as well as playing the piano I am also composing, and that in your opinion I should receive an increase?'

'Well,' said Haydn steadily. 'Maybe. Maybe. Tell me, what is your salary now? You don't mind me asking?'

'Five hundred florins.'

Haydn raised his eyebrows. 'It is not much, I agree.' He clapped his hands. 'Here is what we will do. I will send these manuscripts to the Elector as proof of your industry and—'

'No! Just tell him. I want to keep them. I want to do more work on them.'

'I will have them copied. That way he will be able to read them! No, no, do not take offence. I will do as you ask, Ludwig.'

Chapter 4

Haydn's room was in disorder. There were bags on the floor, some with clothes spilling out. Papers were piled on the table in different folders. There was an unusual air of chaos in the room.

Ludwig looked quickly round. He was in buoyant mood. He had put the piano concerto he was working on to one side and had begun a major new composition, a trio for piano, violin and cello. He intended it to be on a scale unlike anything he had written before. Two trios; maybe even three. It was a similar combination of instruments to that which had attracted such criticism in Bonn. Then it had been a piano quartet. It had never been done, they said. They were wrong. They had not known Mozart himself was working on just such a combination at that very time, when Ludwig was composing his. A coincidence, but what a portentous one. Mozart and Beethoven, using the same unusual combination of instruments at the same time as each other . . .

Ludwig's good humour was compounded by his discovery that Prince Lichnowsky had arrived back in Vienna. He had seen the gilded coach outside the building in the Alstergasse. Servants were carrying boxes and cases through the double front door and up the stairs to the apartment which covered the entire first floor. He thought of the letter of introduction to the Prince from Count Waldstein. How pleased he was that the improvisation contest against Gelinek had happened before the Prince's return to Vienna. Someone would surely have told him about it – or would do soon.

He did not at first hear Haydn enter the room. When he turned Haydn was standing stock still, glowering at him.

'Ludwig, you have been less than honest with me. You have maltreated me. You have abused my . . . my . . . kindness towards you.'

Ludwig said nothing, but clamped his lips together. He looked at the floor.

'I have the reply His Grace sent to my letter,' Haydn continued. 'I must admit I was surprised he replied, given the awful problems that lie on his doorstep. But when I read his letter my surprise vanished. For you have abused his kindness too.'

Ludwig let out a sigh, but still he said nothing.

'Here, I shall not spare your blushes. Sit down. This is what His Grace has written. "The music of young Beethoven which you sent me I received with your letter. Since, however, this music, with the exception of the fugue, was composed and performed here in Bonn before he departed on his second journey to Vienna, I cannot regard it as progress made in Vienna."'

Haydn looked at Ludwig, who sat in a chair, his chin cupped in his hands. 'I'll continue. "As far as the allotment which he has had for his subsistence in Vienna is concerned, it does indeed amout to only five hundred florins. But in addition to this five hundred florins his salary here of four hundred florins has been continuously paid to him. Thus he receives nine hundred florins for the year. I cannot, therefore, very well see why he is as much in arrears in his finances as you say." And what he says next I know will affect you most. "I am wondering therefore whether he had not better come back here in order to resume his work. For I very much doubt that he has made any important progress in composition and in the development of his musical taste during his present stay, and I fear that, as in the case of his first journey to Vienna, he will bring back nothing but debts."'

Ludwig was now sitting bolt upright. 'I'm not going back. I can't. I won't.'

'You might have to. Otherwise what will you live on? If nine hundred florins a year is not enough for you?' Haydn's tone was unforgiving.

'I will publish my compositions. That will earn me money.'

'Very optimistic of you. But it may be your only hope. If you want my opinion, it is that if you do not return to Bonn, the Elector will stop your payments.'

'Why? He can't do that. It's my salary.'

'My dear Ludwig,' Haydn said, exasperation in his voice, 'you may consider yourself to be free of tutelage, free of the kind of serfdom I lived under for so many years. But you are still an employee of the Electoral court at Bonn. That is where you derive your income from. And the Elector has the right to do what he pleases with it.'

Ludwig felt the anger rise in him, but he suppressed it. He felt guilt that he had caused his teacher anguish, that he had embarrassed him. He wondered if he should apologise.

'I take it the Elector is not mistaken? About your compositions, I mean?'

Ludwig nodded. 'I . . . I'm sorry I have embarrassed you. It was not my intention.'

Haydn's face softened. 'You should not have done it, Ludwig. I had confidence in you. Trust in you. It was I who persuaded Baron Swieten to champion you in the improvisation contest. I did it because you are a remarkable musician. But you have repaid me with deceit.'

'I apologised,' said Ludwig, regretting the sharpness in his voice, but not adjusting it. 'The Elector . . . I . . . I felt I was justified in asking what I did. I just shouldn't have pretended the compositions were new. But he should not have reacted the way he did.'

Haydn shook his head. 'You have a lot to learn, Ludwig, about how to handle people. And like it or not, as a musician you will have to learn. You cannot exist in isolation. Now I must ask you to leave. I have a lot of preparation to do. And packing. I leave for London in a matter of days.'

Ludwig stood, his mood dampened utterly from the euphoria he felt earlier.

'I was not going to mention this, Ludwig. But it might help you to understand how the effect of your actions can be detrimental to yourself as well as to others. It was my intention to take you to London with me. I feel I cannot do that now. I'm not sure how long I will be away. Several months at least. I will look for signs of progress on my return. Assuming you have not returned to Bonn.'

There was a knock on Ludwig's door, and he opened it to find the landlord, Wenzel Glaser, standing there, dressed in his black houserobe. Ludwig's face sank as he looked into the long, sour face of the man who had condemned him to a small attic room and who had tossed his head sceptically every time Ludwig had mentioned the name of Prince Lichnowsky.

'The rent. Yes, I shall . . .'

'Herr Beethoven, I am commanded by His Imperial Highness

the Prince Lichnowsky to bid you come to his apartment on the first floor of this building at the hour of eleven this morning.' Then, in an entirely different voice, the one Ludwig was more used to hearing, he snapped, 'And I suggest you make yourself as respectable as possible, which probably isn't saying very much.' And he turned on his heel and walked away.

Ludwig tried to drag a wide-toothed comb through his hair but gave up the task, throwing it down in disgust. Cursorily brushing the sleeves of his jacket with his hands, he slammed the door to his room and descended the stairs to the first floor. Long before he reached the ornate door into the Lichnowsky apartment, he heard the piano. Pausing outside the door he listened intently. He recognised the Clementi sonata, and judged by its gentleness that it was played by a woman's hands. He waited for the playing to stop and lifted his hand to knock. Changing his mind, he turned the handle, pushed against the heavy door and entered the apartment.

For a moment he remained still, allowing his eyes to rove over the sumptuous interior: heavy brocade curtains hung from the ceiling to the floor, gathered back to reveal full-length windows with ornate wrought-iron balconies beyond; portraits hung on the walls; the furniture was gilt-topped and clearly in the French style, if not actually from Paris; thick rugs with Chinese designs covered the polished wood floor. And in the far corner of the room stood the most beautiful piano Ludwig had seen. At it a woman was seated. She had a fine alert face, which showed the concentration with which she was playing. She was dressed richly, her hair piled high. Rows of pearls hung round her neck, and precious stones sparkled on her ear lobes.

Suddenly she looked up. 'Who . . . who . . . ?'

'Beethoven. Ludwig van Beethoven.'

It took a few seconds for the name to register. Then it was Ludwig's turn to recoil slightly as the Princess flung her arms in the air, emitted a cry and came striding across the room to him.

'You poor, poor boy!' she cried, throwing her arms round him and pulling his untidy head to the jewel-encrusted bodice of her dress. 'There, there. Do not upset yourself.' And she rocked him gently. 'Now,' she said, taking him by the shoulders and holding him at arm's length, 'let me look at you. So you are young Ludwig von Beethoven.'

'Van.'

'So different. So different from my divine Wolfgang. Ah, how

I miss him. Dear Wolfi. But they say you are as fine a musician. Is it possible? Goodness, your hair. You must let me do something. And this jacket. Oh, you poor, poor boy. Come, you must let me look after you, you must let me be a mother to you. So far from home, and parents both dead. Oh, life can be so cruel. So cruel.'

As she uttered the last words a door closed sharply.

'Ludwig von Beethoven. Ludwig von Beethoven!' The deep voice intoned the words as if to accustom itself to the sounds the name made. Ludwig winced, not just at the incorrect prefix, but at hearing his name pronounced again with the stress on the second syllable: 'Beet*hov*en'. It was not the first time he had heard it pronounced this way since his arrival in Vienna. At first he had tried to correct it to the familiar pronunciation he had grown up with, the stress on the first syllable. But it seemed this was how the Viennese pronounced his name, and he would have to become accustomed to it. Unconsciously, Ludwig squared his shoulders just a little and turned to face Prince Karl Lichnowsky.

The Prince was a man approaching his fortieth year, of tall stature and regal bearing. His thinning hair was brushed forward, framing a large, angular face with a prominent, albeit uneven nose. He had full lips and sensitive, surprisingly kindly eyes. He was dressed in the most expensive attire, his velvet frockcoat perfectly brushed; a white upturned collar seemed to support his jowls; a white cravat was knotted at the neck. His beige waistcoat strained slightly where it covered his full stomach; his breeches were tucked neatly into white stockings and his black shoes were set off by sparkling silver buckles. He stood with his hands behind him, tucked underneath the tails of his coat.

Ludwig stood fixed to the spot, straining to overcome his fear at the sight of this formidable aristocrat. Sensing Ludwig's discomfort, the Prince smiled and held out his arms. 'Come. Shake my hand. Let us be friends.' Still Ludwig did not move. With an audible chuckle, Prince Lichnowsky walked across to the young composer, shook his hand, then guided him by the shoulders to a sofa. The Princess sat alongside him, the Prince in a high-backed chair opposite.

'Well, young man,' said the Prince, 'it is a privilege and honour to meet you. Your fame has spread before you. I have heard from the good Baron Swieten of your prodigious talent. Prince Lobkowitz too. You have certainly made your mark with him.'

Ludwig said, 'I have a letter here for you from Count

Waldstein.' He passed the letter he had guarded so carefully to the Prince.

'Hah! My old friend. It has been years. Is he well?'

Ludwig nodded.

The Prince read the letter. 'I will not reveal its contents to you, young man. You would surely blush. I have to tell you, your name is being talked of in the best salons of the city. It is even gaining some currency in the walls of the Hofburg itself. You have Herr Haydn to thank in large measure.'

'I am grateful to him.'

'And the business with Gelinek!' Lichnowsky laughed out loud. 'The whole of Vienna is still talking about it. How the proud Abbé was pulled down a peg by the untidy country boy from the Rhine!' He laughed out loud again and then drew in his breath sharply. 'Oh, my dear Beethoven. I am so sorry. I had not meant to be rude. Will you forgive me?'

Ludwig nodded, but said nothing. The Princess spoke. 'You know, Ludwig, we were aware of you even before you came to Vienna. Word had travelled. Already some of your compositions are well known.'

'Indeed they are,' the Prince said. 'My dear, why don't you . . . ?'

The Princess rose swiftly from her chair and swept across the room, holding her long dress clear of the ground. 'I do hope you approve of my playing, Ludwig.'

Ludwig nodded, a smile on his face.

The Princess sat at the piano and from memory gave a perfect rendition of the piano part of the 'Se Vuol Ballare' variations, the piece for piano and violin on the aria from *The Marriage of Figaro*, which Ludwig had told Mozart himself he intended writing.

At the last flourish, the Prince applauded lightly, his arms held out in front of him and just the tips of his fingers meeting. 'Such a devilish difficult piece to play, and there it was, not a note out of place. I must say, er, Ludwig, I have tried many times to play that piece, but it is beyond me. For me, well, there is an earlier piece of yours that I greatly admire.'

As the Princess returned to her chair, her cheeks flushed and gently rubbing her hands in front of her, the Prince walked to the piano, his heavy step contrasting with the lightness of his wife's. At the piano he leafed through a pile of manuscripts and extracted the one he was seeking.

'Here now,' and he read from the elaborately printed title

page, '"Three Sonatas for Pianoforte, dedicated to the Most Worthy Archbishop and Prince Elector of Cologne, Maximilian Friedrich, my Most Gracious Lord. Composed by Ludwig van Beethoven, eleven years old." Eleven years old, by Jove! Well, I shall play just the first one.' He sat, pushing the chair a little further from the instrument, opened the manuscript, and peering intently at it, his eyes slightly screwed up, he played.

Ludwig sat entranced, a half-smile on his face as he heard the notes he had composed more than a decade before. Delicate, gentle notes in the treble clef over an easy, throbbing bass line. So like Mozart's music, he thought, realising in the same instant how greatly his compositional style had developed since those youthful days in Bonn.

'We must introduce you to some of our dearest friends who are musicians,' said the Prince, as he brought the piece to a gentle close. 'Have you met Schuppanzigh?'

Ludwig shook his head. 'I don't think so.'

'Well, if you had you would not have forgotten it. A stouter, fatter man you will not find in the whole of Vienna!' he said, laughing. 'But what a fine violinist. He makes the instrument sing. He is my quartet leader.'

'Your . . . your quartet . . . ?'

'Yes. I have my own quartet. Every Friday I hold a matinée here in my apartment. Or I did before we went away to our country estate, and I intend starting again. My quartet plays, with Schuppanzigh on first violin. Kraft is the cellist. Anton Kraft. Charming chap. Tall and thin. Schuppi and Anton, fat and thin. But what music! You must play too at a matinée. I do hope you will.'

'No, dear, do not be too insistent. You must not impose your will on this poor young man. Do forgive him, Ludwig. He gets carried away with his love for music.'

Ludwig smiled. 'I would be . . . One day, when I—'

Suddenly the Princess stood. 'Come, Karl, let us show Ludwig his apartment.'

The Prince at first looked bemused, but then said, 'Ah, yes. What a splendid idea, my dear. Come, Ludwig. Come with us.'

The Prince and Princess, among the highest-born of the Viennese aristocracy, into whose home there came usually only those of a similar status or those commanded to be there, took this ill-dressed and awkward young Rhinelander and walked him to an imposing set of double doors. These they threw open to reveal a sizeable salon, adequately albeit not abundantly furnished. Off it was a smaller room, with a bed, several chairs, a table and a washstand.

Entering the salon the Prince said, 'This will be your apartment, Ludwig. My wife and I have to leave Vienna again, unfortunately, but not for long. When we return I will arrange for Glaser to move your things here. I will not expect payment. I will ask only that you play a part in my Friday musical matinées. And get rid of your old piano. You shall have a new one.'

The Prince's offer was timely. Ludwig's head was full of music as he walked past the Burgtheater and under the huge arch at the entrance to the Hofburg palace in the Michaelerplatz. Work on the piano trios was going well. He had not finally decided, but he wanted them to form his Opus Number One. There would be three, a substantial work and worthy of bearing his first opus number.

But that was not the composition he carried now under his arm. He had completed a string trio, in no fewer than six movements. Sketches had been made some years before, back in Bonn, but after the humiliation of the Elector's reply to Haydn's letter, Ludwig had worked on it furiously. A six-movement string trio! What better proof of his industry? With the piano trios well advanced – and he had resumed serious work on a piano concerto as well as making sketches for a set of piano sonatas – the Elector would surely then agree to increase his salary.

He turned left under the Schweizertor, pushed open a heavy wooden door, climbed the staircase to the first floor, knocked on a door bearing the Electoral shield and the words 'Exchequer of the Electorate and Archbishopric of Cologne and Münster', and entered.

'I've come to collect my salary. It's due now. Beethoven. And I want to send this manuscript to the Elector.'

The clerk continued shuffling the papers in front of him for a few moments, then opened a drawer to his right and wordlessly put a sheet of paper in front of Ludwig.

'This isn't what I normally . . . I just sign a receipt and take it to the cashier's desk.'

'Read it. The payments have been stopped.'

Ludwig saw the Elector's seal on the document.

'But I wasn't told. Why wasn't I . . . ?'

The clerk looked up. 'You weren't? I'm surprised. The

Elector himself was here earlier in the year and made the decision then. But we've only just received the paperwork from Bonn.'

'But could there be a mistake? I'm sure he wouldn't—'

'Listen, young man. It may have escaped your attention, but we are at war with the French. Our homeland – yours and mine – has been overrun by French soldiers. All able-bodied young men are being put into uniform to join the imperial army. That's why you have to go back. To fight the French.'

'I am a musician. I—'

'As for His Grace, he has twice been forced to leave Bonn. It's likely he will have to leave soon for good. So you can understand the question of your salary is not uppermost in his mind.'

'Can I not draw one last payment? The one due now? I expected it. I—'

'Read what it says,' the clerk said, irritation creeping into his voice. 'No further payments.'

'Could you send this to the Elector? It's important.'

'Important, is it? Is it to do with the war? The deployment of soldiers? The supply of weapons to the front?' The clerk took the manuscript and looked at it. 'Music. A piece of music.'

Ludwig was about to snatch it back when he saw the clerk's face suddenly soften.

'Music. Ah, yes. When will we ever have time again to listen to it?' He looked up at Ludwig. 'Listen, Herr Beethoven, I'm sorry for how it has worked out. I can tell you this. The Elector spoke very highly of you while he was here. He regretted having to stop your payments. I, too, have heard some of your music and I admire it greatly.' He leaned forward. 'Take my advice. Do not fight this. It is impossible. We are at war. But do not go back, or you will find yourself exchanging your piano for a musket. And I will send this,' he added, waving the manuscript. 'I can't guarantee it'll get through, but I'll send it anyway.'

Everywhere the talk was of the war against the French. The humiliation of the defeat at Jemappes had faded. Austria was no longer facing the revolutionary army on its own; Britain and Prussia had pledged support, though for the moment it was Austrian soldiers in the front line. Some months before, the British had suffered a humiliation of their own. They had been forced to evacuate their fleet from the impregnable southern French port of Toulon. And now a new name was on British lips – and being talked of by officers in Vienna – that of a young French artillery major who had secured victory at Toulon against apparently impossible strategic odds: a Corsican by the name of Napoleon Bonaparte.

Another word was on people's lips. The terror of the Guillotine had spread. With horror the people of Vienna had learned of dozens, then hundreds, then thousands of people climbing the steps to come under the blade.

Aristocrats at first, men and women; then it seemed anyone who had made a success of their lives, anyone who had wealth, however it had been acquired. The Viennese had grieved for the French Queen, but her memory had faded as the numbers which followed her grew inexorably.

Ludwig was concerned for his homeland. The words of the clerk at the Electoral office had saddened him – not just because he was now without a salary, but because the Rhineland had been taken over by the French.

He wondered about Bonn; his brothers Caspar and Nikola. Were they safe? What of the Breuning family and Franz Wegeler? And Franz Ries and his family? Even if he wanted to, there was now no prospect of him returning home. The journey alone would be unsafe, and the prospect of joining the army . . .

A small item at the bottom of a newssheet had caught his eye.

Many flee in the German lands from the advancing French. They travel south or east, relying on the imperial forces to prevent their pursuit by the French. We grieve with them for their homeland.

It made Ludwig sad to think of the turmoil back in the Rhineland. But he was in Vienna now. He was Viennese. He could share in the pride of the Viennese that they were part of a grand coalition that would restore peace to Europe; that they lived in the capital of the great Habsburg Empire, the thousand-year dynasty that nothing could destroy – certainly not a murderous rabble from the land to the west of the Rhine.

On the Bastion, the great city wall now used as a promenade by the Viennese, Ludwig mingled with the strollers. And like them, in the early-summer morning, he walked across the city to the great public park, the Augarten, to indulge in the city's favourite cultural pursuit, music.

When, some years back, word had first reached Bonn that in

Vienna in the summer months concerts began at six o'clock in the morning, the court musicians had not believed it. But it was true. Wolfgang Mozart himself had played at them. Twelve in number, to run through the summer on Thursdays, they quickly established themselves not solely as an opportunity to begin the day with music, but as an essential meeting-place for the city's wealthy to gather and exchange news.

For Ludwig the Augarten concerts were the most overt proof of the love of the Viennese – its aristocracy at least – for music.

The sun was already rising over the flat Hungarian plains to the east of the city when Ludwig walked across the Augarten bridge over the Danube Arm. He could already hear the bright sound of the music on the clear, cool air.

Six o'clock on a summer's morning, and already the city was bathed in the sounds of music! Ludwig's step lightened and his heart quickened. He recognised the notes immediately. The overture to Christoph Gluck's opera *Alceste*.

Christoph Gluck, Ludwig thought, a musician I would like to have met. A German, who chose to come and live in Vienna, like me; who, the story goes, insulted the King of France while dining at the home in Paris of a duke – just as I insulted the Elector Maximilian Friedrich by refusing to play for him . . . Dead these last six years, a composer whose operas might have been the greatest heard had it not been for *The Marriage of Figaro*, *The Magic Flute*, *Don Giovanni* . . .

Ludwig passed under the ornamental gate at the entrance to the park. 'To All Men This Place Is Dedicated By Their Protector' read the round, embossed shield above his head. A royal garden, given to the people by the late Emperor Joseph. Tasting summer on the air, he walked along the Lindenallee, the path lined with tall, thin linden trees, their tops trained to meet high above in an arch of foliage. And at the end of the path the low, wide garden pavilion, built on the ruins of the old palace destroyed a century before by the Turks.

Outside stood groups of people; others sat at round tables drinking steaming coffee. Children played together, heeding their parents' occasional admonitions to make less noise. The music flowed out of the tall open windows.

Ludwig walked into the pavilion. There was a low buzz of conversation, the air redolent with the aroma of coffee and sweet cakes. The small orchestra sat on a raised platform at one end of the room.

Ludwig smiled, despite his instincts which inclined towards irritation. Here was music being well played by competent musicians, and the audience was more intent on eating breakfast and discussing, no doubt, the latest developments in the war against France!

The men were mostly dressed in military uniform, their great cockaded bicorn hats either held stiffly under their arms or placed ostentatiously on the table. The women wore long hooped dresses, one hand poised on a brightly decorated parasol; they sported the latest hair fashions, butterfly wings currently the most popular.

He looked at the orchestra. It was small, just eight players: two violins, two cellos, a single double bass, clarinet, flute and horn. It was led by the first violin, who sat upright in his chair, his head nodding the beat for the other players to follow.

Ludwig walked along the side wall, found an empty chair and sat and listened to the musicians. They were competent. They played fluently and easily. But there was something missing. Dynamics. There was no variation in loudness and softness. That was why their playing never really engaged the attention; that was why people were content to hear with one ear while listening to conversation with the other. It will not be that way with my music, Ludwig thought. My music will demand total concentration on the part of the players, and the audience will recognise that and do likewise.

He looked at the lead violinist. He admired the way his fingers moved so lightly up and down the strings, the way his bow touched the strings in perfect coordination with his fingers. It was all the more remarkable given the corpulence of the man. His sheer girth made the violin look like a toy in his hands, and gave the impression he would be heavy-handed, ponderous in his playing. But he was the opposite. He was a fine musician.

Ludwig knew who he was. Ignaz Schuppanzigh, the leader of Prince Lichnowsky's string quartet. Just from looking at him Ludwig knew he would like him. He waited for the music to stop and the musicians to leave the platform for a short break, their heads nodding in recognition of the sprinkling of applause, and he walked towards them.

'Herr Schuppanzigh. I'm Beethoven. Ludwig van Beethoven. Prince—'

'Beethoven! At last we meet. Word has spread. I have heard about you.' His face, already smiling, suddenly lit up with enthusiasm. 'You must play for us. Today. Now. The audience would be thrilled.'

'No, no. Really. I . . . Anyway,' Ludwig said, looking round with relief in his voice, 'there is no piano.'

Schuppanzigh, just as suddenly despondent, said, 'Yes, you're right. But another time. Do you promise?'

Ludwig smiled and nodded. 'Prince Lichnowsky is giving me rooms in his apartment. When he returns to Vienna.'

'Ha! Then you are honoured. He is back very soon. He wrote to me. He says he wants to start his Friday matinées again and told me to start work on them.'

'I promised I would play at them. In return for the rooms.'

'Capital. Capital. First class. Then we shall meet again before long. And I will introduce you to Kraft and the others. We've all heard about you, you know.' He leaned forward and spoke with a conspiratorial smile. 'Poor old Gelinek. He speaks very highly of you, though, I can assure you. Excellent. Now do excuse me. Back to entertaining this discerning and attentive crowd! Herr . . .'

'Ludwig.'

'. . . Ludwig. Ignaz. Delighted again.'

Walking back across the city, Ludwig reflected on his good fortune. He had been in Vienna for less than two years, and already he had established himself as a pianist of repute, even if his compositions were not yet known. And now he was about to move into rooms in the sumptuous apartment of the city's most senior patron of the arts.

Most important of all, he was meeting musical patrons and musicians, moving in musical circles, talking of music. It was what he had dreamed of back in Bonn: to be rid of family worries and constraints and concentrate on the one pursuit that really mattered. One day he would return to Bonn and see his brothers again. For now the freedom to live the life of a musician was all he had ever sought; and it was his.

Soon after he returned to his rooms, there was a knock on the door. He opened it to find Wenzel Glaser standing there.

'Herr Beethoven,' he said, bowing his head slightly and adopting a deferential tone of voice that he had used since learning that Ludwig was to move into the Lichnowsky apartment. 'A gentleman came to see you. He said he would return at noon. Your brother, sir. Herr Carl Beethoven.'

BOOK SEVEN

Chapter 1

The small group of young men sat round a table in a corner of the inn Zum Weissen Schwan, the White Swan, in the Schwangasse, a narrow street which linked the Neuer Markt to the busy Kärntnerstrasse. A cloud of tobacco smoke hung below the ceiling, from the pipes ready stuffed with tobacco which some drinkers ordered with their beer.

The table, on which stood a mixture of wine goblets and beer mugs, set the men away from the main body of customers. It was intentional. The men were Rhinelanders, their accents and appearance – less formal, more colourful clothes – immediately identifying them as non-Viennese. They kept their voices low, so as not to draw attention to themselves; but it was not easy, given the story one of their number had to tell.

'But in your position, rector of the university, surely you were safe?'

'That's exactly the point. It was my position that made me unsafe. They're suspicious of anyone with authority, anyone with a title to their name,' said Doktor Franz Wegeler.

'But you upset them too, didn't you? I heard you did something that made them angry.'

Wegeler nodded. 'It was so ridiculous. The Academic Senate passed a unanimous resolution to forbid the medical students from going to see any of the French soldiers taken prisoner at Quesnoi and Landrecies. The students wanted to go to examine their wounds – also,' he said, leaning forward and lowering his voice, 'although it was never said so, to get a new supply of fresh cadavers to dissect. But the Senate was worried about the spread of hospital fever. Quite reasonably, in my view. So I signed the decree.'

'Why were they so worried?'

'Ah, Andreas,' said Wegeler, 'you've come from Augsburg. So far from all the fighting. You can't know what it's like in

Bonn and the Rhineland. French soldiers everywhere, and with all the fighting, the wounded, disease is spreading fast. In Bonn people have been dying in the streets. It's dreadful.'

Andreas Streicher shook his head. 'I had no idea it was that bad. Nor did Nanette. She'll be upset when I tell her.'

'How is Nanette?' asked Ludwig van Beethoven. 'It's so long since I saw her.'

'I know. She says she hasn't seen you since before we were married. She often talks about when you came to Augsburg and met her family. Do come and see us. We're in the Landstrasse suburb beyond the Stubentor gate. I'd like you to see some of the pianos I'm working on.'

Ludwig nodded. 'I will. I will.'

'But, Wegeler, why were the French so upset? You were telling us,' said Carl Beethoven impatiently.

'Somehow or other a revolutionary newssheet in Paris called the *Moniteur* heard about this decree and published it. They interpreted it as German doctors refusing to treat wounded French soldiers who, they said, were guardians of the revolution. And they branded all of us as enemies of the Republic. Because my signature was at the bottom of the decree, they mentioned me by name and ordered my immediate arrest.'

There was a collective exclamation of surprise around the table and heads shook in disbelief.

'One of my students who has a relative in Paris heard about this and warned me. He said it was only a matter of time before the People's Representative – as he is called – in Bonn acted on the order. He said that although the worst of the dreadful guillotining was now over, it still wasn't safe. In Paris or anywhere.'

'I thought all that was finished.'

'So did I. But they're saying in Paris that the head of that vile man Robespierre is just as dangerous now as it was when it was still attached to his body. There's still fear everywhere. Even in Bonn all they have to do is mention the word "guillotine" and it seems they can get what they like.'

There were a few moments' silence while the group contemplated the horrors that had befallen their homeland. They drank gloomily.

Ludwig was the first to speak. 'How are the Breunings? What news of them?'

'Fine. Fine. Frau Breuning still keeps the most elegant salon in the city. The People's Representative said there was no more aristocracy, in France or Germany, and nobody was to behave as if there were. Frau Breuning simply ignored this. So did her servants. They continue as usual.'

'And Steffen? And Eleonore?'

'All well, and asked to be remembered to you. Steffen might be moving soon to Mergentheim to take up an appointment with the Teutonic Order.'

Ludwig smiled as he remembered his trip with the court orchestra.

Streicher drained his beer mug and stood. 'Forgive me, friends. Work calls. I will see you all soon.'

'Yes,' said Wegeler, 'I must go too.'

'Can I walk with you?' asked Ludwig. 'I would like to talk to you.'

'Of course. I'm going to the university medical school. Is that . . . ?'

'Yes, yes. It doesn't matter. As long as I can talk.'

There were more farewells and Ludwig and Wegeler left together.

'Well, Ludwig, from what I hear you are moving in high circles.'

Ludwig nodded.

'How's Carl settling in?'

'Hmm. I still can't get used to that name. He's still Caspar to me.'

'Why has he insisted on using his middle name?'

Ludwig shrugged. 'He says coming to Vienna is a new start for him.'

'What's he doing?'

'He's giving piano lessons. He earns a bit of money from it. And he's dealing with publishers for me. Contracts. At least it leaves me free to concentrate on my music.'

'Keep an eye on things, though. He upsets people easily. His manner is . . . offputting.'

'Let's stop for a moment. Here. Sit for a few minutes.'

The two men climbed the narrow steps and sat on the edge of the fountain in the middle of the Neuer Markt, among the lead figures surrounding it. Ludwig slapped the naked backside of the largest figure, a full-sized statue of a man bestriding the rim.

'Some Viennese have a sense of humour. The sculptor placed this figure so his backside faced the home of a man who owed him money. That house there.' He pointed and both men laughed.

In the silence that followed the laughter, Wegeler said, 'Eleonore sends you her best wishes. She asks after the waist-coat.'

Ludwig smiled. 'Tell her I have worn it so often it is almost in threads. And tell her I am still sorry for missing her lessons.'

'I will,' said Wegeler, laughing. 'Ludwig. I have some happy news. Lorchen and I are to become engaged.'

Ludwig clapped his old friend on the shoulder. 'I am pleased for you, Franz. You are marrying into a good family.'

'Thank you for saying that.'

'I still remember the day you took me to their house on the Münsterplatz for the first time. I was so nervous.'

Wegeler laughed. 'Ludwig, do you mind if we walk? I have to be at the university in ten minutes.'

The two men stood and walked towards the top of the square.

Wegeler said, 'Did you hear about young Ferdi Ries?'

'No. What?'

'Tragic. He was struck down with smallpox. It must have been soon after you left. He seemed to be recovering well, but then it attacked his left eye. Try as we might, nothing seemed to arrest it. Finally he lost the sight in that eye. So sad. And he's little more than a child. Eleven or twelve, that's all.'

Ludwig shook his head. 'That's sad. Poor boy. I had smallpox as a child. I know the misery. Franz, may I mention something to you about my own health? I am suffering dreadfully from stomach pains. Is there anything . . . ?'

'When did it start? Is it recent?'

'Yes. And it seems to be connected with . . . I was told a week ago by Prince Lichnowsky that I am to play in public for the first time. At a concert. Not a soirée in a salon, but a concert in the Burgtheater. I can play my own composition, my first piano concerto . . .'

'But that's wonderful, Ludwig. Congratulations. You must be—'

'But ever since he told me, I have been struck with this dreadful pain in my stomach and my bowels give me problems. I can't work. The concerto is not completed. I still have the Rondo to write. I am not going to be able to—'

'It is just nervousness, Ludwig. Nothing more. I am sure of

it. I will bring you some powders to take. They will relieve the pain.'

Ludwig stopped walking and took his old friend's arm, turning him to face him.

'Franz, this is the first time I have had this sort of problem. Will it always happen before an important performance?'

'No, Ludwig. I can assure you it will not. You are a robust young man. You have a long and healthy life ahead of you.'

The pains did not improve despite the powders. Ludwig tried to work on the piano concerto but the ideas revolving in his head seemed to collide with each other. He could not cut through them to find what he wanted, and the reason was the debilitating pains in his stomach – unpredictable and sharp.

Prince Lichnowsky was concerned for him. With only two days to go, the Rondo was not yet completed. He knew how important the occasion was. The concert, on 29 March, was organised by the Musicians' Society for the benefit of its members' widows and orphans. The audience, therefore, consisting not just of family members but also the committee of the Society and its guests, was one which understood and appreciated music. Its verdict on the young musician from Bonn would be crucial to his future. The music critic of the *Wiener Zeitung* would also be there.

The Prince saw how distressed Ludwig was and discussed with Wegeler if there was anything more he could do for him.

'Well I'll get the copyists to come here to the apartment to take some of the workload off him. At least when he does write something they'll be able to start work on it right away. And it will avoid the correction stage.'

Lichnowsky contacted Vienna's foremost copyist, Wenzel Schlemmer, and asked him to provide four copyists to come and work at the apartment. They sat patiently in the anteroom while Ludwig passed each sheet to them as soon as he completed it.

Clenching his teeth against the pain, and obediently taking the powders Wegeler regularly administered to him, Ludwig finished the last movement of the concerto in the early hours of the morning of the twenty-eighth – leaving just one day for rehearsal.

Tired from the monumental effort – in fact, Wegeler believed, on the verge of exhaustion – Ludwig was in no frame of mind to receive an unexpected visitor on the morning of the final day. Lichnowsky, in fact, tried to send her away, agreeing finally, when his servant assured him that Ludwig was up and dressed, to send in her card.

Despite his tiredness Ludwig hurried from his room, still plastering down his wet, unruly hair with the palms of his hands.

'Frau Mozart. I am honoured that you have come to see me.'

Constanze Mozart still had a lively and pretty face, framed with ringlets which were not quite as lustrously dark as when Ludwig had seen her last.

Lichnowsky and Wegeler bowed to her and left the room. Ludwig guided her to a chair.

'Are you in good health? Do you—?'

'I am, young man, and I thank you for asking.'

'I . . . I . . . your husband, Herr Mozart. I played for him once.'

'I remember it well. And it is the reason I am here. First, I owe you an apology. Long overdue. I was impolite to you when you came to see Wolfi.'

'You said my name was harsh. It did not have . . . it would not be great.'

'And you must forgive me. It was just . . . When I heard it, it made me think of a garden of beet growing . . .'

Ludwig winced to hear what he had not heard since his schooldays. But when he saw the genuine and contrite smile on Constanze's face, he smiled with her.

'I did not take offence, Frau Mozart.'

'That is good. Do you remember what my husband said about you? That you would give the world something to talk about? And I disagreed.'

Ludwig nodded. 'I have never forgotten what he said.'

'From what I hear, it is already beginning to be true. Süssmayr told me about the contest between you and Abbé Gelinek.' She chuckled. 'I don't know who he heard it from, but he said he would have given anything to be there.'

'It . . . it was nothing. Your husband would have done better. Is Herr Süssmayr well?'

Constanze nodded. 'But hurt by the criticism of the work he did on Wolfi's Requiem. Particularly by that awful man Salieri. He was always jealous of Wolfi anyway. He knew he was a better musician. I am grateful to Süssmayr for finishing the Requiem. It is what Wolfi would have wanted.'

Ludwig nodded. 'No one could have done better.'

'Now, let me tell you why I have come to see you. On the thirty-first, three days from now, I am arranging a performance of Wolfi's opera *La Clemenza di Tito*. It is the one Süssmayr helped him with. He wrote the recitatives. It will be in the Burgtheater. At the end of part one, I would like you to play his Piano Concerto in D minor. In memory of him. Would you do that? You do know the one I mean?'

Ludwig nodded again. 'I have written a cadenza for it. But it is too soon, Frau Mozart. Tomorrow I play my own piano concerto, also at the Burgtheater. There will be no time to rehearse it.'

'Oh, Ludwig, I know my husband would have wanted it. He admired you. He talked about you after you had left. He said what a tragedy it was you had had to return home so suddenly. He was looking forward to teaching you.'

'He spoke about me?'

'He most certainly did. He said, "At last, a pianist who wants to compose." He was impressed that you did not just want to entertain people with fireworks on the keyboard.'

'He gave me advice I have never forgotten. And never will. That great music is built with simple themes. It is what the composer does with those themes which makes the music great. Poor composers write complicated themes.'

'Well, he was as sad as you were that you couldn't stay in Vienna. You will play the concerto, won't you?'

'Of course, Frau Mozart. It will be an honour.'

Prince Lichnowsky invited all the musicians to his salon and provided food and drink. The sumptuous surroundings, not to mention the abundant refreshments, contributed to a general atmosphere of bonhomie. The Prince knew there had been some murmurings among the orchestral players – the wind in particular – about the difficulty of some passages, but there was no evidence of it when they settled down at their music stands to rehearse.

At the first note of the piano's solo entry a cry of despair went up from the orchestra. Ludwig glared disbelievingly at the keys in front of him. Then he struck the A key and the instrumentalists played A to tune their instruments.

A ghastly discord sounded. Ludwig struck the key harder, as

if to will it into tune. It was clear to everyone that the piano was tuned a semitone flat.

Prince Lichnowsky fussed around the instrument, wringing his hands.

'I don't understand it. It was tuned . . . Oh dear, what are we going to do? Ludwig, I do apologise, I . . .'

Ludwig stood and addressed the orchestral players. 'Retune your instruments to B flat. I will transpose the piano part up a semitone to C sharp.'

Noisily the players did as Ludwig asked, while he played a few runs in the new key.

The rehearsal began again, and to the surprise of everyone present – and the incalculable relief of Prince Lichnowsky – proceeded satisfactorily.

Only the first tier of boxes in the Burgtheater was reserved on the night of the concert for the committee of the Musicians' Society and its guests. The rest of the auditorium, normally divided strictly according to class, was available equally to all members of the Society and their families. It was the only occasion of the year when these ordinary members of the public – through their musical connections – could sit in the second and third tier of boxes and the centre stalls, and there was a buzz of anticipation in the hall.

In the centre box of the first tier – normally reserved for the Emperor and his family – the cream of Vienna's aristocratic patrons of music mingled. Prince and Princess Lichnowsky, the senior among them, moved easily through the group, the Prince giving his opinion on the progress of the war with France and soliciting others' views; the Princess lamenting with the ladies how the wretched state of affairs in France had put an end – temporarily, she trusted – to the export to Vienna of the latest Paris fashions.

Baron Swieten was listening to an animated Prince Lobkowitz, who banged the floor with his crutch to emphasise his point. They were joined by a tall, elegantly dressed man wearing distinctive jewel-encrusted star-shaped brooches on the left side of his tunic. This was Count Andreas Kyrillovitch Razumovsky, Russian ambassador to the imperial court, a music-lover and like Prince Lobkowitz an accomplished violinist.

'So, Prince, is the rumour I hear true? That you are considering establishing your own orchestra?'

'I am. I am.' Lobkowitz nodded firmly and banged his crutch again. 'To give concerts at my palace. But don't go and talk to my good wife about it.' He looked round to establish that his wife was in animated conversation with the other ladies. 'Maria Karolina is not entirely in favour of such expense. Ha! But a small ensemble to begin with. Twenty players, maybe. Not more than twenty-five.'

'A capital project, Prince,' said Swieten. 'And no doubt you'll ask young Beethoven to play for you?'

'Certainly. Certainly. If he's as good in front of an orchestra as he is in a salon. And we're about to find that out.'

'He's playing for the widow Mozart in a few days' time as well.'

'Yes. Remarkable. I hope he hasn't taken on too much. It would be disastrous for him if one or the other performance was a failure.'

'Let's hope his health holds up. I hear he's had a bit of stomach trouble.'

'It's just nerves, according to his friend Wegeler. I understand the good doctor is with him now, administering more powders.'

As they spoke a small figure darted from one group to another, as if unable to settle. The truth was no group wanted to engage him in conversation. He was not elegantly dressed and he moved with a furtiveness that made people instinctively wary of him. His red hair was not auburn enough to be attractive, having a paleness that made it look as if the sun had bleached it. Already he had acquired a nickname. People referred to him when he was out of earshot as 'the hyena' – drawings of which, showing the predator on the vast African plain, had recently appeared in Artaria's print shop on the Kohlmarkt.

He resembled that animal now, as he moved between the groups, his shoulders sloping forwards, his head darting one way, then another. He gave the impression that if he had a tail, it would have been pointing down, curving between his legs. There was no doubting that had he not shared the same name as the musician who was about to make his first public performance, Carl van Beethoven – as he now styled himself – would not have gained admittance to the prestigious first tier.

By now the orchestra had tuned up and the choir was on stage, and the audience settled down to hear the popular two-part oratorio, *Gioas, Re di Giuda*, by the Prussian composer of Italian extraction, Antonio Cartellieri.

The audience, given its musical connections, was highly educated to the nuances of the performance, and was liberal with its applause, several times calling for a particularly popular chorus to be repeated. Cartellieri, his right hand across his heart, acknowledged the applause and made several fulsome bows to the first tier, then blew kisses with his hands to the stalls.

After the briefest of intervals, the audience reconvened and Ludwig van Beethoven walked out on to the stage for the first time in his career. The applause was polite but prolonged, his reputation already known to the audience.

With barely an acknowledgement to the audience, and none to the first tier, he called the orchestra to order and raised his hands. Only when the opening long *tutti* was well under way did he cross the stage to the piano, continuing to nod the beat with his head.

On either side of the piano were tall candles, their flames dancing in the air to the movement of bows across strings. Beethoven blew them out, causing a gasp of astonishment in the audience, compounded when he closed the manuscript which stood on the piano stand, then collapsed the stand itself. Finally he sat, still nodding the beat with his head.

At the piano's first solo entry Beethoven played the notes not just with his hands but his whole body. His face was etched with concentration, his hair flying as he played, his shoulders one moment hunched, the next held squarely back.

In the imperial box Prince Lobkowitz leaned across to Swieten and said as quietly as he could, 'Intensity. Such intensity. My breathing has nearly stopped!'

Swieten nodded without turning, not wishing to take his eyes off the stage.

There was barely a movement or a sound in the auditorium as Beethoven played his Piano Concerto in C, his first. The cadenza in the first movement, beginning deceptively simply but ending in a rush of notes and the trill in the treble that was the cue for the orchestra to re-enter, seemed to call naturally for applause and an encore, but Beethoven nodded to the orchestra to continue.

The hymn-like Largo, with its simple, expressive beauty, was received with an almost pious silence, and the final movement, with its welter of notes cascading to the finish, acted as a release for the audience's emotions.

At the final chord the auditorium erupted in applause, with loud cries for an encore. Beethoven bowed to the stalls first, then the first tier, then stood in with the orchestra, his arms outstretched in a command to them to acknowledge the applause with him.

Before the applause was finished he left the stage and to the disappointment of every person present did not return.

The next day, in a glowing review of the entire concert, the *Wiener Zeitung* wrote: 'The famous Herr Ludwig van Beethoven reaped the wholehearted approval of the public.'

The next night, by popular demand, the concert was repeated. It was a different Ludwig van Beethoven who this time acknowledged the approbation of the audience. It was as a musician who had proved himself to the musical cognoscenti of Vienna, not just as virtuoso pianist, but – of greater importance to him – as composer too.

When the applause finally died down, Beethoven turned to the orchestra and told them to put their instruments down. He then returned to the piano and improvised on it for a full half-hour, to the delight of the audience.

The evening after that, 31 March, Frau Constanze Mozart took over the Burgtheater to put on the performance she had promised of *La Clemenza di Tito*.

After the interval Beethoven took to the stage again and played Mozart's Piano Concerto in D minor, with the cadenza he had written himself.

As the final notes sounded and the audience rose to their feet in appreciation, Beethoven sat still, his head bowed, for a full minute. Then, without looking up, he left the stage.

Chapter 2

Carl van Beethoven walked down the wide Kohlmarkt, his hands thrust deep into his coat pockets. He was looking forward to the next hour, but had a nervous feeling in his stomach which gave a slight spring to his step. Streicher had warned him about Carlo Artaria – a gentleman of the old school, courteous, formal, refined, proper, but with a heart of steel. Artaria was without question the leading music publisher in Vienna, with many works by Mozart and Haydn to its name.

He looked at the imposing four-storey building, the name ARTARIA & COMPANY spelled out in large gold letters above the three arched windows of the ground floor. Behind the glass, discreetly positioned, were old maps and prints, giving the appearance that the building housed a library rather than a shop.

Carl entered, his nose wrinkling at the musty smell of old paper. He enjoyed saying, 'Artaria. Carlo Artaria. Expecting me,' to the stony-faced man who asked him what he was looking for in particular, and ignored the implied slight in the reply, '*Signor* Artaria is in his office on the first floor.'

He mounted the stairs at the back of the shop and without knocking opened the imposing door that faced him.

Carlo Artaria looked up, his hands adjusting his wig, and the look of irritation which came over his face at the unannounced interruption immediately giving way to a warm smile.

'Herr Beethoven, I believe? It is a pleasure to welcome you to my humble office.'

Carl's eyes quickly swept the room, taking in the paintings of Artaria's native Italy, the dark, wood-panelled walls, the sumptuous curtains which hung in a graceful sweep on either side of the three tall windows.

He shook Artaria's hand and sat down before being invited to do so, taking some papers from a folder, which he put in front of him on the wide desktop. Artaria went round the desk and sat in his chair facing Carl.

'Herr Beethoven, I am delighted at the reports I hear of your brother. He—'

'Right. The piano trios. My brother has decided they will be his Opus Number One. There are three of them. Very substantial. And as Opus Number One very important. These are the terms he wants . . .'

'Herr Beethoven,' said Artaria, holding his hands up and smiling, 'let us not talk of terms just yet. Tell me first how—'

'Artaria, I am a busy man. After I have seen you I have to go to the office of Breitkopf and Härtel to see their representative here.'

Artaria's smile left his face at the mention of the renowned Leipzig publisher he regarded as his rival.

'Herr Beethoven,' said Artaria with an edge to his voice, 'before you came to Vienna, I had the honour of publishing your brother's variations for violin and piano on Herr Mozart's aria from *The Marriage of Figaro*, "Se Vuol Ballare".' He gave the Italian vowels their full resonance. 'I was rather expecting that—'

'You wouldn't have had them if I had been here. You paid him a pittance. It's not happening again. Now, the piano trios. I want them offered for subscription. Advertised, at your expense, for subscription.'

'I'm really not sure that is wise, Herr Beethoven. For subscription to be successful – by which I mean for the publication costs to be recouped – it requires at least fifty subscribers, ideally more. Assuming each buys one copy, and assuming the usual price per copy of three florins. It might be a little optimistic to expect that—'

'Artaria, there are three trios here. Each one consisting of four movements. And they are Opus Number One. Already they have been played at Prince Lichnowsky's Friday matinée – more than once – and have excited great interest. His Royal Highness himself has declared them to be the finest such works he has heard, and he is passing his opinion on to his aristocratic colleagues.'

Artaria leaned forward and put his fingers to his lips. The name of Lichnowsky, deliberately dropped at that moment by Carl, had found its mark.

'Then if we issue them by subscription at three florins and . . .'

Carl shook his head vigorously. 'No, no, Artaria. One ducat. One ducat per copy. Five florins.'

Artaria brought his hands down on to the desktop in an uncharacteristically impulsive gesture. 'They will not sell at that price. Three florins per copy, on equal terms, namely one and a half florins to your brother, one and a half to this house, which are the normally accepted terms, and there is a chance, a possibility, we might recoup—'

'One ducat per copy. And divided four to one. Four florins to my brother, one to you.'

'Herr Beethoven, if I may say so, you betray a certain lack of understanding about the publishing business. Your brother is a musician, a fine musician, and seeks to earn a living. I run a publishing house, and seek to make a profit. Without it, the house will not survive. I will agree to one ducat per copy, split three to two in favour of your brother. If we fail to recover the cost of publication, you will find me rather more difficult to deal with next time.'

'Four to one, Artaria. Otherwise the trios go to Breitkopf in Leipzig.'

Artaria looked across the desk at Carl van Beethoven. Carl returned his condescending gaze unflinchingly. Nor did his expression change when Artaria gave a tiny, almost imperceptible nod. He simply pushed the top sheet of paper across the desktop for the publisher to sign.

When Artaria announced that the subscription to Beethoven's Opus Number One was available, Prince and Princess Lichnowsky swung into action. While the Prince quietly let his fellow aristocrats and friends in the diplomatic service know about the offer, the Princess was indefatigable in her efforts on Ludwig's behalf. She organised a series of morning gatherings for the wives of her husband's influential friends, not allowing the ladies to leave without a firm promise to insist on their husbands subscribing.

The result – to Carlo Artaria's astonishment – was that no fewer than one hundred and twenty-three of the most illustrious names in Vienna bought a subscription, committing themselves to buy, between them, more than two hundred and forty copies of the manuscript. Prince Lichnowsky, when he heard that Ludwig intended dedicating the trios to him, bought twenty copies. 'For the musicians at my residence in

Silesia,' he said. Prince Lobkowitz bought six copies and Baron Swieten three.

With free lodgings in the Lichnowsky apartment, and the income from the subscription – particularly given the extraordinarily favourable terms negotiated by his brother – the financial strain caused to Ludwig by the cessation of his salary from Bonn was over. He could at last devote himself to composition.

He was grateful for that, because the compositional process was not going as well as he wanted. He decided that the string trios he had sent to the Elector needed some revision. The piano sonatas which he was also working on – like the piano trios a set of three – were giving him problems. And although the work on the piano trios was complete and the manuscript with Artaria, he was not yet satisfied with them.

He was therefore not in an appropriately receptive mood when Prince Lichnowsky spoke to him one morning in August.

'My dear Ludwig, such a success, the subscription for the piano trios. We are so delighted for you, the Princess and I.'

'There's something . . . I'm not finished with them yet. There's still a problem.'

'Problem? What do you mean? When you and Schuppanzigh and Kraft played them at the matinée last week, they were delightful. My guests were enchanted.'

'Delighted. Enchanted. I do not write music to enchant or delight people.'

'Come now, Ludwig. You are being too hard on yourself. How many subscribers?' Lichnowsky asked, secretly hoping for some gratitude from Ludwig for the efforts he had made on his behalf. 'Mmh? Over a hundred, wasn't it? Mmh?'

Ludwig nodded wearily. He looked at the Prince's eager face, eyebrows raised, so expectant. This was Prince Lichnowsky, no less, aristocrat, confidant of the Emperor, wealthy beyond imagining – and yet here am I, he thought, a young Rhinelander, a musician, just beginning to earn a small amount of money, without influence . . . and he, the Prince, wants my gratitude, my approval.

'Ludwig,' said the Prince, leaning closer to him, 'do forgive me for what I am about to say. It's . . . it's really . . . the Princess has asked me to mention it to you . . . I wouldn't . . . I don't mind myself . . .'

Ludwig knew before the words were out what he was about

to hear. He cupped his chin in his hand. He was surprised the matter had not been mentioned before.

'It's really only for the servants . . . so they know. But she . . . the Princess . . . has noticed that you have stopped taking dinner with us. At six o'clock. She so enjoyed it when you joined us. Could you . . . ? Would you consider . . . ?

A surge of anger shot through Ludwig. 'I have my own life to lead. I'm not . . . I'm not . . . You mustn't treat me as if you own me.'

A look of extreme embarrassment came over the Prince's face. 'Of course. Of course. I do understand. The Princess too. You must forgive me. You mustn't think . . . Now listen. There is something I have to discuss with you. Totally different. Music. Music. Let's discuss that. Mmh?'

Ludwig nodded. 'Have you heard,' the Prince continued, 'that Haydn is back? Dear old Joseph is back in Vienna?'

Ludwig sat up straight, the memory of his last meeting with Haydn causing a pang of nervousness to shoot through his stomach. He hoped Haydn had not harboured resentment against him over the matter of the compositions he had sent to the Elector.

'Is he?'

'He is, and after another triumphant stay in London. They say he is as much loved in London as—'

'I wonder why he didn't send me a note to say he was back?'

'Oh, he's so busy. You mustn't mind that. I haven't even seen him yet myself. Now listen, Ludwig. Here is what I propose. I would like to arrange a soirée to welcome him back. A large gathering of the most important people in Vienna. And do you know who I will invite? The people who subscribed to your piano trios. And you will perform the trios for them. All three. Your Opus Number One. Played by you, Schuppanzigh and Kraft. With Herr Haydn as guest of honour. Now what do you say, Ludwig? You do agree, don't you?'

'They're not completely ready yet. I need to do more work on them.'

'You will have time. It will take a while to organise things. Don't worry. And believe me, if you change nothing, they will still be fine.'

Ludwig shook his head. 'No. Herr Haydn will know. If they're not right. He will know. They must be right.'

'But you will agree to it, Ludwig? Christiane and I will be so happy.'

'Yes, Prince. If you want me to.'

Franz Wegeler was excited. 'Come, Ludwig, there is someone I want you to meet.'

'Franz. I have work to do. My piano trios are to be performed and—'

'Later. But come with me now.'

'I need more of your powders too. The stomach pains have come on again.'

'It is the tension. When you know you have to perform. Remember, you are in a new city, making a name for yourself, proving yourself. It takes its toll on the body. Once you are established it will be different.'

The two friends turned into the wide Graben and walked past the ornate Baroque monument to the Great Plague that had decimated the city.

'Who are we going . . . ? It's not Steffen, is it? He's not in Vienna?' asked Ludwig excitedly.

'No. But someone who'll be able to tell you about him. Here. Taroni's coffee house. Let's go in. Ludwig, tidy your hair. Quick. Flatten it with your hands.'

The two entered Taroni's and Wegeler walked to a small, round table at the back. Carl was sitting there, talking animatedly to a woman whose face was turned towards him. Ludwig could not see who she was. The nervous feeling in his stomach at seeing it was a woman was compounded by his irritation at his brother's presence.

Wegeler hailed Carl and put one hand on the woman's shoulder. She turned.

'Franz. How good to see you. Have you brought . . . ? Ludwig. Ah, Ludwig. Dear friend.'

Magdalena Willman stood up quickly and encircled Ludwig with her arms. She kissed him firmly on the cheek. He breathed in the scent of her perfume and it made his head slightly dizzy. As she kissed him, her soft, tumbling hair caressed his forehead. He felt her thigh momentarily touch his and it sent a bolt of desire through him.

'Leni,' he said, hoping his voice sounded normal. 'I had no idea. No idea you were . . .'

'Isn't it exciting?' she said, as they all sat at the table, amid much shuffling to make room. 'I've been on tour. Singing. Venice, Berlin, then Graz here in Austria, and now Vienna. And what do I find in Vienna? My old friends. It's so wonderful.' She leaned forward and briefly put her hand on Ludwig's.

'How long . . . ? How long are you in Vienna?'

'I don't know. But I certainly cannot go back yet. Ludwig, it's dreadful. There are French soldiers everywhere. The Elector and his court have had to leave. They're in Münster.'

'And the Breunings? Are they all right?'

'Yes. So far. Their main problem is the house. The French officers wanted to seize it, to house themselves. So far they haven't succeeded.'

'The fighting is over, isn't it?'

'Mercifully, yes. But the streets are full of . . . It's so sad. There are wounded men everywhere. Austrian and German soldiers. You see them in the streets. They've lost a leg, or an arm. Or they're blind. They've become beggars. It's so sad. And the French soldiers patrol the streets as if they owned our city.'

'What news of Steffen? What is he doing now?'

'He's fortunate. He's going to Mergentheim, away from all the trouble. I'm not sure when. Soon, anyway. He's worried about leaving his mother. And Lorchen, of course,' she said, looking at Wegeler. 'But things are peaceful now, even if life is . . . rather different.'

Carl turned to Ludwig. 'Leni says she spoke to Nikola before she left. He's talking about coming to Vienna.'

Ludwig could not disguise his sigh. 'What will he do here? He'll just . . . just . . .'

'He'll be able to work in an apothecary's shop here. More reliable than earning a living as a musician. He could be the most successful of the three of us.'

Ludwig scowled. 'He's too lazy.'

Carl raised his voice. 'Don't insult our brother—'

'Carl, quiet. Stop,' said Wegeler. 'This is not the time for a family dispute. Have some manners. There is a lady at the table. A dear lady. Now, Leni. Tell us more. May I ask about a certain young man? A certain cellist by the name of Bernhard Romberg?'

Ludwig, grateful that Wegeler had intervened, looked up quickly, eager for Leni's response.

Magdalena blushed slightly, bringing her hand to her cheek. 'Fine. Well. And his cousin. I . . . I . . . haven't heard from

Bernhard since I left Bonn. We don't . . . correspond. He's a dear man. We are still friends.'

'I understand,' said Wegeler consolingly. 'Do forgive my appalling lack of tact. Now, let us order more coffee and you must tell us more about your plans.'

'No, no,' Leni said animatedly. 'Ludwig, I want to hear about you. I haven't heard much, but I believe you are making quite an impression.'

'With my help,' said Carl, 'he is beginning to earn a respectable living. I deal with his publishers and make sure he is well treated. He couldn't do that himself. Could you, Ludwig?'

Leni pursed her lips and turned to face Ludwig. 'Tell me, Ludwig. Tell me about your music. Your compositions.'

'I have written three piano trios, and they are to be performed at Prince Lichnowsky's. In front of Herr Haydn in one week from now. I have work to do on them.'

'Why didn't you tell me?' exclaimed Carl. 'What are the terms? Did you . . . ? You should have let me—'

'Carl!' said Wegeler sharply. 'Will you stop interrupting and let Ludwig speak. Out of politeness, if nothing else.'

'We are rehearsing on Thursday. And again on the morning of the soirée. And as well as Herr Haydn there will be princes and counts and barons . . .'

'Oh, Ludwig, how wonderful for you,' said Magdalena. 'Do you think I could possibly be there? And Franz?'

'Of course. I'll speak to Prince Lichnowsky. Do you really want to be there?'

'Oh yes. Yes. I'll be so proud of you. All of us. From the little town of Bonn. Rhinelanders. Among all these important, aristocratic Viennese.'

'You mustn't let them intimidate you.'

'No,' said Carl. 'They're all so pompous. They treat us like . . . like . . . as if we had no sophistication whatsoever.'

Wegeler turned to Ludwig. 'How is it in the Alstergasse?'

Ludwig let out a long sigh. 'Comfortable. Luxurious . . .'

'More than I can say for my rooms,' said Carl.

'But . . . but . . . I don't know. Sometimes I feel . . . stifled.'

'Stifled? You should be grateful . . .'

Magdalena put a restraining hand on Carl's arm. She and Franz looked at Ludwig, concern on their faces.

'I know it sounds ungrateful, but they treat me almost as

their son. Dinner is punctual. Six o'clock. And I am expected
to be present, shaven and cleanly dressed. And the Princess fusses
around me, straightening my coat, flattening my hair . . . I've
stopped being there, and I know it's upset them.'

'I spoke to the Prince,' said Wegeler. 'He hasn't said
anything.'

'The Prince even told his servant when I started living there
that if ever he and I rang at the same time, the servant should
come to me first. It just makes me feel . . . under pressure all
the time. I'm afraid sometimes I decide I can't take any more,
and I do something . . .'

'What? What have you done?'

'The Princess's mother was there one afternoon. Countess
Thun. I was working on my piano trios. I didn't even know
what time of day it was, I was so involved in what I was doing.
But there was a knock on the door and the servant told me I was
commanded to attend upon His and Her Imperial Highnesses.

'I went into the salon and they were all sitting there, sipping
coffee out of those tiny china cups. I can barely hold them,
the handles are so small. The Countess . . .' he looked down,
slightly embarrassed by what he knew he was about to say, '. . .
she started comparing me to the Greek gods, saying my music
was immortal and my powers divine. I . . .'

'Are you complaining?'

'She's so . . . so . . . eccentric. It annoyed me more than
anything. She doesn't even know my music. It's just what she's
heard, been told by the Princess. Anyway, it made me angry. She
asked me to play the piano. Demonstrate my "divine powers". I
refused.'

Carl laughed again. 'My brother, the humble outsider from
Bonn, refuses to play for the nobility of Vienna . . .'

Ludwig looked up, a mischievous smile creeping across his
face. 'Do you know what she did then? She threw herself on to
her knees in front of me, hands held out as if she were praying,
begging me, imploring me to play. There were actually tears in
her eyes.'

'And did you? What did you do?'

'The Prince was actually rather embarrassed. I could tell
from his face. Even the Princess was embarrassed by her
mother.'

'What did you do? Tell us.'

'I still refused.'

Carl clapped his hands. Franz and Magdalena could not resist broad smiles.

'I said no. And I got up and left the room.'

There was laughter around the table. 'I'll have to leave sooner or later. Comfortable though it is. I need to be able to . . . to breathe. But these salons are important to me. The piano trios, for instance. The Prince, as I said, is letting me perform them in front of Haydn. That way important people will hear my music.'

'It's wonderful for you, Ludwig,' said Magdalena. 'You are such a dear, clever man.'

She leaned forward and stroked her hand lightly across Ludwig's cheek. The perfume from her wrist wafted across his face. Suddenly he was transported to the deck of the boat on the Rhine, on that trip to Mergentheim. He remembered how she had kissed him on the cheek then, how their lips had touched, just for an instant.

He looked at her now, his breathing quickening and warmth flowing through his body. He thought she was the most beautiful woman he had ever known.

Chapter 3

Ludwig worked hard on revising the piano trios. He saw them as a way of putting himself back in Haydn's favour after the business with the compositions and the Elector. He even thought of dedicating them to his teacher, but decided against it – he owed Prince Lichnowsky too much not to give him the dedication of his Opus Number One.

He reworked certain passages and adjusted the balance between the instruments, but mostly he meticulously wrote in a great many more dynamic markings. He already knew that in this he differed from his great predecessors, Mozart and Haydn. His compositions would bristle with dynamic markings, from double *pianissimo* if he required it, to double *fortissimo*, and everything in between. He knew exactly how loudly or softly he wanted every bar played, and he would ensure his players respected it. Dynamic markings, he had long ago decided, were as essential to music as the notes.

He paid particular attention to the very first bars of the first movement of the first trio. The key signature was E flat. He had written a conventional chord in the home key, a sort of call to attention to the audience. But what followed it was unconventional in the extreme. As soon as the third bar, with violin and cello still shaping the home key, the piano made a descent to D flat. E flat and D flat! It was a startling effect which had shocked the audience at one of the matinée performances.

On that occasion the chord was played *fortissimo*. But Ludwig had not been happy with it. Its existence alone was enough to shock. To compound it by playing it *fortissimo* was unnecessary. A lesser composer would do that – though he smiled at the knowledge that a lesser composer would never have descended to D flat in the third bar! – and the effect was all the better for not being exaggerated. That chord, repeated twice in the very next bar, became a more integral part of the music when played *piano*.

He marked the opening chord *forte*, then the very next note – the first of the rising arpeggio – *piano*. He wrote *piano* again in the next bar, so the players could not mistake it.

He smiled to himself. He was pleased with what he had written. There was only one outstanding problem with the trios, one that had been at the back of his mind since the matinée and had not been solved at subsequent rehearsals. It concerned the final movement of the second trio. It was a galloping theme, led off by semiquavers on a single string by the violin, accompanied by piano chords.

At the matinée performance the theme somehow had failed to take wing. Ludwig's intention was that it would drive along, not heavily, but skip lightly, as if dancing before a wind. But it had remained anchored to the ground. Ludwig discussed it with Schuppanzigh later. He had urged him to play the sequence of semiquavers in the top half of the bow, so that it bounced slightly on the string. Together they had rehearsed. Still the movement had not quite taken flight.

The musicians gathered for the final rehearsal at Prince Lichnowsky's before the performance. There was an air of expectation in the salon. Servants were already making preparations. Curtains were being brushed down, the carpet swept and the windows cleaned. Chairs were being arranged. Princess Lichnowsky had to order the servants to stop what they were doing so the rehearsal could go ahead.

She – and her husband – were no less nervous than the musicians. Most of the important subscribers to the piano trios had accepted invitations to attend the performance. Count Razumovsky, the Russian ambassador, and of course Prince Lobkowitz and Baron Swieten. Prince Charles of Lichtenstein, Prince Josef Poniatowski and Prince and Princess Schwarzenberg had all indicated they would be present. So had Count Wielhorsky, Count Künigel and the Hanoverian envoy Count von Hardenberg.

The Hungarian Chancellor Count Palfy would also attend, which accounted for the presence at the final rehearsal of a secretary at the Hungarian Chancellery, Nikolaus Zmeskall von Domanovecz.

'Ludwig,' said Ignaz Schuppanzigh, 'I'd like you to meet a

good friend of mine, and, I might add, a very fine musician, Nikolaus Zmeskall.'

Ludwig found himself looking at a mass of white hair, since the Hungarian was already bowing formally, and as he returned to an upright position Ludwig was confronted by a face wearing the thickest-lensed spectacles he had ever seen. The effect was to magnify the eyes behind them, which Ludwig realised were blinking as they struggled to focus on his face.

Ludwig could not stop the broad smile spreading across his face. He half bowed in return, to show that the gesture had not been lost on him. The two men stood looking at each other, neither one wishing to be the first to speak.

'Maybe I should have said Count, or is it Baron?' Schuppanzigh asked. 'Nikola owns land in Hungary, much of it, I am pleased to say, vineyards, and with the land comes a title. Baron, is it not?'

'Yes,' said Zmeskall, 'but please do not use it to me. Herr . . . Herr Beethoven, it really is the greatest honour . . .' And he bowed again.

'My pleasure, I assure you,' said Ludwig, not returning the bow this time. 'And you are a musician too?'

Zmeskall shook his head and laughed. 'No, not really. Schuppi does me too much honour. I try to play the cello. Once I was quite good. But I am afraid I did not practise enough, and if you do not practise . . . But Schuppi has told me of your music. And I must say I have heard you play myself. At Baron Swieten's soirées. Always I wanted to meet you, but I never . . . I never . . .' He hung his head modestly.

Ludwig liked Zmeskall immediately. His modesty was appealing and his respect for Ludwig's music obvious. The fact that he was clearly very short-sighted somehow added to his equability.

'Ludwig, Nikola has asked if he can listen to our rehearsal. I assured him you would not mind.'

'Of course not. I want to work on the Presto of number two before we do anything else. I am still not happy with it.'

As he spoke Anton Kraft entered the salon, nodded to everyone in turn and began unpacking his cello.

The three musicians tuned their instruments, while Zmeskall pulled a chair to the front of the room to listen, his arms folded.

On a cue from Ludwig they began the final movement of the second trio, the galloping theme that Ludwig had thought about so much echoing around the room.

Ludwig stopped playing before the second theme was reached. He sat silent at the piano. After a few moments he looked up, shaking his head.

'It hasn't . . . It doesn't . . . I don't know. It's better. But it's not quite what I want.'

Kraft, who was some years older than both Ludwig and Schuppanzigh and the composer of some cello sonatas himself, spoke. 'Maybe it is simply a question of taking it faster? That way it would—'

'I would not be able to get the bouncing effect with the bow if we took it faster,' Schuppanzigh interrupted, 'unless you rewrite them as demisemiquavers, Ludwig. Then I could play the whole sequence with one bow movement.' He demonstrated what he meant.

'No. No,' Ludwig said. 'It makes the theme too . . . unsubstantial. I want more drive, not more speed. It's the second half of each bar that seems to lose emphasis.'

Zmeskall coughed, the sort of cough that is meant to draw attention. All three men looked at him.

He blinked behind his thick spectacles a few times, cleared his throat again and spoke.

'Please do forgive my impertinence, but I have not heard the piece before and maybe a fresh pair of ears will help. And my ears are better than my eyes! From the way you have played it, it seems to me it must be written in four-four time. Yes?'

The three nodded.

'Play it as if it was in two-four time,' Zmeskall said. 'That way both halves—'

'Yes. Yes!' Ludwig exclaimed before he had finished. 'Yes! Ready? On my cue. One, two . . .'

The three played the opening of the movement again and the music seemed to take flight. It was a simple adjustment, but played in 2/4 time the music had an entirely different quality. It gave the impression of going much faster; in fact it was the same speed as before, but by giving the second half of each bar as much accent as the first half, the theme acquired a momentum.

'Yes! Yes!' Ludwig called again as they played on. Without warning, at the end of the first exposition, Ludwig leaped up from his chair, ran the few steps to Zmeskall, who also rose, and gave him a huge embrace.

'Baron Zemskallity. Count Zmeskall of Zmeskalls. Most

Honoured Zmeskallovitch. You are hereby – and for all time
– appointed chief musical adviser to Ludwig van Beethoven,
composer.'

There was an air of expectancy in the Lichnowsky salon. Even
the servants moved with an added urgency as the most aristocratic and influential people in Vienna began arriving. Prince
and Princess Lichnowsky flitted among the guests, making sure
no one was left out. But there was no need. The princes, counts,
barons moved easily among one another. Their wives likewise,
accompanying each greeting with a quick sweep of the eye to
appraise each other's dress.

The guests were not strangers to each other. Most met nightly
at one soirée or another, or during the day in the offices of the
Hofburg palace. After formal welcomes, conversations would be
picked up where they had left off the previous day or evening.

Ludwig, Schuppanzigh and Kraft sat in the corner of the room
with Wegeler, Magdalena Willman and Nikolaus Zmeskall.
There was a tenseness about the musicians, knowing that
they would soon be called on to perform for a distinguished
audience.

Ludwig had a sharp pain in his stomach, which Wegeler had
done his best to ease. He rejected the glass of wine which
Zmeskall pushed towards him.

'There is no shame in being nervous,' Zmeskall said in a
kindly voice. 'In fact I believe it leads to a better performance.'

'Thank you, Nikola,' said Schuppanzigh with a cynical edge
to his voice. 'Most reassuring. It's strange. I'm far more nervous
than when I'm playing at the Augarten. Although the audience
there is much bigger.'

'The public,' said Ludwig. 'General public. And bigger. This
is more intimate. No wrong notes tonight, gentlemen.' He
smiled weakly.

There was a bustle around the double doors which gave on
to the salon, and a sprinkling of applause as Prince Lichnowsky
led in his guest of honour.

Haydn, although considerably smaller than most of the men
he moved amongst, walked with a leisurely, wide step, which
gave the impression of a larger, more powerful man. The fact
that he was the centre of attention increased the impression that
he was bigger than he actually was.

When he was sure Haydn was fully engaged in conversation,

the Prince looked round the salon until his eyes fell on the small group in the corner. He hurried over to them.

'Ludwig. Gentlemen,' he said nervously, wringing his hands. 'All in order, I trust?'

The meaningless question elicited no response.

'My plan is that in a few minutes I will call for silence and formally welcome Herr Haydn. After that, Ludwig, I will introduce your Opus Number One, and thank the guests for subscribing to it. Is that all right?'

Ludwig nodded.

'Good. Good. I must say, everyone is . . . Well, I'll get back to Haydn now. Do you think you should take your places? That way we can start whenever I judge the moment to be right.' He hurried away.

Ludwig looked across at the group of men surrounding Haydn. He could not see his teacher among them, but he hoped that the adulation he was clearly receiving would ensure he was in good humour. Ludwig wanted Haydn's approval tonight for his Opus Number One.

Nodding at the good-luck wishes that accompanied them, the three musicians stood and walked towards their instruments, which lay on the raised floor that the servants had specially laid down. As they did so, Prince Lichnowsky began ushering his guests to their seats.

In the general hubbub, Ludwig, Schuppanzigh and Kraft tuned their instruments and arranged their scores on the music stands. Giving the A to his colleagues, Ludwig's eyes swept the audience. He acknowledged Prince Lobkowitz's encouraging nod and saw Baron Swieten sitting not far from him, engaged in animated conversation with someone immediately behind. Prince Kinsky sat near the back; his young son sat next to him, his corpulence already much greater than when Ludwig had last seen him. He saw Count Razumovsky raise his hand in greeting and he nodded in reply.

Suddenly, and with a pang in his stomach, he caught Haydn's eye. It was unavoidable. Haydn was sitting in the centre of the front row of chairs. Haydn, it seemed to him, took a moment to focus, his face looking stern as he did so. Ludwig's heart sank. But in the same instant a benevolent smile came to Haydn's lips and he stood.

He walked the few paces to the raised floor, carefully stepped on to it and clapped his hand on Ludwig's shoulder.

'So, how goes it with our young Mogul?' he said in a loud voice.

The other musicians laughed, as did a few people in the front row who heard Haydn's words.

'Good luck, my boy. Good luck. Good luck to you all.' He returned to his seat.

Lichnowsky clapped his hands for silence. 'Most illustrious guests,' he said, a slightly obsequious smile clamping itself on to his face, 'how delighted my wife and I are that you have chosen to grace our humble salon. Such an illustrious gathering! Such nobility! Such . . . such . . . I know I scarcely need to introduce my guest of honour to you. He is known not only to every one of you, but to all the music-lovers of Europe. In London they fêted him as never before. His new symphonies were played to universal . . .'

Haydn, a look of embarrassment on his face, frowned at Lichnowsky and raised his palms to try to stem the flow of compliments. But it was to no avail.

'I ask him now to stand to acknowledge your appreciation of him. Europe's greatest composer and musician!'

Reluctantly, and as swiftly as he could, Haydn stood and, holding the back of his chair, bowed slightly as the audience applauded, before resuming his seat.

Lichnowsky clapped for a few seconds longer after the general applause had died down, then raised his palms in an unnecessary call for silence.

'Most of you, I am sure, are familiar with our musicians this evening. Herr Schuppanzigh and Herr Kraft you have surely all heard at the Augarten pavilion. And if you have not heard our young pianist play, you have certainly heard reports of him. Ludwig van Beethoven, who hails from the Rhineland, so sadly under the occupation of the French enemy at present – until, that is, our gallant forces liberate his homeland . . .' a smattering of applause, '. . . he has proved himself worthy of the greatest praise for his performances not just in this humble salon, but others of more improtance. Tonight he is going to play for you his Opus Number One, a set of three piano trios in four movements each, a work to which you have all been kind enough to subscribe. A work which . . . aha! . . . I am fortunate enough to find – most unworthily, I assure you – is dedicated to me.' More applause, and Prince Lichnowsky took his seat.

Ludwig looked at the two string players, raised his head, and brought it down instantly. The three played the opening chord in perfect unison.

Joseph Haydn shook his head gently and a faint smile crossed his face at the audacious move to D flat in the third bar. He wondered how many in the audience would appreciate the daring of what this young musician had written.

He too had done something similar, in his own E flat Piano Sonata, but he had been less bold about it, less assertive. He doubted whether his pupil had consciously copied it; in fact he suspected the reverse. If Ludwig had known he had used such an unconventional transition, he might even have deliberately avoided it!

What an extraordinary young man he is, Haydn thought. He remembered the first time he had met him, in Bonn, and how impressed he had been with the two cantatas he had written for the Elector. And what a remarkable pupil he was. Argumentative and stubborn, yet with the skill on the piano to support the most outrageous ideas.

It can't be done that way, Haydn would patiently explain. You will produce a discord that will cause people to clasp their hands over their ears. Yes, yes, he would reply, and play the sequence in such a way that the discord seemed to have a natural place.

How Haydn wished Ludwig had been able to take lessons with Mozart. He smiled wistfully at the memory of the great musician. A born rebel, thought Haydn, who revolted at the thought of producing music to order and who finally escaped from the tyrannical Archbishop of Salzburg. Ah, if only I had been similarly able to escape from Prince Esterhazy, he thought. But he knew he was from an older generation, set in his ways, in the conventions of the day.

And if Mozart and Beethoven had studied together? What might they have produced? But Mozart was gone; he himself was in his sixties. Was Ludwig van Beethoven to be the one to carry the art of music forward into a new era?

Frankly, even in his most charitable mood, he doubted it. Ludwig's music was remarkable. Strong, resolute, defiant even. But it lacked discipline. It was as if every time an unconventional idea came into Ludwig's head, he wrote it down. He had tried to explain to him that there was more to writing music than that, but he had not listened. He did not want to listen.

Haydn shuffled in his seat. He was weary. The London stay

had tired him more than he had realised. Three trios, four movements each. Twelve movements. Why so long, Ludwig? he wanted to ask him. Is there so much to say that you could not say it in nine movements, three movements each? Three was enough for Mozart and me. But not for you. Or in two trios, instead of three?

He liked the galloping Presto of the second trio. It was a perfect end to the piece. In fact a perfect end to the two trios. Why on earth had Ludwig decided a third trio was necessary? he wondered. His heart sank as the gloomy minor opening began the third trio and he shuffled again in his seat.

It was an hour and a half after the music had begun that the final movement of the third trio brought the entire work to a close, and as he had done at the beginning Haydn could not suppress a smile at the audacity Ludwig had shown. No final flourish, no *fortissimo* passage to rouse the audience to a spontaneous burst of applause. Just a softly stroked *pianissimo* chord that was so quiet that some in the audience did not realise the work was over, taking their cue only from the fact that Schuppanzigh rested his violin on his lap.

Haydn led the applause, guiltily hoping no one – his pupil least of all – would realise the large measure of relief inherent in it. He decided in that instant that when Ludwig next came to see him, if he were to be asked for his advice then he would give it.

Chapter 4

'Oh, Ludwig, you cannot know how proud we were of you, Franz and I. And Nikolaus. He is so nice. To see such important people swarming around you like bees to a honeypot, all wishing to shake your hand.'

'It makes me happy to know that I pleased you.'

'No, no. You mustn't think of just pleasing me. Everybody was so pleased for you.'

'Leni, I want you to know that . . . that . . .'

'Ludwig, you are such a dear friend. Now we must listen. The final act is about to start.'

Ludwig paid little attention to Paisiello's *La Molinara*. Instead he looked at the profile of the woman he had come to realise he was in love with. After the success of the soirée at Prince Lichnowsky's he had made an important decision. He was going to propose marriage to Magdalena Willman. He had wanted to discuss it with Franz Wegeler first, to ask his opinion. Had Leni said anything to him? Had she indicated she might be receptive to a proposal? But the moment had not arisen.

In fact the three of them were supposed to be together this very evening at the Kärntnertor theatre, sitting in the box Prince Lichnowsky had hired but had been unable to take up. An emergency at the university hospital had kept Wegeler away too.

It was the perfect opportunity, Ludwig decided, to press his suit. After the performance ended and they walked in the shadow of the great Bastion, Magdalena shivered and slipped her arm through his, clasping her hands together around his arm. Her move made him instinctively broaden his shoulders.

'Will you . . . will you come to my apartment? There is something I want to give you.'

'Ludwig. It is late. Do forgive me, but . . . it is late, and . . .'

'It will only take a moment. It is something I have written for you. I want you to have it.'

She smiled and nodded. 'But I will not stay long. You do understand, don't you?'

In the apartment Ludwig shuffled through a pile of manuscript papers until he found what he was looking for.

'There. You see, I did not forget.'

'What is it?' she asked, taking the papers he was holding.

She read the title page. It was a set of variations for piano on the aria 'Nel cor più non mi sento' from *La Molinara*. She laughed.

'It is for you,' he said. 'I composed them for you.'

'Oh, Ludwig, how kind you are. But how did you . . . how did you know . . . ?'

'Don't you remember? You told Franz and me one evening that you had a set of piano variations on the song that you had found in Berlin, but that you had lost them. So I wrote these for you, to take their place. There are six. They are quite simple. You will be able to play them.'

Magdalena stood shaking her head gently. 'That is so kind of you, Ludwig, I will treasure them with—'

'Leni,' said Ludwig, 'there is something I want to ask you.'

Magdalena walked quickly forward and put her finger on his lips. 'No, Ludwig. Do not ask it. Do not be angry with me. But do not ask it. We are good friends, you and I. I am fond of you. I have been since that boat trip to Mergentheim. I will always be fond of you. More than that, I admire you. You are a fine musician. One day, I believe, you will be a great musician. You must not be distracted by . . . by . . . anything.'

Ludwig looked at her, speechless. What did she . . . ? Why did she . . . ?

'Leni, I . . .'

She leaned forward and kissed him on the lips. He felt fire rush through his body. He put his hands on her shoulders and pulled her towards him. She did not resist. He kissed her passionately. She returned his kiss, but only for a moment. Then she pulled her head back.

'Dear Ludwig. I will think of you while I am away.'

'Away?'

She nodded. 'I should have told you earlier. I am going back to Venice. My brother Max and his wife are there. It is a good thing. And remember, Ludwig. I believe one day, one day soon, you will be grateful for the way things have worked out. You may not think so now. But you will do one day.'

*   *   *

Ludwig was in no mood to listen to criticism.

'I must disagree with you, Herr Haydn. The applause surely was enough to prove you wrong.'

'Ah, Ludwig, a word of advice from an older musician. Never let the applause deceive you.'

'But if your only criticism is that the piece is too long . . .'

'Of course I will need to listen to it again, as I assure you I will do. But remember, Ludwig. You must bear your audience in mind. Three trios, an hour and a half of music. Is it really necessary to—'

'I do not compose music just for the audience. I compose it because I have to.'

'But you do not object to the applause.'

Ludwig smiled, aware that Haydn had exposed the inconsistency in his argument. He looked at his teacher, nearly forty years older than he, immaculately dressed and coiffed – just like his music – a gentleman musician, servant of a prince for most of his life, a man of the eighteenth century.

He did not underestimate Haydn's music as he had once done. It was Mozart who had first told him to study it and learn from it, and who was he to disagree with that master? But he felt instinctively that Haydn's music was rooted in a bygone age, an era when the composer was little more than a tradesman in music, at the behest of a wealthy patron.

Mozart had changed that. He had escaped from Archbishop Colloredo. Haydn owed his freedom to the timely death of Prince Esterhazy and the enlightened attitude of his successor. Ludwig determined that he would emulate neither man. He would never be in a position where he either needed to escape or longed for the demise of a patron. He was a free musician. He belonged to a new era, a new century.

'I believe . . . I believe . . . My Opus Number One is ready. Artaria has it.'

'Look, Ludwig. Here is a suggestion. Withdraw the third trio from publication. Two substantial pieces are surely enough to constitute an opus. Each one runs longer than most of my symphonies! Take the third one back and we will work on it together.'

'No!' There was a sharpness in Ludwig's voice that he could not suppress. 'No. I am not having . . . I do not want . . . They are my trios and I am satisfied with them.'

'As you wish, my boy. As you wish. Why do we not talk of

other matters. Are you working on any other compositions?'

'Yes. Piano sonatas. Three.'

'Three again,' said Haydn with an unmistakable weariness to his voice. 'You must think the number three brings you luck.'

'My second opus. I have decided. And . . . and . . . another piano concerto. I am writing another piano concerto.'

'Are you indeed? I heard about the success of the first. You played it at the Burgtheater, didn't you?'

Ludwig nodded. 'It was well received.'

'So I heard. Prince Lichnowsky told me about it. How far advanced are you with the second?'

Ludwig's face perceptibly brightened. 'The first movement. I'm revising the first. But the other three are written. I began working on it in Bonn, but I put it aside. When I returned to it, I found it better than I remembered. I reworked it substantially. But it has gone well.'

'Key?'

'B flat major.'

Haydn smiled. 'A good key. Gentle. Soft. But not easy for the soloist. A mix of black keys and white keys. Difficult. Well, I wish you luck with it. When you are ready, I would like to look at it with you. And, Ludwig, the trios. You must be prepared to listen to advice, you know. That is the relationship a pupil has with a teacher.'

Ludwig suddenly felt a flash of anger shoot through his body. He did not want to talk any more about the trios. He did not want to talk any more about his music. Haydn's calm, reasonable voice grated on his nerves. He had had enough of being told what to do.

'I am not your pupil!' he said, standing quickly. 'No more. I am a composer now. I will make my own way.'

Ludwig sought out Franz Wegeler at the university. He needed comforting words. Wegeler was in the small office he had been given near the hospital building. He was clearly busy.

'Ludwig. Good to see you. You must forgive me. I have a lecture and—'

'I have had an argument with Haydn.'

'You shouldn't have done that. He's a distinguished man. He deserves respect.'

'I know that. But he . . .'

Wegeler was opening the drawers of a cabinet, one after another. 'I know I put it in one of these drawers. Ten sheets, bound together. My lecture. If I can't find it . . .'

'He wants me to withdraw my third piano trio from publication.'

'You should listen to him.'

'I am not going to listen to anyone,' Ludwig said with anger in his voice.

'Then don't come here asking me for advice. Look on that table for me, will you? Are they in that folder?'

'Also . . . also . . . I . . . I was going to ask Leni Willmann . . . I wanted . . .'

'She's gone. Left yesterday for Venice.' He stopped what he was doing and turned to Ludwig. 'I heard. She told me. In secrecy. She was very touched. But, Ludwig, I think her decision is the right one.'

There was anguish in Ludwig's face. 'But if she . . . and now Haydn. Why is everyone deserting me?'

'They're not, Ludwig. Don't be so ridiculous. Leni had to leave. And it sounds as if you're deserting Haydn, not the other way round.'

'Ridiculous? Are you calling me ridiculous?'

'Ludwig. Forgive me. I am late for a lecture. I cannot find my notes. Now is not the time for a long discussion about your personal problems. I will come and see you this evening.'

'No. I need to be alone.'

'As you wish, Ludwig. As you wish.'

For several days Ludwig closeted himself in his apartment, telling the servant to admit no one. Furiously he worked on his compositions. He brought the piano concerto to fruition, leaving only the orchestration to complete. He made final revisions to the string trio he had sent to the Elector. And to his own surprise, he told his brother Carl to get the third piano trio back from Artaria.

He did not intend altering it. He only wanted to look at it. Haydn's objections to it seemed to be based on nothing more than its length. He looked at the second movement, the Andante con Variazioni. The opening theme was simple, song-like. Too simple, too light for the third of three trios? No. No. Remember Mozart's words. Simple themes. It is what the composer does with them that is important.

He leafed through the pages. The variations on the theme. Ten of them. The longest movement of the trio. The longest of all three trios. Too long! Yes, too long. It unbalanced the piece. Really, once he realised it, he could not understand why Haydn had not simply said, 'The second movement is too long'.

And it was so easy to amend. Fewer variations, that was all. He examined the variations, remembering clearly the compositional process. He remembered too where the sixth variation began – an explosive key change which Schuppanzigh had said was almost impossible to carry off. 'Not in the natural progression of the music,' he had said. Ludwig had insisted.

Taking a crayon, he drew a vertical line down the bar division. He turned to the end of the movement, a recapitulation of the theme. No. Why recapitulate? There's a fourth movement to come. It is not the end of the piece. He drew another line down the final bar of the movement. He joined the two lines up with a long horizontal line through six pages of manuscript – five variations and the recapitulation.

The second movement now consisted of a theme and five variations. A tighter, more balanced movement. Was that what Haydn had intended him to do? He doubted it. He would have said so. Still, it would please him.

He gave the amended manuscript back to Carl and then turned to the set of three piano sonatas. He did so with an enormous sense of relief. It was like putting a familiar coat back on.

The piano sonata, since his earliest days his favourite musical form. He remembered how gladly he had worked on the three sonatas for Elector Maximilian Friedrich. Since then he had written so many more, but all little more than jottings, experiments. Preparation. He would turn to many other forms, he knew that. Symphonies were still to come; string quartets. He had already made a youthful – abandoned – attempt at a violin concerto.

But always the piano sonata would be there to return to. It would be the constant factor of his musical life. And he knew it, even now in his mid-twenties as he embarked on his career.

Three piano sonatas, the first to be given an opus number. They would be large-scale; he made that decision early on. Four movements each. Haydn might complain about the length again, but his mind was made up. Also he would incorporate material from his early piano quartets – the compositions both Neefe and Franz Ries had criticised back in Bonn. The material was worthwhile – he did not want to abandon it – and it would speed up the composition.

Work progressed well. Ludwig found that by giving instructions to the servant not to be disturbed, he could immerse himself in composing in a way he had never done before. The emotional disappointment of Magdalena Willmann's rejection of his suit had not left him in a deep depression, as he had feared it would. In a curious way he felt liberated. It left his emotions free to concentrate on music.

Even more liberating was the effect of his break with Joseph Haydn. He was no longer a pupil. He had made that decision. His Opus Number One was completed and with the publisher. His Opus Number Two would soon be ready. And there was the string trio, the piano concerto . . .

Haydn, surely, was nearing the end of his career; Ludwig was grateful for what the elderly composer had done for him. Counterpoint, fugue, canon, the relationships of instruments to one another, balance . . . He had learned a lot. But he was ready now, ready to make his own mark.

He looked again at the opening of the first movement of the first sonata. More than any other passage he had thought about this one. Should he announce it with a flourish? A dramatic gesture? A huge chord? No. Time and again he had rejected that idea. The opening of the first sonata, he decided, would be a simple rising theme in the right hand.

But what promises the theme holds, thought Ludwig. In the minor key, and the first expression of it lasting a mere eight bars. But in those eight bars no fewer than seven naturals; and when the theme is taken up again in the left hand, more accidentals, almost one to a bar, some bars with several. How many rules does that break? he wondered. Haydn would surely shake his head.

Instead of allowing the theme to flourish, Ludwig progressively foreshortened it. The effect: tension. The sudden and unexpected key changes, sometimes in consecutive bars, driving the music forward. That was the effect Ludwig wanted more than any other: momentum. The drive of the music carrying the listener forward.

After the first subject, four bars of semiquaver triplets. The second subject an inversion of the first: a falling theme in the left hand. Right hand to left hand, like an acrobat taking the stage and juggling balls in the air. Throwing them away he performs a series of somersaults, then walks on his hands.

On the music drives, not a note wasted, not a bar too few or too many. Until finally Ludwig cries, 'Enough! The theme is exhausted,' and brings the movement to an end with a series of staccato *sforzando* chords off the beat, followed by three *fortissimo* chords ending in the home key of A flat.

Ludwig was satisfied with his work.

The note from Prince Lichnowsky brought a smile to Ludwig's face.

> Dear Ludwig
>   Should you wish to end your self-imposed exile, the Princess and I would be delighted to welcome you to our dinner table this Thursday evening. There is a matter of great importance to discuss with you.

He shook his head as he reread the note. How differently the Prince treated him now! He no longer expected him to conform to the strict timetable he and the Princess observed. If he wished to be alone, he was left alone. Still, it was Ludwig's intention to leave the Lichnowskys' apartment, as final evidence of his freedom. It was just a matter of timing.

On Thursday evening, at the appointed hour, Ludwig was ushered into the Lichnowskys' drawing room. The Princess swept across the room to him and clasped her arms round his neck.

'Ludwig. Oh, Ludwig. Have you been unwell? How glad we are to see you again? Let me look at you. Are you all right?'

'My dear, I am sure he is,' said the Prince, coming to the rescue. He extended his hand, which a grateful Ludwig shook.

'Sir. I have been working. I apologise if . . .'

'Not at all, my boy. Come and sit down. There is a glass of wine already poured for you.'

The Prince and Ludwig sat; Princess Christiane bustled out of the room to give the cook instructions for dinner.

'And how has the work gone, if I may ask?'

'Well, I think. I have made considerable progress. A piano concerto. And three sonatas for piano.'

'Bravo!' The Prince clapped his hands. 'Excellent. I shall tell you why I am so pleased in a minute. And the trios, you know. My trios, if I may be so bold. They are still talked of admiringly.

That performance you gave was splendid. I . . . I . . . I believe Joseph Haydn—'

'He was critical of the third trio. I have amended it. I think he will approve.'

Lichnowsky's eyes opened wide in astonishment. 'You have amended it?'

'I have shortened the second movement. The variations. It is better.'

Again Lichnowsky clapped his hands.

'Ludwig. Dear Ludwig. I have so much good news to tell you. First, on the subject of my dear friend Joseph. He has told me . . . I understand . . . you have decided to take no more lessons with him.'

'I need to spend my time composing, not taking more lessons.'

'I understand. I understand completely. And so does Herr Haydn. He has asked me to tell you he thinks you have made the right decision. And he supports you and will continue to do so.'

'I am pleased. I owe him a lot.'

'And, Ludwig . . .' Lichnowsky could hardly contain his glee. 'As a token of his esteem for you, he has asked me to tell you that he invites you to perform your new piano concerto at a concert he is giving in the small Redoutensaal in the Hofburg palace.'

Ludwig leaned forward. 'He has? Really? That is good of him. I will be very pleased to do so.'

'Ludwig.' The Prince's face was expectant. 'He asks only one thing. One . . . favour. As a token of your gratitude for his teaching, will you write "Pupil of Haydn" at the top of your next work to be published? So the world will know of his part in your musical education? The piano sonatas, I believe, are next?'

Ludwig thought for a moment. 'No. Kindly tell Herr Haydn that I do not wish to be known as his pupil, or anybody's pupil. But I am grateful to him. I will offer him the dedication of the piano sonatas. If he wishes.'

'Oh yes. Yes. He will, I am sure, be even more pleased.'

The Princess entered the room. 'Have you told him, Karl? Have you told him?'

'No. Not yet, my dear. Sit down. Sit down. I will tell him now.

'Ludwig, I have something to tell you which I am sure will make you very happy indeed. In the new year I have to travel to Prague. I would like to take you with me. To perform your music. Just as I once took poor Wolfgang Mozart, so many years ago. Your first tour, Ludwig. Your first tour.'

Chapter 5

The Redoutensaal concert was a success, the threat of a breach between Ludwig and his illustrious teacher avoided by Prince Lichnowsky's intervention. Haydn was fulsome in his praise of the new piano concerto. He kept from Ludwig his disappointment at Ludwig's refusal to put 'Pupil of Haydn' at the top of the piano sonatas, but thanked him for the dedication. He also told him he thoroughly approved of the amendment to the third piano trio, and he wished him well on his forthcoming trip with Prince Lichnowsky to Prague.

Ludwig was in the midst of preparations for the trip when Nikolaus Zmeskall called round to see him one evening, eagerly clutching a small bag in his left hand.

'See, Ludwig. Look. You will not tell a soul?' He put his hand into the bag and pulled out a clutch of goose-feathered quills. He held them towards Ludwig, blinking behind his thick spectacles. 'From the Chancellery. No one knows.'

'Nikola, you most splendid of Zmeskalls. How can I thank you enough?'

'No need, Ludwig. Just write me some music.'

'Ba-ron! Ba-ron!' Ludwig chanted. 'Or is it Count? I never remember.'

Zmeskall laughed. 'Either will do. So when do you leave, Ludwig?'

'Soon. Very soon. And there is so much to do. The blood is racing round my veins. I feel . . . I feel . . . Sometimes I think I will burst.'

'Come, Ludwig. Put on your coat. Let us walk together.'

The two friends walked towards the Bastion, through the Schottentor and into the city. It was a chill December night and they walked with their hands thrust deep into their pockets and scarves wound tightly round their necks.

A light sprinkling of snow lay on the streets, matching the

scenes of Christmas in shop windows. It was late evening and a few people were still in the streets, most carrying parcels that were Christmas gifts and hurrying home with heads bent down against the cold.

Ludwig saw the Kärntnertor theatre and for a moment his mind flashed back to Magdalena Willmann. To his relief the thought was not accompanied by sadness; instead it made him smile. The huge Bastion wall loomed on their right, a sentry standing guard at the Kärntnertor gate.

In the dark shadow of the wall the air was icy and still. The two men pulled their scarves up high around their necks and thrust their hands deeper into their pockets. Their breath made white shafts in the flickering lights that lined the top of the Bastion.

Ludwig expected Zmeskall to turn left into the broad Kärntnerstrasse. Instead he headed for a narrow alley which ran to the right alongside the wall. The Walfischgasse was barely wide enough for two carriages to pass, and the buildings were four or five storeys high, intensifying the blackness which enveloped them and giving an echo to their voices.

'Where are we going?'

'To a fortress I know.'

'A fortress?'

'A fortress, Ludwig my friend. What is a fortress? A fortress is a firm and solid erection.' He looked at Ludwig and smiled.

For a moment Ludwig did not understand what his friend meant. Then he let out a sigh. He wanted to turn back. He wanted to say that this was not what he needed, that he was an artist and artists must keep their minds pure and unsullied. But he said nothing. Instead he felt his breathing quicken and a tight, constricting – yet not unpleasant – feeling come into his chest. Despite the chill air his cheeks became suddenly hot.

A little way down the Walfischgasse, on the right, a candle in a small wire cage flickered on the wall at first-floor level, throwing a dancing light on the sign above it, which hung motionless in the still air. Ludwig could see that it showed a soldier, a hussar, his sabre curved upwards and seeming to come from between his legs. 'Zum blauen Säbel', 'At the blue sabre', the words above him said.

Zmeskall stopped outside the door and turned to Ludwig. He had a smile on his face, but a different smile from the one Ludwig was used to seeing. This was more a look of anticipation, of excitement. Behind his thick spectacles his eyes were open wide and unblinking.

'Our secret, Ludwig. We are visiting our secret fortress. Here you do not have to give explanations, or make promises. You do not have to wonder what the reply will be, or worry that you might have said the wrong thing. Here you are in charge. You say what you want, and it is given to you. Come.'

He pushed open the heavy door. Wordlessly Ludwig followed him in. He was breathing in short gasps, his cheeks now warm as if he were standing in front of an open fire. Ahead of them, at the end of a long, narrow passage, a flight of stairs led up, lit by a single flickering candle.

They climbed it, turning on the landing halfway up. At the top another door, lit by another candle. On it, underneath a grille, a small, round medallion depicting the hussar and his tumescent sabre.

Zmeskall knocked twice, paused and knocked a third time, using the ring on his finger. The grille slid back silently and moments later come the sound of bolts sliding and the door was opened.

Zmeskall nodded and pointed to Ludwig behind him. He gave Ludwig another of those expectant smiles and the two went in, removing their coats and scarves and leaving them on a table by the door.

Ludwig was struck first by the aroma – heavy and sweet. It pervaded his nose and his senses. He breathed deeper and it filled his lungs. He did not know what it was. There was an exotic quality to it. Turkish. Yes – similar to the aroma he remembered from his grandfather's clothes.

After a few seconds his eyes grew accustomed to the light. It was dim, with a dark-reddish hue. Single candles flickered behind deep-red glass. He saw figures moving and heard the rustle of lace, but it was as if they were floating noiselessly. He noticed there was something strange about the faces. All similar, all unmoving. Then he realised why. Everyone was holding a mask to their face.

He became aware of a woman standing to his left, holding out an arm. He saw Zmeskall reach into his pocket and put several notes into the pouch which hung from the woman's arm. Zmeskall then put his hand on Ludwig's shoulder and motioned him to take what she was offering, as he had. Ludwig reached out. It was a mask. The woman was holding one too.

He followed Zmeskall's example and held the mask to his face.

Zmeskall leaned towards him and whispered in his ear. 'Everyone here wears one. Everyone. It's so no one knows who anyone is. It's said some of the most important men in Vienna come here, and no one knows. And do you know what else?' He leaned even closer. 'It's said some of the women here who . . . who offer their services are princesses and duchesses. And no one knows. Not even their husbands.

'And barely a word is said. Just silence. Come with me.'

He led Ludwig to the back of the room. A woman brushed against Ludwig. He saw that her breasts were naked and that she lingered slightly as she passed him so he could feel her flesh press against him. He felt the burning in his loins.

He saw Zmeskall smile at him as he reached out and stroked the naked breasts of another woman, who dallied for a few seconds, then moved away, rubbing her hand along his loin as she did so.

Ludwig felt a tap on his shoulder. He turned. A woman moved her mask away, moved Ludwig's too, and placed her lips on his, forcing them open with her tongue. Making little gasping noises she explored the inside of his mouth with her tongue. He felt her thighs rub against his. Her hand reached behind his head and pulled it down on her breasts. With her other hand she cupped her breast and squeezed her nipple into his mouth. As he stood upright again, she put her mask back in place and moved silently away.

He looked round. Zmeskall had gone. In the dimness he saw the head of another woman turn and her mask gaze expressionlessly at him. She floated towards him. He saw that her dress cut diagonally across her chest, exposing one breast. The nipple was deep red against her white skin. He looked at her breast and could see that it was powdered white and the nipple rouged red.

Silently she took his hand and led him through a narrow doorway at the back of the room, down a small corridor where she opened the last door on the left. She led him in.

A single candle threw a flickering light across the tiny room. On the floor was a thick mattress, a blanket thrown across it. Two huge pillows were propped against the wall. Above the bed a painting hung. It showed a woman naked and on her knees, performing fellatio on a man who was standing, his body arched forward and his hands on his hips.

Before he could fully take in his surroundings, Ludwig felt the woman untie his trousers. Without speaking she slipped them down, knelt and took him in her hands, then her mouth, letting her tongue roam over his groin. He felt a weakness in his legs, as if his knees were not going to be able to support him. With little gasping noises she caressed him with her hands, her mouth and tongue, until he could no longer tell which was which.

An intoxicating wave of pleasure swept over him; from his own throat sounds came to match hers. Her movements around him intensified. He felt her reach round with one hand and pull his buttocks towards her. With the other she now drove the length of him, the sound of her saliva wet on him mingling with the sounds from both of them.

Finally the sensation overwhelmed him. With his hands he gripped her head to support himself. He arched his back as he pressed himself against her face. Her hot saliva extended the length of him as he drove himself forward into her mouth and felt himself explode.

She continued to caress him, ever more tenderly. As his breathing subsided she released him, pulling his trousers back up and tying the cord around them. She stood, putting the mask back in front of her face as she did so.

His knees still felt as if they were about to give way, but the woman pulled a chair from the wall and gently pushed down on his shoulder.

'Just a few minutes. To rest. Then you must leave,' she said.

Ludwig sat, waiting for his breathing to return to normal. Images floated into his mind. His mother, first, her face as always uncomprehending. Elenore Breuning, Magdalena Willmann . . . they were smiling at him. He knew he should feel disgust, revulsion. But curiously he did not. He had not chosen to come here: his friend Zmeskall had brought him. He had not upset or hurt the woman: the contrary was true. And he had liked it, enjoyed it. Just as every man here seemed to. Why else would they be here? If Zmeskall was right, there were Princes here, and Counts. And possibly their wives! To his own surprise, he even felt a sense of achievement. He had behaved *normally*, like a *normal* man.

Ludwig stood, allowing his knees a few seconds to become

reaccustomed to his weight. He walked back along the corridor and into the main room. This time no women approached him, knowing that by his emerging into the room by the back door and heading for the main entrance the purpose of the visit had been accomplished. Now the heady smell of Turkish incense offended his nose, its sweetness cloying.

He found his coat, and as he put it on he heard Zmeskall's voice close by him.

'We must hurry. It's late. The sentries close the Bastion gates at ten. Come on.'

Ludwig went out with him, down the steps and into the Walfischgasse, gulping down the chilly air as if it was iced water and he was slaking his thirst.

The next time Ludwig saw Zmeskall was at the Schwan Inn. Schuppanzigh and Carl were also there. Zmeskall greeted Ludwig in the normal way, no hint in his greeting or his smile of the experience they had shared together. Nor, Ludwig was relieved to find as the conversation began, had anyone at the table noticed any change in him, as he rather thought they might. In the days after the visit to the 'fortress' Ludwig had expected to feel guilt. But he had not. The sense of achievement he had experienced immediately afterwards had diminished, but not vanished; a vestige remained.

Carl had an animated look on his face. 'I have some news, Ludwig. I have some news.'

Ludwig sipped the hot coffee and felt its welcoming warmth spread through him. 'Mmh? What? What news?'

'I have heard from our brother. Nikola. He is definitely coming to Vienna. Do you remember I told you he might? He arrives on the day after Christmas.'

Ludwig put down his cup and sighed. 'Where will he live? He can't stay with me. Anyway, I'm going away, and I'm not staying with the Lichnowskys when I return. I want to be on my own. I can only afford somewhere small.'

'You don't have to concern yourself,' Carl said with an ill grace. 'You can concentrate on your music. I am making the necessary arrangements. He'll stay with me to begin with, then get a place on his own.'

'What work will he do?'

'He already has a position. That is why he is coming. At the apothecary shop Zum Heiligen Geist in the Kärntnerstrasse. He will only be earning a small salary to begin with, but there are prospects.'

There was a pause. Then Carl asked, 'Where is Wegeler? I haven't seen him for more than a week.'

The question sent a pang of guilt through Ludwig. 'I . . . No . . . I haven't seen him either. I saw him at the university. We . . . I must write to him.'

By coincidence, when he returned to his apartment Ludwig found a letter from Wegeler, begging him not to let their friendship suffer any longer, and apologising if he had caused him sadness. He wrote that he must soon return to Bonn, although the date had yet to be decided, and he implored him to get in touch soon, so they could meet and he could tell all their friends in Bonn the very latest news about Ludwig's progress in Vienna.

Ludwig, overcome with remorse, wrote a long letter to his old Bonn friend, apologising for the way he had behaved to him and the sharp words he had used when they last met. The fault, he wrote, lay entirely with him. He would, of course, come to see him, where he would throw himself into his arms and plead for his forgiveness.

But Nikola's imminent arrival and his own forthcoming trip to Prague with Prince Lichnowsky distracted him, and he did not fulfil his promise to Franz Wegeler.

BOOK EIGHT

Chapter 1

Ludwig shielded his face against the rain and gazed up in wonder at the medieval statues, their flashes of gold leaf glinting despite the greyness in the air. He turned and looked at the bridge tower with its high arch which guarded the entrance to the Lesser Town.

'It's . . . everything seems smaller than in Vienna. And more . . . ornate.'

Prince Lichnowsky walked with him, holding a wide umbrella over their heads. 'I know what you mean. It's a smaller city, narrower streets, less . . . imperial. I always feel more relaxed here than in Vienna.'

They walked under the tower, up the slight incline of a street lined with irregular houses, some embellished with small but elaborately decorated statues, and took the first turning to the left into Lazenska Street. The rain beating on the umbrella made conversation difficult, and so Ludwig looked around him at the unfamiliar architecture.

He thought of his home town, Bonn. Such an ordered town; neat houses in regular rows, many painted white – like the Electoral palace – similar shutters and windows, similar gabled roofs. And his adopted home town, Vienna: broad streets lined with grand houses, many four or five storeys high; ornate buildings crowned with imperial regalia, a globe here, an eagle there.

Prague, though, seemed to have grown from the bottom up. There was a lack of symmetry, no two neighbouring buildings alike; statues smaller than in Vienna, less portentous and mostly depicting saints. And practically every street, it seemed, having a church, from the small to the grand.

And the people. Here in Prague they somehow seemed less hurried. Even in the rain Ludwig noticed how they stood in small groups on the street, talking animatedly; arguing but with good humour, arms waving to make a point, heads nodding or shaking, frequent bursts of laughter. They looked as if they were discussing not the latest French victories on the battlefield, but the relative merits of the Roman Catholic and the Protestant views of the Eucharist. Their clothes too were less formal and more colourful than those seen on the streets of Vienna. And it struck Ludwig that there was not a wig to be seen.

They reached the Golden Unicorn Hotel, on the corner of Lazenska Street and the square, where Lichnowsky had taken two rooms.

'Spend the rest of the day in your room, Ludwig. Rest. It's too wet to go out. I have appointments arranged this afternoon. Tomorrow there is someone I want to introduce you to.'

Ludwig stood at the window and looked down into the square. The rain was still falling steadily. In the far corner a small number of carriages waited, their horses standing forlornly and their drivers sheltering in a doorway, one gesticulating animatedly while the others listened.

Prague. The Bohemian capital. Even back in Bonn it had been talked of as a city apart, as if it belonged to a different continent. The city that had taken Wolfgang Mozart to its heart long before the imperial capital, Vienna.

Ludwig had wondered then if he would ever go to Prague, or even Vienna. Yet he was now living in one and visiting the other. He was the guest of one of the most senior aristocrats in Vienna and he was moving in circles he had once only dreamed of. Counts, dukes, princes . . . Yet he was a musician, first and foremost, and he must never forget that, never allow his head to be turned.

He pulled his coat around his shoulders and walked down into the square.

It was a moment before the carriage-drivers allowed themselves to be interrupted, and when one of them replied to Ludwig's question he did so pointedly in the Czech language before switching to German.

'Across the bridge to Charles Street. Behind the Church of St Gall. You'll see it. Anyway, it's closed.'

Ludwig nodded his thanks, ignoring the driver's final words: 'You'll get soaked. I'll take you . . .'

He followed the driver's instructions, asking directions once or twice more, and finally stood in front of the building he sought.

The Nostitz theatre, bearing the name of the music-loving nobleman who had commissioned it, was – like everything about this city, it seemed – smaller than Ludwig had expected. In fact he had twice walked past it before realising what it was. It had a certain grandeur to it, but a restrained grandeur. Two sets of pillars stood either side of the tall, curved window above the large entrance doors. But – unlike what Ludwig had become used to seeing in Vienna – there were no allegorical statues on its roof, no ornate friezes depicting scenes from antiquity.

Ludwig found the doors into the building were bolted shut. How different the Nostitz was to the Burgtheater in Vienna; so much less impressive, so much more intimate. It was hard to believe that this was where the first performances of Mozart's *Don Giovanni* and *La Clemenza di Tito* had taken place, and where *The Marriage of Figaro* had been rapturously received while in Vienna it was talked of in dismissive terms.

As he turned away from the theatre and began retracing his steps, Ludwig found his thoughts taking a direction he had not expected. *The Marriage of Figaro. Don Giovanni.* Music which from the moment he had studied the scores Ludwig knew was great music, destined to endure. But the stories Mozart had chosen to set to music were trivial. Worse than that, they were immoral. *Don Giovanni* was a wretched tale of seduction and murder; *The Marriage of Figaro* trivialised the institution of marriage; what was *Così fan Tutte* but a sordid tale of infidelity and immorality?

Ignoring the rain which was soaking through his clothes, his hands plunged deep into his coat pockets, Ludwig pondered the paradox of Mozart. Why had he chosen such plots for his glorious music? There was one obvious answer: to amuse the public, to give audiences what they wanted, namely entertainment. But would he have chosen different plots if circumstances had been different, if for instance he had been a wealthy man with no need to pander to the trivial desires of the public?

He stopped on the Charles Bridge and looked at the water below, the gently flowing Vltava. So different from the Rhine. No turbulence, no mystery, no legend, no Drachenfels. How he wished Mozart was alive so he could talk to him, ask him these important questions. Ludwig clenched his fists. I will not pander to the public, he thought; I will never write music just to please them.

My music will speak to people's souls, thought Ludwig. In it they will hear truths. It will teach them that they are free, that their souls and minds are free, even if their bodies are enslaved by tyranny.

He walked into the huge-domed church of St Nicholas and looked up at the organ in front of the west window. Above it was a fresco of Cecilia, patron saint of music. He could not see the keyboard, but he could see the two sets of organ pipes on each side of the gallery. He climbed the short, circular staircase to the organ loft. What he saw took his breath away.

The organ was unlike any other he had seen. Instead of being made of wood, the framework, pillars and ornaments were all of white marble. He stroked the smooth surface with his finger. The keyboard was smaller than he expected and he ran his finger gently along it. Had Mozart sat here and played on these keys? He sat on the hard bench that ran the length of the organ and rested his fingers on the keys, without depressing them.

He longed to play on the beautiful instrument, but he knew he must not. He went back down into the nave and looked again at the high altar, surmounted with a sumptuous copper and gilt statue of St Nicholas. Candles flickered on either side of it, heating the incense containers which hung above.

More people were coming into the church to sit and pray. He looked at them and he was overwhelmed by a feeling of oneness with them. He wanted to tell them that he understood what they were searching for and to reassure them that there was an answer to their questions. But he knew he could not explain in words what he meant. His music would do that for them. Through it he would express his faith in humanity, and his unshakeable faith in the liberty of individual human beings.

'Ludwig, I'd like you to meet a friend of mine, a musician with a very fine reputation in this city. An organist. Jan Vaclav Tomaczek.'

Ludwig found himself looking up into a lively, roundish face, with full cheeks, a broad nose and sparkling eyes. The man's hair was cut short and came forward in uneven points over his broad forehead.

'Very pleased. Very pleased,' Tomaczek said, stepping lightly from one foot to the other with an ease which belied his considerable bulk. 'But,' and he put his fingers to his lips, 'Tomaschek might be wiser. Johann Wenzel.'

'No, my dear friend!' said Lichnowsky dismissively. 'I've no time for that nonsense. Anyway, I hardly think they would dare clap *me* behind bars!'

Ludwig looked confused. Tomaczek lowered his voice. 'Czech names are forbidden, by order of the Hofburg palace in Vienna. But I'm bound to say it is not an easy law to enforce. So with the Prince's permission I will use the names I was born with.'

'Glad to hear it, my friend,' Lichnowsky said.

'I do not know how much you know about our city or our country,' Tomaczek continued to Ludwig. 'But we are used to rules imposed on us by others. Already this century we have been occupied by French and Bavarian soldiers. We have been besieged by Prussian forces. Now it is the Habsburgs who run our lives. Who knows what the next century will bring?'

'More peaceful times, I hope,' said Lichnowsky.

Ludwig found himself looking through the window at a mill which was gently turning, water dripping off its blades.

'Yes. Beautiful, isn't it?' said Tomaczek. 'It is no wonder so many people invade us. We are actually on an island here. Kampa Island. Formed by a branch of the Vltava which breaks away from the main river. We are at the top end, almost under the Charles Bridge. The rest of the island is mostly gardens. I will show you more one day. Many artists live on Kampa. For the peace.'

'Vaclav knew Mozart, Ludwig. Knew him well, did you not, Vaclav?'

'Indeed I did. Heard him play. The Prince tells me you met him too, Ludwig.'

'Once only. I had to return to Bonn and he died before I returned to Vienna.'

'Sad. Sad. And now look at him, buried in a common grave and unmourned. Unmourned in Vienna, at any rate. Here in Prague we mourn him greatly. We took him to our hearts far more readily than our Viennese friends, you know.'

Lichnowsky shook his head sadly. 'It is true. It is true.'

'So, Ludwig,' said Tomaczek with enthusiasm in his voice. 'We know your music here in Prague.'

Ludwig looked up sharply.

'Yes. It is true. Your piano trios. Opus Number One, are they not? The music has indeed reached this far-flung outpost of the Holy Roman Empire, and has been played to much acclaim.'

'I am pleased,' said Ludwig. 'I did not know.'

'Oh yes. Your reputation was assured here from the day of the improvisation contest against the Abbé Gelinek.'

Ludwig looked surprised. 'But that was . . .'

'Yes. Some time ago. But word has travelled. You see, Gelinek is a Bohemian and much respected in this city. But his reputation suffered somewhat after he was humbled by a certain young man from the Rhineland.'

Tomaczek and Lichnowsky laughed. Ludwig smiled and lowered his head modestly.

'And so, will we hear you play during your stay here in Prague?'

'I . . . I . . . I would like to compose while I am here. I do not know whether . . .'

'You have written two piano concertos, I understand, which you have performed in public in Vienna. Is that true?'

Ludwig nodded.

'And very well received,' added Lichnowsky.

'Then should they not be heard here in Prague? Would you play them for us?'

Ludwig looked at Lichnowsky, whose eyebrows were raised in expectation. He nodded. 'If you wish.'

'Excellent. Excellent. I will arrange it. I will speak to the manager at the Konviktsaal in the Old Town. I know him well.'

'And, Vaclav, you must introduce Ludwig to Josefa Duschek. She is a fine soprano, Ludwig. The best in Prague, would you not say, Vaclav?'

'Without question. In fact, my good friend Josephine Clary is holding a small soirée at her fiancé's palace. She herself is a pianist of considerable skill. I do believe it would be a good opportunity for you to meet musicians and patrons alike, Ludwig. Would you and the Prince come as my guests? And, Ludwig, would you play for us? I can assure you, you would have a very attentive and appreciative audience.'

Ludwig looked again at Lichnowsky, who was already nodding on his behalf.

The coach dropped off Ludwig and Lichnowsky sooner than Ludwig had expected, in a narrow street. Ludwig looked around him, wondering how far they would need to walk to reach the palace.

'It's there. Right in front of you,' said Lichnowsky with a smile.

Ludwig found himself looking at a wide wooden doorway, set off by two huge pairs of statues, one on either side. Each of four figures represented a muscular Hercules, their faces contorted with pain as they bore the massive stone portals. He stepped back to look at them, but there was not enough space in the street.

'The street. It's too narrow for this . . . this . . . It's not really a palace at all. It's not very different from the other houses, except for the statues.'

'It doesn't appear to be. But I think you'll be impressed when we go inside. That's typical of the Bohemians. They don't like to flaunt their riches. They're more . . . subtle about it than us Viennese.'

A servant opened the heavy double doors. The two men crossed a closed-in courtyard and went through another door. The staircase that faced them bore out the Prince's words. It was wide and grand, flanked on both sides by more heavy stone figures from antiquity. On the ceiling a magnificent fresco looked down.

'Don't be daunted,' said Lichnowsky. 'You'll find everyone very friendly. A more . . . relaxed atmosphere than in Vienna.'

A slim woman with dark hair, the curls framing her face, came out of a room to greet them at the top of the staircase. The dress she wore was less full than Ludwig was used to seeing in Vienna, and followed the contours of her body more naturally. It did not reach the ground as was the style he was used to, and he noticed she had no decoration in her hair and just a single strand of pearls around her neck.

'My dear Prince. Welcome back to our fair city. I am so glad Vaclav invited you on my behalf. And this is Herr Beethoven.'

Ludwig bowed his head and took her hand.

'A great pleasure. I have heard much about you, Herr Beethoven.'

'Ludwig,' said Lichnowsky, 'this is the Countess Clary, and although she will not admit it, she is one of the city's finest pianists.'

'No, no. You flatter me too much. A dilettante, I fear. Nothing more than that. But you must call me Josephine.'

Ludwig nodded, as she led them into the salon. Ludwig looked quickly round the room, which was richly furnished and larger than he expected. The chairs and sofas seemed soft and inviting; the portraits, mostly depicting faces that were smiling, less forbidding than Ludwig had grown used to seeing. He spotted the piano, which to his surprise was built of light-coloured wood with decorations painted on it.

A man came towards them. 'Prince, Herr Beethoven.'

'My dear Count. A pleasure as always. Ludwig, this is Count Clam-Gallas. Ludwig Beethoven, Count.'

'My fiancée has told me about you, sir. I am no musician myself, but since I am shortly to marry one who is, I am determined to learn something of that noble art.'

'Ludwig,' said Josephine, 'I would like you to meet a far better musician than I.'

She led another woman to Ludwig. 'This is my good friend Josefa Duschek, without doubt the finest soprano in Prague.' Josefa was shorter and fleshier than her host, plump almost, and was dressed entirely differently, with a white shawl thrown casually around her shoulders and a bonnet which held her hair away from her head.

Josefa smiled uncontradictingly, as if she was used to hearing the compliment. Both men bowed slightly.

'Karl. Good to see you. And you, Ludwig. So glad you could both come,' Vaclav Tomaczek said as he approached, shaking both their hands.

'And, Prince,' said the Countess. 'This is Councillor Kanka, a lawyer of great repute. And, I must tell you, a lawyer who is also a composer, with several musical works to his name.'

Ludwig looked at Kanka, feeling an initial resentment towards him. Composition was not something to be indulged in as an adjunct to other work. But he was disarmed by the lawyer's smiling face and shaking head, and the words he spoke with sincerity.

'No, Countess. I would not presume to the name of composer. It is far too illustrious a title for me. All the more so since I find myself in the presence of a genuine composer. Herr Beethoven, I have studied your piano trios and I believe them to be works of genius.'

Ludwig smiled. Given the strange surroundings and new faces he felt surprisingly at ease. He looked from one to the other as Countess Clary brought wine glasses over, which she had filled at a sideboard along one wall. Occasionally a servant – a young woman in a black dress and white apron – would bring in a new bottle, or a jug of water. But she left it on the sideboard for Josephine Clary to deal with.

The conversation was light and punctuated with laughter. Ludwig felt happy to be brought into the conversation whenever anyone chose to do so, particularly since there seemed to be an affinity with the fact that he was not a Viennese.

'Tell us about Bonn. I have heard it is beautiful. Small, like Prague. But cleaner and brighter. Is that true?'

Ludwig nodded. 'Little more than a village, really. Compared with Vienna. Only two squares, the Marktplatz and Münsterplatz. Not as many churches as here in Prague. We have the Rhine, of course. But it is not as wide as the Danube. Or the Vltava. But what we have most is the countryside. If I walk from the Marktplatz I am soon in the countryside. The hills. The Siebengebirge.'

'How wonderful,' said Countess Clary. 'My dear,' she said, turning to her fiancé, 'I would so love to go to Germany. May we go next year, when the wedding is over?'

Count Clam-Gallas smiled. 'I am afraid the French are rather preventing that. So sad for you and your family, Ludwig. Have you heard from them? Are they all right?'

'My family is no longer in Bonn. My parents are dead and both my brothers have come to Vienna.'

'Oh, that's nice for you, to have them in Vienna. You must be so pleased. What are they doing?'

Ludwig said nothing for a moment. Then, 'Caspar – Carl, he calls himself now – gives music lessons. He helps me with publishers. He is . . . he's not . . . he may have to take other work soon. He doesn't earn enough from lessons. Nikola, the youngest, is an apothecary, and works in a shop near the Kärntnertor. He only arrived in Vienna a little while ago.'

'Is he staying? Are they both staying?'

'They say so. At the moment it is not safe to return to Bonn. If they do, they would be conscripted by the French.'

Josephine Clary clapped her hands. 'Tell me of our good friend Franz Lobkowitz. Is he well? How is his leg, the poor man?'

'He is well,' said Lichnowsky. 'I saw him shortly before we left Vienna. His leg pains him, though. He asked me to send his regards to you and say how much he wishes he could be here.'

'Yes, the dear man. You know the Prince of course, Ludwig?

A great music-lover and patron of musicians. He is a Bohemian, like us. His palace is in Hradcany, inside the castle walls. I do hope we will see him soon.'

'And the happy event,' said Lichnowsky. 'Is all going according to plan?'

Josephine looked down, a slight blush colouring her face.

'Yes indeed,' said the Count. 'So many arrangements to make. Josephine is making most of them. And Josefa will of course be singing for us. In fact, let us have some music now. Before we eat. Josefa, you will sing for us now, won't you?'

There was a general nodding of heads and words of encouragement.

'Herr Beethoven. Would you be so kind as to accompany me on the piano?'

Ludwig rose and walked to the piano. The music was already set on it. He recognised the aria from the start of Act Two of *The Marriage of Figaro*, where the Countess pleads to be allowed to die, if the alternative is to lose her lover. It was a gentle, lyrical piece, with long, sustained notes that sounded simple to achieve but which tested the singer to the utmost.

With a nod to Josefa, he began the long, gentle introduction. When Josefa's voice first came in, Ludwig felt his skin tingle. It was an utterly pure and beautiful sound. There was none of the dramatic vibrato that so many singers used. He knew the aria well. It was a masterstroke of Mozart's: in a comic opera whose plot was, frankly, farcical, Mozart stopped the momentum to give his soprano one of the most graceful and beautiful arias he ever wrote.

He watched Josefa Duschek's chest rise and fall, but barely. He was aware that she was using only a small proportion of her voice. But it was exactly the right amount, and it filled the room, echoing off the walls and ceiling.

As he stroked the quiet chords which ended the aria, he was unable to restrain himself. There was polite applause, but Ludwig stood quickly and applauded loudly.

'Bravo, madame!' he said. 'Bravo!' Crossing quickly to her, he took both her hands and raised them to his lips. Suddenly realising what he had done, he turned to the others, a look of embarrassment on his face. 'Forgive me, but . . .'

'No, my dear Ludwig, you have nothing to apologise for,' said Josephine Clary. 'I have rarely heard anything so beautiful.'

Ludwig sat down, joining in the encouragements to Josefa

to sing more. She obliged with two unaccompanied songs by a Bohemian composer unknown to Ludwig. Again he was aware she was restraining herself. He suspected her voice was powerful, even perhaps with a wild quality. He began to form an idea; to write a piece of music to explore her voice, to stretch it.

His thoughts were interrupted by calls to play the piano. He did not want to. He wanted to think instead. But he knew he had no choice. He also knew the small audience was appreciative.

He sat at the piano and played the Rondo from the second of the three piano sonatas he had dedicated to Joseph Haydn. The explosive opening brought an immediate smile from the small audience, followed by looks of wonder as Ludwig's fingers flew faultlessly over the keys. The smiles vanished at the central passage, doom-laden minor chords accompanied by virtuosic chromatic runs. The intensity of Ludwig's playing, the obvious depth of his concentration held the listeners enthralled, seeming scarcely to breathe. And each one of them – although it was familiar to Lichnowsky – breathed out in surprise at the unexpectedly peaceful ending.

There was warm-hearted applause, accompanied by smiles. Kanka was the first to speak. 'Extraordinary, my dear Ludwig. Quite extraordinary. And it is one of your own compositions?'

Ludwig nodded. Tomaczek said, 'I swear, Ludwig, Mozart himself would have been impressed. You are like . . . like . . . a furious comet streaking through the sky. As for me, I shall not play my own piano for several days.'

'Will you give us something else?' asked Josephine.

'This is a rondo I composed recently.' He played again, this time less virtuosically, allowing the gentle theme in the right hand to flow out of the instrument and hang in the air. His body swayed as he played and he half closed his eyes. As he brought the short piece to a close, he hesitated before playing the final chord, and suddenly both hands flew out in opposite directions in massive chromatic runs, returning to meet in the centre of the keyboard. Finally he played the closing chord.

This time cheers accompanied the applause, as everyone rose.

'Wonderful, wonderful,' said Josephine. 'Now, let us eat. Supper is laid out on the buffet. Come. Ludwig, what a fine musician you are.'

The mood was relaxed and convivial as the guests returned to their seats and ate with their plates on their laps. There was no formality, no servants to be seen.

Ludwig saw that Josefa Duschek had pulled up a chair to sit next to him.

'Ludwig, I have not thanked you for accompanying me so perfectly. You were most sensitive. It was as if you understood my voice immediately.'

'You have a fine voice. It is a strong voice, is it not? You have much more power than you displayed.'

Josefa nodded vigorously and smiled. 'I rather wish there was more music which suited it.'

'I would like to compose a song for you.'

'Ludwig! Would you do that? You understand what my voice requires, what it is capable of.'

'Do you have a text? Is there something you particularly like? It would be better that way.'

Without hesitation Josefa replied, 'Do you know the poem "Ah, Perfido! Spergiuro", by the Italian poet Metastasio?'

Ludwig shook his head. 'What is the subject?'

'It is about the conflict which rages in a woman's breast after the man she loves has left her. One moment she calls down the wrath of the gods upon him. The next she is begging fate to spare him . . .'

'Conflict. Yes. I need to see the text.'

'I will send it to you. Where are you staying?'

'At the Golden Unicorn.'

Unnoticed by both of them, everyone present was listening to their conversation.

'How exciting!' said Josephine. 'You will compose a work specially for Josefa, and it is because you have met each other in this house.' She turned to her fiancé. 'Are you not proud, Christian?'

'Indeed I am.'

'And, Ludwig,' said Tomaczek, 'may I make a suggestion to you and Madame Duschek? I have spoken to my friend who manages the Konviktsaal. He would like to discuss with you the possibility of putting on a concert in his hall. I told him you would play your two piano concertos, which have been so well received in Vienna. Why not also perform the new song you are about to write. With Madame Duschek. Madame? Would you oblige?'

Josefa Duschek looked at Ludwig, registered his agreement, and said, 'It would be an honour, sir. I shall look forward to it very much.'

Chapter 2

Ludwig threw himself into preparations for the concert at the Konviktsaal. Lichnowsky and Tomaczek took him to meet the manager of the hall, who made a small room with a piano available to him to practise and compose. The hall itself, which was in the Old Town and just a ten-minute walk from the Clam-Gallas palace, seated no more than five hundred people – the Burgtheater in Vienna held more than a thousand – and was of simple, almost austere design, betraying its former role as a Jesuit seminary.

On his first visit there Ludwig asked for the piano to be wheeled on to the low stage, where he played a few sequences, varying the dynamics, then he asked Prince Lichnowsky to do the same while he stood at various points in the hall. Satisfied, he confirmed that he would perform his first and second piano concertos, improvise on a theme, and accompany Madame Duschek in the concert aria he was composing.

The manager, clasping his hands to his chest in delight, assured him he would assemble an orchestra in time for rehearsals. The date was fixed for one month hence.

Ludwig threw himself into composing the aria. At the same time he rehearsed his piano concertos, refining the cadenzas of each. Neither work had yet been published – Ludwig had resisted Carl's urging to let him invite offers – and Prince Lichnowsky sent to Vienna for a set of orchestral parts. At the same time as working on the aria and the concertos, Ludwig composed a number of small piano pieces for Josephine Clary. It seemed that his mind was overflowing with too many ideas for the main works alone.

The poem by Pietro Metastasio appealed to Ludwig from the moment he read it. The opening stanza was full of fury. The first line set the tone. *Ah, perfido! spergiuro, barbaro traditor, tu parti?* Ah, faithless! liar, vile deceiver, you are to leave me?

The spurned woman vents her rage against her lover, warning him that he will not escape the wrath of the gods. Everything, she warns him, will conspire to punish him. Vengeance. Vengeance is all she demands.

But as suddenly as her fury explodes, it dies. No, no, she pleads to the gods, spare him. And to him she implores his return, or else she will die of grief. And finally, in the closing stanza, once more her fury returns, but this time accompanied by an appeal not to the gods but directly to him, her faithless lover. Do I not deserve your pity? she pathetically implores him.

Ludwig saw immediately the full potential of the verse. It would be a concert aria, but performed as if in an opera, with all the drama and gestures that that required. He knew Josefa Duschek was capable of it.

The first decision he made – and he settled on it before he had written a note – was that the song would have an orchestral accompaniment, and the orchestra would play a full part in the drama. It would be like a chorus, adding its voice to his.

He composed quickly. The orchestral opening, fast, furious, ending on an expectant discord, then silent as the soprano sang alone. The music moved along swiftly, the soprano executing leaps and varying dynamics almost from bar to bar. He was writing for the voice as if it were an instrument and this a concerto.

The central section he marked *adagio* and wrote a beautiful, lyrical passage, with long, sustained notes from the singer held over pizzicato strings. After the leaps of the opening section, the sustained notes demanded perfect voice control. It ended in quiet harmony, and then the soprano introduced the final section – rage once more – with full power. Ludwig wrote in descending chromatic scales – so easy for a pianist to play, but for the voice liable to become a discordant slide, especially after ten minutes at least of virtuoso singing.

Ludwig was pleased with his work. It had drama and pathos, tension and beauty. He was delighted with the ease with which he had set an Italian text to music, enjoying the florid vowels and expressive consonants. But he knew he had set Josefa a difficult task. In an opera the aria would be less hazardous to accomplish – the singer would already have been on stage for some time, her voice lubricated and settled. He decided it was time for Josefa to start work on it.

The first rehearsal was long and arduous. Josefa concentrated on the dangerous opening leap, then tried to accustom herself to the tempestuous passage which followed.

'Ludwig, why are you making me perform such vocal acrobatics? I have so little time to learn it, yet I do not believe I have ever sung anything as difficult.'

'You are capable of it, Josefa. Remember what I told you before. Conflict. There must be conflict in your voice. Conflict, because you rage against your faithless lover. But a deeper conflict, because you are in conflict with yourself. You love him. You want to punish him, yet you want him to return. That must come through in your voice. Now, from the opening again.'

Gradually Josefa began to feel the inner force of the music Ludwig had written. Imperceptibly – paradoxically – she began to relax as she sang. She realised that the conflict Ludwig was talking about was in the music itself, inherent in it. She simply had to give it expression.

'Yes, yes!' he called, as she began to understand the relation between the words and the notes. 'Now, the Adagio. Gentle. Lyrical. Do not hurry.'

Josefa arched the top of her body forward and held her hands out in supplication. The sustained notes carried above the pizzicato accompaniment.

'Good. Slow. Hold the notes. Wait for the piano. Wait. And . . . *Allegro*! *Allegro*! Fury again. But this time frustration. Anger at yourself . . .'

Ludwig wanted to rehearse the central section again, but Josefa resisted. 'Ludwig, I will have no voice left.'

'No. You can do it. Once more. And, Josefa. Listen. The final word. *Moriro. Moriro.*' He repeated it. 'Think of its meaning. "I will die". She says, "Of grief I will die."' He said it again, more slowly. '"I will die." It is the moment for the singer. You are in control. The orchestra will wait for you. Hold it. Sustain it.'

They worked on, Josefa no longer singing out, but becoming ever more familiar with the piece.

Finally Ludwig said, 'Good, Josefa. You will do it. I know you will. Let your voice rest now. I will play for you.'

She sat gratefully and Ludwig played again the main theme from the Adagio, then began to vary it. There was no tempestuous virtuosity, instead gentle, serene lines which seemed to take flight in the upper register of the piano.

Josefa watched him playing, marvelling at how so many ideas could come to him so spontaneously. A lesser musician, she knew, would be hurrying to scribble each idea down before it evaporated, for each different variation was worthy of preserving. But Ludwig showed no regard for it. He moved seamlessly from one variation to the next.

Josefa found the music enveloping her, her voice accompanying it in a barely audible hum. She had no control. Her voice was responding naturally to the music.

Ludwig's first rehearsal with the orchestra was less successful. For one thing the manager of the Konviktsaal had had trouble securing enough players. So far he could only find three violinists and two cellists. And one of those violinists complained about some of the string passages. They were not just difficult, he said, but unnecessarily so. He made the mistake of saying that Wolfgang Mozart would never have written such music.

Ludwig stood up from the piano. 'What do you know of Mozart?' he asked with anger in his face. 'What do you know of Beethoven?'

'And what, may I ask, does Herr Beethoven know of the violin?'

Ludwig walked over to the violinist and held out his hands. A look of doubt crept over the violinist's face, but he handed his instrument to Ludwig.

Ludwig put the violin under his chin. 'Like this!' And he executed a furious run on the E string, causing the resin to fly in clouds from the bow. 'And this. Third position.' He played again. 'Do you understand? Do you see? It cannot be any other way. That is why I have written it like that. Because it cannot be any other way.'

'Maybe you should play violin instead of piano, Herr Beethoven,' said a cellist, and the laughter that accompanied the remark defused the tension.

Ludwig worked furiously in the days before the concert, but Prince Lichnowsky knew he was not using his time well. He was concentrating on the cadenzas for the two piano concertos, and still writing small pieces for Josephine Clary. The Prince decided to speak to Ludwig.

'Do forgive me for interrupting you, Ludwig. But Madame Duschek has asked me to speak to you. She wants to rehearse with the orchestra. She says—'

'Yes, yes. I know that. I haven't written the orchestra parts yet. Tell her—'

'There are not many days left, Ludwig. She needs—'

'I know! Lichnowsky, leave me. I must work.'

Lichnowsky reported back to Josefa, who wrung her hands and paced the floor with nervousness.

Ludwig grew increasingly tense as the concert approached. Predictably his stomach pains returned. He wished Franz Wegeler could be there to give him some powders. He thought of his old friend with a pang of guilt. He hoped Franz would still be in Vienna when he returned.

His stay in Prague was lasting longer than he had envisaged, and he was not sorry. There was little incentive for Ludwig to return to Vienna. His brothers' presence would put a strain on him, affecting his work. And Nikola had made an announcement when he arrived in Vienna that had shocked Ludwig.

Echoing Caspar's decision to call himself Carl, Nikola had decided to use his second name. Johann.

The sound of his father's name had made Ludwig shiver. He had not realised the effect it would have on him. In the days that followed, Ludwig had tried to come to terms with it, but he could not bring himself to utter his father's name.

There was an added problem – one that had stayed with him in Prague. Prince Lichnowsky treated him like a son, behaving himself like an overprotective father. Ludwig had begun to find it wearing in Vienna, and was continuing to do so in Prague.

That was why he had not listened when Lichnowsky had come to him with Josefa's plea for more rehearsal. He knew she was right, but he did not want to hear it from Lichnowsky. He found the Prince's constant questions burdensome. How was the composition going? Was he comfortable in his room? Was he eating enough? Be sure to dress warmly when you go out.

At the same time Ludwig was conscious of how much he owed the Prince. A day or two earlier the Prince had told him he would shortly have to leave Prague to return to Vienna. But Ludwig could stay on as long as he liked – Lichnowsky would make sure all his expenses were covered.

Furthermore, the Prince had suggested that Ludwig should extend his tour.

'Why do you not go on to Berlin and Leipzig?' he said. 'Madame Duschek is going there. Go with her. She will introduce you at court. King Friedrich, I am told, is a capable cellist. Dresden, too. Go there if you wish. Consider it. Let me know. If you wish to, I will send letters and make sure you have introductions.'

Ludwig did not wish to be any more in the Prince's debt than he already was, but he could not afford to miss such an opportunity. How better to introduce his music to new audiences? Plus he would be away from the Prince. That would make it easier, on his return to Vienna, to leave the apartment on the Alstergasse.

'Then I will accompany her on the piano. The orchestra is useless anyway.'

Lichnowsky and Tomaczek breathed a collective sigh of relief.

Josefa smiled when the two men relayed the information to her. 'Then it will be all right. When he plays I find it easier to sing. Somehow he is able to communicate what he wants, even if I am not looking at him. I can feel it in his music.'

Ludwig's stomach pains gave him severe discomfort in the twenty-four hours before the concert. But then, after the final rehearsal, when he knew there was no more work that could be done, as he changed for the performance he realised that the pains had gone.

The small hall of the Konviktsaal was filled to capacity. Ludwig looked out at the audience and knew these were people who had heard Mozart's music, who had seen him conduct his own works, and who had taken him and his music to their hearts. He could see the look of anticipation on their faces. There was not, it seemed to him, a single person present who had come for any other purpose than to listen to his music; they were not there to be seen, preening themselves in the latest Paris fashions, trying to outdo each other with the amount of wine and champagne being served in their private box.

Even the orchestra seemed to sense the special nature of the occasion: the first performance in the Bohemian capital of the music by a young German whose name was already talked about excitedly in Vienna, and was known too in Prague. A worthy successor to Wolfgang Mozart, who had died so tragically young? There were those who believed so.

Ludwig knew from the opening bars of the *tutti* of the Piano

Concerto in C that the concert would be a success. Conducting the small orchestra from the piano, he played without music. The cadenza, on which he had worked so hard, went flawlessly. At the resounding end of the work, the audience cheered and stamped their feet.

How Ludwig wished they could be so unrestrained in Vienna, where applause was invariably muted by white gloves!

As much for his own relaxation as for their pleasure, he played a simple rondo, smilingly refusing to repeat it. After a short interval he performed his Piano Concerto in B flat, again revelling in the unrestrained applause which greeted it.

This time he jumped up from the chair and personally shook the hand of every member of the orchestra, thanking them for their playing. To the violinist who had earlier complained, he gave an extra pat on the shoulder and a knowing nod.

It remained only for him and Madame Duschek to perform the concert aria, 'Ah! Perfido, spergiuro'.

Josefa was waiting for him by the side of the stage. As he took her hand and led her to the centre of the stage, the audience erupted in a cheer of welcome.

Of course! thought Ludwig. She is one of them, born in Prague. He smiled to himself.

Josefa's voice was flawless. He marvelled at the sureness of the leaps she executed, glorying in the wonder of hearing his music as he had intended it.

In strength her voice never went shrill, nor slightly above the note as lesser singers seemed unable to avoid. In the central *adagio* she sang with a quiet and stillness that he could tell had the audience spellbound. As he played the gentle pizzicato passage, she held her voice like an angel singing in heaven. He felt the tears start at the beauty with which she moulded the notes he had written. He did not hurry her. She held the notes beyond what he believed possible.

And the final section, the *allegro assai*, passion and rage again, but with a pathos this time even he had not intended or expected. The last desperate plea of a doomed woman.

As the audience rose to their feet, he walked towards her and embraced her. She took his hand and raised it, turning him to the audience.

Prague, Ludwig knew, had taken him and his music to its heart, as it had done Wolfgang Mozart.

Chapter 3

The make-up of the group of friends from Germany who sat round their usual table at the Schwan Inn had changed slightly. Franz Wegeler had left Vienna and returned to Bonn, and Johann van Beethoven, as he was now called, had taken his place. His brother Carl was with him. Andreas Streicher was on one of his regular visits to the city to see the piano-dealer in the Schlossergassel, and also at the table was Bernhard Romberg, and Nikolaus Zmeskall.

Carl stood. 'I need a smoke. Would anyone else like a pipe?'

Johann looked up, his face smiling. 'Yes, I'll have one.'

'Give me five kreutzer then.'

Johann dug into his pocket and brought out the coins, counting them carefully.

'So, Bernhard,' said Streicher, 'how was Italy?'

Romberg shook his head. 'It is going badly for the Austrians. I was in Rome and Naples and there are French soldiers everywhere. They swagger around like they did in Bonn. It's terrible.'

'What are their aims?'

'Simple, in my view. To drive the Austrians out of Italy. They've already practically succeeded. That's why I've come north. It's not safe to speak German any more in Italy. I'm going back to Bonn. I have to anyway, to see my family. I'm leaving one French–occupied country for another.'

'It's this devil of a Corsican, isn't it?'

Romberg nodded. 'You hear his name everywhere. You can't escape it. Napoleon Bonaparte.'

'He cannot take on the Empire,' said Zmeskall. 'Don't underestimate our manpower. I have seen the figures at the Chancellery. And there's Britain. Not to mention Prussia, Russia . . .'

'It won't come to that,' said Carl, returning to the table with two pipes and handing one to Johann. 'He'll be defeated, this Napoleon, and there'll be no French army left, and we'll get our city of Bonn back again.'

'I saw Austrian soldiers drilling on the Glacis and the Paradeplatz,' said Streicher. 'They're highly disciplined. It's quite a frightening sight.'

'Not to the French,' said Romberg. 'Drilling on the Glacis is one thing. Fighting in the Italian hills is another. And the French are more used to that kind of terrain. But let's not talk of war any more. Let's talk of home, Bonn. Nikola . . .'

'Johann.'

'Johann. Forgive me. You were the last of us to be there. What news of old friends? Is Stephan Breuning there? I heard . . .'

'No. He's in Mergentheim now. But Frau Breuning and her family are well.'

'And Eleonore? Is she still engaged to Franz Wegeler?'

Johann nodded. 'But they are postponing marriage, with all the trouble going on. Also, Wegeler may be moved to a hospital somewhere else. Koblenz, possibly.'

'And what about Neefe? I often think of him. Such a nice man.'

'I didn't know him well. But I heard things went badly for him. He had to give up music and took some post under the French. People started to call him a traitor. I believe his wife and daughters suffered because of it, but I understand he really thought the French would improve things for everybody. The last I heard was he had to leave Bonn – feelings were running high. I think he went to Dessau. I'm not sure. At any rate, he's no longer in Bonn.'

'Hasn't Count Waldstein left also?'

'Yes. Strange what happened to him. Apparently he fell out of favour with the Elector. He encouraged Max Franz to raise a local militia and fight the French. Max Franz said his heart would willingly do that, but he could not hold himself responsible for the loss of life that would ensue. Waldstein himself started carrying out minor attacks on the French. Nothing serious. He was caught hobbling a horse and the French threatened to lock him up, but Max Franz told them he would take care of it. I don't know what happened, but Waldstein said he was leaving Bonn for England where he was going to raise a regiment to fight the French. I heard a rumour he had come here to Vienna. In disguise.'

There was laughter and a shaking of heads. 'Rumours, rumours,' said Streicher. 'This city is full of them. I heard the other day that Napoleon had crossed the Alps and was marching through southern Austria.'

'It may yet happen.'

'Keep your voice down. There are spies everywhere.'

'Then let us talk of a subject which can be of no interest to them at all,' said Romberg. 'Music. How is my old friend, my old fellow kitchen scullion, Ludwig Beethoven?'

Carl, with a slight sneer in his voice, said, 'Moving in rather more exalted circles than kitchens. In fact, I doubt he has seen the inside of a kitchen for some years. He's been in Prague, where apparently he managed to persuade them his name was really Wolfgang Amadeus. He's now in Berlin, as guest of a certain gentleman named Friedrich Wilhelm, who happens to be the King of Prussia . . .'

'I can assure you he's making quite a name for himself here in Vienna,' said Streicher. 'Mind you, he's still not exactly fastidious about the way he dresses. Prince Lichnowsky, I'm told, has had to order his wife to stop trying to make him dress more smartly for soirées and concerts.'

'He spoke to Nanette before he left for Prague,' said Streicher. 'He told her he wanted to move. She's been looking for somewhere for him. She has always felt rather . . . motherly towards him. I don't mean to criticise your mother in any way, but whenever Nanette saw him, he was away from home. And she wanted to help him, look after him. Princess Lichnowsky doesn't know it, but Nanette often goes to his apartment and brings his washing back to our place to do it!'

'He's a fortunate man,' said Carl.

'Anyway, I think she has found rooms for him. In Petersplatz. Off the Graben. Very central. Quite noisy, though.'

'Well, if you'll excuse me, I have a desk laden with paper to attend to,' said Zmeskall.

'Me too. I must go,' said Streicher. 'I have an appointment in the Schlossergassel.'

They all stood, shook hands and went their separate ways.

Ludwig van Beethoven, on his return from his tour, was a very different individual from the one who had left Vienna only months earlier. Fêted in Prague, Dresden, Berlin and Leipzig, his music was played to universal acclaim, and he was able to call himself a friend of the King of Prussia. In Berlin he had composed sonatas for cello and piano, which he dedicated to the King. He had also composed a number of songs, a piano sonata, and had begun work on a quintet for piano and wind.

Ludwig was himself surprised at the amount of composing he had managed to do while away from Vienna. It was as if being out of the city had liberated him. He was not under obligation to a patron like Prince Lichnowsky, and although he performed at salons, there were no concerts to prepare for, and if he declined an invitation in order to continue work, no offence was taken.

The trip gave Ludwig an understanding of his own status as a musician – a status he determined to maintain on his return to the imperial capital. He now moved in his own illustrious circles; he would not allow his brothers to encroach on his life more than was absolutely necessary. It was a pity Wegeler had already left, but there was nothing he could do about that.

When Nanette Streicher pointed out that the rooms on the third floor of a building on Petersplatz were the best she could find, and that the church bells in the centre of the square were not far from his window, and that there was a militia barracks on the corner with orders shouted at early-morning drill . . . he dismissed her protestations and took them immediately.

He went to take his leave of Prince and Princess Lichnowsky, aware of how much he owed them. Not just the apartment but the introductions to the city's leading patrons of the arts, the matinées and soirées at which his music had first become generally known and admired, the enthusiasm with which the Prince had promoted his music, and, of course, the trip to Prague and beyond.

But he was also innately sure that even without the Lichnowskys' help, his own genius for music would have manifested itself. What the Lichnowskys had done was speed the process. Nevertheless, he acknowledged that he owed them a debt of gratitude.

'I have decided now to live on my own. I am grateful . . .'

'You poor dear boy,' said the Princess, putting her arm round him. 'How on earth will you manage? How will you eat?'

'My dear,' said the Prince assuagingly, 'you are talking to a young man, a very assured young man and one making quite a name for himself. I am sure he is capable . . .'

'Yes. But, Ludwig, wouldn't you rather be rid of domestic cares?'

'Maybe you will marry soon, Ludwig. Mmh? That would solve the problem.'

'No,' said Ludwig sharply, frustrated that the conversation was taking the course he feared. 'I have found rooms. I shall move into them next week. Of course, I shall still see you. I hope to play at your matinées, with Schuppanzigh and the others. But I need . . . I need . . .'

'Of course, Ludwig. My wife and I are only delighted that we have been able to be of some assistance to you. I will get my servants to move your things into your new rooms. Are you lacking for anything there?'

'No. Everything is provided. I am grateful to you both.' He bowed to each of them and quickly left the room.

Ludwig worked on the Quintet for Piano and Wind. From the start he intended it to be a homage to Wolfgang Mozart, whose own quintet for a similar combination of instruments he had admired since he had first heard it in Bonn. His work, like Mozart's, would be in E flat, but he intended to give the piano a more important role. He wanted his quintet to be less an ensemble piece, more a display for the piano with wind accompaniment.

In his new rooms, and composing, Ludwig's mood was good. At last he could work without unwanted interruptions and instructions to dress for dinner.

He was in the final stages of composition – and in particularly good spirits – when Ignaz Schuppanzigh came to see him in the Petersplatz. He entered the room puffing from the three flights of stairs and sat heavily in a chair.

'Ludwig, if we are to remain friends, you will have to move to a ground-floor apartment.'

'Schuppi, you're monstrous fat. Monstrous fat.' Ludwig started dancing from one foot to the other, shifting his own weight with surprising ease. 'Schuppanzigh-you're-a-fat-man,' he sang. 'Schuppanzigh-you're-a-fat-man. A-fat-man. A-fat-man. Schuppanzigh-you're-a-fat-man.'

Schuppanzigh shook his head slowly. 'Ludwig, I am known for my fatness, I cannot deny it. I am also known for my even and good-natured temper, for which you should be grateful. Otherwise you might find yourself with one friend fewer.'

'Schuppanzigh-you're-a-fat-man, a-nice-man, a-kind-man, a-nice-man, a-kind-man.' He raised his voice. 'And-a-fiddler-unexcelled-in-the-whole-of-this-fair-city!'

Schuppanzigh waved his arms to quieten Ludwig down. 'Shh. If you go on like that, you'll find yourself moving out of here whether you like it or not.'

'Schuppi, have you got your breath back? I need to walk. Will you come with me. Not far. Just on the Bastion. The air is clearer up there.'

'Ludwig, look at me. There is sweat on my brow. I am barely recovered from that climb and you want to drag me out again.'

'Get your breath back and then we'll go. Here, have a glass of wine.' Ludwig went to a carafe on the table and poured a glass, but Schuppanzigh waved it away.

'Remind me. There is something I have to talk to you about. When I can talk, that is,' Schuppanzigh said, his breathing still heavy.

Ludwig walked to the window. 'Fine view, don't you think, Schuppi? Look. The dark-grey walls of a church. You could almost reach out and touch it. Do you know why it's called St Peter's Church? I read that it's because it's modelled after St Peter's in Rome. Same shaped dome. Except there there's light. And sun. Here, just darkness. And greyness.'

'Why did you move here then? Your apartment at the Lichnowskys' was superb. Light, spacious, airy, and beyond the wall. You had space.'

Ludwig turned away from the window and sat on a lumpy sofa opposite Schuppanzigh. 'It was more stifling there than here. Not the apartment, the Lichnowskys.'

'They mean well. They admire you greatly.'

'I must be on my own, Schuppi. I cannot work if people are always coming in and asking to see what I have written. And telling me my meal is ready. And asking me to spend the evening with them. It is . . . oppressive.'

'They were upset, you know. They wouldn't say anything, but they were upset. They looked on you almost as—'

'A son. That's the point. I am not their son. Anyway, I have left, and that is that.'

'And now you have only church bells to disturb you . . .'

'And soldiers drilling in the street outside . . .'

'And a staircase which will be the death of me.'

'Schuppanzigh-you're-a-fat-man,' Ludwig sang again. 'Come on. Let us walk on the Bastion.'

The friends descended the ornate spiral staircase and went out into the street. Two sentries stood guard at the entrance to the barracks, their muskets shouldered with bayonets fixed and their eyes darting in all directions. A couple of men were sweeping the cobbled pavement outside the main entrance to the church, and a stream of people moved in both directions in the short, narrow street that led to the busy Graben.

'Can we not go to Taroni's, Ludwig? A coffee would be a gift from heaven. I can smell it already.'

'After. Come. I need to walk. My legs need to stretch. Maybe we will walk beyond the wall and—'

'No. Ludwig, no. I will walk on the wall with you. Stroll on it. And then we will go to Taroni's. If you want to go on one of your long walks in the suburbs, you can go alone.'

From the Graben they walked into the narrow Nagler Gasse. The Bastion loomed some distance ahead of them.

'Spring,' said Ludwig. 'Can you smell it in the air? The blossoms are beginning. I need to get into the country, Schuppi. Out of this city. In the summer I will go.'

'Where?'

'I don't know. Into the country.'

They walked from the Nagler Gasse into the small open square known as the Freyung.

'That's Prince Kinsky's palace,' said Schuppanzigh, pointing to the left. 'You've met him, haven't you?'

Ludwig frowned. 'I think so. Yes, only once. He was at the soirée when I played against Gelinek. He was impolite to me. Said I was ill dressed or something. Soldier. With a son.'

'Yes, that's him. He's a typical military man. Thinks anyone who is not a soldier is not worth bothering with. But his son is in a different mould.'

'But just as fat,' said Ludwig.

Schuppanzigh ignored the comment. 'Unlike his father he loves music. It's said he loves it more than anything. He's going into the army, obviously, but I'm told he talks of little else but music.'

'Does he play an instrument? Or compose?'

'No. He just loves listening to it. In fact I can tell you he has heard your music more often than you are aware. He was at the Burgtheater when you played your piano concertos, and he has attended some matinées at Prince Lichnowsky's. Because of his age, he usually sits near the back and leaves soon after it is over.'

Ludwig looked at the palace. 'Not as grand as Lobkowitz's.'

'Prince Lobkowitz's palace is one of the finest in all Vienna. But then he is one of the wealthiest noblemen in the city. He inherited a fortune. Some of the Bohemian aristocracy are wealthier than the Viennese, though few people are aware of it. Prince Lobkowitz has a palace too in Prague.

'Yes. I saw it when I was there. They speak highly of him there.'

'Not surprising. He is one of the most senior of their aristocrats, as well as being one of the most wealthy. And he has high standing here in the imperial capital. That gives him a lot of prestige at home. Mind you, he spends his money with scarcely a thought. His wife, I believe, has trouble keeping him in check.'

They climbed the steps by the Schottentor and began walking along the broad top of the Bastion.

Although it was a pleasant spring day there were not as many strollers as usual on the wall, and there was a noticeable lack of uniformed soldiers. Those that there were walked more purposefully than before, the usual rather smug look on their faces now replaced by something approaching consternation. The stalls were quiet. No sideshows; a forlorn juggler or two and the occasional running child. All so different from when Ludwig first came to Vienna.

'Rather sad, isn't it?' said Schuppanzigh. 'No one seems to smile any more, and we have this wretched Corsican to thank for it. The great imperial army is in tatters. The French are in control of all of northern Italy, they've crossed the Alps and it's said they've begun taking towns in southern Austria.'

'Will they head for Vienna? Will they come to these city walls?'

'Unlikely, so it's said. We don't have the forces to defend the city, believe it or not. They're all out in the field, and suffering defeat after defeat.'

'What'll happen?'

'Napoleon will offer peace terms and the Emperor will have

to accept. Humiliating, but he has no choice. The price will be our Italian possessions. Better than losing Vienna.'

Ludwig stopped and looked out across the Glacis. 'Look, Schuppi. So cultivated. So civilised. What are those villages? Grinzing. Heiligenstadt. Nussdorf. And look at the Kahlenberg. So . . . so . . .'

'It's very fine, isn't it, the way it stands guard over the city? Did you know, it's where the Polish soldiers charged down from to relieve the Turkish siege?'

'Then I'm surprised they succeeded. Such a gentle slope. Have you ever been to Bonn? To the Rhine?'

'No.'

'You must go one day. I will take you. I will show you our Kahlenberg. It's called the Dragon Mountain. Rough, rugged . . .'

'Like you, Ludwig,' and he laughed.

Ludwig began laughing too. 'Maybe you are right.'

'Come on,' said Schuppanzigh, taking advantage of the moment. 'Time for that coffee. To Taroni's.'

Ludwig turned round uncomplainingly and the two retraced their steps.

In the coffee house on the Graben, Schuppanzigh made sure Ludwig was relaxed and enjoying his coffee, then he took a deep breath and spoke.

'Ludwig, I have a favour to ask of you.'

'Granted, my good friend. Granted.'

'Excellent. Then what will you play?'

Ludwig jerked his head up from his coffee, a bead of frothy milk on his upper lip. 'The Augarten? One of your concerts at the Augarten?'

'Actually, no, though there is a connection. Do you know Ignaz Jahn?'

Ludwig shook his head.

'He runs a restaurant in the Himmelpfortgasse, off the Kärntnerstrasse.'

'Jahn's restaurant? I've heard of it. Zmeskall mentioned it. There something about it. I can't remember . . .'

'Jahn's Hungarian . . .'

'That's why Zmeskall knows him then . . .'

'He was head chef to the Empress Maria Theresa in the Schönbrunn palace, and when Emperor Joseph opened the Augarten to the public, he ran the restaurant in the pavilion, where we have the early-morning concerts. In fact, you know the sign over the entrance to the Augarten, about this place being dedicated to the enjoyment of all people by their protector? Jahn claims credit for the words.'

'So?'

'Well, through his connections with the Emperor he came to know all the important people in Vienna and he opened his restaurant in the Himmelpfortgasse. But he wanted it to be more than just a restaurant, so he started having entertainment there. Conjurors and dancers at first, things like that. But then it changed. Writers came and read passages from their books, actors performed scenes, philosophical debates took place. And, of course, music was played.'

'Music?'

'There's a large room on the first floor of the restaurant. It looks out up the Rauhensteingasse. Jahn encouraged musicians to perform there. I'm talking of some time ago now. Ten or fifteen years. And do you know who performed there?'

'Who?'

'Wolfgang Mozart, no less. Yes, Mozart himself. He played a pastorale by Handel, apparently. I was a child, but I remember my father talking about it.'

'Mozart played in a restaurant?'

'Yes. And in the year he died he played his last piano concerto there. The B flat. I think it was his last public concert. Then, a year or so later, his Requiem was sung there. Constanze wanted it performed. Baron Swieten organised it with Süssmayr, you know, who completed it after Mozart died.'

'All this happened at Jahn's?'

Schuppanzigh nodded. 'But there's been virtually no music there since.'

'That's why I haven't heard of it, then.'

'Yes. Apparently Mozart did not like performing there. He didn't get on with Jahn. But more than that, he didn't think his works should be played while people were eating.'

'He's right. He's right. Music is more . . .'

'That's why he stopped playing at the Augarten concerts as well. He said people weren't there to listen to the music, just to be seen in the latest fashions.'

Ludwig nodded.

'But, Ludwig, this is what I am getting at,' said Schuppanzigh, leaning forward enthusiastically. 'It's been a while since any music was played there. But Jahn wants to start it up again, and he's asked me to organise a concert.'

'But you said yourself it's not the right place . . .'

'I know, but Jahn has said he'll make the first floor into a proper concert area. No food or drink, the chairs arranged properly, so people have to listen. I think it's a good idea.'

Ludwig shook his head. 'No. It's still a bad idea. Anyway, what do you want from me? Is this the favour which you asked for?'

'And which you said was granted!'

'No, Schuppi. Not in a restaurant. Anyway, why involve me? You can play with Weiss and Kraft . . .'

'The reason, dear Ludwig, is that Jahn knows your music and believes you to be the successor to Mozart. He wants to offer you his concert room for the first performance of a new work.'

'Is he commissioning a piece from me?'

Schuppanzigh nodded and smiled. 'He wanted to tell you himself. He asked my advice. I said I would mention it to you first. Sound you out.'

'Ha!' Ludwig leaped suddenly from his chair. 'Schuppan-zigh-you're-a-fat-man,' he sang, dancing from foot to foot, 'Schuppanzigh-you're-a-fat-man . . .'

'Ludwig. Stop. Sit down,' said Schuppanzigh anxiously, pull-ing at Ludwig's sleeve and looking nervously round the room. 'I take it from this response that you are not averse to Herr Jahn's offer?'

'If that is how you take it, Schuppanzigh, you are entirely mistaken. In Berlin my new cello sonatas were performed at the court of King Friedrich of Prussia. In Dresden and Leipzig I was admitted into the most exclusive salons. And in Prague. The same is true here in Vienna. I am not going to perform my music in a restaurant.'

Chapter 4

Ignaz Jahn would not take no for an answer.

'But did you explain about the concert room? That I won't serve food in it? That I want the whole first-floor area to become . . . as it was when . . . ?'

Schuppanzigh nodded wearily. 'Herr Jahn, my friend Beethoven is a man of strong opinions, especially when it comes to music. If he has made up his mind, it would take a more powerful force than the French army to change it.'

'Did you tell him who would be there? That I am personally acquainted with Baron Swieten, Prince Lobkowitz, Prince Lichnowsky, Count—'

'That is probably the least . . .' Schuppanzigh's eyes suddenly lit up. 'Have you spoken to Zmeskall? Nikola Zmeskall?'

'Zmeskall?' asked Jahn with a disdainful tone to his voice. 'Why should I speak to him? He is an underling at the Hungarian Chancellery. What—?'

'Because he has Beethoven's ear. He is probably his closest friend. They get on better than Beethoven gets on with his own brothers. He might be able to persuade him. And since he is Hungarian too, he might be willing to help.'

'Herr Schuppanzigh, may I remind you that I was head chef to the Empress Maria Theresa at Schönbrunn. She chose me personally. Few were as close to her as I was. On political matters, that is. I do not now need to enlist the services of a junior diplomat to achieve what I desire. You, forgive my bluntness, cannot have explained to Herr Beethoven the importance of the occasion. I shall write to him myself. Meanwhile, I shall expect you to continue making the other musical arrangements. April the sixth is not that far away.'

*   *   *

Ludwig screwed the letter into a ball and tossed it to the corner
of the room, where it joined several others. Ignaz Jahn was
beginning to wear him down.

He was looking forward to the summer. He was determined
to get away. Not far, but away. Mödling perhaps, just to
the south of Vienna. Or Baden, a little further. Or maybe
Heiligenstadt to the north, or Döbling. He could not go far,
anyway. The French were now firmly in control of southern
Austria, and Vienna was seething with rumours that they were
advancing north.

There was a knock on the door. Ludwig glanced at it wearily,
but a smile crossed his face as Nikolaus Zmeskall walked in.

'Baron Zmeskall, Zmeskallovich. Enter my humble apartment. Did the soldiers stop you at the entrance and ask you
your business? Listen, the church bells. They toll your arrival.'

Zmeskall smiled broadly, his eyes narrowing and blinking
behind his thick spectacles. 'Ludwig, you are mad. Delightfully,
utterly mad. If you were not such a capable musician, they would
lock you up.'

'Capable! Capable! You, my dear Baron, my most excellent
Count of Music, my highly distinguished Muck-cart Driver,
you are a capable musician. On that splendid instrument that
you grasp between your legs, you are truly a capable musician.
But please do not rank me in that category.'

'As you wish, Ludwig. What should I call you instead?'

'Oh, I don't know, Nikola. Nikola. Splendid name that.
You are not ashamed of it, are you? Then why should my
wretched brother wish to rid himself of it? All my life I
have had two brothers, Caspar and Nikola. Now, suddenly,
I have two different brothers, Carl and Johann. They are
both . . . both . . . Oh, I want to be rid of them. Everything. Sometimes everything is too much.' He walked to
the window and gazed out at the church wall just across the
narrow street.

'Ludwig, come back. Sit down. Here, let me pour you a glass
of wine. Shall we go the Schwan?'

'No. Their wine is muck. Anyway, the war is making
everyone tense. And there are spies everywhere. As soon as
you speak a dozen pairs of eyes turn to look at you.'

'I know. It's a wretched business. The imperial army is not
used to defeat. And by the French! A wretched, dastardly race of
people who cut off their King's head. And his wife's a Habsburg,

for God's sake. And if they defeat the imperial army, what then for our own royal family. Cut their heads off too? Wretched business. Wretched business.'

'Nikola, I have finished my piano quintet. I think it is . . . It's on the same model as Wolfgang Mozart's. Piano and wind instruments. But the piano is more . . . more . . .'

'Excellent. I am delighted. When are we going to hear it?'

'I don't know. One of the Augarten concerts in the summer?'

'It's not certain they'll take place, because of the war.'

'No music in Vienna? The capital of music? The people will die of starvation.'

'It'll depend on salons and the few individuals who are able to put on performances.'

'Yes, that would be the answer,' Ludwig said excitedly. 'But are there any? Would they be interested in my music?'

'One or two,' said Zmeskall, his voice remaining calm and affecting an air of disinterest. 'I think they would be interested in your music. Might be, rather. In fact, there is one who I happen to know . . .'

'Who . . . ?'

'He has an excellent reputation. Mozart played for him. His concert room is first class, patronised by the best . . .'

'Who?'

Zmeskall smiled. 'A fellow Hungarian of mine. I can vouch for him totally.'

Ludwig stood quickly. 'Ba-ron!' he sang. 'Ba-ron . . . Ba-ron, Ba-ron, Ba-ron!'

Schuppanzigh promised he would engage the finest oboe, clarinet, horn and bassoon players in Vienna and assemble them as soon as possible for rehearsal in the concert room on the first floor of Jahn's restaurant in the Himmelpfortgasse.

Ludwig, as he knew he would, took an instant dislike to the fawning Jahn, who, when he was not talking loftily of his closeness to Empress Maria Theresa and her son the late Emperor Joseph, was bustling around Ludwig asking him if there was anything further he required.

The rehearsals went well. The instrumentalists were as accomplished as Schuppanzigh promised they would be, though one or two complained that the piano part in the quintet was of far greater prominence than any of theirs.

'That is because I composed the piece, and I am a pianist.'

'So was Mozart, and he did not—'

Ludwig was patient with them, recognising that they were accomplished musicians. 'Gentleman, my name is not Mozart, it is Beethoven. Now, if you would be so kind. The opening again. It is a powerful introduction. A call to attention. I wrote it so that nobody could be in any doubt that the piece they are about to hear is important. Not a trivial divertissement, a piece of salon frippery. An important work. So. The opening. In unison. On the notes of the tonic chord. Perfect unison. You must all watch me for the beat. Then the piano solo, which grows out of it. Then again unison, *fortissimo*. And again watching me for the beat.'

Two days before the performance, Schuppanzigh came to see Ludwig in his rooms on Petersplatz and the two sat drinking wine.

'I hear the rehearsals have been successful.'

Ludwig nodded. 'They are good musicians. I think the piece will go well.'

'Excellent. Excellent. Now, Ludwig, I want to talk to you about the introductory piece.'

'What do you mean?'

'Your work, your quintet, is obviously the main work of the evening. It's four movements, isn't it? That's good. But I have decided to have one extra piece, as a . . . a . . . sort of introduction. To put the audience in the right frame of mind for the quintet.'

Schuppanzigh drained his glass. Ludwig refilled it, topping up his own at the same time. Schuppanzigh drank again, then leaned forward, a look of slight apprehension on his face.

'Ludwig, I think a song, a gentle song, a beautiful soprano voice . . . In that room, just a voice with soft piano accompaniment . . . would that not be the perfect . . . ? It would contrast . . .'

Ludwig nodded. 'Yes. It would prepare people. You are right. Who will sing? And what song?'

'Ludwig, do you know who is back in Vienna? From Venice, I think.'

Ludwig shook his head.

'Magdalena Willmann. Your friend from Bonn, the singer in the Electoral chorus. She has a beautiful voice. Soft. Gentle.'

Ludwig looked up sharply. 'Is she in Vienna? You're right

about her voice. Why have you chosen her? In a city of a thousand singers?'

'To be absolutely honest with you, it was her idea. She approached me through your brother Carl.'

'She wants to sing?'

Schuppanzigh nodded enthusiastically. 'She heard that your quintet was being played at Jahn's. She wants to sing, and I think it is a good idea. Don't you?'

Ludwig allowed a small smile to creep across his face. 'She wants to. She asked to. Well, why not? All right. What will she sing?'

'She has chosen an aria from *La Molinara*. "Nel cor più".'

'Has she? And who will accompany her?'

'Carl.'

Ludwig took a long draught of wine. 'No. No, Carl will not accompany her.'

'Ludwig, it is arranged. They have rehearsed.'

'Tell Leni I would like her to sing a song I composed. It's from a poem by Bürger. Gottfried Bürger. It's called "Love Requited". Carl has the manuscript. Ask him for it.'

Ludwig wished he could quell his churning stomach. At least the atmosphere in Jahn's restaurant was less formal than the Burgtheater or the Redoutensaal at the Hofburg palace, but still the sharp pains were there – the constant accompaniment, it seemed, to any public performance he was to give.

He was less apprehensive, though, than he might have been. The quintet rehearsals had gone well. So had the two brief rehearsals he had had with Leni Willmann. She had behaved in a delightful way towards him; no hint of what had been said when they last met. She behaved as she had done on that trip to Mergentheim: friendly, relaxed, no hint of tension. She kissed him on the cheek, put her arm on his, nodded vigorously at his instructions from the piano, and sang, Ludwig thought, beautifully.

'My dear boy, how good to see you again,' said Baron Swieten. 'Must admit, my duties have kept me away, but I've followed your progress. Prague and Berlin, eh? What did they say about Abbé Gelinek in Prague? Mmh?'

Ludwig smiled but said nothing.

'Remember this young lad? Old Prince Kinsky's son. Ferdinand.'

Ferdinand Kinsky nodded.

'How is your father?' Ludwig asked.

'Not well, sir, I regret to say. Otherwise he would have been here. He sends you his compliments.' Ferdinand Kinsky pulled his shoulders back as he spoke, his already large stomach straining against his waistcoat, exactly as his father's had, Ludwig remembered. 'What are we hearing?'

'Herr Beethoven's new Quintet for Piano and Wind,' said Swieten quickly, noticing the flash of irritation on Ludwig's face at the abruptness of the question from the young man who was not yet twenty.

Kinsky nodded slowly. 'You know, Herr Beethoven,' he said with a disarming smile, 'I heard that Herr Haydn did not approve of one of your piano trios. The third, I think it was. Damn-fool notion, if you ask me. My opinion is that it is the strongest of the three. Very fine works for your Opus Number One. Damned fine. And the third the finest.'

Ludwig found himself smiling at the young man's precociousness. He turned to Swieten. 'And how is Herr Haydn? It is a while since I have seen him.'

'Very overworked, I am afraid. Very overworked. I did not even mention to him about your performance tonight. He would not have had time. And I am afraid it is my fault.'

'Why?'

'I finally gave him the text – the Biblical text – I had been working on. *The Creation*, it is called. He is to set it to music. An oratorio. He was reluctant at first; he said his life's work was done. But I persuaded him. Actually, I think he needed very little persuading.'

The sound of a stick hitting the floor made Ludwig turn round.

'Prince Lobkowitz. I am pleased to see you.'

'Pleasure's mine. Pleasure's mine. Swieten. Kinsky. Good gathering. Fine job Jahn has made of this place, eh? Like it was before. I bring Prince Lichnowsky's regrets. His wife the Princess is unwell.'

Ignaz Jahn bustled up to the group, carrying a tray of low glasses of heavy, sweet wine and small round cakes.

'Gentlemen, such a pleasure to welcome you to my humble establishment. May I . . . ?'

Ludwig bowed slightly to everyone and took the opportunity to leave the group. He sought out Carl and took him into the concert room at the back, where a waiter was arranging chairs into straight rows.

'Do you have all the music? Is it all in order? Where are the wind parts?'

'Will you calm down, Ludwig? I have everything.'

'Is Leni Willmann here yet?'

'Yes. I have seen her. She's with a friend.'

'We should start soon. Go and tell Jahn. I want to start soon.'

'I told Jahn he should be paying you for this performance tonight. He said no. You should have brought me in on this sooner. Let me do the negotiations. I've told you before—'

'Go!' said Ludwig sharply. 'Tell Jahn I want to start.' He walked to the piano and arranged his chair in position. Still standing, he played a few chords and looked into the top of the piano. He plucked a string or two to test their strength and played the chords again. Satisfied, he turned to leave the room.

Leni Willmann and her friend were standing there.

'Hello, Ludwig. I'd like you to meet my friend Antonie Birkenstock. She lives in the Erdbeergasse in the Landstrasse.'

Ludwig bowed his head. 'I have friends in the Landstrasse. The Streichers. Do you know them?'

Antonie shook her head and smiled. Ludwig found himself smiling with her. He liked the openness of her face and the way it lit up when she smiled. It was framed by tumbling auburn curls, and her lips were wide and sensuously curved. Her nostrils flared almost imperceptibly. What struck Ludwig most of all was that despite her smile, there seemed to be a sadness to her eyes; they were dark and deep, and Ludwig felt instinctively that they had known tears.

'Toni is so happy,' Leni said. 'She has just become engaged. You don't mind me telling Ludwig, do you, Toni? He's such a good friend. She's to marry a very important businessman from Frankfurt. His name's Franz. I forget . . .'

'Brentano,' said Toni softly.

'Congratulations,' said Ludwig. 'I wish you happiness.'

'Thank you.' And Ludwig was struck again by how dark her eyes were.

He was distracted by Schuppanzigh, who hurried up to him, breathing hard. There were beads of sweat on his forehead.

'I am so sorry to be late. I was detained. Is everything in

order? Jahn is telling people now to be seated. Will you begin right away with the song? Leni?' he asked anxiously.

'Do not worry, Ignaz. It will be all right. Calm yourself. You are making me nervous!'

Antonie wished them both luck and took a seat at the back of the room. Then the other guests came in and began taking their seats. Schuppanzigh hurried Ludwig and Leni off to the side.

'I will introduce you,' he said in a loud whisper. 'And then you can start. Then the quintet. The wind players have just arrived. They're in one of the small rooms downstairs where they'll warm up. All right? Ready?'

Ludwig looked across the room and felt his stomach constrict. It was an impressive gathering. Pity Lichnowsky was not here, or Haydn to give the evening a certain musical authority. No, thought Ludwig, perhaps it was better Haydn was not here. This was not the kind of occasion which called for analysis, and he suspected that the venerable old composer still harboured a slight resentment over their disagreement regarding the third piano trio – even though it had been resolved successfully. The three trios had achieved enormous popularity in the city – the third being the most often performed and praised.

At the side of the room he saw his brothers with Zmeskall. Carl was gesticulating angrily towards the gentle Hungarian. Always arguing, thought Ludwig, always driving his point home as if the person he was talking to was some kind of idiot. Johann – Nikola, he will always be Nikola to me, he thought – was looking round the room, a vacant smile on his face. He was lowering his head to the men he knew were aristocrats, but was receiving no response.

At the back of the room he watched Antonie Birkenstock. She caught his eye and gave him an encouraging nod. He smiled back.

Schuppanzigh waited for Jahn and a waiter to clear the room of glasses, after which Jahn closed the double doors and nodded at him. Schuppanzigh cleared his throat, looked at Ludwig and Leni for their assurance that they were ready, then walked to the front of the room and raised his hands for quiet.

'Your Imperial Highnesses, ladies and gentlemen. A great pleasure to welcome you here to Jahn's establishment for an evening of music by my friend, who is known to all of you, Herr Beethoven from Bonn. He will first accompany Fräulein Willmann in one of his own songs. And then you will hear his new Quintet for Piano and Wind. It has not been heard in public before. I am sure you will take it to your hearts as readily as you have taken his other compositions.'

He cleared his throat again, noticing the anxious signals from Ignaz Jahn in the corner of the room.

'And, yes, of course, let me say how good it is of Herr Jahn to make his fine establishment available to us this evening. I am sure you know of his illustrious past, as head chef to the late Empress and her son the Emperor. Also that Herr Mozart himself performed in this very room. Yes, and of course after tonight's performance, Herr Jahn invites you all to stay for drinks and an excellent supper, which will be served downstairs.'

A general nodding of heads accompanied light clapping.

'So without further words from me, allow me to introduce Herr Beethoven and Fräulein Willmann. They are going to sing for you the song "Love Requited", set to music by Herr Beethoven from a poem by Gottfried Bürger.'

There was applause, more sustained this time, as Ludwig sat at the piano and Leni took her place in front of the audience, her hands held across her chest.

Ludwig began the short piano introduction. He had written the song as one of a pair, with no pause between the two. But he and Leni had agreed at their first rehearsal only to perform the second. It suited her voice perfectly, with its gentle and instantly memorable theme. It was a wistful verse, the plaintive yearning of a lover that her love might be requited. Ludwig had given it a delicate theme, which Leni's pure voice had instantly taken to. And though she smiled at him as he took her through it, there was no hint in her face at what might have been between them. They were two musicians, making music together.

Now she faced the audience, the top half of her body leaning slightly towards them. Even though he could not see her face, Ludwig knew she was smiling as she sang the words.

> If I had known you loved me even though
> Your love was just a hundredth part of mine,
> If I had known your heart would
> Even half as my heart pine,
> If I had known your lips would kiss me
> Willingly and kiss again;
> Then, Oh God, my heart would surely
> Burst. My life and soul I'd give to you.

> From simple favours love comes forth
> And love will nurture love requited.
> What would once the smallest spark have stayed
> Becomes an everlasting fire of love
> Ne'er to fade. Ne'er to fade.

He played the few quiet bars which brought the song to an end and held the final chord.

There were cries of 'Bravo!' Not loudly, as in a concert hall, but conversational almost. The applause, similarly, was polite but sustained. Ludwig allowed Leni to take her bow, not going to join her in front of the audience, even when she beckoned to him to do so.

The applause continued, growing in intensity, and predictably the shouts of 'Bravo!' turned to 'Encore!' Leni looked at Ludwig, her eyebrows raised. He nodded and smiled, waited for the applause to subside, and began playing again.

More relaxed this time, Leni allowed herself a little more emotion in her voice, held the top notes a fraction longer. Ludwig sensed her increased confidence immediately and adapted his accompaniment accordingly.

She sang the song beautifully and the renewed applause reflected it. As it finally began to die down, Ludwig walked to her, took her hand in both of his, raised it to his lips and kissed it. Flushed, Leni walked to the back of the room and took her seat next to Antonie, who encouragingly patted her on the shoulder.

Schuppanzigh, beaming broadly, stood again in front of the audience.

'A fine, fine performance, ladies and gentlemen, as I know you will agree. Indeed, as your applause most generously acknowledged. A small pause now, while we set up the music stands. I suggest you remain in your seats . . .'

Even as he spoke, the wind players were arranging their stands and seats. None had his back to the piano; the clarinet player sat in front of Ludwig, so he – as leader of the winds – could coordinate timing with the piano. As soon as they were seated they began tuning their instruments – clarinet, horn, oboe and bassoon – to the A that Ludwig gave them.

'Your Imperial Highnesses, ladies and gentlemen,' said Schuppanzigh, raising his voice slightly over the tuning, 'the Quintet for Piano and Wind, by Herr Ludwig Beethoven.'

With barely a pause, Ludwig ascertained from the clarinettist that all four were ready, raised his head and brought his hands down on the keys for the opening unison bars.

It was a critical opening, demanding total accuracy of timing from all four wind instruments and piano. Indeed, the bassoonist had pleaded with Ludwig to make it otherwise. Too much at stake too early in the piece, he had said. And as if that wasn't enough, a repetition of the unison sequence, *forte*, just a few bars later. If that didn't work, he said, the whole piece would fail.

Ludwig had rehearsed the opening again and again, more than any other passage in the work. He made each player play it alone with the piano, then in pairs. Finally they played it together, Ludwig and the clarinettist coordinating the timing.

Now, with the added tension of performing before an audience, the players were alert to a greater degree than was possible in a rehearsal, and the opening sequence – and its repeat – were played in perfect unison.

Ludwig could sense from the start that the audience was receptive. He was pleased with his composition – he had not hesitated in giving it an opus number. It was true he had modelled it on Mozart's work for a similar combination of instruments, but his intention was to take it further. The players themselves had been quick to see that of all the instruments it was the piano that had the most exposed and difficult sequences, but Ludwig had been careful to give each instrument solo passages. They knew of his reputation as a virtuoso; they knew too that the quintet was his composition. To persuade him to make alterations was out of the question. They had quickly decided among themselves to accept what he had written and play it to the best of their ability.

The work was not long. Ludwig wondered as he played the Andante Cantabile whether he had made the movement too short. After the briefest of pauses he began the piano solo at the start of the Rondo, the final movement. It was a simple theme – simple, the word Mozart himself, who had played in the very room, had used – light and easy to listen to. The wind players entered perfectly; Ludwig increased the pace slightly.

A glance over their heads told him that the audience was hanging on every note. Ludwig decided on the spur of the moment that it deserved more.

A third of the way into the Rondo, the music slowed to an almost complete halt. The piano had a run in the right hand, after which it took up the main theme again and was then joined by the other instruments.

Ludwig played the run as he had written it, and as he began the main theme again the other players raised their instruments to their lips. But Ludwig did not play the theme as written. He began varying it. The players lowered their instruments. As the variation neared its end, they raised their instruments again. But Ludwig began another variation, this time louder and faster. Again they lowered their instruments, a look of some frustration crossing the face of the oboist. Ludwig went straight into another variation, this time solid chords, and after that a skeletal variation in the minor key. The wind players left their instruments in their laps.

Ludwig was smiling, clearly enjoying what he was doing. This communicated itself to the audience, who had smiled at the obvious discomfort of the wind players, but were reluctant to show too much enjoyment for fear of offending either Ludwig or the players. Now they smiled openly, exchanging looks and nods of the head. This was one of the improvisations for which Ludwig was famous, but which he was notoriously reluctant to perform to request. They sat back and enjoyed it.

When finally Ludwig decided to bring the variations to an end, he began playing the theme again in its original form and nodded to the clarinettist, who raised his clarinet to his lips. The other musicians followed. All came in perfectly and resumed the music.

The trills in the right hand of the piano, while the wind instruments threw fragments of the theme between them, signalled the approaching end of the work. In perfect unison the musicians played the seven chords which ended it.

The audience erupted into applause. Any irritation on the part of the players at Ludwig's unscheduled and unprepared variations dissipated in the warmth of the reception. Ludwig encouraged the players to stand while he remained seated at the piano. Then he joined them, pushing them further forward with his arms.

He looked at the faces, upturned and smiling. He saw Lobkowitz holding his crutch high and shaking it. The young Prince Kinsky was clapping with his hands held above his head. Swieten was smiling broadly and clapping. In the back row Leni was leaning towards Antonie and whispering something; they were both smiling. He could see Zmeskall blinking behind his thick spectacles. He saw his brothers. Johann was clapping loudly and looking around him to encourage the applause. Ludwig knew he should feel grateful; instead he felt a wave of irritation. Johann did not understand music; he was simply clapping because it was expected. Carl was applauding, but half-heartedly and with no smile.

Ludwig knew his quintet was a success. Afterwards, drinking wine and eating chicken legs, he enjoyed the compliments that were directed at him. He sought out Leni, to congratulate her again on her performance of his song. He asked after Antonie, but unfortunately she had had to get back to her father's house, leaving Leni to tell Ludwig how impressed she was with his playing.

The next day Ludwig slept late and was awoken by an insistent knocking on the door. Blearily he opened it to see Zmeskall standing there.

'Ludwig, get dressed quickly. You must come and see. On the Paradeplatz.'

'What? What's going on? Has anyone spoken about the quintet? Said anything?'

'I don't know. I'm sorry, Ludwig. I'm afraid people's minds are elsewhere today. Come to the Paradeplatz. You'll see. The militia's been called out.'

The friends hurried to the open space between the rear of the Hofburg Palace and the Bastion, where they joined a growing crowd.

The militia were drilling, the sun glinting off their bayonets and silver helmets. In front of them stood twelve soldiers, each carrying a different regimental banner. In response to commands, the militia separated into two lines and marched off in different directions, wheeling on a further command and joining up again. The crowd applauded with excitement.

'Where are the French now?' someone asked.

'They've taken all of Tyrol and Carinthia. I heard they've captured Leoben.'

'Leoben? But that's in Styria. It means they're heading for Vienna.'

'Apparently an advance guard is close to Semmering. That's only a day's march from here. Two at most.'

'But look at this wall. It withstood the Turks. It'll withstand the French.'

'The Turks didn't have cannon like the French have.'

'Or a general with a Corsican name.'

'But our forces are prepared. Look at them. Aren't they a splendid sight?'

The confidence being displayed on the Paradeplatz was not shared in the Hofburg palace. Emperor Franz knew that if he did not make peace with Napoleon Bonaparte, the French would invade Vienna and most likely take it. It would be a defeat – and humiliation – from which the Holy Roman Empire might not recover.

The Emperor sent a team of diplomats to the Bishop's palace at Leoben, where the French General had made his headquarters, to offer peace terms. To his huge relief Napoleon Bonaparte agreed. Franz ceded Belgium and the Rhine frontier, as well as Lombardy, in return for receiving Venice.

There was a certain sense of anti-climax in Vienna at the realisation that the war against France was over. But cooler heads pointed out that Napoleon's aims were larger than he had himself admitted. He wanted nothing less than the destruction of the empire, and was unlikely to rest until he had achieved it. That meant that the fighting was very unlikely to be over.

Round the table in the Schwan Inn the conversation was similarly gloomy. By giving up Germany as far as the Rhine, the Elector had confirmed the French as conquerors of the Rhine valley. Bonn was now under French rule, with the acquiescence of the empire.

Ludwig told his brothers he was going to Mödling for the summer and did not want to be disturbed.

BOOK NINE

Chapter 1

Ludwig walked through the Stubentor gate on the east side of the city, past the huge hospital building on the left and out on to the Landstrasse. There was an autumn chill in the air and his body ached. His head throbbed with a pain which had been with him for days and which he seemed unable to shake. He wished he had worn his coat. He was not looking forward to winter. He clutched the folder of papers tighter to his body. As he emerged from the shadow of the hospital he felt himself unexpectedly bathed in warmth. The sun, a pale and weak yellow, retained just a vestige of its summer strength, enough to dispel the chill he had felt around the cold stone of the city wall.

He looked up. Ahead of him the Landstrasse suburb stretched into the distance, a gently rising incline lined with linden trees, the open countryside beyond. He breathed in the air and enjoyed its freshness. If it had been spring instead of autumn, he knew that the warmth and the green leaves, flowers and singing birds would have cured his aching body. But there would be no more warmth now for perhaps six months. The thought depressed him.

He turned into a small road to the right, then left into the Ungargasse, which ran parallel to the Landstrasse and like it out into the country. The Ungargasse was narrower than the Landstrasse, the houses closer together. It had a comfortable feel about it. Ludwig liked the quietness, disturbed only by the occasional passing carriage clattering on the cobbles and the clucking directions of the driver to his horse. Small groups of children played in the open fields behind the houses, a happy infantile cry piercing the air momentarily.

He walked under the arch of the house known as the Red Rose and across the small courtyard. Even before he reached the workshop he could smell the sawdust and wood shavings which irritated his nose. He became aware of a harsh sound, a jarring noise which caused vibrations in his head and increased the pain. It was the single key of a piano being struck forcefully and repeatedly.

Ludwig sat on a stool, pulled a handkerchief from his pocket and wiped his forehead. He looked at the broad back of Andreas Streicher crouched over the piano, one hand on the keys, the other reached over inside holding a tuning instrument.

The sawdust was now hurting his lungs and the sound from the piano seemed to be growing harsher, painful even.

'Stop! For God's sake, Streicher. Enough! You'll burst my head with that noise.'

Andreas Streicher turned round, a look of shock on his face at the interruption. It broke into a warm smile when he recognised his friend.

'Ludwig. How good to see you. You gave me quite a start. How are you?' He stood, slipping the instrument into the pocket of his leather apron and wiping his hands on its front.

'I don't know. Not well. A chill or something. My head hurts.'

'It's the change of season, that's all. It'll pass. Now tell me, how was Mödling? I haven't seen you since you got back.'

'All right to begin with. I was able to compose. I took a room on the square. It's beautiful. Quiet. But I became ill. A fever. I think it's still with me. I haven't shaken it off.'

'Oh dear. You poor man. Nanette will be so sorry too. Let me get her. No, even better. Come into the front room. Away from all this mess.'

Ludwig nodded, grateful for the suggestion.

'We'll have some tea. Or coffee. Whatever you like. But if you don't mind, we'll come back out here afterwards. There's something I want to show you.'

Ludwig nodded and followed Andreas into the house.

'Nanette, my dear. Ludwig's come to see us.'

Nanette came hurrying out of the scullery, drying her hands on a cloth.

'Dear Ludwig. How are you?' She kissed him on both cheeks. 'Have you brought me some clothes to wash for you? Here. Come into the front room. Sit down. You look tired. Can I get you some tea?'

'Thank you.'

'You must tell me all your news. You were in Döbling, weren't you?'

Ludwig shook his head. Andreas answered for him. 'Mödling. South of the city. It was restful. But he was unwell.'

'Unwell? Oh dear, I'm so sorry to hear that. You must tell me about it. But let me get the tea first.'

Ludwig leaned back in the chair, allowing his head to rest against the back of it, and closed his eyes. He wished the throbbing in his head would stop. At least he could breathe more easily away from the piano workshop. For a moment his mind drifted back to Mödling.

How enchanting the main square was. The town hall on one side, with its onion-domed clock tower; hay wagons rumbling across the uneven ground, laden down with bales which had been harvested from the fields. On the side of the square adjacent to the town hall a tavern with tables and chairs outside, where he would sit and drink wine as he watched the summer sun sinking on the horizon. He did not seek company or conversation and was not offered any.

He had taken a room on the first floor of the humble pension alongside the tavern. There was no piano but he did not mind. He was composing without one. He had decided to do more work on the musical form which still interested him most: the piano sonata. He was pleased with the two small sonatas he had composed after the trip to Prague, but he regarded them almost as exercises – preparations for something more substantial.

He had made good progress. The broad outline of a major piano sonata was now committed to paper – in fact he had the sheets in the folder he was now holding in his lap. He knew what he wanted the sonata to say, how he wanted the movements to sound. He had only to write the final manuscript. But there were some questions he wanted to ask Streicher . . .

Remembering suddenly that he was sitting in Streicher's front room, he opened his eyes to see both Andreas and Nanette smiling at him.

'I . . . I'm sorry. I was thinking . . .'

'Here, dear Ludwig,' said Nanette. 'Have some tea. You didn't hear us talking to you.'

'No. I'm sorry. I was thinking. My sonata. It's here. I'd like to play you the opening later. It's . . . it's different. I need to speak to you about the instrument, Andreas.'

'Of course. We'll go through afterwards. I'm looking forward to hearing it.'

'You look refreshed from your little sleep,' said Nanette, handing him a cup.

'I wasn't asleep,' said Ludwig, immediately regretting the harshness in his voice. 'I . . . I just didn't hear you.'

'Well, anyway, how was Mödling? Did you say you were unwell?'

Ludwig nodded. 'It was my own fault. My own stupidity. I went for a long walk one afternoon. In the Hinterbrühl. It was hot. The sun was strong. When I got back to my room I threw open the shutters, opened the window, took off my shirt and stood there, letting the air cool my body. It was so refreshing, I can feel it now.'

'But you were naked to the waist?'

'Yes. To the amusement of the urchins in the square. But the air was cooling, and I was damp with sweat. From the long walk.'

'How long did you stand there?' asked Nanette, concern in her voice.

'Maybe half an hour. Maybe an hour. I pulled up a chair and sat there. The sun was low across the square and still warm, but already the air was chill. I fell asleep. When I woke up I was shivering and my body was cold.'

'Ludwig, I'm not surprised you became ill.'

'It was strange. I didn't seem to be able to warm up. I climbed under the bedcovers. I even told them to bring me an extra blanket. But I was still cold. I shivered all night. I hardly slept. The next morning I had a throbbing pain in my head. It's still there, I can feel it now. Though it's not as bad.'

'Oh, Ludwig, how awful for you. Can I get you something? I have some powders which always . . .'

'Thank you, Nanette, but no. Nothing. Just the tea.'

'Did you have a fever?'

'Yes. For two or three days.'

'Did you call a doctor?'

'No. I didn't want any fuss. Anyway it passed. And I was working. I didn't want interruptions.'

'Working? You mean composing? How could you do that with pains in your head?'

'I had to work. I needed to work. And I found I could. I got used to the pain. After a while it is just a dull ache. It does not throb so much.'

'What work did you do?' asked Andreas.

Ludwig held up the folder. 'A piano sonata. It is different from the rest. I think . . . I think . . . I would like to play it for you. Will you let me?'

'Of course, of course,' said Andreas, standing quickly. 'In fact, it could not be better. Do you remember I said I had something to show you. Come into the workshop. Nanette, will you come too?'

All three went out to the workshop. The large room held a variety of pianos of different shapes and sizes. A long workbench ran along one wall, pieces of wood and tools lying on it. Sawdust covered the floor.

Ludwig coughed and covered his mouth and nose with his hand.

'The sawdust. It irritates my throat.'

'Yes, I'm sorry. But come with me. Through here.'

Andreas led Ludwig into a small room off the end of the workshop. 'Come in, come in. Both of you. I'll close the door. That should keep out the sawdust.'

A sheet covered a piano. Andreas gently pulled it off.

'There. My new baby. What do you think? What's your first impression? The first thing that strikes you?'

'It's . . . it's . . . bigger. It *is* bigger, isn't it?'

Andreas nodded vigorously. 'Look at the keyboard. Six and a half octaves. I think I'm the first to build six and a half octaves. What did your father build, Nanette? Five octaves and two notes, wasn't it?'

Nanette nodded.

'This is six and a half. And I am the first. Walter here in Vienna. Erard in Paris. Neither has yet done it. They say it would be too big and heavy for the legs. But look what I have done.'

He bent down and held the legs. They were solid and chunky. 'See? Rounded and thicker. And I've moved them in slightly, so the weight is better distributed. Now look in here.' He opened the lid.

'See how I have improved it. I am still using buckskin for the hammers. It is the best. Nanette's father is responsible for that. But look what I have done with the action. I have simplified it. Made it lighter to the touch. The mechanism is less . . . not so many hinges. And the tone . . . Listen.'

Andreas played a few notes. They seemed to resonate more, hang in the air a little longer than Ludwig had heard before.

'Here, Ludwig. Will you play on it? It is not complete yet. I have more work to do on the frame. But I want to see how it holds up. Where the weak points are. And there is no one I can think of who would test its strength better than you.'

Ludwig nodded. He raised the music stand and placed his folder on it, opening it to the first sheet. He sat in the chair Andreas moved to the piano, wiped the palms of his hands on his trousers, and closed his eyes for a few moments.

He stretched his hands over the keys and played a crashing chord of C minor. The piano shook. Andreas bent quickly down, checking one of the joins where the leg supported the frame. He smiled and nodded to himself.

After a short dotted semiquaver rhythm played softly, and a demisemiquaver, almost a grace note, in the bass, another loud minor chord, followed again by the dotted semiquaver rhythm. Another demisemiquaver in the bass, more dotted chords, followed by a solo run of semi–demisemiquavers – and demi–semi–demisemiquavers! – in the right hand.

Andreas looked at Nanette and they both smiled. Ludwig played several bars more of dotted semiquaver rhythms, and then the right hand repeated its solo run, only this time it was a descending chromatic scale, semi–demisemiquavers followed by demi–semi–demisemiquavers, no fewer than twenty-eight notes covering two and a half octaves.

Again Andreas and Nanette glanced at each other, their faces more serious this time. Both were aware this was virtuoso play-ing – and composition – unlike anything they had heard before. Unlike anything that had been heard in Vienna before.

The chromatic run led into an explosive section, the main body of the first movement, still in the minor key, which Ludwig played at a furious pace. It seemed to have its own momentum. Ludwig was not driving it; it was driving itself. The momentum came from within it.

The dotted rhythm again, which Ludwig played more slowly this time, savouring the tempo change. It was as if he was saying there were no rules, nothing to say 'I must obey the time signature'. No, the time signature is only there as a formality; I must play the notes at the tempo they demand of me.

Again the central section, *crescendo*, then unexpectedly *pianis-simo*. Andreas had never heard such dynamic contrasts before; Nanette stood almost holding her breath. She did not know the piano was capable of such fury.

The dotted rhythm yet again, but this time foreshortened, creating drive, more momentum, leading to a series of *fortissimo* chords which brought the movement to an end.

Ludwig sat looking at the keys. Andreas and Nanette exchanged glances. Both were aware that what they were hearing was exceptional, unique. In their humble workshop. A new work for piano which would surely . . .

Without looking up at the music, which was still open to the first page, Ludwig began playing a gentle Adagio Cantabile. To a simple accompaniment he played a theme which sang across the small room. Andreas could see that Ludwig was now playing in the key of A flat, the warmest of all keys. He felt a frisson of joy at the warmth of tone that came from the black keys.

Andreas frowned. The theme seemed so familiar. Had Mozart used it? No. Why was it so familiar then? Yet at the same time it was not familiar. Andreas knew he had never heard it before. Such a simple theme. So beautiful. He watched Ludwig's hands. After such a tempestuous and virtuoso first movement, now a section so gentle a child could play it. He knew this Adagio would achieve instant popularity, not just for its beauty, but for the ease with which it could be played.

He looked up at Nanette. She was nodding slowly and he could see tears glistening in her eyes.

Ludwig played the brief second subject, still with the gentle beat of semiquavers under it, before returning to the main theme, unembellished. No variation, no ornamentation. Just the theme so perfectly self-contained that it needed nothing more.

A *pianissimo* ending, and Ludwig began the Rondo that was the final movement. Again, as in the first movement, the notes seemed to contain their own momentum. It sounded simple, but Andreas noted how the main theme was thrown from one hand to the other, at times both hands seeming to be competing with each other.

He again looked at Nanette, who was a far better pianist than he. She was frowning, studying the movement of Ludwig's hands. They both knew this was fiendishly difficult to play.

The central section was extraordinary. After alternate staccato quaver runs in the left then the right hands, six bars of what appeared to be semiquaver arpeggios, alternately in the bass and treble, each going in the opposite direction! It was like turbulent water, currents pulling against each other. Another furious descending run in the right hand, a held minim, and then the main theme again, but played now so fast that both Andreas and Nanette marvelled at how Ludwig struck each note cleanly and in its proper place. The sonata ended with a *fortissimo* quaver run in the right hand and a chord in the home key of C minor.

Andreas and Nanette looked at each other, their faces like masks of wonder. Neither wanted to speak, understanding instinctively that it was for Ludwig to break the silence.

Ludwig sat still for a moment, looking at the keys. Then he reached forward again and played the sublime theme of the slow movement, the Adagio Cantabile. Tunelessly he sang with it. His two friends smiled.

He stopped at the end of it, before the central section.

'Mozart would have approved. Simple themes, he told me. Always simple themes.'

'Why have you not varied it?' asked Andreas. 'It has such potential.'

Andreas and Nanette were surprised that Ludwig did not reply. They looked at each other. Andreas put his finger to his mouth to signal that Ludwig needed a few more seconds of quiet. Then he put the question again, more loudly. Still Ludwig did not reply, only this time it was as if he hadn't heard them. After another full minute Ludwig turned round and gasped when he saw his friends standing behind him.

'I . . . I'm sorry. I didn't hear you. I thought . . . Forgive me . . .'

'No, no, dear Ludwig,' said Nanette, 'it was wonderful. Beautiful. It is the most beautiful sonata I have ever heard.'

Ludwig frowned and turned to Andreas. 'Beautiful, Ludwig. Beautiful. We are very privileged.'

Ludwig frowned again. 'What? What are you saying?'

'Just how beautiful it is. It is a beautiful sonata.'

Ludwig stood, steadying himself on the piano frame. He looked down at the piano. There was a slight hoarseness in his voice.

'It is a good piano, Andreas. A good piano. It has . . . power. It has the strength I need.'

'I have more work to do on it, but it was good to see how you played on it. How it stood up to you!' he said, clapping Ludwig on the shoulder. 'You shall have it when it is ready. I will bring it to your apartment.'

Ludwig nodded his thanks. His face looked unsettled. 'I need to get back now. To the city.'

Nanette and her husband exchanged looks. 'Let me come with you,' Nanette said. 'I need to come into the city anyway. We'll take a carriage.'

'Ludwig, thank you again for letting us hear your new sonata. Will it have a name? Have you thought of a name for it? It is too grand to have only an opus number.'

Ludwig shook his head.

'It is a grand sonata. Why do you not name it that? The Grand Sonata.'

'Yes. Maybe.'

As they walked towards the Landstrasse Nanette slipped her arm through Ludwig's. 'My dear old friend. We have known each other for so many years. Who would have thought we would both be here together in Vienna?'

They stood on the Landstrase and waited for a carriage. Once seated inside Ludwig held the handle tightly. The unmade road beyond the Bastion was bumpy and every jolt caused his head to throb.

The carriage passed through the Kärntnertor gate and into the Kärntnerstrasse, the cobbles at least making the jolting even. Ludwig looked at the bustling figures in the street. Small groups of people talking and gesticulating, but most hurrying, heads down, anxious looks on their faces. At the top of the street, as the carriage turned around St Stephansdom, Ludwig saw street vendors and strained to hear their hoarse cries. The first chestnuts of autumn were burning on red coals.

The wide Graben was lined with opulent carriages. The coffee houses were busy. Ludwig knew what the conversation in Taroni's would be about. The French victories in Italy and the Netherlands. Austria's humiliation at giving up territory. At least Vienna has not been invaded like Bonn, he thought. No French troops strolling along the Graben as they were in the Münsterplatz and the Marktplatz in Bonn.

They dismounted and walked into St Petersplatz, dominated by its church. Soldiers drilled outside the barracks on the corner.

Ludwig walked quickly past. Nanette said something to him. He knew he should ask her to repeat it, but he did not.

The coolness of the building made him shiver slightly. They climbed the stairs to the third floor and entered the apartment.

Ludwig went immediately to the chair in the main room and sat down gratefully.

Nanette busied herself around the apartment. 'Ludwig, really. You must look after yourself better.' She swept clothes off the floor and arranged them in cupboards and drawers. She made his bed. He saw her go to the kitchen cupboard and take out a broom.

'No. No. Not now. It'll make me cough. Too much dust.'

'I'll keep it down, don't worry. But I must clean up a bit for you. I'll make some coffee in a moment. And I'll take your dirty clothes back out with me. You just sit and rest.'

Ludwig smiled as he watched her. The pain in his head was beginning to subside. The stillness of the room, so high above the street, was calming him. He closed his eyes and in his head he heard the sounds of his piano sonata. Not the furious opening, but the gentle theme of the Adagio Cantabile.

He knew that theme would be liked. But he would be asked why it was so simple and why he did not vary it. Was that not what his reputation as a musician was built on? His ability to vary a theme endlessly, to explore it, to embellish it, to reduce it. Why then in this sonata was it played only once, followed by a central section, then played again?

He knew why. Because it was a simple theme – small and perfect. Oh, he could vary it, perhaps at a soirée, if he were asked. But not in his sonata. There it would remain untouched.

They would ask him how the theme had come to him. So beautiful, they would say, so serene. What were you thinking about when you wrote it? A woman? Love?

No, it is never as simple as that, he thought. How can I make them understand that my inspiration is everywhere – in nature, beauty, the sound of a bird, the face of a woman? I do not seek it out; it comes to me, unbidden. And when it comes, I reach out and seize it with my hands . . . All I have to do is give it life.

He took the coffee gratefully from Nanette and sipped it. The warmth suffused him and made him feel good.

'I wrote my sonata while I was ill. While I was sad and lonely and ill. I want to give it the name Pathétique. To remind me of that. And to help people understand.'

'But they will not know that,' Nanette said. 'It makes it sound too sad. It is such a . . . a . . . noble work. Grand Sonata is better.'

'Then I will give it both names. In French. Grande Sonate Pathétique.'

As he spoke the clock on the church outside the window struck the hour. Ludwig winced as the sound cut through his head. He dropped the cup and clasped his hands to his head, letting out a yell of pain as he did so.

'Ludwig! Are you all right?' Nanette hurried forward. She fell to her knees and turned Ludwig's face up to hers. It was a mask of despair.

'Nanette, the clock. It's so piercing. It has never done that to me before. And did you speak to me? You spoke to me, didn't you?'

Nanette nodded.

'Nanette,' Ludwig said, reaching out with his hand for support, 'I think . . . I think . . . My hearing . . . Something is happening to my hearing . . .'

Nanette tried to smile reassuringly and took his hand. 'Do not worry. I noticed at our house that sometimes you did not hear what Andreas or I said. I assumed it was because you were concentrating on your music. But I'm sure it is nothing. It is your illness. You are still not completely better.'

Ludwig looked at her. 'Do you think so? Really? I can hear you now. When you speak. It is only . . . I don't know . . . if there is a lot of noise, or sudden noise.'

'I know what we'll do. We'll get you proper advice. Professor Frank is a good friend of mine. He is director of the General Hospital. On the Landstrasse. He is a wonderful doctor. Will you let me speak to him?'

Ludwig nodded, his breathing steadier now and his noice calmer. 'And I must leave these rooms. I cannot bear all the noise. The clock. And the damned soldiers always drilling. It is too much noise.'

'I understand. Leave it to me. I will find something for you. Outside the Bastion? Do you want to move out to the Landstrasse near us, where it is quieter?'

'No. In the city. I need to be in the city.'

'All right. And, Ludwig, do not worry about your hearing. Do you promise me? You have nothing to worry about. I promise. And that wonderful sonata. Your Grande Sonate Pathétique. You are so talented.'

Ludwig looked as her, and was grateful for her calming smile.

Chapter 2

Ludwig's heart sank the moment he saw his brother Carl's handwriting, but lifted when he read the note.

> Come to the Schwarzen Kameel on Bognergasse. Six o'clock. A welcome surprise awaits you.

The surprise did not interest Ludwig. He knew better than to put his faith in anything his brother promised. There was trouble with him even now over the piano sonata, the Grande Sonate Pathétique. Carl had promised it to the publisher Joseph Eder; Ludwig wanted it to go to Franz Hoffmeister, whose reputation was better. Not for the first time Ludwig decided he must stop Carl meddling in his affairs, but he did not know how to go about it, and the truth was that Carl did take some of the strain of dealing with publishers off his shoulders.

The reason he was pleased to read the note was because he welcomed any opportunity to leave his rooms. He could not blame Nanette: she had done her best. But the Tiefer Graben was a dark, narrow street, with high buildings on each side. It seemed that the sun never reached the ground and that the street was always in shadow. To make matters worse, the house in which she had found rooms was only two storeys high, so it was dwarfed by those around it, which increased the sense of oppression.

But it was quiet, by and large. The exception was early in the morning, when the wagon came round to empty the rubbish bins. The shouts of the driver and the clatter of the bins on the pavement were funnelled upwards by the buildings. The noise hurt Ludwig's ears just as the chiming clock in St Petersplatz had done, but he learned to stifle it somewhat by sleeping with the pillow over his head.

He had been to see Professor Frank, as Nanette had advised.

The doctor had given him medicines. More importantly he had assured him his hearing problems were only temporary, a direct result of the illness he had contracted in Mödling. A chill of the kind he had suffered, particularly when followed by fever, often affected the ear canals, the professor said comfortingly. Take the medicines – and no more standing half-naked by open windows.

The medicines seemed to be working – to a point. The pain in his head had subsided, but in its place were intermittent noises. His ears seemed sometimes to hum and when they did, he found it difficult to hear. He had reported this to the professor, who had merely shrugged, telling him to be patient. It would take time for the organs damaged by the fever to repair themselves.

He stepped out on to the pavement, up the incline to the top of the Tiefer Graben, and turned into the open Am Hof Square, relishing the sudden light that bathed him. As he crossed the square towards the Bognergasse he thought of the work he was now engaged on, the music he was composing, and it gave his step a lift.

At last, a symphony! He had tried before, four or five years ago. But it had not worked and he had abandoned it. It had been in C, as was the one he was working on now. This time, though, the ideas were evolving well. He was able to try them out on Streicher's new piano, which stood in the corner of the room, and he was pleased with the results.

At the same time, he had begun work on a set of string quartets. The contrast was perfect. A symphony for full orchestra; quartets for just four strings – two violins, a viola and a cello. It was at Schuppanzigh's urging that he had begun work on the quartets, but the idea had been in his mind for some time. Mozart and Haydn had both taken the string quartet and changed it from a melodious salon ensemble to a work of drama, and Ludwig was determined to continue the process. Just four voices, engaged in conversation; discussion, argument, agreement . . .

He was engaged on a third work as well, a piece for strings and wind, a septet. Not as sparse as a quartet, not as full as a symphony. He had it in mind to give it six movements. Six! That would surprise the audience. Probably draw complaints from the players as well.

His mind was still absorbed with his compositions as he

crossed the Bognergasse and entered the Schwarzen Kameel. The familiar aroma of the freshly cut ham and cheese on the open counter reminded him of where he was and why he was there. He knew the establishment well, often buying food and wine at the shop but he had less often gone there with friends and it took him a moment to remember that he needed to go through to the room on the right where the small round tables stood.

Still he could not see Carl. The light coming through the window from the street illuminated only the two or three tables close by. He looked towards the back of the room, where a sudden burst of laughter came from a table in the corner. He saw Carl gesticulate towards him and he made his way over.

'Steffen!'

'Hello, my old friend,' said Stephan von Breuning, standing and holding out his arms.

The two boyhood friends embraced warmly.

'How are you? From what I hear, you are making quite a name for yourself here in Vienna. You must tell me all about it. Here, sit. I kept the chair for you.'

Ludwig looked round the group, nodding to his two brothers and leaning across to shake Nikolaus Zmeskall's hand.

'Will you have a drink? I am buying drinks for my old friends, the Beethoven brothers, and my new friend, Herr Zmeskall here.'

'The Baron,' said Ludwig. 'The blind baron! But a fine cellist all the same. In fact that is why he is a fine cellist. Because his eyesight is so bad he cannot see to play the wrong notes.'

Zmeskall laughed, shaking his head. 'Or the right ones. How are you, Ludwig? Are you recovered from that fever?'

'Were you ill?' asked Stephan. 'I didn't know. Carl didn't . . .'

'I'm better now. More or less. A chill. It went to my head.'

'We'll drink to celebrate your recovery. What do you want? A beer?'

'I'd prefer red wine. It's better here than in the Schwan, if I remember correctly.'

'You do,' said Zmeskall.

'Steffen, it's so good to see you. What brings you to Vienna?'

'Not the happiest of reasons. Our Grand Master, His Grace the Elector Maximilian Franz, is ill. Very ill.'

'Max Franz? Ill?' asked Ludwig, surprise in his voice. 'What's the matter with him?'

'I'm afraid Max Franz, as you call him, Ludwig – I forgot you knew him rather well – is very ill indeed. His old leg wound has blown up badly. His leg became very swollen, and the swelling passed to the rest of his body. He's now huge, but it's all poisonous fluid and it's affecting his breathing. It's said the condition might prove fatal.'

'Fatal! But . . . Where is he now? He moved the court to Münster, didn't he?'

'Oh, that didn't last long. The French wouldn't allow him to stay there. They wanted him right out of the way. He's here. In Vienna. Hetzendorf, to be precise. The other side of the Schönbrunn palace. In honourable exile.'

'Can I go and see him?'

'I should imagine, dear Ludwig, you would be one of the few people he would be prepared to see. You had a special place in his affections, if I remember rightly.'

'But you haven't told us why *you* are here,' said Johann.

'As our Grand Master is ill, we have to elect a successor. That means convening a Grand Chapter, and that can only happen in the capital of the Holy Roman Empire, namely here in Vienna.'

'How long will you stay?'

'Well,' said Stephan, talking a sip of wine, 'I am pleased to inform you that I am about to become a permanent member of the Rhinelanders-in-exile here in Vienna. I have decided to leave the Order. Although it still does good work looking after the poor and needy, it is much smaller now and it certainly is not the organisation it once was. So I am going to work here. In the war office at the Hofburg palace.'

Ludwig clapped his hands. 'Shall I write a symphony in celebration? Or an oratorio? Or a piano concerto?'

'Your renewed friendship will be sufficient reward. Though I hear your friends and acquaintances now come from a rather higher social stratum.'

'Bah! What are princes and counts? Or kings, even, compared with friends?'

'What news of anyone else I might know?' asked Stephan.

'Do you remember Magdalena Willmann? The court singer?' asked Carl.

'I most certainly do.'

Ludwig looked up sharply, but said nothing.

'She's married, she married an Italian. Galvani, I think his name is.'

'Married?' said Ludwig in spite of himself. 'I didn't know.'

'That's because you were away,' said Carl with something approaching contempt in his voice. 'If you choose to spend whole months away, things will happen which you don't know about.'

'Carl, Carl,' said Stephan soothingly, motioning with his hands. 'Well, I am delighted for her. I must go and pay my respects. Franz Wegeler was here, wasn't he?'

'Yes, but he left some time ago,' said Johann. 'He's back in Bonn, but he might be moving to Koblenz once things have quietened down.'

'How is Eleonore?' asked Ludwig.

'From what I hear, very well. Just wishing, like everybody else, that the war would end, so she and Franz can go ahead and plan their wedding.'

'So,' Stephan said, 'I have to get used to my new Beethoven friends. Ludwig, of course. But now Carl and Johann. All right. So be it. Carl and Johann I will call you both from now on.'

Ludwig winced at the mention of his father's name but said nothing.

The small group drank happily, occasionally motioning at one another to keep their voices down. Their accents immediately identified them as outsiders, and in any tavern or coffee house in the city there would be at least one person whose duty it was to report back what he had heard to the Hofburg.

'I must go home. I have work to do,' said Stephan finally.

'Where are you living?' asked Ludwig.

'In the Rothes Haus in the Alsergrund.'

'The Alsergrund? That's where I lived when I first came to Vienna. In an attic room to begin with. Then with Prince Lichnowsky.'

'It's not grand. The Rothes Haus is a large block of apartments near the infantry barracks. But it's spacious.'

'May I walk there with you?'

'Of course. I would like you to. We can talk some more.'

The two old friends said their farewells and left. They walked up to the Freyung, past Prince Kinsky's palace and towards the Schottentor gate.

'Ludwig, I do have one piece of sad news. I didn't want to

mention it in the Schwarzen Kameel. I'm afraid that your old teacher, Herr Neefe, died.'

'Neefe? Dead? But that's impossible. He was still young.'

'I know. Regretfully I don't know how he died but apparently he lost his mother, then his wife became seriously ill, and the French allowed them to leave Bonn. It wasn't his home town anyway, was it?'

'No. He was from Saxony. Chemnitz, I think.'

'Well, he moved to Dessau, where he got a job as conductor at the theatre. His wife died soon after the move. And his own health was broken. He died a year or two ago. The daughters are orphans. So sad.'

'Yes. I had no idea. I owe him a lot. He always supported me, you know. He always believed in me. He was a kind and caring man. He used to talk to me about Bach and Handel. Like my grandfather did.'

Ludwig felt the tears prick behind his eyes. It was a long time since he had thought about his grandfather, and with that came a pang of guilt. Now, suddenly thinking of him again made him realise how much he missed him, what a void his death had left in his life.

He suddenly felt overwhelmed. So much work to do, music to write. If only his grandfather had still been alive. If only he had lived and I could have talked to him about music, Ludwig thought. Played him my sonatas.

If he could have told his grandfather about the concerts, and the tours. That he had met the King of Prussia – written cello concertos for him. That he played his music in the most aristocratic salons in Vienna. That he was talked about in the same breath as Mozart. Even as Bach and Handel.

And he could have talked to him about something else too. Something that was beginning to worry him more and more.

The two men reached the Alsergrund and entered the Rothes Haus, climbing the staircase to Stephan's apartment. The walk had put Ludwig in a melancholy mood, his pleasure at seeing Stephan dimmed by the news first about the Elector, then Neefe, then by his own thoughts about his grandfather. Ludwig looked around the room, but he said nothing.

'Sit down, Ludwig. And cheer up. No need for gloom. Let me get you a glass of wine.'

He sat down and took the wine from Stephan, sipping it gratefully.

'Ludwig, do you remember the portrait of your grandfather that used to hang in your home? You remember my mother was looking after it?'

'Of course. It was she who retrieved it for me from the broker's. Where my wretched father had pawned it. I won't forget her kindness.'

'Well, in her last letter to me she told me that she had asked Wegeler to look after it, as apparently it'll be safer up at the university. Don't know if you're aware but the French tried to seize our house for their officers, and Mother fears if things get worse they will try again . . . It makes me so sad to think of the French in that lovely house of ours. Anyway, it seems they are more interested in beautiful homes than academic institutions, so my mother has asked Wegeler to put the painting in one of his rooms at the university.'

Ludwig nodded. 'I will write to Wegeler.' He cleared his throat and leaned towards his friend. 'Steffen, I am worried about something.'

'What, Ludwig? Financial problems?' Ludwig shook his head. 'I know. A woman?' said Stephan, smiling.

'No,' said Ludwig sharply. 'It's my hearing. There's something wrong with it.'

'Your hearing? It seems fine to me. I haven't noticed—'

'That's just it. It's not always there. But when it is . . . It was all right in the Schwarzen Kameel, for example. It's all right now. But then suddenly . . . I've got . . . I've got a ringing, and noises, all the time. They don't seem to go away. Even now.'

'What do you mean?'

'It began in the summer when I was ill. After I had this lingering pain in my head. When it finally went, I was left with a ringing. Or a hum. A buzz sometimes. And sounds become deadened. It's as if there's wool in my ears. Then it clears.'

'Have you seen a doctor?'

'Yes. Professor Frank at the university. He says it'll go. He's given me almond oil. He says I should soak wool in it and put it in my ears. The canals are blocked, that is all it is.'

'I'm sure he's right. Are you doing what he says?'

'I can't walk around like that. People will know something is wrong. Can you imagine it? A musician with a hearing problem? It would be the end. I put it in at night. But it does no good.'

'You must give it time.'

'Time, time. There isn't time.'

'Ludwig, calm yourself. You're young. What are you? Not yet thirty? You have a life of music ahead of you.'

'Do I, Steffen? Do I? If I go . . . If my hearing . . .'

'Are you composing now?'

Ludwig nodded, and despite himself a slight smile turned up the corners of his mouth. 'That's the remarkable thing. I can work. I hear the sounds in my head. I hear the music before I play it on the piano.'

'And you can still hear the piano?'

Ludwig nodded again. 'It's just voices. In a crowd. In company.'

'I'm sure it's nothing to worry about. You must be patient. And listen, I know another doctor. A surgeon. Doktor von Vering. If you want another opinion . . .'

'Thank you. You are a good friend. Steffen, do you promise not to say anything about this to anyone? Especially my brothers. I do not want them to know. Or Zmeskall even.'

'Of course not. Does anyone know?'

'Only Nanette Streicher. She spoke to Professor Frank.'

'Do not worry. I will keep your secret. But I am sure there will be no secret to keep for much longer.'

Ludwig smiled and finished his glass of wine. 'Do you remember when we climbed the Drachenfels, Steffen? You and I?'

'How could I forget it? I thought you were mad then and I still think you were mad.'

'I told you then you were my best friend, didn't I?'

Stephan nodded and smiled. 'You had just heard you were going to Vienna. You were so excited. What about your opera? It was about the Rhine legends, Siegfried and the dragon, wasn't it? Siegried, Hero of the Rhine. That was it, wasn't it? I remember.'

Ludwig shook his head. 'Buried for ever in the soil of the Drachenfels. But, Steffen,' he said excitedly, 'shall we go back? Shall we go back and climb the Drachenfels again?'

'One day, old friend. One day. When the French have gone. And when it's not raining!'

Chapter 3

At first Ludwig did not recognise the vast bulk of the man on a wooden bench under the low branches of a spreading oak tree. But then he saw the figure lean forward, grimacing, to massage the knee of his half-straightened right leg. Memories of Bonn filled his mind.

Was this really the lively spirited man who had had such a profound influence on his life? He looked now like a lumbering animal, his body swollen, his face puffed out, as if someone had inflated him with air. This man, Maximilian Franz, Elector of Cologne and Archbishop of Cologne and Münster, who once ruled over thousands of people and vast tracts of land, looked now as if he could not have ruled over a pet dog. He was clearly a sick man. Sick and, it seemed, helpless.

Ludwig wanted to turn around and leave, but he knew he could not. He walked towards the bench. Max Franz was half lying on it now, his injured leg stretched out, his head moving up and down with the effort of gulping in air.

Ludwig stood gazing down at him. Without looking up, Max Franz spoke.

'Don't stare at me so, boy. It only makes me feel worse. I know I look dreadful, but it will pass. Pull up a seat. There. There.' He pointed to a small wooden chair under the tree, which Ludwig moved so he could face the Elector.

'Your . . . Your Grace . . .'

'Oh, cut it out, for God's sake, Ludwig. Here, let me look at you. Hah! Quite a name you're making for yourself, I hear. I've been following your progress.'

'But you've been in Münster, haven't you?'

'Yes. Damned French. But we kept our eye on you, you know.'

He began coughing. The cough racked his body as he lost control of it. His face coloured with the effort. Finally he snatched a handkerchief from his sleeve and clasped it to his mouth. Ludwig saw his lips pucker into the handkerchief. Folding it in on itself, he wiped his brow and sat back, exhausted by the effort. Ludwig saw that his eyes were watering. But a smile spread slowly across his face.

'There. That's better. Maybe they're right, these damn-fool doctors. Once I get that wretched fluid up, everything seems better. Now, tell me about yourself. Your fame has reached even here to far-flung Hetzendorf.'

Ludwig smiled. 'I gave a concert at the Burgtheater. I played my piano concertos. That was some time ago now. But it was a success, and after that . . .'

Max Franz nodded. 'Yes, I think I remember that. Old Franz Ries told me. He's a great admirer of yours, you know. Talked about you as if you were his son.'

'He was very kind to me. Especially after my mother died. I owe him a lot. How's his son? Ferdinand. I heard he became ill.'

'Smallpox. Ries was very worried. I gave him leave to be with the boy. He recovered, but he lost an eye. I remember. The court was distraught.'

'Is he a musician now?'

'Don't know. Haven't seen the family for some time. Since the orchestra was disbanded. Everyone suffered, you know. My exchequer was depleted, courtesy of my brother, the Emperor here in Vienna. That's why I disbanded the orchestra. And the theatre.'

'That finished Herr Neefe. He lived for the theatre.'

'Neefe. Now there's a name I had forgotten. He taught you, didn't he? Yes, I remember now. From Saxony. Young family. I wonder what's happened to him.'

'He died. He left Bonn with his family after the invasion, but both he and his wife died.'

Max Franz shook his head. 'So sad. These damn French. Damn French. My poor sister.' He began to cough again, slowly at first, but then it consumed him. Again he puckered his lips into the handkerchief. Ludwig waited for his breathing to settle.

'Will you return to Bonn?' Ludwig asked.

'Not while the French are there. And there's no prospect of them leaving. They say the territory on the left bank of the Rhine belongs to them.'

Max Franz smiled. 'Do you remember Heller, Ludwig?' Ludwig looked down, but a smile crept across his face. 'That wretched, pompous Heller? And how you threw him off the note when he was singing . . . Lamentations of Jeremiah, wasn't it? Hah, I remember it so well. He complained to Kapellmeister Lucchesi and that venerable gentleman made an official complaint to me. I chuckled when I heard what had happened. What you had done. I had to reprimand you. But after that I took an interest in you, you know. I watched your progress. There were some who said I should not have allowed you to come to Vienna when I did. You were only, what, sixteen?' The Elector thumped his chest with his fist, as a sudden shaft of pain shot through him.

Ludwig nodded. 'You know I am grateful to you. If I had not come, I would never have met Mozart. Until I die I will remember the day I met Mozart. And talked with him about music. And played for him.'

'Ludwig, you are a determined young man. You get what you want. But not always. Sometimes you go a little too far in your efforts to get what you want.'

'What do you mean?'

'Do you think I have forgotten the business with Herr Haydn? He wrote asking me to increase your salary . . .'

Ludwig looked down, clasping his hands between his knees, knowing what the Elector was going to say next.

'. . . and sent me some fine examples of your work. Very fine indeed. Except that I had heard them all in Bonn . . .'

'Not the fugue. That was new.'

'Ah, the fugue. Yes, that was new.'

'Anyway, you cut off my salary.'

'I was going to bring you back to Bonn.'

'I wouldn't have come. I sent you another manuscript. The clerk at the Hofburg said he—'

'Didn't get it.'

'It doesn't matter. It needed changes anyway.'

Another long, racking cough convulsed the Elector's body, and ended with him spitting fluid into the handkerchief. He picked up a small bell and rang it.

'Take this away. Bring me a clean handkerchief.'

The servant held out a silver platter with a clean handkerchief already on it. Without speaking, Max Franz put his sodden handkerchief on the platter and took the clean one.

'Anyway, enough of that. You are not a child any more. I should not speak to you like one. Tell me about Herr Haydn. How is he?'

'I . . . I don't see much of him any more. I stopped being his pupil some time ago.'

'Nothing wrong with that. Can't be a pupil for ever. Have to make your own way.'

'He . . . He was not pleased with me. He wanted me to put "Pupil of Haydn" at the top of my work. I refused. I don't want to be known for ever as Haydn's pupil.'

'Dedicate a piece to him. That'll keep him happy.'

'I have. My three piano sonatas. Opus Two. But he criticised my trios. My first opus.'

'But, Ludwig, he is a venerable old man. A great composer.'

'I know. I admire his music. Especially the oratorio he has written. *The Creation*. Baron Swieten wrote the text. It is a great work. But Haydn's music is Haydn's. Beethoven's is Beethoven's.'

Max Franz smiled. Suddenly he looked very tired. His breathing became laboured.

'Ludwig,' he said in a quieter voice, 'I am pleased you came to see me. So pleased. You must leave now because I am tired. Will you come again? It does me good to hear the accent of the Rhineland and talk of Bonn. Even though I am an Austrian, I felt at home there. I was looking forward to a long and happy life in Bonn, on the banks of the Rhine. Away from all the intrigues of Vienna. The gossip. The court. The formalities. Now it would appear my life will be neither long nor happy.'

Ludwig frowned. 'No. You must not say that. You must not give up. The French will be driven from the Rhineland. One day. They can defeat the German army, or the Austrian army, but if all France's enemies join together, they will be defeated.'

'I shall not live to see it. Ludwig, you know I am fond of you. I am pleased with what you have accomplished.'

'I am grateful to you too.'

Max Franz smiled. 'Ludwig, I am not asking you to put "Pupil of Maximilian Franz" on top of your work, because you are not my pupil. But if ever you were to wish to dedicate a piece of your music to me, I would not order you not to.'

Ludwig smiled. He stood, bowed slightly to the man who had done so much for him, and left.

Ludwig sat in a chair near the window and contemplated the future. Over and over in his mind he turned the problem. He tried to look at it positively; he reasoned with himself; he could cope with it, surely? But try as he might he kept returning to the basic, unalterable fact. He was losing his hearing. He, a musician, was losing his hearing.

The thought made him smile. The absurdity of it. A deaf musician! It was impossible!

But then maybe he would not go deaf. Maybe Professor Frank was right and the strengthening medicine and the almond oil ... Bah! Frank was a charlatan. He had admitted himself he was baffled, that was why he had agreed to refer Ludwig on to Doktor von Vering.

And what had his solution been? Ludwig was to fill a bath with lukewarm water from the Danube, introduce strengthening solutions into it, and sit in the water.

Was the man mad? There had, of course, been no improvement in his hearing, though Ludwig had to admit that the warm water seemed to relieve his sharp stomach pains. But there was so much work involved in having a servant bring water to his room, heat it and transfer it to the bath, that it was simply not worth the effort.

But Doktor Vering had said one thing to Ludwig, one fateful thing that Ludwig could not get out of his mind. 'Your hearing may or may not improve, but I can't guarantee that you will ever be free of hearing problems.'

What did he mean? Ludwig had thought. Will I go deaf? he asked him. Is that what you mean? Vering had simply shrugged his shoulders and spoken about the possibility of a deformity in the inner ear which might be irreversible. But it would not necessarily get worse.

So. A deaf musician. He walked to the piano, sat down and played some chords. He could hear them perfectly, despite the other noises in his ear. A high-pitched whistle, that was what he was hearing at the moment. But he was used to it; it was not such a hardship. Sometimes a rushing sound; even that was not so bad. Like the sea. The hum and the buzz were worst. But there was no telling when they would come. Usually when his stomach was hurting particularly.

But as long as I can hear my music, he thought. As long as I can go on playing and composing. He looked across at the piles of manuscript papers on the table. The symphony. The Septet for Strings and Wind. The quartets. Progress on all three. He was composing, despite his problems. As long as that could go on . . .

I'll go to Mödling again, he thought. So peaceful there. To be alone. Away from Vienna, the pressure, the demands. Rest my ears.

He played on. It was the opening movement of the Grande Sonate Pathétique, the great C minor sequence with its furious runs of semi-demisemiquavers in the right hand. He threw his head back, savouring the sounds.

Only when he opened his eyes did he see the servant standing facing him. The servant's lips moved soundlessly; he bowed and left the room, leaving two men standing there.

Ludwig wondered for a moment why he had not heard what the servant had said, then suddenly the whistling in his ear intensified, as if filling the void left by the sounds of the piano. He could not help the grimace of pain which spread across his face. He felt a hand on his shoulder.

'Ludwig, are you all right? Come over here.' Ludwig allowed himself to be led to a chair. Finally he looked up, to see the concerned face of Baron Swieten.

'Baron? I'm sorry . . . I . . . My head . . . I . . .'

'It's all right, my dear boy. I'm sorry I took you by surprise.' Swieten's kindly face wore a smile which was a mixture of pleasure and concern. 'I've brought Hummel. He wanted to meet you. Or more precisely, I wanted you to meet him.'

Ludwig nodded. He looked at the rather dandified figure sitting opposite him, a green velvet jacket with its high collar turned up, a gold pin holding a white cravat at the neck. Hummel's hands were folded across his chest; a ring was on every finger except his thumbs. Despite himself Ludwig smiled. He had heard about Hummel.

The first time was all those years ago, on his first trip to Vienna and his meeting with Mozart. Hummel was Mozart's pupil – his best, he remembered Mozart saying. And he remembered that Mozart, after hearing Ludwig play, had said Hummel was a better pianist. He had heard talk of him too in Vienna; he knew people compared him with Hummel, some saying he was better, some not. But he had never met him. Hummel had spent a lot of time on tour. When in Vienna, their paths had simply not crossed.

'Hummel, a pleasure. Mozart spoke to me of you. He was highly complimentary.'

'Ah, my dear teacher. So sad. Such a dismal fate. Such a loss to our divine art. But may I return your kind remark. I have heard of your exceptional powers.'

Ludwig shrugged. He turned to Swieten. 'You did well with *The Creation*, sir. The text is good. And Haydn has written fine music. It is a great oratorio.'

'You are kind, Ludwig. Did you hear the performance? It was held at Prince Lobkowitz's palace.'

'No, I regret not. But I have studied the score. Haydn has not lost his powers.'

'I think I have given him the taste. We are now working on another oratorio. It's to be called *The Seasons*. We work well together!'

'May I offer . . . ? Would you . . . ? I can ask my servant . . .'

Swieten held up his hands. 'No, no. We will not disturb you for long. I only wanted to extend an invitation to you. Do you know of Dragonetti? Domenico Dragonetti?'

Ludwig shook his head.

'He is an Italian. From Venice. He is living in London because of the war. But he is here in Vienna now. Just briefly. He is a virtuoso of the double bass.'

'The double bass? How can you be a virtuoso of the double bass?'

'Well, I would like to invite you to find out. He gives a recital tomorrow evening, and my good friend Hummel here will be accompanying him on the piano. Would you come? And would you perhaps play something? After Hummel and Dragonetti, of course.'

A pang of anxiety shot through Ludwig's stomach. Play? In public? He dared not. What if people realised . . .

'No,' said Ludwig with a sharp tone to his voice. 'No. I . . . No. I'm sorry.'

'Herr Beethoven,' said Hummel, with a note of condescension in his voice, 'I heard how you took on Abbé Gelinek in an improvisation contest. I would very much like—'

'No! I told you both. I do not want to play.'

'It will be said you turned down a challenge. People will draw their own conclusions.'

Ludwig leaped from his chair. 'Look, Hummel. Do not talk to me of challenges. Do you hear? I am not a musician to be challenged. Listen. Here. Listen.'

He strode to the piano. He played a gentle theme in the right hand, accompanied by chords in the bass. 'So! Now!' Thunderously he varied the theme. Streicher's sturdy six-and-half octave piano shook under the strain. The theme was now tempestuous, now sinister, now gentle again. He threw it between bass and treble. Crashing chords were followed by gentle chords, minor by major. Finally he brought it to a rushing end, sitting with his hands held above the keys until the final sounds died away.

He stood, his face drained, supporting himself on the piano.

'My dear boy!' exclaimed Swieten. 'Wonderful. A privilege to hear.'

Hummel clapped gently and smiled. 'Just as I had heard. A master of the piano. I congratulate you, Herr Beethoven. Now, will you listen to me?'

Hummel stood, straightening his jacket by pulling down on the sides. He walked to the piano, stood for a moment with one hand on the frame, then sat.

'I shall play a few notes, just to test the pressure of the keys . . . Mmm. Interesting. Quite a heavy touch. But a nice deep sound. Made here in Vienna? Excellent. So, Herr Beethoven. First, your theme.'

Hummel played Ludwig's opening theme. His touch was extraordinarily light. Ludwig immediately sat upright and looked across at him. Hummel's hands were arched high, his rings catching the light. His long fingers were touching the keys with an exquisite delicacy.

Suddenly he played a *fortissimo* minor chord in both hands. Then his variation began. It was in total contrast to Ludwig's. Instead of the tempestuousness and thunder, it consisted of extraordinarily fast runs. Hummel's fingers moved so swiftly they were almost a blur. In opposite directions his hands flew over the keys seemingly at random. Yet hidden in the runs Ludwig could hear the occasional accented note which picked out his original theme.

He leaned forward to watch more closely. He had never witnessed the piano played this way. Suddenly the runs became chromatic, a drastic change of key, then arpeggios, and still the theme was hidden in there, hidden but discernible.

Finally, his head thrown back, Hummel played the original

theme again, first in the bass accompanied by treble chords, then in the treble with the left hand crossed over to play the chords on the even higher treble keys, then in its original setting.

As the final chord died away, Ludwig leaped up from his chair and ran across to the piano. As Hummel stood, Ludwig threw his arms around him and patted him on the back.

'Hummel! You are a genius! Such playing. I have not heard it before. I congratulate you.'

The two men shook hands. Ludwig felt Hummel's rings against his fingers. Swieten smiled contentedly. 'So, Ludwig. Here I am in the company of two great pianists. Beethoven and Hummel. Hummel and Beethoven. I am indeed a fortunate man. Will you now come to hear Hummel and Dragonetti?'

'Where is it?'

'In the Mehlgrube in the Neuer Markt. You know it, the hall next to the Schwan. At seven thirty. Or maybe nearer eight.'

'I will come. But, Swieten, do not ask me to play. Do you understand? Hummel, it has been a pleasure to hear you play. I look forward to hearing you again tomorrow night. But I will not play. You must understand.'

The two men nodded, both knowing that further argument would only harden Ludwig's resolve. They took their leave, Ludwig and Hummel again clasping each other by the shoulder.

Ludwig went to the window. As he looked down into the dark Tiefer Graben, his body was tingling with excitement. He knew he should look on Hummel as a rival; people had talked of them both in that way, but he had paid no attention. Now he realised why Hummel's playing was so popular in Vienna. There was less . . . less . . . what was the right word? Passion. Yes, passion. There was less passion in it than in his own playing. And it was therefore easier to listen to. But that did not detract from the brilliance of Hummel's playing. He was a dandy, with his velvet jacket and rings on his fingers, but Ludwig found he liked him, and he admired him as a pianist.

It took Ludwig a few moments to realise it, but from the moment he had begun talking to Swieten and Hummel, he had had no problem with his hearing. Even the dreadful noises in his head had stopped. When he had played, and when Hummel had played, he had heard normally, and afterwards, he had heard every word Hummel and Swieten had said.

He closed his eyes and listened carefully. He could hear the runs Hummel had executed so brilliantly. He could hear his own thunderous chords. But where was that whistling sound? Or the buzz? They were not there. Could it be . . . could it be . . . ? He dared not think it.

He felt the blood race through his veins. His skin felt as if it was on fire. His face he knew was burning, but not with fever.

He turned sharply away from the window and went to the table. Pulling a sheet of paper towards him, he dipped the quill in ink and hurriedly wrote:

Baron Zmeskall of Zmeskallity

I require your presence at my lodgings this very hour. Delay is not acceptable. There is a fortress to be stormed.

L. van B.

Chapter 4

It was one of the mysteries of Vienna that the Mehlgrube, the flour pit, still retained the aroma of flour, although the building that had been the centre of Vienna's medieval flour trade had been pulled down more than a hundred years before. And there were few in the hall – certainly none of the ladies, heavily bewigged and powdered in the dresses they reserved for city soirées – who were aware that as well as being the storage house for flour, the building had at the same time served as a brothel, the professional women parading in the gallery, and disappearing at regular intervals with tradesmen and suppliers to the first-floor rooms.

Now there was a contrived ornateness to the hall, as if it were trying to shed its past. Windows from floor to ceiling allowed the light to stream in from the Neuer Markt; chandeliers hung in clusters from the high ceiling; there were elaborately framed paintings high on the wall, angled sharply downwards. And still there was the aroma of flour. It was said that a severe storm two hundred years ago, which had brought the roof crashing down, had saturated the earthen floor, causing the flour to seep deep down into it. At any rate the sweet, rather heavy atmosphere provided guests – however many times they might have encountered it before – with a perfect topic to accompany the pleasantries which opened conversation.

Prince Lichnowsky, bulky in his tight-fitting waistcoat but surprisingly light on his small feet, came quickly over to Ludwig.

'My dear Ludwig, how pleased I am that you have come. You will not regret it. We must talk before the evening is out. Do you understand? You will not leave before we have done so? There is something I have to speak to you about. Most important.'

Ludwig was already regretting that he had come, his optimism of the night before dashed. The steady hum of conversation was growing progressively louder as the hall filled with people, and it was becoming clear to him that this was exactly the kind of gathering which affected his hearing most. In his own room, or with a small number of people, there was no real problem, but when there was a background noise, he found it difficult to hear anyone talking to him. If they raised their voice, as they were bound to, it was painful to him. As yet, though, nobody seemed to notice that he was having any difficulty, that he had developed the technique of leaning forward just slightly and closing his eyes a fraction to concentrate a little harder.

Ludwig took a glass of red wine from a proffered tray and drank gratefully. There was a roughness to it that bit at the back of his throat and made his eyes water slightly. He cleared his throat, feeling immediately better.

'So, Ludwig,' said Baron Swieten, 'good to see you. Good to see you.'

Ludwig had seen Swieten approaching him as he drank. So different in appearance to Lichnowsky, he thought. Heavy, lumbering almost, the flesh of his neck quivering; his wig not quite in place, his tailcoat straining to remain buttoned across his bulging front but threatening at any moment to give up the battle.

Ludwig knew immediately the identity of the small, thin man with the mop of dark curly hair at Swieten's side.

'Signor Dragonetti, Ludwig. Signor Domenico Dragonetti. From Venice. And if I have pronounced your name incorrectly, sir, I beg your eternal forgiveness.'

Dragonetti inclined his head and spoke. 'Enchanted, sir. Signor B'thofen. Your fame has reached even my city. It is mostly a pleasure to assume your acquaintance.'

Ludwig was pleasantly surprised that Dragonetti's voice was quite high and sharp; his heavy Italian accent and awkward command of German made it quite difficult for Ludwig to understand him, but in that he was not alone, and it was a problem of which Dragonetti himself was well aware.

Ludwig smiled, taking immediately to the diminutive Italian whose eyelids fluttered when he spoke. He wondered how this man could be a virtuoso of the double bass, an instrument which it seemed must be entirely wrong for him in size as well as temperament. Bass players in general, Ludwig had observed, were much like their instrument – tall, heavily built, deep-voiced, even inclined to speak in short, definitive words, anchoring the conversation in much the same way as they anchored the orchestra. But Dragonetti, clearly familiar with the reaction his appearance caused, preempted Ludwig's curiosity.

'I am called Il Drago. The Dragon. Strange for one so small. But when I play, the fire is coming from my nostrils, as you will see. And you are wondering, surely, of how such a small man to play the giant instrument?'

Ludwig smiled again, almost subconsciously registering the fact that if he failed to hear what Dragonetti was saying, the lapse would be put down to the Italian's language, not his hearing. But he was having no problem, and that lightened his mood.

'Indeed, Signor, that was exactly my thought. How is it possible to . . .'

'Arms, Signor. Arms. Look at my arms.' He lifted both arms high in the air. 'You see how long are my arms. And my instrument. Come, sir, I show you.'

Eagerly Dragonetti led him through the rows of seats to the platform at the right-hand end of the hall, leaving Swieten smiling at the two musicians. Dragonetti's double bass case was lying horizontally at the side of the platform. Swiftly he unclasped it and took out the huge instrument. He stood it upright, handling it with surprising ease, as if it weighed half what it actually did.

He stood alongside it, his right arm stretched high up on the fingerboard, his left hand steadying the body, a look of triumph on his face. Several people standing and conversing near the platform turned to watch him, smiles on their faces.

Ludwig looked at the instrument, astonishment frozen on his face. He had never seen a double bass like it. It was taller than any he had seen, with a huge body and above it a relatively short fingerboard. The effect was of a massively stout man with a short, thin neck and a small head above it. And most extraordinary of all, it had only three strings.

Dragonetti's small frame was dwarfed by his instrument.

'Bigger, you see,' said Dragonetti. 'I have it made especially that way. The body – deeper, broader, taller. The sound it is deeper. But also the people think it is more impossible to play. So they applaud harder. And it is made of . . . what is the word? Yes, sycamore wood.'

Ludwig continued to look hard at the instrument. 'Three strings,' he said to himself. 'Just three strings. Why three strings instead of four?' he asked Dragonetti.

Dragonetti leaned forward conspiratorially. 'Three strings. Yes, only three strings.' And he smiled expectantly. 'Can you know why?'

Ludwig looked bemused and shook his head.

'The height is more, so four strings they are not needed. But there is another reason. Like this it is more difficult to play. The hands they must move further. So the audience they must applaud even more hardly.'

Ludwig laughed. 'A pity I cannot do the same with the piano. I will ask Streicher to make the keys larger. So my hands must move more! But can you play this giant, this monster?'

Dragonetti allowed a look of triumph to cross his face. He leaned forward again until his head was nearly touching Ludwig's.

'I can play the Sonata for Cello by the famous Signor Luigi B'thofen.'

'Sonata for . . . Cello? You can play it? On this?'

'*Si, si, si!* I play Sonata for Cello on my double bass.'

'Impossible. Even cello players complain my sonatas are too difficult.'

'You will see, my friend. I demonstrate to you. Tonight. You will hear.'

There was a sudden increase in the hum of conversation, and a scattering of applause, signifying the arrival of Hummel. This sociable man, so ready to demonstrate his skills at the piano and happy to accommodate the audience's every wish, was one of the most popular instrumentalists in Vienna. His showmanship – from his brilliant flourishes on the keyboard to his fine clothes and sparkling rings – always drew an enthusiastic response, and yet the audience was sophisticated enough to appreciate the great talent that lay behind it.

Dragonetti gently laid down his instrument and hurried to meet his accompanist. Ludwig decided to take a seat. He saw that the chairs each had a white name-card on them, and he saw that between Prince Lichnowsky and Baron Swieten was a card on which was written Hr L. van Beethoven.

When the audience finally settled down and Hummel and Dragonetti took their places on the platform, Hummel told the audience that Signor Dragonetti had asked him to explain that the music they were to hear this evening was written for the cello. The double bass regrettably was a much-neglected instrument, and it was his hope that his performance tonight would convince them of its value as an instrument in its own right.

They began with a Sonata for Cello and Piano by Johann Sebastian Bach. Ludwig folded his arms and watched Dragonetti. The little Italian with the long arms had an extraordinary technique. His left hand flew up and down the fingerboard, his fingers bent at the joints to hold down the heavy strings. The sound was deeply sonorous.

Ludwig joined enthusiastically in the applause. Another Sonata for Cello and Piano by J. S. Bach received equally appreciative applause.

Dragonetti then announced, 'Now, I play this music I myself compose for my instrument. I give Herr Hummel a little rest.'

And before the audience had stilled their chuckles, Dragonetti threw himself into a furious piece. It had no structure or identifiable theme, but it involved more frenetic movement up and down the fingerboard than anything Bach had composed.

Ludwig concentrated on the instrument. Dragonetti was a superb performer, of that there was no doubt. But Ludwig was not convinced of the instrument's value on its own, or even with piano accompaniment. It was not designed for solo performance. That was not to say it could not be used as such, as Dragonetti was using it now. But that was more for curiosity and virtuosity, for the amusement of the audience.

Its real value, Ludwig knew, was in the orchestra as an anchor. But what he was learning tonight was that that could involve far more than simply providing the keynote in the bass, the foundation rock for the rest of the orchestra. In its own way the double bass – a pair of double basses – in the orchestra could furnish a piece of music with drama. If such playing as Dragonetti's was possible, it meant that scoring for the double bass could be more adventurous, more stimulating than before.

Drama. That was it. Not just an anchor, but drama – that was what the double bass could provide. He pulled a scrap of paper from his pocket and scribbled on it *Basso profundo dramatico!!!*

He was aware that the applause had stopped and for a moment he did not hear Dragonetti's voice. He sensed rather than saw heads turn towards him. He looked up. The Italian was smiling at him.

'And so, ladies and gentlemen, I play you now a very famous piece of music. The music is written by my good friend who sits here among you, Signor Luigi B'thofen. It is his Sonata for Cello, which he publishes already as his Opus Number Five. I choose the sonata number two, which I learn here in my head so I do not need the music. Herr Hummel he has the piano part and will accompany me.'

There was applause, and Ludwig felt Swieten pat him on the shoulder. Hummel suddenly stood and walked to the front of the platform. He whispered in Dragonetti's ear; Dragonetti nodded vigorously.

'Most gracious ladies,' Hummel said, addressing the audience, 'most noble gentlemen. With such an illustrious musician among you, no less a personage than the composer of the very piece you are about to hear, I cannot possibly take his place. I therefore yield my seat at the keyboard to one who is known to you all, Herr Ludwig van Beethoven.'

There was vigorous applause. Ludwig felt his stomach churn. He looked around. All faces were turned to him, smiles in abundance. Hummel and Dragonetti were leading the applause. Ludwig knew he had no choice but to comply.

He stood, and the applause intensified. Hummel thrust out his hands, the lights from the chandeliers catching the rings on his fingers. Ludwig nodded to Hummel and took the seat Hummel had yielded at the piano. He looked across at Dragonetti.

'We play the opening chord together when I bring my head down, then you take the time from the solo piano bars which follow. The same in the Rondo. I will set the time with the opening bars.'

Dragonetti's face was serious and his eyebrows heavy over his eyes. 'I understand. I follow you. At your speed I play.'

Ludwig took the music off the stand. He looked at the first page, turned it, turned it again, then turned to the opening of the Rondo, the second and last movement. Satisfied, he closed the music and put it to one side.

He looked at the audience. They were silent and all looking towards the platform. He looked at Dragonetti and raised his eyebrows. Dragonetti nodded and with a wide arc brought his bow into position a fraction above the strings. There was total silence in the hall.

They played the opening chord in perfect unison. From that moment Ludwig knew with a musician's instinct that the performance would be a success. He looked across at the small Italian as he played the brief piano solo, a half-smile on his face and his mouth slightly open. Dragonetti did not match his smile. His face was a mask of intense concentration, belying his normally sunny disposition.

Ludwig watched him as he played, marvelling at the way his arms negotiated their way around the huge machine. Occasionally he looked at the audience. Every face was fixed on Dragonetti and from his brief glance it seemed every face was wearing an expectant smile. There was certainly something slightly comic about the wiry Italian playing his huge instrument – maybe they were thinking he resembled a bear-tamer and his animal, one of the sights that was once common outside this very hall in the Neuer Markt.

Towards the end of the Rondo, Ludwig had written a devil-ishly difficult passage of arpeggios for the cello. He remembered how in Berlin, where he had gone after Prague, King Friedrich Wilhelm – the capable but amateur cellist for whom he had written this and another sonata, and to whom he had dedicated them both – had thrown down his bow in frustration. Using his authority as King of Prussia, he had ordered Ludwig to simplify the passage. Ludwig had taken great pleasure, in front of the audience, in announcing he would not obey the royal order.

Dragonetti negotiated the arpeggios perfectly. Ludwig saw how he looked up at the fingers of his left hand as he did so. Ludwig – again with a musician's instinct – knew there was no need for him to do this. If they had been playing together in private he would not have done so. He did it now, Ludwig knew, to draw the audience's attention to what he was doing, to emphasise how difficult the passage was. Ludwig admired his musicianship – and his showmanship. Why not? An audience wants to be impressed; it is up to a performer not to disappoint it.

With a flourish of notes both players brought the sonata to a perfectly timed end. Ludwig, without looking at the audience, strode across to Dragonetti, his arms wide. Dragonetti had not moved from his final position, his bow still poised across the strings, his left hand still high on the fingerboard.

Ludwig embraced Dragonetti. The audience added cheers to their vociferous applause. Ludwig was oblivious to the audience. He stood in front of Dragonetti, his back turned to them. Dragonetti nodded with satisfaction.

'Bravo, Dragonetti!' someone shouted from near the front.

The sound cut into Ludwig's ears, reminding him suddenly of

the existence of the audience and that he was standing between them and the object of their admiration. He stepped to one side and applauded with the audience. He turned his head and looked at them: they were smiling, all of them. Dragonetti now stood to the side of his instrument, his left hand holding it by the fingerboard, his right arm held out wide with the bow in it. He bowed once, deeply, then nodded at the audience. In between nods he looked at the double bass, as if wanting his instrument to share in the applause.

Hummel, when he sensed that the applause was dying down, joined Ludwig and Dragonetti on the platform, and the three took the applause together.

When they stepped down from the platform they were surrounded by admirers.

Ludwig tried to melt away to the side of the room, but knew it was impossible. This, more than any other, was the moment he dreaded. He had learned already that if his hearing was giving him problems, it was always at its worst immediately after he had played music. The notes were still in his head; the sounds still revolved there. If someone spoke to him, the noise of their voice was harsh and dissonant. It hurt his ears and he could not always make out what they were saying.

Ludwig felt the beads of perspiration break out on his forehead. He reached into his sleeve for a handkerchief and cursed as he realised he had not brought one. He ran the back of his hand across his forehead. He wished he could walk away from the noise. It was so harsh. His heart sank as he felt a hand on his shoulder.

'Splendid, my dear Ludwig! Absolutely splendid!' He turned to see Prince Lichnowsky's face close to his. Ludwig felt a sudden surge of irritation that he could not be left alone.

'I need a handkerchief,' he snapped.

'Yes, yes. Of course, of course,' said Lichnowsky, taking a silk one from his sleeve, shaking it and giving it to Ludwig.

Ludwig wiped his forehead, put the handkerchief in his own sleeve and said, 'He is a fine player. I must pay him my respects and leave.'

'No, Ludwig. I must talk to you. Do not leave yet.'

Ludwig winced at the harshness of the voice. It had a slight high-pitched edge to it. It was not usually like that. Lichnowsky was speaking more loudly than normal to make himself heard above the crowd, and the raised pitch of his voice was causing Ludwig great pain. He screwed his eyes against it.

'Are you all right, Ludwig? You must be exhausted after that. Come and sit down.'

Ludwig allowed the Prince to lead him to a chair. He looked up and saw with satisfaction that Dragonetti had a cluster of people around him. To the side, Hummel too was being lauded.

'Rest here,' said the Prince. 'I have to speak to Swieten. I will be back in a minute.'

Ludwig smiled gratefully. He looked quickly round, and seeing that he was alone, he stood and walked half crouching to the back of the hall, hoping to be as inconspicuous as possible. There, in the shadow of the chandelier, he sat and leaned his head back against the wall. A window was open and the cool air bathed his face like a balm.

He looked again towards the front of the hall at the groups of admirers around Dragonetti and Hummel. Occasionally a face would look up and eyes would sweep the room; he knew they were looking for him. In the shadow he could not be seen and he was pleased.

He closed his eyes and thought about the music he had just played. He remembered writing it in Berlin. He had been given a room at the palace and all the facilities he needed. A guest of the King of Prussia! The young man from the Rhineland.

He knew why he was fêted. For the same reason he had always been. From the first Elector, Maximilian Friedrich, on. It was because he could play the piano in a way they had never heard before. And in a way no one could match. And that was why he was applauded tonight. Not for the piece of music, his composition, but for the way he could play.

That was why Dragonetti was applauded as he was. And Hummel. Because they were both fine players. An audience will always applaud fine playing. But I do not seek the applause as they do, he thought. I do not crave the recognition. I do not need it.

I am a composer, Ludwig thought to himself. I play my compositions, but I am a composer of music. A creator. That alone does not bring applause. The audience thinks it is applauding the composer, but it is not. It is applauding the skill of the players, or the singers. The music itself it takes for granted.

But compositions endure. And with them the name of the

composer. He looked again at the group around Dragonetti. Will the name of Domenico Dragonetti live on after his death? No. Who will remember that he was capable of playing cello sonatas on his double bass?

But they will remember the cello sonatas. Cellists not yet born, and their children, and their children beyond them . . . My music will be heard, he thought, long after they have forgotten that I was also a virtuoso pianist.

He saw Swieten and Lichnowsky talking to each other, gesturing. Lichnowsky looked up, concern on his face. Swieten shook his head. Ludwig knew they were talking about him. He knew it instinctively. In a moment they would come to find him. He breathed deeply. Away from the clamour of voices, he felt better. The pain in his head had subsided. The music no longer revolved. When they came to speak to him he was certain he would hear them with no difficulty.

Performances like tonight's . . . they were the problem. If he continued performing, it would only be a matter of time before someone realised his problem. And then the word would get out. Beethoven, the musician who cannot hear properly. But people would expect him to perform his own music. How could he avoid it? He did not know. But at least he could control those occasions. He could play just what he wanted, and no more. It was evenings like this one – with other musicians involved – that he must avoid.

He looked straight ahead, his head still leaning back against the wall, as Lichnowsky and Swieten approached. As they came up to him, he allowed his eyelids to close. He heard them pull up two chairs and knew they were sitting facing him.

He smiled and opened his eyes. 'Gentlemen. Forgive my . . . I needed some quiet. Peace. Let the others enjoy the praise.'

'We were worried about you,' said Lichnowsky.

'You don't need to be, Prince,' Ludwig said, a little more sharply than he had intended. 'I can look after myself.'

'Ludwig,' said Swieten, 'it was superb. The performance of your cello sonata. Did you ever expect to hear it played on the double bass?'

Ludwig smiled and shook his head. 'That Italian has opened my ears to his instrument. His successors may one day have cause to regret it.'

'What do you mean?'

'Bass players. All they are used to is playing the keynote in the bass. They concentrate when they play that note, because if they play it in the wrong place, the whole orchestra is thrown off. But when they are not playing that note . . . I have seen them whispering to each other. I have seen them with a folded newspaper on their music stand, passing it to each other. When they are required to play their note, they play it. Then they relax again. Maybe I will give them something to think about. When they play my music there will be no time for anything else. And they can blame Signor Dragonetti.'

The two noblemen laughed. Prince Lichnowsky said, 'Tell me, Ludwig, have you heard of Steibelt? Daniel Steibelt?'

'Yes. I think so. A Frenchman. Schuppanzigh has mentioned him. A pianist.'

'And composer.' The word made Ludwig look up. 'A composer of growing renown. But first and foremost a pianist, as you say. Not a Frenchman. Prussian actually. But he lived in Paris. Then in London.'

'What has he composed?'

'An opera. *Romeo and Juliette*. That's what he's best known for. Very successful in Paris. Apparently it secured him an interview with the First Consul, the Corsican.'

'Bonaparte. Napoleon Bonaparte.'

'Yes. He's also composed several piano concertos. The most recent – I think it is his third – has become instantly famous.'

'Why?' asked Ludwig with a touch of petulance in his voice.

Lichnowsky looked at Swieten, who nodded encouragingly. 'The finale has an imitation of a storm. It has thunder and rain and flashes of lightning. I have seen the score. There are so many notes for the piano you can barely see the white page underneath. It has not been played yet here in Vienna because no one can play it. Only Steibelt can play it.'

Ludwig said nothing.

'Whenever he plays it,' said Swieten, 'the audience stands and cheers. It is said . . . I am only repeating what I have heard . . . it is said he is the foremost piano virtuoso in Europe.'

Ludwig looked wearily at the two men. When will it end? he thought. When will they leave me alone? To compose. When will I not have to prove myself any more?

'And he is coming to Vienna,' said Ludwig.

Lichnowsky nodded enthusiastically. Swieten put out a restraining hand and spoke more gently. 'He is on a tour, and he is coming here, yes. Also Hamburg, Dresden and Berlin. I think he is going to Prague too. I am not sure.'

'And you want me to play against him. Like I did against Gelinek.'

'Oh, yes,' said Lichnowsky. 'Think of it. What a contest! Two great pianists . . .'

Again Swieten put out a restraining hand. 'It was an idea, that was all. But of course, Ludwig, the decision is yours. I can tell you that he has a full schedule here. He will give several recitals. I believe he is to be received at the Hofburg. The Empress has asked him to perform his music for her.'

Ludwig felt a surge of anger. 'No! No more contests. I will not perform again like a dancing bear. I am not a puppet for you to . . . to . . . pull the strings. I am not a circus animal who . . . who . . .'

'Ludwig, dear Ludwig, of course not,' said Swieten consolingly. 'Do not think of it again. The Prince and I quite understand. But at least let us introduce you to him. You two musicians will have much to talk about, I am sure. I will speak to Prince Lobkowitz and find out more details of his schedule.'

'Why Prince Lobkowitz?'

'He is his host here in Vienna. Steibelt will stay at his palace in the Michaelerplatz.'

'No. I won't play against this man, Steiberg, whatever his name is. No more improvisation contests. No more. Do you understand?'

Both men nodded.

Chapter 5

'What do you think of this man Bonaparte appointing himself First Consul of France?' asked Stephan von Breuning as he and Ludwig walked up the Kärntnerstrasse.

Ludwig shrugged. 'Statesmen, politicians, diplomats, soldiers. Charlatans, all of them. Only artists have purity in their hearts.'

Stephan chuckled. 'Thank you, my old friend. You have just dismissed practically everyone I respect. Including me. Since I work in the war office, I must be counted a diplomat.'

'And you then,' said Ludwig, but added a loud laugh. 'You and the Emperor. And everyone involved in this damned war.'

The two turned into the wide Himmelpfortgasse. 'This man Bonaparte,' said Ludwig. 'He seems to secure victory on the battlefield and off it.'

'What do you mean?'

'He's victor at Marengo. Is that the right name? And practically anywhere else he chooses to fight. And he's First Consul of France. He's commander of the military, and commander of the country.'

'He won't last as both. He'll have to choose.'

'Do you think so? I don't. He'll go on winning on the battlefield, and because of that he'll be given greater honours at home.'

'He can't go on winning. The whole of Europe will fight him. It's only a matter of time before his enemies unite. Imagine Austria, England, Prussia, Russia . . .'

Ludwig chuckled. 'You think he can do what centuries of living on the same continent have failed to do? Unite old enemies? If he does, he'll truly have something to be proud of.'

They turned left into the Rauhensteingasse, a narrower, quieter street lined by high buildings which led up to the Stephansplatz.

'Where are we going?' asked Ludwig suddenly.

'To see some old friends. Zmeskall and Schuppanzigh. At the Blumenstock. They wanted to see you. Now tell me about your work. How is it going?'

Ludwig nodded slowly. 'The septet is finished. For wind and strings. I am satisfied with it. And I think I am at last learning how to write quartets. String quartets.'

He stopped walking and turned to his old friend, who had stopped with him. 'There is so much to learn, Steffen. The quartet, for example. I thought it would be simple. Straightforward. Just four voices. But it is more difficult than anything I have done. I see Mozart, even old Haydn, in a new light because of what they have done with the quartet.'

An expectant smile settled on Stephan's face. 'Ludwig, do you realise we are talking normally? As friends do. Your hearing . . . You are not having a problem. Even in the open air.'

Ludwig smiled and began walking again. 'Sometimes it is all right. Just talking to you, one person, even though I am not looking at you. I am learning how to cope. If I am with a lot of people, I can tell by gestures, expressions, what they mean. But, Steffen, I have no desire to be in company any more. That evening at the Mehlgrube with Dragonetti. It was painful.'

'But successful. I heard so many good reports of it. I am afraid as a musician, Ludwig, a performer, you will not be able to hide yourself away.'

'Composer, Steffen. Composer. That is what I am.'

'Does anyone else know of the problem?'

Ludwig shook his head. 'Still only Nanette Streicher. So far. And the doctors. The damned useless doctors. If they had their way, everyone would know. "Wear this wool in your ears, soaked in yellow oil." How could I walk around like that?'

'But you can hear me,' said Stephan, smiling.

They turned right into the Ballgasse, a dark, narrow street, little more than an alley. Candles burned above doorways, even though it was still daylight.

Stephan took a letter from his pocket. 'Zum alten Blumenstock. Number nine-eight-six. I don't know it. Do you?'

Ludwig shook his head. 'I've heard Schuppanzigh talk about it. What do they want to see me about?'

Stephan shrugged his shoulders. 'I think just for company. I'll stay for one glass of wine, but then I shall have to leave you.'

The candle outside the Blumenstock was brighter than the

others and a warm glow came from the windows, throwing yellow light on to the cobbles outside.

Stephan and Ludwig walked through a side door and into the front room. A heavily gilded mirror hung on the back wall, shelves of bottles containing various coloured liquids lined up beneath it. Small, round tables filled the centre of the room; along the walls there were comfortably upholstered chairs and sofas. Two young women looked up and smiled as the men walked in.

Stephan glanced quickly round, a slightly embarrassed look on his face. There was no sign of Zmeskall or Schuppanzigh. A sudden burst of laughter caused him to look towards the back of the room, where a doorway led to a second room. He walked towards it, gesturing Ludwig to follow. With some relief, he saw the two friends at a table. There was no one else in the small room.

Ludwig glanced back once more as he followed Stephan. The women were still smiling at him. He felt a sudden shaft of heat course through his body. The air had about it an aroma of wine and wood, which permeated his senses. As he passed the counter he took a filled pipe from the rack, smelled the tobacco in the bowl and put it back.

He nodded at Zmeskall and Schuppanzigh.

'At last,' said Schuppanzigh, smiling broadly. 'Come on in. Sit down. Your glasses are ready and waiting.' He reached for the carafe of red wine and filled glasses for Stephan and Ludwig.

'I cannot stay,' said Stephan. 'Forgive me. I am needed at the war office.'

'Even at this time? It is evening.'

'I know. But unfortunately we are at war.'

'True,' said Zmeskall, taking off his thick spectacles, breathing on them and polishing them. 'But just for once it is not my people you are at war against.'

'Far from it,' said Stephan, laughing. 'You Hungarians are now our ally. And allies are what we need.'

Ludwig sipped the wine, enjoying its familiar flavour. He looked up. Above the doorway was a dark oil painting. He could just make out the shape of a woman reclining. A naked woman. Again he felt the warmth in his veins. He took another sip of the wine.

'The quartets, Ludwig,' said Schuppanzigh eagerly, 'how are

they going? When are you going to let me see them? Play them through?'

Ludwig smiled. 'Patience, Schuppi. They are progressing. I completed them some time ago, but I was not happy. I have started again.'

'Started again? Ludwig, I—'

'Started again, Schuppi. And it will not be a pair of quartets, as I intended. Or three. Or four.'

Schuppanzigh lowered his glass. 'Ludwig, I don't understand.'

'Six quartets, Schuppi. Six. I will write six. I have ideas for them all. And I will write them. All with a single opus number. And then I will wait.'

'What do you mean, wait?'

'When they are completed, I will not write more quartets until I have learned more. The Quartet is new to me and there is much to learn.'

'Weren't you writing something else?' asked Zmeskall. 'For six instruments, or seven, was it?'

'Seven. String quartet and three wind. A septet.'

'I have seen the score, Nikola,' said Schuppanzigh. 'Six movements, no less. And a beautiful Adagio. You will have great success with it, Ludwig. You would have had even more if you had given the opening solo of the Adagio to the violin instead of the clarinet!'

'Ha! Schuppi. You want the solo, do you? If I had given it to you, I would have had to write a big fat theme to go with the player!'

A look of hurt crossed Schuppanzigh's face at the apparent cruelty of the remark, but Ludwig's smile – and a cry of sympathy and support from both Breuning and Zmeskall – took away any pain he might have felt.

Stephan put down his glass. 'Gentlemen, you must excuse me. I shall take my leave of you. Ludwig. Nikola. Ignaz.' He bowed his head slightly and left, looking straight ahead until he reached the front door.

'I heard about the soirée with the Italian bass player, Ludwig,' said Schuppanzigh. 'I wish I had been there.'

Ludwig nodded. 'He plays like the devil. Like a dragon, I should say. They call him Il Drago.'

'Is it true he played one of your cello sonatas on the double bass?'

'And not just any ordinary double bass. I have never seen a machine like it. A monster. And only three strings.'

'That's what I heard. And you accompanied him?'

'It wasn't the intention. But Hummel yielded his place.'

'Nice man, Hummel. Fine pianist. Despite all those rings encrusting his fingers. Good thing he's not a violinist. He'd put the rings through the wood!'

Zmeskall refilled their glasses. Deliberately turning away from Ludwig to look straight at Schuppanzigh, he said, 'Tell me about this man Steibelt. When is he coming here?'

'In a week. Europe's finest piano virtuoso. They say he is the best. What have you heard, Ludwig?'

'Nothing. Only that he's coming.'

'Will you meet him? Hear him play?'

'No.'

Schuppanzigh pushed Ludwig's glass nearer to him. 'I was talking to Prince Lichnowsky the other day. After one of his Friday matinées. He said an interesting thing.'

'What did he say, Schuppi?' asked Zmeskall, blinking behind his thick spectacles to give his question greater weight.

'He said . . . He said . . . Ludwig, this will interest you . . . He said that you were now generally accepted as the finest piano virtuoso in Vienna and that—'

'Hummel is as good as I am. I heard him the other night. In private. He has exceptional gifts.'

'That is true. But Hummel is saying openly that he is inferior to you.'

'I have not heard that. From him or anyone else.'

'Well, you are now. I am telling you, and it is the truth.'

'What about Wölffl? And Cramer? Clementi even, in London.'

'Wölffl as you know does not even claim to match you. The same goes for Cramer. He is in London. He told me so when he was last here. Hummel I have already mentioned. Clementi I can't speak about, but word reaches me that he is concentrating more on building up his music publishing business than performing. He, too, is in London. He now no longer gives recitals, or very few at any rate.'

'Then he is not stupid. I wish to do the same. Give up playing so I can compose.'

Schuppanzigh and Zmeskall exchanged worried glances.

'I haven't finished telling you what Prince Lichnowsky said. He said that if you were to take Steibelt on – and no one doubts who would win – you would be universally regarded as the finest pianist in Europe.'

'I don't need that kind of recognition. What I want is recognition for my composing; it is compositions that endure.'

'But, Ludwig,' said Zmeskall enthusiastically, 'don't you see? If you were known as the finest in Europe, it would make your compositions better known. They would receive even greater attention.'

'Exactly,' said Schuppanzigh. 'Your compositions would benefit from your skill as a pianist.'

Ludwig drank down the wine and pushed his glass forward for more. He drank again from the refilled glass. 'A conspiracy. Do you think I can't see that? Even my old friend Steffen. Bring Ludwig to the . . . whatever this place is called . . . We'll give him wine, we'll tell him he's the greatest in Vienna . . .'

Both his friends held up their hands in protest. 'No, Ludwig, you mustn't . . .'

Ludwig brought his glass down hard on the table. Some wine splashed over the top of the glass and seeped into the rough wood of the table. He looked at his friends, his face red. He stood.

'Schuppanzigh and Zmeskall. My two good friends. Schuppanzigh, Schuppanzigh. Schuppanzigh-you're-a-fat-man!' he sang. 'Schuppanzigh-you're-a-fat-man!' Turning to Zmeskall, 'Ba-ron, Ba-ron, Ba-ron. *Baron Muck-Cart Driver and the Fat Man.* An opera by Ludwig van Beethoven. *The Fat Man and the Blind Man.* Blink at me, Nikola. Baron Zmeskallovitch.'

He sat down again, both friends gesturing at him to lower his voice.

'Steibelt,' said Ludwig. 'Steiberger. Steifung. Steigruber. Steigelberg. Steiteufel. Yes, that's it. Steiteufel. Steibelt the devil. To be struck down, torn asunder, destroyed, by the Dragon of the Rhine, the monster of the Drachenfels. Me. Il Drago. Der Drachen.'

'Shh!' said Schuppanzigh. 'You'll get us thrown out. Anyway, I must leave you. Do you know what I need, Ludwig? Do you know what I need to feel? The skin of a woman against mine. The scent of her perfume in my nostrils. An artist must live for art. And with it. And a woman is art, Ludwig. Do you not agree?'

'My dear Schuppi,' said Ludwig. 'To disagree with you would condemn me to eternal damnation.'

'It's too soon for that. Too soon for any of us. We'll all be damned one day. But not yet. And in the meantime ... Ludwig, the Muck-Cart Driver will look after you. I will see you tomorrow, probably. And, Ludwig, you have made the right decision.'

He looked conspiratorially at Zmeskall and left. Ludwig watched his bulk move towards the main room, marvelling not for the first time at the ease with which he carried it. He noticed that instead of walking to the door, he turned into the room. Moments later came the sound of female laughter.

Zmeskall looked at him, his face flushed with anticipation. 'The fortress, Ludwig.'

'Not that place again. Walfischgasse. Too many people. No, no. We are not going anywhere. We are staying just where we are.'

Ludwig leaned his head back against the wall and allowed his eyes to close. His senses were reeling. The wine was making his head swim, but with a lightness that was overwhelmingly pleasant. He felt as if he had no problems in the world. His ears had begun to ring, but he assured himself it was only the effect of the wine and he smiled at the realisation that it was nothing to worry about.

Steibelt. Had he agreed to an improvisation contest against Steibelt? He thought he had. He knew perfectly well from the moment Steffen had asked him to come here tonight that they were going to try to persuade him. He had been determined to resist, not to yield.

Was it too late to change his mind? Of course it wasn't. It was only Zmeskall and Schuppanzigh he had spoken to, and if he told them he had changed his mind, then that was that. They would have to agree.

But did he really want to? He would defeat Steibelt, he knew that. He was not in the slightest doubt about it. And then he would be the greatest pianist in all Europe. Perhaps then they would leave him alone to compose. He would insist on it. He would have earned it.

He became aware of a sweet aroma, a scent of perfume in the air. His skin was on fire, his cheeks burning. He knew without opening his eyes that Zmeskall was no longer there. He felt a soft cheek brush against his and the velvet touch of soft lips on his own. A hand massaged his groin and he stretched up into it. Then his hands felt a mass of fine, silky hair. Without opening his eyes, he pushed down on the woman's head and felt dampness around him. He pushed up into her mouth and arched his back, pressing his head against the wall, until a feeling of utter joy and relief flooded through him and he knew his destiny. Unmistakably, unequivocally. He was the greatest pianist in Europe and he would be the greatest composer. Who was there to touch him?

Chapter 6

There was a grating edge to Carl's voice which irritated Ludwig. It was an ugly sound, but worse than that it seemed to be at a pitch that Ludwig found difficult to hear, or at least understand.

'Can't you hear me, Ludwig? Or are you deliberately being difficult?'

'I . . . I was playing the piano before you arrived. It takes me a while . . .'

'Yes, yes. I know. I am a musician too, you know. And a rather successful one, I might add.'

Johann nodded. 'Carl is clever. He teaches music and makes money out of it. More than you do by writing it.'

Ludwig looked at him. It was an unworthy thought, but he did despise his two brothers. He always had done, from as early as he could remember. What did he have to say to them? How could he tell them about the *isolation* he felt?

Caspar and Nikola, his two brothers. Now they were Carl and . . . Carl and . . . He could not bring himself to say the name. Their father's name. The name that in his childhood he had grown to loathe. The name that meant misery to him. Pain, suffering, anger.

A look of smugness settled on Carl's face. 'Yes, you'd be surprised, Brother Ludwig, what the name Beethoven can do. "Oh, is this how your brother plays it, Herr Beethoven?" "Two such talented brothers. Is he as proud of you as you are of him?" "You must make such wonderful music together" . . .'

'Sometimes,' said Johann, 'they even think Carl is you and he doesn't—'

'Enough, Johann!' Carl snapped.

The contempt Ludwig felt for his brothers turned to pity. What were they? Nothing, really. Carl was a mediocre musician, a pianist whose talents did not rise one tiny level above those of thousands of other pianists. And the other brother? An apothecary; nothing better than a charlatan who pandered to the imagined needs of sick people; a quack, really, without the medical training that would have allowed him to call himself a doctor. He would never get anywhere, never earn a satisfactory living.

Carl was talking again, in that grating voice of his.

'I shall make some good money out of it.'

'What? Money? What are you saying?'

Carl brought his hand down on his thigh in exasperation. 'For God's sake, Ludwig. Are you deaf? It's like talking to a deaf man. Johann, can't you give him something for his ears? I said, I shall make good money out of your contest against Steibelt.'

'What do you mean?'

'The pawnshop in the Dorotheegasse is taking wagers on the outcome.'

'Wagers? What are you talking about? I still don't understand.'

Carl looked at Johann, who willingly took up the narrative, while Carl sat back, his arms folded, his legs crossed, the smug look still on his face.

'Carl told Müller about it, the man who runs the pawn shop. That you were taking Steibelt on. He said Steibelt had already performed twice since he arrived here, and people were saying he could not be matched, anywhere in Europe. Carl persuaded him to take wagers.'

Ludwig sunk his head on his hand. 'You see it as sport, as a game, don't you, Carl?'

'No, Ludwig. Business. Money to be made.'

'Carl told Müller,' Johann continued, 'that you had been unwell and that your playing had suffered . . .'

Ludwig jerked his head up. Carl said quickly, 'It's true, Ludwig. You were ill. Some time ago perhaps, but you were ill when you came back from Mödling. Anyway, it worked with Müller.'

'He gave Carl a good price,' said Johann. 'Five florins to one. Both of us have put forward fifty florins.'

'And I'll do it for you, Ludwig. If you give me the money. I'll make the wager in my name. Because you are going to win, aren't you? We all know that.'

Ludwig paused a moment. 'You are, aren't you, Ludwig?' Johann echoed Carl's question.

John Suchet

Ludwig looked from one brother to the other, then spoke in a steady, calm voice. 'If it were not for my reputation, I would allow Steibelt to win, just to see the two of you ruined. I despise you both. Now leave my room immediately. And, Carl. Caspar. Whatever you call yourself. You are to give up music once and for all. No more teaching. You are to have nothing more to do with publishers on my behalf. If you do not do as I say, I will ruin your reputation. Remember, I have powerful friends. Do you understand?'

As Ludwig approached the palace of Prince Lobkowitz, his mood darkened. He wished he had not agreed to play against Steibelt; it was not the way he wanted to display his musical skills. But that was what they did in Vienna. Really he could consider himself fortunate that it had not happened to him more often. Well, this would be the last time. He had vowed that to himself, and he would make sure everyone understood it. Lichnowsky, Swieten, Lobkowitz, everybody. He would see off this charlatan Steibelt. His supremacy would never be challenged again. And he could devote himself to composition.

As long as my hearing does not let me down, he thought as he climbed the staircase. All night he had lain with wool in his ears, wool soaked in almond oil. He had stayed awake to ensure his head did not fall to the side. It had left him tired and his pillow was still badly stained in the morning – he must have fallen asleep several times – but his ears did not seem to be troubling him. And his stomach was settled. That was one area in which Doktor Vering was having undoubted success.

The staircase was less ornate than he had expected, the ceiling paintings less decorative. He noticed that the plaster patterns around the ceilings had been shaped at intervals to take on the face of an old man.

A large set of double wooden doors, intricately carved, stood open across the wide first-floor landing and a steady hum of conversation came from inside the room. It was punctuated by a loud laugh and Ludwig winced as the harsh sound hit his ears. He was, he knew, walking into the worst sort of situation he could imagine. Get it done, he thought to himself. Get through it.

He walked into the room and gasped with astonishment. It was much larger and more splendid than he had imagined. It was wider than it was deep, with tall, oval-topped windows on the far side which gave out on to the Spiegelgasse below.

The ceiling was adorned with richly coloured frescoes, figures from antiquity, women with elaborate gowns slashed to reveal naked breasts, naked cherubs playing at their feet. The theme that united them all was music. In each set of figures a harp or lyre was being played.

Ludwig took the pictures in and forced his eyes down. Most of the people in the room were clustered in the centre, surrounding one figure who was clearly the object of their interest. At last I shall meet this Steibelt, Ludwig thought. He saw Lobkowitz, talking vociferously, his head nodding jerkily forward to emphasise his words, banging his crutch against the floor for added emphasis. Lichnowsky was there, Swieten too, several people he did not know in wigs and rich costumes.

He saw the young Prince Kinsky, his girth matching that of anyone there. He was in military uniform, standing rigidly erect, his right hand resting on his sword pommel. Ludwig remembered now that his father, the old Prince, had died suddenly a year or two before. The young man's bearing demonstrated that he had taken the weight of his newly elevated standing upon his shoulders.

Prince Lichnowsky saw him first and came straight over to him.

'Dear boy, dear boy! Are you on good form? Such a gathering! You will not regret your decision. Everyone is talking of you in the highest possible terms. Even the great Master himself, who was only just saying . . .'

'Who? Who is here?'

'Herr Haydn, Ludwig. Your old teacher. He was just saying how so often the pupil surpasses the teacher. Come. Come. I will introduce you.'

He took Ludwig by the elbow and led him towards the group.

Ludwig grimaced. That sudden sharp stab of pain in the stomach which he had believed himself rid of shot through him. And, almost like an old friend, the buzz in his ears returned.

He was pleased to see that Haydn's smile was genuinely friendly. He bowed to the old man.

'I keep in touch with your progress, Ludwig. It gives me such pleasure to learn of your successes. And tonight, surely, will be another to add to them. What will you play?'

'I haven't . . . I don't know. It depends on what he plays.'

'I think we can be sure,' said Swieten, 'that we will have a storm in here tonight. Thunder and lightning and rain. Courtesy of Herr Steibelt!'

'Hah! I can guarantee it. No Steibelt performance is complete without the famous storm,' said Lobkowitz.

'Is he here?'

'Not yet. But he will be soon.'

'Ludwig,' said Lichnowsky, 'do you know Prince Schwarzenberg? And Count Fries? Hummel of course you know.'

'Ludwig. I would not have missed this evening for the world. I shall sit back and admire a master at work.'

Haydn laughed. 'So you see, Ludwig. You are already called a master. Not so long ago you were my pupil, now you are acknowledged as a master, and quite rightly so, if I may say so. Your compositions are exceptional. I have studied the scores of your piano concertos. They are indeed masterly.'

Gloved hands applauded delicately at Haydn's fine compliment. Ludwig lowered his head in acknowledgement. As he did so the buzz in his ears intensified. When he looked up again it became a sharp whistle, but to his relief it immediately subsided.

'You have good friends here tonight, Ludwig,' said Lichnowsky, gesturing to a corner of the room.

Ludwig looked across and saw the vast bulk of Ignaz Schuppanzigh. Zmeskall and Stephan Breuning were with him. Stephan saw him look across and gave him a smile. Ludwig wanted to go over and talk to his friends, but he knew he could not. Anyway Carl his brother was with them. He wished he had not come. At least his other brother was not here. Too busy mixing quack medicines, no doubt, he thought.

He winced as a sharp voice cut through the room. Ludwig could not immediately tell where it came from. But all eyes turned to the door and he realised it was a footman speaking.

'My noble lords, dukes, counts and gentlemen. His Excellency Herr Steibelt.'

Ludwig looked at the figure poised in the doorway. A tall powdered wig, lavishly embroidered coat, white cravat – obviously of double length and thickness – knotted elaborately at the neck, hose to below the knee and fastened with a golden buckle, white stockings and shining black court shoes with a slight heel. He stood with one hand on his hip, the other held out suggestively, a folder of manuscripts in it.

There was a ripple of applause, and Prince Lobkowitz, Steibelt's patron for the evening, went to the door to bring him in.

Ludwig looked at Steibelt and his stomach turned over. The poise; the natural authority. He glanced down at his own clothes, dark wool, the cravat which he knew he had not knotted properly, a button missing on the jacket – he had meant to tell Nanette about it – his shoes stained from the street.

Suddenly Ludwig felt hopelessly inadequate. This man was not just a great pianist, but a composer too. Could he – so elegant, so confident – be a finer musician than Ludwig? Could it be that for the first time in his life he was about to suffer public humiliation? He, Ludwig, humiliated as a musician. He knew he would not be able to bear it. There would be no point in living. Damn my ears, he thought, as the whistling made him wince. Damn my wretched stomach. Damn everything. He just wanted to be on his own. In the country, where it was peaceful, where he could hear the birds sing, smell the hay, feel the freshness of the country air on his face. Away from all this. Why could they not just leave him alone? His self-pity turned to anger.

'And where is the man who is to become my victim?' asked Steibelt, eliciting laughter from those around him. 'Ah, Herr Haydn,' he said, before anyone could answer, 'what a great pleasure. What a great privilege.' He bowed low, and Haydn acknowledged the courtesy.

'Fine gathering we've got for you here tonight, Herr Steibelt,' said Prince Lobkowitz, giving the floor a couple of taps with his crutch. 'Cream of society. Cream of society. Lichnowsky, Schwarzenberg, Fries. This is Kinsky. Succeeded to the title after the unfortunate death of his father. D'you know Baron Margelick?' he said, gesturing to a late arrival. 'Chief secretary to His Majesty the Emperor . . .'

Steibelt and Margelick bowed to each other.

Steibelt said. 'And now where is my poor victim? A young man from the Rhineland, I am told. Is he here yet?'

'Yes, indeed,' said Lobkowitz, looking round.

Ludwig stood slightly away from the group, knowing it was only a matter of time before all heads turned towards him. He looked again at the other small group, and Stephan Breuning gave him a nod of encouragement.

When he turned back, Prince Lichnowsky was walking towards him.

'Well, Ludwig. How are you feeling? Come. Let me introduce you to Herr Steibelt.'

Unsmiling, as if secretly hoping that his serious expression would increase his standing, Ludwig followed the Prince.

'Herr Steibelt,' Lichnowsky said, 'it is my honour to sponsor this young gentleman tonight. May I present Herr Ludwig Beethoven, of the city of Bonn by Cologne in the German Rhineland.'

Ludwig registered the deliberately curt nod of the head he received from Steibelt, who introduced himself solely as, 'Steibelt. Berlin.'

Steibelt looked at him for a moment, then said, with a tone more of disbelief than condescension, 'I have seen your music, sir. Your scores have reached me. Can you really have written them? They are . . . different.'

Hummel spoke. 'As a musician myself, sir, I can assure you they are written by Herr Beethoven. And remarkable they are too, as you rightly—'

'Herr Haydn,' said Steibelt, turning to the old composer, who was supporting his small, now rather frail body on a stick, 'will you confirm it to me, as Europe's foremost composer?'

Haydn smiled. 'Indeed I will, sir. The young man was once my pupil. I am fortunate to be the dedicatee of his first piano sonatas. I can assure you I long since realised I had nothing more to teach him.'

'So, sir,' said Steibelt, turning back to Ludwig, 'you have high praise lavished on you. And tonight you encounter Steibelt. We shall see what transpires.'

Ludwig took a deep breath. What an odious man this Steibelt was. Pompous and arrogant. Was there any worse quality? Ludwig wanted to make a cutting remark, which would silence him. But words, he knew, were not his weapon. His weapon was something else and he was about to wield it.

Lobkowitz said eagerly, 'Well, Lichnowsky. Is your man ready? Shall we set them at each other?'

There was a general murmuring of agreement and the guests quickly took their seats, leaving four chairs in the front row empty for the four men still standing – Lobkowitz, Lichnowsky and their champions.

Prince Lobkowitz waved his crutch in the air to command

silence. 'The rules are well established. As Herr Steibelt is an honoured guest in our city, he shall be regarded as the challenger. Herr Beethoven will play first. A theme of his own choosing. Herr Steibelt will be asked to improvise on it. The roles will then be reversed. Both gentlemen will then repeat the procedure, with different themes. After that . . . well, we shall see how the evening goes. And may I remind you all, my servants have laid a lavish table in the adjoining room – through those doors at the end,' he pointed to the far end of the room, 'and you will all, I hope, be my guests.'

There was applause. Ludwig walked towards the piano. It was set between two of the large windows overlooking the street below. On the wall between the two windows was a portrait of an old man in court dress. Ludwig looked at it, and in his mind he saw the face of his grandfather, his dear grandfather, with that familiar turban on his head and the velvet cloak on his shoulders. How his grandfather had inspired him – and how just the thought of him inspired him now. Yes, the spirit of his grandfather was here, in the room with him.

He touched the frame of the piano as he reached it. The anger which had been in his body subsided. My world, he thought. This is where I belong. The piano, the king of instruments, and I am its master. This is my language. Through it I can speak to people. Through it I can open their souls. I can give them art and beauty.

He sat at the keyboard and after a momentary pause stretched his hands forward over the black keys and began playing the Adagio Cantabile from his Grande Sonate Pathétique. The gentle, lyrical theme floated across the room. Ludwig closed his eyes. He was playing the theme more slowly than he usually did, allowing its grandeur to come through.

He did not see the worried looks in the corner of the room, where his friends sat. Hummel, who had joined them, shot a look at Schuppanzigh. Ludwig was playing one of the most simple pieces of music he had written. Beautiful, maybe, but simple to play. The object of the improvisation contest was to demonstrate virtuosity. Carl shook his head, his lips pulled back over his teeth in anger. Stephan gave them reassuring looks, as if to say, don't worry, the fireworks will come any moment.

But Ludwig played on, performing the short movement exactly as he had written it and it had been published. When he reached the end, he stood and went to his chair in the front row. The applause was polite.

Steibelt, a look of quiet satisfaction on his face, walked to the piano, placed his folder of manuscripts on it and turned to the audience.

'A fine rendering, if I may say so. The piece is known to me, your Pathétique Sonata, and I am bound to tell you it has achieved considerable popularity. Especially the movement you have just played. Not, I must say, because of its beauty, its undoubted beauty. But because it is so simple that anyone can play it! I shall now demonstrate what a master pianist can do with it.'

Steibelt sat at the piano and began playing the Adagio. Ludwig saw immediately that he was playing in the key of C major. No black keys. It gave the theme a harsher sound. At the end of the eight-bar theme, Steibelt played the repeat an octave higher, as Ludwig had written it, but on each note of the theme he added a trill. Ludwig winced to hear what was happening to his music, his beautiful music.

Instead of then moving into the second subject, Steibelt repeated the theme, this time with trills in the treble and the bass. The piano was suddenly alive with sound. It began to shudder.

Ludwig wanted to scream at him to stop, to leave his music alone. It was hurting his ears and he shut his eyes tightly against it. He felt Lichnowsky's hand pat him reassuringly on the thigh, as if to say that he understood.

Now Steibelt's hands were flying in different directions up and down the keys. The theme was nowhere to be heard. Suddenly he stopped, and there was the theme played again, and again adorned with furious trills. There was a chuckle from the audience. The theme stopped and Steibelt played shuddering chords, all in the minor key for added drama. He stopped suddenly again, and there was the now familiar theme, in a different key this time. Then chromatic runs in both hands, beginning on the extreme bass notes of the piano and running to the top treble.

Steibelt was demonstrating his skills to the audience. The theme he was supposed to be improvising on was incidental. In between the shows of virtuosity the theme returned, always with those trills. When the final chord sounded and Steibelt threw his head back, eyes closed, there was an eruption of applause from the audience.

Steibelt stood, removed a handkerchief from his sleeve and mopped his brow. He did not bow. Instead he raised his head, eyes still closed. He paused a moment longer, after the applause had subsided.

'Thank you. You are most kind. You shall have your reward now by witnessing the famous Steibelt storm.'

His words were greeted with more applause, and he removed the manuscripts from his folder and propped them up on the stand. He began playing.

The theme was a jaunty rondo. Suddenly he broke it off and played with both hands in the bass register. Where before trills had been the main characteristic of his playing, now it was tremolos. The approach of storm clouds. They faded away and the rondo theme returned. But suddenly the tremolos came back, this time in the treble. Then in both bass and treble. Storm clouds, the rumble of thunder. Then the thunder burst over the countryside. Crashing chords from Steibelt in the bass and treble, first one after the other, then in unison.

The storm was in full flow. Steibelt threw his head back one moment, leaned forward right over the keys the next. The piano frame shuddered. Slowly he decreased the intensity. The storm was subsiding. The tremolos became weaker. The piano frame steadied. A final rumble in the bass.

Steibelt lifted both hands off the keys. A moment later he brought them gently down and the rondo resumed. There were smiles of relief in the audience. The storm had passed. Faces turned towards each other. What extraordinary playing! What virtuosity!

Ludwig looked at Steibelt. Was he the only person in the room who could see the man for what he was? A . . . a . . . charlatan. There was nothing impressive about what he had just done. Effects, that was all. Tremolos, trills. Effects. Not music, real music.

Steibelt stood to acknowledge the applause, again mopping his damp brow. Without looking at Ludwig, he walked slightly unsteadily back to his chair. Lobkowitz clapped him on the shoulder, then stood, leading another round of applause.

Ludwig sat, breathing quickly. His body felt on fire. The pain in his stomach had subsided. The noise in his ears was still there, but through it he could hear music. He could hear the sounds he wanted to make. He became aware of Prince Lichnowsky's voice.

'It's up to you now, Ludwig.' Ludwig turned and looked at the corner of the room. His brother Carl sat with his head in his hands. Schuppanzigh had a worried frown, biting his lower lip. Stephan sat with both fists clenched. Hummel was leaning forward, his chin resting on his hand.

'Will you go and play something? Anything?' asked Lichnowsky.

Ludwig stood, and every face turned to him. Steibelt was the last to look at him. He raised his eyebrows, as if to say, 'Well?'

Again that familiar surge of anger shot through Ludwig, but this time he welcomed it. His skin tingled. He knew what he had to do, what he was about to do. He owed it to his friends. He owed it to himself. But most of all he owed it to his art. His great art. He needed to rescue it from charlatans like Steibelt.

He walked to the piano. He knew his walk was clumsy, not refined like Steibelt's. He snatched Steibelt's folder off the music stand and opened it. He pulled the last sheet of paper from it and put the folder down. He went to put the sheet on the stand but at the last moment held it up and made an elaborate display of turning it upside down. There was a gasp from the audience, followed by laughter. Ludwig did not look to see Steibelt's reaction.

He picked out four notes on the piano. E flat, B flat above it, B flat an octave lower, and E flat again. He played them again.

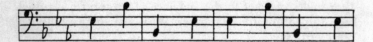

Ludwig paused a moment, as if trying to assess the implication of the notes. A third time he played them. Then very gently in the right hand, accompanied by runs in the left; then runs in both hands, but in the right accenting the four notes each time, even though they were off the beat. Then he accented them in the left. Then both.

A torrent of notes was now pouring from the piano; Ludwig's hands were moving up and down the keys in different directions, just as Steibelt's had a few moments before. But the difference was that however fast Ludwig played, those four notes kept coming through, now in the treble, now in the bass, now in both; on the beat, off the beat.

Slowly a new theme emerged from under Ludwig's fingers, a

singing, soaring melody in the treble. Hesitant at first, quaver, dotted crotchet, quaver, dotted crotchet, quaver, dotted

And while he played that, still the same four notes sounded in the bass.

He alternated the four-note theme and the soaring melody above it, left hand and right hand, right hand and left hand. He changed keys, major to minor, minor to major.

Slowly, imperceptibly at first, he slowed the two themes down, playing ever more quietly, knowing that the audience would be straining forward to hear every note.

He turned to them and shouted, 'Take cover! Storm! Storm! Storm *à la* Steibelt!'

And he began playing furious tremolos in both hands, deliberately throwing in some wrong notes, half crouching above the chair and looking wildly at the audience. 'Storm! Storm!' he cried.

On he played, in a merciless parody of Steibelt's technique. Suddenly he stopped, hands poised above the keys. 'Calm,' he said to the audience. 'Calm after the storm.' And he played Steibelt's jaunty rondo, exactly as Steibelt had played it, note perfect. The audience burst into laughter.

'Storm! Storm! Take cover!' Tremolos again. More laughter from the audience. Applause from Ludwig's small group of friends at the back of the room.

'Calm! Calm! Storm gone!' The rondo theme again, now sounding ever more trivial and banal.

'And now, to end,' he shouted, 'the upside-down music of Herr Steibelt.'

E flat, B flat, B flat, E flat. The soaring theme above it, now taking flight as Ludwig found its pace. Finally he brought the music to a gentle and graceful end.

He held his hands poised above the keys. A smile suffused his face.

'Storm! Storm! Take cover! Take cover! No, enough storms for one evening, and not a single real one. Look, not a drop of rain anywhere!'

There was a burst of laughter, faces turned mockingly towards Steibelt.

Steibelt's face was red with rage. He stood, and without a glance to the side or a single word, he strode from the room.

Lobkowitz went hurrying after him, as quickly as he could with the impediment of his crutch.

Lichnowsky leaped to his feet, leading the applause. Every person in the room stood, applauding Ludwig.

Moments later Lobkowitz came hurrying back in. He raised his arms for silence.

'I have to tell you that Herr Steibelt has decided to leave Vienna forthwith. He says it is unlikely he will return to our city again. Herr Ludwig van Beethoven, you are the champion of the evening. You are the champion of Vienna. Let your position never again be challenged.'

BOOK TEN

Chapter 1

There was a light sprinkling of snow in Mödling. The air was chilly but bright with the sun of late winter. It would soon be spring. The birds sensed it; they were beginning to emerge hesitantly from their winter hibernation. The ground would soon begin to soften; in a matter of weeks they would no longer need to peck through the thin ice covering the little patches of water that had collected in hollows. Life was beginning to return to the main square. In the late morning and early afternoon the warmth of the sun was enough for people to stop and exchange greetings and information. It would not be long before sowing could begin. If the fine weather persisted into spring, it would give the crops a good chance; the cattle would eat well and be healthy . . .

Ludwig took the same room on the first floor of the pension next to the tavern. He liked it because when the sun sank low it flooded the room with light. And he had discovered that there was a piano in a small room at the back of the town hall. It was enough. He could compose in his room. If he needed to hear the effect of what he had written, he could cross the square and play it on the piano. The room was usually locked but he had persuaded the caretaker to show him where the key was kept. In return, Ludwig had promised not to play it when any town meetings were in progress.

The caretaker was one of the few people Ludwig had spoken to. As on his last stay here, people left him alone. He would eat his meals at the tavern next to his lodgings, becoming a familiar sight at the same table on its own in the corner. He always had a notebook open and a pencil in his hand. The look of intense concentration on his face was enough to deter would-be conversationalists.

The same applied on his walks. As he strode up from the square, past the church of Othmar and into the woods, his face was set in thought. His arms waved. He would stop for a moment to take the notebook from his coat pocket to scribble something down. Other walkers kept away from him. It was obvious that although he was alone he was fully occupied with his own company and did not desire any other. Ludwig was at last working on a composition that had been on his mind for a long time: his first symphony.

How they had wanted him to remain in Vienna after his triumph against Steibelt! Prince Lobkowitz in particular, who had said he would arrange performances in his concert room any time Ludwig wished. No, Ludwig had replied. Enough performing. He wanted to get away, out of Vienna, into the country, to compose.

The idea of a symphony had been revolving in his mind for some time. The Septet for Wind and Strings was now complete. So were the string quartets. Ah, yes, the quartets. Ludwig thought of them often as he walked in the woods above Mödling. There were six in all. He had surprised himself by writing so many. Initially he had intended a single quartet, then a pair, then three. He had realised early on that it would exceed three, and once he had decided to write as many as six it seemed to clear the way for him. But they had not been easy. He had thought he'd completed them; he'd even shown them to Schuppanzigh, who declared them enthusiastically to be the equal of anything Haydn or Mozart had written, and asked Ludwig to allow him to play them with Louis Sina, Franz Weiss and Anton Kraft, the other members of Prince Lichnowsky's string quartet.

Ludwig had refused. At first he'd been bemused by his own reluctance to hear them, but he knew they were not yet right. He was unable to see, though, what was wrong with them. Perhaps there was nothing wrong. He decided to put the scores to one side and come fresh to them at a later date.

It was a friend of Schuppanzigh's, Karl Amenda, an amateur violinist from Courland in the Baltic, who unwittingly gave Ludwig the clue when he looked at the score of the first of the six.

'So many notes, Herr Beethoven,' he said. 'It is as if you have tried to put everything in at once.'

Ludwig had ignored the remark, but it revolved in his mind. So many notes. So many notes. Could Amenda be right? There was a temptation to ignore his own doubt and simply offer the quartets for publication, to capitalise on the successful publication of his Grande Sonate Pathétique, and his enhanced reputation after the Steibelt contest.

But he could not do it. The quartets were not right. Looking again at the scores, he could see what Amenda meant. He had – and it struck him in an instant – written orchestral pieces for four string instruments. Small symphonies, in fact. That was the problem. Amenda, though he had put it crudely, was right. These were full-scale orchestral works, reduced for a quartet. That was not what a string quartet should be.

Four voices. Just four voices talking to each other. Listening, agreeing, interrupting. Persuading, assuaging, cajoling, pleading. A pure sound. But above all, simplicity. Remember Mozart's words, Ludwig reminded himself. Simple themes. It is not the theme that counts, but what the composer does with it.

Knowing he had the answer, he rewrote the quartets. It was not just a revision, it was a reworking. And the optimism and comparative ease with which he did it was proof to him that it was right. Before, he had struggled with the new combination of instruments. Now, he was their master, for the moment at least. He was satisfied with his first quartets.

He knew, though, that there were many more worlds to explore with these four instruments; the purest combination of instruments it was possible to have, producing the simplest yet at the same time most complex conversation. He would return to the string quartet again; it was only a matter of time.

But the experience of the first version of the quartets pushed him towards composing a symphony. A full orchestra. The prospect excited him – and intimidated him. Here he was, an established composer, yet he had so seldom composed for full orchestra. The cantatas – the ill-fated cantatas he had written when Emperor Joseph had died and been succeeded by Leopold. That was ten years or more ago, in Bonn. It seemed that a lifetime had passed since then. His two piano concertos – even those were five years ago now. As if to emphasise the fact, with the exception of those piano concertos, he had given his first twenty opus numbers to chamber works.

There had been songs; sonatas for piano, violin, cello, even horn; trios, quartets, a quintet, a septet. And there had been a failed attempt to write a symphony about five years ago.

The notes, the many scribbled notes for the symphony, he had put to one side. Now, with relish, he returned to them.

There was his original idea for the opening. A rising scale of quavers. Four different ways he had jotted it down. Rising quavers followed by descending crotchets and minims. He remembered now. Why would it not take flight? Why did that rising scale seem rooted to the ground?

On a beautiful spring morning, with the birds singing their joy that the winter was over, he walked across the square to the town hall. In the small room at the back he sat and played the piano. He set the notebooks – the one with the original sketches, and a new one – on the table next to the piano. He began by playing one of Bach's fugues from the Well-Tempered Klavier. Then he moved on to his own sonatas. The small, intimate pair he had published as his Opus Fourteen, which had served as a prelude to the mighty Pathétique Sonata.

As he played, he looked at the notebook open on the table. The rising scale that had given him so much trouble. He could abandon it, start again. But no, he knew it was right. It was the way he wanted to begin his first symphony. He brought the Scherzo of the second sonata to a close, with its repeat of the delicate opening motif of rising quavers and semiquavers, this time descending in the treble, ending with two semiquavers and a quaver in the deep bass.

It was a quiet, gentle ending. He sat and thought for a moment. He played again the opening of the Scherzo, the final of the sonata's three movements. A simple rising scale in the treble, just four bars. Then a repeat an octave higher. He remembered his satisfaction when he composed it. 'Beethoven writes violent music', someone had said in Vienna. 'Angry, tempestuous.' Let them listen to this, he had thought. No tempestuous ending here. This is the other Beethoven.

That rising scale, which gave him so many possibilities, which opened up such opportunities; the perfect ending to the piece. The perfect ending . . . He smiled quietly to himself. He looked again at the notebook with his earlier sketches. Straight scales, all of them. Regular. On the beat.

He played the opening three notes of the sonata Scherzo. B, middle C, D. Two semiquavers and a quaver. He played them again, this time as a dotted semiquaver, demisemiquaver and quaver. Rhythm. Again he played them, only instead of moving up the scale, as the piano sonata did, he played them on the same note, G. He intensified the rhythm. Three notes, dotted semiquaver, demisemiquaver, quaver. Four notes:

demisemiquaver, dotted semiquaver, demisemiquaver, quaver. Five notes: two demisemiquavers, two semiquavers, quaver. Then six: five semiquavers and a quaver.

He played the sequence again. It was like a springboard. At the end of it, he played a simple scale, a full scale. The scale of the notebooks. Only this time it took flight. Staccato semiquavers in a rising scale, leading into a jaunty theme of crotchets, quavers and semiquavers.

He scribbled more sketches, underlining them. He did not need to write out in full what he had just played. He would have no problem remembering it. It was already lodged securely in his mind. He jumped up from the piano and went outside. On a seat in the small garden behind the town hall, two elderly men sat. Ludwig saw that they were smiling at him. He hoped they would not talk.

'We hope you do not mind. We were listening. You play beautifully, Herr Beethoven.'

To his relief their voices carried easily on the still, warm air.

'Thank you. I did not know you knew . . .'

'We know of you, sir,' said the other man. 'Your name has travelled south from Vienna. Your music is known to us. Well, some of it. Our local pianists have struggled long and hard . . .'

The first man, who saw the troubled look on Ludwig's face, said, 'Please do not be concerned, Herr Beethoven. You will not be disturbed here. We will respect your desire to be left alone. Herr Winkler and I – I am Herr Seliger – we sit on the governing council of Mödling. We have made it known that you are not to be disturbed . . .'

'In fact, sir, may I say that we are proud you have chosen our humble village for your sojourn. You must let us know if there is any further way we can be of help to you.'

Ludwig nodded at both men. 'Thank you. I . . . I am grateful. I appreciate . . .'

He turned quickly and walked away. He would have preferred the men not to have spoken to him. He thought he had anonymity. He knew now he did not. So be it. He had had no cause for complaint so far; there was no reason why it should not stay that way.

Instead of taking his usual walk past the church and up through the woods, he walked down from the town hall towards the fields. They were vineyards, and there were workers in them, planting out the young vines and tending to the mature ones, making sure the supports were in place for the heavy bunches of grapes that were to come.

Ludwig followed a small cart track, humming his theme to himself and waving his arms to accent it.

He did not hear the soft female voice at first.

'Hello,' it said insistently.

He stopped and turned, again resenting the interruption as he had done when he left the town hall. What he saw caused his stomach to turn over, and he immediately felt his pulse quicken. A full-hipped peasant girl stood, one hand on a wooden stake, the other provocatively on her hip. Her hair tumbled in ringlets on to naked shoulders. Her full breasts rose and fell in time with her breathing. Ludwig saw immediately that her bodice was low, so that her breasts bulged over the top. A thin film of sweat glistened on them; some sprigs of vine were sticking to them.

As if suddenly noticing the impediment, she looked down, clucked, and lifted the sprigs clear with her fingers. She had allowed them to rest on the top of her breasts fractionally longer than was necessary. She looked up and smiled at Ludwig.

He felt the blood rush through him. He decided not to try to speak. He nodded and smiled.

She beckoned him to come nearer. He was grateful. It meant he would be able to hear her.

'Are you the famous musician? My name is Rosamunde. Yours is Ludwig, isn't it? I cannot pronounce the rest.'

Ludwig nodded and smiled. 'Hello, Rosamunde. That is a pretty name.'

The girl threw her head back, shaking her long hair and running her hand through it.

'So warm, and it's not yet summer. I'll soon have to wear less clothing.'

She pulled the front of her bodice forward and blew cool breath down on to her breasts.

Ludwig felt the blood rush through his body again. He wanted to seize her where she stood and feel her body against his. He wanted to press her large, soft breasts against his chest. He knew exactly how they would feel, soft, malleable, and the skin and nipples would be dark.

She smiled at him. Was she sending him a message, he wondered? What was she trying to say? Could it be, could it possibly be, that she wanted him too? No, it was impossible, he thought. It is only because she knows who I am that she is behaving like this.

There was a sudden flurry of leaves close to the girl. Her head darted round and a look of irritation crossed her face. An older woman, her greying hair piled on her head, her forearms scratched and bruised, hurried up to her.

'What are you doing standing there, girl? Get back to work.' She saw Ludwig. 'Who are you? Be on your way. The girl has work to do.' She took Rosamunde's arm and tried to pull her away, but the girl shook her free. The woman bustled back into the foliage.

As she turned to follow the woman, Rosamunde said to Ludwig, 'I am here every day at this time.' She smiled invitingly and walked away.

Ludwig stood where he was for a few moments, feeling the heat in his body slowly subside. Then he turned and walked on down the track.

The sun was warm now. Ludwig took off his jacket and slung it over his shoulder. To his right the vineyards stretched up gentle slopes. Figures were bent over, tending the vines. He looked to the left and saw that the ground sloped down to a stream. A small track led to the water and he followed it.

He walked along the bank, watching the flowing water, listening to the birds' song. He found a grassy rise and sat on it, laying his jacket beside him. He took out the notebook and looked at the sketches he had underlined.

He began to sing the sequence, the rising rhythmic sequence. Laa–la–laaa, la–laa–la–laaa, la–la–laa–laa–laaa, la–la–la–la–la–laaa. He scribbled a fifth sequence, six demisemiquavers and a sustained quaver. The springboard was complete. Then came the rising scale that he had first sketched several years before and abandoned. Now it fitted perfectly. He wrote *adagio*, then *allegro vivace*. The rising sequence, the springboard, would be played slowly, then the scale, the theme which would run through the movement, would be played *allegro*. *Allegro molto e vivace*.

He listened again to the birds, singing so beautifully. No effort. Perfect. They were incapable of a wrong note. Nature's musicians! He lay back and rested his head on the grass, feeling the sun warm on his face. Not hot yet, not oppressive as it would be in summer; just perfectly warming, and already enough to release the rich smell of the grass.

Unbidden, the image of the girl came into his mind. He could see her standing there, provocative, hand on hip, laughing face, swelling breasts. He saw her again pull the bodice forward and blow on to her breasts. But in his mind, instead of putting the bodice back, she looked up at him, smiled and pulled down the bodice, allowing her breasts to fall free. They were bigger and fuller than he had imagined, and he could feel their soft flesh against his face.

He smiled to himself and thought of Zmeskall. He wanted to tell Zmeskall about the girl. He wanted to ask his advice. Should he storm this fortress? Was the girl inviting him to do so?

A look of frustration suddenly came to his face. Why did women so often send out signals, obvious signals, but with messages that they did not mean? This girl appeared to be sending him a clear message, but he knew instinctively she was not. He did not know how he knew it, but he did. If he took those few steps towards her and seized her in his arms, he knew she would push him away. He just knew it.

He thought of Magdalena Willmann, the woman he had decided to propose marriage to. Had she not given him all the signals? From the first time they had met, on the boat to Mergentheim. Then it transpired that she and Romberg were to get engaged. After that proved unsuccessful, did she not send him the signals again? And when finally he made the decision to propose to her, she had not even let him say the words.

Music. Music. Music. Just music, he thought. Nothing must come between me and my music. How could I give myself to my music *and* a wife. Or a woman, even. No. Rosamunde was a joy to behold, a creature of beauty. As an artist I will appreciate her beauty. That is all.

He sat up quickly. My symphony. I have the opening movement, do I not? He heard a bird sing, not a tuneful song this time, but a screech of warning. The bird had seen his sudden movement. He snatched up his notebook. The movement must begin positively.

He scribbled a chord of G. He crossed it out and wrote a single G. Positive. Definite. And because the symphony will be in C, he thought, to use the dominant will create an air of expectancy. He wrote a single C. The final note. The home key. He wrote *ff* under both notes.

Yes. The beginning and ending of the first movement. Why,

then, the frown? Was there something wrong? He looked up angrily and the sun momentarily blinded him.

He thrust the notebook and pencil back into his pocket and stood. Picked up his jacket and retraced his steps. He walked up the small track and turned on to the larger track that led back to the village. He looked up as he passed the spot where he had seen Rosamunde, but there was no sign of her.

Something was worrying him and he could not put his finger on it. It was to do with the movement for his symphony, the opening movement which he was so pleased with. He was still happy with it. Then why was it causing him concern? Was it perhaps that there was something too definite about it, too final? That it was answering questions instead of posing them? He put the thought to the back of his mind.

In the Hofburg palace, Stephan von Breuning sat in the ornate antechamber, waiting to be summoned into the office of the Chief Secretary to the Emperor. He smiled wryly at the thought that he was about to enter a room he would never normally have entered, and it was thanks to his childhood friend, Ludwig van Beethoven!

He remembered the untidily dressed, often impolite boy his mother had welcomed into their house At first he had wondered why she had done it. He and his sister Eleonore joked about Ludwig, sometimes playing games together in which one would take the part of Ludwig, refusing to answer a question, or snapping back a querulous reply.

Now look at him, thought Stephan. He moves in the very highest circles. He met the King of Prussia in Berlin and composed cello sonatas for him. The aristocrats of Vienna compete to sponsor him and be his patron. I do not know if he has met the Emperor, the highest in the land, Stephan mused, but if he hasn't, that might be about to be rectified.

Stephan knew why Baron Margelick had summoned him. Prince Lichnowsky had already warned him. Margelick had spoken first to the Prince, to see whether he thought the idea was appropriate and to secure his assistance in making the necessary arrangements. Prince Lichnowsky had considered it prudent to speak to Stephan, so Ludwig's friend could think it over. Stephan spoke to Schuppanzigh. All agreed the idea was splendid.

Stephan followed the bewigged courtier into the sumptuous

chamber of the Chief Secretary. What a contrast to the Electoral palace at Bonn! thought Stephan. Yet as a young man he had considered that to be ornate, in fact the grandest place he had ever seen. It paled by comparison with the Hofburg, seat of the empire, focal point of a thousand-year dynasty.

Stephan waited for Baron Margelick to look up from the document he was reading. When he did so, Stephan bowed his head. 'Baron. Sir.'

'Sit down, Breuning,' Margelick said with a wave of the hand. There was a touch of impatience in his voice, as if he knew that under normal circumstances this lowly secretary from the war office would not be sitting across the desk from him.

Stephan caught the tone and was not surprised by it. The truth was he too felt uncomfortable finding himself face to face with the Chief Secretary. He waited while Margelick added a few words to the document – probably more for effect than any useful purpose, Stephan thought uncharitably – and then tensed slightly as Margelick laid down his quill and leaned back in his chair.

'Well, Breuning, your young friend from the Rhineland is making quite a stir here in the capital. They're still talking of what he did to Steibelt.'

Stephan smiled and nodded. He thought it prudent not to speak, and was pleased with his decision when Margelick immediately continued.

'I believe he has said he will never come to our fair city again. At least, not as long as your friend remains here. It will be our loss, since he is a fine musician. Mind you, after such a humiliation, mmmh . . . ?'

'Yes, sir. We were all very proud of Ludwig. All his friends, that is. We had no doubt of the outcome. Although sometimes . . . It depends very much on his mood.'

'Quite. So I hear. Which is why I spoke to Lichnowsky, and I know he has spoken to you. Tell me what he told you.'

'Only, sir, that you considered that in light of what happened at the Steibelt contest, you were in favour of granting Ludwig his first benefit concert. To mark his victory, so to speak.'

'And? What is your view?'

'An excellent idea, sir. Excellent. I spoke with Schuppanzigh about it. The violinist. And he agreed. You see, sir, I know that Ludwig seeks recognition as a composer as much as a pianist.

More, in fact. I know he would welcome the opportunity to perform his own works.'

'As well as a piece by Haydn and Mozart, of course. It will be expected.' He paused. 'He doesn't know yet, does he? He's away, isn't he?'

'Yes. He's in Mödling. I believe he's working on a symphony. It will be his first. One of the few musical forms he has not yet explored, he told Schupp—'

'Yes, yes,' said Margelick, the touch of impatience still in his voice. 'Well, the original idea has changed somewhat. So that you are in command of the facts, let me tell you what has happened.'

A slightly worried look crept over Stephan's face. He hoped Margelick was not about to tell him that the idea had been judged impractical, that the offer was to be withdrawn.

'The original idea came from Prince Lobkowitz. Hardly surprising, really, given that it was his man Steibelt whom your friend humiliated. Lobkowitz believes that your friend – rough edges though he may have – is destined for greatness. I'm not sure I entirely agree. Music is more than just nice sounds. A musician needs a certain . . . a certain *savoir-faire*. Like Herr Haydn, for instance. However, putting that to one side for the moment. The Prince offered to put on a benefit concert in his salon, the same room where your friend and Steibelt met. He asked me if the imperial exchequer would make a contribution to cover costs, since a benefit concert would leave him without income. We discussed it. I pointed out that the Prince's own orchestra is small. The room even is not large. Given your friend's growing reputation, I would imagine the concert would attract many people. Especially if he performs a piano concerto. He is quite interesting – amusing, some say – to watch.'

'I'm sure it would prove very popular, sir.'

'I suggested the Kärntnertor theatre. The Prince pointed out that it had a production running and would not allow the necessary interruption. Rehearsals, performance, and so on.'

'Sir, I am sure the Prince's palace would be quite—'

'I then happened to mention the idea to no less a personage than Her Imperial Majesty the Empress Maria Theresa, who, as you will surely know, is a great lover of music. Greater than her husband, His Imperial Majesty the Emperor. Greater than many of her subjects.'

Stephan's eyes opened wide and his eyebrows rose.

'Her Imperial Majesty was extremely interested. She has heard of your friend. She immediately offered the Redoutensaale here in the palace. I pointed out to her that only the smaller of the two was available. She immediately said, "Why not the Burgtheater?" It was a stroke of genius on the part of Her Majesty. The current production ends in a few weeks' time. It is the largest hall in Vienna.'

Stephan nodded vigorously. 'He knows the hall. Ludwig. Beethoven, I mean. He performed there some years ago, I believe. Before I came to Vienna. He loved the hall, because of its associations with Mozart.'

'Indeed. Her Majesty mentioned that too. With Her Majesty's authority I spoke to Herr Hartl, who manages the imperial theatres. We have set a date just one month hence.'

'One month. I must alert Ludwig immediately.'

'Indeed you must. And, Breuning. You had better tell him everything is arranged. He is no position to refuse. Her Majesty has said she will grace the concert with her presence.'

Chapter 2

Ludwig wanted to tell Rosamunde about the concert: It meant he would have to go back to Vienna as soon as possible. He had come to look forward to his morning walk down to the stream. He found that when he awoke, it was already with anticipation to see her. Rosamunde – as she had said she would be – was always there. Ludwig stopped and watched her for a few minutes. She did not stop working. He did not talk to her.

As she worked she frequently turned and smiled at him. She made no attempt to hide her body from him. If her breasts needed wiping, she drew her hand sensuously across the top of them. As the weather became warmer she lifted her skirt high on her legs and tucked it in.

Then there was almost an invisible signal between them. She would smile at him and turn away. He would walk on. When he turned back a few paces later she would be gone.

The work on the First Symphony was progressing, but Ludwig was not satisfied. He had written two more movements. The second was a slow movement, an Andante Cantabile. He was pleased with the main theme, a graceful and lyrical melody which he had given to the second violins alone to open the movement. That would annoy the players, he knew. Second violinists were not supposed to be so exposed, but he needed to hold the first violins back.

The opening was a small fugue. Second violins first; then violas and cellos; then double basses and bassoons. All gave only half the theme. Only the fifth entry, that of the first violins, flute and oboe in the home key, gave the whole theme. Ludwig knew the audience would think they were hearing a fugue. But he did not want a fugue. He wanted the movement to be graceful and delicate. And simple.

He had thought of Mozart when he wrote it. This was a

simple theme, rising regular quavers followed by descending rhythmic semiquavers. He would state it; allow the second subject to grow from it, then return to it and develop it.

Ludwig wanted the movement to be tribute to the man who had so nearly become his teacher. It was the sort of movement he would have written for Mozart's approval. It obeyed the rules. The home key was established throughout. When the music moved away from it, it quickly returned. Only in his dynamic markings – from *pianissimo* to *fortissimo* and *sforzando-forte-piano* – did he give it touches of his own. He was aware as he wrote it that he was looking back, to Mozart, Haydn, even Bach. He was certain he would not do so again.

The very next movement, the third, was proof of that. A swift Allegro, opening with a rising scale of staccato crotchets and minims covering one and a half octaves, then descending with slurred crotchets. Ludwig then moved the music through a number of keys alien to the home key. He peppered the score with accidentals. More cause for annoyance from the players!

Ludwig knew that what he was really writing was a Scherzo. But a scherzo in a symphony was unheard of. He even wrote a trio section in the middle – steady chords in the wind, chromatic runs in the strings – which he used to send all the instruments cascading towards a *fortissimo* and *sforzando* end.

No more looking back. This was looking forward, and Ludwig knew it. Why then, he thought to himself, cursing as he did so, did he take his pencil and write 'Menuetto' at the top of the movement? It was not a minuet. But a minuet was what audiences were used to hearing in the third movement of a symphony. Prepare them by stages, he thought. A minuet that is really a scherzo this time. A scherzo that is called a scherzo next time.

Three movements complete. The fourth and final one still to be written, and he would have his First Symphony. But why that doubt that had nagged at him since he had written the first movement? What was it about the first movement that worried him – that movement which answered so many questions?

He would perform his First Symphony at the concert in the Burgtheater. His first benefit concert! He clutched the letter from Stephan in his hand and left his room to take the familiar walk down to the stream. He felt the sun bathe him in warmth as he crossed the square.

'Sir. Herr Beethoven. If you will forgive me, sir.'

Ludwig, deep in thought, did not hear the voice, but he felt the slight tug at his sleeve. It was one of the two men who had spoken to him two or three weeks previously when he had left the town hall after playing the piano.

'Herr Beethoven. Would you step into the hall with me? Just for a moment. Seliger, sir. Herr Seliger. Town councillor. We spoke before.'

Ludwig frowned, irritated at the interruption, but he followed Seliger the few steps into the entrance of the town hall.

'Sir. I will not detain you. Forgive my impertinence. The girl you see in the vineyard. You stop and . . . I believe you . . . Well, sir, she is not of good character. She has a . . . a reputation. Her family is not respected. If I may humbly suggest, sir . . .'

'What are you saying, Seliger? Is that your name?'

'Indeed, sir. Only that your reputation is of the most excellent . . . I would not want . . . My colleagues felt I . . .'

'Thank you for your concern, Seliger,' said Ludwig gruffly. 'I assure you I can look after myself. Good day.'

Ludwig walked quickly through the square and on to the track which led out to the vineyards. What on earth was Seliger talking about? More importantly, what was he implying? Was it any of his business, or anybody's business, if he chose to watch a girl working in the field? And if he admired her beauty, was that somehow wrong?

He thrust the interruption to the back of his mind and unfolded the letter from Stephan. He read it as he walked. He had no need to. He knew it by heart.

Ludwig, my friend

You should return to Vienna soon. You are to hold a concert for your benefit in the Burgtheater. You may choose the works to be performed, which will of course include your own, as well as works by Herr Mozart and Haydn. It is the intention of the Empress to attend.

There are arrangements to be made. Your presence is required here.

Your friend Stephan B.

'A concert for your benefit . . . the Empress to attend . . . You may choose the works to be performed'! He would tell Rosamunde. He wanted to see the smile his words would bring.

He knew it would be a broad smile. That she would speak to him. That she would say . . . That she might say . . . He would walk towards her . . .

He realised now how much he wanted her, how he desired her body. He followed the track. He found – and he could not suppress a slight smile – that Seliger's words had excited him. If Rosamunde really was such a girl, really did have such a reputation . . .

She was not there. *She was not there!* He stood rooted to the spot, the same spot where he always stood. He was suddenly aware of a pain in his head. It began to throb, and with it came that dreadful whooshing in his ears. He had not experienced it for some time now. The peace and calm of Mödling had quietened his ears and he had begun to hope that maybe . . . maybe . . .

He put his hand to his ear and lowered his head. The whooshing became more like a rustle. He had not heard such a sound before. He looked up. More rustling and then she was there. In front of him. Rosamunde. Her back was turned to him, but he saw that her shoulders were heaving. She was crying. He knew it immediately.

Should he reach forward? Should he turn her round? Should he comfort her? But before he could decide she turned. Her face was streaked with tears. Her eyes were red and puffy.

'Ludwig. Ludwig. You must help us.'

'What? What do you mean?' He leaned his head towards her.

'My father. He was in a fight last night. At the tavern near here. He has been arrested and put in prison. It wasn't his fault. I know it wasn't. You must help us.'

'In prison? But they can't do that without . . . Will he go before the magistrates?'

She shrugged her shoulders. 'I don't know what is going to happen. But with him locked up, we will lose our livelihood. We won't be able to eat. They are saying we will have to leave.'

'Leave?'

She nodded and sniffed, drawing the back of her hand across her upper lip. 'Leave this town. If we go, it will be the end for us. I don't know how . . . how . . . And it wasn't his fault. I know it. It wasn't.'

'What happened?'

'I don't know. My mother said he was trying to break up a fight. There were two men. Drunk. And my father stepped in. But he was the one they arrested. It's not fair.'

Ludwig thought quickly. He would help. He had to. There was no choice. Anyway, he wanted to. He thought of Seliger's rather smug face, the warning he had uttered. Now it is my turn, he thought.

He put his arm out but Rosamunde moved a step away.

'Is there anything you could do? I know you're a kind man. I . . . I . . . would be so grateful. If you could do something . . .'

'I will speak to . . . to . . . I know one of the councillors. I will speak to him.'

Rosamunde darted forward and placed a kiss swiftly on his cheek. Then she turned and hurried away, her billowing skirt rustling against the vines.

Ludwig walked swiftly back into the town and into the main entrance of the town hall.

'Sir?' said a voice. It belonged to the caretaker.

'Where is Seliger? And the other man. I forget . . . Winkler. Town councillors.'

'Sir, they will not be here until two o'clock. That is when the council meets. Two o'clock, sir.'

Ludwig hurried across the square and climbed the stairs to his lodgings. He threw his jacket angrily on the chair and went to the window.

Rosamunde, he thought. Injustice. And in his mind revolved the opening theme of the first movement of his symphony. That introduction; that rising scale, the rapid theme it led into. What was it . . . ? What was it . . . ? I must fight for Rosamunde, he thought. He paced the floor. His mind was racing. Laa–laa–laaa–laa, laa–laa–laa la–la–la–la laaa–la.

To the end. Racing to the end. Providing the answers! That movement provided the answers! So obvious, so simple. The movement he had written first should in fact be the final movement. Realising that, everything dropped into place. I have the final movement of my First Symphony, he thought. And it is right. Now it is right. All the doubts that had been revolving in his mind evaporated. He had the second, third and fourth movements. It remained only to write the first. Pose the questions.

He hurried to his pile of manuscripts and pulled out the sheets of the first movement. Ahead of that opening phrase, the first *pianissimo* rising sequence – dotted semiquaver, demisemiquaver, quaver – he wrote the firm chord of G. In octaves. Just G. And he marked it *fortissimo*. He put a huge vertical bracket around it. Every instrument in the orchestra was to play it. From flutes, oboes, clarinets, bassoons, horns, trumpets, to violins, violas, cellos and double basses. Accompanied by the timpani. Just G. A solid opening call. A call to attention. The symphony is entering its last climactic stage.

A smile crossed his face. Hah, yes! Let them wonder what is coming. Let their faces show their shock. And now the first movement. I will give them a first movement that they will talk about, wonder about, argue about, marvel at. The opening to Beethoven's First Symphony. A sign of what is to come.

He pulled a clean sheet of manuscript paper towards him and wrote at the top:

SYMPHONY NO. 1 IN C MAJOR

With a smile which an onlooker would have had no difficulty in describing as mischievous, he wrote a chord which was the dominant seventh of the key of F. Sustained *fortepiano* for the wind, pizzicato for the strings.

His lips stretched into a grin as he resolved the chord into the key of F. The key of F in the first bar of a Symphony in C! He did not expect the audience to realise he had used the 'wrong' key, but he knew that the effect of the dominant seventh would unsettle them.

His mouth stretched into a grin as he wrote another dominant seventh, again sustained in the wind, pizzicato for the strings, but this time resolving into the home key of C.

And if that placated them slightly, let them prepare for another surprise. He wrote yet another dominant seventh, this time resolving into the key of G!

Three dominant sevenths – the most disturbing and 'pregnant' chord in all music, Haydn had once told him – in the first three bars. The musicians would complain, of course. Players always did. The audience would shuffle in their seats. Mozart had never done this, they would say. They would be right. Not a single one of Mozart's symphonies began with any doubt as to the home key. You could not open a Symphony with doubt as to its tonality. It was a fatal mistake from which the piece in its entirety would never recover. Haydn had told him that so long ago.

Beethoven could! he thought. Beethoven could and would write as no musician had ever written before. And if the players and audience were shocked, so be it.

He sketched in another nine bars of introduction, more key changes, another dominant seventh, and finally the establishment of the home key of C.

He wrote the main theme, a jaunty rhythmic theme of dotted quavers and staccato crotchets. He composed swiftly. Since taking the decision to make the original first movement the fourth and final movement, everything had dropped into place. He allowed the movement to skip along, almost under its own momentum. He did not need to hear what he was composing on the piano, he could hear it in his head. And he knew it was right.

A third of the way through the movement he slowed the music down, giving the oboe a lovingly gentle phrase to sing out above the other instruments. But then he picked up the momentum again and wrote furiously on.

He stopped suddenly, in the middle of a bar. He saw Rosamunde's face, the tears on her cheeks. Justice. He would fight on her behalf, on her father's behalf. He remembered Seliger's words. What did he have against Rosamunde and her family? Why had he spoken about them in such a way? Yes, he would fight for her, to see justice done. He hummed the theme of the movement to himself, punching his clenched fist into his other hand. He paced the room, his mind full of music.

He returned to the desk and wrote on. Sustained chords in the wind, semiquaver runs in the strings. His First Symphony. Almost complete. Just the recapitulation and coda. And the final, positive, unequivocal statement of the home key, *fortissimo* chords in all instruments in the key of C.

He looked out of the window. One o'clock. An hour to go. He pulled on his jacket and went down to the tavern next door. He sat at his usual table in the corner and was grateful that no one tried to start a conversation with him. He ordered roast lamb and potatoes and a carafe of red wine.

He drank the wine thirstily. When the food came he only picked at it. His furious work on the symphony had left him tired, very tired; almost too tired to eat. But his thirst raged. He finished the carafe and ordered another, as well as a larger carafe of water. He drank the water in a single draught. He took a few more mouthfuls of the food and pushed away his plate. He drank some more wine, slower this time, savouring the effect it was already having on his head.

He felt the familiar sensation the wine induced, relaxing him. He closed his eyes and he saw the notes of his symphony. He was satisfied. He had come to Mödling to write his First Symphony and it was completed. It was almost ready to go to the copyist. He would conduct its first performance at the benefit performance at the Burgtheater. What else should he perform? He would need to think about that. Get back to Vienna first, then make the decisions.

He soon finished the second carafe of wine. Then he stepped outside to look at the clock. His legs felt slightly unsteady. It was the work he had done, the concentration. He knew that. He returned to his seat and ordered a single glass of red wine. A large glass.

When finally he knew it was time to go, he left money on the table and stood. A wave of pain shot through his head. It throbbed, and the whooshing sound came back into his ears. He leaned against the doorpost. The whooshing was accompanied now by that dreadful high-pitched whistle, which he had not suffered since he had left Vienna. Why? Why? Why could the doctors not stop it? All their potions, their ridiculous remedies, yet he was suffering more than ever.

True, his stomach pains seemed to have subsided. But his hearing, that was what mattered to him most. He was a musician, damn it! Why could they not cure it?

He strode out of the tavern and crossed the square as steadily as he could. The bright sun blinded him momentarily. His head hurt. The throbbing. The whistling. He entered the town hall, waving the concierge's restraining arm away.

He walked towards the big double doors and threw them open. A dozen shocked faces turned to him.

Look at them, he thought to himself. Idiots, all of them. What are they? Just petty officials bloated with their own self-importance.

He walked to the heavy oak table in the middle of the room around which the town councillors sat. He saw that Seliger was at the head of the table, in an ornate chair with a crest on the top crossrail.

'You. Seliger. Are you in charge here?'

'Herr Beethoven, if I may say so, this is most improper. I must ask you—'

'Seliger, what do you have against that girl and her family? You know who I mean. Why are you doing this to them?'

'Herr Beethoven, if you are not going to leave the chamber, would you please be seated. It is not right that you should stand there in a threatening manner.'

Ludwig strained to hear him. Why were his words not cutting through the noise in his head? His head was aching now, aching badly. The damned wine. Rough peasant wine. Worse than the wine in the Schwan. His head was spinning. And the noises. The whistling. The whooshing.

'Seliger,' he said hoarsely, 'you must let her father go. Release him. I know what happened. I can tell you.'

Seliger stood, his demeanour suddenly angry. He said in a loud, determined voice, 'Herr Beethoven. Be seated. This moment. Or I shall summon an usher to escort you from the chamber.'

The chair at the end of the rectangular table opposite Seliger was empty. Ludwig's movement was closer to collapsing into it than sitting in it.

'Herr Beethoven,' Seliger continued, 'it is highly improper of you to come into the chamber like this, while a meeting of the town council is in session. It is only because of your rank and status in society, and undoubted fame as a musician of the first rank, that I will recommend to my fellow councillors that you say what you have to say. We will consider your words and then you will have to leave.'

He looked to his colleagues for their assent, and there was a general nodding of heads.

Ludwig looked around the table. To Seliger's right he recognised Winkler, whose face was set in an angry scowl. He looked at the other councillors. All were palpably angry at the interruption. Every face was turned towards Ludwig, waiting for him to speak.

Ludwig's breathing had steadied now. His head still swam from the wine, but he had heard what Seliger said. He wished he had not come into the chamber, but it was too late. He had to speak. So they knew of his fame as a musician. He would tell them something they did not know.

'I have completed my First Symphony. Here, in Mödling. I am to perform it before the Empress . . .'

Seliger spoke, an edge to his voice. 'Herr Beethoven, on another occasion we would be very pleased to hear of your musical progress. For the moment, would you please confine your words to the case you have raised, and we will then consider them.'

Ludwig looked round at the men again. How could they be so petty? Did music count for nothing? Did they not understand what it meant, to hear that he had completed . . . ?

'I shall assume, Herr Beethoven, that you have nothing to say. I will summon an usher . . .'

Ludwig could not bear the complacency any longer. He knew he should restrain himself, but he was not capable of it. He brought his right fist down on the table.

'Do you realise you will ruin that family? If you send them away, they will be ruined. The father is innocent, do you hear? Innocent.'

'Innocent, Herr Beethoven?' It was Winkler speaking. 'You say he is innocent? Please explain.'

'There was a fight in the tavern. He tried to stop it. To separate the two . . . the men who were fighting, and . . .'

Winkler spoke clearly. Ludwig wondered for a brief moment if he knew about his hearing problem. But how could he?

'You were there, were you, Herr Beethoven? You witnessed this fight?'

'No. I . . . I was not there. I have been told . . .'

'By whom, sir? Who told you of the fight?'

'The girl. His daughter. I see her in the field. The vineyard. When I go . . . When I go . . .'

'We know that, Herr Beethoven. We are aware of that.' It was Seliger who was speaking now. He leaned forward, clasping his hands in front of him, and spoke distinctly.

'Now, Herr Beethoven, I must ask you to listen to me carefully. I wish to explain certain things to you, that I think will help you to . . . to . . . understand the position a little more clearly. Will you listen fully?'

Ludwig frowned. Why was the man talking to him like this? Did he know? Was that it? It was impossible. He couldn't know. No one knew, apart from Stephan and Nanette. And the doctors, but they . . .

'The family in question, Herr Beethoven, the Zoltanys, are from Hungary. A Romany family. Gypsies. Why they chose to come here, we do not know. The father rents a field in which he has planted vines. It was a bad choice of crop. The soil is not right. He was warned but ignored the advice. He soon fell into financial difficulties, because he had borrowed considerable amounts of money . . .'

Ludwig listened intently. He heard what Seliger was saying but he was having difficulty understanding it. It was the pain in his head, and the noises. If only they would stop.

He waved his hands at Seliger. 'Slower, Seliger. My head. I . . .'

Seliger nodded and spoke even more distinctly and at a slower pace.

'As I was saying, he fell into financial difficulties. In order to alleviate these problems, he . . . How shall I say this delicately? . . . He put his daughter to work. Do you understand what I am trying to say? His daughter offered her . . . her favours in return for payment . . . And she set about her task with relish, approaching some of our most respected . . . I can tell you, several of us around this table have been insulted by . . .'

'A common whore!' said a voice from one side of the table.

'A blot on our town,' said another, to Ludwig's left. 'An insult to our wives.'

Ludwig could scarcely believe what he was hearing. He knew he had heard correctly. It could not be. It simply could not be.

'The girl? Rosamunde? A . . . a . . . Are you saying . . . ?'

'Indeed I am, Herr Beethoven. And more than that. The reason for the fight which you seem to think the father was nobly trying to stop was rather different. A man to whom the wretch owes money, a man known to us all here, a gentleman of impeccable standing in our community . . . This ignoble wretch accused him in front of his friends of availing himself of the services of his daughter and refusing to . . . to . . . to pay.'

'It is not the sort of behaviour we wish to see in our town, Herr Beethoven,' said Winkler, 'and that is why the family is being told to leave. Ordered to leave. The fight was a wilful breach of the peace. The girl's behaviour is immoral. It is enough. They have been ordered to go and they will go.'

Ludwig wanted to speak. He tried to speak, but the words would not come. Was it true? Could it be true? Was Rosamunde a whore? Was the father trying to extort money? It had to be true. These men would not invent it. He thought for a moment. He pictured Rosamunde in his mind: her sensuous body, the way she almost displayed it for him, wiping the perspiration from the tops of her breasts, showing her legs as she lifted her skirt . . .

'I . . . I . . . I have to return to Vienna soon. There is to be a concert. I am to give a concert. The Empress is to attend.'

'Herr Beethoven,' said Seliger in a more conciliatory voice. 'We are all aware of how hard you have been working. Also, to put it frankly, and I hope you will not consider that I am speaking out of turn, but we are all men in this room, and we all understand how someone of Rosa— that girl's – appearance can . . . beguile a man . . . a temptress, nothing more. I did try to warn you, sir, but you were not . . .'

'No. I . . . I . . . I will be leaving soon.'

Winkler spoke, his face having now lost the anger it carried earlier. 'And, Herr Beethoven, as I myself once said to you, we are proud that you chose our humble town for your stay.'

'And indeed, sir, it is our hope that you will come and stay here again,' said another voice. 'You will be most welcome.'

Ludwig stood. The movement increased the throbbing in his head, and the dizziness that accompanied it made him sway.

'Gentlemen.' He inclined his head. 'I will leave in the morning. I must return to Vienna. I have important work to do.'

Chapter 3

Ludwig looked across the desk at Baron Peter von Braun, his face etched in despair.

'Braun, do you realise what you are saying? Do you realise what this means?'

'I am sorry, Herr Beethoven. There is nothing I can do, as I have already explained. It was always planned that the orchestra of the Burgtheater, when the production finished, would disband for a month. The players have other commitments. I could not gather them together even if I wished to. Most have already left the city.'

'Braun, the Empress herself, Her Imperial Majesty, is to attend this concert. Shall I tell her there is to be no concert, because there is no orchestra?'

Braun shrugged. 'Can you change the date?'

'The advertisements have already been printed. Tickets sold.'

'There are other orchestras in the city. At the Kärntnertor theatre. Have you . . . ?'

'They have engagements already. That was why the Burgtheater was chosen. It is clear.'

'Too clear, I regret to say. If you restrict the pieces to small ensembles, you could find enough musicians to—'

'My First Symphony. It is to be given its first performance. It is important for it to be heard.'

Braun suddenly clapped his hands. 'Wait. There may be one last possibility.' He opened a drawer and took out a leather-bound book. 'Let me check the dates. Yes, here we are. The orchestra of the Italian opera is in Vienna, and as far as I know their performances finish very shortly. Then they stay here until a new programme begins. In between they could play at your concert.'

'The Italian opera? How could they play my music?'

'They are very accomplished, so I am told. Their conductor

and director is a Signor Conti. A capable musician, by all accounts.'

'No. I must have Wranitzky. Paul Wranitzky. He will conduct the Mozart and Haydn pieces. I will conduct my own.'

'An ambitious programme. I wish you luck. Would you like me to make contact with Signor Conti for you?'

'Yes. But tell him Wranitzky will conduct.'

Prince Lichnowsky and Baron van Swieten sat opposite Ludwig in the Prince's richly furnished drawing room.

'You know you can move back here any time you wish, Ludwig. My wife would be so happy to have you living here again.'

Ludwig shook his head. 'It's better for me to be in the city. Thank you.'

'Tell us about the symphony, Ludwig,' said Swieten. 'Are you pleased with it?'

'Yes. It is the best I can do. It is different. The opening will cause surprise.'

'How? What have you done?'

'You will hear it at the concert. If the concert ever takes place.'

'Is there a problem?' asked Lichnowsky, concern on his face.

'Not just one. Two, three, I have lost count.'

'What do you mean?'

'First of all we have no orchestra. But it seems that even if we had one, there would be no music for it to play.'

'I don't understand.'

'The Burgtheater orchestra is not available. They have disbanded. Left the city. Wenzel Schlemmer the copyist has my manuscript of the symphony. He says he would be hard pressed to make one good copy in time, let alone enough for all the players.'

'What about Prince Lobkowitz's orchestra?' said Swieten.

Lichnowsky shook his head. 'A lot of them are Burgtheater players.'

'The Italian opera orchestra is in Vienna. Braun is speaking to their director.'

'I will speak to Schlemmer,' said Lichnowsky. 'I will tell him to take on more copyists. Don't worry. They'll be ready.'

Swieten coughed into his hand. 'Have you . . . Have you

decided on a dedication for your symphony, Ludwig? Who will the lucky person be whose name will sit above the first movement?'

'The Elector Max Franz. The man who first sent me here to Vienna. Without him I would never have met Mozart. My First Symphony will be dedicated to him.'

'At least it all ended satisfactorily,' said Zmeskall. 'But, Ludwig, from what I hear, you took rather too much of an interest in the girl and her family.'

Ludwig leaned across the table, moving the carafe of wine out of the way. 'She was provocative, Nikola . . . when I was watching her she appeared not to notice, but all the time she knew I was standing there . . . and she flaunted her body.'

'And you allowed yourself to get involved.'

'I thought they were being unjust to her. To her father. But, Nikola, how did you . . . ? How did word . . . ? Does anybody else . . . ?'

Zmeskall leaned forward. 'Do not worry. I have sorted matters out. One of my colleagues at the Chancellery lives in Mödling. He heard, obviously. He's spoken to the councillor. What's his name? Seliger. I told him to say you were under a lot of strain. This concert. The Empress, and so on.'

'I told Seliger that myself.'

'He understands. At the next meeting he is explaining more fully to the other councillors. He apparently said your fame as a musician allows you to behave in a way others wouldn't. The matter is closed. And the girl's family has left. They've gone back to Hungary. You won't be hearing from them again. And, Ludwig.' He moved further forward. Ludwig turned his head to make sure he could hear. 'Remember. Take care, some fortresses are dangerous.'

Ludwig smiled and drank from his glass. 'Thank you, Nikola. You are a good friend. Why do we come to the Schwan? Wretched place. The wine is dreadful. Raw. It hurts my throat.'

'But it improves the head. If you drink exactly the right amount, that is. How is your head? You were complaining of pains before you went to Mödling.'

Ludwig snapped his head up. 'All right. Sometimes. I get . . . When I have a pain in my head it makes noises. I . . .'

'The wine will cure that! Ludwig, has Schuppi spoken to you?'

Ludwig shook his head. 'What about? The septet? Yes. He is to play it at the concert. He is rehearsing with the others already.'

'No, not that. About Carl. Your brother.'

'No. What's happened?'

'I'll let Schuppi tell you. Nothing serious. Just something you ought to know about.'

Schuppanzigh was still breathing heavily from the effort of climbing the stairs.

'The septet is going well, Ludwig. It is a fine piece. But difficult to play. When will you write something simple?'

'What news on the orchestra? Have you heard?'

'Good news. Braun has spoken to Conti. The Italian orchestra is engaged. Rehearsals have begun. They are starting with the Mozart and Haydn. Then the parts for your symphony will be ready. If not, you can begin with the piano concerto.'

'Good. I will go and see Wranitzky.'

'Wranitzky?'

'He is conducting. I told Braun.'

Schuppanzigh shrugged. 'Maybe. But from what I saw, it was Conti who was conducting. Very interesting, the Italian sound. Not quite right for our Viennese music, in my opinion.'

Ludwig sunk his head in his hands. 'It cannot be. Conti does not know my music. It *must* be Wranitzky.'

'Ludwig,' Schuppanzigh said, 'there is something I have to tell you. That you should know about. Did Zmeskall say anything to you?'

Ludwig looked at him. 'Only that it concerned my brother. What has happened?'

'Well, it may not be a problem. But we felt you ought to know. Carl has published some compositions.' He took a piece of newspaper from his pocket. 'They were advertised in the *Wiener Zeitung*. Here. See for yourself.'

Ludwig took the scrap of paper. 'New compositions by Beethoven,' he read. 'Eighteen entirely new compositions of the first quality, comprising six minuets, six Deutsche Tänze, six contredances. Subscriptions are invited.'

Ludwig looked up. 'New compositions by Beethoven,' he said again, and let out a long sigh. 'Have you seen them?'

Schuppanzigh nodded. 'I am afraid so. They are . . . I don't know what the right word is. Ordinary. Banal. I wouldn't say worthless, but they do not deserve your illustrious name above them.'

'What is being said? Have people noticed?'

'I am afraid so. I have heard it said . . .' he was speaking clearly but more quietly '. . . that you have exhausted your talent for composition and that you are having to fall back on this kind of work to earn money.'

Ludwig sunk his face in his hands again. He stood and walked to the window, looking down into the dark street below. 'This place is like a prison. The Tiefer Graben. That's exactly what it is. A deep ditch. I must get out.'

'Move somewhere with fewer stairs.'

'Schuppi, how much more must I take? My first benefit concert. The orchestra I want is not available. The wrong conductor is directing them. It's possible the orchestral parts of my symphony will not be ready. And now I discover my brother is usurping my name.'

'It will be all right. I am sure—'

'And all the time my head hurts. As if sometimes it is going to burst.'

'The Schwan's red wine. That's probably all it is. It'll pass.'

'I hope so, Schuppi.'

The two brothers stood confronting each other in the small living room of Carl's lodgings.

'You are a damned impudent fool, Carl. You deliberately set out to blacken my name.'

'*Your* name? *Your* name? It happens to be my name too, Ludwig. Or had you forgotten that?'

'You put Beethoven because you knew it would attract attention. Just Beethoven. No first name. That was deliberate, wasn't it?'

Carl smiled a small, crooked smile. 'Was it a lie? Was the music not by Beethoven?'

'Damn you, Carl. You, you . . . you hyena.'

'What did you say? What did you call me?'

'A hyena. That is what they call you. Didn't you know? A hyena, because you are a dishonest scavenger. You . . .'

Carl grabbed Ludwig by the shoulders. 'Don't you ever . . . Do you hear? Don't you ever . . .' He began shaking Ludwig. Ludwig brought his hands up and pushed Carl away with all his strength. Carl staggered back, hit the side of an armchair and collapsed into it.

Ludwig stood looking down at him, breathing heavily. Carl remained where he was, his face redder than his hair. Ludwig, grateful that Carl had decided not to fight back, slumped into a chair at the table. He rested his head in his hands. A feeling of sadness overwhelmed him. He felt the tears rise into his eyes and he could not prevent them. He pulled a handkerchief from his pocket, wiped his eyes and mopped his brow.

'We are brothers, Carl. We should not fight.'

'We have always fought. You have always . . . always put yourself apart. As if the rest of the family was not good enough for you. Poor Mama. She could never understand you.'

Ludwig's head had begun to throb. A sharp whistle resonated between his ears and made him close his eyes. He said nothing.

'She tried, you know. She used to tell me about it. But she felt she could not get through whatever it was you seemed to cloak yourself in. An invisible barrier. Even when she was dying. She knew she was dying. She wanted to talk to you. She felt you somehow blamed her for making you leave Vienna. Making you come back to Bonn.'

Ludwig looked at Carl. He wanted his brother to stop talking. His head was hurting. He could hear what Carl was saying, but he did not want to hear any more.

'She had Johann and me. We looked after her. We—'

The sound of his brother Nikola being called by his father's name seemed to cause an added shaft of pain to shoot through Ludwig.

'Enough! I will not hear any more.'

Carl rose quickly and leaned across the table menacingly. 'You say enough, and expect me to obey. Why should I? I have lived in your shadow for long enough. If I want to talk about our family, why should I not? Our mother, our dear mother, who you ignored. Father. He tried. He tried so hard. But he too was in your shadow. What is it, Ludwig? What is it that makes you think you are different from everyone else? Better than everyone else?'

Ludwig breathed deeply. He looked at his brother. That same hunted look that had always been there lodged on his face. How he loathed him. How he wanted him to go away. Both his brothers.

'Why did you have to come to Vienna? Both of you. You and Nikola. Why could you not leave me alone?'

'Why? You ask why? Do we somehow have to apologise for taking the same course of action as you? Are you the only one with the right to do as you please? My God, Father was right. He said you were selfish.'

'Enough, Carl! Stop!' Ludwig banged the table with his fist. 'If you insist on talking of our family, then let us talk of our grandfather. You never knew him. He died before you were born. He is the one I miss most. He was a musician. A real musician. A fine musician. Not like Father. And you. Useless musicians, both of you. And the tragedy is you do not realise it.' He was unable to stop the words. 'That is your great tragedy, Carl. You are a worthless musician, yet you do not know it. You think you are somehow ... somehow ... Yet you are worthless. Do you hear me? Worthless?'

He braced himself for an onslaught from his brother. Instead a smile slowly crept across Carl's face, a smile of triumph. 'You think I am worthless, do you? Then let me tell you something that will help change your mind. I have been promoted. I am now a financial officer in the Tax and Revenue office of the exchequer. My salary is now two hundred and fifty florins and I have excellent prospects for promotion.'

'I am pleased for you,' said Ludwig with some relief in his voice.

'It means that two of the Beethoven brothers are now gainfully employed. Johann has qualified as an apothecary and is earning a regular salary. It seems only Ludwig, the genius of the family, is still unable to earn money on a regular basis.'

With fatigue in his voice, Ludwig said, 'Now that you have a good position, you will be able to give up your musical pursuits.'

'Probably. I shall see. I still have pupils, who give me an extra source of income. But I shall not need to compose. I shall leave that to you, and much good it is likely to do you. It will bring you nothing but debt. But you, of course, do not have the intelligence to see that.'

Ludwig slumped back wearily in the chair. He wondered if he would ever be free of his brother, Caspar Carl.

Ludwig looked wearily at Braun, who sat behind his imposing desk.

'I am sorry, Herr Beethoven, there is nothing more I can do. The players refuse to play under Herr Wranitzky.'

'Then, Herr Braun,' Ludwig said in a calm and measured voice, 'you must make them. You are the director of the imperial theatres. You must order them.'

'Herr Beethoven, it is my experience that musicians do not take well to being given orders. Would you not agree?'

'Braun, I must have Wranitzky. He is used to conducting Mozart and Haydn. Also, I have decided to play one of my piano concertos. He is familiar with it.'

'I have tried my best to accommodate your wishes, Herr Beethoven. I have spoken to the leader of the orchestra on your behalf. He in turn has spoken to his colleagues. I believe a vote was taken. The players – Italians, all of them – voted to play under the direction of Signor Conti. A further vote was taken, which declared that if Herr Wranitzky were forced on them, they would refuse to play. The matter really is closed.'

Ludwig realised there was nothing more he could say. He left Braun's office and entered the auditorium, where the orchestra of the Italian opera, under the baton of Signor Conti, was rehearsing the Mozart symphony which was to open the concert. He walked down a side aisle so as not be seen, and sat at the end of a row in the *parterre noble*, the front part of the stalls that was reserved for the nobility.

Conti was talking to the orchestra volubly in Italian. He raised his baton and brought the orchestra in with the middle section of the Andante of the Symphony in D that Mozart had written for the Haffner family of Salzburg – a work which Ludwig knew had first been heard in this very hall nearly twenty years before. It was a gentle theme, woven of musical threads as delicate as the threads of a spider's web.

Ludwig knew before he had heard half a dozen bars that the concert – his first benefit concert – would be a failure.

Chapter 4

'More tickets would have been sold had it not been for this dreadful war, Beethoven,' said Prince Lobkowitz. 'In fact, if it were not for my damned leg, I'd be on the battlefield myself. That's where young Kinsky is, I know for a fact. I apologise for his absence on his behalf. And Count Razumovsky has been recalled to Moscow, temporarily, I believe.'

'Yes, Ludwig, I'm afraid it's only the older generation like myself who can be here,' said Baron Swieten, who seemed to have aged suddenly as he approached his seventieth year. 'Mind you, I should not condemn everyone here to the same great age as myself. You're a young man, Lobkowitz, and I can give Lichnowsky more than twenty years.'

Prince Lichnowsky smiled. The cream of Viennese society had gathered in the imperial box on the first tier, as it had several years before for Ludwig's first public concert in Vienna.

'You wear your years well, Baron,' said Lobkowitz. 'So, Beethoven, will you triumph again tonight? As you did against Steibelt?'

'What a triumph!' said Prince Schwarzenberg. 'If our army could have a victory on the battlefield to match our young friend's victory against Steibelt, the war against the French would quickly be over.'

'What is the latest from the battlefield?' asked Count Fries.

'Genoa has been retaken by the French. Prince Hohenzollern was forced to surrender to General Suchet. He was outnumbered. English reinforcements were apparently in sight of the port, but Suchet attacked before they could arrive. Another feather in the cap of the dreadful Corsican.'

'At least tonight we can forget the war and think only of music, the noblest of the arts,' said Prince Lichnowsky. He pulled a watch from his pocket. 'Her Imperial Majesty should be here any moment. Tell us, Ludwig, how did the rehearsals go?'

Ludwig shook his head. 'The orchestra is Italian. When they heard of the victory at Genoa they were more interested in that than the music.'

There was laughter. 'I thought Wranitzky was going to conduct,' said Lobkowitz.

'I wanted him to. The orchestra refused to play under him. If you want the truth, gentlemen, the pieces have been under-rehearsed. I fear for the performances. I wish the concert had been cancelled.'

'I am sure your fears are misplaced. I . . .'

A voice cut through the hubbub of conversation.

'Her Imperial Majesty the Empress. His Imperial Highness the Archduke.'

All present bowed – except Ludwig, who stood looking at the Empress. She was a larger woman than he had imagined, her stature increased by the vast amount of hair that was piled upon her head.

'My dear Prince,' said the Empress, moving towards Lichnowsky, confirming his status as the most senior aristocrat present. 'How good to see you again. I do hope your dear wife the Princess is here tonight.'

'Regrettably not, Your Majesty. Christiane, I regret to say, has taken to her bed with a chill.'

'Oh, I am so sorry to hear that. I do hope it is nothing serious.'

'I fear so, Your Majesty. Nothing trivial would have prevented her being here to pay her respects to Your Majesty.'

The Empress smiled. 'You are too kind. Do wish her a speedy recovery.'

'Is His Majesty well?'

'As well as can be expected, given the strain he is under. The war does not go well and I fear it is taking a toll on his health.'

Ludwig did not at first notice Archduke Rudolph standing at the Empress's side. When he did, he assumed he was a page. The boy's eyes were fixed on Ludwig, and Ludwig saw at once that he had an extraordinarily sensitive face. It was thin and pale. His nose was long and fine, his lips full, the lower lip having the extra fullness characteristic of the Habsburgs. The rosiness of his lips stood out in contrast to the paleness of his face. His hair was parted in the middle and neatly combed to each side, and Ludwig saw that he could not have been far into his teenage years.

The boy began to move towards Ludwig, but at the same time Lichnowsky took Ludwig by the arm.

'Your Majesty, may I present Ludwig van Beethoven, for whose benefit the concert tonight is being given.'

'Beethoven, at last I can meet you. I assure you your reputation has breached the walls of the Hofburg.'

There was a ripple of laughter. Ludwig bowed his head, raising it again a little quicker than convention dictated.

'In fact,' the Empress continued, 'it is largely due to my young brother-in-law here. He is a great disciple of your music. Indeed, he insisted on coming here tonight.'

Ludwig turned to Archduke Rudolph, wondering if he should bow – indeed if he could bow – to one so young, but found Rudolph bowing to him.

'Herr Beethoven,' he said in a voice that had not yet broken but which had a clearness to it, 'my admiration for your music is second to none in this city. I flatter myself that I can play your piano sonatas, although not as well as I would wish. Maybe when my hands have grown a little larger . . .'

There was more laughter but Rudolph did not smile. 'Will you teach me, Herr Beethoven? Not just to play but about composition. Fugue, counterpoint . . . How different keys . . .'

Ludwig saw the unmistakable earnestness in the young Prince's eyes. He was used to being asked to give piano lessons, and generally delighted in refusing. But he had never been asked before to teach composition. He remembered Mozart's story about the boy who had asked him to recommend a book to teach him to compose, and how he had pushed him out of the door. But this boy – Archduke or not – was clearly sincere. He wondered what to say but the Empress saved him from having to decide.

'My dear Rudolph, this is not the time to ask Herr Beethoven for music lessons. He has an important evening ahead of him, and more pressing things to think about.'

Ludwig smiled. He judged the moment right to absent himself.

'Your . . . Your Majesty. Sir. Gentlemen. If you will excuse me, I will attend to musical matters.'

'Of course,' said the Empress, 'and I am sure we all wish you a splendidly successful evening.'

There was a ripple of applause. Ludwig hurried out of the imperial box, down one of the side aisles and through a door that led to the rooms behind the stage. He could not help noticing as he went that the *parterre noble* was nowhere near full; the second *parterre* behind it, for ticket-holding members of the public, was hardly more full.

The musicians were tuning their instruments. Few glanced at him. The rehearsals had not been a success. In the Piano Concerto in B flat the orchestral entries had been scrappy and the musicians had played without enthusiasm. There was a residual resentment among them that Ludwig had tried to foist Wranitzky on them, instead of allowing them to play under the director they knew well. The votes they had taken had left a bitter taste.

Ludwig quickly spotted Schuppanzigh, his bulk standing out among the other musicians.

'Schuppi, I fear the worst.'

'Do not worry, Ludwig. I have heard good reports. Of the Mozart, especially.'

'I hope it is better than the Beethoven,' Ludwig said with a wry smile.

'The septet will be fine,' Schuppanzigh said. 'Rehearsals went well.'

'Good, since I am making a present of it to the Empress afterwards. Too many wrong notes and she will give it back to me.'

Schuppanzigh chuckled. 'You need not worry about your septet, Ludwig. I have secured the top players. Nickel the clarinettist. I even found Matauschek and Dietzel. I thought they had left the city, but they had not.'

'A pity they can't play in the orchestra as well. It is in the wind section that the Italians are at their poorest. They play their wretched instruments as if they were parading in Naples on a summer's afternoon.'

Ludwig clapped Schuppanzigh on the shoulder and turned away to find Conti.

'Signor Conti. Your players should take the stage. The Empress is here. We should begin.'

Giving the Italian no time to reply, Ludwig left the room and went back into the auditorium. He sat on a chair against the wall and surveyed the scene.

The imperial box and the boxes to either side of it on the first tier were full. All the boxes on the second tier were unoccupied. The two sections of the *parterre* were still half-empty. Ludwig now knew his first benefit concert would be a financial, as well as a musical, failure.

The most important piece of music to be played was his First Symphony. The rehearsals had been a disaster. The opening of the first movement, the three dominant seventh chords in three bars, the players were convinced was nothing more than a mistake by the copyist.

'He has put the chords in the wrong key,' said the leader of the violins. 'We all realised that. Also, you surely do not mean to open a symphony with such a chord. So here is what you surely intended to write.' He nodded at his fellow players and the orchestra played a unison chord of C major.

Ludwig, angry at their assumption and in no mood to reason with them, said simply, 'There is no mistake. Play it as it is written.'

Several times the wind players had complained that passages were unplayable. They had refused Ludwig's implorings to try to play them. In the end he had been forced to accept that where they considered the music to be unplayable, they simply would not play it.

Ludwig sat now watching the musicians file on to the stage, wishing he could just get up and leave.

After the formalities in honour of the Empress were over, Signor Conti raised his baton to begin Mozart's Symphony in D major.

The first sound of the music – the famous octave leaps which had so stunned the audience in this same hall – hit Ludwig's ears and made him wince. Immediately the high-pitched whistle returned, so vividly that he thought at first that the oboist was responsible.

Why on earth had he chosen this symphony to open the concert? He shook his head at his own folly. The octave leaps were difficult enough for the Burgtheater orchestra; but they, with their natural affinity for Wolfgang Mozart, their fellow Austrian, had worked at the movement until they could play it perfectly. The Italians could only make, at best, an attempt at it.

He knew perfectly well why he had chosen this symphony: precisely because of the opening. It was startlingly bold. It said to the listener, 'Pay attention, what you are about to hear is important.' It obeyed the rules of key, opening in the home key of D major, but was none the less extraordinary for that.

What his choice was actually saying was, 'Listen to the opening of Mozart's symphony. Then listen to the opening of mine and you will see that what Mozart began I am continuing.'

The Italian orchestra settled down and were making an attempt to play the Symphony in D as Mozart had written it. Their worst fault, Ludwig realised, was that they were ignoring the music's dynamics. *Forte* and *piano* were indistinguishable. The music was played with no variations; a constant flow somewhere between loud and soft. The delicate second theme of the Andante, where the bows should bounce off the strings to give it lightness, was played as if it was part of an overture to an Italian comic opera.

Nevertheless they reached the end of the work without serious mishap, and Ludwig was surprised at the warmth of the reception. He went through the door again to the area behind the stage to prepare himself for the performance of his piano concerto, while the orchestra were joined on stage by two solo singers for the Adam and Eve duet from the third part of Haydn's *Creation* – chosen by Ludwig because he knew Baron Swieten would be in the audience.

He remembered how – it seemed so many years ago, yet it could only have been five or six – he had played his first piano concerto in this hall, and how well it had been received! The audience had called for an encore, but he had decided against it. He wanted to remember just the reception they had given to the concerto.

And he remembered how, two nights later, again in this same hall, he had played Mozart's great Piano Concerto in D minor, at the request of Constanze Mozart. It had been a sudden decision of his to sit quietly at the piano, his head bowed, after the final notes. His tribute to the man he regarded as the master.

He heard the applause now for the duet from *The Creation*, pleased that it, like the Mozart symphony, was receiving appreciation from the audience. He had never been particularly worried about the Haydn piece. The soloists were the father and daughter Saals, popular with the audience and regular performers in the imperial theatres.

Ludwig walked out on to the stage to supervise the positioning of the piano. He glanced across the auditorium at the imperial box. The Empress was engaged in animated conversation with Lichnowsky and several others. He saw Archduke Rudolph. The boy was apart from the others, standing and leaning on the velvet-covered rail. He was watching the action on the stage intently.

Ludwig spoke to the leader of the orchestra. 'You take your time from me in the opening *tutti*. I will conduct from the piano. Do you understand?'

'Do we understand?' said the violinist, turning to his colleagues.

'*Si, si,*' several voices said.

'And remember, the slow movement, the Adagio, not too slow. It is not a hymn.'

Ludwig's eyes swept the players, looking for signs of dissent. But there were none. It must be that they were pleased with the progress of the concert so far, thought Ludwig. All to the good.

Ludwig realised as he sat at the piano and gave the orchestra the A to tune to that the dreadful whistling in his head had gone. It had happened like this before. It was always in the preparation that the pain in his head and the sounds were worst. Once he had begun playing they seemed to evaporate.

The orchestra played better than he had feared after the rehearsals. He mentally congratulated himself on allowing Mozart and Haydn to begin the concert. If he had chosen to open it with his piano concerto it could have been a disaster. They played accurately, but without feeling and without contrast.

The three chords which introduced the second subject of the *tutti* were almost in unison, but the slurred phrases in the strings which immediately followed it were ragged. The *tutti* ended with two *fortissimo* chords in the home key of B flat. But they were crotchets, and after just a semiquaver rest the piano solo entered. Ludwig had wanted the piano entry to emerge from the orchestra, as if it was almost another instrument of the orchestra. It was impossible now, as the orchestra held on to the final chord for at least a minim. Well, they did not play any wrong notes, Ludwig thought, as he brought the solo piano in.

Ludwig soon found that rather than the orchestra following his nod of the head, he was following them. They had set their own speed, slower than he wanted, and try as he might he could not move them on.

The same was true in the second movement, so that it sounded exactly as Ludwig had warned against – a hymn, almost a dirge. When, towards the end of the movement, the piano and orchestra engaged in a dialogue, which he had scored *pianissimo*, it sounded, he thought to himself, more like a one-sided conversation.

The final movement, the Rondo, was surprisingly successful. The jaunty theme, accented off the beat, appealed to the Italians. Ludwig soon found he was having to hold them back as they accelerated through the movement. The strings heeded him but the wind did not. More than once Ludwig feared the piece would collapse. But each time a solo passage on the piano allowed him to re-establish the tempo.

The ending was supposed to be one of contrasts. Ludwig had deliberately slowed the music down to increase anticipation. He had alternated a *crescendo* passage with a *decrescendo* passage, *pianissimo* chords on the piano followed *pianissimo* by the orchestra, then a *fortissimo* chord from the orchestra and the final four bars *fortissimo* from them alone.

True to form the Italian players ignored all Ludwig's dynamic markings. The music hurried along at a steady *forte*. Ludwig at first used the solo sequences to try to establish the contrast, but he realised that by doing that the piano would simply not be heard. So, as he had done almost throughout the concerto, he followed the orchestra.

It was with a considerable measure of relief that he heard the orchestra strike the final chord of B flat in unison and with not a single instrument out of tune.

Even more to his relief, the audience responded enthusiastically. Archduke Rudolph, Ludwig saw, rose to his feet, encouraging those around him to do the same. The Empress, as her status dictated, remained seated.

So far the concert, although Ludwig knew it could not be described as a *succès fou*, was at least not a failure. The next piece to be performed was Ludwig's Septet for Wind and Strings, led by the inimitable Ignaz Schuppanzigh. Ludwig knew that that could not fail. Schuppi had rehearsed it successfully and he had confidence in his fellow players – they were Austrian, not Italian!

He went to the back of the hall to hear the septet. How well the sound carried across the auditorium! The piece was to be published soon by Anton Hoffmeister, who had recently moved from Vienna to Leipzig. There he had established a new publishing firm with Ambrosius Kühnel and had asked Ludwig for pieces for publication. Without hesitation – and making sure his brother Carl knew nothing of it and so could not interfere –

he gave Hoffmeister and Kühnel the Piano Concerto in B flat which he had just performed, as well as the septet and the First Symphony.

The First Symphony! That was still to come tonight. The final piece to be performed. How would the orchestra behave? Would they appreciate the pause that the septet gave them and return to the platform refreshed? Or would they resent the fact that there was yet one more piece to be played, and a piece that in rehearsal they had treated with disdain? Ludwig did not know what to expect. And what if the reception for the symphony was bad? His first symphony. What if it was not well received? Would it damage his reputation as a composer? His fear was that with the orchestra already against the work, it could not help but fail. The question was how seriously.

He stood at the back of the hall, the half-empty hall. Just as well, he thought. If my reputation is going to suffer tonight, it is just as well. If I do not make money out of the evening, so be it. There will be other occasions.

He folded his arms and smiled. It was – whatever the circumstances – a wonderful experience for a composer to hear his work being performed. It was not an event he had experienced too often, since by far the greatest number of his works had involved the keyboard and he himself had performed.

Look at Schuppanzigh! How fond Ludwig was of this over-sized violinist. He held his instrument under his chin, his huge arms encircling it, the vast bulk of his chest and stomach seeming to support it, making it look like a child's toy, an instrument belonging to the island of Lilliput. Yet how easily Schuppi moved his bulk, how delicately he moved his head to give the other players the beat, how expressive his eyebrows which rose and fell with the cadence of the music.

He was an ensemble player, thought Ludwig. A perfect ensemble player. Some violinists wanted only to impress an audience with their solo skills, to perform pyrotechnics which always seemed more difficult than they were. Not Schuppi. He was a natural group player, and a natural group leader.

How well Ludwig remembered writing these notes – and how he remembered the consternation his choice of instruments had caused. Even Schuppi had been bemused. 'A septet? Which seven, and why?' he had asked. 'Violin, viola, cello, double bass; clarinet, horn, bassoon,' Ludwig replied. 'To see what they sound like.' 'Why not call it a small orchestra? An *orchestre piccolo*?'

Ludwig had had another surprise in store for Schuppi. Six movements! But it was another of Schuppi's admirable qualities that he respected Ludwig's musical judgement and never queried it. And as soon as the parts came back from Schlemmer the copyist and Schuppi played the violin part, he became the work's greatest advocate.

He and Ludwig had discussed the opening of the second movement, the Adagio Cantabile, at great length. Ludwig had written a gloriously lyrical opening solo for the clarinet, which the violin then took up. Schuppanzigh wanted to take the opening as well for the violin. 'I can make it soar,' he said. 'No. I want the contrast in texture between clarinet and violin,' Ludwig replied.

There had been a private performance of the work at the palace of Prince Schwarzenberg – more an extended rehearsal. The unfortunate clarinettist had failed to give the solo the quality Ludwig required, that he demanded.

For tonight's performance Schuppanzigh had sought out the city's foremost clarinettist, Gottfried Nickel, and he played the solo now exactly as Ludwig had envisioned it, taking wing above the other instruments, plaintive, lyrical, gentle yet firm.

Ludwig closed his eyes. Schuppi took up the theme and it remained in flight like a bird. Yes, the music was right. The little minuet which formed the third movement Ludwig had taken from an earlier piano sonata, not yet published. Would anyone notice? It did not matter. How well it worked now for this *orchestre piccolo*.

He smiled as the musicians played the jaunty Andante with its variations. Someone had said to him after the performance at Prince Schwarzenberg's that he had taken this simple theme from a street singer. It was an old folk song, they said accusingly. 'Really? Then the folk song will become immortal,' he had replied, a smile defusing the remark of any arrogance. The fact was that the man might well have been right. Ludwig did not know, he honestly did not know. But the tune was perfect for his purposes. And it was, as his accuser had said, simple. As Mozart had instructed him.

After the Scherzo, which Ludwig had written to provide a variation of mood, a punctuation mark almost between two lengthy movements, came the final Andante and Presto. The solemn nature of the opening of the last movement was soon replaced by the Presto, carried along now as if on an invisible wave, Schuppi's body bouncing slightly on the chair, all the players' eyes turned to him for the beat.

He positively relished the skittish arpeggios with which the violin dominated the closing section of the movement, and of the work. As the last chord sounded, Ludwig looked at the audience. They were applauding, but it was half-hearted. There were some smiles, but some heads were shaking too. Why? Why? Why could they not see? One day they would, he thought angrily. One day. If not this audience, then another audience. Another generation.

He felt a hand on his shoulder. He turned to see Stephan Breuning standing behind him, with Johann Hummel.

'Congratulations, Ludwig,' said Stephan. 'Delightful.'

'A septet!' said Hummel. 'Well, Beethoven, you always have something to teach us other musicians. The combination would never have occurred to me.'

The sudden buzz of conversation in the auditorium had affected Ludwig's ears. There was no pain in his head, but rather a dullness which made it difficult for him to hear. But he could tell from the smiles that both men were complimenting him.

'. . . the symphony,' said Hummel, his eyebrows raised in expectation.

Ludwig nodded to both of them and went down the aisle towards the stage. My First Symphony, he was thinking to himself. Before such an audience. A half-empty hall. The Empress and the important musical patrons of the city; some of them, anyway. This was not what he had wanted, what he had expected for the first performance of his First Symphony. And worst of all, an orchestra which not only did not appreciate the piece, but which had clearly done enough playing for one evening.

Ludwig watched the musicians tramp out on to the stage. Weariness was etched in their faces. They wanted to go home. He saw Schuppanzigh come up to him.

Despite the tension he felt, he smiled encouragingly.

'Ah, Schuppi, you did it justice. What I would give for you now to lead the Burgtheater orchestra in the symphony.'

'It is a fine piece, your septet. We enjoyed playing it. Nickel especially. He sings your praises. Good luck with the symphony.'

Ludwig waited for the musicians to be seated and finish adjusting their music stands. He did not glance at the audience. He simply stood in front of them, swept his eyes across them, raised his arms, his hands held high, and brought them down.

The first chord sounded, the dominant seventh. Was that a gasp he could hear from the audience behind him, or was it his ears playing tricks on him? He held his arms out to sustain the chord, but the orchestra resolved the chord almost immediately. Too quick, too quick! They did so again, and again for a third time. The three dominant seventh chords, his entrée into the world of the symphony, thrown away, played as if they were a mistake.

After the twelve-bar introduction, into the first main theme, launched by the dotted quaver and semiquaver motif. Now they were playing too slowly. It should almost hop, this theme, bounce along. The orchestra were playing the notes heavily, as if they were tied to the floor. Ludwig tried to induce them to play faster, but it was to no avail.

He made a decision. He needed to reach the end of the symphony without mishap. In order to do that, it was quite clear that the orchestra would have to play at its own pace. Where the woodwind found passages too difficult, they would not play. Where the strings found similar problems, they would play slowly. So be it.

Ludwig relaxed slightly, having decided that this performance, the first time his Symphony had been heard, would be little better than a run-through; a rehearsal without pauses. There were worse fates.

The second movement, the Andante Cantabile, curiously benefited from the orchestra's sluggish playing. It lacked sparkle; it lacked the sprightliness Ludwig wanted. But the pace was right. Not so in the swift third movement, the deliberately misnamed Menuetto, with its rising scale of staccato crotchets and minims. This Ludwig wanted to spring along, carried by its own momentum. The violins' bows should have bounced off the strings, but the Italians played the notes as if lead weights were tied to the ends of their bows.

The same was true of the last movement, with its rapidly turning semiquaver phrases. Momentum, that was the key. The music must never falter, never stumble. And it did not. It just never once moved at the right pace.

It was with relief in every pore of Ludwig's face that the

orchestra played the closing set of chords in unison and on his beat. The relief on his face was matched on theirs, for different reasons. For them, this unwanted concert was over.

Ludwig nodded towards the leader of the violins, but did not shake his hand. Nor did he turn to acknowledge the applause. The sudden cessation of sound had hurt his ears. The applause sounded like a whooshing – in fact he was not sure if it was applause or the dreadful noise in his ears.

He walked from the stage, his head down and his eyes screwed half-shut. He wanted to go home, back to his lodgings. Drink some wine. Just put the whole experience behind him. Had it been dreadful? No. Had it been a success? No.

He walked up the side aisle, ignoring glances in his direction. He knew he had to go and speak to the Empress, see Prince Lichnowsky and the others. There was something he wanted to say to the Empress. Should he go ahead with it? What would her reaction be? Yes, it was the right decision. It could only be of help to him in the long run.

'Bravo, my dear Beethoven,' said Prince Lichnowsky, hurrying forward and clasping his hand in both his. 'Splendid. Splendid. Was it not splendid?' He turned and smiled at the heads which nodded in agreement.

'Fine septet, sir. Very fine indeed, though I confess the combination is new to me,' said Prince Lobkowitz.

'The symphony,' said Swieten. 'Most impressed. Most impressed.'

The Empress stood. Ludwig moved a little nearer to her to be sure he could hear what she was saying.

'Herr Beethoven, a delightful evening. May I say how much I enjoyed the music. Your . . . septet . . . Is that what you call it? Most enjoyable.'

Ludwig was aware of the weariness in his voice as he spoke. 'Your Imperial Majesty, it gives me in that case even more pleasure to dedicate it to you, if you would be so kind as to accept my humble dedication.'

The Empress smiled. 'How charming of you, Herr Beethoven. Quite charming. I shall of course accept. I thought it a particularly fine piece.'

There was applause from all those present in the imperial box.

Count Fries spoke. 'Unusual opening to the symphony, Beethoven, if you don't mind my saying so. Those chords.

Most unusual, though I couldn't quite put my finger on it.'

'Dominant sevenths,' said a small voice to Ludwig's right. He turned. It was Archduke Rudolph who had spoken. 'Weren't they, sir? Dominant sevenths.'

'Yes,' said Ludwig. 'Not the usual way to open a symphony, I admit. But I wanted . . . I wanted . . .'

'And in the wrong key, were they not?' Rudolph said. 'I am not sure what key they were in, but they were not in the home key of C. You did not establish that until the end of the introduction. G, was it?'

Ludwig smiled at the boy. 'Yes. You're right. Did you think . . . ?'

'Sounded a bit strange to me, Beethoven,' said Lobkowitz. 'Can't say I've heard anything like that before.'

'It was a little unusual, Ludwig,' said Lichnowsky. 'Are you sure you meant . . . ?'

Ludwig turned to the young Archduke. 'What did you think, sir?'

'My opinion, Herr Beethoven,' said Archduke Rudolph, a smile playing around his full lips, 'is that you have taken us into a new century.'

BOOK ELEVEN

Chapter 1

'Oh, Ludwig, isn't it sad? Just look. Those poor men.'

Nanette Streicher stood with Ludwig on the corner of the Landstrasse, only a street away from her husband's piano factory, and watched the wounded being carried into the hospital.

'It is not the end of it,' said Ludwig. 'If the fighting goes on there may soon be French soldiers in the streets of Vienna, just as there are in Bonn.'

The Battle of Hohenlinden had been a disaster for Austria. Napoleon Bonaparte, refusing to consider how nearly he had been defeated at Marengo, followed up the victory by pushing north from the Italian plain and engaging the imperial forces at Hohenlinden. Sixty thousand French defeated seventy thousand Austrians. As many as twenty thousand wounded Austrian soliders were carried back to Vienna.

Nanette hurried forward and lifted the bloody and dangling arm of a soldier back on to the stretcher as he was carried into the hospital.

She turned to Ludwig. 'Come to the house, Ludwig. I will give you your clothes. They're all ready for you. But I will not stay. I must get back here to see if I can be of any help. So many good men cut down.'

In the house on the Ungargasse Ludwig could hear Andreas Streicher playing single notes on a piano in his workshop. They alternated with blows from a hammer as he tuned the instrument. Ludwig sat in an easy chair while Nanette bustled around, gathering up his clothes, folding them and putting them into a large bag.

The bag full, she tied the top of it with cord and tested its weight. 'There, not as heavy as I thought. Come on. I will go home with you. Let's get a carriage.'

In Ludwig's rooms on the Tiefer Graben Nanette busied herself, tidying up, putting away his clothes for him and cleaning dirty dishes. Ludwig watched her. He knew he was lucky to have such a dear friend.

Finally, wiping her hands on a towel, she sat down. 'Now, Ludwig. Tell me, how is your hearing?'

'I . . . It is strange. Sometimes I have a problem, sometimes I don't. It is worst in company. If there is a lot of noise, I cannot hear what someone is saying to me. And sometimes I have a dreadful high-pitched whistle, always with a throbbing pain in my head.'

'You poor dear,' said Nanette, putting her hand for a moment on his arm. 'But now, for instance, you don't seem to be having any trouble.'

'No. We are alone. There's no other noise. When I am alone with someone, it is all right. Almost.'

'What do you mean?'

'There always seems to be some noise in my head. Even now, there is a hum. I can hear something all the time, although it's not that bad at the moment. It's not affecting my hearing. But if someone shouts . . . If you were suddenly to shout at me, it would make my ears want to burst.'

'Do you have trouble with both ears? Or just one?'

'To begin with it was only my left ear, but now it is the same with both. When I hear the whistle, or the buzzing, or sometimes a whooshing noise, it is as if it is in the middle of my head. That is why I cannot concentrate on anything. And why, more and more, I need to be alone.'

'And the doctors? You've left Professor Frank, haven't you?'

Ludwig nodded. 'I am seeing Doktor Vering. He makes me take tepid baths. It helps my stomach pains, but does nothing for my ears. He said if my stomach got better, my hearing would too. But it hasn't. And he says I should put almond oil in my ears, like Frank did. But it's useless.'

'But, Ludwig, if both doctors . . .'

Ludwig's face crumpled. 'Frank said my hearing would be cured. But Vering . . . Vering said . . .'

'Yes . . . ?'

'Vering said it will improve if I use the oil all the time, not just at night. But . . . but . . . it may never be completely right.'

'Ludwig, I'm sure . . . I'm sure . . . If it's just a simple blockage . . .'

'It's not, Nanette. If it was I wouldn't suffer from these

dreadful noises. Sometimes it's like an orchestra is in my head, so many different sounds. And all out of tune.'

'But, Ludwig, a blockage of earwax would cause that. It happens to children all the time, and they complain of noises.'

'Why then did he say it would never be completely cured?'

'I'm sure he didn't mean that. He meant if you don't use the oil it won't be cured. The blockage won't go away. That's what he meant. He was trying to encourage you to use it. Now you must use it. Where is it? I'll prepare some for you. I insist.'

Ludwig gestured with a resigned look on his face. 'In the cupboard over there. By the door. But it will just end up on my clothes, or my pillow.'

Nanette bustled round. She took a copy of the *Wiener Zeitung* that was lying on the floor and spread it on the table. She tore a small piece of cotton from a large roll, unstopped the oil container and poured some drops on to it. She squeezed the cotton to make sure it absorbed the oil.

'Now, lean your head that way.' She placed the cotton at the entrance to Ludwig's ear and gently pushed it in. With a cloth she wiped away a small trickle of oil that ran down his lobe. 'There. Now keep your head like that for a few seconds.'

She repeated the process with another piece of cotton, moved Ludwig's head in the other direction and put it in his ear. She made sure that no oil was running down on either side.

Ludwig felt a deadening sensation in his head. 'Nanette, I cannot hear at all. Just the noises. You must take them out.'

Nanette smiled and held her finger to her mouth. 'Shhh. Don't talk for a moment.' She sat close to Ludwig and spoke to him in a clear and firm voice.

'Now, Ludwig, it will take a while for you to get used to it. But soon you will forget the cotton is there. You must wear it, as Doktor Vering says. If both doctors recommended it, you must do it. You must wear it all the time. Do you promise me you will?'

Ludwig grimaced.

'You should change it two or three times a day, say at lunchtime and in the early evening. Then again when you go to bed.'

'People will notice. They will ask me what is wrong.'

'Just tell them you have some earwax. It's common. They won't think anything of it. Have you told any of your friends about the problem? Does anyone already know?'

'Only Stephan Breuning. He's the only one. I'm surprised no one else has noticed, because sometimes I have to get close to them to hear them, especially if it is noisy. But they just put it down to my absent-mindedness. I am famous for it. But . . . because of the problem I go out less. I don't go to the Schwan so often, or the Schwarzen Kameel.'

'That's sad for you. You need to see your friends. But I am sure it will get better. Especially if you do what Doktor Vering says. You do promise me, don't you?'

Ludwig nodded. Nanette said, 'Ludwig, I hope you don't mind me asking, but what about money? I know your benefit concert didn't . . . wasn't . . . Are you all right? Do tell me.'

Ludwig smiled. 'Dear Nanette, you are so kind, but you do not need to be concerned about me. Prince Lichnowsky has been very generous. After the concert he said he would pay me an annuity of six hundred florins – fifty a month – until I find a permanent position. He said he didn't mind how long that took.'

'Oh, the dear man. That's so good of him. I've heard he admires you very much, you know.'

'He also made me a gift of four stringed instruments. Two violins, viola and cello. They're valuable. Italian, and a hundred years old.'

'How kind of him. Why . . . ?'

'He knows my love for the string quartet. He admires the set of six I wrote.'

'Did you dedicate them to him?'

'No. I was going to but he advised me to dedicate them to Prince Lobkowitz. He says the Prince is keen for my music to be heard in his concert room. So I said I would. I have to let the publisher know.'

'Look at you, Ludwig, friend of Princes, even the Empress. Famous throughout Vienna. I'm so proud of you, Ludwig.'

Ludwig smiled. 'I want to leave my rooms in the Tiefer Graben. They're too dark and depressing. Do you know of anywhere?'

Nanette shook her head. 'There is an apartment in the Landstrasse. But it's further away from the city. You don't want to move beyond the Bastion, do you?'

'No. Although I don't like it in the city, I need to be there. It's convenient.'

'Wait. I do know of somewhere. I heard only yesterday.

One of the elderly ladies I buy food for is having to move to a smaller apartment, lower down. She can't manage the stairs any more . . .'

'Then I can't take it. Schuppi would never forgive me. He always complains about the stairs.'

'It would be perfect, Ludwig. On the Wasserkunstbastei, near the Seilerstätte. It is on the third floor. The windows have wonderful views across the Bastion and the Glacis.'

'The Wasserkunstbastei? What number?'

'One two seven five.'

Ludwig thought for a moment. 'The house owned by Councillor Hamberger?'

'Yes.'

Ludwig smiled. 'Herr Haydn used to live there. It's where I went for lessons with him when I first came to Vienna. He had an apartment on the first floor.'

'Then it's doubly perfect. You'll feel quite at home. And do you realise something, Ludwig? We've been speaking to each other perfectly normally. You've already forgotten about the cotton in your ears.'

Prince Lobkowitz directed Prince Lichnowsky up the stairs of his palace, holding on to the ornate banister to keep his balance.

'Damn leg. Curse of my life. Sometimes I wonder what I would have been able to do with my life if I hadn't been afflicted by this infirmity.'

'My dear Franz, it may sound an odd thing to say, but you can count your blessings. Were it not for your leg you would probably be on the battlefield now, dying for the empire. If I were ten years younger, that would be my fate.'

'Yes, you're right. I shouldn't complain. I'm in the fortunate position of being able to pursue my interests, chief of which . . .'

He threw open the double doors to his concert room, the room which had witnessed Steibelt's humiliation.

'There! The Lobkowitz concert room. Is there a finer one in Vienna?'

'I doubt that there is a finer one in the empire,' said Lichnowsky, still breathing heavily from the climb up the staircase.

'Do you see, I've added new music stands. And my plan is to

build a bank of seats over here,' he said, gesturing to the back wall, 'rising to the back. I'll put a low railing in front of the first row' – he pointed in a sweeping movement with his crutch – 'to separate the audience from the orchestra. And I'll have the seats stuffed and covered with red linen. Won't it be splendid? What do you think, Lichnowsky, eh?'

'Very impressive, my friend. Very impressive. Tell me, I do not wish to be inquisitive, but this will cut rather heavily into your funds, won't it?'

Lobkowitz looked round. 'Don't raise your voice. I don't want Karolina to hear. She says we cannot afford it. But I'm telling you we can. I have funds in Prague. I can easily get them transferred.'

'Then you're fortunate. My own position . . . As you know, we've had to leave our lovely apartment on the Alstergasse. The Schottentor is comfortable, but we do not have the space we had in the Alstergasse. But it's this wretched war, it's a drain on finances. You're fortunate that you don't have to contribute, not being Austrian.'

'Hah! You see, you Austrians, you highborn noblemen look down on us Bohemian peasants, but it does have some advantages. But, Lichnowsky, if you have a problem, why have you made over this annuity to Beethoven? You have, haven't you? Six hundred a year?'

Lichnowsky nodded. 'Actually it was Christiane's idea. She is so fond of the boy. She feels almost like a mother to him, although he must be around thirty now. Your age. And I must admit, I have a tender spot for him. He is such a . . . such a . . . genius. When he plays the piano, it is as if . . . as if . . .'

'I know what you mean. And from one who appears so unsophisticated. Look at the way he dresses. I will never forget Steibelt's face. In this very room! He thought we were playing some sort of practical joke on him. He said to me afterwards he thought Ludwig was one of the servants who had forgotten to put on a uniform for the evening! I think in the end he was quite frightened. He told me he believed Ludwig had the devil in him. He had never heard such playing.'

'Curious. That's what Abbé Gelinek said after he had come up against him.'

Both men laughed.

'Did you know I gave him a quartet of instruments too? Two violins, a viola and a cello. Italian. Worth a lot of money.'

Lichnowsky made a dismissive gesture with his hands. 'Well, they've been in my family for years. I don't even know how we acquired them. And what use are they to me? His face when Christiane and I presented them to him. It lit up.'

'You really are generous.'

'I just cannot bear to see him struggle. The benefit concert made him no money. His brother Carl has ruined his relationships with most of the publishers, though I understand he's told Carl not to meddle in his affairs again. If you want my opinion, most of the money that should have gone to Ludwig went straight into his brother's pocket. Though perhaps I shouldn't say that. There's no proof.'

'Well, it's generous of you, Lichnowsky. I'd like to be able to do the same for him one day.'

Ludwig looked down into the Tiefer Graben, dark and gloomy as ever, and felt a lightness of mood he had not experienced for a long time. Nanette, God bless her, was right. There was something curiously comforting about the cotton soaked in almond oil which he now had in his ears day and night. The humming and buzzing were still there, but certainly not as sharp as before. And the fact that he had the cotton in his ears was evidence that something was at last being done to correct the problem.

She was right too about his friends. No one had mentioned it. He knew they had seen it; he learned to notice how their eyes would flit to his ears. But no one had said a word. There was the occasional small smile, as if they were thinking, Poor Ludwig, a childhood ailment. Earwax. But no questions.

And soon he would leave the Tiefer Graben. Nanette had taken him to see the apartment in the Wasserkunstbastei. He liked it immediately. The windows at the back of the living room looked out – as Nanette had said – over the Bastion and the Glacis and the Belvedere Palace beyond. The light streamed in; so different from the Tiefer Graben.

For the moment at least his money problems were over. The annuity from Prince Lichnowsky meant he had a steady guaranteed income, which he had never before had. He smiled when he thought of the instruments Lichnowsky had given him. Schuppanzigh had begged Ludwig to allow him and his colleagues in the Lichnowsky Quartet to play them. Ludwig had refused. They were too precious. He had given them to

Stephan Breuning for safekeeping. At least he had the space in his apartment.

How could he express his thanks to Prince Lichnowsky? Simple. How fortunate a composer was to have the means at hand. He would dedicate a piece of music to him. He had already dedicated the Opus One piano trios to him, as well as the Grande Sonate Pathétique. Now Ludwig knew exactly what piece he would dedicate.

He would compose a Second Symphony. He was ready for it. Already he had ideas and had made jottings in a notebook. The result might even help people to understand the first. It would be clear to them that without the first, he could not have composed the second. And the Second Symphony he would dedicate to Prince Lichnowsky.

Already in anticipation of the move to the Wasserkunstbastei, Ludwig was composing again. He had written a new romance for violin and orchestra and rewritten another romance he had composed some years before. Schuppanzigh had helped him with the compositions, advising on technique.

Ludwig had rewarded him by presenting him, in the new romance, with an opening passage of double-stopping that made Schuppi turn white when he saw it on the manuscript. He had still not mastered it, and all his supplications to Ludwig to simplify it – 'Why *double*-stopping? Is a single note at a time not enough?' – had been ignored.

Ludwig turned away from the window. Yes, his mood was lighter than for some time. At least – thanks to Nanette's insistence – he was now doing something about his hearing. Maybe . . . maybe . . . And with the move to the Wasserkunstbastei imminent, perhaps . . .

He felt the vibration of footsteps on the stairs outside his rooms. He was actually looking forward to seeing this young boy. How many times in the last few years had he refused to see young pianists? He had lost count. Always they had come with the highest recommendation. A letter extolling their talent. 'Once you hear my son, you will know that your genius has passed to him . . .', 'You alone will see in my son the genius with which you are blessed . . .'

Genius. Always they used the word. How he hated to hear it. So often he had heard his Father use it about him. And what did it mean? Nothing. What was genius? Who could tell? Bach and Mozart had it. Does Haydn have it? Do I have it? he wondered. It is not for this generation to say; future generations will decide.

But when old Wenzel Krumpholz had come to him and said he really ought to hear this young lad, he had been responsive. Krumpholz was fortunate and Ludwig made him aware of it.

'You know my views on young geniuses,' he had said. 'If each one who was described to me as a genius were one, the world would be full of them. And it is not.'

'I did not say he was a genius, Ludwig,' said the elderly mandolin player patiently. 'I just said you ought to hear him.'

'"Krump-Krump-Krumpholz, king of the mandolin, You surely don't know what a good mood you find me in." There, a new composition for you. Just you. Should I give it a dedication and an opus number?'

'I think that won't be necessary, Ludwig. However, if you wish to score it for mandolin and sign the sheet of music for me, I shall be eternally grateful.'

Ludwig had smiled. 'No, old man. Maybe it is not quite up to my usual exacting standards. However, bring the boy to me and we shall see what he can do. I shall get a couple of colleagues to come as well, and he can entertain us all. What is his name again?'

'Czerny,' Krumpholz said. 'Carl Czerny.'

There was a knock on the door. Without waiting for a reply, Schuppanzigh came in, followed by Paul Wranitzky, the court music director the Italian opera orchestra had refused to play under at Ludwig's benefit concert.

'Ah, gentlemen, the very essence of Viennese music enters my humble apartment, soon not to be my apartment any longer.'

'Really?' said Schuppanzigh. 'Where are you . . . ?'

'To the Wasserkunstbastei. Where light comes into the rooms. Light. Something I have never seen here. There is a carafe of wine in the corner. Help yourselves.'

'We don't see you at the Schwarzen Kameel so much now, Ludwig. Or the Schwan.'

'What, Schuppi? Work. Always so much work to do. But you won't find me without a carafe of wine in the house. Go on, pour some glasses.'

'When is the boy arriving?' asked Wranitzky.

'When you raise your baton and command him to, Maestro Wranitzky. Unlike the perfidious Italians, who need to be taught a thing or two about discipline. And Austrian music-making.

Otherwise for ever they will just play trivial, light-hearted music, and it will be left to us to create the music that endures.'

Schuppanzigh poured out three glasses and handed them around.

'How are you, Ludwig?'

Ludwig saw Schuppi's eyes flit to the cotton in his ears but he made no comment about it. The noises were in Ludwig's head, but still less severely than before. The dullness the cotton induced seemed to take the edge off them. And there was no pain or throbbing.

'My health is greatly improved, thank you, Schuppi. Unlike your violin-playing, I am quite sure. How fares the opening to my romance. The one in G. Quite dreadfully, I have no doubt.'

'It is difficult to play, Ludwig, as you well know. You took lessons on the violin once, didn't you? In Bonn? You should know how difficult it is. And so easy to change. Or just have the double-stopping on the opening note to give it emphasis. That would be . . .'

'Hah, Schuppi!' Ludwig clapped his hands. 'Schuppanzigh-you're-a-fat-man. Schuppanzigh-you're-a-fat-man. And you cannot play the vi-o-lin. And you cannot play the vi-o-lin.'

All three men laughed. 'It'll be good to see old Krumpholz again,' said Schuppanzigh.

Wranitzky nodded. 'How is he? I haven't seen him for a long time.'

'Krumpholz?' said Ludwig. 'He came to see me about this boy. Fine pianist, apparently.'

'Why are you seeing him, Ludwig?' asked Schuppanzigh. 'You don't usually . . .'

'What's that, Schuppi?'

'Why did you agree to see him?' asked Schuppi again in a louder voice.

'To make the old man happy. To see a smile cross the face of the world's greatest exponent of that delightful but obscure instrument of music, *il mandolin*.'

Ludwig drank from the glass and smiled at his friends. It was a long time since he had felt so buoyant, so optimistic. It had to do with his hearing, with the fact that his friends were in the room, talking to him, and there appeared to be nothing wrong. God bless Nanette, he thought to himself. Only she has the power to raise me from my melancholy and lift my spirits.

Schuppanzigh stood quickly at the knock and opened the door. Wenzel Krumpholz, only a little above fifty years of age but appearing much older because of his stooped shoulders, entered, his arm on the shoulder of a small, dark-haired boy.

'Krump-Krump-Krumpholz, my old friend,' said Ludwig. 'Help yourself to wine. Young man, you remind me of a boy I taught in Bonn.'

'Sir?'

'Ries, his name was. Ferdinand Ries. We called him Ferdi. His father was a violinist, leader of the Electoral orchestra. He taught me violin, until I had the good sense to leave the playing to others. You've got the same dark curly hair.'

'You taught him, sir?'

'What, boy? Come nearer and speak louder.' Ludwig saw the boy's eyes take in the cotton in his ears. Nothing to worry about, thought Ludwig. Boys' voices are always softer anyway.

'You taught him, sir?'

'I did. Yes, I did. A fine pianist. He's older than you. How old are you?'

'Just ten, sir.'

'Ten? Well, I'd say Ferdi's about seven or eight years older than you. Now, tell me your name.'

'Czerny, sir. Carl Czerny. My father says you're to give me lessons.'

There was laughter from Schuppanzigh and Wranitzky. Ludwig looked round at them enquiringly.

Schuppanzigh said in a firm voice, 'He says his father is hoping you will give him lessons, Ludwig.'

Ludwig looked back at the boy. 'Czernsky, did you say?'

'Czerny, sir.'

'Well, Czernskoy, Czernovich, Czernevsky. Come to the piano right away. Schuppi, more wine. Here, boy, look at this. Herr Streicher's finest. Strong. See? Good tone. Listen.' He sat and played some runs. 'Now, play something for us.'

Ludwig turned back to his friends and took the glass Schuppanzigh held towards him. 'Reminds me of Ferdi,' he said to no one in particular. 'Well, let's hear what he can do.'

Czerny looked nervously at the men, rubbing the palms of his hands on his trouser legs.

'Don't be nervous, Carl,' said Krumpholz with a kindly smile. 'You are among friends. Play the sonata by Herr Beethoven that you play so well. The one . . .'

Czerny shook his head slightly. 'I . . . I'll begin with Mozart.' He reached forward and played magisterial chords.

'No, no, not the introduction,' said Ludwig immediately. 'Play the piano part.'

A strange feeling came over Ludwig as the boy played the delicate runs that opened one of the C major piano concertos by Mozart. The words he had just uttered resonated in his head, though not with his own voice but that of his great predecessor Wolfgang Mozart. He felt suddenly that he was back in his youth. He remembered clearly how he had played for Mozart, how Mozart had told him to compose simple themes. But what else had he said? So often he had tried to remember, but he could not. Sometimes he wondered if the meeting really had happened. Had he really played for the great man?

Yes, he had. He had played for Mozart, the god of music, the finest composer who had ever lived. Greater even than Bach and Handel. And Mozart had been impressed and agreed to teach him.

Now he, Ludwig, was listening to a young boy play, a nervous young boy, just as Mozart had listened to him. And without realising it he had echoed Mozart's words. Why had that happened?

Because we are both musicians, Ludwig said to himself. Another flash of memory shot through his mind. *Mozart had said it.* 'We are musicians, you and I.' For the first time he remembered it clearly. Mozart's words.

Wolfgang Mozart, Ludwig thought to himself. I wear your mantle. I am the protector and defender of our great art. I will not fail you.

He stood, enjoying the slight light-headedness the wine induced in his brain. He moved his chair and put it to Czerny's left. The boy continued playing. Ludwig reached his left hand forward and began playing the orchestral accompaniment in the bass register.

Czerny, emboldened, played as if inspired. Ludwig judged the accompaniment perfectly, not playing it too loudly and stripping it down to its essentials. When the moment came for the piano cadenza he moved away, lifted his chair and carried it back to its original place.

At the end of the cadenza Ludwig applauded. 'Bravo! Stop there. Very fine. Very fine indeed.' He turned to his friends and noted that they were all smiling and applauding with him.

The dullness in his ears seemed to increase the moment the music stopped, as if filling a void. But almost immediately the pleasant sensation of the wine seemed to subdue it. He heard Krumpholz's voice.

'Play the sonata by the master here, Carl. The one you played for me earlier today.'

Ludwig saw the nervous look on Czerny's face. He waved his arm expansively. 'Do not be nervous, young man. After Mozart comes Beethoven. What will you play for me?'

'Your Grande Sonate, sir. The one that is called the Pathétique. With your permission, sir.'

'What? Say it louder.'

Schuppanzigh, who was nearest to Ludwig, spoke. 'The Pathétique Sonata, Ludwig. The Sonata in C minor.'

Ludwig nodded, settled back in his chair and drank more wine. He was enjoying the occasion. This boy was a remarkable pianist and it gave him comfort to know it. He was not sure why. Maybe he should have felt the reverse. Jealousy, perhaps. But no; to discover another musician was reassuring, exciting. Would this boy become great? Ludwig did not know. But as he listened now to those great C minor chords which opened the sonata he knew the boy possessed extraordinary talent.

He lacked the power in his hands, of course. The chords needed more weight. That would come. But the drama Ludwig had intended was there. Czerny, his head stretched forward, played the enormous two-and-a-half-octave chromatic run that led into the first main subject. There was not a note out of place.

Ludwig smiled at the way Czerny changed pace. He liked that. Too many pianists set a pace at the beginning and stuck to it rigidly, as if they were counting their way through every bar. That was not the way music should be played. Hummel played like that, Ludwig thought mischievously. A fine pianist, but too ordered. Predictable, that was the word.

Carl Czerny straightened his back as he played the lyrical Adagio Cantabile.

'Yes,' Ludwig called out. 'Let it sing. Let it sing. From your heart, not your head.' He held out his glass for Schuppanzigh to refill.

The Rondo Czerny played with exactly the delicacy of touch it required. Ludwig sat back and listened to his music. The piano sonata, he thought. A single voice, yet many voices. The piano.

There was no other instrument that could do what it could do. My instrument. Already they call me a master. But I am not. I will never be the master of the piano. It is too great an instrument for any man to master. And when any man believes he has done so, that is when he will be proved wrong.

I am its servant and I will serve it, compose for it and play my compositions. But I will never consider myself greater than it.

Czerny played the final descending *fortissimo* scale and the chord of C minor which ended the work. Ludwig led the applause.

He stood, steadying himself on the chair. The wine had now made him feel quite intoxicated, but in a pleasurable way.

'My boy, you are a fine pianist. Come, sit down with us here. Schuppi, can we give him some wine?'

Schuppi smiled. 'I will get him a drink from the cupboard. A lemon drink, Carl?'

Ludwig looked at the boy as he stood. His body seemed to shrink. At the piano his small body seemed to have power. His face had a determination that could be seen in the way his cheek muscles were set. Now, as he walked to his chair, he was like any other ten-year-old boy again, small, shy and unsure of himself.

He sat in his chair and looked down at his hands, saying nothing.

'Krump-Krump, you did not deceive me about your young protégé here. I will teach him. Give him lessons. Does that please you, Czernsky? Mmh?'

'Yes, sir. Thank you.'

'Czerny,' said Schuppanzigh distinctly as he handed the boy his drink. 'Carl. Why do you not call him Carl, Ludwig?'

'What? Carl? Is he here? My damned brother?'

Schuppanzigh smiled and looked at Wranitzky, who said, 'You can call him Carl, Ludwig. That is his name.'

The wine was now causing Ludwig's head to spin. He was not sure who was talking. He could hear voices, but he could not make out the words. He looked from one face to another.

Carl Czerny had a concerned look on his face. He spoke in a loud voice, the force he put into it giving it a shrill edge. Ludwig heard it clearly.

'Are you deaf, sir? Is that why you have those pieces of cotton in your ears?'

Chapter 2

Stephan von Breuning climbed the steps to the top of the Bastion and walked over to the news vendor to buy a copy of the *Wiener Zeitung*. He moved to the edge of the rampart and stood for a moment to read the front page, and his heart sank.

He knew from his colleagues in the war office the broad outline of what had happened. By the Treaty of Lunéville Austria had made peace with France. An end to the fighting – at last. But at what a cost. Humiliation for the seat of the empire at the hands of a Corsican soldier. Austria had given up Belgium and Luxembourg, all of northern Italy except Venice, and – Stephan could barely bring himself to read it – Germany up to the west bank of the Rhine.

Bonn was now formally occupied by the French. He feared for his family. As if the war was not enough of a strain, his youngest brother Lenz had died at a tragically early age. He hoped his mother was bearing up. At least Eleonore was there to comfort her, as long as she and Wegeler had not yet left for Koblenz. He decided to write to Wegeler immediately for news. If the letter was able to get through.

He hurried along the Herrengasse and turned into the Kohlmarkt. He had arranged to meet Nikolaus Zmeskall in Milani's coffee house opposite Artaria's. He had been working long hours every day in the war office and not seen his friends for some time. He wanted news of them – especially Ludwig.

'The last I heard there was concern about his health. What exactly was wrong?'

'There's seems to be something the matter with his ears,' said Zmeskall. 'I don't know how serious it is, but he's wearing cotton in them and it's yellow. Soaked in oil, I think. The doctor told him to do it.'

'Is it working?'

'Difficult to say. He seems not to hear very well, always asking you to repeat yourself. But if you had cotton in your ears, you might not hear very well either! Have you noticed anything?'

Stephan thought for a moment, his jaws clenched. Then he said, 'He told me some time ago he was having trouble with his hearing.'

Nikolaus nodded. 'I guessed as much. In fact we all guessed as much. Schuppanzigh noticed it too. But perhaps it's not serious.'

'No, and if he's wearing cotton in his ears he can't be trying to hide it.'

'He was at first; I think he really thought no one would notice. But then apparently a young musician he's taking on as a student saw it and asked him outright if he was going deaf.'

'My God! How did Ludwig react?'

'I wasn't there. Schuppi said, though, he took it surprisingly well. I think, in a funny way, it's more of a relief not to have to try to hide it.'

'Yes, I see that. How is it affecting his work?'

Nikolaus took a sip of his coffee and replied enthusiastically. 'Well, the extraordinary thing is, he seems to be composing more than ever. Have you heard about the Prometheus ballet?'

'No.'

'Vigano, Salvatore Vigano, the ballet master at the Hofburg, asked him to compose the music for a ballet, *The Creatures of Prometheus*. None of us thought he'd accept, particularly given Vigano's reputation.'

'What do you mean?'

Nikolaus leaned across the table and lowered his voice. 'His wife is rather ... rather ... attractive, shall we say. She's Spanish. Dark and fiery and a reputation to match. She's a dancer and she danced in one of his productions. He made her wear a flesh-coloured tunic. *And nothing else*. She appeared to be totally naked. She did not try to hide anything. In fact she flaunted herself.'

'That wouldn't please Ludwig. We all know how he is about things like that.'

'That's right. But he accepted the commission. I gather it's going very well. Vigano's pleased. It's going to open at the Mehlgrube very soon. Or maybe it's the Kärntnertor theatre. I can't remember.'

'Is Vigano paying him well?'

'I'm not sure what the arrangement is but I don't think he's paying him in advance. It'll be a share of the receipts. I gather Carl tried to interfere. He wanted to do the negotiations in return for a percentage but Ludwig apparently told him to mind his own business.'

'Good. I shouldn't say it, but Carl causes problems wherever he goes. Whatever he does. You know he's working in the finance department in the Hofburg? It's a lowly job, cashier I think. But already he's making enemies. The less he has to do with Ludwig's affairs, the better.'

'I agree. Anyway the Prometheus piece isn't the only thing Ludwig is working on. Schuppi told me he composed a piece especially for him for solo voices – male voices – and full chorus. You will never imagine what it's called.'

Stephan shook his head. 'Something sacred? I know he once—'

'Not exactly. It's called "In Praise of the Fat One".'

Both men laughed out loud.

'But also,' Nikolaus continued, 'he's composed a sonata for violin and piano that Schuppi says is extraordinarily beautiful. He played it with Ludwig and could not believe how calm and . . . simply beautiful it is. Apparently. Hard to believe a man of Ludwig's temperament – especially with his hearing problem – could compose something so . . . serene. Yes, that's the word Schuppi used. Serene.'

'I must ask him to play it for me.'

'Yes. Schuppi said that he played it with Ludwig for the first time with the sun streaming through the window, the smell of blossom in the air, and it should therefore be called the Spring Sonata.'

'Sun streaming in? In the Tiefer Graben?'

'No, no. He's moved. Didn't you know? I'm sorry. I should have told you. He's taken rooms on the Wasserkunstbastei. Three floors up. Windows at both ends. Magnificent views. Gets the sun most of the day.'

Stephan shook his head slowly. 'What a restless man he is. He was like that as a boy, you know. Not moving, obviously, but never seeming able to settle. Never satisfied. He's been in Vienna, what, not ten years yet, and I've lost count of the number of times he's moved.'

'Yes, well, I hope he'll settle this time. Though I have to tell you, it may not last.'

'Why?' asked Stephan with concern in his voice.

'He's composing furiously, as I said. He's even asked me for more quills. I get them for him from the Chancellery. The trouble is, he often composes in the middle of the night. Three o'clock in the morning. Four o'clock, even. His neighbours are not exactly happy with the situation. He doesn't just play the piano, apparently, he bangs on the wall to keep time.'

Stephan could not resist a smile. 'I can just picture him doing that. But how can we stop him? He won't take any notice of us, I know that.'

'At the moment it's all right. He's really quite famous now. The neighbours are rather proud to have him in the building. Let's hope it remains that way.'

'Yes. Let's hope.'

Ludwig opened the letter and smiled with satisfaction as he read it. It was from the poet Friedrich von Matthisson in Stuttgart.

Most honoured sir!

My lyric fantasies have been blessed with the attention of many composers, to the great enhancement of my humble words. But none, sir, has so thrown the text into the shade as you with the music you have written to accompany my 'Adelaïde'.

I can only hope, sir, that this will not be the last time that you will cast the genius of your music towards my verse.

I am your sincere admirer as you profess yourself to be mine.

Fried. v. Matthisson

He folded the single sheet and tossed it on to the table. He sat at the piano and began playing. He smiled at the rough sound of his own voice in his head. A-de-la-ï-de, A-de-la-ï-de. He remembered the first time he had read the verse. It was in Bonn. He returned to it in Vienna, at a time when Magdalena Willmann had been in his thoughts.

He had completed the setting two or three years ago and Artaria had published it. It was an instant success in Vienna, the staple of many a soirée.

He had heard it sung once or twice himself, and always smiled as the singer failed to negotiate the small pitfalls he had written in, the sudden twists, the unexpected key changes. Once he had heard Leni herself sing it, her Italian husband accompanying her on the piano. How beautifully she had executed it. At the difficult passages she had slowed her voice almost imperceptibly, forcing the pianist to slow with her. That was the way! It was for the singer to lead the accompanist, not the other way round.

In a sudden inspiration he went to the table and wrote a short note to Stephan Breuning. There had been a series of concerts held recently – Ludwig, Leni Willmann, even Haydn had taken part – to raise money for the soldiers wounded at the Battle of Hohenlinden.

Why not hold another, of just his own music? He had begun work on two new compositions, a quintet for strings – two violins, two violas and a cello – and a piano sonata. Why the unusual combination of instruments for the quintet? Because he was not aware that it had been used before, even by Mozart, and when he had mentioned it to Schuppanzigh, the violinist had replied that the result would be, as he put it, 'tonal confusion'.

Ludwig had written the first movement in the key of C quickly and without difficulty – a flowing Allegro with an opening almost in unison. But – even to his own surprise – he had soon introduced some radical key changes. Instead of progressing in the traditional way to the dominant, G, he had taken the music a step higher to A. The momentum that produced! But how the musicians would complain, he knew. Let them complain, just as they had done over the opening to his First Symphony.

He had realised after that that the quintet would be a more substantial work than he had at first intended, so he put it aside. Not so the piano sonata. He had chosen the key of D, perhaps the brightest key of all. The initial inspiration had come on a beautiful sunny evening as the light streamed into his new apartment. The scene was almost pastoral, and when he had played the opening movement to Schuppanzigh and Zmeskall, the Hungarian had remarked how it made him think, wistfully, of his homeland and the pastoral themes of his youth.

Would Prince Lobkowitz make his concert room available? Ludwig wrote to Stephan. He would play his new piano sonata and improvise on the piano as well. Schuppanzigh, he was sure, would gather his string players and perform one, or even two, of the set of six string quartets which were about to be published by the firm of T. Mollo (how angry Carl had been at being excluded from the negotiations!). And, to crown the evening, let Magdalena Willmann – Magdalena Galvani, he must get used to her new name – sing 'Adelaïde' to his accompaniment on the piano.

Yes, he thought to himself, an excellent idea. He folded the letter and rang for the servant. How his fortunes had changed since he moved into this apartment on the Wasserkunstbastei. Almost immediately the Italian Vigano had presented him with a commission for a ballet; he was aware his friends had been surprised when he had accepted, but if they knew him better, they would not have been.

The Italian's timing had been fortuitous, coming so soon after the cool response to his benefit concert. He thought of his First Symphony. No one really understood how hard he had worked to bring it to fruition. To what end? What had the *Allgemeine Musikalische Zeitung* said? Ludwig knew it off by heart:

> . . . One of Beethoven's symphonies was performed in which there is considerable art, novelty and a wealth of ideas. The only flaw was that the wind instruments were used too much, so that there was more harmony than orchestral music as a whole.

The only flaw? His music did not contain flaws. He did not write flaws. One day everyone would realise that, including critics. What did they know of music anyway? *Really* know? Nothing. Nothing!

He rang for the servant again, stepping out into the corridor and shaking the bell louder, ignoring the jarring effect it had on his ears.

He crossed to the smaller table alongside the window, where several sheets of manuscript were strewn. Sixteen separate pieces, as well as an overture and introduction. His music for Vigano's ballet, *The Creatures of Prometheus*. And what a suitable subject, Ludwig had thought right from the beginning. Not frivolous, as he had to admit so many of even Mozart's chosen subjects were. This was noble, heroic. The hero Prometheus, elevated by his selfless behaviour to take his place among the gods.

It was perfect in every respect. His friends might wonder why he had accepted the commission; he was in no doubt.

He sifted through the sheets until he found the one on top

of which he had written 'Finale'. That was all there remained to write, and he knew – he had known for some time – where he wanted the theme to come from.

Ludwig looked at the twinkling lights coming from the buildings of the other side of the Glacis. He thought of Daniel Steibelt. What an odious, despicable, pretentious and arrogant man. Worst of all, he called himself a musician. And a composer! Ludwig smiled to himself. Take cover, here comes a storm! A Steibelt storm, unlike any you have seen or heard. The man was a charlatan, and Ludwig had exposed him for what he was.

But ... but ... Ludwig sat at the piano. E flat, B flat, B flat, E flat. And then ... and then ... Da–daaa–da–daaa, da–daaa–da–daaa, the soaring theme above it which Ludwig had invented that moment and improvised upon.

He played the theme again, and again. This time, instead of varying it, he played on ... Da–daaa–da–daaa, da–daaa–da–daaa, then up to three notes repeated, da–da–da, and down again in triplet runs, da–da–da, da–da–da, and sustained to the end, daaa–da.

He smiled with satisfaction. There was his theme. He repeated it. Now a response to it. A run up the scale to three repeated notes again; up the scale again to a sustained note, up a further semitone to launch into four bars of coda, returning to the keynote.

The theme and its response. He smiled and played it again. Twenty-four bars in all. The opening to the finale of *Prometheus*.

He stood up from the piano and walked across to the table. As he did so, he let out a gasp of fright and his stomach turned over. A shadowy figure was standing in the doorway.

'What ... ? Who ... ?'

Ludwig saw the man's facial muscles move as he spoke, but he could hear nothing. The sounds of the music were still vibrating in his head.

'What? Speak up. Who in God's name ... ?'

Ludwig peered at the man and realised it was his servant. Angry at the interruption, he pulled the cotton out of his ears and threw the pieces down on the table. Immediately there was a harshness in his ears, a rawness.

The servant spoke again, but the words hurt Ludwig's ears and he covered them with his hands. Suddenly he remembered why the servant was there. What had taken the wretched man so long?

'At last. Here. This letter. Take it—'

'Sir!' The servant was standing with his hands on his hips. He spoke in a loud voice. 'It is three o'clock in the morning. I am not taking anything anywhere. You must not ring for me in the middle of the night. And another thing. You must stop playing that instrument of yours. People are trying to sleep. Do you understand?'

Ludwig winced as the force of the servant's voice hit his ears. He had not heard every word but he had understood what the servant meant.

'Three o'clock? In the night? Morning. It cannot be. I . . . It cannot be . . .'

'It is, sir. And I will ask you to respect other people's wishes and let them sleep. And that includes me, sir.'

The servant turned on his heels and left the room, closing the door softly behind him.

Ludwig's ears were ringing with pain. The music he had played was still vibrating in his head, mingled with the harsh edge of the servant's voice. He clasped his hands to his ears and sank into a chair, his elbows resting on the table.

God, what is happening to me? he thought. Am I truly going deaf? If I am . . . if it is true . . . I am finished.

Chapter 3

'Congratulations on *Prometheus*, Ludwig,' said Stephan Breuning as the two of them walked up from St Stephansdom along the Haarmarkt.

Ludwig nodded and smiled. 'More performances are planned. Braun is angry that Vigano put it on at the Kärntnertor and then the Mehlgrube and not one of the court theatres. Hah! Serves him right. He's so pompous. And it's made more money than it would have done at the Burgtheater or one of the Redoutensaals in the Hofburg.'

'I'm pleased for you. And the music is wonderful. Better, I might say, than the ballet. Those movements and poses. I find them rather . . . rather . . . I don't know . . . contrived.'

'The ballet will be forgotten, but not the music. Beethoven's music.'

'Where would you like to have lunch, Ludwig? What about the fish restaurant in the Rotenturmgasse? It's very near to where Leni lives, so it won't be far to walk afterwards. And it's Friday; the fish is always good on Friday.'

Ludwig nodded.

Over lunch Stephan decided to broach a subject he knew Ludwig would not want to talk about. But he needed to know the situation. He decided to lead up to it gently.

'How are your new lodgings? Zmeskall says you like them.'

'I'm happy there. So much light. I can breathe.'

'I must come and see them.'

'Only the neighbours are fools. And the servant. Damned man comes knocking on the door at all hours. The neighbours have complained about the noise.'

Stephan smiled. 'Maybe you shouldn't play the piano in the middle of the night. By the way, I see you've stopped putting cotton in your ears. A good sign, I hope.'

'Damned doctors. Quacks, with quack remedies. All it did was cover my clothes with almond oil. And my pillow.'

'But your fears about . . . You're obviously hearing very well. Normally, in fact.'

Ludwig's face fell. 'That's not the case, Steffen. It's not bad all the time. Now it's bearable, though if people in here talk a bit louder I will find it hard. Or if someone suddenly laughs out loud, or shouts, it will cut into my head. The worst . . . the worst is after I play music, or hear it. Once the music stops, there's a . . . a . . . void in my head. Something has to fill it, and it's usually a rushing sound. That's not so bad, but it can also be a sharp whistle, and my head throbs.'

Stephan said nothing.

'Sometimes it is worst at night, when there are no other sounds. Then all I hear are the sounds in my head. That is why I often work at night.'

'Have you noticed it getting worse?' Stephan said, unconsciously moving his lips more distinctly and speaking clearly.

'That's the most upsetting part. It's definitely getting worse, not better.'

The two men ate in silence. Stephan's face suddenly brightened.

'Ludwig, let me write to Franz about it. He's still in Bonn. You know he's professor of medicine at the university now. Dean. He's the most respected medical man in the city. I'm sure he'd be able to help.'

Ludwig shrugged. 'But tell him to keep his counsel. I don't want . . .'

'Of course. Of course.'

They continued eating and Stephan decided enough had been said on the subject.

After the meal, as they walked the short distance to Magdalena Willmann's house, Stephan said, 'It was a nice idea of yours to give a charity soirée with Leni, but I think you'll see rather soon why it was not possible. By the way, there was another reason. Prince Lobkowitz is in Prague at the moment, so his concert room is not available. And I didn't think you would want anywhere smaller.'

Ludwig shook his head. 'There have been enough charity concerts. Now it is time to earn money from my music.'

The servant admitted them and showed them up an elegant staircase to the first floor. There, he knocked on a set of double doors, opened them without waiting for a response, and announced, 'Your guests, madame.'

'Dear Leni,' said Stephan. 'No, no, do not get up. Stay exactly where you are. How well you look. Radiant, if I might say so.'

He walked over to the large easy chair, took Leni's hand and kissed it.

'And dear Ludwig,' said Leni. 'How good to see you.'

Ludwig looked at Leni, whom he had first met all those years ago. How he had loved her! How he had wanted her! But it was not to be. He bore her no ill will. It would have been wrong, he knew it. She had seen it too.

He too kissed Leni's proffered hand, and he and Stephan sat down. Leni rang a small bell on a side table and asked the servant to bring coffee and cake.

'Doesn't Leni look well, Ludwig?'

Ludwig looked at Leni's face, the cheeks flushed pink. He looked at her hands, folded across her extended stomach.

'I am pleased for you and your husband, Leni,' he said. 'I give you my congratulations. When . . . ? When . . . ?'

'I feel as if it could be any minute. But the doctor says at least a month, maybe six weeks. It is very tiring. I shall be pleased when it is over, and God willing Luigi and I will be proud parents.'

'Is Luigi here this afternoon?' asked Stephan.

'Unfortunately he could not be. But he asks me to give you his regards.'

'Do give ours to him.'

When the servant returned, Leni poured some coffee for Stephan and Ludwig, and the servant put the cups on small tables by each of them, together with a slice of chocolate cake.

'Ah, you are spoiling us, Leni. I fear we are eating better – and I might say more comfortably – than our poor friends and families in Bonn.'

Leni shook her head. 'Isn't it sad? So sad. How long will it last, do you think?'

Steffen said, 'Until this tyrant is defeated once and for all and Europe can return to normal. He must be defeated, that is the only solution.'

'More bloodshed,' said Leni. 'Men must die because of one man's ambitions. Are your family all right, Steffen? What news of your dear mother?'

'She's well, thank you. I received a letter from Wegeler. The French are billeted outside Bonn, and apparently behaving properly. So our house is all right. But the menfolk stay in at night, he says. The Zehrgarten on the Marktplatz has only French soldiers in it in the evening. Hard to believe, isn't it?'

'Let's talk of nicer matters,' said Leni. 'Ludwig, Stephan told me of your wonderful idea for a charity concert. I'm so sorry I can't . . . As you can see, I'm . . .'

Ludwig smiled and nodded. 'I understand, Leni. There was a problem anyway. Prince Lobkowitz is away. I had the idea because I received a letter from Matthisson the poet. The author of "Adelaïde".'

'Oh, Ludwig, it is such a beautiful song. Such tender words, and you have made them so . . . so . . . Your music is so . . .'

Stephan interrupted, 'Well, I have to make a guilty confession. Ludwig, Leni, I have not heard the song. I know you have sung it before an audience, Leni. I have heard talk of how beautiful it is. But I have never heard it.'

'Then you shall hear it, Stephan. Right now. Ludwig, will you accompany me?'

Ludwig nodded vigorously. 'But, Leni, are you sure? Can you . . . ?'

'I shall certainly try. Here, Stephan, just give me your hand.'

With an effort Leni stood, wincing slightly as her legs took the weight of her body. 'There, just let me get my balance. That's better. Now, would you walk me to the piano, Steffen? Thank you.'

Ludwig sat at the piano and looked at the keys, rubbing the palms of his hands on his thighs. He looked up at Leni, who stood with one arm supporting herself on the piano, the other around and slightly underneath her stomach. She smiled at him and nodded.

Ludwig played the gentle introduction of the song, then Leni's voice – a clear, crystal soprano with a rapid and perfectly pitched *vibrato* – began singing.

> Lonely do I wander in the green grassy glade,
> Bathed in the magical light of your love
> That filters through every trembling blade,
> Adelaïde!

In the glint of the tide, in the shimmering snow,
In the golden-hued clouds at the end of the day,
E'en in the stars does your beauteous face glow,
Adelaïde!

And on my grave let a purple flower grow
Nurtured by the ashes of my heart,
And let each single leaf my trembling love show,
Adelaïde! Adelaïde!

Ludwig kept his fingers on the keys as the final sounds died away. He shut his eyes, bracing himself for the noises he knew would fill the void. He heard voices but could not distinguish the words. The sound of rushing, whooshing filled his head, followed, as he knew it would be, by a sharp whistle and the throb of pain.

He wanted to stretch his hands forward again and play more music. Speak his language. Tell Stephan and Leni what it was like, in musical notes not words. How when he played his music his head was clear, alive, alert. And how when he stopped . . .

He felt a hand on his shoulder.

'That was beautiful, Ludwig,' said Stephan close to his ear. 'Come and sit down. I'll help Leni.'

Mercifully Ludwig felt the pain in his head begin to subside, more quickly than usual. He knew it was because he did not have to hide it, pretend there was nothing wrong. Stephan knew and now Leni would know. But they were friends. They would protect him.

Ludwig wanted to tell Leni how beautifully she had sung. But he did not know what words to use. He looked at her and smiled. 'It was . . . was . . .'

'Dear Ludwig, you play so beautifully. I had almost forgotten how beautifully. And how do you keep all that music in your head?'

Stephan laughed. 'Leni is right, Ludwig. You have a touch on the keys that . . . that . . . to put it frankly, one does not expect. I have heard people remark that they are not surprised when you play loudly and dramatically, but they do not expect to hear such gentle music from you.'

'Hah! Steibelt's storm. Anyone can play it. Just as with words. It is easy to get angry and shout. Not so easy to talk of . . . love.'

Leni was mopping her brow with a lace handkerchief. Suddenly she looked up. 'Did I tell you, I heard recently from my friend Toni? You know, Antonie Birkenstock. Brentano now. Do you remember, Ludwig, you met her at that wonderful performance you gave at Jahn's in the Himmelpfortgasse?'

Ludwig nodded.

'How is she?' asked Stephan. 'I have heard you talk about her so often but I never met her. She left Vienna before I arrived.'

'She is well. Married now to Franz Brentano and living in Frankfurt. But it has not all been happiness for her.'

'Oh dear, what happened?'

'She gave birth to a daughter two years ago, Mathilde Josefe. But the poor soul died before her first birthday. Toni was distraught. She so wanted to come to Vienna to see her old friends and her old house, but Franz said she was needed in Frankfurt. But there is some good news. She now has a healthy son, Georg Franz. He was born at the beginning of the year.'

'And he is in good health?'

'From her letters it seems so. Apparently, he already has a voice with the strength of one much older. Poor Toni, I don't believe she is getting much sleep.'

'I am afraid, dear Leni, that is a condition you will yourself soon have to become accustomed to!' said Stephan, with a kindly smile on his face.

Ludwig felt a tug in the pit of his stomach as he read Franz Wegeler's letter. All the familiar names . . . Helene von Breuning, Eleonore – 'my dear Lorchen', as Wegeler called her – old Father Ries, Reicha, Romberg . . .

A sudden wave of nostalgia swept over him as he recalled his childhood friends. It was so long since he'd seen many of them. He remembered how Romberg had passed through Vienna . . . how long ago was it? Five years? Ludwig had been away on tour but he had seen Romberg on his return to Vienna. They had even played a recital together.

Five years. How different his life was then. He had had no problems with his ears. How blissful it must have been, to be able to hear everything anyone said, in company or alone, without difficulty. Was he really ever like that? Had he once really had no difficulty in hearing?

He realised now that his hearing was beginning to dominate

his life. He was dividing his life into before and after his problem started: his childhood and youth when he could hear; his adulthood when he could not.

He clenched his fists and strode around his room. He must not let his hearing dominate his life in this way. He was in the hands of a doctor, one of the most respected in Vienna. Maybe the treatment Doktor Vering had given him would work. Nanette was right. He must persevere, that was all.

He returned to Wegeler's letter. Stephan had told him about Ludwig's hearing. 'Tell me more about the symptoms,' Wegeler wrote. 'It is my opinion that the problem is very unlikely to be anything worse than a surfeit of earwax.'

A burst of optimism shot through Ludwig. My good old friend Wegeler, he thought. Professor Wegeler. The most respected doctor in Bonn. With both him and Vering involved, it was only a matter of time, surely . . .

'And for your colic and stomach I recommend that you should apply herb extract to your belly. Your brother the pharmacist will make up the correct mixture for you, I am sure.'

My brother the pharmacist, thought Ludwig with contempt. Nikola. Johann. How can I ask him for help? He will not even speak to me if I use his rightful name, the name he was christened with.

The last paragraph of Wegeler's letter came as such a surprise to Ludwig that he had to read it twice.

> . . . Father Ries tells me his son Ferdinand, to whom you imparted your love of music, has been trying to make a living as a pianist in Munich and wishes to come to Vienna, where he would of course renew his friendship with you. Ries asks what you consider his prospects might be for earning a living as a teacher of the piano. His skills at that instrument have progressed beyond anything his father dared hope . . .

Ludwig tried to suppress the irritation he felt. He knew it was an unworthy sentiment, but the fact was, he did not wish the encumbrance of a young man whom he had known in Bonn, particularly a musician. Ferdinand Ries was probably not yet twenty years of age. He would be heavily dependent on Ludwig, he would want more lessons, seek advice. And Ludwig knew he could not turn him away. Old Father Ries had been so kind to him when his mother had died, he would be obliged to help Ferdinand. And the reality was that there were so many musicians in Vienna, so many players trying to earn a living, that Ferdinand would not find it easy.

Ludwig re-read Wegeler's letter. How it made him long for his homeland. To return to the Rhineland again, see the great river meandering past his home town, stroll along its bank, walk in the Siebengebirge hills, climb the Drachenfels . . .

He crossed to the window and looked out over the Bastion. It was early evening and the sky was a beautiful blue. The sun was setting on the other side of the city, which caused the wall and the buildings beyond to throw deep shadows. He saw groups of people standing and talking, their arms waving in gesticulation. Ordinary people, exchanging pleasantries, news, gossip.

Why am I not like them? Why can I not go down on to the Glacis and stand and talk with other people? Ordinary, unimportant – trivial, even – conversations? But I cannot. That is not my purpose in life. God gave me a gift, a divine gift.

The whooshing came into his ears as if by some preordained command. He thought of his great gift – had God sent him this to remind him he was only mortal? The Lord giveth and the Lord taketh away. Was that not what the Bible said?

He turned towards the table alongside the wall. He poured himself a glass of red wine, took it to the table in the centre of the room and sat down. He pulled a piece of paper towards him, dipped the quill in ink and began to write to his old friend Franz Wegeler.

. . . How I long for my fatherland, the beautiful country where I first opened my eyes to the light, which still appears as clearly before me as when I left you. In short, I shall look upon the day when I can see you again and greet Father Rhine as one of the happiest moments in my life . . .

He drank some wine and considered that this was the first letter he had written to Wegeler for years – at least three or four. But his life seemed to have become so busy.

After writing words of apology he explained to Wegeler how his compositions were now earning him money, that Prince Lichnowsky had settled an annuity of six hundred florins on him, and that he had given concerts and expected to give more.

> . . . If it were not for that jealous demon, my wretched
> health . . .

There it was, he thought, that familiar sound in his head,
to remind him of his debility, his fallibility. And was that
the beginnings of the throbbing pain, that would soon be
accompanied by the high-pitched whistle?

He poured himself more wine. He had to tell Wegeler about
it. He had to have help.

> . . . For the last three years my hearing has become weaker
> and weaker . . . My ears continue to hum and buzz day
> and night. I must confess that I lead a miserable life . . .

He gulped another mouthful of wine, gripped the quill firmly
in his hand and wrote:

> I am deaf

He looked at the words. *I am deaf.* He felt a sudden light-
headedness, as if a weight had been lifted from his shoulders.
I am deaf.

He stood, swaying slightly and enjoying the numbness in his
head induced by the wine. I am deaf. *I am deaf.* So what? Does
it matter? Look at the wounded from Hohenlinden, men with
one arm or no legs. Blind men. Deaf men, their ear drums
blown away by exploding shells.

But I am a deaf musician. Can a more tragic fate befall a
musician? He sat and took up the quill again.

> . . . It is surprising some people have never noticed my
> deafness, but since I have always been liable to fits of
> absent-mindedness, they attribute my hearing problem to
> that. Sometimes I can barely hear a person who speaks
> softly. I can hear sounds, but cannot make out the words.
> But if anyone shouts I cannot bear it. Heaven alone knows
> what is to become of me . . . Already I have often cursed
> my Creator and my existence . . .

He threw down the quill and drank more wine. What if Wegeler
could not help him? It did not bear thinking about.

He would write no more of his deafness. His *deafness* . . . He would not be frightened of the word again.

He wrote some words about Steffen and how they met nearly every day. How nostalgic it made him, to be writing to Wegeler about Stephan. Oh, those far-off days in Bonn. He stood, steadying himself on the back of the chair, and walked towards the piano.

What was missing? What was it he wanted to see but was not there? He sat at the piano and played some chords, gently. What had he loved most about his youth?

What he had loved most was so long ago he could remember only tiny fragments. No coherent memory, just impressions. He had been little more than an infant, but the impressions were strong. Even now as he sat at the piano, allowing his fingers to roam aimless over the keys, they flooded over him.

The deep, resonant voice, the familiar aroma. The feel of the strong hand clasping his. The pride as he pulled his little shoulders back, walking alongside the giant of a man. His grandfather, the Kapellmeister.

He wanted him with him now. He wanted him with him for the rest of his life.

. . . Send me my grandfather's portrait. Send it by the first available mail coach. Do this as swiftly as possible, dear Wegeler . . .

As soon as it arrived he would hang it on the wall above the piano, so that whenever he sat at the keyboard he would be under the eye of the man he had loved more dearly than anyone in the world. He had understood his grandfather and his grandfather had seen – foreseen – what the future would hold for him.

He closed his eyes tightly and he could feel the thick, coarse hair that he stroked as his grandfather lay dead. How he had shaken him but his grandfather had not moved. He had gone, left him. From that moment Ludwig was on his own.

He felt the tears well up, but he fought them back. He clenched his fists. If he was to be alone, so be it. Alone to compose his music. But he would not be totally alone; his beloved grandfather would be with him always.

He did not need anybody else. He did not want anybody else. In a moment of petulance he snatched up the pen again.

. . . As for Ries, to whom I send cordial greetings, I think his son could make his fortune more easily in Paris than in Vienna.

He looked at the words. He underlined Paris and Vienna. A few final words of farewell to Wegeler and he signed the letter. Just Beethoven. He regretted it the moment he had written it. He should have signed it Ludwig. But no. He was a different man now. An artist recognised and respected by the cognoscenti of Vienna. A friend of the imperial royal family. He was Beethoven.

Chapter 4

At first Ludwig regretted agreeing to take the young Carl Czerny on as a pupil. He had always detested teaching; and now more than ever he wished to concentrate on composing. But he soon discovered that Czerny was a remarkable pianist. He was astounded at the way in which he seemed able to play scales, broken chords, arpeggios in perfect unison in both hands, never a note out of place.

The natural aversion Ludwig had developed to teaching was partly due to the fact that pupils always wanted to play pieces which would demonstrate their prowess. They wanted to be able to show off. When he insisted on the rudiments coming first it always met with wails of protest.

Carl Czerny was entirely different. He seemed to relish the mechanics of music-making. He seemed almost to prefer that to playing pieces. As a result Ludwig found, to his surprise, that for the first time he was enjoying teaching.

The enjoyment was enhanced by the fact that Czerny was an infrequent visitor. Because of his young age and the fact that he lived across the river in Leopoldstadt, his father insisted on accompanying him into the city, and his father only came into Vienna when he had a meeting to attend. These meetings were irregular and rare. Ludwig complained to the boy, telling him to remonstrate with his father, but secretly he was relieved not to have to teach too often.

Curiously his hearing did not seem to trouble him when he was teaching. He had stopped wearing the inconvenient and messy cotton in his ear, but Czerny had seen it and remarked on it at that first meeting, so Ludwig felt he had nothing to hide. The boy – with a child's instinct – accepted it without question, making sure he spoke clearly. He soon learned to let the music die down and wait a few seconds before speaking.

Ludwig appreciated his behaviour and soon grew to like him.

After a while he tried to give him some of his own sonatas to play. The boy was enthusiastic, immediately understanding the music in a way that Ludwig had not seen in adults. But his hands were too small and lacked the power to do justice to the music.

Ludwig found himself wishing Czerny were that little bit older and more experienced. He could teach him to play his sonatas exactly as he wanted them played. Not as Hummel, for instance, played them, lightly and without portent; or as he had heard amateurs like Prince Lichnowsky play them, subtly omitting passages that were too difficult.

One morning in the middle of summer, towards the end of a lesson, Czerny turned to Ludwig and pointed.

'Who's that man, sir?'

'That man, Carl? That's my grandfather. Kapellmeister Beethoven.'

'Why is he wearing a fur turban?'

'Do you know, I do not know the answer to that? I never asked him. He was a great musician, Carl. A fine singer.'

'And your father was a singer too, sir, wasn't he?'

'Yes. But his voice . . . he lost his voice. At the height of his career. He never . . . He might have been Kapellmeister otherwise.'

'Why did you not stay in Bonn and become Kapellmeister?'

Ludwig smiled. 'I was going to at one time. But . . . I needed to come to Vienna. It was where Mozart was. It is the home of music.'

'Sir, I hear someone at the door. Shall I open it?'

'What? The door. Was that a knocking? Yes, go on. I am not expecting anybody. If it is the servant, send him away.'

Stephan Breuning came into the room. His face was unsmiling. He nodded at Czerny.

'Ludwig, I bring sad news. The Elector Maximilian Franz has passed away.'

Ludwig heard the words and listened to them a second time in his head. The corners of his mouth set.

'Max Franz. My old benefactor. He knew he was dying when I went to see him. Did he suffer?'

'I only know that when it happened it was sudden. Despite his illness his courtiers were taken by surprise. It is a sad day for us Rhinelanders, Ludwig. There is unlikely to be a successor.'

'No Elector of Cologne? Is this true?'

'Under French occupation there is no possibility of such a thing. And after . . . if there is an after . . .'

Ludwig walked to the window and thought of Max Franz. He shook his head slowly. 'Sad. So sad. He was a good man. I will never forget his kindness to me. Where was he when he died?'

'In the Schönbrunn palace. They moved him in from his residence in Hetzendorf. It was only a short distance.'

'Hetzendorf. Coincidence. I have to go there this afternoon.'

'Why?'

'To see Doktor Vering. Damnably inconvenient. But he will not come to me.'

Breuning glanced quickly at Czerny, who was standing with his gaze directed out of the window, uninterested in the conversation.

'How . . . how are you?'

'My stomach pains me less and I can hear you clearly. But your voice is not the only sound I hear, I regret to say. It is competing with all sorts of other noises. Ugly ones.' He shrugged his shoulders. 'Vering says he has a new remedy. So I have to stop my work, cancel my plans, to attend upon him.'

'It sounds hopeful.'

'I doubt it, Steffen. I doubt it.'

The carriage jolted on the cobbles as it passed under the Kärntnertor gate and out on to the Glacis. Soldiers drilled – what was the point? Ludwig wondered.

The carriage made a right turn to run alongside the Wien river. Ludwig looked out of the window to the right to see the newly opened Theater an der Wien. It was an imposing building, two sets of double pillars setting off an ornate entrance. Competition for the other private theatres, but more so for the imperial court theatres – and therefore a headache for Baron Braun, Ludwig thought mischievously.

Practically an hour later, as the carriage rounded the east wing of the Schönbrunn palace, Ludwig saw that the windows were draped in black to mark the death of Max Franz.

When the young Habsburg prince had arrived in Bonn it had all begun with so much promise. His love for learning and the arts soon manifested itself, and the people of Bonn loved and respected him for what he did for the city. Who was to foresee that it would end like this? An early death in exile, his court disbanded, the city he had loved so much occupied by foreign soldiers.

Ludwig's head was filled with sadness for his old benefactor – and pain from the jolting of the carriage – as he climbed the steps which led up from a courtyard to the rooms of Doktor Vering.

He lifted his arm to pull the bell but stopped when he heard a bell ring on the other side of the door. He frowned. He had not rung. Why would a bell sound inside? He heard it again, more distinctively this time. It was not a bell. It was the gentle cadence of a woman's laughter.

He pulled the bell and entered. He saw immediately that Vering was standing talking to a woman, who was seated in a large easy chair. Both heads turned towards him.

'I . . . I'm sorry. I'll . . .'

'My dear Beethoven, come in, come in,' said Vering warmly, walking towards him and guiding him in with his arm round Ludwig's shoulder. Vering was a large man, with a full but immaculately trimmed white beard framing a florid face.

'May I introduce Mademoiselle Giulietta Guicciardi, a friend of my daughter Julie.'

Ludwig felt a pang of panic shoot through his stomach as he found himself looking at the lively, pert and sparkling face which was turned up towards him. A gloved hand was held out.

Ludwig took it and bowed his head. 'Madame.'

'No, no, not so formal. You must call me Julia, like everyone.' She gave her head a slight toss, so that the curls which fell on to her forehead seemed to dance. Her cheeks were high-boned and rosy, her eyes sparkling, and most strikingly her lips were blood-red, full and curved. She had a sensuous face and behaved with the self-confidence of one who was aware of her attributes.

Ludwig looked at her and felt his mouth go dry. He nodded. 'Julia,' he said, aware that the sound was strangulated. He cleared his throat and said her name again. He wanted desperately to say something else, to glide easily into conversation, as Zmeskall would, or even Stephan. But no words came.

Vering and Julia both began speaking at the same moment. Vering yielded to Julia.

'Herr Beethoven. You are such a famous musician. I hear your name spoken everywhere. And always with such respect and admiration. When will you allow me to hear you play the piano?'

'I . . . I . . . Will you come to see me in my lodgings? On the Wasserkunstbastei. The Seilerstätte side. I will play for you there.'

'Oh, Doktor Vering, isn't he a dear, kind man? How good of you, Ludwig.' Her face suddenly fell. 'But . . . but why have you come here to see Doktor Vering? I do hope nothing is wrong.'

'I sometimes have trouble with my hearing. Not serious. I'm sure—'

'Nothing serious, nothing serious at all,' said Vering in a booming voice. 'In fact I have a new remedy which I am sure will cure it once and for all.'

'I wish you luck. I do hope it is successful, Ludwig. I must leave you now, but I look forward to seeing you in the Wasserkunstbastei.'

Julia Guicciardi stood and Vering handed her the parasol she had leaned against the wall.

'Goodbye, Doktor Vering. So good to see you again. Will you tell Julie that I will be in touch soon? Until our next meeting, Ludwig.'

As she passed him she raised her gloved fingers to brush his cheek. They barely touched him but he felt the warmth which came off them permeate his skin.

'Such a charming young lady,' said Vering, closing the door behind her. 'And, Ludwig, what she did not tell you – in fact I am rather surprised she did not – is that she is a capable pianist herself. You must ask her to play for you when she comes to see you.'

Vering walked round to the other side of his desk. 'Now, Ludwig, come and sit here. I need to talk to you.' He shuffled through some papers until he found what he was looking for. 'How good is your botany?'

Ludwig looked confused. 'I don't know . . . What do you . . . ?'

'Well now, see here.' He waved a sheet of paper at Ludwig. 'An article in a medical journal published in Berlin. Have you ever seen a plant like this?'

He passed the paper to Ludwig, who looked at a coloured drawing of a shrub, small but with tightly clustered pink blossoms spreading out from a narrow trunk, with even narrower branches

Nikola, I miss my homeland more than I believed I would. Bonn. The Rhine. The Siebengebirge . . .'

'Oh my goodness!' exclaimed Zmeskall, with an embarrassed smile on his face. 'I almost forgot why I came to see you. I have a message from Stephan. He asks you to come to the Schwarzen Kameel tonight at seven for dinner. He will have someone with him – someone from Bonn who you will be very happy to see again.'

'See again, did you say? Someone I know? Who?'

Zmeskall shrugged. 'I don't know. But I soon shall. Stephan has invited me too. Schuppi will be there. He never turns down an invitation to dinner. Your brothers are coming too. So whoever it is, it must be someone important.'

'I don't want to go to the Kameel. It always . . . When I am with a group of people . . .'

'Ludwig,' said Zmeskall, blinking behind his thick spectacles, his thick, white hair quivering slightly, 'may I suggest a little . . . shall we say . . . relaxation to put you in the right mood?'

'No, Nikola!' Ludwig said sharply. 'Leave me now. If you hear any word from Julia, let me know.'

Ludwig walked along the wide Graben and turned up towards the Bognergasse. Why had Julia not told him she was going away? Surely she must know how he was waiting to see her? Surely she must aware of what he had in mind, the question he wanted to put to her? She must have known for some time she was going away. In fact, he dreaded to think, she must even have known when she last came to see him.

He pushed the thought to the back of his mind. He wished he had not accepted Stephan's invitation. He did not want to be sociable. He did not want to meet anybody. He was fairly certain he knew who the person from Bonn was. Christoph, Stephan's elder brother.

The truth was Ludwig had no particular desire to see Christoph. He had barely known him in Bonn. Alone among the Breuning children, Christoph had had no interest in music at all. The last Ludwig had heard, he had gone off to Göttingen to study law.

He wrinkled his nose as he walked into the warm, smoky atmosphere of the Schwarzen Kameel. He turned to the right and entered the dining room. His eyes swept the room and at first he thought he had come to the wrong place. Had Zmeskall said the Schwan? Then he spotted the broad expanse of back that he knew belonged to Schuppanzigh.

Opposite him sat a young man whom Ludwig did not recognise. He was wearing an eye patch, and his hair was a mass of tight black curls. Was there something familiar about him? No, there could not be. He did not know who he was; but he knew immediately it was not Christoph von Breuning. And there, he realised with a sinking feeling, were his two brothers, largely obscured by other people.

He walked over. 'Ludwig,' said Schuppanzigh. 'Here, sit down.' He pulled out a chair and poured Ludwig a glass of red wine. Ludwig nodded at Schuppanzigh, then at his two brothers.

'The herbal remedy,' said Johann. 'Is it effective? Did it work?'

Ludwig frowned. As he expected, the noise in the dining room made it difficult for him to hear. But before he could ask his brother to repeat what he had said, he clearly heard Carl's sharp-edged voice.

'Why? Were you ill? What was the matter?'

Ludwig sighed and shook his head. He turned to Schuppanzigh. 'The rondo. Have you mastered the double stops yet?'

Schuppanzigh nodded, a smile on his face. 'Yes,' he said. 'So now you will write something even more difficult, I suppose.' He laughed heartily and Ludwig smiled with him. 'Now, since Stephan is not here yet, allow me to do the introduction. Ludwig, I believe you know this young man.'

Ludwig, relieved that his ears were adjusting to the sound, looked across the table and shook his head. 'I'm sorry. I . . .'

'Shame on you, Ludwig,' said Carl. 'Your very own pupil, son of a man well known to us all. This is Ferdinand Ries. Ferdi.'

In an instant Ludwig remembered Wegeler's letter. Old Father Ries had wanted his son to come to Vienna, and didn't I try to dissuade him? thought Ludwig.

He looked at Ferdinand. Was this young man really the tousle-haired child he had taught the piano all those years ago in Bonn? Ludwig looked at the eye patch and felt a twinge of pity for the young man. But what should he say to him?

He put down the glass and saw that all faces were turned to him. Ferdinand had an expectant look. Ludwig knew he had to say something, some words of greeting.

'Ferdinand Ries. How well I remember your father. How much I owe him. Is he in good health?'

'Thank you, sir, I believe so. I have not seen him these past ten months. But he has written to me and my family is well.'

To Ludwig's relief, Ries had a deep, resonant voice, and he found he could hear his words well. Encouraged, he continued the conversation.

'Your eye. The patch. Smallpox, wasn't it?'

'Yes. It infected my eye. The surgeon had to remove it.'

'You poor boy,' said Johann. 'The pain . . .'

'Strangely enough, it wasn't like that. Even when it was infected, my eye didn't hurt. But I lost sight in it. The surgeon said if he did not remove it, it might spread to my other eye. I protested because I was not in pain. Even the operation did not hurt. Strange. But I am fortunate. My other eye is good.'

'I had smallpox as a child,' said Ludwig.

'Yes. None of us came near you,' Carl retorted. 'How old are you now, Ferdi?'

'Eighteen, sir.'

'Tell us about Munich. You were in Munich, weren't you?'

Ludwig watched Ferdi talking and felt a certain empathy with him. It was the eye patch. In a curious way he envied him, as he did Lobkowitz. An obvious disability, there for all to see. Unlike his own wretched hearing.

'. . . After the French invaded it all changed. The orchestra was dispersed. You know, sir,' he said, looking at Ludwig, 'Herr Neefe left Bonn and tragically died. His wife too. My father tried to help his daughters, but with the French occupation it became impossible.'

'I heard he had died,' said Ludwig. 'He was a good man.'

'My father suffered too,' Ferdi continued, 'though thankfully not with his health. All the court musicians lost their jobs, which meant there was no income. My father earned a little giving music lessons, but there was barely enough for us to live on. So I left Bonn. I went first to Arnsberg and then Munich.'

'Why did you go to Munich?'

'To study composition with Winter.'

'Composition?' asked Ludwig. 'Who's Winter?'

Schuppanzigh interjected. 'I know of him. German composer. Peter von Winter. He has written pieces for the violin. But mainly he has written operas. He knew Mozart.'

Ferdi nodded. 'That's right. But he was too busy to give me

in front of his chest, put his head down against the wind and walked swiftly to the small house on the Herrengasse.

Stephan Breuning looked across the table at his young friend with a concerned expression on his face.

'What news of your family, Ferdi? How is you father?'

'He's well, thank you, sir. My mother and sister too. My father writes that people are getting used to the French now. There is still tension in the air, but they are adapting.'

Both men spoke quietly, not wishing their Rhineland accents to identify them as foreigners.

Stephan shook his head. 'I ought to return to see my mother. I . . .'

'No, sir,' Ferdi Ries said quickly. 'It is not safe to travel. And I can assure you, Frau Breuning is pleased you are in the safety of Vienna. She told me so several times before I left. And your sister and Doktor Wegeler will soon be safe in Koblenz.'

'Yes,' said Stephan, managing a smile.

'In his last letter my father asks how you are progressing on the violin, sir. Whether you are keeping up your practising.'

Stephan laughed. 'Oh dear. Then you must either ignore his question or tell him a small lie. I regret to say I have not picked up my instrument for some years now.'

'I am sure he will understand, sir. He knows what an important position you have at the imperial palace. I have written and told him so.'

Stephan frowned. 'Ferdi, how much older am I than you?'

'I . . . I don't know, sir. At least ten years, I believe.'

'Wrong, Ferdi. Only ten years. *Only*. Do you understand? And will you take an order from an older man?'

'Yes, sir. Of course, sir,' said Ferdi, a fearful look flitting across his face.

'You are never to call me sir again. Do you understand?'

'Yes. Yes, Herr Breuning. I . . .'

'Ferdi, my name is Stephan. My close friends call me Steffen. You may number yourself among them. Do you understand?'

Ferdi nodded and smiled.

'And talking of close friends . . .' Stephan continued. 'What news of our mutual friend Ludwig Beethoven, pianist and composer? I regret I have not seen or spoken to him for some time.'

'I know, sir. Stephan. Steffen. He did not behave very . . .

have to choose. And because you can play the piano better than anyone else, people always admire you. That is why they think highly of your compositions. You are such a fine pianist, that your works must be good. That is what they believe.'

'Then they are wrong. It is the other way round: I am a composer first, a pianist second. It is my compositions that matter; they are what will endure.'

'You are wrong again, Ludwig. It is because you are the best pianist in Vienna that you have friends in the aristocracy. In the Hofburg palace, even. You can walk into Prince Lichnowsky's salon. Or Prince Lobkowitz's. The Empress knows you by name. Swieten, Kinsky, Fries, Schwarzenberg, they are all your friends. When you play the piano you are their equal. No, you are better than them. They wonder how this . . . this foreigner in his clothes that don't fit is transformed when he sits at the piano. And so they accept you. I dress better than you. I behave better than you. But I cannot do what you do. And so I am not accepted. To the aristocrats of Vienna I will always just be a rough Rhinelander. An unsophisticated peasant. But you . . .'

Ludwig gazed across at the opposite bank and was silent for a moment. Carl spoke again, his voice a little louder.

'Ludwig, is it true you are going deaf?'

Ludwig looked sharply at Carl. 'No. No, it is not. I had problems but . . . How did you . . . ? I didn't want to tell anyone . . .'

'I would have expected you to want to tell your brother. But you didn't. That's up to you. But I found out. People are talking. How bad is it?'

Ludwig looked down at the gushing water. There's no point in trying to keep it a secret from Carl, he thought. Anyway, if it is improving as it seems to be it will not matter if he knows.

'I did have problems, as I told you. I saw various doctors. Imbeciles. But my doctor now is Doktor Schmidt and he's very good. He told me to come here for the summer. Into the country. To rest. And it has worked. My hearing is normal again.'

'Is it really, Ludwig? I've noticed once or twice you don't . . .'

'It's normal, I'm telling you,' Ludwig snapped. 'We are having a normal conversation.'

'If it got bad again and it affected your music . . . If you couldn't play the piano, or compose . . .'

Ludwig took a deep breath. 'Carl, no more talk of it. If I could not play my music, there would be no point in living. I . . . I could not live without music. Unlike you. That is the difference between us. You enjoy music. You play the piano. But for you it is an entertainment. For me, it is my life.'

'I think I understand that. You really are fortunate. I am a musician, but not a good enough one to earn my living by it. But I have a good job now, with a good salary. Johann, too, is earning a good living.'

Ludwig, despite himself, winced at the sound of his father's name.

'Why do you make that face, Ludwig? Why can you not accept he is Johann? It is his name. Nikolaus Johann.'

'It's . . . it's . . . It makes me . . . Father was . . . cruel to me. When I was small – before you were born maybe, or you were a baby, I don't know – he used to wake me in the night and force me to play the piano. Sometimes all night, until dawn. He was always drunk.'

Carl's face was incredulous. 'He what? He did what? Are you inventing that? You *must* be.'

'He beat me. Hit my wrists if I played a wrong note.' Ludwig felt the emotion well up in him. He forced the tears back down, but there was a catch in his throat. 'It was after Grandpa died. You didn't know him. He was . . . He was . . .'

'The Kapellmeister. I wish . . .'

'He was a fine man. A great musician. I loved him. He loved me. He *loved* me, Carl. More than Father ever did. I can still remember the day he died. He was lying on the bed. So still. Absolutely still. And his head . . . his head it was . . . smaller than it had been. I . . . I kissed him, but he would not move. I got angry with him. I didn't understand. I wanted . . .'

Ludwig felt a vast wave of emotion sweep over him. He knew he could not suppress it. His whole body began to convulse with the tears that welled up in him. He gave in and sobbed out loud. All the years of frustration, the rejections he had suffered. His mother, who he was sure had never really loved him. His father, who had been so cruel. Then there were Leni and Julia. Neither, it was obvious, had wanted him.

Only one person. Only one.

'If only Grandfather had lived,' Ludwig said between his sobs, 'everything would have been so different.'

Slowly he brought his emotions under control. He saw that

Carl was holding out a handkerchief for him. For the first time that he could remember he felt a sense of closeness to his brother.

'I . . . I'm sorry. I couldn't control . . .'

'I am sorry for what I said about Ludwig. The other Ludwig. I should not have said it.'

As before, Ludwig heard Carl's words but could not at first make them out. His head was not hurting and there were no noises in his ears, but there was a new kind of dullness, heaviness.

Neither man spoke as they walked back along the stream. Ludwig listened to the rushing water, but the noise stayed in his head after they had left the stream and turned down the path that led away from the Kahlenberg. And where was the birdsong that always filled the air? Ludwig looked anxiously around him.

They turned into the Herrengasse and under the arch of the small house, across the courtyard and up the wooden staircase. Ludwig threw his jacket over a chair and slumped gratefully into it. Carl stood, his breathing heavy.

Ferdi Ries came quickly into the room. 'I'm sorry. I was sorting through your papers, sir, Herr Ludwig, and I went into the kitchen to boil some . . .' Suddenly his eyes opened wide. 'Whatever . . . ? Are you all right? Herr Ludwig? Herr Carl? What happened? Your clothes, Herr Carl. There's mud . . .'

'Nothing,' said Carl. 'We had words. But it's fine now.'

Ferdi turned anxiously to Ludwig.

Ludwig looked at him. His breathing was still heavy and the noises in his ear sharp. He knew the pain would follow soon. And then . . . then . . .

'Yes,' he said, his voice hoarse. 'Tell the woman to make coffee. No, better, pour me some wine.'

Ferdi did as Ludwig asked. Ludwig took the wine and gulped it gratefully.

'Sir?' He handed Carl a glass, but Carl waved it away.

'No. I must leave. Take the stage back to Vienna. I need to be back by this evening. I will write to Breitkopf. Tell him there was a mistake about the sonatas. Nägeli can have them.'

'Oh, that's very good, Herr Carl,' said Ferdi, relief in his voice. 'I'm grateful. So, sir, the problem is at an end,' he said, turning to Ludwig.

Ludwig had closed his eyes and his head was tilted back,

resting against the chair. He had heard Carl's words. Not clearly, but he had heard them and understood them. What did it matter anyway? Let Ferdi and Carl sort it out, he thought. I am a composer. I compose music. Let others deal with publishers.

Although the rushing noise had filled his head and the pain had begun, he heard clearly the four notes, E flat, B flat, B flat, E flat, and the theme above it.

'It is so clear, Ferdi. The variations. I will start on them in the morning.'

'Sir?'

'The variations, Ferd'nand. The variations.'

'Oh good, sir. Excellent.'

'And we will let Breitkopf have them. You may tell him, Carl.'

Carl smiled, turned and left.

'Herr Ludwig,' said Ferdi, coming a little closer to him, 'I really should go back too. But I need your manuscripts. The symphony and the sonatas. I have tried to find all the pages, but . . .'

'Stay tonight, Ferdi. Stay tonight. Tell the woman. There is another room. She will give you a bed. We will sort out the papers together tomorrow.'

Chapter 5

The next morning Ludwig rose early. He had slept badly, dreaming fitfully of his mother and father. He had seen their faces clearly, but they would not look at him. Instead they looked at each other, shaking their heads dolefully. He knew that he was the cause of their despair. At one point his father came up close to him, his face almost touching him. He smelled the alcohol and it made his stomach heave. He tried to force the smell from his head but it persisted. Finally, together, his mother and father turned to him, fixed him with their stare, and shouted at him. But he could not hear what they were saying, only the dreadful noises in his head.

He was relieved to wake early, to escape his dreams. He smiled to himself when he saw the wine glass on its side on the small table by the bed, the wine having stained the wood. The same pungent smell that had invaded his dream . . .

He did not know what time it was. Before six, certainly. He wanted some hot coffee, but it was too early. He remembered that Ferdi Ries had stayed the night. Good, he thought. We'll sort out the manuscripts today, go for a long walk together, then after he's gone I'll compose.

He went to the piano in the middle room. He picked out the four notes that had been in his mind for so long. Again he played them, adding the four bars which brought the phrase to an end. Then the theme that rose above the phrase.

The variations. I will begin the variations today, he thought. When Ferdi has gone. He stood up from the piano and as he did so he felt the heaviness in his head. No, no ringing noise, no rushing noise, he pleaded. Let it not come back. He sang the four notes out loud. Yes, he could hear them. There was no problem. It would be all right.

He started slightly as the door opened. It was the young girl carrying a tray of coffee. The aroma wafted into the room with her.

'Thank you, young lady. Will you thank your mother?'

The girl did not look at him. As she moved some papers to put down the tray, he asked, 'What's your name? I've never asked you your name.'

Still she did not look at him. The moment the tray was safely deposited she turned away and hurried from the room. Ludwig smiled. He poured a cup of coffee, savoured its aroma and drank. The coffee scalded the roof of his mouth, but he swallowed it quickly and took another mouthful.

He sat down and pulled a notebook and quill towards him. E flat, B flat, B flat, E flat. He was about to start writing the notes when another thought occurred to him. He crossed quickly to the other table, the one that stood by the window. He lifted several sheets of clean unlined paper from it and went back to the main table.

He drank more coffee, dipped the quill in the inkpot and began writing.

My dear friend Stephan

Your letter, which Fd. Ries passed to me, brought me much pleasure, though I am sorry for the state of affairs in our home town.

If Bonaparte declares himself Consul for life, he is a rascal like them all. He will declare himself King next.

Please tell Nanette that my rooms are small but comfortable. I have composed several pieces, among them a new symphony. Ries will return with them. Please ensure Schlemmer sets to work on them. He alone can distinguish my notes from the ink stains that accompany them!

The wine here is very passable. I see the grapes growing on the hill and thank them for the pleasure they give me as I pass them. The Kahlenberg does not compare with the Drachenfels. Shall we return home and climb the rock again?

My hearing improves. Doktor Schmidt is a fine physician. I will drink to his health today, and to yours, my dear old friend.

Ludwig v.B.

steady himself. The frame of the instrument trembled. He walked to the chair and sat, placing the glass on the table in front of him.

Julie looked at him questioningly. He attempted a smile.

'Thank you, Julie. I must work now. Alone. Go back to your mother. Come and see me again.'

Julie did not speak. In a whirl of movement, she turned and left the room.

Ludwig drank more wine. Then he pulled a sheet of manuscript towards him and wrote the A–B flat discord Julie had played, the bars filled with the chords he had used as accompaniment. He wrote the segment Julie had been unable to play, ending it with the accented top E flats.

He wanted to go back to the piano and play the whole variation, but he knew it would hurt his ears too much. Soon there would be only the last variation to write. He knew what it would be. A huge fugue, combining both themes. The four notes and the *Prometheus* theme. As a fugue. It would be difficult to play, coming at the end of a long work. They would complain. The pianists. Virtuosos.

But I will play it and show them how it must sound. If only my wretched ears will allow me, he thought.

Ferdi Ries sent him a note.

> . . . Your rooms are ready. I have arranged everything. Herr Streicher's piano sits in the main room. Your grandfather's portrait hangs on the wall above it. People are saying winter has arrived, without an autumn. I expect you will return any day. Inform me, and I will come and help you pack your things . . .

Yes, I must return to Vienna, he thought. My work here is done. Just write the fugue, to end the variations. Then I will leave.

The opening to the fugue was straightforward. The four notes, but for the first time the fourth, the return to E flat, would have a shorter value than the other three. Three minims, but the E flat a dotted crotchet. Dotted crotchet, followed by running semiquavers and the fugue in motion.

Sforzando. Sforzando. Sforzando. Fortissimo. Sempre piu forte. He struck the keys of the piano hard, shaking the frame. Each time he stopped to write the notes down, his ears howled with sound. He was scrawling rather than writing. He knew it. I'll play it to Ries when I return. He can help Schlemmer decipher it.

'End the fugue suddenly, for effect,' Haydn had once told him. 'It is a device. Do not slow it down. Stop unexpectedly. Like suddenly pulling on the reins and bringing the horses and carriage to a halt, to avoid someone who has walked into your path.'

A *fortissimo* sustained minim chord. A *sforzando* sustained minim arpeggio, and a third sustained chord. Then ... then ... *piano*, two gentle chords, just quavers, a huge chromatic run, still *piano* – *still* piano, *Herr Steibelt; no storms here* – the *Prometheus* theme. Gentle and lyrical, but slowly developing into a fugue. Trills in the right hand below the theme. Thumb and forefinger for the trills, third, fourth and fifth fingers for the theme. *Impossible to play, Steibelt, isn't it? Yes, impossible. But I can play it, can't I? Prometheus. Teach him fire. Lead him to the Temple of Apollo.*

Rushing onwards to the end. Ludwig played two *fortissimo* chords, B flat and E flat. The fugue was complete. The variations were ended.

As suddenly as summer had come, winter took its place. The onion dome of St Michael's Church no longer shimmered in the heat, but danced once again behind the wall of rain. Rivulets of water ran down the small windows of Ludwig's rooms, and large black drops of it fell once more into the firegrate.

Ludwig pulled the box away from the wall. He stacked all the sheets of paper on the table and pushed them into his leather bag. He pulled one sheet back out and scrawled a note on it.

Ries

I am ready to return to Vienna. You must come tomorrow. I will need your help. Warn Doktor Schmidt I will need to see him.

Beethvn

He walked to the Pfarrplatz and down the small street that led to the baths. He went into the office of the mail coach.

'This must go to Vienna on the next stage.'

'I'm sorry, sir, there won't be another one until next week.'

'What?'

'Next week, sir. Next week. The summer schedule is over. Anyway the roads are too wet. Monday at the earliest. It may be Tuesday.'

Ludwig noticed the man back away slightly as he leaned towards him. He could not hear him. Why did the wretch not speak more clearly? The room was small and oppressive and it had a dank smell. The rushing sound had come into his ears as soon as he entered it. What had the man said? Obviously a problem, from the look on his face.

Ludwig wanted to ask him to repeat himself, but he knew it would do no good. He threw the letter on to the desk, along with a few coins, and turned and left.

There was a steady drizzle with just the hint of a chill to it. Ludwig pulled up his collar. He wanted to be warm. He wanted to be still and relaxed, so the noise in his ears would go.

He turned towards the bath house. He should have come here more often. It was warming, comforting. He pushed on the door, but it would not open. He pushed harder. It was locked.

He cursed and walked back up to the Pfarrplatz and along the Herrengasse. The rain was falling steadily. His jacket was soaked and water ran from his hair down his forehead. The rain was splashing noisily on to the street. Yet he knew it was not heavy enough to make such noise. His ears, his damned ears.

He turned into the courtyard of the small house, crossed it, and mounted the wooden staircase to his rooms.

A letter lay on his table. He tore it open.

Sir

I am unexpectedly detained. I must go to Krems to give lessons. I will stay there for two weeks. I will write to you on my return, then I will come to assist your return to Vienna.

Yr pupil, Fd. Ries

Ludwig threw down the letter in frustration. He wanted to be back in Vienna. He had had enough of these small rooms. In the summer they had been bearable. He could walk along the stream, climb the slopes of the Kahlenberg . . .

That damned shepherd, he thought, slumping into a chair. Why was that damned shepherd playing his pipe and singing? If it had not been for that . . . Ferdi had said he could not hear him either. He was lying, for my sake.

But I can hear the piano. I can hear speech. Sometimes. He walked to the piano and struck a chord. It jarred in his head. His head began to throb with pain. Oh no. Not my music going. Not going from me. He sat and played a run with both hands. The sounds clashed in his head. They were not clear. They were not as they should be.

Frowning, he stood and looked into the top of the piano. He hoped to see broken strings, frayed hammers. No, it was in order. He brought his hands crashing down on the notes again. Dreadful, cacophonous, harsh sounds. Not music.

He stood quickly. He went to the table by the window to pour himself a glass of wine. The carafe had little more than a dribble in it. He cursed out loud.

He turned and looked at the wall. It was blank. Where was his grandfather? He wanted to speak to his grandfather.

What shall I do, Grandfather? What shall I do? Is it enough? Have I written enough music for you? My variations are good. My symphonies, piano concertos, sonatas . . . Are you proud of me? Have I achieved what you wanted from me?

The whistling in his ears hurt. His head throbbed. He wanted to go to the piano again. Play more notes. Assure himself it was not true, that he could still hear his music. But he dared not.

He looked at the carafe again. Damn it, why was it empty? He went out on to the landing of the wooden staircase and called out, 'Wine! Julie, are you there? Bring me wine.'

Without waiting for a response he went inside again. Everything was in disarray. Waiting for Ries to come and pack it up. How can I cope? he thought. How can I cope? If I cannot hear . . .

He paced the room, his heavy boots clumping on the floor. He wrung his hands. He looked at the piano; it seemed to return his gaze defiantly.

He started as Julie tugged on his sleeve. The full carafe was on the table. She was trying to pull him to the piano.

'No . . . No, Julie. Not now.'

She ran to the piano and struck the discord, the discord he had encouraged her to play. The pain shot through his head, the throbbing terrible.

'Stop! I can't hear any more. I can't hear.' He clasped his hands to his ears and sank his head down on his chest.

Julie stood looking at him, horrified. Gently she took his arm and led him to the chair. She poured him a glass of wine and handed it to him. He drank it down and handed the glass back to her to refill. She did so, then looked around the room quickly. She went to the box that was lying on the floor, picked a book off the top of it, and handed it to Ludwig with a smile.

He took it and nodded his thanks. She looked at him for a few moments longer, smiled and skipped from the room.

The book was the collected poems of Friedrich Schiller that he had asked Ries to find for him before he left for Heiligenstadt. He had meant to read it several times. It reminded him of his youth. Neefe had told him to read Schiller, hadn't he? What had he said? All men are free and equal under God. You will learn that from Schiller.

Ludwig laughed out loud. The wine had given his head a pleasant dizziness. The absurdity of it all. The sheer, utter absurdity of it all. He laughed again. A musician who could not hear his music! A deaf musician!

He looked at the blank wall and saw his grandfather's face. The familiar face that he had looked up into as a child. So real. So real.

He sat upright. There was his grandfather's portrait on the wall and there . . . the smell of his Turkish tobacco. And there . . . there . . . listen! The sound of his voice. The deep, mellifluous sound of his voice.

And I am his grandson. His blood. I am a musician like him, and I will make him proud.

He picked up the book and opened it. He read. It was a poem he had read when he was a boy. Not long before his first trip to Vienna. He remembered how fond of it Neefe had been. 'Learn it,' he had said. But Ludwig hadn't.

He poured himself another glass of wine and read it now, remembering the words, the cadences from his youth.

To Joy

Be joyful, Oh ye children of th'Almighty
Daughters of the Elysian field.
Bathe us in the fire of your Glory
To your Kingdom we gladly yield.